CHARL

THE

KNIGHT OF GWYNNE

Elibron Classics
www.elibron.com

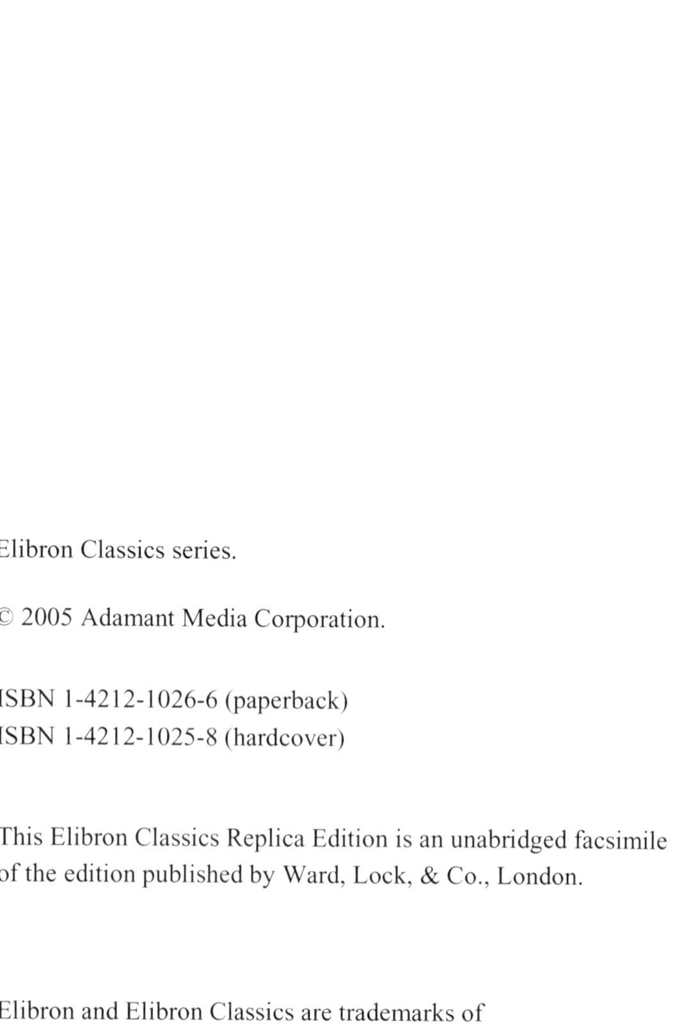

Elibron Classics series.

ISBN 1-4212-1026-6 (paperback)
ISBN 1-4212-1025-8 (hardcover)

This Elibron Classics Replica Edition is an unabridged facsimile of the edition published by Ward, Lock, & Co., London.

THE KNIGHT OF GWYNNE

THE

KNIGHT OF GWYNNE.

BY

CHARLES LEVER.

AUTHOR OF

"CHARLES O'MALLEY," "JACK HINTON," "DODD FAMILY ABROAD,"
"ONE OF THEM," ETC., ETC.

NEW EDITION.

LONDON:
WARD, LOCK, & CO., WARWICK HOUSE,
SALISBURY SQUARE, E.C.

PREFACE.

I WROTE this story in the Tyrol. The accident of my residence there was in this wise: I had travelled about the Continent for a considerable time in company with my family, with my own horses. Our carriage was a large and comfortable caleche, and our team, four horses; the leaders of which, well-bred and thriving-looking, served as saddle horses when needed.

There was something very gipsy-like in this roving uncertain existence, that had no positive bent or limit, and left every choice of place an open question, that gave me intense enjoyment. It opened to me views of Continental life, scenery, people and habits I should certainly never have attained to by other modes of travel.

Not only were our journeys necessarily short each day, but we frequently sojourned in little villages, and out of the world spots; where, if pleased by the place itself, and the accommodation afforded, we would linger on for days, having at our disposal the total liberty of our time, and all our nearest belongings around us.

In the course of these rambles we had arrived at the town of Bregenz, on the lake of Constance; where the innkeeper, to whom I was known, accosted me with all the easy freedom of his calling, and half-jestingly alluded to my mode of travelling as a most unsatisfactory and wasteful way of life, which could never turn out profitably to myself, or to mine. From the window where we were standing as we talked, I could descry the tall summit of an ancient castle, or schloss, about two miles away; and rather to divert my antagonist from his argument than with any more serious purpose, I laughingly told my host if he could secure me such a fine old chateau as that I then looked at, I should stable my nags and rest where I was. On the following day, thinking of nothing less than my late conversation, the host entered my room to assure me that he had been over to the castle, had seen the baron, and learned that he would have no objection to lease me his chateau, provided I took it for a fixed term, and with all its accessories, not only of furniture but cows and farm requisites. One of my horses, accidentally pricked in shoeing, had obliged me at the moment to delay a day or two at the inn, and for want of better to do, though without the most remote intention of becoming a tenant of the castle, I yielded so far to my host's solicitation—to walk over and see it.

If the building itself was far from faultless it was spacious and convenient, and its position on a low hill in the middle of a lawn finer than anything I can convey; the four sides of the schloss commanding four distinct and perfectly dissimilar views. By the north it looked over a wooded plain, on which stood the Convent of Mehreran; and beyond this, the broad expanse of the lake of Constance. The south opened a view towards the upper Rhine, and the valley that led to the Via Mala. On the east you saw the Gebhardsberg and its chapel, and the lovely orchards that bordered Bregenz; while to the west rose the magnificent Lenten and the range of the Swiss Alps—their summits lost in the clouds.

I was so enchanted by the glorious panorama around me, and so carried away by the thought of a life of quiet labour and rest in such a spot, that after hearing a very specious account of the varied economies I should secure by this choice of a residence, and the resources I should have in excursions on all sides, that I actually contracted to take the chateau, and became master of the Rieden Schloss from that day.

Having thus explained by what chance I came to pitch my home in this little-visited spot, I have no mind to dwell further on my Tyrol experiences than as they concern the story which I wrote there.

If the scene in which I was living, the dress of the peasants, the daily ways and interests had been my promptors, I could not have addressed myself to an Irish theme; but long before I had come to settle at Predeislarg, when wandering amongst the Rhine villages, on the vine-clad slopes of the Bergstrasse, I had been turning over in my mind the Union period of Ireland as the era for a story. It was a time essentially rich in the men we are proud of as a people, and peculiarly abounding in traits of self-denial and devotion which, in the corruption of a few, have been totally lost sight of; the very patriotism of the time having been stigmatised as factious opposition, or unreasoning resistance to wiser counsels. That nearly every man of ability in the land was against the Minister, that not only all the intellect of Ireland, but all the high spirit of its squirearchy, and the generous impulses of its people, were opposed to the Union,—there is no denying. If eloquent appeal and powerful argument could have saved a nation, Henry Grattan or Plunkett would not have spoken in vain; but the measure was decreed before it was debated, and the annexation of Ireland was made a Cabinet decision before it came to Irishmen to discuss it.

I had no presumption to imagine I could throw any new light on the history of the period, or illustrate the story of the measure by any novel details; but I thought it would not be uninteresting to sketch the era itself; what aspect society presented; how the country gentleman of the time bore himself in the midst of solicitations and temptings the most urgent and insidious; what, in fact, was the character of that man whom no national misfortunes could subdue, no Ministerial blandishments corrupt; of him, in short, that an authority with little bias to the land of his birth has called—*The First Gentleman of Europe.*

I know well, I feel too acutely, how inadequately I have pictured what I desired to paint; but even now, after the interval of years, I look back on my poor attempt with the satisfaction of one whose arm was not ignoble. A longer and deeper experience of life has succeeded to the time since I wrote this story, but in no land nor amongst any people have I ever found the type of what we love to emblematise by the word Gentleman, so distinctly marked out as in the educated and travelled Irishman of that period. The same unswerving fidelity of friendship, the same courageous devotion to a cause, the same haughty contempt for all that was mean or unworthy; these, with the lighter accessories of genial temperament, joyous disposition, and a chivalrous respect for women, made up what I had at least in my mind when I tried to present to my readers my Knight of Gwynne.

That my character of him was not altogether ideal, I can give no better proof than the fact that during the course of the publication I received several letters from persons unknown to me, asking whether I had not drawn my portrait from this or that original, several concurring in the belief that I had taken as my model The Knight of Kerry, whose qualities I am well assured fully warranted the suspicion.

For my attempt to paint the social habits of the period, I had but to draw on my memory. In my boyish days I had heard much of that day, and was familiar with most of the names of its distinguished men. Anecdotes of Henry Grattan, Flood, Parsons, Ponsonby, and Curran, jostled in my mind with stories of their immediate successors, the Bushes and the Plunketts, whose fame has come down to the very day we live in. As a boy, it was my fortune to listen to the narratives of the men who had been actors in the events of that exciting era, and who could even show me in modern Dublin the scenes where memorable events occurred, and not unfrequently the very houses where celebrated convivialities occurred. And thus from Drogheda Street, the modern Sackville Street, where the beaux of the day lounged in all their bravery, to the Circular road where a long file of carriages, six in hand, evidenced the luxury and tone of display of the capital. I was deeply imbued with the features of the time, and ransacked the old newspapers and magazines with a zest which only great familiarity with the names of the leading characters could have inspired.

Though I have many regrets on the same score, there is no period of my life in which I have the same sorrow for not having kept some sort of note-book instead of trusting to a memory most fatally unretentive and uncertain. Through this omission I have lost traces of innumerable epigrams, and *jeus d'esprit* of a time that abounded in such effusions, and even where my memory has occasionally relieved the effort, I have forgotten the author. To give an instance, the witty lines—

"With a name that is borrowed, a title that's bought,
Sir William would fain be a gentleman thought;
His wit is but cunning, his courage but vapour,
His pride is but money, his money but paper."

which, wrongfully attributed to a political leader in the Irish house, were in reality written by Lovel Edgeworth on the well-known Sir William Gladowes, who became Lord Newcomen; and the verse was not only poetry but prophecy, for in his bankruptcy some years afterwards the sarcasm became fact,—"his money was but paper."

This circumstance of the authorship was communicated to me by Miss Maria Edgeworth, whose letter was my first step in acquaintance with her, and gave me a pleasure and a pride which long years have not been able to obliterate.

I remember in that letter her having told me how she was in the habit of reading my story aloud to the audience of her nephews and nieces; a simple announcement that imparted such a glow of proud delight to me that I can yet recall the courage with which I resumed the writing of my tale, and the hope it suggested of my being able one day to win a place of honour amongst those who, like herself, had selected Irish traits as the characteristics to adorn fiction.

For Con Heffernan I had an original. For Bagenal Daly, too, I was not without a model. His sister is purely imaginary, but that she is not unreal I am bold enough to hope, since several have assured me that they know where I found my type. In my brief sketch of Lord Castlereagh I was not, I need scarcely say, much aided by the journals and pamphlets of the time, where his character and conduct were ruthlessly and most falsely assailed. It was my fortune, however, to have possessed the close intimacy of one who had acted as his private secretary, and whose abilities have since raised him to high station and great employment; and from him I came to know the real nature of one of the ablest statesmen of his age, as he was one of the most attractive companions, and most accomplished gentlemen. I have no vain pretence to believe that by my weak and unfinished sketch I have in any way vindicated the Minister who carried the Union against the attacks of his opponents, but I have tried at least to represent him such as he was in the society of his intimates; his gay and cheerful temperament, his frank nature, and what least the world is disposed to concede to him, his sincere belief in the honesty of men whose convictions were adverse to him, and who could not be won over to his opinions.

I have not tried to conceal the gross corruption of an era which remains to us as a national shame, but I would wish to lay stress on the fact that not a few resisted offers and temptations, which to men struggling with humble fortune and linked for life with the fate of the weaker country, must redound to their high credit. All the nobler their conduct, as around them on every side were the great names of the land trafficking for title and place, and shamelessly demanding office for their friends and relatives as the price of their own adhesion.

For that degree of intimacy which I have represented as existing between Bagenal Daly and Freney the robber, I have been once or twice reprehended as conveying a false and unreal view of the relations of the time; but the knowledge I myself had of Freney, his habits and his exploits were given to me by a well-known and highly-connected Irish gentleman, who represented a county in the Irish Parliament, and was a man of unblemished honour, conspicuous alike in station and ability. And there is still, and once the trait existed more remarkably in Ireland, a wonderful sympathy between all classes and conditions of people: so that the old stories and traditions that amuse the crouching listener round the hearth of the cottage, find their way into luxurious drawing-rooms; and by their means a brotherhood of sentiment was maintained between the highest class in the land and the humblest peasant who laboured for his daily bread.

I tried to display the effect of this strange teaching on the mind of a cultivated gentleman when describing the Knight of Gwynne. I endeavoured to show the "Irishry" of his nature was no other than the play of those qualities by which he appreciated his countrymen and was appreciated by them. So powerful is this sympathy, and so strong the sense of national humour through all classes of the people, that each is able to entertain a topic from the same point of view as his neighbour, and the subtle equivoque in the polished witticism that amuses the gentleman is never lost on the untutored ear of the unlettered peasant. Is there any other land of which one could say as much?

If this great feature of attractiveness pertains to the country and adds to its adaptiveness as the subject of fiction, I cannot but feel that to un-Irish ears it is necessary to make an explanation which will serve to show that which would elsewhere imply a certain blending of station and condition, is here but a proof of that wide-spread understanding by which, however divided by race, tradition, and religion, we are always able to appeal to certain sympathies and dispositions in common, and feel the tie of a common country.

At the period in which I have placed this story the rivalry between the two nations was, with all its violence, by no means ungenerous. No contemptuous estimate of Irishmen formed the theme of English journalism; and between the educated men of both countries there was scarcely a jealousy that the character which political contest assumed later on, changed much of this spirit and dyed nationalties with an amount of virulence which, with all its faults and all its shortcomings, we do not find in the times of the Knight of Gwynne.

CHARLES LEVER.

TRIESTE, 1872.

THE KNIGHT OF GWYNNE.

CHAPTER I.

A FIRESIDE GROUP.

It was exactly forty-five years ago that a group, consisting of three persons, drew their chairs around the fire of a handsome dinner-room in Merrion-square, Dublin. The brilliantly lighted apartment, the table still cumbered with decanters and dessert, and the sideboard resplendent with a gorgeous service of plate, showed that the preparations had been made for a much larger party, the last of whom had just taken his departure.

Of the three who now drew near the cheerful blaze, more intent, as it seemed, on confidential intercourse than the pleasures of the table, he who occupied the centre was a tall and singularly handsome man, of some six or seven-and-twenty years of age. His features, perfectly classical in their regularity, conveyed the impression of one of a cold and haughty temperament, unmoved by sudden impulse, but animated by a spirit daringly ambitious. His dress was in the height of the then mode, and he wore it with the air of a man of fashion and elegance.

This was Lord Castlereagh, the youthful Secretary for Ireland, one whose career was then opening with every promise of future distinction.

At his right hand sat, or rather lounged, in all the carelessness of habitual indolence, a young man some years his junior, his dark complexion and eyes, his aquiline features, and short, thin upper lip almost resembling a Spanish face. His dress was the uniform of the Foot Guards, a costume which well became him, and set off to the fullest advantage a figure of perfect symmetry. A manner of careless inattention in which he indulged contrasted strongly with the quick impatience of his dark glances and the eager rapidity of his utterance when momentarily excited, for the Honourable Dick Forester was only cool by training, and not by temperament, and, at the time we speak of, his worldly education was scarcely more than well begun.

The third figure—strikingly unlike the other two—was a man of fifty, or thereabouts, short and plethoric. His features, rosy and sensual, were lit up by two grey eyes, whose twinkle was an incessant provocative to laughter. The mouth was, however, the great index to his character. It was large and full, the under lip slightly projecting—a circumstance, perhaps, acquired in the long habit of a life where the tasting function had been actively employed, for Con Heffernan was a gourmand of the first water, and the most critical judge of a vintage the island could boast. Two fingers of either hand were inserted in the capacious pockets of a white vest, while his head jauntily leaning to one side, he sat the very ideal of self-satisfied ease and contentment. The *aplomb*—why should there be a French word for an English quality?—he possessed was not the vulgar ease of a presuming or under-bred man—far from it, it was the impress of certain gifts which gave him an acknowledged superiority in the society he moved in. He was shrewd, without over-caution; he was ready-witted, but never rash; he possessed that rare combination of quick intelligence with strong powers of judgment; and, above all, he knew men, or at least such specimens of the race as came before him in a varied life, well and thoroughly.

If he had a weak point in his character, it was a love of popularity; not that vulgar mob worship which some men court and seek after—no, it was the estimation of his own class and set he desired to obtain. He was proud of his social position, and nervously sensitive in whatever might prejudice or endanger it. His enemies—and Con was too able a man not to have made some—said that his low origin was the secret of his nature; that his ambiguous position in society demanded exertions uncalled for from others less equivocally circumstanced; and that Mr. Heffernan was, in secret, very far from esteeming the high and titled associates with whom his daily life brought him in contact. If this were the case, he was assuredly a consummate actor. No man ever went through a longer or more searching trial unscathed, nor could an expression be quoted, or an act mentioned, in which he derogated, even for a moment, from the habits of "his order."

"You never did the thing better in your life, my Lord," said Con, as the door closed upon the last departing guest. "You hit off Jack Massy to perfection; and as for Watson, though he said nothing at the time, I'll wager my roan cob against Deane Moore's hackney—long odds, I fancy—that you find him at the Treasury to-morrow morning, with a sly request for five minutes' private conversation."

"I'm of your mind, Heffernan. I saw that he took the bait; indeed, to do the gentlemen justice, they are all open to conviction."

"You surely cannot blame them," said Con, "if they take a more conciliating view of your Lordship's opinions, when assisted by such claret as this—this is old '72, if I mistake not."

"They sold it to me as such, but I own to you I'm the poorest connoisseur in the world as regards wine. Some one remarked this evening that the '95 was richer in bouquet."

"It was Edward Harvey, my Lord. I heard him; but that was the year he got his baronetcy, and he thinks the sun never shone so brightly before; his father was selling Balbriggan stockings when this grape was ripening, and now, the son has more than one foot on the steps of the Peerage." This was said with a short, quick glance beneath the eyelids, and evidently more as a feeler, than with any strong conviction of its accuracy.

"No Government can afford to neglect its supporters, and the acknowledgments must be proportioned to the sacrifices, as well as to the abilities of the individuals who second it."

"By Jove! if these gentlemen are in the market," said Forester, who broke silence for the first time, "I don't wonder at their price being a high one; in consenting to the 'Union,' they are virtually voting their own annihilation."

"By no means," said the Secretary, calmly; "the field open to their ambition is imperial and not provincial; the English Parliament will form an arena for the display of ability, as wide surely as this of Dublin. Men of note and capacity will not be less rewarded; the losers will be the small talkers, county squires of noisy politics, and crafty lawyers of no principles; they will, perhaps, be obliged to remain at home, and look after their own affairs; but will the country be the worse for that, while the advantages to trade and commerce are inconceivable?"

"I agree with you there," said Con; "we are likely to increase our exports, by sending every clever fellow out of the country."

"Why not, if the market be a better one?"

"Wouldn't you spare us a few luxuries for home consumption?" said Con, as he smacked his lips and looked at his glass through the candle.

His Lordship paid no attention to the remark, but taking a small tablet from his waistcoat-pocket, seemed to study its contents. "Are we certain of Cuffe; is he pledged to us, Heffernan?"

"Yes, my Lord, he has no help for it; we are sure of him; he owes the Crown eleven thousand pounds, and says, the only ambition he possesses is to make the debt twelve, and never pay it."

"What of that canting fellow from the north?—Newland."

"He accepts your terms conditionally, my Lord," said Con, with a sly roll of his eye; "if the arguments are equal to your liberality, he will vote for you, but as yet, he does not *see* the advantages of a Union."

"Not *see* them!" said Lord Castlereagh, with a look of irony; "why did you not let him look at them from your own windows, Heffernan? the view is enchanting for the Barrack Department."

"The poor man is short-sighted," said Con, with a sigh, "and never could stretch his vision beyond the Custom House."

"Be it so, in the devil's name; a commissioner more or less shall never stop us!"

"What a set of rascals," muttered Forester between his teeth, as he tossed off a bumper to swallow his indignation.

"Well, Forester, what of your mission? Have you heard from your friend Darcy?"

"Yes; I have his note here. He cannot come over just now, but he has given me an introduction to his father, and pledges himself I shall be well received."

"What Darcy is that?" said Heffernan.

"The Knight of Gwynne," said his Lordship; "do you know him?"

"I believe, my Lord, there is not a gentleman in Ireland who could not say yes to that question; while west of the Shannon, Maurice Darcy is a name to swear by."

"We want such a man much," said the Secretary, in a low, distinct utterance; "some well-known leader of public opinion is of great value just now. How does he vote usually? I don't see his name in the divisions."

"Oh, he rarely comes up to town, never liked Parliament, but when he did attend the House, he usually sat with the Opposition, but, without linking himself to party, spoke and voted independently, and, strange to say, made considerable impression by conduct which in any other man would have proved an utter failure."

"Did he speak well, then?"

"For the first five minutes you could think of nothing but his look and appearance; he was the handsomest man in the House, a little too particular, perhaps, in dress, but never finical; as he went on, however, the easy fluency of his language, the grace and elegance of his style, and the frank openness of his statements, carried his hearers with him; and many who were guarded enough against the practised power of the great speakers, were entrapped by the unstudied, manly tone of the Knight of Gwynne. You say truly, he would be a great card in your hands at this time."

"We must have him at his own price, if he has one. Is he rich?"

"He has an immense estate, but, as I hear, greatly encumbered; but don't think of money with him, that will never do."

"What's the bait, then? Does he care for rank? Has he any children grown up?"

"One son and one daughter are all his family; and, as for title, I don't think that he'd exchange that of Knight of Gwynne for a Dukedom. His son is a lieutenant in the Guards."

"Yes; and the best fellow in the regiment," broke in Forester. "In every quality of a high-spirited gentleman, Lionel Darcy has no superior."

"The better deserving of rapid promotion," said his Lordship, smiling significantly.

"I should be sorry to offer it to him, at the expense of his father's principles," said Forester.

"Very little fear of your having to do so," said Heffernan, quickly; "the Knight would be no easy purchase."

"You must see him, however, Dick," said the Secretary; "there is no reason why he should not be with us on grounds of conviction. He is a man of enlightened and liberal mind, and surely will not think the worse of a measure because its advocates are in a position to serve his son's interests."

"If that topic be kept very studiously out of sight, it were all the more prudent," said Con, dryly.

"Of course; Forester will pay his visit, and only advert to the matter with caution and delicacy. To gain him to our side, is a circumstance of so much moment, that I say *carte blanche* for the terms."

"I knew the time that a foxhound would have been a higher bribe than a blue ribbon with honest Maurice; but it's many years since we met, now, and Heaven knows what changes time may have wrought in him. A smile and a soft speech from a pretty woman, or a bold exploit of some hair-brained fellow, were sure to find favour with him, when he would have heard flattery from the lips of Royalty without pride or emotion."

"His colleague in the county is with us; has he any influence over the Knight?"

"Far from it. Mr. Hickman O'Reilly is the last man in the world to have weight with Maurice Darcy, and if it be your intention to make O'Reilly a Peer, you could have taken no readier method to arm the Knight against you. No, no; if you really are bent on having him, leave all thought of a purchase aside; let Forester, as the friend and brother officer of young Darcy, go down to Gwynne, make himself as agreeable to the Knight as may be, and when he has one foot on the carriage-step at his departure, turn sharply round, and say, 'Won't you vote with us, Knight?' What between surprise and courtesy, he may be taken too short for reflection, and if he say but 'Yes,' ever so low, he's yours. That's *my* advice to you. It may seem a poor chance, but I fairly own I see no better one."

"I should have thought rank might be acceptable in such a quarter," said the Secretary, proudly.

"He has it, my Lord—at least as much as would win all the respect any rank could confer; and besides, these new Peerages have no prestige in their favour yet a while; we must wait for another generation. This claret is perfect now, but I should not say it were quite so delicate in flavour the first year it was bottled. The squibs and epigrams on the new promotions are remembered, where the blazons of the Heralds' College are forgotten: that unlucky Banker, for instance, that you made a Viscount the other day, both his character and his credit have suffered for it."

"What was that you allude to?—an epigram, was it?"

"Yes, very short, but scarcely sweet. Here it is:

> With a name that is borrow'd, a title that's bought,—

you remember, my Lord, how true both allegations are—

> With a name that is borrow'd, a title that's bought,—
> Sir William would fain be a gentleman thought;
> While his Wit is mere cunning, his Courage but vapour,
> His Pride is but money, his Money but paper."

"Very severe, certainly," said his Lordship, in the same calm tone he ever spoke. "Not your lines, Mr. Heffernan?"

"No, my Lord; a greater than Con Heffernan indited these: one who did not scruple to reply to yourself in the House in an imitation of your own inimitable manner."

"Oh, I know whom you mean—a very witty person indeed," said the Secretary, smiling; "and if we were to be laughed out of office, he might lead the Opposition. But these are very business-like, matter-of-fact days we're fallen upon. The Cabinet that can give away blue ribbons may afford to be indifferent to small jokers. But to revert to matters more immediate: you must start at once, Forester, for the west, see the Knight, and do what ever you can to bring him towards us. I say *carte blanche* for the terms; I only wish our other elevations to the Peerage had half the pretension he has; and, whatever our friend Mr. Heffernan may say, I opine to the mere matter of compact, which says, so much for so much."

"Here's success to the mission, however its negotiations incline," said Heffernan, as he drained off his glass, and rose to depart. "We shall see you again within ten days or a fortnight, I suppose?"

"Oh, certainly; I'll not linger in that wild district an hour longer than I must." And so, with good night and good wishes, the party separated—Forester to make his preparations for a journey which, in those days, was looked on as something formidable.

CHAPTER II.

A TRAVELLING ACQUAINTANCE.

Whatever the merits or demerits of the great question, the legislative Union between England and Ireland—and assuredly we have neither the temptation of duty nor inclination to discuss such here—the means employed by Ministers to carry the measure through Parliament were in the last degree disgraceful; never was bribery practised with more open effrontery, never did corruption display itself with more daring indifference to public opinion; the Treasury Office was an open mart, where votes were purchased, and men sold their country, delighted, as a candid member of the party confessed,—delighted "to have a country to sell."

The ardour of a political career, like the passion for the chase, would seem in its high excitement to still many compunctious murmurings of conscience, which in calmer moments could not fail to be heard and acknowledged: the desire to succeed, that ever-present impulse to win, steels the heart against impressions which, under less pressing excitements, had been most painful to endure, and, in this way, honourable and high-minded men have often stooped to acts which, with calmer judgment to guide them, they would have rejected with indignation.

Such was Dick Forester's position at the moment; an aide-de-camp on the staff of the Viceroy, a near relative of the Secretary, he was entrusted with many secret and delicate negotiations, affairs in which, had he been a third party, he would have as scrupulously condemned the tempter as the tempted: the active zeal of agency allayed, however, all such qualms of conscience, and every momentary pang of remorse was swallowed up in the ardour for success.

Few men will deny in the abstract the cruelty of many field sports they persist in following, fewer still abandon them on such scruples; and that while Forester felt half ashamed to himself of the functions committed to him, he would have been sorely disappointed if he had been passed over in the selection of his relative's political adherents.

Of this nature were some of Dick Forester's reflections as he posted along towards the west; nor was the scene through which he journeyed suggestive of pleasanter thoughts. If any of our readers should perchance be acquainted with that dreary line of country which lies along the great western road of Ireland, they will not feel surprised if the traveller's impressions of the land were not of the brightest or fairest. The least reflective of mortals cannot pass through a dreary and poverty-stricken district without imbibing some of the melancholy which broods over the place. Forester was by no means such, and felt deeply and sincerely for the misery he witnessed on every hand, and was in the very crisis of some most patriotic scheme of benevolence, when his carriage arrived in front of the little inn of Kilbeggan. Resisting, without much violence to his inclinations, the civil request of the landlord to alight, he leaned back to resume the broken thread of his lucubrations, while fresh horses were put to. How long he thus waited, or what progress his benign devices accomplished in the mean while, this true history is unable to record; enough if we say, that when he next became aware of the incidents then actually happening around him, he discovered that his carriage was standing fast in the same place as at the moment of his arrival, and the rain falling in torrents as before.

To let down the glass and call out to the postilions was a very natural act; to do so with the addition of certain expletives not commonly used in good society, was not an extraordinary one. Forester did both; but he might have spared his eloquence and his indignation, for the postilions were both in the stable, and his servant agreeably occupied in the bar over the comforts of a smoking tumbler of punch. The merciful schemes, so late the uppermost object of his thoughts, were routed in a moment, and vowing intentions of a very different purport to the whole household, he opened the door and sprang out. Dark as the night was, he could see that there were no horses to the carriage, and with redoubled anger at the delay, he strode into the inn.

"Holloa, I say—house here! Linwood! Where the devil is the fellow?"

"Here, sir," cried a smart-looking London servant, as he sprang from the bar with his eyes bolting out of his head from the heat of the last mouthful, swallowed in a second. "I've been a trying for horses, sir; but they've never got 'em, though they've been promising to let us have a pair this half-hour."

"No horses! Do you mean that they've not got a pair of posters in a town like this?"

"Yes, indeed, sir," interposed a dirty waiter in a nankeen jacket, for the landlord was too indignant at the rejection of his proposal to appear again, "we've four pair, besides a mare in foal; but there's a deal of business on the line this week past, and there's a gentleman in the parlour now has taken four of them."

"Taken four! Has he more than one carriage?"

"No, sir, and a light chariot it is; but he likes to go fast."

"And so do I—when I can," muttered Forester, the last words being an addition almost independent of him. "Couldn't you tell him that there's a gentleman here very much pressed to push on, and would take it as a great favour if he'd divide the team?"

"To be sure, sir; I'll go and speak to him," said the waiter, as he hurried away on the errand.

"I see how it is, sir," said Linwood, who, with true servant dexterity, thought to turn his master's anger into any other channel than towards himself, "they wants to get you to stop the night here."

"Confound this trickery! I'll pay what they please for the horses, only let us have them. Well, waiter, what does he say?"

"He says, sir," said the waiter, endeavouring to suppress a laugh, "if you'll come in, and join him at supper, you shall have whatever you like."

"Join him at supper! No, no; I'm hurried—I'm anxious to get forward, and not the least hungry, besides."

"Hadn't you better speak a word to him, anyhow?" said the waiter, half opening the parlour door. And Forester, accepting the suggestion, entered.

In the little low-ceilinged apartment of the small inn, at a table very amply and as temptingly covered, sat a large, and, for his age, singularly handsome man. A forehead both high and broad surmounted two clear blue eyes, whose brilliancy seemed to defy the wear of time; regular and handsome teeth; and a complexion the very type of health appeared to vouch for a strength of constitution rare at his advanced age. His dress was the green coat so commonly worn by country gentlemen, with leather breeches and boots, nor, though the season was winter, did he appear to have any great-coat, or other defence against the weather. He was heaping some turf upon the fire as Forester entered, and laughingly interrupting the operation, he stood up and bowed courteously.

"I have taken a great liberty, sir, first, to suppose that any man at this hour of the night is not the worse for something to eat and drink; and, secondly, that he might have no objection to partake of either in my company." Forester was not exactly prepared for a manner so palpably that of the best society, and at once repressing every sign of his former impatience, replied by apologising for a request which might inconvenience the granter. "Let me help you to this grouse-pie, and fill yourself a glass of sherry; and by the time you have taken some refreshment, the horses will be put to. I am most happy to offer you a seat."

"I am afraid there is a mistake somewhere," said Forester, half timidly. "I heard you had engaged the only four horses here, and as my carriage is without, my request was to obtain two, if you——"

"But why not come with me? I'm pressed, and must be up, if possible, before morning. Remember, we are forty-eight miles from Dublin."

"Dublin! But I'm going the very opposite road. I'm for Westport."

"Oh, by Jove! that is different. What a stupid fellow the waiter is! Never mind—sit down. Let us have a glass of wine together. You shal have two of the horses. Old Wilkins must only make his spurs supply the place of the leaders."

There was a hearty good-nature in every accent of the old man's voice, and Forester drew his chair to the table, by no means sorry to spend some time longer in his company.

There is a kind of conversation sacred to the occupations of the table—a mixture of the culinary and the social, the gustatory with the agreeable. And the stranger led the way to this, with the art of an accomplished proficient, and while recommending the good things to Forester's attention, contrived to season their enjoyment by a tone at once pleasing and cordial.

"I could have sworn you were hungry," said he, laughing, as Forester helped himself for the second time to the grouse-pie. "I know you did not expect so appetising a supper in such a place; but Rickards has always something in the larder for an old acquaintance, and I have been travelling this road close upon sixty years, now."

"And a dreary way it is," said Forester, "except for this most agreeable incident. I never came so many miles before with so little to interest me."

"Very true: it is a flat, monotonous-looking country, and poor besides; but nothing like what I remember it as a boy."

"You surely do not mean that the people were ever worse off than they seem now to be?"

"Ay, a hundred times worse off. They may be rack-rented and over-taxed in some instances, now—not as many as you would suppose, after all—but, then, they were held in actual slavery, nearly famished, and all but naked; no roads, no markets; subject to the caprice of the landowners on every occasion in life, and the faction fights—those barbarous vestiges of a rude time—kept up, and encouraged by those who should have set the better example of mutual charity and good feeling. These unhappy practices have not disappeared, but they are far less frequent than formerly; and however the confession may seem to you a sad one, to me there is a pride in saying, Ireland is improving."

"It is hard to conceive a people more miserably off than these," said Forester, with a sigh.

"So they seem to your eyes; but let me remark, that there is a transition state between rude barbarism and civilisation which always appears more miserable than either; habits of life which suggest wants that can rarely, if ever, be supplied; the struggle between poverty and the desire for better, is a bitter conflict, and such is the actual condition of this people. You are young enough to witness the fruits of the reformation; I am too old ever to hope to see them, but I feel assured that the day is coming."

"I like your theory well; it has Hope for its ally," said Forester, as he gazed on the benevolent features of the old squire.

"It has even better, sir, it has Truth; and hence it is that the peasantry, as they approach nearer to the capital—the seat of civilisation—have fewest of those traits that please or attract strangers; they are in the transition state I speak of; while down in *my* wild country, you can see them in their native freshness, reckless and improvident, but light-hearted and happy."

"Where may the country be you speak of, sir?" said Forester.

"The far west, beside the Atlantic; you have heard of Mayo?"

"Oh, that is my destination at this moment; I am going beyond Westport, to visit one of the chieftains there. I have not the honour to know him, but I conclude that his style of living and habits will not be a bad specimen of the gentry customs generally."

"I know that neighbourhood tolerably well. May I ask the name of your future host?"

"The Knight of Gwynne is his title—Mr. Darcy——"

"Oh! an old acquaintance—I may almost say an old friend of mine," said the other, smiling. "And so you are going to pass some time at Gwynne?"

"A week or so; I scarcely think I can spare more."

"They'll call that a very inhospitable visit at Gwynne, sir; the Knight's guests rarely stay less than a month. I have just left it, and there were some there who had been since the beginning of the partridge shooting, and not the least welcome of the party."

"I am sorry I had not the good fortune to meet you there," said Forester.

"Make your visit a fortnight, and I'll join you, then," said the old man, gaily. "I'm going up to town to settle a wager; a foolish excursion, you'll say, at my time of life, but it's too late to mend."

"The horses is put to, sir," said the waiter, announcing the fact for something like the fourth time, without being attended to.

"Well, then, it is time to start. Am I to take it as a pledge that I shall find you at Gwynne this day fortnight?"

"I cannot answer for my host," said Forester, laughing.

"Oh! old Darcy is sure to ask you to stay. By the way, would you permit me to trouble you with five lines to a friend, who is now stopping there?"

"Of course; I shall be but too happy to be of any service to you."

The old gentleman sat down, and, tearing a leaf from a capacious pocket-book, wrote a few hurried lines, which, having folded and sealed, he addressed, "Bagenal Daly, Esquire, Gwynne Abbey."

"There that's my commission; pray add my service to the Knight himself, when you see him."

"Permit me to ask, how shall I designate his friend?"

"Oh! I forgot, you don't know me," said he, laughing. "I have half a mind to leave the identification with your own descriptive powers."

"I'd wager five guineas I could make the portrait a resemblance."

"Done, then, I take the bet," said the other; "and I promise you, on the word of a gentleman, I am known to every visitor in the house."

Each laughed heartily at the drollery of such a wager, and, with many a profession of the pleasure a future meeting would afford to both, they parted, less like casual acquaintances, than as old and intimate friends.

CHAPTER III.

GWYNNE ABBEY.

When Forester parted with his chance companion at Kilbeggan, he pursued his way without meeting a single incident worth recording, nor, although he travelled with all the speed of posters, aided by the persuasive power of additional half-crowns, shall we ask of our reader to accompany him, but, at one bound, cross the whole island, and stand with us on the margin of that glorious sheet of water which, begirt with mountain, and studded with its hundred islands, is known as Clue Bay.

At the southern extremity of the bay rises the great mountain of Croagh Patrick, its summit nearly five thousand feet above the sea; on the side next the ocean, it is bold and precipitous, crag rising above crag in succession, and not even the track of a mountain goat visible on the dangerous surface; landward, however, a gentle slope descends about the lower third of the mountain, and imperceptibly is lost in the rich and swelling landscape beneath. Here, sheltered from the western gales, and favoured by the fertility of the soil, the trees are seen to attain a girth and height rarely met with elsewhere, while they preserve their foliage to a much later period than in other parts of the country.

The ruins of an ancient church, whose very walls are washed by the Atlantic, show that the luxuriant richness of the spot was known in times past. They who founded these goodly edifices were no mean judges of the resources of the land, and the rich woods and blossoming orchards that still shelter their ruined shrines, evidence with what correctness they selected their resting-places.

The coast road which leads from Westport skirts along the edge of the bay, and is diversified by many a pretty cottage, whose trellised walls and rose-covered porches vouch for the mildness of the climate, and are in summer resorted to as bathing-lodges by numbers from the inland counties. The high road has, however, a grander destiny than to such humble, though picturesque dwellings, for it suddenly ceases at the gate of an immense demesne, whose boundary wall may be seen stretching away for miles, and at last is traced high up the mountain side, where it forms the enclosure of a deer park.

Two square and massive towers connected by an arch form the gateway, and though ivy and honeysuckle have covered many an architectural device which once were looked on with pride, a massive armorial escutcheon in yellow stone forms the key of the arch, while two leopards supporting a crown, with the motto "Ne la touchez pas!" proclaim the territory of the Knight of Gwynne.

Within, an avenue wide enough for a high road led through a park of great extent, dotted with trees single or in groups, and bounded by a vast wood, whose waving tops were seen for miles of distance. If a landscape gardener would have deplored with uplifted hands the glorious opportunities of embellishment, which neglect or ignorance had suffered to lie undeveloped within these grounds, a true lover of scenery would have felt delighted at the wild and picturesque beauty around him, as, sometimes, the road would dip into a deep glade, where the overhanging banks were clothed with the dog-rose and the sweet-briar, still and hushed to every sound save the song of the thrush, or the not less sweet ripple of the little stream that murmured past; and again, emerging from the shade, it wound along some height, whence the great mountain might be seen, or, between the dark foliage, the blue surface of the sea, swelling and heaving with ever restless motion. All the elements of great picturesque beauty were here, and in that glorious profusion with which Nature alone diffuses her wealth—the mountain, the forest, and the ocean, the green sward, the pebbly shore, the great rocks, the banks, blue with the violet and the veronica—and all diversified and contrasted to produce effects the most novel and enchanting.

Many a road and many a pathway led through these woods and valleys, some grass-grown, as though disused, others bearing the track of recent wheels; still, as you went, the hares and the rabbits felt no terror, the wood-pigeon sat upon the branch above your head, nor was scared at your approach, for, though the Knight was a passionate lover of sport, it was his fancy to preserve the demesne intact, nor would he suffer a shot to be fired within its precincts. These may seem small and insignificant matters to record, but they added indescribably to the charms of the spot, completing, as they did, the ideas of tranquillity and peace suggested by the scene.

The approach was of some miles in extent, not needlessly prolonged by every device of sweep and winding, but in reality proceeding by its nearest way to the house, which, for the advantage of a view over the sea, was situated on the slope of the mountain. Nor was the building unworthy of its proud position: originally an abbey, its architecture still displayed the elaborate embellishment which characterised the erections of the latter part of the sixteenth century.

A long façade, interrupted at intervals by square towers, formed the front, the roof consisting of a succession of tall and pointed gables, in each of which some good saint stood enshrined in stone; the windows, throughout this long extent, were surmounted by pediments and figures, not rudely chiselled, but with high pretension as works of art, and evidencing both taste and skill in the designer; while the great entrance was a miracle of tracery and carving, the rich architraves retreating one within another to the full depth of twelve feet, such being the thickness of the external wall.

Spacious and imposing as this great mass of building appeared at first sight, it formed but a fragment of the whole, and was in reality but the side of a great quadrangle, the approach to which led through one of the large towers, defended by fosse and drawbridge, while overhead the iron spikes of a massive portcullis might be seen, for the Abbot of Gwynne had been a "puissance" in days long past, and had his servitors in steel, as well as his followers in sackcloth. This road, which was excessively steep and difficult of access, was yet that by which carriages were accustomed to approach the house, for the stables occupied one entire wing of the quadrangle; the servants, of whom there were a goodly company, holding possession of the suite of rooms overhead, once the ancient dormitory of the monks of Gwynne.

In the middle of the court-yard was a large fountain, over which an effigy of St. Francis had formerly stood; but the saint had unhappily been used as a lay figure, whereupon to brush hunting-coats and soiled leathers, and gradually his proportions had suffered grievous injury, till, at last, nothing remained of him save the legs, which were still profaned as a saddle-tree; for grooms and stable-boys are irreverent in their notions, and, probably, deemed it no disgrace for a saint to carry such honourable trappings.

The appearance of the abbey from within was even more picturesque than when seen from the outside, each side of the quadrangle displaying a different era and style of architecture, for they had been built with long intervals of time between them; and one wing, a low two-storied range, with gaol-like windows and a small, narrow portal, bore, on a three-cornered stone, the date 1304.

We shall not ask of our readers to accompany us further in our dry description, nor even cast a glance up at that myriad of strange beasts which, in dark grey stone, are frowning or grinning, or leaping or rearing from every angle and corner of the building, a strange company, whose representatives in real life it would puzzle the zoologist to produce; but there they were, some with a coat of arms between their paws, some supporting an ornamental capital, and others actually, as it seemed, cutting their uncouth capers out of pure idleness.

At the back of the abbey, and terraced on the mountain side, lay a perfect wilderness of flower-gardens and fish-ponds, amid which a taste more profane than that of the founders had erected sundry summer-houses in rock-work, hermitages without hermits, and shrines without worshippers, but all moss-grown, and old enough to make them objects of curiosity, while some afforded glorious points of view over the distant bay and the rich valley where stands the picturesque town of Westport.

The interior of this noble edifice was worthy of its appearance from without. Independent of the ample accommodation for a great household, there was a suite of state apartments running along the entire front and part of one wing, and these were fitted up and furnished with a luxury and costliness that would not have disgraced a royal palace. Here were seen velvet hangings and rich tapestries upon the walls, floors inlaid with tulip and sandal-wood, windows of richly stained glass threw a mysterious and mellow light over richly carved furniture, the triumphs of that art which the Netherlands once boasted; cabinets, curiously inlaid with silver and tortoiseshell, many of them gifts of distinguished donors, few, without their associations of story; while, one chamber, the ancient hall of audience, was hung round with armour and weapons, the trophies of long-buried ancestors, the proud memorials of a noble line; dark suits of Milan mail, or richly inlaid cuirasses of Spanish workmanship, with great two-handed swords and battle-axes, and, stranger still, weapons of Eastern mould and fashion, for more than one of the house had fought against the Turks, and crossed his broadsword with the scimitar.

There were objects rare and curious enough within these walls to stay and linger over, but even if we dared to take such a liberty with our reader, our duty would not permit the dalliance, and it is to a very different part of the building, and one destined for far other uses, that we must now for a brief space conduct him.

In a small chamber of the ground-floor, whose curiously groined roof and richly stained window showed that its occupancy had once been held by those in station above the common, now sat two persons at a well-garnished table, while, before them, on the wide hearth, blazed a cheerful fire of bog deal. On either side of the fireplace was a niche, in which formerly some saintly effigy had stood, but now, such are Time's chances, an earthenware pitcher, with a pewter lid, decorated each, of whose contents the boon companions drank jovially to each other. One of these was a short, fat old fellow of nigh eighty years; his bowed legs, and wide, round shoulders, the still surviving signs of great personal strength in days gone by; his hair, white as snow, was carefully brushed back from his forehead, and tied into a "queue" behind. Old as he was, the features were intelligent and pleasing, the hale and hearty expression of good health and good temper animated them when he spoke, nor were the words the less mellow to an Irish ear, that they smacked of the "sweet south," for Tate Sullivan was a Kerry man, and possessed in full measure the attributes of that pleasant kingdom; he was courteous and obliging, faithful in his affections, and if a bit hasty in temper, the very first to discover and correct it. His failing was the national one, the proneness to conceal a truth, if its disclosure were disagreeable; he could not bring himself to bear bad tidings, and this tendency had so grown with years, that few who knew his weakness could trust any version of a fact from his lips without making due allowance for blarney.

For eight-and-forty years he had been a butler in the Knight's family, and his reverence for his master went on increasing with his years; in his eyes he was the happy concentration of every good quality of humanity, nor could he bring himself to believe that his like would ever come again.

Opposite to him sat one, as unlike him in form and appearance as he was in reality by character; a gaunt, thin, hollow-cheeked man of sixty-six or seven, rueful and sad-looking, with a greenish grey complexion, and a head of short, close grey hair, cut horseshoe fashion over the temples; his long thin nose, pointed chin, and his cold green eye, only wanted the additional test of his accent to pronounce him from the north. So it was, Sandy M'Grane was from Antrim, and a keener specimen of the "cold countrie" need not have been looked for.

His dress was a wide-skirted, deep-cuffed brown coat, profusely studded with large silver buttons richly crested, one sleeve of which, armless and empty, was attached to his breast; a dark crimson waistcoat, edged with silver lace, descending below the hips; black leather breeches, and high black boots—a strange costume, uniting in some respects the attributes of in-door life and the road. On the high back of his oaken chair hung a wide-brimmed felt hat and a black leather belt, from which a short straight sword depended, the invariable companion of his journeys, for Sandy had travelled in strange lands, where protective police were unknown, and his master, Mr. Bagenal Daly, was one who ever preferred his own administration of criminal law, when the occasion required such, to the slower process of impartial justice.

Meagre and fleshless as he looked, he was possessed of great personal strength, and it needed no acute physiognomist to pronounce, from the character of his head and features, that courage had not been omitted among the ingredients of his nature.

A word of explanation may be necessary as to how a western gentleman, as Bagenal Daly was, should have attached to his person for some forty years a native of a distant county, and one all whose habits and sympathies seemed so little in unison with his own part of the country. Short as the story is, we should not feel warranted in obtruding it on our readers, if it did not to a certain extent serve to illustrate the characters of both master and man.

Mr. Daly, when a very young man, chanced to make an excursion to the northern part of the island, the principal object of which was, to see the Giant's Causeway, and the scenery in the neighbourhood. The visit was undertaken with little foresight or precaution, and happened at the very time of the year when severe gales from the north and west prevail, and a heavy sea breaks along that iron-bound coast. Having come so far to see the spot, he was unwilling to be baulked in his object; but still, the guides and boatmen of the neighbourhood refused to venture out, and notwithstanding the most tempting offers, would not risk their lives by an enterprise so full of danger.

Daly's ardour for the expedition seemed to increase as the difficulty to its accomplishment grew greater, and he endeavoured, now, by profuse offers of money, now, by taunting allusions to their want of courage, to stimulate the men to accompany him; when, at last, a tall, hard-featured young fellow stood forward and offered, if Daly himself would pull an oar, to go along with him. Overjoyed at his success, Daly agreed to the proposal, and although a heavy sea was then running, and the coast for miles was covered with fragments of a wreck, the skiff was soon launched, and stood out to sea.

"I'll ga wi' ye to the twa caves and Dunluce, but I'll no engage to ga to Carrig-a-rede," said Sandy, as the sea broke in masses on the bow, and fell in torrents over them.

After about an hour's rowing, during which the boat several times narrowly escaped being swamped, and was already more than half full of water, they arrived off the great cave, and could see the boiling surf, as, sent back with force, it issued beneath the rock, with a music louder than thunder, while, from the great cliffs overhead, the water poured in a thick shower, as each receding wave left a part behind it.

"The cobble" (so is the boat termed there) "is aye drawing in to shore," said Sandy; "I trow we'd better pull back, noo."

"Not till we've seen Carrig-a-rede surely," said Daly, on whom danger acted like the most exciting of all stimulants.

"Ye may go there by yersel," said Sandy, "when ye put me ashore I tauld you, I'd no ga so far."

"Come, come, it's no time to flinch now," said Daly; "turn her head about, and lean down to your oar."

"I'll no do it," said Sandy, "nor will I let you either." And as he spoke, he leaned forward to take the oar from Daly's hand. The young man, irritated at the attempt, rudely repulsed him, and Sandy, whose temper, if not as violent, was at least as determined, grappled with him at once.

"You'll upset the boat—curse the fellow!" said Daly, who now found that he had met his match in point of strength and daring.

"Let go the oar, man," cried Sandy, savagely.

"Never," said Daly, with a violent effort to free his hands.

"Then swim for it, if ye like better," said Sandy; and placing one foot on the gunwale he gave a tremendous push, and the next instant they were both struggling in the sea. For a long time they continued, almost side by side, to buffet the dark water, but at last, Daly began to falter, his efforts became more laboured, and his strength seemed failing; Sandy turned his head and seized him in the very struggle that precedes sinking. They were still far from shore, but the hardy northern never hesitated; he held him by the arm, and after a long and desperate effort succeeded in gaining the land.

"Ye got a bra wetting for your pains, anyhow," said Sandy; "but I'm no the best off either: I'll never see the cobble mair."

Such were the first words Bagenal Daly heard when consciousness returned to him; the rest of the story is soon told. Daly took Sandy into his service, not without all due thought and consideration on the latter's part, for he owned a small fishing-hut, for which he expected and received due compensation, as well as for the cobble and the damage to his habiliments by salt water; all matters, of which, as they were left to his own uncontrolled valuation, he was well satisfied with the arrangement; and thus began a companionship which had lasted to the very moment we have presented him to our readers.

It is but fair to say, that in all this time no one had ever heard from Sandy's lips one syllable of the adventure we have related, nor did he ever, in the remotest degree, allude to it in intercourse with his master. Sandy was little disposed to descant either on the life or the character of his master; the Scotch element of caution was mingled strongly through his nature, and he preferred any other topic of conversation than such as led to domestic events. Whether that he was less on his guard on this evening, or that, esteeming Tate's perceptions at no very high rate, so it is, he talked more freely and unadvisedly than was his wont.

"Ye hae a bra berth o' it here, Maister Sullivan," said he, as he smacked his lips after the smoking compound, whose odour pronounced it mulled port; "I maun say, that a man wha has seen a good deal of life might do far war' than settle down in a snug little nook like this; maybe, ye hae no journeyed far in your time either."

"Indeed, 'tis true for you, Mr. M'Grane, I had not the opportunities you had of seeing the world, and the strange people in foreign parts; they tell me you was in Jericho, and Jerusalem, and Gibraltar."

"Further than that, Maister Sullivan. I hae been in very curious places wi' Mr. Daly; this day nine years we were in the Rocky Mountains, among the Red Indians."

"The Red Indians! blood alive! them was dangerous neighbours."

"Not in our case. My master was a Chief among them, I was the Doctor of the tribe—the 'Great Mystery Man,' they cau'd me; my master's name was the 'Howling Wind.'"

"Sorra doubt, but it was not a bad one—listen to him now;" and Tate lifted his hand to enforce silence, while a cheer loud and sonorous rang out, and floated in rich cadence along the arched corridors of the old abbey; "'tis singing he is," added Tate, lower, while he opened the door to listen.

"That's no a sang, that's the war-cry of the Manhattas," said Sandy, gravely.

"The saints be praised it's no worse!" remarked Tate, with pious horror in every feature. "I thought he was going to raise the divil. And who was the man-haters, Mr. M'Grane?" added he, meekly.

"A vara fine set o' people; a leetle fond o' killing and eating their neighbours, but friendly and ceevil to strangers; I hae a wife amang them mysel."

"A wife! Is she a Christian, then?"

"Nae muckle o' that, but a douce good-humoured lassie for a' that."

"And she's a black?"

"Na, na; she was a rich copper tint, something deeper than my waistcoat here, but she had twa yellow streaks over her forehead, and the tip o' her nose was blue."

"The Mother of Heaven be near us! she was a beauty by all accounts."

"Ay, that she was; the best-looking squaw of the tribe, and rare handy wi' a hatchet."

"Divil fear her," muttered Tate between his teeth. "And what was her name, now?"

"Her name was Orroawaccanaboo, the 'Jumping Wild Cat.'"

"Oh, holy Moses!" exclaimed Tate, unable any longer to subdue his feelings, "I wouldn't be her husband for a mine of goold."

"You are no sae far wrong there, my auld chap," said Sandy, without showing any displeasure at this burst of feeling.

"And Mr. Daly, had he another—of these craytures?" said Tate, who felt scruples in applying the epithet of the Church in such a predicament.

"He had twa," said Sandy, "for by'e, ane in the mountains, that was too auld to come down; puir lone body, she was unco' fond of a child's head and shoulders wi' fish gravy!"

"To ate it! Do you mane for ating, Mr. M'Grane?"

"Ay, just so; butchers' shops is no sae plenty down in them parts.—But what's that! dinna ye hear a ringing o' the bell at the gate there?"

"I hear nothing—I can think of nothing! sorra bit! with the thought of that ould baste in my head, bad luck to her!" exclaimed Tate, ruefully—"a child's head and shoulders!—Sure enough that's the bell, and them that's ringing it knows the way, too." And with these words Tate lighted his lantern and issued forth to the gate tower, the keys of which were each night deposited in his care.

As the massive gates fell back, four splashed and heated horses drew forward a calèche, from which, disengaging himself with speed, Dick Forester descended, and endeavoured, as well as the darkness would permit, to survey the great pile of building around him.

"Coming to stop, yer honour?" said Tate, courteously uncovering his white head.

"Yes. Will you present these letters and this card to your master?"

"I must show you your room, first, that's my orders always. Tim, bring up this luggage to 27. Will yer honour have supper in the hall, or in your own dressing-room?"

There is nothing more decisive as to the general tone of hospitality pervading any house, than the manner of the servants towards strangers, and thus, few and simple as the old butler's words were, they were amply sufficient to satisfy Forester that his reception would be a kindly one, even though less ably accredited than by Lionel Darcy's introduction; and he followed Tate Sullivan with the pleasant consciousness that he was to lay his head beneath a friendly roof.

"Never mind the supper," said he; "a good night's rest is what I stand most in need of. Show me to my room, and to-morrow I'll pay my respects to the Knight."

"This way then, sir," said Tate, entering a large hall, and leading the way up a wide oak staircase, at the top of which was a corridor of immense extent. Turning short at the head of this, Tate opened a small empanelled door, and with a gesture of caution moved forwards. Forester followed, not a little curious to know the meaning of the precaution, and, at the same instant, the loud sounds of merry voices laughing and talking reached him, but from what quarter he could not guess, when, suddenly, his guide drew back a heavy cloth curtain, and he perceived that they were traversing a long gallery, which ran along the entire length of a great room, in the lower part of which a large company was assembled. So sudden and unexpected was the sight, that Forester started with amazement, and stood uncertain whether to advance or retire, while Tate Sullivan, as if enjoying his surprise, leaned his hands on his knees and stared steadily at him.

The scene below was indeed enough to warrant his astonishment. In the great hall, which had once been the refectory of the abbey, a party of about thirty gentlemen were now seated around a table covered with drinking vessels of every shape and material, as the tastes of the guests inclined their potations. Claret, in great glass jugs holding the quantity of two or three ordinary bottles; port, in huge square decanters, both being drunk from the wood, as was the fashion of the day; large china bowls of mulled wine, in which the oranges and limes floated fragrantly; and here and there a great measure made of wood and hooped with silver, called a "mether," contained the native beverage in all its simplicity, and supplied the hard drinker with the liquor he preferred to all—"poteen." The guests were no less various than the good things of which they partook. Old, young, and middle-aged; some, men stamped with the air and seeming of the very highest class; others, as undeniably drawn from the ranks of the mere country squire; a few were dressed in all the accuracy of dinner costume; some wore the well-known livery of Daly's Club, and others were in all the easy negligence of morning dress; while, scattered up and down, could be seen the red coat of a hunter, whose splashed and stained scarlet spoke rather for the daring than the dandyism of its wearer. But, conspicuous above all, was a figure who, on an elevated seat, sat at the head of the table, and presided over the entertainment. He was a tall—a very tall—and powerfully-built man, whose age might have been guessed at anything from five-and-forty to seventy, for though his frame and figure indicated few touches of time, his seared and wrinkled forehead boded advanced life. His head was long and narrow, and had been entirely bald were it not for a single stripe of coal-black hair which grew down the very middle of it, and came to a point on the forehead, looking exactly like the scalp-lock of an Indian warrior. The features were long and melancholy in expression—a character increased by a drooping moustache of black hair, the points of which descended below the chin. His eyes were black as a raven's wing, and glanced with all the brilliancy and quickness of youth, while the incessant motion of his arched eyebrows gave to their expression a character of almost demoniac intelligence. His voice was low and sonorous, and, although unmistakably Irish in accent, occasionally lapsed into traits which might be called foreign, for no one that knew him would have accused him of the vice of affectation. His dress was a claret-coloured coat, edged with narrow silver lace, and a vest of white satin, over which, by a blue ribbon, hung the medal of a foreign order; white satin breeches and silk stockings, wi.. shoes fastened by large diamond buckles, completed a costume which well oecame a figure that had lost nothing of its pretension to shapeliness and symmetry. His hands, though remarkably large and bony, were scrupulously white and cared for, and more than one ring of great value ornamented his huge and massive fingers. Altogether, he was one whom the least critical would have pronounced not of the common herd of humanity, and yet whose character was by no means so easy to guess at from external traits.

Amid all the tumult and confusion of the scene, his influence seemed felt everywhere, and his rich solemn tones could be heard high above the crash and din around. As Forester stood and leaned over the balcony the noise seemed to have reached its utmost. One of the company—a short, square, bull-faced little squire—being interrupted in a song by some of the party, while others—the greater number—equally loud, called on him to proceed. It was one of the slang ditties of the time—a lyric suggested by that topic which furnished matter for pamphlets, and speeches, and songs, dinners, debates, and even duels—the Union.

"Go on, Bodkin—go on, man! You never were in better voice in your life," mingled with, "No, no; why introduce any party topic here?"—with a murmured remark: "It's unfair, too. Hickman O'Reilly is with the Government."

The tumult, which, without being angry, increased every moment, was at last stilled by the voice of the chairman, saying:

"If the song have a moral, Bodkin——"

"It has—I pledge my honour it has, your 'Grandeur,'" said Bodkin.

"Then finish it. Silence there, gentlemen."

And Bodkin resumed his chant.

"Trust me, Squire," the dark man cried,
"I'll follow close and mind you,
No however high the fence you ride,
I'll ever be far behind you."

And true to his word, like a gentleman
He rode, there's no denying,
And though full twenty miles they ran,
He took all his ditches flying.

The night now came, and down they sat,
And the Squire drank while he was able,
But though glass for glass the dark man took,
He left him under the table.

When morning broke, the Squire's brains,
Though racking, were still much clearer
"I know you well," said he to his guest,
"Now, that I see you nearer.

"You've play'd me a d—d scurvy trick:
Come, what have I lost—don't tease me.
Is it my soul?" "Not at all," says Nick,
"Just vote for the Union to please me."

Amid the loud hurras, and the louder laughter that followed this rude chant, Forester hurried on to his room, fully convinced that his mission was not altogether so promising as he anticipated.

Undeniable in every respect as was the accommodation of his bedchamber, Forester lay awake half the night, the singular circumstances in which he found himself occupying his thoughts, while, at intervals, came the swelling sounds of some loud cheers from the party below, whose boisterous gaiety seemed to continue without interruption.

CHAPTER IV.

THE DINNER PARTY.

It was late on the following day when Forester awoke, nor was it for some time that he could satisfy himself how far he had been an actor, or a mere spectator, in the scene he had witnessed the preceding night. The room and the guests were vividly impressed upon his memory, and the excitement of the party, so different in its character from anything he had seen in his own country, convinced him that the sea, narrow as it was, separated two races very unlike in temperament.

What success should he have in this, his first mission? was the question ever rising to his mind; how should he acquit himself among persons to whose habits of life, thought, and expression, he felt himself an utter stranger? Little as he had seen of the party, that little showed him that the Anti-Union feeling was in the ascendant, and that, if a stray convert to the Ministerial doctrines was here and there to be found, he was rather ashamed of his new convictions, than resolute to uphold and defend them. From these thoughts he wandered on to others, about the characters of the party, and principally of the host himself, who in every respect was unlike his anticipations. He opened his friend Lionel's letter, and was surprised to find how filial affection had blinded his judgment—keen enough, when exercised without the trammels of prejudice. "If this," thought he, "be a fair specimen of Lionel's portrait-painting, I must take care to form no high-flown expectations of his mother and sister; and as he calls one somewhat haughty and reserved in manner, and the other a blending of maternal pride with a dash of his father's wilful but happy temperament, I take it for granted that Lady Eleanor is a cold, disagreeable old lady, and her daughter Helen a union of petted vanity and capriciousness, pretty much what my good friend Lionel himself was when he joined us, but what he had the good sense to cease to be very soon after."

Having satisfied himself that he fairly estimated the ladies of the house, he set himself, with all the ingenuity of true speculation, to account for the traits of character he had so good-naturedly conferred on them. "Living in a remote, half-civilised neighbourhood," thought he, "without any intercourse save with some country squires and their wives and daughters, they have learned, naturally enough, to feel their own superiority to those about them, and possessing a place with such claims to respect from association, as well as from its actual condition, they, like all people who have few equals and no superiors, give themselves a license to think and act independent of the world's prescription, and become, consequently, very intolerable to every one unaccustomed to acknowledge their sovereignty. I heartily wish Lionel had left these worthy people to my own unassisted appreciation of them; his flourish of trumpets has sadly spoiled the effect of the scene fo. me;" and with this not over gracious reflection he proceeded to dress for the day.

"The squire has been twice at the door this morning, sir," said Linwood, as he arranged the dressing apparatus on the table; "he would not let me awake you, however, and at last said, 'Present my cordial respects to Mr. Forester, and say, that if he should like to ride with the hounds, he'll find a horse ready for him, and a servant who will show him the way.'"

"And are they out already?" said Forester.

"Yes, sir, gone two hours ago; they breakfasted at eight, and I heard a whipper-in say they'd twelve miles to go to the first cover."

"Why, it appeared to me that they were up all night."

"They broke up at four, sir, and except two gentlemen that are gone over to Westport on business, but to be back for dinner, they're all mounted to-day."

"And what is the dinner hour, Linwood?"

"Six, sir, to the minute."

"And it's now only eleven," said Forester to himself, with a wearied sigh "how am I to get through the rest of the day? Are the ladies in the drawing-room, Linwood?"

"Ladies! no, sir; there are no ladies in the house as I hear of."

"So much the better then," thought his master; "passive endurance is better any day than active boredom, and with all respect for Lady Eleanor and her daughter, I'd rather believe them such as Lionel paints them, than have the less flattering impression nearer acquaintance would as certainly leave behind it."

"The old butler wishes to know if you will breakfast in the library, sir?" asked Linwood.

"Yes, that will do admirably; delighted I am to hear there is such a thing here," muttered he; for already he had suffered the disappointment the host's appearance had caused him to tinge all his thoughts with bitterness, and make him regard his visit as an act of purgatorial endurance.

In a large and well-furnished library, with a projecting window, offering a view over the entire of Clue Bay, Forester found a small breakfast-table laid beside the fireplace. From the aspect of comfort in everything around, to the elegance of the little service of Dresden, with its accompaniment of ancient silver, the most fastidious critic would not have withheld his praise and the young Englishman fell into a puzzled reverie how so much of taste for the refinements of daily life could consort with the strange specimen of society he had witnessed the preceding evening. The book-shelves, too, in all their later acquisitions, exhibited judgment in the works selected, and as Forester ran his eye over the titles, he was more than ever at fault to reconcile such readings with such habits. On the tables lay scattered the latest of those political pamphlets which the great contested question of the day evoked, many of them ably and powerfully written, and abounding in strong sarcasm; of these, the greater number were attacks on the meditated Union; some of them, too, bore pencil-marks and annotations, from which Forester collected that the Knight's party leanings were by no means to the Government side of the question.

"It will be hard, however," thought he, "but some inducement may be found to tempt a man whose house and habits evidence such a taste for enjoyment; he must have ambitions of one kind or other, and if not for himself, his son, at least, must enter into his calculations. Your ascetic or your anchorite may be difficult to treat with, but show me the man with a good cook, a good stable, a good cellar, and the odds are there is a lurking void somewhere in his heart, to discover which is to have the mastery over him for ever." Such were the conclusions the young aide-de-camp came to after long and mature thought, nor were they very unnatural in one whose short experience of life had shown him few, if any, exceptions to his theory. He deemed it possible, besides, that, although the Knight's politics should incline to the side of opposition, there might be no very determined or decided objection to the plans of Government, and that, while proof against the temptations of vulgar bribery, he might be won over by the flatteries and seductions of which a Ministry can always be the dispensers. To open the negotiation with this view was then the great object with Forester, to sound the depth of the prejudices with which he had to deal, to examine their bearings and importance, to avoid even to ruffle the slightest of national susceptibilities, and to make it appear that, while Government could have little doubt of the justice of their own views, they would not permit a possibility of misconstruction to interfere with the certainty of securing the adhesion of one so eminent and influential as the Knight of Gwynne.

The old adage has commemorated the facility of that arithmetic which consists in reckoning "without one's host," and there are few men of warm and generous temperament who have not fallen, some time or other, into the error. Forester was certainly not the exception; and so thoroughly was he imbued with the spirit of his mission, and so completely captivated by the force of his own argument, that he walked up and down the ample apartment, repeating aloud, in broken and disjointed sentences, some of those irrefutable positions and plausible inducements by which he speculated on success. It was already the dusk of the evening, the short hours of a wintry day had hurried to a close, and except where the bright glare of the wood fire was reflected on the polished oaken floor, all was shrouded in shadow within that spacious library. Now pushing aside some great deep-cushioned chair, now removing from his path the projecting end of a table, Forester succeeded in clearing a space in which, as he walked, he occasionally gave vent to such reflections as these:

"The necessities of the Empire, growing power and influence of England, demand a consolidation of her interests and her efforts—this only to be effected by the Act of Union—an English Parliament, the real seat of legislation, and, as such, the suitable position for you, Sir Knight, whose importance will now increase with the sphere in which you exercise your abilities. I do not venture," said he, aloud, and with a voice attuned to its most persuasive accents—"I do not venture to discuss with you a question in which your opportunities and judgment have given you every advantage over me; I would merely direct your attention to those points on which my relative, Lord Castlereagh, founds the hopes of obtaining your support, and those views, by which, in the success of the measure, a more extended field of utility will open before you. If I do not speak more fully on the gratitude which the Ministry will feel for your co-operation, and the pledges they are most ready and willing to advance, it is because I know—that is, I am certain that you—in fact, it is the conviction that—in short——"

"In short, it is because bribery is an ugly theme, sir, and, like a bad picture, only comes out the worse the more varnish you lay on it." These words, uttered in a low, solemn voice from a corner of the apartment, actually stunned Forester, who now stood peering through the gloom to where the indistinct figure of a man was seen seated in the recess of a large chair.

"Excuse me, Captain Forester," said he, rising, and coming forward with his hand out; "but it has so seldom been my fortune to hear any argument in defence of this measure, that I could not bring myself to interrupt you before. Let me, however, perform a more pleasing task, in bidding you welcome to Gwynne Abbey. You slept well, I trust, for I left you in a happy unconsciousness of this world and its cares." It required all Forester's tact to subdue the uncomfortable sensations his surprise excited, and receive the proffered welcome with becoming cordiality. But in this he soon succeeded, not less from his own efforts than from the easy and familiar tone of the speaker. "I have to thank you for a very pleasant note you were kind enough to bring me," continued he, as he seated himself beside the fire. "And how have you left Dublin? Is the popular excitement as great as some weeks ago? or are the people beginning to see that they have nothing to say to a measure which, like venison and turtle, is a luxury only to be discussed by their betters?"

"I should say that there is more of moderation in the tone of all parties of late," said Forester, diffidently, for he felt all the awkwardness of alluding to a topic in which his own game had been so palpably discovered.

"In that case, your friends have gained the victory. Patriotism, as we call it in Ireland, requires to be fed by mob adulation, and when the *canaille* get hoarse, their idols walk over to the Treasury benches.—But there's the bell to dress; and I may as well tell you that we are the models of punctuality in this house, and you have only fifteen minutes for your toilet." With these words the old gentleman arose and strode out of the room, while Forester hastened, on his side, to prepare for the dinner-hour.

When the aide-de-camp had accomplished his dressing, he found the party at table, where a vacant place was reserved for himself at the right hand of the host.

"We gave you three minutes' grace, Captain Forester. I knew a candidate lose his election in the county by very little more"—and here he dropped his voice to a whisper, only audible to Forester—"and I'd rather contract to keep the peace in a menagerie full of tigers than hold in check the passions of twenty hungry fox-hunters while waiting for dinner."

Forester cast his eyes over the table and thought he perceived that his delay had not prepossessed the company in his favour. The glances which met his own round the board bore an expression of very unmistakable dissatisfaction, and, although the conversation was free and unrestrained, he felt all the awkwardness of his position.

There was, at the time we speak of—has it quite disappeared even yet? —a very prevalent notion in most Irish circles, that Englishmen, in general, and English officials, in particular, assumed airs of superiority over the natives of the country, treating them as very subordinate persons in all the relations in which good breeding and social intercourse are concerned; and this impression, whether well or ill founded, induced many to suspect intentional insult in those chance occurrences which arise out of thoughtlessness and want of memory.

If the party now assembled manifested any portion of this feeling, it was not sufficient to interrupt the flow of conversation, which took its course in channels the most various and dissimilar. The individuals were intimate, or, at least, familiar with each other, and through all the topics of hunting, farming, politics, and horse-racing, ran a tone of free and easy raillery, that kept a laugh moving up and down the table, or occasionally occupying it entirely. The little chill which marked Forester's first entrance into the room wore off soon, and ere the dinner was over he had drunk wine with nearly every man of the party, and accepted invitations to hunt, course, and shoot in at least a dozen different quarters. Lionel Darcy's friend, as he was soon known to be, was speedily made the object of every attention and civility among the younger members of the company, while even the older and less susceptible reserved their judgments on one they had at first received with some distrust.

Forester had seen in the capital some specimens of those hard-drinking habits which characterised the period, but was still unprepared for the determined and resolute devotion to the bottle which at once succeeded to the dinner. The claret-jugs coursed round the table with a rapidity that seemed sleight of hand, and few refrained from filling a bumper every time. With all his determination to preserve a cool head and a calm judgment, Forester felt that, what between the noisy tumult of the scene, the fumes of wine, and the still more intoxicating excitement of this exaggerated conviviality, he could listen to tales of miraculous performances in the hunting field, or feats of strength and activity more than mortal, with a degree of belief, or, at least, sufferance, he could scarcely have summoned a few hours earlier.

If wine expands the heart, it has a similar influence on the credulity; and belief, when divested of the trammels of cool judgment, takes a flight which even imagination might envy. It was in a frame of mind reduced to something like this, amid the loud voices of some, the louder laughter of others, strange and absurd bets as eagerly accepted as proffered, that he became suddenly mindful of his own wager made with the stranger at Kilbeggan, and the result of which he had pledged himself to test at the very first opportunity.

No sooner had he mentioned the fact than the interests of the company, directed before into so many different channels, became centred upon the circumstance, and questions and inquiries were rapidly poured in upon him to explain the exact nature of the wager, which in the then hallucination of the party was not an over easy task.

"You are to describe the stranger, Captain Forester, and we are to guess his name, that I take it is the substance of the bet," said a thin-faced, dark-eyed man, with a soft silkiness of accent very unlike the others. This was Mr. Hickman O'Reilly, member for the county, and colleague of "the Knight" himself.

"Yes, that is exactly what I mean. If my portrait be recognised, I've won my bet."

"May I ask another question?" said Mr. O'Reilly; "are we to pronounce only from the evidence before us, or are we at liberty to guess the party, from other circumstances known to ourselves?"

"Of course, from the evidence only," interrupted a red-faced man of about five-and-thirty, with an air and manner which boded no small reliance on his own opinion; then mimicking the solemnity of a judge, he addressed the assembled party thus: "The gentlemen of the jury will dismiss from their minds everything they may hear touching the case outside this court, and base their verdict solely on the testimony they shall now hear." These few words were delivered in a pompous and snuffling tone, and it was easy to see, from the laughter they excited, were an accurate imitation of some one well known to the company.

Mr. Alexander Mac Donough was, however, a tolerably successful mimic, and had practised as an attorney until the death of an uncle enabled him to exercise his abilities in the not less crafty calling of a Squireen gentleman; he was admitted by a kind of special favour into the best county society, for no other reason as it seemed, than that it never occurred to any one to exclude him. He was a capital horseman, never turned from a fence in his life, and a noted shot with the pistol, in which his prowess had been more than once tried on "the ground." Probably, however, these qualities would scarcely have procured him acceptance where he now sat, if it were not that he was looked upon as the necessary accompaniment of Mr. Hickman O'Reilly and his son Beecham, not indeed to illustrate their virtues and display their good gifts, but as a species of moral blister, irritating and maddening them eternally.

They had both more money and ambition than Mac Donough, had taken higher and wider views of life, and were strenuously working up from the slough of a plebeian origin to the high and dry soil of patrician security. To them, Mac Donough was a perfect curse; he was what sailors call "a point of departure," everlastingly reminding them of the spot from which they had sailed, and tauntingly hinting how, with all their canvas spread, they had scarcely gained blue water.

Of the O'Reillys a few words are necessary. Three generations were still living, each depicting most strikingly the gradations by which successful thrift and industry transmute the man of humble position into the influential grade of an estated gentleman; the grandfather was an apothecary of Loughrea; the son, an agent, a money-lender, and an M.P.; and the grandson, an Etonian and a fellow commoner of Baliol, emerging into life with the prospect of a great estate, unencumbered with debt, considerable county influence, and not least of all the *ricochet* of that favour with which the Government regarded his pliant parent.

To all of these, Mac Donough was insupportable, nor was there any visible escape from the insolent familiarity of his manner. Flattery had been tried in vain; all their blandishments could do nothing with one who well knew that his own acceptance into society depended on his powers of annoying; if not performing the part of torturer, he had no share in the piece; a quarrel with him was equally out of the question, for even supposing such an appeal safe—which it was very far from being—it would have reflected most disadvantageously on the O'Reillys to have been mixed up in altercation with a man so much beneath themselves as Alexander Mac Donough of "the Tenement," for such, in slang phrase, did he designate his country residence.

Let us now return from this long but indispensable digression to the subject which suggested it.

So many questions were put, explanations demanded, doubts suggested, and advices thrown out to Forester, that it was not until after a considerable lapse of time he was enabled to commence his description of the unknown traveller, nor even then was he suffered to proceed without interruption, a demand being made by Mac Donough, that the absent individual was entitled to counsel, who should look after his interests, and, if necessary, cross-examine the evidence. All this was done in that style of comic seriousness to which Forester was so little accustomed, that, what with the effect of wine, heat, and noise, combined with the well-assumed gravity of the party, he really forgot the absurdity of the whole affair, and became as eager and attentive as though the event were one of deep importance.

It was at last decided that Mac Donough should act as counsel for the unknown, and the company should vote separately, each writing down on a slip of paper their impression of the individual designated, the result being tested by the majority in favour of any one person.

"Gentlemen of the Jury," said the host, in a voice of deep solemnity, "you will hear and well weigh the evidence before you touching this case, and decide with truth and conscience on its merits; so fill a bumper and let us begin. Make your statement, Captain Forester."

The sudden silence succeeding to the tumultuous uproar, the directed gaze of so many eager faces, and the evident attention with which his statement was awaited, conspired to make Forester nervous and uneasy, nor was it without something of an effort that he began the recital of his adventure at Kilbeggan; warming as he proceeded, he told of the accident by which his acquaintance with the unknown traveller was opened, and at length, having given so much of preliminary, entered upon the description of the individual.

Whatever Forester's own impression of the stranger, he soon felt how very difficult a task portrait-painting was, and how very unlike was his representation of the individual in question. The sure way to fail in any untried career is to suspect a failure; this he soon discovered, and cut short a most imperfect description by abruptly saying, "If you guess him now, gentlemen, I acknowledge the merit is far more in *your* perspicuity than in *my* powers of description."

"Only a few questions before you leave the table, sir," said Mac Donough.

addressing him with the mock sternness of a cross-examining barrister. "You said the unknown was gifted with a most courteous and prepossessing manner, pray what is the exact meaning of your phrase, for we uncouth inhabitants of a remote region have very imperfect notions on such subjects; my friend Dan Mahon here would call any man agreeable who could drink fourteen tumblers, and not forget the whisky in mixing the fifteenth: Tom Callaghan, on the other hand, would test his breeding by what he knew of a wether or a 'short-horn:' Giles, my neighbour here, would ask, did he lend you any money? and Mr. Hickman O'Reilly would whisper a hope, that he came of an old family."

The leer by which these words were accompanied, gave them an impertinence even greater than their simple signification, but however coarse the sarcasm, it suited well the excited tone of the party, who laughed loud and vociferously as he uttered it.

Stranger as he was to the party, Forester saw that the allusion had a personal application, and was very far from relishing a pleasantry whose whole merit was its coarseness; he therefore answered in a tone of rather haughty import, "The person I met, sir, was a gentleman, and the word, so far as I know, has an easy signification, at least to all who have had opportunities to learn it."

"I have no doubt of that, Captain Forester," replied Mac Donough, "but if we divided the house on it here, some of us might differ about the definition. Your neighbour there, Mr. Beecham O'Reilly, thinks his own countrymen very far down in the scale."

"A low fellow—nobody pays attention to him," muttered young O'Reilly in Forester's ear, as with a cheek pale as death he affected to seem totally indifferent to the continued insolence of his tormentor.

"I beg your pardon, Mr. Beecham O'Reilly," interposed Mac Donough, with a significant smile, "but your observation was, I think, meant to apply to me."

The young man made no answer, but proceeded to fill his glass with claret, while his hand trembled so much that he spilled the wine about the table. Forester stared at him, expecting each instant to hear his reply to this appeal, but not a word escaped him, nor did he even look towards the quarter from which the taunt proceeded.

"Didn't I tell you so, sir?" exclaimed Mac Donough, with a triumphant laugh. "There are various descriptions of gentlemen: some are contented with qualities of home growth, and satisfied to act, think, and deport themselves like their neighbours; others travel for this improvement, and bring back habits and customs that seem strange in their own country; now, I don't doubt but in England that young gentleman would be thought all that was spirited and honourable."

"I have nothing to say to that, sir!" replied Forester, sternly; "but you would like to hear the opinion my countrymen would have of yourself, I could perhaps favour you."

"Stop, stop, where are you hurrying to? no more of this nonsense," cried the host, who had suddenly caught the last few words, while conversing with a person on his left.

"I beg your pardon most humbly, sir," said Mac Donough, whose face was flushed with passion, and whose lip trembled, notwithstanding all his efforts to seem calm and collected, "but the gentleman was about to communicate a trait of English society. I know you misunderstood him."

"Perhaps so," said the host; "what was it, Captain Forester? I believe I did not hear you quite accurately."

"A very simple fact, sir," said Forester, coolly, "and one that can scarcely astonish Mr. Mac Donough to hear."

"And which is——?" said Mac Donough, affecting a bland smile.

"Perhaps you'd ask for a definition, if I employ a single word."

"Not this time," said Mac Donough, still smiling in the same way.

"You are right, sir, it would be affectation to do so; for though you may feel very natural doubts about what constitutes a gentleman, you ought to be pretty sure what makes a blackguard."

The words seemed to fall like a shell in the company; one burst of tumultuous uproar broke forth, voices in every tone and accent of eagerness and excitement, when suddenly the host cried out, "Lock the doors; no man leaves the room till this matter is settled; there shall be no quarrelling beneath this roof so long as Bagenal Daly sits here for his friend."

The caution came too late—Mac Donough was gone.

CHAPTER V.

AN AFTER-DINNER STORY.

The unhappy event which so suddenly interrupted the conviviality of the party scarcely made a more than momentary impression. Altercations which ended most seriously were neither rare nor remarkable at the dinner tables of the country gentlemen, and if the present instance caused an unusual interest, it was only because one of the parties was an Englishman.

As for Forester himself, his first burst of anger over, he forgot all in his astonishment that the host was not "the Knight" himself, but only his representative and friend, Bagenal Daly.

"Come, Captain Forester," said he, "I owe you an *amende* for the mystification I have practised upon you. You shall have it. Your travelling acquaintance at Kilbeggan was the 'Knight of Gwynne;' and the few lines he sent through your hands contained an earnest desire that your stay here might be sufficiently prolonged to admit of his meeting you at his return."

"I shall be extremely sorry," said Forester, in a low voice, "if anything that has occurred to-night shall deprive me of that pleasure."

"No, no—nothing of the kind," said Daly, with a significant nod of his head. "Leave that to me." Then, raising his voice, he added: "What do you say to that claret, Conolly?"

"I agree with you," replied a rosy-cheeked old squire in a hunting dress; "it's too old—there's little spirit left in it."

"Quite true, Tom. Wine has its dotage, like the rest of us. All that the best can do is to keep longest; and, after all, we scarcely can complain of the vintage that has a taste of its once flavour at our age. It's a long time since we were schoolfellows."

"It is not an hour less than——"

"Stop, Tom—no more of that. Of all scores to go back upon, that of years past is the saddest."

"By Jove! I don't think so," said the hearty old squire, as he tossed off a bumper. "I never remember riding better than I did to-day. Ask Beecham O'Reilly there which of us was first over the double ditch at the red barn."

"You forget, sir," said the young gentleman referred to, "that I was on an English-bred mare, and she doesn't understand these fences."

"Faith, she wasn't worse off, in that respect, than the man on her back," said old Conolly, with a hearty chuckle. "If to look before you leap be wisdom, you ought to be the shrewdest fellow in the country."

"Beecham, I believe, keeps a good place in Northamptonshire," said his father, half proudly.

"Another argument in favour of the Union, I suppose," whispered a guest in Conolly's ear.

"Well, well" sighed the old squire, "when I was a young man, we'd have thought of bringing over a dromedary from Asia as soon as an English horse to cross the country with."

"Dick French was the only one I ever heard of backing a dromedary," said a fat, old farmer-like man, from the end of the table.

"How was that, Martin?" said Daly, with a look that showed he either knew the story, or anticipated something good.

"And by all accounts, it's the devil to ride," resumed the old fellow; "now, it's the head down and the loins up, and then, a roll to one side, and then to the other, and a twist in the small of your back, as if it were coming in two. Oh, by the good day! Dick gave me as bad as a stitch in the side just telling me about it."

"But where did he get his experience, Martin? I never heard of it before," said Daly.

"He was a fortnight in Egypt, sir," said the old farmer. "He was in a frigate, or a man-of-war of one kind or another, off—the devil a one o' me knows well where it was, but there was a consul there, a son of one o' his father's tenants—indeed, ould French got him the place from the Government—and when he found out that Dick was on board the ship, what does he do but writes him an invitation to pass a week or ten days with him at his house, and that he'd show him some sport. 'We've elegant hunting,' says he; 'not foxes or hares, but a big bird, bigger nor a goose, they call——' By my conscience, I'll forget my own name next, for I heard Dick tell the story at least twenty times."

"Was it an ostrich?" said Tom.

"No; nor an oyster either, Mr. Conolly," said the old fellow, who thought the question was meant to quiz him.

"'Twas an ibis, Martin," cried Daly—"an ibis."

"The devil a doubt of it, that's the name. A crayture with legs as long as Mr. Beecham O'Reilly's, and a way of going—half-flying, half-walking—almost impossible to catch; and they hunt him on dromedaries. Dick liked the notion well, and as he was a favourite on board, he got lave for three days to go on shore and have his fun; though the captain said, at parting, 'It's not many dromedaries you'll see, Dick, for the Pasha has them all up the country at this time.' This was true enough; sorra a bit of a camel or dromedary could be seen for miles round. But however it was, the consul kept his word, and had one for Dick the next morning—a great strapping baste, all covered with trappings of one kind or other; elegant shawls and little hearth-rugs all over him.

"The others were mounted on mules or asses, any way they could, and away they went to look after the goose—the 'ibis,' I mean. Well, to be short with it, they came up with one on the bank of a river, and soon gave chase; he was a fine strong fellow, and well able to run. I wish you heard Dick tell this part of it; never was there such sport in the world, blazing away all together as fast as they could prime and load, at one time at the goose, more times at each other; the mules kicking, the asses braying, and Dick cantering about on his dromedary, upsetting every one near him, and shouting like mad. At last he pinned the goose up in a narrow corner among some old walls, and Dick thought he'd have the brush, but sorra step the dromedary would stir; he spurred and kicked, and beat away with a stick as hard as he could, but it was all no good—it was the carpets, maybe, that saved him—for there he stood fast, just for all the world as if he was made of stone.

"Dick pulled out a pistol and fired a shot in his ear, but all to no use; he minded it no more than before. 'Bad luck to you for a baste,' says Dick, 'what ails you at all—are you going to die on me? Get along now.' 'The divil receave the step I'll go till I get some spirits and wather!' says the dromedary, 'for I'm clean smothered with them b——y blankets,' and with them same words the head of the baste fell off, and Dick saw the consul's own man wiping the perspiration off his face, and blowing like a porpoise. 'How the divil the hind legs bears it I can't think,' says he, 'for I'm nigh dead though I had a taste of fresh air.'

"The murther was out, gentlemen, for ye see the consul couldn't get a raal dromedary, and was obliged to make one out of a Christian and a black fellow he had for a cook, and sure enough in the beginning of the day Dick says he went like a clipper, 'twas doubling after the goose destroyed him."

Whether the true tale had or had not been familiar to most of the company before, it produced the effect Bagenal Daly desired, by at first creating a hearty roar of laughter, and then, as seems the consequence in all cases of miraculous narrative, set several others upon recounting stories of equal credibility. Daly encouraged this new turn of conversation with all the art of one who knew how to lead men's thoughts into a particular channel without exciting suspicion of his intentions, by either abruptness or over zeal: to any ordinary observer, indeed, he would have now appeared a mere enjoyer of the scene, and not the spirit who gave it guidance and direction.

In this way passed the hours long after midnight, when, one by one, the guests retired to their rooms, Forester remaining at the table in compliance with a signal which Daly had made him, until atlength Hickman O'Reilly stood up to go, the last of all, save Daly and the young Guardsman.

Passing round the table, he leaned over Forester's chair, and in a low, cautious whisper, said, "You have put down the greatest bully in this country, Captain Forester; do not spoil your victory by being drawn into a disreputable quarrel! Good night, gentlemen, both," said he, aloud, and with a polite bow left the room.

"What was that he whispered?" said Daly, as the door closed and they were left alone together.

Forester repeated the words.

"Ah, I guessed why he sat so late; he sees the game clearly enough. You, sir, have taken up the glaive that was thrown down for his son's acceptance, and he knows the consequence—clever fellow, that he is. Had you been less prompt, Beecham's poltroonery might have escaped notice; and even now, if you were to decline a meeting——"

"But I have no intention of doing any such thing."

"Of course, I never supposed you had; but were you to be swayed by wrong counsels and do so, Master Beecham would be saved even yet. Well, well, I am sorry, Captain Forester, you should have met such a reception amongst us, and my friend Darcy will be deeply grieved at it. However, we have other occupation now than vain regret, so to bed as fast as you can, and to sleep; the morning is not very far off, and we shall have some one from Mac Donough here by daybreak."

With a cordial shake hands, like men who already knew and felt kindly towards each other, they separated for the night.

While Forester was thus sensible of the manliness and straightforward resolution that marked Bagenal Daly's character, he was very far from feeling satisfied with the position in which he found himself placed. A duel under any circumstances is scarcely an agreeable incident in one's life, but a meeting whose origin is at a drinking-bout, and where the antagonist is a noted fire-eater, and, by that very reputation, discreditable, is still a great aggravation of the evil.

To have embroiled himself in a quarrel of this kind would, he well knew, greatly prejudice him in the estimation of his cold-tempered relative, Lord Castlereagh, who would not readily forgive an indiscretion that should mar his own political views. As he sat in his dressing-room, revolving such unpleasant reflections, there came a gentle tap at the door; he had but time to say, "Come in," when Mr. Hickman O'Reilly entered.

"Will you excuse this intrusion, Captain Forester?" said he, with an accent in which the blandest courtesy was mingled with a well-affected cordiality, "but I really could not lay my head on a pillow in tranquillity until I had seen and spoken to you in confidence. This foolish altercation——"

"Oh, pray don't let that give you a moment's uneasiness! I believe I understand the position the gentleman you allude to occupies in your country society; that licence is accorded him, and freedoms taken with him, not habitually the case in the world at large."

"You are quite right, your views are strictly accurate. Mac Donough is a low fellow of very small fortune, no family—indeed, what pretension he has to associate with the gentry I am unable to guess, nor would you have ever seen him under this roof had 'the Knight' been at home; Mr. Daly, however, who, being an old schoolfellow and friend of Darcy's, does the honours here in his absence, is rather indiscriminate in his hospitalities. You may have remarked around the table some singular-looking guests—in fact, he not only invites the whole hunting field, but half the farmers over whose ground we've ridden, and, were it not that they have sense and shame enough to see their own place with truer eyes, we should have an election mob here every day of the week—but this is not exactly the topic which led to my intruding upon you. I wished, in the first place, to rest assured that you had no intention of noticing the man's impertinence, or of accepting any provocation on his part; in fact, were he admissible to such a privilege, my son Beecham would have at once taken the whole upon himself, it being more properly his quarrel than yours."

Forester, with all his efforts, was unable to repress a slight smile at these words. O'Reilly noticed it, and coloured up, while he added: "Beecham, however, knew the impossibility of such a course—in fact, Captain Forester, I may venture to say, without any danger of being misunderstood by you, that my son has imbibed more correct notions of the world and its habits at *your* side of St. George's Channel than could have fallen to him had his education been merely Irish."

This compliment, if well meant, was scarcely very successful, for Forester bit his lip impatiently, but never made any answer. Whether O'Reilly perceived the cause of this, or that, like a skilful painter, he knew when to take his brush off the canvas, he arose at once, and said, "I leave you, then, with a mind much relieved. I feared that a mistaken estimate of Mac Donough's claims in society, and probably some hot-brained counsels of Mr. Bagenal Daly——"

"You are quite in error there; let me assure you, sir, his view of the matter is exactly my own," interrupted Forester, calmly.

"I am delighted to hear it, and have now only one request—will you favour us with a few days' visit at Mount O'Reilly? I may say, without vanity, that my son is more likely to be a suitable companion to you than the company here may afford; we've some good shooting, and——"

"I must not suffer you to finish the catalogue of temptations," said Forester, smiling courteously; "my hours are numbered already, and I must be back in Dublin within a few days."

"Beecham will be sorely disappointed; in fact, we came back here to-day for no other reason than to meet you at dinner. Daly told us of your arrival. May we hope to see you at another opportunity:—are your engagements formed for Christmas yet?"

"I believe so—Dorsetshire, I think," muttered Forester, with a tone that plainly indicated a desire to cushion the subject at once; and Mr. O'Reilly, with a ready tact, accepted the hint, and wishing him a most cordial good night, departed.

CHAPTER VI.

A MESSAGE.

While Forester slept soundly and without a dream, his long, light breathing scarce audible within the quiet chamber, a glance within the room of Bagenal Daly would have shown that, whatever the consequences of the past night's troubles, he, at least, was not likely to be taken unprepared.

On the table in the middle of the apartment two wax candles burned, two others, as yet unlighted, stood ready on the chimney-piece, a pistol-case lay open, displaying the weapons whose trim and orderly appearance denoted recent care, a fact attested by certain cloths and flannels which lay about; a mould for bullets, and about a dozen newly-cast balls most carefully filed and rubbed smooth with sand-paper, were flanked by a small case of surgical instruments, with an ample supply of lint and ligatures, such as are used to secure bleeding vessels, in the use of which few unprofessional persons could vie with Bagenal Daly. A few sheets of paper lay also there, on which appeared some recent writing; and, in a large, deep arm-chair, ready dressed for the day, sat Daly himself, sound asleep; one arm hung listlessly over the chair, the other was supported in the breast of his waistcoat. The strong, stern features, unrelaxed by repose, had the same impassive expression of cold defiance as when awake, and if his lips muttered, the accents were not less determined and firm than in his moments of self-possession. He awoke from time to time and looked at his watch, and once threw open the sash, and held out his hand to ascertain if it were raining; but these interruptions did not interfere with his rest, for, the minute after, he slept as soundly as before. Nor was he the only one, within that house, who counted the hours thus anxiously. A lantern in the stable beamed brightly, showing three horses ready saddled, the bridles on the neck of each, and ready at a moment's notice to be bitted; while, pacing slowly to and fro, like a sentinel on his post, was the tall figure of Sandy M'Grane, wrapped in a long cloth cloak, and his head covered by a cap, whose shape and material spoke of a far-off land and wild companionship; for it was the skin of a black fox, and the workmanship the product of a squaw's fair fingers.

Sandy's patrole was occasionally extended to the gateway, where he usually halted for a few seconds to listen, and then resumed his path as leisurely as before. At last, he remained somewhat longer at the gate, and bent his head more cautiously to hear; then, noiselessly unbarring and unlocking the door, he leaned out. To an ear less practised than his own the silence would have been complete. Not so with Sandy, whose perceptions had received the last finish of an Indian education. He retired hastily, and approaching that part of the court beneath his master's window, gave a long, low whistle. The next moment the casement was opened, and Daly's head appeared.

"What now, Sandy? It is but a quarter past five."

"It may be so; but there's a horse coming fast up the lower road."

"Listen again, and try if you hear it still."

Sandy did so, and was back in a few moments. "He's crossing the bridge at 'the elms' now, and will be here in less than three minutes more."

"Watch the gate, then—let there be no noise—and come up by the back stairs." With these words Daly closed the sash, and Sandy returned to his post.

Ere many minutes elapsed, the door of Mr. Daly's chamber was opened, and Sandy announced Major Hackett, of Brough. As Bagenal Daly rose to meet him, an expression of more than ordinary sternness was stamped upon his bold features.

"Your servant informed me that I should find you in readiness to receive me, Mr. Bagenal Daly," said the Major, a coarse-looking, carbuncled-faced man of about forty; "but, perhaps, the object of my visit would be better accomplished if I could have a few minutes' conversation with a Captain Forester, who is here."

"If you can show me no sufficient cause to the contrary, sir," replied Daly, proudly, "I shall act for him on this occasion."

"I beg pardon," said Hackett, smiling dubiously. "The business I came upon induced me to suspect that, at your time of life——"

"Go on, sir—finish your speech," said Daly, with a fixed and steady stare, which, very far from reassuring, seemed only to increase the Major's confusion.

"After all, Mr. Daly," resumed he, more hurriedly, "I have nothing whatever to do with that. My duty is to convey a message from Mr. Alexander Mac Donough to a gentleman named Forester, here. If you will accept the proposition, and assist in the necessary arrangements——"

"We are ready, sir—quite ready. One of the consequences of admitting dubious acquaintances to the intimacy of the table is such a case as the present. I was guilty of one fault in this respect, but I shall show you I was not unprepared for what might follow it." And as he spoke he threw open the window, and called out, "Sandy! awaken Captain Forester. I suppose you are ready, Major Hackett, with your friend?"

"Yes, sir. Mr. Mac Donough expects us at Cluan Point."

"And bridle the horses, Sandy," continued Daly, speaking from the window.

"I conclude, from what I see," said Hackett, "that your friend is not only decided against offering an apology for his offence, but desirous of a meeting."

"Who said so, sir?—or what right have you to suppose that any gentleman of good family and good prospects should indulge such an unnatural caprice as to wish to risk character and life in a quarrel with Mr. Alexander Mac Donough?"

"Circumstanced as that gentleman is at this moment, your observations are unsuitable, sir," replied the Major.

"So they are," said Daly, hastily; "or, rather, so they would have been if not provoked by your remark. But, hang me! if I think it signifies much; if it were not that some of our country neighbours were good-natured enough to treat this same Mr. Mac Donough on terms of equality before, I'd have advised Captain Forester not to mind him. *My* maxim is, there are always low fellows enough to shoot one another, and never come trespassing among the manors of their betters."

"I must confess myself unprepared, sir, to hear language like this," said Hackett, sternly.

"Not a whit more than I feel at seeing myself negotiating a meeting with a man turned out of the army with disgrace," said Daly, as his face grew purple with anger. "Were it not that I would not risk a hint of dishonour on this young Englishman's fame, I'd never interchange three words with Major Hackett."

"You shall answer for this, sir, and speedily, too, by G—d!" said Hackett, moving towards the door.

Daly burst into an insolent laugh, and said, "Your friend waits us at Cluan?" The other bowed. "Well, within an hour we'll be there also," continued the old man; and Hackett retired without adding a syllable.

"We've about five miles to ride, Captain Forester," said Daly, as they issued forth beneath the deeply arched gate of the abbey, "but the road is a mountain one, and will not admit of fast riding. A fine old place it is," said he, as, halting his horse, he bestowed a gaze of admiration on the venerable building, now dimly visible in the grey of the breaking dawn. "The pious founders little dreamt of men leaving its portals on such an errand as ours." Then, suddenly, with a changed voice, he added, "Men are the same in every age and country; what our ancestors did in steel breastplates, we do now in broadcloth; the Law, as they call it, must always be subservient to human passions, and the Judge and the Jury come too late, since their function is penalty, and not prevention."

"But surely you do not think the world was better in the times when might was right?" said Forester.

"The system worked better than we suspect," said the old man, gravely, "there was such a thing as public opinion among men in those days, although its exponents were neither pamphlets nor scurrilous newspapers. The unjust and the cruel were held in reprobation, and the good and the charitable had a fame as pure, although their deeds were not trumpeted aloud, or graven on marble. Believe me, sir, we are not by any means so much wiser or better than those who went before us, and even if we were both, we, certainly, are not happier. This eternal warfare, this hand to hand, and foot to foot struggle, for rank, and wealth, and power, that goes on amongst us now, had no existence then, when a man's destiny was carved out for him, and he was all but powerless to alter or control it."

"That alone was no small evil," said Forester, interrupting him; "the humbly born and the lowly were debarred from all the prizes of life, no matter how great their deserts, or how shining their abilities."

"Every rank and class had wherewithal to supply its own requirements," answered Daly, proudly, "and the menial had more time to indulge affection for his master, when removed from the temptation to rival him. That strong bond of attachment has all but disappeared from amongst us." As he spoke, he turned in his saddle and called out, "Can we cross the sands now, or is the tide making, Sandy?"

"It's no just making, yet," said the servant, cautiously, "but when the breakers are so heavy off the point, it's aye safer to keep the road."

"The road be it, then," muttered Daly to himself; "men never are so chary of life as when about to risk it."

The observation, although not intended, reached Forester's ears, and he smiled and said, "Naturally enough, perhaps we ought not to be too exacting with fortune."

Daly turned suddenly round, and after a brief pause, asked, "What skill have you with the pistol?"

"When the mark is a shilling I can hit it, three times out of four, at twenty paces, but I never fired at a man."

"That does make a difference," said Daly, musingly; "nothing short of an arrant coward could look calmly on a fellow-creature while he pointed a loaded pistol at his heart. A brave man will always have self-possession enough to feel the misery of his position. Had the feat been one of vengeance and not of love, Tell had never hit the apple, sir. But there—is not that a fire yonder?"

"Yes, I see a red glare through the mist."

"There's a fire on Cluan Point," said Sandy, riding up to his master's side; "I trow it's a signal."

"Ah! meant to quicken us, perhaps: some fear of being surprised," said Daly, hastily; "let us move on faster." And they spurred their horses to a sharp trot as they descended the gentle slope, which, projecting far out to sea, formed the promontory of Cluan.

It was at this moment the glorious panorama of Clew Bay broke forth before Forester's astonished eyes. He looked with rapture on that spacious sheet of water, which, in all the majesty of the great ocean, came heaving and swelling against the rocky coast, or pouring its flood of foam through the narrow channels between the islands. Of these, the diversity seemed endless, some, rich and verdant, teeming with abundance and dotted with cottages; others, less fertile, were covered with sheep or goats; while some, rugged and barren, frowned gloomily amid the watery waste, and one, far out to sea, a bold and lofty cliff, showed a faint twinkling star upon its side, the light for the homeward-bound ships over the Atlantic.

"That's Clare Island yonder," said Bagenal Daly, as he observed the direction of Forester's gaze; "I must show you the great cliff there. What say you if we go to-morrow?"

"To-morrow!" repeated Forester, smiling faintly; "perhaps so."

CHAPTER VII.

A MOTHER AND DAUGHTER.

WHEN speaking of Gwynne Abbey to our readers, we omitted to mention a very beautiful portion of the structure—a small building which adjoined the chapel, and went, for some reason or other, by the name of the "Sub-Prior's house." More recent in date than the other parts of the abbey, it seemed as if here the architect had expended his skill in showing of how much ornament and decoration the Gothic was capable. The stone selected was of that pinkish hue that is seen in many of the cathedrals in the north of England—a material peculiarly favourable to the labours of the chisel, and, when protected from the rude influence of weather, possessing qualities of great endurance. This building was surrounded on three sides by a flower-garden, which descended by successive terraces to the edge of a small river pursuing its course to the sea, into which it emerged about a mile distant. A very unmindful observer would have been struck at once with the aspect of greater care and cultivation bestowed here than on other portions of the abbey grounds. The trim and orderly appearance of every thing, from the flowering shrubs, that mingled their blossoms with the rich tracery of the architraves, to the bright gravel of the walks, denoted attention, while flowers of rare beauty, and plants of foreign growth, were seen blending their odours with the wild heaths that shed their perfume from the mountain side. The brilliant beauty of the spot was, indeed, heightened by the wild and rugged grandeur of the scene, like a diamond glittering brighter amid the dark dross of the mine.

On the side nearest to the bay, and with a view extending to the far-off Island of Achill, an apartment opened by three large windows, the upper compartments of which exhibited armorial bearings in stained glass. If the view without presented a scene of the most grand and varied loveliness, within this chamber art seemed to have vied in presenting objects the most strange and beautiful. It was furnished in all the gorgeous taste of the time of Louis XV The ceiling, a deep mass of carving relieved by gold, presented masses of fruit and flowers fantastically interwoven, and hanging, as though suspended, above the head. The walls were covered with cabinet pictures of great price, the very frames objects of wonder and admiration. Large vases of Dresden and Sèvres porcelain stood on brackets of massive silver, and one great cabinet of ebony, inlaid with gold and tortoiseshell, displayed an inscription that showed it was a present from the great Louis XIV. himself.

It is not, however, to linger over the objects of rare and costly excellence which here abounded, that we have conducted our reader to this chamber, and whither we would beg of him to accompany us about two hours later than the events we have narrated in our last chapter.

At a breakfast-table, whose equipage was, in price and elegance, in exact keeping with all around, were two ladies. The elder of the two was advanced in life, and although her hair was perfectly white, her regular features and finely pencilled brow bore, even yet, great marks of beauty. If the expression of the face was haughty, it was so without anything of severity; it was a look of pride that denoted rather a conscious sense of position and its duties, than any selfish assumption of personal importance. Habitual delicacy of health contributed to strengthen this expression, lending to it a character which, to an incautious observer, might convey the notion of weariness or *ennui*. The tones of her voice were low and measured, and perfectly devoid of any peculiar accent. If to those more familiar with the cordial familiarity of Irish manner, Lady Eleanor Darcy might seem cold and frigid, such as knew more of the world at large, and were more conversant with the general habits of society, could detect, through all the seeming impassiveness of her air, that desire to please, that anxiety to make a favourable impression, which marked the character of one who, in early life, had been the beauty of her circle. Even now, as she lay back indolently within the deep recess of a cushioned chair, her attitude evinced a gracefulness and an ease which long habit seemed to have identified with her nature.

At the opposite side of the table, and busy in the preparation of the breakfast, stood a young girl whose age could not have been more than eighteen. So striking was the resemblance between them, that the least acute of physiognomists must have pronounced her the daughter. She was dressed with remarkable simplicity, but not all the absence of ornament could detract from the first impression her appearance conveyed, that she was one of birth and station. Her beauty was of that character which, although attributed peculiarly to the Celtic race, seems strangely enough to present its most striking examples among the Anglo-Irish. Rich auburn hair, the colour varying from dark brown to a deep golden hue as the light falls more or less strongly on it, was braided over a brow of classic beauty; her eyes were of blue, that deep colour which, in speaking or in moments of excitement, looks like dark hazel or even black; these were fringed with long dark lashes, which habitually hung heavily over the eyes, giving them a character of sleepy, almost indolent beauty. The rest of her features, in unison with these, were of that Greek mould which our historians attribute to the Phœnician origin of our people—a character by no means rare to be seen to this day among the peasantry. If the mild and gentle indications of womanly delicacy were told in every lineament of her face, there were traits of decision and determination when she spoke not less evident. From her mother she inherited the placid tenderness of English manner, while, from her father, her nature imbibed the joyous animation and buoyant light-heartedness of the Irish character.

"And there are but two letters, mamma," said Helen, "in the bag this morning?"

"But two," said Lady Eleanor; "one of them from Lionel."

"Oh, from Lionel!" cried the young girl, eagerly; "let me see it."

"Read this first," said Lady Eleanor, as she handed across the table a letter bearing a large seal, impressed with an Earl's coronet; "if I mistake not very much, Helen, that's my cousin Lord Netherby's writing, but what eventful circumstance could have caused his affectionate remembrance of me, after something nigh twenty years' silence, is beyond my power of divination."

Helen Darcy well knew that the theme on which her mother now touched was the sorest subject on her mind, and, however anxiously she might, under other circumstances, have pressed for a sight of her brother's letter, she controlled all appearance of the wish, and opened the other without speaking.

"It is dated from Carlton House, mamma, the 2nd——"

"He is in waiting, I suppose," said Lady Eleanor, calmly; and Helen began

"'My dear Cousin——'"

"Ah! so he remembers the relationship at least," muttered the old lady to herself.

"'My dear cousin, it would be a sad abuse of the small space a letter affords, to inquire into the cause of our long silence; faults on both sides might explain much of it; I, was never a brilliant correspondent, you, were always an indolent one; if I wrote stupid letters, you sent me very brief answers; and if you at last grew weary of giving gold for brass, I can scarcely reproach you for stopping the exchange. Still, at the risk of remaining unanswered, once more——'"

"This is intolerable," broke in Lady Eleanor; "he never replied to the letter in which I asked him to be your godfather."

"'Still, at the risk of remaining unanswered, once more, I must throw myself on your mercy. In the selfishness of age—don't forget, my dear coz, I am eleven years your senior—In the selfishness of age——'"

The old lady smiled dubiously at these words, and Helen read on:

"'I desire to draw closer around me those ties of kindred and family, which, however we may affect to think lightly of, all our experiences in life tend to strengthen and support. Yes, my dear Eleanor, we are the only two remaining of all those light-hearted boys and bright-eyed girls that once played upon the terrace at Netherby. Poor Harry, your old sweetheart at Eton, fell at Mysore. Dudley, with ability for anything, would not wait patiently for the crowning honours of his career, took a Judgeship in Madras, and he, too, sleeps in the land of the stranger! And our sweet Catherine! your only rival amongst us, how short-lived was her triumph!—for so the world called her marriage with the Margrave—she died of a broken heart at two-and-twenty! I know not why I have called up these sad memories, except it be in the hope that, as desolation deals heavily around us, we may draw more closely to each other.'"

Lady Eleanor concealed her face with her handkerchief, and Helen, who had gradually dropped her voice as she read, stopped altogether at these words.

"Read on, dear," said the old lady, in a tone whose firmness was slightly shaken.

"'A heart more worldly than yours, my dear Eleanor, would exclaim that the *parti* was unequal—that I, grown old and childless, with few friends left, and no ambitions to strive for, stood in far more need of *your* affectionate regard, than you, blessed with every tie to existence, did of *mine;* and the verdict would be a just one, for, by the law of that Nemesis we all feel more or less, even in this world, *you*, whom we deemed rash and imprudent, have alone amongst us secured the prize of that happiness we each sought by such different paths.'"

A heavy sigh that broke from her mother made Helen cease reading, but at a motion of her hand she resumed: "'For all our sakes, then, my dear cousin, only remember so much of the past as brings back pleasant memories. Make my peace with your kind-hearted husband. If I can forgive *him* all the pangs of jealousy he inflicted on *me*, *he* may well pardon any slight transgressions on *my* part, and Lionel, too—but first, tell me how have I offended my young kinsman? I have twice endeavoured to make his acquaintance, but in vain. Two very cold and chilling answers to my invitations to Netherby, are all I have been able to obtain from him; the first, was a plea of duty which I could easily have arranged; but the second note was too plain to be mistaken—"I'll none of you," was the tone of every line of it. But I will not be so easily repulsed: I am determined to know him, and, more still, determined that he shall know me. If you knew, my dear Eleanor, how proudly my heart beat at hearing his Royal Highness speak of him—he had seen him at Hounslow at a review. It was a slight incident, but I am certain your son never told it, and so I must. Lionel, in passing with his company, forgot to lower the regimental flag before the Prince, on which Lord Maxwell, the Colonel, the most passionate man in England, rode up, and said something in an angry tone. "I beg pardon, Colonel," said the Prince, "if I interfere with the details of duty, but I have remarked that young officer before, and trust me, he'll come off 'with flying colours,' on more occasions than the present." The *mot* was slight, but the flattery was perfect; indeed, there is not another man in the kingdom can compete with his Royal Highness on this ground. Fascination is the only word that can express the charm of his manner. To bring Lionel more particularly under the Prince's notice, has long been a favourite scheme of mine; and, I may say, without arrogance, that my opportunities are not inferior to most men's in this respect; I am an old courtier, now, no small boast for one who still retains his share of favour. If the son have any of his father's gifts, his success with the Prince is certain. The manner of the highly-bred Irish gentleman has been already pronounced by his Royal Highness as the type of what manner should be, and, with your assistance, I have little doubt of seeing Lionel appointed on the staff, here.

"'Now, I must hazard my reputation a little, and ask what is the name of your second boy, and what is he doing?'"

Helen burst into a fit of laughter at these words, nor could Lady Eleanor's chagrin prevent her joining in the emotion.

"This, he shall certainly have an answer to," said the old lady, recovering her self-possession and her pride; "he shall hear that my second boy is called Helen."

"After all, mamma, is it not very kind of him to remember even so much?"

"I remember even more, Ellen," interrupted Lady Eleanor, "and no great kindness in the act either"

"Shall I read all the possible and impossible chances of pushing my fortune in the Army or the Navy, mamma?" said Helen, archly, "for I see that his Lordship is most profuse in offers for my advancement; nay, if I have a clerical vocation, here is a living, actually waiting my acceptance."

"Let us rather look for something that may explain the riddle, my dear," said Lady Eleanor, taking the letter in her own hand, while she lightly skimmed over the last page. "No, I can find no clue to it, here——Stay, what have we in this corner?—'Politically speaking, there is no news, here; indeed, in that respect, *your* side of the Channel engrosses all the interest; the great question of the "Union" still occupies all attention. Virtually, *we* know the Ministry have the majority, but there will be still a very respectable fight, to amuse the world withal. How does the Knight vote? with us, I hope and trust, for although I may tell you, in confidence, the result is certain, his support would be very grateful to the Government, and, while he himself can afford to smile at Ministerial flatteries, Lionel is a young fellow whom rapid promotion would well become, and who would speedily distinguish himself, if the occasion were favourable. At all events, let the Knight not vote *against* the Minister; this, would be a crime never to be forgiven, and personally offensive to his Royal Highness, and I trust Darcy is too good a sportsman to prefer riding the last horse, even, should he not wish to mount the winner.'"

Here, the letter concluded, amid protestations of regard most affectionately worded, and warm wishes for a renewal of intimacy, only to cease with life. Across this was written, with a different ink, and in a hurried hand: "I have this moment seen Mr. Pitt—the Knight's vote is most important. He may make any terms he pleases—Pitt spoke of a Peerage, but I suppose that would not be thought advisable; let me hear *your* opinion. Lionel has been gazetted to a company this morning, *en attendant* better."

Lady Eleanor, who had read these last lines to herself, here, laid down the letter without speaking, while the slight flush of her cheek, and the increased brilliancy of her eyes, showed that her feelings were deeply and powerfully excited.

"Well, mamma, have you found the solution of this mystery?" said Helen, as she gazed with affectionate solicitude on her mother's features.

"How unchangeable a thing is Nature!" muttered Lady Eleanor, unconsciously, aloud; "that boy was a crafty tufthunter, at Eton."

"Of whom are you speaking, mamma?"

"Lord Netherby, my dear, who would seem to have cultivated his natural gift with great success; but," added she, after a pause, and in a voice scarcely above a whisper, "I am scarcely as easy a dupe now, as when he persuaded me to take ash-berries in exchange for cherries. Let us hear what Lionel says."

"As usual, mamma, four lines in each page, and the last, a blank," said

Helen, laughing: "'My dear mother, what blandishments have you been throwing over the War Office? they have just given me my company, which, by the ordinary rules of the service, I had no pretension to hope for, these five years to come! Our Colonel, too, a perfect Tartar, overwhelms me with civilities, and promises me a leave of absence on the first vacancy. Have you seen Forester, of ours? and how do you like him? A little cold or so, at first, but *you* will not dislike that. His riding will please my father. Get him to sing, if you can; his taste and voice are both first-rate. Your worthy relative, Lord Netherby, bores me with invitations to his houses, town and country. I say "No;" but he won't be denied. Was he not rude, or indifferent, or something or other, once upon a time, to the ancient house of Darcy? Give me the *consigne,* I pray you, for I hear he has the best cock shooting in England; and let my virtue, if possible, be rewarded by a little indulgence. Tell Helen they are all giving up powder, here, and wear their hair as she does; but not one of them half as good-looking.

"'Yours, as ever,

"'LIONEL DARCY.

"'Hounslow, January 1st, 1800.'"

"Is that Sullivan, there?" said Lady Eleanor, as her daughter finished the reading of this brief epistle. "What does he mean by staring so at the window? The old man seems to have lost his senses!"

"Ochone arie! ochone! ochone!" cried Tate, wringing his hands with the gestures of violent grief, as he moved up and down before the windows.

"What has happened, Tate?" said Helen, as she threw open the sash to address him.

"Ochone! he's kilt—he's murthered—cut down like a daisy in a May morning. And he, the iligant, fine young man!"

"Whom do you mean? Speak plainly, Sullivan," said the commanding voice of Lady Eleanor. "What is it?"

"'Tis the young officer from England, my Lady, that came down the night before last to see the master. Oh, murther! murther! if his honour was here, the sorra bit of this grief we'd have to-day—ochone!"

"Well, go on," said his mistress, sternly.

"And if he came down for joy, ''tis sorrow he supped for it,' the young crayture! They soon finished him."

"Once for all, sir, speak out plainly, and say what has occurred."

"It's Mr. Bagenal Daly done it all, my Lady—divil a one of me cares who hears me say it. He's a cruel man, ould as he is. He made him fight a duel, the darling young man—the 'moral' of Master Lionel himself; and now he's kilt—ochone! ochone!"

"Can this dreadful story be true, Helen?" said Lady Eleanor, as the faint colour left her features. "Call Margaret; or, stay——Sullivan, is Mr. Daly here?"

"That he is, never fear him. He's looking at his morning's work—he's in the room where they carried the corpse; and the fine corpse it is."

"Go tell Mr. Daly that Lady Eleanor desires to see him at once."

"Go, and lose no time, Tate," said Helen, as, almost fainting with terror, she half pushed the old man on his errand.

The mother and daughter sat silently gazing on each other for several minutes, terror and dismay depicted in the face of each, nor were they conscious of the lapse of time when, the door opening, presented Mr. Bagenal Daly before them. He was dressed in his usual suit of dark brown, and with all his accustomed neatness. His long cravat, which, edged with deep lace, hung negligently over his waistcoat, was spotless in colour and accurate in every fold, while his massive features were devoid of the slightest signs of emotion or excitement.

For an instant Lady Eleanor was deceived by all these evidences of tranquillity, but a glance at old Tate's face, as he stood near the door, assured her that from such signs she had nothing to hope. Twice had Mr. Bagenal Daly performed his courteous salutations, which, in the etiquette of a past time, he made separately to each lady, and still Lady Eleanor had not summoned courage to address him. At last, he said,

"Have I been mistaken—and must I apologise for a visit at an hour so unseemly? But I heard that your Ladyship wished to see me."

"Quite true, Mr. Daly," interrupted Lady Eleanor, her habitual tact supplying a courage her heart was far from feeling. "Will you be seated? Leave the room, Sullivan. My daughter and I," continued she, speaking with increased rapidity, to cover the emotion of the moment, "have just heard something of a dreadful event which is said to have occurred this morning. Old Sullivan so often exaggerates, that we indulge the hope that there may be little or no foundation for the story. Is it true, sir, there has been a duel fought near this?" Her voice grew fainter as she spoke, and at last became a mere whisper.

"Yes, madam," replied Daly, with an air of perfect calmness. "Two gentlemen met this morning at Cluan Point, and both were wounded."

"Neither of them killed?"

"Wounded, madam," reiterated Daly, as if correcting a misconstruction.

"Are the wounds deemed dangerous, sir?"

"Mr. Mac Donough's, madam, is not so. The inconvenience of using his left hand on any similar occasion, in future, will be probably the extent of the mishap. The other gentleman has not been equally fortunate—his life is in peril." Mr. Daly paused for a second, and then, perceiving that Lady Eleanor still awaited a further explanation, added, with gravity,

"When taking his position on the ground, madam, instead of standing half front, as I took pains to point out to him, Captain Forester—— "

"Forester!—is that his name, sir?" interrupted Helen, as, in a hand trembling with terror, she held out Lionel's letter towards her mother.

"A friend of my son's—is he in the same regiment with Lionel?" asked Lady Eleanor, eagerly.

Daly bowed, and answered, "The same, madam."

A low, faint sigh broke from Lady Eleanor, and, covering her eyes with her hand, she sat for some moments without speaking.

"Has any one seen him, sir?" asked Helen, suddenly, and in a voice that showed energy of character had the mastery over every feeling of grief,—"is there a surgeon with him?"

"No, Miss Darcy," said Daly, with a certain haughtiness of manner. "I believe, however, that, although not a professional person, my knowledge of a gun-shot wound is scarcely inferior to most men's. I have sent in two directions for a surgeon; meanwhile, with my servant's aid, I have succeeded in extracting the ball——I beg pardon, ladies, I think I hear the noise of wheels; it is probably the doctor." And, with a deep bow, and a measured step, Mr. Bagenal Daly withdrew, leaving Lady Eleanor and her daughter speechless, between grief and terror.

CHAPTER VIII.

THE "HEAD" OF A FAMILY.

When Bagenal Daly reached the court-yard, he was disappointed at finding that, instead of the surgeon, whose arrival was so anxiously looked for, the visitor was no other than old Dr. Hickman, the father of Hickman O'Reilly, M.P. for the county, and grandfather of that very promising young gentleman slightly presented to our reader in an early chapter.

If the acorn be a very humble origin for the stately oak of the forest, assuredly Peter Hickman, formerly of Loughrea, "Apothecary and Surgeon," was the most unpretending source for the high and mighty house of O'Reilly. More strictly speaking, the process was only a "graft," and it is but justice to him to say, that of this fact no one was more thoroughly convinced than old Peter himself. Industry and thrift had combined to render him tolerably well off in the world, when the death of a brother, who had sought his fortunes in the East—when fortunes were to be found in that region—put him in possession of something above two hundred thousand pounds. Even before this event, he had been known as a shrewd contriver of small speculations, a safe invester of little capital, was conversant, from the habits of his professional life, with the private circumstances of every family of the country, where money was wanting, and where repayment was sure; the very temperament of his patients suggested to him the knowledge by which he guided his operations, and he could bring his skill as a medical man into his service, and study his creditors with the eye of a physiologist. When this great accession of wealth so suddenly occurred, far from communicating his good fortune to his friends and neighbours, he merely gave out that poor Tom had left him "his little savings," "though God knows in that far-away country, if he'd ever see any of it." His guarded caution on the subject, and the steady persistence with which he maintained his former mode of life, gave credence to the story, and the utmost estimate of his wealth would not have gone beyond being a snug old fellow, "that might give up his business any day." This was, however, the very last thing in his thoughts, the title of "Doctor," so courteously bestowed in Ireland on the humbler walks of medicine, was a "letter of marque," enabling him to cruise in latitudes otherwise inaccessible. Any moneyed embarrassment of the country gentry, any severe pressure to be averted by an opportune loan, or the sale of landed property, was speedily made available by him, as a call, to see whether "the cough was easier;" or "how was the gouty ankle;" if the "mistress was getting better of the nerves," "and the children gaining strength by the camomile." And in this way he made one species of gain subservient to another, while his character for kindness and benevolence was the theme of the whole neighbourhood.

For several years long he pursued this course without deviating, and in that space had become the owner of estated property to a very great extent, not only in his own, but in three neighbouring counties. How much longer he might have persisted in growing rich by stealth, it is difficult to say, when accident compelled him to change his *tactique*. A very large property had been twice put up for sale in the county Mayo, under the will of its late owner, the trustees being empowered to make a great reduction in the price to any purchaser of the whole; a condition which, from the great value of the estates, seemed of little avail, no single individual being supposed able to make such a purchase.

At last, and, as a final effort to comply with the wishes of the testator, the estate was offered at ten thousand pounds below the original demand, when a bidder made his appearance, the offer was accepted, and the apothecary of Loughrea became the owner of one of the most flourishing properties of the West, with influence sufficient to return a member for the county.

The murder was now out, and the next act was to build a handsome hou-

unpretentious dwelling-house on a part of the estate, to which he removed with his son, a widower with one child. The ancient family of O'Reilly had been the owners of the property, and the name was still retained to grace the new demesne, which was called Mount O'Reilly, while Tom Hickman became Hickman O'Reilly, under the plea of some relationship to the defunct, a point which gained little credence in the county, and drew from Bagenal Daly the remark, "that he trusted they had a better title to the acres than the arms of the O'Reillys." When old Peter had made this great spring, he would gladly have retired to Loughrea once more, and pursued his old habits, but, like a blackleg who has accidentally discovered his skill at the game, no one would play with him again, and so he was fain to put up with his changed condition, and be "a gentleman," as he called it, in spite of himself.

He it was who, under the pretence of a friendly call to see the "Knight," now drove into the court-yard of Gwynne Abbey. His equipage was a small four-wheeled chair close to the ground, and drawn by a rough mountain pony, which, in size and shape, closely resembled a water-dog. The owner of this unpretending conveyance was a very diminutive, thin old man, with a long, almost transparent nose, the tip of which was of a raspberry red; a stiff queue, formed of his wiry grey hair carefully brushed back, even from the temples, made a graceful curve on his back, or occasionally appeared in front over his left shoulder. His voice was a feeble treble, with a tremulous quiver through all he said, while he usually finished each sentence with a faint effort at a laugh, a kind of acknowledgment to himself that he was content with his opinion, and this, on remarkable occasions, would be followed by the monosyllable "ay," a word which, brief as it was, struck terror into many a heart, intimating, as it did, that old Peter had just satisfied himself that he had made a good bargain, and that the other party was "done."

The most remarkable circumstance of his appearance was his mode of walking, and even here was displayed his wonted ingenuity. A partial paralysis had for some years affected his limbs, and particularly the muscles which raise and flex the legs; to obviate this infirmity, he fastened a cord with a loop to either foot, and by drawing them up alternately he was enabled to move forward, at a slow pace, to be sure, and in a manner it was rather difficult to witness, for the first time, with becoming gravity. This was more remarkable when he endeavoured to get on faster, for then the flexion, a process which required a little time, was either imperfectly performed, or altogether omitted, and consequently he remained stationary, and only hopped from one leg to the other after the fashion of a stage procession. His dress was a rusty black coat with a standing collar, black shorts, and white cotton stockings, over which short black gaiters reached half way up the leg; on the present occasion he also wore a spencer of light grey cloth, as the day was cold and frosty, and his hat was fastened under his chin by a ribbon.

"And so he isn't at home, Tate," said he, as he sat whipping the pony from habit, a process the beast seemed to regard with a contemptuous indifference.

"No, docther," for by this title the old man was always addressed by preference, "the Knight's up in Dublin; he went on Monday last."

"And this is the seventh of the month," muttered the other to himself; "faith, he takes it easy, anyhow! And you don't know when he'll be home?"

"The sorra know I know, docther; 'tis maybe to-night he'd come—maybe to-morrow—maybe it would be three weeks or a month; and it's not but we want him badly this day, if it was God's will he was here!" These words were uttered in a tone that Tate intended should provoke further questioning, for he was most eager to tell of the duel and its consequences, but the "Doctor" never noticed them, but merely muttered a short "Ay."

"How do you do, Hickman?" cried out the deep voice of Bagenal Daly at the same moment. "You didn't chance to see Mulville on the road, did you?"

"How d'ye do, Mister Daly? I hope I see you well. I didn't meet Dr. Mulville this morning—is there anything that's wrong here? Who is it that's ill?"

"A young fellow, a stranger, who has been burning powder with Mr. Mac Donough up at Cluan, and has been hit under the rib here."

"Well, well, what folly it is, and all about nothing, I'll engage."

"So your grandson would tell you," said Daly, sternly; "for if he felt it to be anything, this quarrel should have been his."

"Faix, and I am glad he left it alone," said the other, complacently; "'tis little good comes of the same fighting. I'll be eighty-five if I live to March next, and I never drew sword nor trigger yet against any man."

"One reason for which forbearance is, sir, that you thereby escaped a similar casualty to yourself. A laudable prudence, and likely to become a family virtue."

The old doctor felt all the severity of this taunt against his grandson, but he merely gave one of his half-subdued laughs, and said, in a low voice, "Did you get a note from me about a fortnight ago?—Ay!"

"I received one from your attorney," said Daly, carelessly, "and I threw it into the fire without reading it."

"That was hasty—that was rash, Mr. Daly," resumed the other, calmly; "it was about the bond for the four thousand six hundred——"

"D—n me if I care what was the object of it! I happened to have some weightier things to think of than usury and compound interest, as I indeed have at this moment. By-the-by, if you have not forgotten the old craft come in and see this poor fellow. I'm much mistaken, or his time will be but short."

"Ay, ay, that's a debt there's no escaping!" muttered the old man, combining his vein of moralising with a sly sarcasm at Daly, while he began the complicated series of manœuvres by which he usually effected his descent from the pony-carriage.

In the large library, and on a bed hastily brought down for the purpose, lay Forester, his dress disordered, and his features devoid of all colour. The glazed expression of his eye, and his pallid, half-parted lips, showed that he was suffering from great loss of blood, for, unhappily, Mr. Daly's surgery had not succeeded in arresting this symptom. His breathing was short and irregular, and in the convulsive movement of his fingers might be seen the evidence of acute suffering. At the side of the bed, calm, motionless, and self-possessed, with an air as stern as a soldier on his post, stood Sandy M'Grane; he had been ordered by his master to maintain a perfect silence, and to avoid, if possible, even a reply to Forester's questions, should he speak to him. The failure of the first few efforts on Forester's part to obtain an infraction of this rule, ended in his submitting to his destiny, and supplying by signs the want of speech; in this way, he had just succeeded in procuring a drink of water, when Daly entered, followed by Hickman. As with slow and noiseless steps they came forward, Forester turned his head, and catching a glance of the mechanism by which old Peter regulated his progression, he burst into a fit of uncontrollable laughter.

"Ye mauna do it, ye mauna do it, sir," said Sandy, sternly; "ye are lying in a pool of blood this minute, and it's no a time for a hearty laugh. Ech! ech! sir," continued he, turning towards his master, "if we had that salve the Delawares used to put on their wounds, I wadna say but we'd stap it yet."

By this time old Peter had laid his hand on the sick man's wrist, and with a large watch laid before him on the bed, was counting his pulse aloud.

"It's a hundred and fifty," said he, in a whisper, which, although intended for Daly's ear, was overheard by Forester; "but it's thin as a thread, and looks like inward bleeding."

"What's to be done, then—have you anything to advise?" said Daly, almost savagely.

"Very little," said Hickman, with a malignant grin, "except writing to his friends. I know nothing else to serve him."

A brief shudder passed over Daly's stern features, rather like the momentary sense of cold than proceeding from any mental emotion, and then he said, "I spoke to you as a doctor, sir; and I ask you again, is there no thing can be done for him?"

"Well, well, we might plug up the wound to be sure, and give him a little wine, for he's sinking fast. I've got a case of instruments and some lint in the gig—never go without the tools, Mr. Daly—there's no knowing when one may meet a little accident like this."

"In Heaven's name, then, lose no time!" said Daly, "Whatever you can do, do it at once."

The tone of command in which he spoke seemed to act like a charm on the old doctor, for he turned at once to hobble from the room.

"My servant will bring what you want," said Daly, impatiently.

"No, no," said Peter, shaking his head, "I have them under lock and key in the driving-box; there's no one opens that but myself."

Daly turned away with a muttered execration at the miser's suspicions, and then, fixing his eyes steadily on Sandy's face, he gave a short and significant nod. The servant instinctively looked after the doctor, then, slowly moving across the floor, the nod was repeated, and Sandy, wheeling round, made three strides, and catching the old man round the body with his remaining arm, carried him out of the room with the same indifference to his struggles or his cries as a nurse would bestow on a misbehaving urchin.

When Sandy deposited his burden beside the pony-carriage, old Peter's passion had reached its climax, and assuredly, if the will could have prompted the act, he would have stamped as roundly as he swore.

"It's an awfu' thing," observed Sandy, quaintly, "to see an auld carle, wi' his twa legs in the grave, blaspheming that gate; but come awa', tak your gimcracks, and let's get back again, or, by the saul of my body, I'll pit you in the fountain!"

Reasoning on that excellent principle of analogy, that what had happened might happen again even in a worse form, old Hickman unlocked the box and delivered into Sandy's hands a black leather case, bearing as many signs of long years and service as his own.

"Let me walk! let me walk!" cried he, in a supplicating tone.

"Av you ca' it walking," said Sandy, grimly; "but it's mair, far mair like the step o' a goose than a Christian man."

What success might have attended Peter's request it is difficult to say, for at this moment the noise of a horse was heard galloping up the avenue, and, immediately after, Mulville, the surgeon sent for by Mr. Daly, entered the court-yard. Without deigning a look towards Hickman, or paying even the slightest attention to his urgent demands for the restoration of his pocket-case, Sandy seized Mulville by the arm, and hurried him away to the house.

The newly-arrived doctor was an army surgeon, and proceeded, with all the readiness experience had taught him, to examine Forester's wound; while Sandy, to save time, opened old Hickman's case on the bed, and arranged the instruments.

"Look here, Mr. Daly," said the doctor, as he drew some lint from the antiquated leather pocket,—"look here, and see how our old friend practises the art of medicine." He took up, as he spoke, a roll of paper and held it towards Daly: it was a packet of bill stamps of various value, for old Peter could never suffer himself to be taken short, and was always provided with the ready means of transacting money affairs with his patients.

"Here's my d—d old bond," said Daly, laughing, as he drew forth a much-crumpled and time-discoloured parchment; "I'd venture to say the man would deserve well of his country who would throw this confounded pocket-book, and its whole contents, into that fire."

"Ye maybe want some o' the tools yet," said Sandy, dryly, for taking his master's observations in the light of a command, he was about to commit the case and the paper to the flames.

"Take care! take care!" said Mulville, in a whisper; "it might be a felony."

"It's devilish little Sandy would care what name they would give it," replied Daly; "he'd put the owner on the top of them, and burn all together, on a very brief hint;" then lowering his voice, he added, "what's his chance?"

"The chance of every young fellow of two or three-and-twenty, to live through what would kill any man of my time of life. With good care and quiet, but quiet above all, he may rub through it. We must leave him now."

"You'll remain here," said Daly—"you'll not quit this, I hope?"

"For a day or two at least, I'll not leave him." And with this satisfactory assurance Daly closed the door, leaving Sandy in guard over the patient.

"Here's your case of instruments, Hickman," said Daly, as the old doctor sat motionless in his gig, awaiting their reappearance; for, in his dread of further violence, he had preferred thus patiently to await their return, than venture once more into the company of Sandy M'Grane. "We've robbed you of nothing except some lint; and," added he, in a whisper to Mulville, "I very much doubt if that case were ever opened and closed before with so slight an offence against the laws of property."

Old Hickman by this time had opened the pocket-book, and was busily engaged inspecting its contents.

"Ay, that's the bond!" said Daly, laughing; "you may well think how small the chance of repayment is, when I did not think it worth while burning it."

"It will be paid in good time," said Hickman, in a low cackle, "and the interest too, maybe—ay!" And with sundry admonitions from the whip, and successive chucks of the rein, the old pony threw up his head, shook his tail grossly, and with a step almost as measured as that of his master, moved slowly out of the court-yard.

"So much for our century and our civilisation!" said Daly, as he looked after him; "the old miser that goes there has more power over our country and its gentry than ever a feudal chief wielded in the days of vassalage."

CHAPTER IX.

DALY'S."

It was upon one of the very coldest evenings of the memorably severe January of 1800, that the doors of Daly's Club House were besieged by carriages of every shape and description; some, brilliant in all the lustre of a perfect equipage; others, more plainly denoting the country gentleman, or the professional man; and others again, the chance occupants of the various coach-stands, displayed every variety of that now extinct family, whose members went under the denominations of "whiskeys," "jingles," and "noddies."

A heavy fall of sleet, accompanied with a cutting north wind, did not prevent the assemblage of a considerable crowd, who, by the strange sympathy of gregarious curiosity, were drawn up in front of the building, satisfied to think that something unusual, of what nature they knew not, was going forward within; and content to gaze on the brilliant glare of the lustres as seen through the drawn curtains, and mark the shadowy outlines of figures, as they passed and repassed continually.

Leaving the mob, for it was in reality such, to speculate on the cause of this extraordinary gathering, we shall at once proceed up the ample stair, and enter the great saloon of the Club, which, opening by eight windows upon College-green, formed the conversation room of the members.

Here were now assembled between three and four hundred persons, gathered in groups and knots, and talking with all the eagerness some engrossing topic could suggest. In dress, air, and manner, they seemed to represent sections of every social circle of the capital—some, in full Castle costume, had just escaped from the table of the Viceroy, others, in military uniform, or the dress of the Club, contrasted with coats of country squires, or the even more ungainly quaintness of the lawyers' costume. They were of every age, from the young man emerging into life, to the old frequenter of the Club, who had occupied his own place and chair for half a century.

and in manner and style as various, many preserving the courteous observances of the old school in all its polished urbanity, and the younger part of the company exhibiting the traits of a more independent, but certainly less graceful, politeness. Happily for the social enjoyments of the time, political leanings had not contributed their bitterness to private life, and men of opinions the most opposite, and party connexions most antagonistic, were here met, willing to lay aside for a season the arms of encounter, or to use them with only the sportive pleasantry of a polished wit. If this manly spirit of mutual forbearance did not characterise the very last debates of the Irish Parliament, it may in a great measure be attributed to the nature of that influence by which the measure of the Union was carried, for bribery not only corrupted the venal, but it soured and irritated the men who rejected its seductions; and in this wise a difference was created between the two parties, wider and more irreconcilable than all which political animosity or mere party dislike could effect.

On the present occasion, however, the animating spirit of the assemblage seemed to partake of nothing less than a feature of political acrimony; and amid the chance phrases which met the ear, and the hearty bursts of laughter that every moment broke forth, it was easy to collect that no question of a party nature occupied their attention.

At the end of the room a group of some twenty persons stood or sat around a chair, in which a thin, elderly gentleman was seated, his fine and delicately-marked features far more unequivocally proclaiming rank than even the glittering star he wore on his breast. Without being in reality very old, Lord Drogheda seemed so, for, partly from delicacy of health, and partly, as some affirmed, from an affectation of age (a more frequent thing than is suspected), he had contracted a stoop, and walked with every sign of debility.

"Well, gentlemen, how does time go?" said he, with an easy smile. "Are we not near the hour?"

"Yes; it wants but eleven minutes of ten now, my Lord," said one of the group. "Do you mean to hold him sharp to time?"

"Egad, I should think so," interrupted a red-whiskered squire, in splashed top-boots. "I've ridden in from Kildare to-night to see the match, and I protest against any put-off."

Lord Drogheda turned his eyes towards the speaker with a look in which mildness was so marked, it could not be called reproof, but it evidently confused him, as he added, "Of course, if the gentlemen who have heavy wagers on it are content, I must be also."

"I, for one, say 'sharp time,'" cried out a dapperly-dressed young fellow, with an open pocket-book in his hand; "play or pay is the only rule in these cases."

"I've backed my Lord at eight to ten, in hundreds," said another, "and certainly I'll claim my bet if the 'Knight' is one minute late."

"Then you have just three to decide that question," said one at his side. "My watch is with the Post-office."

"Quite time enough left to order my carriage," said Lord Drogheda, rising with an energy very different from his ordinary indolent habit. "If the Knight of Gwynne' should be accidentally delayed, gentlemen, I, for my part, prefer being also absent. It will then be a matter of some difficulty for the parties betting to say who is the delinquent." He took his hat as he spoke, and was moving through the crowd, when a sudden cheer from without was heard, and then, almost the instant after, a confused sound of acclamation as the "Knight of Gwynne" entered, leaning on the arm of Con Heffernan. Making his way with difficulty through the crowd of welcoming friends and acquaintances, the "Knight" approached the end of the room where Lord Drogheda now awaited him, standing.

"Not late, my Lord, though very near it," said he, extending his hand. "If I should apologise, however, I have an excuse you will not reject—Con Heffernan's Burgundy is hard to part with."

"Very true, Knight," said his Lordship, smiling. "With a friend one sees so seldom, a little dalliance is most pardonable."

This sarcasm was met by a ready laugh, for Heffernan was better known as a guest at other tables than a host at his own; nor did he, at whose expense the jest was made, refrain from joining in the mirth, while he added,

"The Burgundy, like one of your Lordship's *bon mots*, is perhaps appreciated the more highly because of its rarity."

"Very true, Heffernan," replied Lord Drogheda; "we should keep our wit and wine only for our best friends."

"Faith, then," whispered the red-whiskered squire who spoke before, "if the liquor does not gain more by keeping than the wit, I'd recommend Con to drink it off a little faster."

"Or, better still," interposed the Knight, "only give it to those who understand its flavour. But we are, if I mistake not, losing very valuable time. What say you to the small room off the library, or will your Lordship remain here?"

"Here, if equally agreeable to you. We are both of us too old in the harness to care much for being surrounded by spectators."

"Is it true, Con," said a friend in Heffernan's ear, "that Darcy has laid fifty thousand on this party?"

"I believe you are rather under than over the mark," whispered Heffernan. "The wager has been off and on these last eight or ten years. It was made at Hutchinson's one evening, when we all had drunk a good deal of wine. At first, whist was talked of, but Drogheda objected to Darcy's naming Vicars as his partner."

"More fool he. Vicars is a first-rate player, but confoundedly unlucky."

"Be that as it may, they fixed on piquet as the game, and, if accounts be true, all the better for Darcy. They say he has beaten the best players in France."

"And what is really the stake? One hears so many absurd versions of it."

"The Bally-dermot property."

"The whole of it?"

"Every acre, with the demesne, house, plate, pictures, carriages, wine—begad! I'm not sure if the livery servants are not included—against fifty thousand pounds. You know Drogheda has lent him a very large sum on a mortgage of that property already, and this will make the thing about double or quits."

"Well, Heffernan," cried the Knight, "are you making your book there? When you've quite finished, let me have a pinch of that excellent snuff of ours."

"Why not try mine?" said Lord Drogheda, pushing a magnificently jewelled box, containing a miniature, across the table.

"'Twould be a bad augury, my Lord," said Darcy, laughing. "If I remember aright, you won this handsome box from the Duke de Richelieu."

"Ah! you know that story, then."

"I was present at the time, and remember the circumstance perfectly. The King was leaning over the Duke's chair, watching the game——"

"Quite true. The Duke affected not to know that his Majesty was there, and when he placed the box on the table, cried, 'A thousand louis against the portrait of the King!' There was no declining such a wager at such a moment, although, intrinsically, the box was not worth half the sum. I accepted, and won it."

"And the Duke then offered to give you twice the money for it back again?"

"He did so, and I refused. I shall not readily forget the sweet, sad smile of the King as he tapped the wily courtier on the shoulder, and said, 'Ah! Monsieur le Duc, do you only value your King when you've lost him?' They were prophetic words! Well, well! we've got upon a sorrowful theme; let's change it."

"Here are the cards, at last," said the Knight, taking a sealed packet from the waiter's hand, and breaking it open on the table. "Now, Heffernan, order me a glass of claret negus, and take care that no one comes to worry us with news of the House."

"It's a Sugar Bill, or a new clause in the Corporation Act, or something of that kind, they're working at," said Lord Drogheda, negligently.

"No, my Lord," interposed Heffernan, slyly; "it's a bill to permit your Lordship's nephew to hold the living of Ardragh with his deanery."

"All right and proper," said his Lordship, endeavouring to hide a rising flush on his cheek by an opportune laugh. "Tom is a capital fellow, and a good parson, too."

"And ought never to omit the prayer for the Parliament!" muttered Heffernan, loud enough to be heard by the bystanders, who relished the allusion heartily.

"The deal is with you, Knight," said Lord Drogheda, pushing the cards across the table.

The moment afterwards, a pin could not have fallen unheard in that crowded assembly. Even they who were not themselves bettors, felt the deepest interest in a game where the stake was so great, and all who could set value on skill and address were curious to watch the progress of the contest. Not a word was spoken on either side as the cards fell upon the table, and although many of the bystanders displayed looks of more eager anxiety, the players showed by their intentness how strenuously each struggled for the victory.

After the lapse of about half an hour, a low, murmuring noise spread through the room, and the news was circulated that the first game was over, and the Knight the winner. The players, however, were silent as before, and the deal went over without a word.

"One moment, my Lord," said Darcy, as he gently interposed his hand to prevent Lord Drogheda taking up his cards—"a single moment. You will call me faint-hearted for it, but I do not care. I beseech you let the party cease here. It is a great favour; but, as I could not ask it if I had lost the game, give me, I pray, so much of advantage for my good luck."

"You forget, Knight, that I, as a loser, could not accede to your proposal; what would be said of any man who, with such a stake at issue, accepted an offer like this?"

"My dear Lord, don't you think that you and I might afford to have our actions canvassed, and yet be very little afraid of the criticism?" said Darcy, proudly.

"No, no, my dear Darcy, I really could not do this; besides, you mus concede something to mortified vanity. Now, I am anxious to have my revenge."

"Be it so, my Lord," said the Knight, with a sigh, and the game began.

The looks and glances which were interchanged by those about during this brief colloquy showed how little sympathy there was felt with the generosity of either side. The bettors had set their hearts on gain, and cared little for the feelings of the players.

"You see he was right," whispered the red-whiskered squire to his neighbour; "my Lord has won the game in one hand." And so it was; in less than five minutes the party was over.

"Now for the conqueror," cried the Knight of Gwynne, who, somewhat nettled at a success which seemed to lessen the generous character of his own proposal, dealt the cards hastily, and as if anxious to conclude.

"Now, Darcy, we have a better opportunity," said Lord Drogheda, smiling; "what say you to draw stakes as we stand?"

"Willingly, most willingly, my Lord. If a bad cause saps courage, I have reason to be low in heart. This foolish wager has cost me the loss of three nights' sleep, and if you are content——"

"But are these gentlemen here satisfied?" said Lord Drogheda; and an almost universal cry of "No" was the reply.

"Then if we are to play for the bystanders, my Lord, let us not delay them," said the Knight, as he took up his cards and began to arrange them.

"Darcy has it, by Jove!—the game is his," was muttered from one to another in the crowd behind his chair; and the report, gaining currency, was soon circulated in the larger room without.

"Have you anything heavy on it, Con?" said a fashionably-dressed man to Heffernan, who endeavoured to force his way through the crowd to where the Knight sat.

"Look at Heffernan," said another; "they say he never oets, but mark the excitement of his face, now."

"What is it, Heffernan?" said the Knight, as the other leaned over his chair and tried to whisper something in his ear. "Is that a queen, my Lord? In that case I believe the game is mine——What is it, Heffernan?" and he bent his ear to listen; then suddenly dashing the cards upon the table, cried out, "Great Heaven! is this true?—the young fellow I met at Kilbeggan?"

"The same," whispered Heffernan, rapidly; "a brother officer of your son Lionel's—a cousin of Lord Castlereagh's—a fine, dashing fellow, too."

"Where is he wounded?" asked Darcy, eagerly.

"Finish your game—I must tell you all about it," said Heffernan, folding up a letter which he had taken from his pocket a few minutes before.

"Your pardon, my Lord," said Darcy, with a look full of agitation; "I have just heard very bad news—I play the knave." A murmur ran through the crowd behind him.

"You meant the king, I know, Knight," said Lord Drogheda, restoring the card to his hand as he spoke, but a loud expression of dissatisfaction arose from those at his side.

"You are right, my Lord, I did intend the king," said the Knight; "but these gentlemen insist upon the knave, and, if you'll permit me, I'll play it."

The whole fortune of the game hung upon the card, and after a brief struggle the Knight was beaten.

"Even so, my Lord," said the Knight, smiling calmly, "you have beaten me against luck; fortune will not do everything The Roman satirist goes even further, and says she can do nothing." He rose as he said these words and looked around for Heffernan.

"If you want Con Heffernan, Knight," said one of the party, "I think he has gone down to the House."

"The very man," said Darcy; "good night, my Lord,—good night, gentlemen all."

"I did not believe anything could shake Darcy's nerve, but he certainly played that game ill," said a bystander.

"Heffernan could tell us more about it," said another; "rely on it, Master Con and the devil knew why that knave was played."

CHAPTER X.

AN INTRIGUE DETECTED.

Of all the evil influences which swayed the destinies of Ireland in latter days, none can compare, in extent or importance, with the fatal taste for prodigality that characterised the habits of the gentry. Reckless, wasteful extravagance, in every detail of life, suggested modes of acting and thinking at variance with all individual, and, consequently, all national prosperity. Hospitality was pushed to profusion, liberality became a spendthrift habit. The good and the bad qualities of the Irish temperament alike contributed to this passion; there was the wish to please, the desire to receive courteously, and entertain with splendour within doors, and to appear with proportionate magnificence without.

A proud sense of what they deemed befitting their station, induced the gentry to vie in expenditure with the richly-endowed officials of the Government, and the very thought of prudence or foresight in matters of expense, would have been stigmatised as a meanness by those who believed they were sustaining the honour of their country, while sapping the foundation of its prosperity.

If we have little to plead in defence, or in palliation of such habits, we can at least affirm, that, in many cases, they were practised with a taste and elegance that shed lustre over the period. Unlike the vulgar displays of newly-acquired wealth, they exhibited, in a striking light, the generous and high-spirited features of the native character, which deemed that nothing could be too good for the guest, nor any expenditure for his entertainment either too costly or too difficult. The fatal facility of Irish nature, and the still more ruinous influence of example, hurried men along on this road to ruin, and as political prospects grew darker, a reckless indifference to the future succeeded, in which little care was taken for the morrow, until, at last, thoughtless extravagance became a habit, and moneyed difficulties the lot of almost every family of Ireland.

That a gentry so embarrassed, and with such prospects of ruin before them, should have been easy victims to Ministerial seduction, is far less surprising than that so many were to be seen who could prefer their integrity to the rich bribes of Government patronage; and it is a redeeming feature of the day, that, amid all the lavish and heedless course of prodigality and excess, there were some who could face poverty with stouter hearts than they could endure the stigma of gilded corruption: nor is it the history of every Parliament that can say as much.

Let us leave this theme, even at the hazard of being misunderstood, for the moment, by our reader, and turn to the Knight of Gwynne, who now was seated at his breakfast in a large parlour of his house in Henrietta-street. Sad and deserted as it seems now, this was, in those days, the choice residence of Irish aristocracy, and the names of Peers and Baronets on every door told of a class which, now, should be sought for in scattered fragments among the distant cities of the Continent.

The Knight was reading the morning papers, in which, amid the fashionable news, was an account of his own wager with Lord Drogheda, when a carriage drove up hastily to the door, and immediately after, the loud summons of a footman resounded through the street.

While the Knight was yet wondering who his early visitor should prove, the servant announced Mr. Con Heffernan.

"The very man I wished to see," cried Darcy, eagerly; "tell me all about this unfortunate business. But, first of all, is he out of danger?"

"Quite safe. I understand, for a time, it was a very doubtful thing; Daly's surgery, it would seem, rather increased the hazard. He began searching for the ball regardless of the bleeding, and the young fellow was very near sinking under loss of blood."

"The whole affair was his doing!" said the Knight, impatiently. "How Mr. Mac Donough could have found himself at *my* table is more than I can well imagine; that, when he got there, something like this would follow, does not surprise me. Daly is really too bad. Well, well, I hoped to have set off for the abbey to-day, but I must stay here, I find; Drogheda is kind enough to let me redeem Bally-dermot, and I must see Gleeson about it. It's rather a heavy blow just now."

"I am afraid I am not altogether blameless," said Heffernan, timidly. "I ought not to have mentioned that unlucky business till the game was over, but I thought your nerve was proof against anything."

"So it was, Heffernan," said the Knight, laughing, "some five-and-twenty years ago; but this shattered wreck has little remains of the old three decker. I should have won that game."

"It's all past and over now, so never think more about it."

"Yes, I should have won the game. Drogheda saw my advantage: he went on with the very suit in my hand, and when he reached over for his snuff-box, his hand trembled like in an ague-fit."

"Come, don't let the thing dwell in your mind. There is another and heavier game to play, and you're certain to win there, if you do but like it."

"I don't clearly understand you," said Darcy, doubtingly.

"I'll be explicit enough, then," said Heffernan, taking a chair and seating himself directly in front of the Knight. "You know the position of the Government at this moment. They have secured a safe and certain majority —the 'Union' is carried. When I say carried, I mean that there is not a doubt on any reasonable mind but that the Bill will pass. The lists show a majority of seven, perhaps eight, for the Ministry; and if they had but one in their favour, Pitt is determined to go through with it. Now, we all very well know how this has been done. Our people have behaved infamously, disgracefully—there's no mincing the matter. You heard of Fox——?"

"No. What of him?"

"He has just accepted the escheatorship of—I forget what or where, but he vacates his seat to make room for Courtenay."

"Sam Courtenay?—Scrub, as we used to call him?"

"Scrub,—exactly so. Well, he comes in for Roscommon, and is to have a place under the new commission of twelve hundred a year. But to go back to what I was saying, Castlereagh has bought these fellows at his price or their own; some were dear enough, some were cheap. Barton, for instance, takes it out in Castle dinners, and has sold his birthright for the Viceroy's venison."

"May good digestion wait on appetite," repeated Darcy, laughing.

"Well, let's not waste more time on them, but come to what I mean. Castlereagh wants to know how you mean to vote; some have told him you would be on his side; others, myself among the number, say the reverse. In fact, little as you may think about the matter, heavy bets are laid at this moment on the question, and——But I won't mention names; enough if I say a friend of ours—an old friend, too—has a thousand on it."

The Knight tapped his snuff-box calmly, and with his blandest smile begged Heffernan to proceed.

"Faith! I've nearly told all I had to say. Every one well knows that, whatever decision you come to, it will be unbiassed by everything save your own conscientious sense of right; and, as arguments are pretty nearly equal on the question—for in truth, after having heard and read most of what has been spoken or written on the point—I'm regularly nonplused on which side to see the advantage. The real question seems to be, can we go on as we are?"

"I think not," observed the Knight, gravely. "A Parliament which has exhibited its venality so openly, can have little pretension to public confidence."

"The very remark I made myself," cried Heffernan, triumphantly.

"The men who sell themselves to-day to the Crown, will, if need be, sell themselves to-morrow to the Mob."

"My own words, by Jové!—my very words."

"A dependent Parliament, attempting separate and independent legislate, means an absurdity."

"There is no other name for it," cried Heffernan, in ecstasy.

"I have known Ireland for something more than half a century now," said the Knight, with a touch of melancholy in his voice, "and yet never before saw so much of social disorder as at present, and perhaps we are only at the beginning of it. The scenes we have witnessed in France have been more bloody and more cruel, but they will leave less permanent results behind them than our own revolution, for such after all it is. The property of the country is changing hands, the old aristocracy are dying out, if not dead; their new successors have neither any hold on the affection of the people, nor a bond of union with each other. See what will come of it. the old game of feudalism will be tried by these men of yesterday, and the peasantry, whose reverence for birth is a religion, will turn on them, and the time is not very distant, perhaps, when the men who would not harm the landlord's dog, will have little reverence for the landlord's self."

"You have drawn a sad picture," said Heffernan, either feeling or affecting to feel the truthfulness of the Knight's delineation.

"Our share in the ruin," said the Knight, rising, and pacing the room with rapid strides—"our share is not undeserved. We had a distinct and defined duty to perform, and we neglected it; instead of extending civilisation, we were the messengers of barbarism among the people."

"Your own estates, I have heard, are a refutation of your theory," interposed Heffernan, insinuatingly.

"My estates——" repeated the Knight, and then stopping suddenly, with a changed voice he said: "Heffernan, we have got into a long and very unprofitable theme; let us try back, if we can, and see whence we started: some were talking of the Union."

"Just so," said Heffernan, not sorry to resume the subject which induced his visit.

"I have determined not to vote on the measure," said the Knight, solemnly; "my reasons for the course I adopt I hope to be able to justify when the proper time arrives; meanwhile it will prevent unnecessary speculation, and equally unnecessary solicitation, if I tell you frankly what I mean to do. Such is my present resolve."

The word solicitation fell from the Knight's lips with such a peculiar expression, that Heffernan at once saw his own game was detected, and, like a clever tactician, resolved to make the best of his forced position.

"You have been frank with *me*, Knight, I'll not be less candid with *you*. I came here to convey to you a distinct offer from the Government—not of any personal favour or advantage, *that*, they well knew, you would reject—but, in the event of your support, to take any suggestion you might make on the new Bill into their serious and favourable consideration; to advise with you, how, in short, the measure might be made to meet your views, and, so to say, admit you into conclave with the Cabinet."

"All this is very flattering," said the Knight, with a smile of evident satisfaction, "but I scarcely see how the opinions of a very humble country gentleman can weigh in the grave councils of a Government."

"The best proof is the fact itself," replied Heffernan, artfully. "Were I to tell you of other reasons, you might suspect me of an intention to canvass your support on very different grounds."

"I confess I'm in the dark—explain yourself more fully."

"This is a day for sincerity," said Heffernan, smiling, "and so, here it is—the Prince has taken a special liking to your son Lionel, and has given him his company."

"His company! I never heard of it."

"Strange enough that he should not have written to you on the subject, but the fact is unquestionable—and, as I was saying, he is a frequent guest at Carlton House, and admitted into the choice circle of his Royal Highness's parties: if, in the freedom of that intimacy with which he is honoured by the Prince, the question should have arisen, how his father meant to vote, the fact was not surprising, no more than that Captain Darcy should have replied——"

"Lionel never pledged himself to control *my* vote, depend upon that, Mr. Heffernan," said the Knight, reddening.

"Nor did I say so," interposed Heffernan. "Hear me out—your son is reported to have answered, 'My father's family have been too trained in loyalty, sire, not to give their voice with what they believe the best interests of the Empire: your Royal Highness may doubt his judgment, his honour will, I am certain, never be called in question.' The Prince laughed good-naturedly, and said, 'Enough, Darcy—quite enough; it will give me great satisfaction to think as highly of the father as I do of the son; there is a vacancy on the Staff, and I can offer you the post of an extra aide-de-camp.'"

"This is very good news—the best I've heard for many a day, Heffernan, and for its accuracy——"

"Lord Castlereagh is the guarantee," added Heffernan, hastily; "I had it from his own lips."

"I'll wait on him this morning. I can at least express my gratitude for his Royal Highness's kindness to my boy."

"You'll not have far to go," said Heffernan, smiling.

"How so?—what do you mean?"

"Lord Castlereagh is at the door this moment in that carriage;" and Heffernan pointed to the chariot which, with its blinds closely drawn, stood before the street door.

The Knight moved hastily towards the door, and then, turning suddenly, burst into a hearty laugh—a laugh so racy and full of enjoyment, that Heffernan himself joined in it, without knowing wherefore.

"You are a clever fellow, Heffernan!" said the Knight, as he lay back in a deep-cushioned chair, and wiped his eyes, now streaming with tears of laughter—"a devilish clever fellow! The whole affair reminds me of poor Jack Morris."

"Faith! I don't see your meaning," said Heffernan, half fearful that all was not right.

"You knew Jack—we all knew him. Well, poor Morris was going home one night—from the theatre, I believe it was—but, just as he reached Ely place, he saw, by the light of a lamp, a gentlemanlike fellow trying to make out an address on a letter, and endeavouring, as well as he could, to spell out the words by the uncertain light. 'Devilish provoking!' said the stranger, half aloud; 'I wrote it myself, and yet cannot read a word of it.' 'Can I be of any service?' said Jack. Poor fellow! he was always ready for anything kind or good-natured. 'Thank you,' said the other; 'but I'm a stranger in Dublin—only arrived this evening from Liverpool—and cannot remember the name, or the street of my hotel, although I noted both down on this letter.' 'Show it to me,' said Jack, taking the document. But, although he held it every way, and tried all manner of guesses, he never could hit on the name the stranger wanted. 'Never mind,' said Jack; 'don't bother yourself about it. Come home with me and have an oyster—I'll give you a bed; 'twill be time enough after breakfast to-morrow to hunt out the hotel.' To make short of it, the stranger complied; after all the natural expressions of gratitude and shame, home they went, supped, finished two bottles of claret, and chatted away till past two o'clock. 'You'd like to get to bed, I see,' said Jack, as the stranger seemed growing somewhat drowsy, and so he rang the bell, and ordered the servant to show the gentleman to his room. 'And, Martin,' said he, 'take care that everything is comfortable, and be sure you have a nightcap.' 'Oh! I've a nightcap myself,' said the stranger, pulling one, neatly folded, out of his coat pocket. 'Have you, by G—d!' said Jack. 'If you have, then, you'll not sleep here. A man that's so ready for a contingency has generally some hand in contriving it.' And so he put him out of doors, and never saw more of him—eh, Heffernan—was Jack right?" And again the old man broke into a hearty laugh, in which Heffernan, notwithstanding his discomfiture, could not refrain from participating.

"Well," said he, as he arose to leave the room, "I feel twenty years younger for that hearty laugh. It reminds me of the jolly days we used to have long ago, with Price Godfrey and Bagenal Daly. By the way, where is Bagenal now, and what is he doing?"

"Pretty much what he always was doing—mischief and devilment," said the Knight, half angrily.

"Is he still the member for Old-Castle? I forget what fate the petition had."

"The fate of the counsel that undertook it is easily remembered," said the Knight. "Bagenal called him out for daring to take such a liberty with a man who had represented the borough for thirty years, and shot him in the hip. 'You shall have a plumper, by Jove!' said Bagenal; and he gave him one. Men grew shy of the case afterwards, and it was dropped, and so Bagenal still represents the place. Good-by, Heffernan—don't forget Jack Morris." And so saying, the Knight took leave of his visitor, and returned to his chair at the breakfast-table.

CHAPTER XI.

THE KNIGHT AND HIS AGENT.

The news of Lionel's promotion, and the flattering notice which the Prince had taken of him, made the Knight very indifferent about his heavy loss of the preceding evening. It was, to be sure, an immense sum; but as Gleeson was arranging his affairs, it was only "raising" so much more, and thus preventing the estate from leaving the family. Such was his own very mode of settling the matter in his own mind, nor did he bestow more time on the consideration than enabled him to arrive at this satisfactory conclusion.

If ever there was an Agent designed to compensate for the easy, careless habits of such a principal, it was Mr. Gleeson—or, as he was universally known in the world of that day, "Honest Tom Gleeson." In him seemed concentrated all those peculiar gifts which made up the perfect man of business. He was cautious, painstaking, and methodical, of a temper which nothing could ruffle, and with a patience no provocation could exhaust; punctual as a clock, neither precipitate nor dilatory, he appeared prompt to the slow, and seemed almost tardy to the hasty man.

In the management of several large estates—he might have had many more if he would have accepted the charge—Mr. Gleeson had amassed a considerable fortune, but so devotedly did he attach himself to the interests of his employers, so thoroughly identify their fortunes with his own, that he gave little time to the cares of his immediate property. By his skill and intelligence many country gentlemen had emerged from embarrassments that threatened to engulph their entire fortunes; and his aid in a difficulty was looked upon as a certain guarantee of success. It was not very surprising if a man, endowed with qualities like these, should have usurped something of ascendancy over his employers. To a certain extent, their destiny lay in his hands. Of the difficulties by which they were pressed he alone knew either the nature or amount, while by what straits these should be overcome none but himself could offer a suggestion. If in all his dealings the most strict regard to honour was observable, so did he seem also inexhaustible in his contrivances to rescue an embarrassed or encumbered estate. There was often the greatest difficulty in securing his services—solicitation and interest were even required to engage him—but once retained, he applied his energies to the task, and with such zeal and acuteness that it was said no case, however desperate, had yet failed in his hands.

For several years past he had managed all the Knight's estates; and such was the complication and entanglement of the property, loaded with mortgages and rent-charges, embarrassed with dowries and annuities, that nothing short of his admirable skill could have supported the means of that expensive and wasteful mode of life which the Knight insisted on pursuing, and all restriction on which he deemed unfitting his station. If Gleeson represented the urgent necessity of retrenchment, the very word was enough to cut short the negotiation; until, at last, the Agent was fain to rest content with the fruits of good management, and merely venture from time to time on a cautious suggestion regarding the immense expense of the Knight's household.

With all his guardedness and care, these representations were not always safe, for though the Knight would sometimes meet them with some jocular or witty reply, or some bantering allusion to the Agent's taste for money-getting, at other times he would receive the advice with impatience or ill-humour, so that, at last, Gleeson limited all complaints on this score to his letters to Lady Eleanor, with whom he maintained a close and confidential correspondence.

This reserve on Gleeson's part had its effects on the Knight, who felt a proportionate delicacy in avowing any act of extravagance that should demand a fresh call for money, and thus embarrass the negotiation by which the Agent was endeavouring to extricate the property.

If Darcy felt the loss of the preceding night, it was far more from the necessity of avowing it to Gleeson, than from the amount of the money, considerable as it was; and he, therefore, set out to call upon him, in a frame of mind far less at ease than he desired to persuade himself he enjoyed.

Mr. Gleeson lived about three miles from Dublin, so that the Knight had abundant time to meditate as he went along, and think over the interview that awaited him. His reverie was only broken by the sudden change from the high road to the noiseless quiet of the neat avenue which led up to the house.

Mr. Gleeson's abode had been an ancient manor-house in the Gwynne family, a building of such antiquity as to date from the time of the Knights Templars, and though once a favoured residence of the Darcys, had, from the circumstances of a dreadful crime committed beneath its roof—the murder of a servant by his master—been at first deserted, and subsequently utterly neglected by the owners, so that at last it fell into ruin and decay. The roof was partly fallen in, the windows shattered and broken, the rich ceilings rotten and discoloured with damp, it presented an aspect of desolation, when Mr. Gleeson proposed to take it on lease. Nor was the ruin only within doors, but without; the ornamental planting had been torn up, or used as firewood; the gardens pillaged and overrun with cattle, and the large trees—among which were some rare and remarkable ones—were lopped and torn by the country people, who trespassed and committed their depredations without fear or impediment. Now, however, the whole aspect was changed; the same spirit of order that exercised its happy influence in the management of distant properties, had arrested the progress of destruction here, and, happily, in time sufficient to preserve some of the features which, in days past, had made this the most beautiful seat in the county.

It was not without a feeling of astonishment that the Knight surveyed the change. An interval of twelve years—for such had been the length of time since he was last there—had worked magic in all around. Clumps had sprung up into ornamental groups, saplings become graceful trees, sickly evergreens that leaned their frail stems against a stake were now richly-leaved hollies or fragrant laurestinas; and the marshy pond that seemed stagnant with rank grass and duckweed, was a clear lake fed by a silvery cascade, which descended in quaint but graceful terraces from the very end of the neat lawn.

In Darcy's eyes, the only fault was the excessive neatness perceptible in everything; the very gravel seemed to shine with a peculiar lustre, the alleys were swept clean, not even a withered leaf was suffered to disfigure them, while the shrubs had an air of trim propriety, like the self-satisfied air of a Sunday citizen.

The brilliant lustre of the heavy brass knocker, the white and spotless flags of the stone hall, and the immaculate accuracy of the staid footman who opened the door, were types of the prevailing tastes and habits of the proprietor. A mere glance at the orderly arrangement of Mr. Gleeson's study, would have confirmed the impression of his strict notions of regularity and discipline: not a book was out of place; the boxes, labelled with high and titled names, were ranged with a drill-like precision upon the shelves; the very letters that lay in the baskets beside the table, fell with an attention to staid decorum becoming the rigid habits of the place.

The Knight had some minutes to bestow in contemplation of these objects before Gleeson entered: he had only that morning arrived from a distant journey, and was dressing when the Knight was announced. With a bland, soft manner, and an air compounded of diffidence and self-importance, Mr. Gleeson made his approaches.

"You have anticipated me, sir," said he, placing a chair for the Knight; "I had ordered the carriage to call upon you. May I beg you to excuse the question, but my anxiety will not permit me to defer it—there is no truth, or very little, I trust, in the paragraph I've just read in Carrick's paper——"

"About a party at piquet with Lord Drogheda?" interrupted Darcy.

"The same."

"Every word of it correct, Gleeson," said the Knight, who, notwithstanding the occasion, could not control the temptation to laugh at the terrified expression of the Agent's face.

"But surely the sum was exaggerated; the paper says, the lands and demesne of Bally-dermot, with the house, furniture, plate, wine, equipage, garden utensils——"

"I'm not sure that we mentioned the watering-pots," said Darcy, smiling; "but the wine hogsheads are certainly included."

"A rental of clear three thousand four hundred and seventy-eight pounds, odd shillings, on a lease of lives renewable for ever—peppercorn fine," exclaimed Gleeson, closing his eyes, and folding his hands upon his breast, like a martyr resigning himself to the torture.

"So much for going on spades without the head of the suit!" observed the Knight; "and yet, any man might have made the same blunder; and then, Heffernan, with his interruption—altogether, Gleeson, the whole was mismanaged sadly."

"The greater part of the land tithe free," moaned Gleeson to himself; "it was a grant from the Crown to your ancestor, Everard Darcy.

"If it was the King gave it, Gleeson, it was the Queen lost it."

"The lands of Corrabeg, Dunragheedaghan, and Muscarooney, let at fifteen shillings an acre, with a right to cut turf on the Derry-slattery bog! not to speak of Knocksadowd! lost, and no redemption!"

"Yes, Gleeson, that's the point I'm coming to; there is a proviso in favour of redemption, whenever your grief will permit you to hear of it."

Gleeson gave a brief cough, blew his nose with considerable energy, and with an air of submissive sorrow apologised for yielding to his feelings. "I have been so many years, sir, the guardian—if I may so say—of that property, that I cannot think of being severed from its interests without deep, very deep regret."

"By Jove! Gleeson, so do I; you have no monopoly of the sorrow, believe me. I acknowledge, readily, the full extent of my culpability. This foolish bet came to pass at a dinner at Hutchinson's—it was the crowning point of a bragging conversation about play—and Drogheda, it seems, booked it, though I totally forgot all about it. I'm certain he never intended to push the wager on me, but when reminded of it, of course I had nothing else for it but to express my readiness to meet him. I must say he behaved nobly all through; and even when Heffernan's stupid interruption had somewhat ruffled my nerves, he begged I would reconsider the card—he saw I made a mistake—very handsome that!—his backers, I assure you, did not seem as much disposed to extend the courtesy. I relieved their minds, however, I stood by my play, and——"

"Lost an estate of three thousand——"

"Quite correct; I'm sure no man knows the rental better. And now, let us see how to keep it in the family."

The stare of amazement with which Gleeson heard these words might have met a proposition far more extravagant still, and he repeated the speech to himself, as if weighing every syllable in a balance.

"Yes, Gleeson, that was exactly what I said: now that we are engaged in liquidating, let us proceed with the good work. If I have given you enlarged occasion for the exercise of your abilities, I'm only acting like Peter Henessy—old Peter, that held the mill at Brown's Barn."

The Agent looked up with an expression in which all interest to learn the precedent alluded to was lost in astonishment at the levity of a man who could jest at such a moment.

"I see, you never heard it, and, as the lawyers say, the rule will apply. I'll tell it to you. When Peter was dying, he sent for old Rush of the Priory to give him absolution; he would not have the parish priest, for he was a 'hard man,' as Peter said, with little compassion for human weakness never loved pork nor 'poteen,' but seemed to have a relish for fasts and vigils. 'Rush will do,' said he to all the family applications in favour of the other—'I'll have Father Rush;' and so he had, and Rush came, and they were four hours at it, for Peter had a long score of reminiscences to bring up, and it was not without considerable difficulty, it is said, that Rush could apply the remedies of the Church to the various infractions of the old sinner. At last, however, it was arranged, and Peter lay back in bed very tired and fatigued, for, I assure you, Gleeson, whatever you may think of it, confessing one's iniquities is excessively wearying to the spirits. 'Is it all right, Father?' said he, as the good priest counted over the roll of ragged bank-notes that were to be devoted to the purchase of different masses and offerings. 'It will do well,' said Rush; 'make your mind easy, your peace is made now.' 'And are you sure its quite safe?' said Peter; 'a pound more or less is nothing now compared to—what you know'—for Peter was polite, and followed the poet's counsel. ''Tis safe and sure, both,' said Rush; 'I have the whole of the sins under my thumb now, and don't fret yourself.' 'Take another thirty shillings then, Father,' said he, pushing the note over to him, 'and let Whaley have the two barrels of seed oats—the smut is in them, and they're not worth sixpence; but, when we are at it, Father dear, let us do the thing complete; what signifies a trifle like that among the rest?' Such was Peter's philosophy, Gleeson, and, if not very laudable as he applied it, it would seem to suit our present emergency remarkably well."

Gleeson vouchsafed but a very sickly smile as the Knight finished, and taking up a bundle of papers from the table, proceeded to search for something amongst them.

"This loss was most inopportune, sir——"

"No doubt of it, Gleeson; it were far better had I won my wager," said the Knight, half testily; but the Agent, scarce noticing the interruption, went on:

"Mr. Lionel has drawn on me for seven hundred, and so late as Wednesday last I was obliged to meet a bill of his amounting to twelve hundred and eighty pounds. Thus, you will perceive, that he has this year overdrawn his allowance considerably. He seems to have been as unlucky as yourself, sir."

Soft and silky as the accents were, there was a tincture of sarcasm in the way these words were uttered that did not escape Darcy's notice, but he made no reply, and appeared to listen attentively as the other resumed:

"Then, the expenses of the abbey have been enormous this year; you would scarcely credit the outlay for the hunting establishment; and, as I learn from Lady Eleanor, that you rarely, if ever, take the field yourself——"

"Never mind that, Gleeson," broke in the Knight, suddenly. "I'll not sell a horse, or part with a dog amongst them. My income must well be able to afford me the luxuries I have always been used to. I'm not to be told that, with a rental of eighteen thousand a year——"

"A rental, sir, I grant you," said Gleeson, interrupting him; "you said quite correctly, the rental is even more than you stated, but consider the charges on that rental, the heavy sums raised on mortgages, the debt incurred by building, the two contested elections, your losses on the turf,—these make sad inroads in the amount of your income."

"I tell you frankly, Gleeson," said the Knight, starting up and pacing the room with hasty steps, "I've neither head nor patience for details of this kind. I was induced to believe that my embarrassments, such as they are, were in course of liquidation; that, by raising two hundred and fifty thousand pounds at four-and-a-half, or even five per cent., we should be enabled to clear off the heavy debts, for which we are paying ten, twelve—ay, by Jove! I believe fifteen per cent."

"Upon my word, I believe you do not exaggerate," said Gleeson, in a conciliating accent. "Hickman's bond, though nominally bearing six per cent., is actually treble that sum. He holds 'The Grove' at the rent of a cottier's tenure, and with the right of cutting timber in Clon-a-gauve wood —a right he is by no means chary of exercising."

"That must be stopped, and at once," broke in Darcy, with a heightened colour. "The old man is actually making a clearing of the whole mountain side; the last time I was up there, Lionel and I counted two hundred and eighteen trees marked for the hatchet. I ordered Finn not to permit one of them to be touched; to go with a message from me to Hickman, saying, that there was a wide difference between cutting timber for farm purposes and carrying on a trade in rivalry with the Baltic. Oaks of twenty, eighty, ay, a hundred and fifty years' growth, the finest trees on the property, were among those I counted."

"And did he desist, sir?" asked Gleeson, with a half cunning look.

"Did he!—what a question you ask me! By Heavens! if he barked a sapling in that wood after my warning, I'd have sent the Derra-hinchy boys down to his place, and they would not have left a twig standing on his cockney territory. Devilish lucky he'd be if they stopped there, and left him a house to shelter him."

"He's a very unsafe enemy, sir," observed Gleeson, timidly.

"By Jove! Gleeson, I think you are bent on driving me distracted this morning. You have hit upon perhaps the only theme on which I cannot control my irritability, and I beg of you, once and for all, to change it."

"I should never have alluded to Mr. Hickman, sir, but that I wished to remark to you that he is in a position which requires all our watchfulness; he has within the last three weeks bought up Drake's mortgage, and also Helson's bond for seventeen thousand, and, I know, from a source of unquestionable accuracy, is at this moment negotiating for the purchase of Martin Hamilton's bond, amounting to twenty-one thousand more; so that, in fact, with the exception of that small debt to Batty and Rowe, he will remain the sole creditor."

"The sole creditor!" exclaimed Darcy, growing pale as marble—"Peter Hickman the sole creditor!"

"To be sure, this privilege he will not long enjoy," said Gleeson, with a degree of alacrity he had not assumed before; "when our arrangements are perfected with the London house of Bicknell and Jervis, we can pay off Hickman at once; he shall have a cheque for the whole amount the very same day."

"And how soon may we hope for this happy event, Gleeson?" cried the Knight, recovering his wonted voice and manner.

"It will not be distant now, sir; one of the deeds is ready at this moment, or at least will be to-morrow. On your signing it, we shall have some very trifling delays, and the money can be forthcoming by the end of the next week. The other will be perfected and compared by Wednesday week."

"So that within three weeks or a month at furthest, Gleeson, we shall have cut the cable with the old pirate?"

"Three weeks, I trust, will see all finished; that is, if this affair of Ballydermot does not interfere."

"It shall not do so," cried the Knight, resolutely; "let it go. Drogheda is a gentleman at least, and if our old acres are to fall into other hands, let their possessor have blood in his veins, and he will not tyrannise over the people; but Hickman——"

"Very right, sir, Hickman might foreclose on the 24th of this month."

"Gleeson, no more of this; I'm not equal to it," said the Knight, faintly; and he sat down with a wearied sigh, and covered his face with his hands. The emotion, painful as it was, passed over soon, and the Knight, with a voice calm and measured as before, said, "You will take care, Gleeson, that my son's bills are provided for; London is an expensive place, and particularly for a young fellow situated like Lionel; you may venture on a gentle—mind, a very gentle—remonstrance respecting his repeated calls for money; hint something about arrangements just pending, which require a little more prudence than usual. Do it cautiously, Gleeson; be very guarded. I remember when I was a young fellow being driven to the Jews by an old agent of my grandfather's; he wrote me a regular homily on thrift and economy, and to show I had benefited by the lesson, I went straightway and raised a loan at something very like sixty per cent."

"You may rely upon my prudence, sir," said Gleeson. "I think I can promise that Mr. Lionel will not take offence at my freedom. May I say Tuesday to wait on you with the deeds—Tuesday morning?"

"Of course, whenever you appoint, I'll be ready. I hoped to have left town this week, but these are too important matters to bear postponement.

Tuesday, then, be it." And, with a friendly shake hands, they parted—Gleeson, to the duties of his laborious life; the Knight, with a mind less at ease than was his wont, but still bearing no trace of discomposure on his manly and handsome countenance.

CHAPTER XII.

A FIRST VISIT.

"Whenever Captain Forester is quite able to bear the fatigue, Sullivan—mind that you say, quite able—it will give me much pleasure to receive him."

Such was the answer Lady Eleanor Darcy returned to a polite message from the young officer, expressing his desire to visit Lady Eleanor, and thank her for the unwearied kindness she had bestowed on him during his illness.

Lady Eleanor and her daughter were seated in the same chamber in which they have already been introduced to the reader. It was towards the close of a dark and gloomy day, the air heavy and overcast towards the land, while, over the sea, masses of black, misshapen cloud were drifted along hurriedly, the presage of a coming storm. The pine wood blazed brightly on the wide hearth, and threw its mellow lustre over the antique carvings and the porcelain ornaments of the chamber, contrasting the glow of in-door comfort with the bleak and cheerless look of all without, where the crashing noise of breaking branches mingled with the yet sadder sound of the swollen torrent from the mountain.

It may be remarked, that persons who have lived much on the seaside, and near a coast abounding in difficulties or dangers, are far more susceptible of the influences of weather than those who pass their lives inland. Storm and shipwreck become, in a measure, inseparably associated. The loud beating of the waves upon the rocky shore, the deafening thunder of the swollen breakers, speak with a voice, to *their* hearts, full of most meaning terror. The moaning accents of the spent wind, and the wailing cry of the petrel, awake thoughts of those who journey over "the great waters," amid perils more dreadful than all of man's devising.

Partly from these causes, partly from influences of a different kind, both mother and daughter felt unusually sad and depressed, and had sat for a long interval without speaking, when Forester's message was delivered, requesting leave to pay his personal respects.

Had the visit been one of mere ceremony, Lady Eleanor would have declined it at once; her thoughts were wandering far away, engrossed by topics of dear and painful interest, and she would not have constrained herself to change their current and direction for an ordinary matter of conventional intercourse. But this was a different case; it was her son Lionel's friend, his chosen companion among his brother officers, the guest, too, who, wounded and almost dying beneath her roof, had been a charge of intense anxiety to her for weeks past.

"There is something strange, Helen, is there not, in this notion of acquaintanceship with one we have never seen; but now, after weeks of watching and inquiry, after nights of anxiety and days of care, I feel as if I ought to be very intimate with this same friend of Lionel's."

"It is more for that very reason, mamma, and simply because he is Lionel's friend."

"No, my dear child, not so; it is the tie that binds us to all for whom we have felt interested, and in whose sorrows we have taken a share. Lionel has doubtless many friends in his regiment, and yet it is very unlikely any of them would cause me even a momentary impatience to see and know what they are like."

"And do you confess to such in the present case?" said Helen, smiling.

"I own it, I have a strange feeling of half curiosity, and should be disappointed if the real Captain Forester does not come up to the standard of the ideal one."

"Captain Forester, my Lady," said Sullivan, as he threw open the door of the apartment, and, with a step which all his efforts could not render firm, and a frame greatly reduced by suffering, he entered. So little was he prepared for the appearance of the ladies who now stood to receive him, that, despite his habitual tact, a slight expression of surprise marked his features, and a heightened colour dyed his cheek, as he saluted them in turn.

With an air which perfectly blended kindliness and grace, Lady Eleanor held out her hand, and said: "My daughter, Captain Forester." And then pointing to a chair beside her own, begged of him to be seated. The unaccustomed exertion, the feeling of surprise, and the nervous irritability of convalescence, all conspired to make Forester ill at ease, and it was with a low, faint sigh he sank into the chair.

"I had hoped, madam," said he, in a weak and tremulous accent—"I had hoped to be able to speak my gratitude to you—to express, at least, some portion of what I feel for kindness to which I owe my life, but the greatness of the obligation would seem too much for such strength as mine. I must leave it to my mother to say how deeply your kindness has affected us."

The accents in which these few words were uttered, particularly that which marked the mention of his mother, seemed to strike a chord in Lady Eleanor's heart, and her hand trembled as she took from Forester a sealed letter which he withdrew from another.

"Julia Wallincourt," said Lady Eleanor, unconsciously reading half aloud the signature on the envelope of the letter.

"My mother, madam," said Forester, bowing.

"The Countess of Wallincourt!" exclaimed Lady Eleanor, with a heightened colour, and a look of excited and even anxious import.

"Yes, madam, the widowed Countess of the Earl of Wallincourt, late Ambassador at Madrid; am I to have the happiness of hearing that my mother is known to you?"

"I had, sir, the pleasure—the honour of meeting Lady Julia D'Esterre; to have enjoyed that pleasure, even once, is quite enough never to forget it." Then turning to her daughter, she added: "You have often heard me speak of Lady Julia's beauty, Helen; she was certainly the most lovely person I ever saw, but the charm of her appearance was even inferior to the fascination of her manner."

"She retains it all, madam," cried Forester, as his eyes sparkled with enthusiastic delight; "she has lost nothing of that power of captivating; and as for beauty, I confess I know nothing higher in that quality than what conveys elevation of sentiment with purity and tenderness of heart; this she possesses still."

"And your elder brother, Captain Forester?" inquired Lady Eleanor, with a manner intended to express interest, but in reality meant to direct the conversation into another channel.

"He is in Spain still, madam; he was Secretary of the Embassy when my father died, and replaced him in the mission."

There was a pause, a long and chilling silence, after these words, that each party felt embarrassing and yet were unable to break; at last Forester, turning towards Helen, asked "when she had heard from her brother?"

"Not for some days past," replied she; "but Lionel is such an irregular correspondent, we think nothing of his long intervals of silence. You have heard of his promotion, perhaps?"

"No; pray let me learn the good news."

"He has got his company. Some very unexpected—I might say, from Lionel's account, some very inexplicable—piece of good fortune has aided his advancement, and he now writes himself, greatly to his own delight it would appear, Captain Darcy."

"His Royal Highness the Prince of Wales," said Lady Eleanor, with a look of pride, "has been pleased to notice my son, and has appointed him an extra aide-de-camp."

"Indeed!" cried Forester; "I am rejoiced at it, with all my heart.

always thought, if the Prince were to know him, he'd be charmed with his agreeability; Lionel has the very qualities that win their way at Carlton House; buoyant spirit, courtly address, tact equal to any emergency, all these are his, and the Prince likes to see handsome fellows about his Court. I am overjoyed at this piece of intelligence."

There was a hearty frankness with which he spoke this that captivated both mother and daughter.

There are few more winning traits of human nature than the unaffected, heartfelt admiration of one young man for the qualities and endowments of another, and never are they more likely to meet appreciation than when exhibited in presence of the mother of the lauded one. And thus the simple expression of Forester's delight at his friend's advancement went further to exalt himself in the good graces of Lady Eleanor, than the display of any powers of pleasing, however ingeniously or artfully exercised.

As through the openings of a dense wood we come unexpectedly upon a view of a wide tract of country, unfolding features of landscape unthought of and unlooked for, so occasionally doth it happen that, in conversation, a chance allusion, a mere word, will develop sources of interest buried up to that very moment, and display themes of mutual enjoyment which were unknown before. This was now the case. Lionel's name, which evoked the mother's pride and the sister's affection, called also into play the generous warmth of Forester's attachment to him.

Thus pleasantly glided on the hours, and none remarked how time was passing, or even heeded the howling storm that raged without, while anecdotes and traits of Lionel were recorded, and comments passed upon his character and temper, such as a friend might utter, and a mother love to hear.

At last Forester rose. More than once during the interview a consciousness crossed his mind that he was outstaying the ordinary limits of a visit, out at each moment some observation of Lady Eleanor, or her daughter, or some newly remembered incident in Lionel's career, would occur and delay his departure. At last he stood up, and warned by the thickening darkness of how time had sped, was endeavouring to mutter some words of apology, when Lady Eleanor interrupted him with—

"Pray do not let us suppose you felt the hours too long, Captain Forester; the theme you selected will always make my daughter and myself insensible to the lapse of time. If I did not fear we should be trespassing on both your kindness and health together, I should venture to request you would dine with us."

Forester's sparkling eyes and flushed cheek replied to the invitation before he had words to say how gladly he accepted it.

"I feel more reconciled to making this request, sir," said Lady Eleanor, 'because, in your present state of weakness, you cannot enjoy the society of a pleasanter party, and it is a fortunate thing that you can combine a prudent action with a kind one."

Forester appreciated the flattery of the remark, and, with a broken acknowledgment of its import, moved towards the door.

"No, no," said Lady Eleanor, "pray don't think of dressing; you have all the privilege of an invalid, and a—friend also."

The pause which preceded the word brought a slight blush into her cheek, but when it was uttered, she seemed to have resumed her self-possession.

"We shall leave you now with the newspapers, which I suppose you are longing to look at, and join you at the dinner-table." And as she spoke, she took her daughter's arm, and passed into an adjoining room, leaving Forester in one of those pleasant reveries which so often break in upon the hours of returning health, and compensate for all the sufferings of a sick-bed.

"How strange and how unceasing are the anomalies of Irish life," thought he, as he sat alone ruminating on the past. "Splendour, poverty, elevation of sentiment, savage ferocity, delicacy the most refined, barbarism the most revolting, pass before the mind's eye in the quick succession of the objects in a magic lantern. Here, in these few weeks, what characters and incidents have been revealed to me! and how invariably have I found myself wrong in every effort to decipher them! Nor are the indications of mind and temper in themselves so very singular, as the fact of meeting them under circumstances, and in situations so unlikely. For instance, who would have expected to see a Lady Eleanor Darcy here, in this wild region, with all the polished grace and dignity of manner the best circles alone possess; and her daughter, haughtier, perhaps, than the mother, more reserved, more timid it may be, and yet with all the elegance of a Court in every gesture and every movement. Lionel told me she was handsome—he might have said downright beautiful. Where were these fascinations nurtured and cultivated? Is it here, on the margin of this lonely bay, amid scenes of reckless dissipation?"

Of this kind were his musings, nor, amid them all, did one thought obtrude of the cause which threw him first into such companionship, nor of that mission, to discharge which was the end and object of his coming.

CHAPTER XIII.

A TREATY REJECTED.

Forester's recovery was slow, at least so his friends in the capital thought it, for to each letter requiring to know when he might be expected back again, the one reply for ever was returned, "As soon as he felt able to leave Gwynne Abbey." Nor was the answer, perhaps, injudiciously couched.

From the evening of his first introduction to Lady Eleanor and her daughter, his visits were frequent, sometimes occupying the entire morning, and always prolonged far into the night. Never did an intimacy make more rapid progress; so many tastes and so many topics were in common to all, for while the ladies had profited by reading and study in matters which he had little cultivated, yet the groundwork of an early good education enabled him to join in discussions, and take part in conversation which both interested at the time, and suggested improvement afterward; and if Lady Eleanor knew less of the late events which formed the staple of London small-talk, she was well informed on the characters and passages of the early portion of the reign, which gave all the charm of a history to reminiscences purely personal.

With the wits and distinguished men of that day she had lived in great intimacy, and felt a pride in contrasting the displays of intellectual wealth so common then, with the flatter and more prosaic habits since introduced into society. "Eccentricities and absurdities," she would say, "have replaced in the world the more brilliant exhibitions of cultivated and gifted minds, and I must confess to preferring the social qualities of Horace Walpole to the exaggerations of Bagenal Daly, or the ludicrous caprices of Buck Whaley."

"I think Mr. Daly charming, for my part," said Helen, laughing. "I'm certain that he is a miracle of truth, as he is of adventure; if everything he relates is not strictly accurate and matter of fact, it is because the real is always inferior to the ideal. The things *ought* to have happened as he states."

"It is, at least, *ben trovato*," broke in Forester; "yet I go further, and place perfect confidence in his narratives, and truly, I have heard some strange ones in our morning rides together."

"I suspected as much," said Lady Eleanor, "a new listener is such a boon to him; so then, you have heard how he carried away the Infanta of Spain, compelled the Elector of Saxony to take off his boots, made the Doge of Venice drunk, and instructed the Pasha of Trebizond in the mysteries of an Irish jig."

"Not a word of these have I heard as yet."

"Indeed! then what, in all mercy, has he been talking of—India, China, or North America, perhaps?"

"Still less; he has never wandered from Ireland and Irish life, and I must say, as far as adventure and incident are concerned, it would have been quite unnecessary for him to have strayed beyond it."

"You are perfectly right there," said Lady Eleanor, with some seriousness in the tone; "our home anomalies may shame all foreign wonders; he himself could scarcely find his parallel in any land."

"He has a sincere affection for Lionel, mamma," said Helen, in an accent of deprecating meaning.

"And that very same regard gave the bias to Lionel's taste for every species of absurdity! Believe me, Helen, Irish blood is too stimulating an ingredient to enter into a family oftener than once in four generations. Mr. Daly's has been unadulterated for centuries, and the consequence is, that, although neither deficient in strong sense or quick perception, he acts always on the impulse that precedes judgment, and both his generosity and his injustice outrun the mark."

"I love that same rash temperament," said Helen, flushing as she spoke, "it is a fine thing to see so much of warm and generous nature survive all that he must have seen of the littleness of mankind."

"There! Captain Forester, there! Have I not reason on my side? You thought me very unjust towards poor Mr. Daly—I know you did; but it demands all my watchfulness to prevent him being equally the model for my daughter, as he is for my son's, imitation."

"There are traits in his character any might be well proud to imitate," said Helen, warmly; "his life has been a series of generous, single-minded actions; and," added she, archly, "if mamma thinks it prudent and safe to warn her children against some of Mr. Daly's eccentricities, no one is more ready to acknowledge his real worth than she is."

"Helen is right," said Lady Eleanor; "if we could always be certain that Mr. Daly's imitators would copy the truly great features of his character, we might forgive them falling into his weaknesses; and now, can any one tell me why we have not seen him for some days past? He is in the abbey?"

"Yes, we rode out together yesterday morning to look at the wreck near the Sound of Achill; strange enough, I only learned from a chance remark of one of the sailors, that Daly had been in the boat the night before, that took the people off the wreck."

"So like him!" exclaimed Helen, with enthusiasm.

"He is angry with me, I know he is," said Lady Eleanor, musingly. "I asked his advice respecting the answer I should send to a certain letter, and then rejected the counsel. He would have forgiven me, had I run counter to his opinions without asking; but when I called him into consultation, the offence became a grave one."

"I declare, mamma, I side with him; his arguments were clear, strong, and unanswerable, and the best proof of it is, you have never had the courage to follow your own determination, since you listened to him."

"I have a great mind to choose an umpire between us. What say you, Captain Forester, will you hear the case? Helen shall take Mr. Daly's side, I will make my own statement."

"It's a novel idea," said Helen, laughing, "that the umpire should be selected by one of the litigating parties."

"Then you doubt my impartiality, Miss Darcy?"

"If I am to accept you as a Judge, I'll not prejudice the Court against myself, by avowing my opinions of it," said she, archly.

"When I spoke of your arbitration, Captain Forester," said Lady Eleanor, "I really meant fairly, for upon all the topics we have discussed together, politics, or anything bordering on political opinions, have never come uppermost; and, up to this moment, I have not the slightest notion what are your political leanings, Whig or Tory."

"So the point in dispute is a political one?" asked Forester, cautiously.

"Not exactly," interposed Helen; "the policy of a certain reply to a certain demand is the question at issue; but the advice of any party in the matter might be tinged by his party leanings, if he have any."

"If I judge Captain Forester aright, he has troubled his head very little about party squabbles," said Lady Eleanor; "and in any case, he can scarcely take a deep interest in a question which is almost peculiarly Irish."

Forester bowed, partly in pretended acquiescence of this speech, partly to conceal a deep flush that mounted suddenly to his cheek, for he felt by no means pleased at a remark that might be held to reflect on his political knowledge.

"Be thou the judge, then," said Lady Eleanor. "And, first of all, read that letter." And she took from her work-box her cousin Lord Netherby's letter, and handed it to Forester.

"I reserve my right to dispute that document being evidence," said Helen, laughing; "nor is there any proof of the handwriting being Lord Netherby's. Mamma herself acknowledges she has not heard from him for nearly twenty years."

This cunning speech, meant to intimate the precise relation of the two parties, was understood at once by Forester, who could with difficulty control a smile, although Lady Eleanor looked far from pleased.

There was now a pause, while Forester read over the long letter with due attention, somewhat puzzled to conceive to what particular portion of it the matter in dispute referred.

"You have not read the postscript," said Helen, as she saw him folding the letter, without remarking the few concluding lines.

Forester twice read over the passage alluded to, and at once whatever had been mysterious or difficult was revealed before him. Lord Netherby's wily temptation was made manifest, not the less palpably, perhaps, because the reader was himself involved in the very same scheme.

"You have now seen my cousin's letter," said Lady Eleanor, "and the whole question is, whether the reply should be limited to a suitable acknowledgment of its kind expressions, and a grateful sense of the Prince's condescension, or should convey——"

"Mamma means," interrupted Helen, laughingly—"mamma means, that we might also avow our sincere gratitude for the rich temptation offered in requital of my father's vote on the 'Union.'"

"No Minister would dare to make such a proposition to the 'Knight of Gwynne,'" said Lady Eleanor, haughtily.

"Ministers are very enterprising now-a-days, mamma," rejoined Helen; "I have never heard any one speak of Mr. Pitt's cowardice, and Lord Castlereagh has had courage to invite old Mr. Hickman to dinner!"

Forester would gladly have acknowledged his relationship to the Secretary, but the moment seemed unpropitious, and the avowal would have had the semblance of a rebuke; so he covered his confusion by a laugh, and said nothing.

"We can scarcely contemn the hardihood of a Government that has made Crofton a Bishop, and Hawes a General," said Helen, with a flashing eye, and a lip curled in superciliousness. "Nothing short of a profound reliance on the piety of the Church, and the bravery of the Army, would support such a policy as that!"

Lady Eleanor seemed provoked at the hardy tone of Helen's speech, but the mother's look was proud, as she gazed on the brilliant expression of her daughter's beauty, now heightened by the excitement of the moment.

"Is it not possible, Miss Darcy," said Forester, in a voice at once timid and insinuating—"is it not possible that the measure contemplated by the Government may have results so beneficial, as to more than compensate for evils like these?"

"A Jesuit, or a Tory, or both," cried Helen. "Mamma, you have chosen your umpire most judiciously; his is exactly the impartiality needed."

"Nay, but hear me out," cried the young officer, whose cheek was crimsoned with shame. "If the measure be a good one—well, let me beg the question, if it be a good one—and yet, the time for propounding it is either inopportune or unfortunate, and, consequently, the support it might claim on its own merits be withheld either from prejudice, party connexion, or any similar cause—you would not call a Ministry culpable who should anticipate the happy working of a judicious act, by securing the assistance of those whose convictions are easily won over, in preference to the slower process of convincing the men of more upright and honest intentions."

"You have begged so much in the commencement, and assumed so much in the conclusion, sir, that I am at a loss to which end of your speech to address my answer; but I will say this much: it is but sorry evidence of a measure's goodness when it can only meet the approval of the venal. I don't prize the beauty so highly that is only recognised by the blind man."

"Distorted vision, Miss Darcy, may lead to impressions more erroneous than even blindness."

"I may have the infirmity you speak of," said she, quickly, "but assuredly I'll not wear Government spectacles to correct it."

If Forester was surprised at finding a young lady so deeply interested in a political question, he was still more so on hearing the tone of determination she spoke in, and would gladly, had he known how, have given the conversation a less serious turn.

"We have been all the time forgetting the real question at issue," said Lady Eleanor; "I'm sure I never intended to listen to a discussion on the merits or demerits of the Union, on which you both grow so eloquent; will you, then, kindly return to whence we started, and advise me as to the reply to this letter."

"I do not perceive any remarkable difficulty, madam," said Forester, addressing himself exclusively to Lady Eleanor. "The Knight of Gwynne has doubtless strong opinions on this question; they are either in favour of, or adverse to the Government views; if the former, your reply is easy and most satisfactory; if the latter, perhaps he would condescend to explain the nature of his objections, to state whether it be to anything in the detail of the measure he is adverse to, or to the principle of the Bill itself. A declaration like this will open a door to negotiation, without the slightest imputation on either side. A Minister may well afford to offer his reasons for any line of policy to one as eminent in station and ability as the Knight of Gwynne, and I trust I am not indiscreet in assuming that the Knight would not be derogating from that station in listening to, and canvassing such explanations."

"Lord Castlereagh, 'aut——,'" said Helen, starting up from her seat, and making a low courtesy before Forester, who, feeling himself in a measure detected, blushed till his face became scarlet.

"My dear Helen, at this rate we shall never——But what is this?—who have we here?"

This sudden exclamation was caused by the appearance of a small four-wheeled carriage drawn up at the gate of the flower-garden, from which old Hickman's voice could now be heard, inquiring if the Lady Eleanor were at home.

"Yes, Sullivan," said she, with a sigh, "and order luncheon." Then, as the servant left the room, she added, "I am always better pleased when the visits of that family are paid by the old gentleman, whom I prefer to the son or the grandson. They are better performers, I admit, but he is an actor of nature's own making."

"Do you know him, Captain Forester?" asked Helen.

But, before he could reply, the door was opened, and Sullivan announced, by his ancient title, "Doctor Hickman."

Strange and grotesque as in every respect he looked, the venerable character of old age secured him a respectful, almost a cordial reception; and, as Lady Eleanor advanced to him, there was that urbanity and courtesy in her manner which are so nearly allied to the expression of actual esteem. It was true, there was little in the old man's nature to elicit such feelings towards him; he was a grasping miser, covetousness and money-getting filled up his heart, and every avenue leading to it. The passion for gain had alone given the interest to his life, and developed into activity any intelligence he possessed. While his son valued wealth as the only stepping-stone to a position of eminence and rank, old Hickman loved riches for their own sake. The Bank was, in his estimation, the fountain of all honour, and a strong credit there better than all the reputation the world could confer. These were harsh traits. But then he was old: long years and infirmity were bringing him each hour closer to the time when the passion of his existence must be abandoned; and a feeling of pity was excited at the sight of that withered, careworn face, to which the insensate cravings of avarice lent an unnatural look of shrewdness and intelligence.

"What a cold morning for your drive, Mr. Hickman," said Lady Eleanor, kindly. "Captain Forester, may I ask you to stir the fire. Mr. Hickman —Captain Forester."

"Ah, Miss Helen, beautiful as ever!" exclaimed the old man, as, with a look of real admiration, he gazed on Miss Darcy. "I don't know how it is, Lady Eleanor, but the young ladies never dressed so becomingly formerly. Captain Forester, your humble servant; I am glad to see you about again; indeed, I didn't think it very likely once that you'd ever leave the library on your own feet; Mac Donough's a dead shot they tell me—ay, ay!"

"I hope your friends at 'The Grove' are well, sir?" said Lady Eleanor, desirous of interrupting a topic she saw to be particularly distressing to Forester.

"No, indeed, my Lady; my son Bob—Mr. Hickman O'Reilly, I mean—

God forgive me, I'm sure they take trouble enough to teach me that name —he's got a kind of a water-brash, what we call a pyrosis. I tell him it's the French dishes he eats for dinner, things he never was brought up to, concoctions of lemon-juice, and cloves, and saffron, and garlic, in meat roasted — no, but stewed into chips."

"You prefer our national cookery, Mr. Hickman?"

"Yes, my Lady, with the gravy in it; the crag-end, if—your Ladyship knows what's the crag-end of a——"

"Indeed, Mr. Hickman," said Lady Eleanor, smiling, "I'm deplorably ignorant about everything that concerns household. Helen affects to be very deep in these matters, but I suspect it is only a superficial knowledge, got up to amuse the Knight."

"I beg, mamma, you will not infer any such reproach on my skill in *ménage*. Papa called my *omelette à la curé* perfect."

"I should like to hear Mr. Hickman's judgment on it," said Lady Eleanor, with a sly smile.

"If it's a plain joint, my Lady, boiled or roasted, without spices or devilment in it, but just the way Providence intended——"

"May I ask, sir, how you suppose Providence intended to recommend any particular kind of cookery?" said Helen, seriously.

"Whatever is most natural, most simple, the easiest to do," stammered out Hickman, not over pleased at being asked for an explanation.

"Then the Cossack ranks first in the art," exclaimed Forester, "for nothing can be more simple or easier than to take a slice of a live ox, and hang it up in the sun for ten or fifteen minutes."

"Them's barbarians," said Hickman, with an emphasis that made the listeners find it no easy task to keep down a laugh.

"Luncheon, my Lady," said old Tate Sullivan, as with a reverential bow he opened the folding-doors into a small breakfast-parlour, where an exquisitely served table was laid out.

"Practice before precept, Mr. Hickman," said Lady Eleanor; "will you join us at luncheon, where I hope you may find something to your liking."

As the old man seated himself at the table, his eye ranged over the cabinet pictures that covered the walls, the richly-chased silver on the table, and the massive wine-coolers that stood on the sideboard, with an eye whose brilliancy betokened far more the covetous taste of the miser than the pleased expression of mere connoisseurship; nor could he recal himself from their admiration to hear Forester's twice repeated question as to what he would eat.

"'Tis elegant fine plate, no doubt of it," muttered he, below his breath; "and the pictures may be worth as much more—ay!"

The last monosyllable was the only part of his speech audible, and being interpreted by Forester as a reply to his request, he at once helped the old gentleman to a very highly seasoned French dish before him.

"Eh! what's this?" said Hickman, as he surveyed his plate with unfeigned astonishment; "if I didn't see it laid down on your Ladyship's table, I'd swear it was a bit of Galway marble."

"It's a *galantine truffée*, Mr. Hickman," said Forester, who was well aware of its merits.

"Be it so, in the name of God!" said Hickman, with resignation, as though to say that any one who could eat it, might take the trouble to learn the name. "Ay, my Lady, that's what I like, a slice of Kerry beef, a beast made for man's eating."

"Mr. Hickman's pony is more of an epicure than his master," said Forester, as he arose from his chair, and moved towards the glass-door that opened on the garden; "he has just eaten the top of your lemon-tree."

"And by way of dessert, he is now cropping my japonica," cried Helen, as she sprang from the room to rescue her favourite plant. Forester followed her, and Lady Eleanor was left alone with "the Doctor."

"Now, my Lady, that I have the opportunity—and sure it was luck gave it to me—would you give me the favour of a little private conversation?"

"If the matter be on business, Mr. Hickman, I must frankly own I should prefer your addressing yourself to the Knight—he will be home early next week."

"It is—and it is not, my Lady—but, there! they're coming back, now, and it is too late;" and so he heaved a heavy sigh, and lay back in his chair, as though worn out and disappointed.

"Well, then, in the library, Mr. Hickman," said Lady Eleanor, compassionately, "when you've eaten some luncheon."

"No more, my Lady; 'tis elegant fine beef as ever I tasted, and the gravy in it, but I'm not hungry now."

Lady Eleanor, without a guess as to what might form the subject of his communication, perceived that he was agitated and anxious; and so, requesting Forester and her daughter to continue their luncheon, she added: "And I have something to tell Mr. Hickman, if he will give five minutes of his company in the next room."

Taking a chair near the fire, Lady Eleanor motioned to "the Doctor" to be seated, but the old man was so engaged in admiring the room and its furniture, that he seemed insensible to all else. As his eye wandered over the many objects of taste and luxury on every side, his lips muttered unceasingly, but the sound was inarticulate.

"I cannot pledge myself that we shall remain long interrupted, Mr. Hickman," said Lady Eleanor, "so pray lose no time in the communication you have to make."

"I humbly ask pardon, my Lady," said the old man, in a voice of deep humility; "I'm old and feeble now, and my senses none of the clearest, but sure its time for them to be worn out; ninety-one I'll be, it I live to Lady-day." It was his habit to exaggerate his age; besides, there was a tremulous pathos in his accents to which Lady Eleanor was far from feeling insensible, and she awaited in silence what was to follow.

"Well, well," sighed the old man, "if I succeed in this, the last act of my long life, I'm well content to go whenever the Lord pleases." And so saying, he took from his coat-pocket the ominous-looking old leather case to which we have already alluded, and searched for some time amid its contents. "Ay! here it is—that is it—it is only a memorandum, my Lady, but it will show what I mean." And he handed the paper to Lady Eleanor.

It was some time before she had arranged her spectacles and adjusted herself to peruse the document, but before she had concluded, her hand trembled violently, and all colour forsook her cheek. Meanwhile, "the Doctor" sat with his filmy eyes directed towards her, as if watching the working of his spell; and when the paper fell from her fingers, he uttered a low "Ay," as though to say his success was certain.

"Two hundred thousand pounds!" exclaimed she, with a shudder; "this cannot be true."

"It is all true, my Lady, and so is this, too;" and he took from his hat a newspaper, and presented it to her.

"The Bally-dermot property! The whole estate lost at cards! This is a calumny, sir—the libellous impertinence of a newspaper paragraphist. I'll not believe it."

"'Tis true, notwithstanding, my Lady. Harvey Dawson was there himself and saw it all; and as for the other, the deeds and mortgages are at this moment in the hands of my son's solicitor."

"And this may be foreclosed——"

"On the 24th, at noon, my Lady," continued Hickman, as he folded the memorandum, and replaced it in his pocket-book.

"Well, sir," said she, as with a great effort to master her emotion, she addressed him in a steady and even commanding voice, "the next thing is to learn what are your intentions respecting this debt? You have not purchased all these various liabilities of my husband's without some definite object. Speak it out—what is it? Has Mr. Hickman O'Reilly's ambition increased so rapidly that he desires to date his letters from Gwynne Abbey?"

"The Saints forbid it, my Lady," said the old man, with a pious horror. "I'd never come here this day on such an errand as that. If it was not to propose what was agreeable, you'd not see me here——"

"Well, sir, what is the proposition? Let me hear it at once, for my patience never bears much dallying with."

"I am coming to it, my Lady," muttered Hickman, who already felt really ashamed at the deep emotion his news evoked. "There are two ways of doing it——" A gesture of impatience from Lady Eleanor stopped him, but, after a brief pause, he resumed: "Bear with me, my Lady. Old age and infirmity are always prolix; but I'll do my best."

It would be as unfair a trial of the reader's endurance as it proved to Lady Eleanor's, were we to relate the slow steps by which Mr. Hickman announced his plan, the substance of which, divested of all his own circumlocution and occasional interruptions, was simply this: a promise had been made by Lord Castlereagh to Hickman O'Reilly that if, through his influence, exercised by means of moneyed arrangements or otherwise, the Knight of Gwynne would vote with the Government on the 'Union,' he should be elevated to the Peerage, an object which, however inconsiderable in the old man's esteem, both son and grandson had set their hearts upon. For this service they, in requital, would extend the loan to another period of seven years, stipulating only for some trifling advantages regarding the right of cutting timber, some coast fisheries, and other matters to be mentioned afterwards, points which, although evidently of minor importance, were recapitulated by the old man with a circumstantial minuteness.

It was only by a powerful effort that Lady Eleanor could control her rising indignation at this proposal, while the very thought of Hickman O'Reilly as a Peer, and member of that proud "Order" of which her own haughty family formed a part, was an insult almost beyond endurance.

"Go on, sir," said she, with a forced composure, which deceived old Hickman completely, and made him suppose that his negotiation was proceeding favourably.

"I'm sure, my Lady, it's little satisfaction all this grandeur would give me. I'd rather be twenty years younger, and in the back parlour of my old shop at Loughrea than the first Peer in the kingdom."

"Ambition is not your failing, then, sir," said she, with a glance which, to one more quick-sighted, would have conveyed the full measure of her scorn."

"That it isn't, my Lady; but they insist upon it."

"And is the Peerage to be enriched by the enrolment of your name among its members? I thought, sir, it was your son."

"Bob—Mr. Hickman, I mean—suggests that I should be the first lord in the family, my Lady, because, then, Beecham's title won't seem so new when it comes to him. 'Tis the only use they can make of me now—ay!" and the word was accented with a venomous sharpness that told the secret anger he had himself awakened by his remark.

"The Knight of Gwynne," said Lady Eleanor, proudly, "has often regretted to me the few opportunities he had embraced through life of serving his country; I have no doubt, sir, when he hears your proposal, that he will rejoice at this occasion of making an *amende*. I will write to him by this post. Is there anything more you wish to add, Mr. Hickman?" said she, as, having risen from her chair, she perceived that the old man remained seated.

"Yes, indeed, my Lady, there is, and I don't think I'd have the heart for it if it wasn't your Ladyship's kindness about the other business; and even now, maybe, it would take you by surprise."

"You can scarcely do that, sir, after what I have just listened to," said she, with a smile.

"Well, there's no use in going round about the bush, and this is what I mean. We thought there might be a difficulty, perhaps, about the vote that the Knight might have promised his friends, or said something or other how he'd go, and wouldn't be able to get out of it so easily, so we saw another way of serving his views about the money. You see, my Lady, we considered it all well amongst us."

"We should feel deeply grateful, sir, to know how far this family has occupied your kind solicitude. But proceed."

"If the Knight doesn't like to vote with the Government, of course there is no use in Bob doing it—so, he'll be a Patriot, my Lady—and why not? Ha! ha! ha! they'll be breaking the windows all over Dublin, and he may as well save the glass!—ay!"

"Forgive me, sir, if I cannot see how this has any reference to my family."

"I'm coming to it—coming fast, my Lady. We were thinking then how we could help the Knight, and do a good turn to ourselves, and the way we hit upon was this—to reduce the interest on the whole debt to five per cent., make a settlement of half the amount on Miss Darcy, and then, if the young lady had no objection to my grandson, Beecham——"

"Stop, sir," said Lady Eleanor; "I never could suppose you meant to offend me intentionally, I cannot permit of your doing so through inadvertence or ignorance. I will, therefore, request that this conversation may cease. Age has many privileges, Mr. Hickman, but there are some it can never confer; one of these is the right to insult a lady and—a mother."

The last words were sobbed rather than spoken: affection and pride, both outraged together, almost choked her utterance, and Lady Eleanor sat down trembling in every limb, while the old man, only half conscious of the emotion he had evoked, peered at her in stolid amazement through his spectacles.

Any one who knew nothing of Old Hickman's character might well have pitied his perplexity at that moment; doubts of every kind and sort passed through his mind as rapidly as his timeworn faculties permitted, and, at last, he settled down into the conviction that Lady Eleanor might have thought his demand respecting fortune too exorbitant, although not deeming the proposition, in other respects, ineligible. To this conclusion the habits of his own mind insensibly disposed him.

"Ay, my Lady," said he, after a pause, "'tis a deal of money, no doubt, but it won't be going out of the family, and that's more than could be said if you refuse the offer."

"Sir!" exclaimed Lady Eleanor, in a tone that to any one less obtusely endowed would have been an appeal not requiring repetition; but the old man had only senses for his own views, and went on:

"They tell me that Mr. Lionel is just as free with his money as his father; throws it out with both hands, horse-racing and high play, and every extravagance be can think of. Well, and if that's true, my Lady, sure it's well worth while to think that you'll have a decent house to put your head under when your daughter's married to Beecham. He has no wasteful ways, but can look after the main chance, as well as any boy ever I seen. This notion about Miss Helen is the only thing like expense I ever knew him take up, and sure"—here he dropped his voice to soliloquy—"sure, maybe, that same will pay well, after all—ay!"

"My head! my head is bursting with blood," sighed Lady Eleanor; but the last words alone reached Hickman's ears.

"Ay! blood's a fine thing, no doubt of it, but faith, it won't pay interest on a mortgage; nor I never heard of it staying the execution of a writ! 'Tis little good blood I had in my veins, and yet I contrived to scrape a trifle together notwithstanding—ay!"

"I do not feel myself very well, Mr. Hickman," said Lady Eleanor; "may I request you will send my daughter to me, and excuse me if I wish you a good morning."

"Shall I hint anything to the young lady about what we were saying?" said he, in a tone of most confidential import.

"At your peril, sir!" said Lady Eleanor, with a look that at once seemed to transfix him; and the old man, muttering his adieu, hobbled from the room, while Lady Eleanor leaned back in her chair, overcome by the conflict of her emotions.

"Is he gone?" said Lady Eleanor, faintly, as her daughter entered.

"Yes, mamma; but are you ill? you look dreadfully pale and agitated."

"Wearied—fatigued, my dear, nothing more. Tell Captain Forester I must release him from his engagement to us to-day. I cannot come to dinner." And so saying, she covered her eyes with her hand, and seemed lost in deep thought.

CHAPTER XIV.

"THE MECHANISM OF CORRUPTION."

"WELL, Heffernan," said Lord Castlereagh, as they sat over their wine alone in a small dining-room of the Secretary's Lodge—"well, even with Hackett, we shall be run close. I don't fancy the thought of another division, so nearly matched; our fellows don't see the honour of a Thermopylæ."

"Very true, my Lord; and the desertions are numerous, as they always will be, when men receive the bounty before they are enlisted."

"Yes; but what would you do? We make a man a Commissioner or a sinecurist for his vote—he vacates his seat on taking office; and, instead of standing the brunt of another election, coolly says, 'That, differing as he must do from his constituents on an important measure, he restores the trust they had committed into his hands——'"

"'He hopes unsullied'—don't forget that, my Lord."

"Yes—'he hopes unsullied—and prefers to retire from the active career of politics, carrying with him the esteem and regard of his former friends, rather than endanger their good opinion by supporting measures to which they are conscientiously opposed.'"

"Felicitous conjuncture, that unites patriotism and profit!" exclaimed Heffernan. "Happy man, that can draw tears from the Mob, and two thousand a year from the Treasury!"

"And yet I see no remedy for it," sighed the Secretary.

"There is one, notwithstanding; but it demands considerable address and skill. You have always been too solicitous about the estimation of the men you bought were held in—always thinking of what would be said and thought of them You pushed the system so far, that the fellows themselves caught up the delusion, and began to fancy they had characters to lose. All this was wrong—radically, thoroughly wrong. When the butcher smears a red streak round a lamb's neck—we call it 'raddling' in Ireland, my Lord—any child knows he's destined for the knife; now, when you 'raddled' your flock, you wanted the world to believe you were going to make pets of them, and you said as much and so often, that the beasts themselves believed it and began cutting their gambols accordingly. Why not have paraded them openly to the shambles? It was their bleating you wanted, and nothing else."

"You forget, Heffernan, how many men would have refused our offers, if we had not made a show, at least, of respect for their scruples."

"I don't think so, my Lord; you offered a bonus on prudery, and hence you met nothing but coyness. I'd have taken another line with them."

"And what might that be?" asked Lord Castlereagh, eagerly.

"COMPROMISE THEM," said Heffernan, sternly. "I never knew the man yet, nor woman either, that you couldn't place in such a position of entanglement, that every effort to go right should seem a struggle to do wrong, and *vice versâ*. You don't agree with me! Well, my Lord, I ask you if, in your experience of public men, you have ever met one less likely to be captured in this way than my friend Darcy?"

"From what I have seen and heard of the Knight of Gwynne, I acknowledge his character has all those elements of frankness and candour which should except him from such an embarrassment."

"Well, he's in the net already," said Heffernan, rubbing his hands gleefully.

"Why, you told me he refused to join us, and actually saw through your negotiation."

"So he did, and, in return for his keen-sightedness, I've COMPROMISED HIM with his party—you didn't perceive it, but the trick succeeded to perfection. When the Knight told me that he would not vote on the Union, or any measure pertaining to it, I waited for Ponsonby's motion, and made Holmes and Dawson spread the rumour at Daly's, and through town, that Darcy was to speak on the division, well knowing he would not rise. About eleven o'clock, just as Toler sat down, Prendergast got up to reply, but there was a shout of 'Darcy! Darcy!' and Prendergast resumed his seat amid great confusion. At that moment I left the bench beside you, and walked over to Darcy's side of the House, and whispered a few words in his ear—an invitation to sup, I believe it was—but while he was answering me, I nodded towards you, and, as I went down the steps, muttered loud enough to be heard, 'All right!' Every eye was turned at once towards him, and he, having no intention of speaking, nor having made any preparation, felt both confused and amazed, and left the House about five minutes afterwards, while Prendergast was bungling out his tiresome reply. Before Darcy reached the Club House, the report was current that he was bought, and old Gillespie was circumstantially recounting how that his title was 'Lord Darcy in England'—'Baron Gwynne in that part of the United Kingdom called Ireland.'"

"Not even success, Heffernan," said the Secretary, with an air of severity—"not even success will excuse a trick of this kind."

Heffernan looked steadily towards him, as if he half doubted the sincerity of the speech; it seemed something above or beyond his comprehension.

"Yes," said Lord Castlereagh, "you heard me quite correctly. I repeat it, advantages obtained in this fashion are too dearly purchased."

"What an admirable actor John Kemble is, my Lord," said Heffernan, with a quiet smile; "don't you think so?"

Lord Castlereagh nodded his assent: the transition was too abrupt to please him, and he appeared to suspect that it concealed some other object than that of changing the topic.

"Kemble," continued Heffernan, while he sipped his wine carelessly—"Kemble is, I suspect strongly, the greatest actor we have ever had on the English stage. Have you seen him in 'Macbeth?'"

"Several times, and always with renewed pleasure," said the Secretary, gradually recovering from his reserve.

"What a force of passion he throws into the part! How terrible he makes the conflict between a great purpose and a weak nature! Do you remember his horror at the murderers who come to tell of Banquo's death? The sight of their bloody hands shocks him, as though they were not the evidences of his own success."

Lord Castlereagh's calm countenance became for a second crimson, and his lip trembled with struggling indignation, and then, as if subduing the temptation of anger, he broke into a low, easy laugh, and with an imitation of Kemble's manner, called out, "There's blood upon thy face!"

"Talking of a bloody hand, my Lord," said Heffernan, at once resuming his former easy jocularity, "reminds me of that Mr. Hickman, or Hickman O'Reilly, as the fashion is to call him; is he to have his baronetcy?"

"Not, certainly, if we can secure him without it."

"And I think we ought. It should be quite sufficient remuneration for a man like him to vote with the Government; his father became a Protestant because it was the gentlemanly faith, and I don't see why the son should not choose his politics on the same principle. Have you ever asked him to dinner, my Lord?"

"Yes, and his father, too. I have had the three generations, but I rather fear the party did not go off well. I had not in those days, Heffernan, the benefit of your admirable counsels, and picked my company unwisely."

"A great mistake with such men as these," said Heffernan, oracularly; "the guests should have been the cream of your Lordship's noble acquaintance. I'd have had an Earl and a Marquis at either side of each of them; I'd have turned their heads with noble names, and pelted them with the Peerage the whole time of dinner; when he had taken wine with a Chamberlain and some Lords in Waiting, if your Lordship would only address him, in a voice loud enough to be heard, as 'O'Reilly,' referring to him on a point of sporting etiquette or country gentleman's life, I think you might spare the Baronetage the honour of his alliance. Do you think, on a proper representation, and with due securities against the repetition of the offence, the Chancellor would let himself be called 'Clare?'—only for once, remember—because I'm satisfied, if this could be arranged, O'Reilly is yours."

"I'd rather depute you to ask the question," said Lord Castlereagh, laughing; "assuredly I'll not do so myself. But when do these people come to town?—to-morrow, or next day, I suppose."

"On Friday next they will all be here. Old Hickman comes up to receive something like two hundred and twenty thousand pounds—for Darcy has raised the money to pay off the incumbrances—the son is coming for the debate, and the grandson is to be balloted for at Daly's."

"You have made yourself master of all their arrangements, Heffernan; may I ask if they afford you any clue to assisting us in our object?"

"When can you give a dinner, my Lord?" said the other.

"Any day after Wednesday; nay, Wednesday itself; I might easily get off Brooke's dinner for that day."

"The sooner the better; time is of great consequence now. Shall we say Wednesday?"

"Be it so: now for the party."

"A small one; selectness is the type of cordiality. The invitation must be verbal, done in your own admirable way: 'Don't be late, gentlemen, for Beerhaven and Drogheda are to meet you, and you know they scold if the soup suffers'—something in that style. Now let us see who are our men."

"Begin with Beerhaven and Drogheda, they are sure cards."

"Well, then, Massey Hamilton—but he's only a commoner—to be sure his uncle's a Duke, but, confound him, he never talks of him! I must draw him out about the Highlands and deer-stalking, and the Christmas revels at Clanschattaghan; he's three—Kilgoff four; he's first-rate, and will discuss his noble descent till his carriage is announced. Loughdooner, five——"

"He's another bore, Heffernan."

"I know he is, my Lord; but he has seven daughters, and will consequently make up to young Beecham, who is a great prize in the wheel matrimonial. We shall want a Bishop to say grace; I think Dunmore is the man; he is the last of your Lordship's making, and can't refuse a short invitation."

"Six, and the three Hickmans nine, and ourselves eleven; now for the twelfth——"

"Darcy, of course," said Heffernan; "he must be asked, and, if possible, induced to come; Hickman O'Reilly will be far more easily managed if we make him suppose that we have already secured Darcy ourselves."

"He'll decline, Heffernan; depend upon it he'll not come."

"You think he saw through my *ruse* in the House—not a bit of it; he is the least suspecting man in Ireland, and I'll make that very circumstance the reason of his coming. Hint to him that rumour says he is coquetting with the Government, and he'll go any lengths to brave public opinion by confronting it: that's Darcy, or I'm much mistaken in my man, and to say truth, my Lord, it's an error I rarely fall into." A smile of self-satisfaction lit up Heffernan's features as he spoke; for, like many cunning people, his weak point was vanity.

"You may call me as a witness to character whenever you please," said Lord Castlereagh, who, in indulging the self-glorification of the other, was now taking his own revenge; "you certainly knew Upton better than I did."

"Depend upon it," said Heffernan, as he leaned back in his chair, and delivered his words in a tone of authority—"depend upon it, the great events of life never betray the man, it is the small, every-day dropping occurrences both make him and mar him. I made Upton my friend for life by missing a woodcock he aimed at; *he* brought down the bird, and *I* bagged the sportsman. Ah! my Lord, the real science of life is knowing how to be, gracefully, in the wrong; how to make those slips that reflect on your own prudence, by exhibiting the superior wisdom of your acquaintances. Of the men who compassionate your folly or deplore your weakness, you may borrow money: from the fellows who envy your abilities and extol your capacity, you'll never get sixpence."

"How came it, Heffernan, that you never took office?" said Lord Castlereagh, suddenly, as if the idea forced itself abruptly upon him.

"I'll tell you, my Lord," replied Heffernan, speaking in a lower tone, and as if imparting a deep secret, "they could not spare me—that's the real fact—they could not spare me. Reflect, for a moment, what kind of thing the Government of Ireland is; see the difficulty, nay, the impossibility of any set of men arriving here fresh from England being able to find out their way, or make any guess at the leading characters about them: every retiring official likes to embarrass his successor—that's all natural and fair; then, what a mass of blunders and mistakes await the newly come Viceroy or Secretary! In the midst of the bleak expanse of pathless waste I was the sign-post. The new players, who took up the cards when the game was half over, could know nothing of what trumps were in, or what tricks were taken. I was there to tell them all; they soon saw that I could do this; and they also saw that I wanted nothing from any party."

"That must be confessed on every hand, Heffernan. Never was support more generous and independent than yours! and the subject reminds me of a namesake, and, as I hear, a nephew of yours, the Reverend Joshua Heffernan—is not that the name?"

"It is, my Lord, my nephew; but I'm not aware of having asked anything for him; I never——"

"But I did, Heffernan, and I do. He shall have the living of Drumslade; I spoke to the Lord-Lieutenant about it yesterday. There is a hitch somewhere, but we'll get over it."

"What may be the obstacle you allude to?" said Heffernan, with more anxiety than he wished to evince.

"Lord Killgobbin says the presentation was promised to his brother, for his influence over Rochfort."

"Not a bit of it, my Lord. It was I secured Rochfort. The case was this. He is separated from his wife Lady Mary, who had a life annuity chargeable on Rochfort's pension from the Ordnance. Cook enabled me to get him twelve thousand pounds on the secret service list, provided he surrendered the pension. Rochfort was only too happy to do so, because it would spite his wife; and the next gazette announced 'that the member for Dunraven had declared his intention of voting with the Government, but, to prevent even the breath of slander on his motives, had surrendered his retiring pension as a Storekeeper-General.' There never was a finer theme for editorial panegyric, and in good sooth your Lordship's press made the most of it. What a patriot!"

"What a scoundrel!" muttered Lord Castlereagh; and it would have puzzled a listener, had there been one, to say on whom the epithet was conferred.

"As for Killgobbin or his brother having influence over Rochfort, it's all absurd. Why, my Lord, it was that same brother married Rochfort to Lady Mary."

"That is conclusive," said Lord Castlereagh, laughing.

"Faith, I think so," rejoined Heffernan; "if you do recover after being hanged, I don't see that you want to make a friend of the fellow that pinioned your hands in the 'press-room.' If there's no other reason against Jos's promotion than this— "

"If there were, I'd endeavour to overcome it," said Lord Castlereagh. "Won't you take more wine?—pray let us have another bottle."

"No more, my Lord; it's only in such safe company I ever drink so freely," said Heffernan, laughing, as he rose to say, "Good night."

"You'll take measures for Wednesday, then; that is agreed upon?"

"All settled," said Heffernan, as he left the room. "Good-by."

"There's a building debt on that same living of seventeen hundred pounds," said Lord Castlereagh, musing; "I'll easily satisfy Killgobbin that we mean to do better for his brother."

"Take office, indeed!" muttered Heffernan, as he lay back in his carriage; "there's something better than that, governing the men that hold office, holding the reins, pocketing the fare, and never paying the breakage when the coach upsets. No, no, my Lord, you are a clever fellow for your years, but you must live longer before you measure Con Heffernan."

CHAPTER XV.

THE KNIGHT'S NOTIONS OF FINANCE.

Heffernan's calculations were all correct, and the Knight accepted Lord Castlereagh's invitation, simply because rumour attributed to him an alliance with the Government. "It is a pity," said he, laughing, "so much good calumny should have so little to feed upon, so here goes to give it something."

Darcy had as little time as inclination to waste on the topic, as the whole interval was occupied in law business with Gleeson, who arrived each morning with a chariot full of parchments, and almost worried the Knight to death by reciting deeds and indentures, to one word of which throughout he could not pay the least attention. He affected to listen, however, as he saw how much Gleeson desired it, and he wrote his name everywhere and to everything he was asked.

"By Jove!" cried he, at last, "I could have run through the whole estate with less fatigue of mind or body than it has cost me to keep a hold of it."

Through all the arrangements, there was but one point on which he felt anxious, and the same question recurred at every moment, "This cannot compromise Lionel in any way?—this will lead to no future charge upon the estate after my death?" Indeed, he would not consent to any plan which in the slightest degree affected his son's interests, being determined that whatever his extravagances, the penalty should end with himself.

While these matters were progressing, Old Hickman studiously avoided meeting the Knight; a sense of his discomfiture at the abbey—a fact he supposed must have reached Darcy's ears—and the conviction that his long-cherished game to obtain the property was seen through, abashed the old man, and led him to affect illness when the Knight called.

A pleasant letter which the post had brought from Lionel routed every other consideration from Darcy's mind. His son was coming over to see him, and bringing three or four of his brother officers to have a peep at "the West," and a few days' hunting with the Knight's pack. Every line of this letter glowed with buoyancy and high spirits; schemes for amusement alternating with the anticipated amazement of his English friends at the style of living they were to witness at Gwynne Abbey.

"We shall have but eight days with you, my leave from the Prince will go no further," wrote he, "but I know well how much may be done in that short space. Above all, secure Daly; I wish our fellows to see him particularly. I do not ask about the stable, because I know the horses are always in condition; but let Dan give the black horse plenty of work every day; and if the brown mare we got from Mullock can be ridden by any one, she must have a saddle on her now. We hope to have four days' hunting; and let the woodcocks take care of themselves in the intervals, for we are bent on massacre."

The postscript was brief, but it surprised Darcy more than all the rest.

"Only think of my spending four days last week down in Essex with a worthy kinsman of my mother's, Lord Netherby: a splendid place, glorious shooting, and the best greyhounds I ever saw run. He understands everything but horses; but I have taken on me to enlighten him a little, and have sent down four greys from Guildfords' yesterday, better than any we have in the Prince's stables; he is a fine fellow, though I didn't like him at first; a great courtier in his way, but *au fond* warm-hearted and generous Keep my secret from my mother, but he intends coming over with us Adieu! dear father. Look to Forester; don't let him run away before we arrive. Cut Dublin and its confounded politics. Netherby says the Ministers have an immense majority—the less reason for swelling or decreasing it.

"Yours ever,

"Lionel Darcy."

"And so our trusty and well-beloved cousin of Netherby is coming to visit us," said the Knight, musing. "Well, Lionel, I confess myself hal of your mind. I did not like him at first—the better impression is yet to come. In any case, let us receive him suitably; and, fortunately, here's Gleeson to help the arrangement. Well, Gleeson, I hope matters are making some progress. Are we to see the last of these parchments soon? Here's a letter from my son. Read it, and you'll see I must get back to 'the West' at once."

Gleeson perused the letter, and when he had finished, returned it into the Knight's hand without speaking.

"Can we conclude this week?" asked Darcy.

"There are several points yet, sir, of great difficulty. Some I have already submitted for counsel's opinion; one in particular, as regards the serving of notice of repayment—there would appear to be a doubt on this head."

"There can be none in reality," said Darcy, hastily. "I have Hickman's letter, in his own handwriting, averring his readiness to release the mortgage at any day."

"Is the document witnessed, and on a stamp?" asked Gleeson, cautiously.

"Of course it is not. Those are scarcely the forms of a note between two private gentlemen."

"It might be of use in equity, no doubt," muttered Gleeson, "or before a jury; but we have no time for these considerations now. The Attorney-General thinks——"

"Never mind the Attorney-General. Have we the money to repay? Well, does Hickman refuse to accept it?"

"He has not been asked, as yet, sir," said Gleeson, whose business notions were not a little ruffled by this abrupt mode of procedure.

"And, in Heaven's name! Gleeson, why pester yourself and me with overcoming obstacles that may never arise? Wait on Hickman at once—to-day. Tell him we are prepared and desirous of paying off these incumbrances. If he objects, hear his objection."

"He will refer me to his solicitor, sir—Mr. Kennedy, of Hume-street—a very respectable man, no higher in the profession, but I may remark, in confidence, one who has no objection to a suit in equity or a trial at bar. It is not money Hickman wants, sir. He is perfectly satisfied with his security."

"What the devil is it, then? He's not Shylock, is he?" said Darcy, laughing.

"Not very unlike, perhaps, sir; but in the present instance, it is your influence with the Government he desires."

"But I have none, Gleeson—actually none. No man knows that better than you do. I could not make a gauger or a tide-waiter to-morrow."

"But you might, sir—you might make a Peer of the Realm if you wished it. Hickman knows this; and whatever scruples *you* might have in adopting the necessary steps, *his* conscience could never recognise them as worthy a moment's consideration."

"This is a topic I'll scarcely discuss with him," said the Knight, proudly. "I never, so far as I know, promised to pay a per-centage in my principles as well as in my gold. Mr. Hickman has a fair claim on the one; on the other, neither he nor any other man shall make an unjust demand. I am not of Christie Ford's mind," added he, laughingly. "He says, Gleeson, that if the English are bent on taking away *our* Parliament, the only revenge we have left is to spoil *their* Peerage. This is but a sorry theme to joke upon, after all; and to come back, what say you to trying my plan? I am to meet the old fellow at dinner, on Wednesday next, at Lord Castlereagh's."

"Indeed, sir!" said Gleeson, with a mixture of surprise and agitation greatly disproportioned to the intelligence.

"Yes. Why does that astonish you? The Secretary is too shrewd to neglect such men as these; they are the rising influences of Ireland."

Gleeson muttered a half assent, but evidently too much occupied with his own reflections to pay due attention to the Knight's remark, continued to himself, "On Wednesday!" then added aloud, "On Monday he is to be in Kildare. He told me he would remain there to receive his rents, and on Wednesday return to town. I believe, sir, there may be good counsel in your words. I'll try on Monday. I'll follow him down to Kildare, and as the papers relative to the abbey property are all in readiness, I'll endeavour to conclude that at once. So, you are to meet at dinner?"

"That same dinner-party seems to puzzle you," said the Knight, smiling.

"No, not at all, sir," replied Gleeson, hurriedly. "You were desirous of getting home next week to meet Mr. Lionel—Captain Darcy I must call him; if this arrangement can be made, there will be no difficulty in your return. But of course you'll not leave town before it is completed."

The Knight pledged himself to be guided by his man of business in all respects; but when they parted, he could not conceal from himself that Gleeson's agitated and troubled manner, so very unlike his usual calm deportment, boded difficulties and embarrassments which to his own eyes were invisible.

CHAPTER XVI.

A HURRIED VISIT.

It was on a severe night, with frequent gusts of stormy wind shaking the doors and window-frames, or carrying along the drifted flakes of snow with which the air was charged, that Lady Eleanor, her daughter, and Forester, were seated round the fire. All the appliances of in-door comfort by which they were surrounded seemed insufficient to dispel a sense of sadness that pervaded the little party. Conversation flowed not, as it was wont, in its pleasant current, diverging here and there as fancy or caprice suggested; the sentences were few and brief, the pauses between them long and frequent; a feeling of awkwardness, too, mingled with the gloom, for, at intervals, each would make an endeavour to relieve the weariness of time, and, in the effort, show a consciousness of the constraint.

Lady Eleanor lay back in her deep chair, and, with half-closed lids, seemed lost in thought. Helen was working at her embroidery, and, apparently, diligently too, although a shrewd observer might have remarked on the slow progress the work was making, and how inevitably her balls of coloured worsted seemed bent on entanglement; while Forester sat silently gazing on the wood fire, and watching the bright sparks as they flitted and danced above the red flame; his brow was clouded, and his look sorrowful; not without reason, perhaps; it was to be his last evening at the abbey—the last of those hours of happiness which seemed all the fairer when about to part with them for ever.

Lady Eleanor seemed grieved at his approaching departure. From the habit of his mind, and the nature of his education, he was more companionable to her than Lionel. She saw in him many qualities of high and sterling value, and even in his prejudices she could trace back several of those traits which marked her own youth, when, in the pride of her English breeding, she would tolerate no deviation from the habits of her own country. It was true, many of these notions had given way since his residence at the abbey; many of his opinions had undergone modification or change, but still he was distinctively English.

Helen, who possessed no standard by which to measure such prejudices, was far less indulgent towards them; her joyous, happy nature—the heirloom of her father's house—led her rather to jest than argue on these topics, and she contrasted the less apt and ready apprehension of Forester with the native quickness of her brother Lionel, disadvantageously to the former. She was sorry, too, that he was going; more so, because his society was so pleasing to her mother, and that, before him, Lady Eleanor exerted herself in a way which eventually reacted favourably on her own health and spirits. Further than this, her interest in him was weak.

Not so Forester: he was hopelessly, inextricably in love, not the less so, that he would not acknowledge it to himself; far more so, because he had made no impression on the object of his passion. There is a period in every story of affection when the flame grows the brighter, because unreflected, and seems the more concentrated, because unreturned. Forester was in this precise stage of the malady; he was as much piqued by the indifference, as fascinated by the charms of Helen Darcy. The very exertions he made for victory stimulated his own passion; while, in her efforts to interest or amuse him, he could not help feeling the evidence of her indifference to him.

We have said that the conversation was broken and interrupted; at length it almost ceased altogether, a stray remark of Lady Eleanor's, followed by a short reply from Forester, alone breaking the silence. Nor were these always very pertinent, inasmuch as the young aide-de-camp occasionally answered his own reflections, and not the queries of his hostess.

"An interesting time in Dublin, no doubt," said Lady Eleanor, half talking to herself; "for though the forces are unequal, and victory and defeat predestined, there will be a struggle still."

"Yes, madam, a brief one," answered Forester, dreamily, comprehending only a part of her remark.

"A brief and a vain one," echoed Lady Eleanor.

"Say, rather, a glorious one!" interposed Helen; "the last cheer of a sinking crew!"

Forester looked up, startled into attention by the energy of these few words.

"I should say so, too, Helen," remarked her mother, "if they were not accessory to their own misfortunes."

"Nay, nay, mamma, you must not remember their failings in their hour of distress; there is a noble-hearted minority untainted yet."

"There will be a majority of eighteen," said Forester, whose thoughts were wandering away, while he endeavoured to address himself to what he believed they were saying, nor was he aware of his error till aroused by the laughter of Lady Eleanor and her daughter.

"Eighteen!" reiterated he, solemnly.

"How few!" remarked Lady Eleanor, almost scornfully.

"You should say, how costly, mamma!" exclaimed Helen. "These gentlemen are as precious from their price as their rarity!"

"That is scarcely fair, Miss Darcy," said Forester, at once recalled to himself by the tone of mockery she spoke in; "many adopted the views of Government, after duly weighing every consideration of the measure; some, to my own knowledge, resisted offers of great personal advantage, and Lord Castlereagh was not aware of their adhesion——"

"Till he had them *en poche*, I suppose," said Helen, sarcastically; "just as you have been pleased to do with my ball of yellow worsted, and which I shall be thankful if you will restore to me."

Forester blushed deeply, as he drew from his coat-pocket the worsted, which, in a moment of abstraction, he had lifted from the ground, and thrust into his pocket, without knowing.

Had any moderately shrewd observer witnessed his confusion, and her enjoyment of it, he would easily have understood the precise relation of the two parties to each other. Forester's absence of mind betrayed his engaged affection, as palpably as Helen's laughter did her own indifference.

Lady Eleanor did not remark either; her thoughts still rested on the topic of which they had spoken, for it was a subject of no inconsiderable difficulty to her. Whatever her sense of indignant contempt for the bribed adherents of the Ministry, her convictions always inclined to these measures, whose origin was from her native country; her predilections were strongly English; not only her happiest days had been passed there, but she was constantly contrasting the position they would have occupied and sustained in that favoured land against the wasteful and purposeless extravagance of their life in Ireland.

Was it too late to amend? was the question ever rising to her mind now if even yet the Knight should be induced to adopt the more ambitious course? Every accidental circumstance seemed favourable to the notion; the Government craving his support; her own relatives, influential as they were from rank and station, soliciting it; the Prince himself according favours, which could no more be rejected, than acknowledged ungraciously. "What a career for Lionel! What a future for Helen!" such were reflections that would press themselves upon her, but to whose disentanglement her mind suggested no remedy.

"'Tis Mr. Daly, my Lady," said Tate, for something like the fourth time, without being attended to. "'Tis Mr. Daly wants leave to visit you."

"Mr. Bagenal Daly, mamma, wishes to know if you'll receive him?"

"Mr. Daly is exactly the kind of person to suggest this impracticable line of policy," said Lady Eleanor, with half-closed eyes; for the name alone had struck her, and she had not heard what was said.

"My dear mamma," said Helen, rising, and leaning over her chair, "it is a visit he proposes; nothing so very impracticable in that, I hope;" and then, at a gesture from her mother, continued to Tate, "Lady Eleanor will be very happy to see Mr. Daly."

Lady Eleanor had scarcely aroused herself from her reverie, when Bagenal Daly entered. His manner was stately, perhaps somewhat colder than usual, and he took his seat with an air of formal politeness.

"I have come, my Lady," said he, slowly, "to learn if I can be of any service in the capital; unexpected news has just reached me, requiring my immediate departure for Dublin."

"Not to-night, sir, I hope; it is very severe, and likely, I fear, to continue so."

"To-night, madam; within an hour, I expect to be on the road."

"Could you defer a little longer, and we may be fellow-travellers," said Forester; "I was to start to-morrow morning, but my packing can soon be made."

"I should hope," said Lady Eleanor, smiling, "that you will not leave us unprotected, gentlemen; and that one, at least, will remain here." This speech, apparently addressed to both, was specially intended for Forester, whose cheek tingled with a flush of pleasure as he heard it.

"I have no doubt, madam, that Captain Forester, whose age and profession are more in accordance with gallantry, will respond to your desire."

"If I could really fancy that I was not yielding to my own wishes only," stammered out Forester.

"Nay, I make it a request."

"There, sir, how happy to be entreated to what one's wishes incline them," added Daly; "you may go through a deal of life without being twice so fortunate. I should apologise for so brief a notice of my departure,

Lady Eleanor, but the intelligence I have received is pressing;" here he dropped his voice to a whisper, "the Ministers have hurried forward their Bill, and I shall scarcely be in time for the second reading."

"All accounts agree in saying that the Government majority is certain," observed Lady Eleanor, calmly.

"It is to be feared, madam, that such rumours are well founded, but the party who form the forlorn hope have their devoirs also."

"I am a very indifferent politician, Mr. Daly, but it strikes me, that a body so manifestly corrupt, give the strongest possible reasons for their own destruction."

"Were they all so, madam, I should join in the sentiment as freely as you utter it," replied Daly, proudly; "but it is a heavy sentence that would condemn the whole crew because there was a mutiny in the steerage; besides, these rights and privileges are held only in trust; no man can in honour or justice vote away that of which he is only the temporary occupant; forgive me, I beg, for daring to discuss the topic, but I thought the Knight had made you a convert to his own opinions."

"We have never spoken on the subject, Mr. Daly," replied Lady Eleanor, coldly; "the Knight dislikes the intrusion of a political matte. within the circle of his family, and for that reason, perhaps," added she, with a smile, "my daughter and myself feel for it all the temptation of a forbidden pleasure."

"Oh, yes!" exclaimed Helen, who heard the last few words of her mother's speech, "I am as violent a partisan as Mr. Daly could ask for; indeed, I am not certain if all my doctrines are not of his own teaching: I fear the Premier, distrust the Cabinet, and put no faith in the Secretary for Ireland; is not that the first article of our creed?—nay, nay, fear was no part of your instruction."

"And yet I have fears, my dear Helen, and very great fears just now," said Daly, in a low whisper, only audible by herself, and she turned her full and beaming eyes upon him for an explanation. As if anxious to escape the interrogatory, Daly arose hastily. "I must crave your indulgence for an abrupt leave-taking, Lady Eleanor," said he, approaching, as he kissed the hand held out to him; "I shall be able to tell the Knight that I left you both well, and under safe protection. Captain Forester, adieu; you need no admonition of mine respecting your charge;" and, with a low and courtly salute, he departed.

"Rely upon it, Captain Forester, he's bent on mischief now. I never saw him particularly mild and quiet in his manner, that it was not the prelude to some desperate ebullition," said Lady Eleanor.

"He is the very strangest of all mortals."

"Say, the most single-minded and straightforward," interposed Helen, "and I'll agree with you."

"When men of strong minds and ambitious views are curbed and held in within the petty sphere of a small social circle, they are, to my thinking, intolerable. It is making a drawing-room pet of a tiger; every step he takes upsets a vase, or smashes a jar. You smile at my simile."

"I'm sure it's a most happy one," said Forester, continuing.

"I enter a dissent," cried Helen, playfully. "He's a tiger, if you will, with his foes, but, in all the relations of private life, gentleness itself: for my part, I can imagine no more pleasing contrast to the modern code of manners than Mr. Bagenal Daly."

"There, Captain Forester, if you would win Miss Darcy's favour, you have now the model for your imitation."

Forester's face flushed, and he appeared overwhelmed with confusion, while Helen went on with her embroidery, tranquil as before.

"I believe," resumed Lady Eleanor—"I believe, after all, I am unjust to him; but much may be forgiven me for being so; he has made my son a wild, thoughtless boy, and my daughter——"

"No indiscretions, mamma," cried Helen, holding up her hand.

"Well, he has made my daughter telle que vous la voyez."

Forester was too well bred to venture on a word of flattery or compliment, but his glowing colour and sparkling eyes spoke his admiration.

Lady Eleanor's quick glance remarked this; and, as if the thought had never occurred before, she seemed amazed, either at the fact, or at her own previous inattention.

"Let us finish that second volume you were reading, Captain Forester," said she, glad to cut short the discussion. And, without a word, he took the book and began to read.

CHAPTER XVII.

BAGENAL DALY'S JOURNEY TO DUBLIN.

It is not our desire to practise any mystery with our reader, nor would the present occasion warrant such. Mr. Daly's hurried departure for Dublin was caused by the receipt of tidings which had that morning reached him, conveying the startling intelligence that his friend the Knight had accepted terms from the Government, and pledged himself to support their favoured measure.

It was a time when men were accustomed to witness the most flagrant breaches of honour and good faith. No station was too high to be above the reach of this reproach, no position too humble not to make its possessor a mark for corruption. It was an epidemic of dishonesty, and people ceased to wonder, as they heard of each new victim to the malady.

Bagenal Daly well knew that no man could be more exempt from an imputation of this nature than the Knight of Gwynne; every act of his life, every sentiment he professed, every trait of his character, flatly contradicted the supposition. But he also knew that though Darcy was unassailable by all the temptations of bribery, come in what shape they might, that his frank and generous spirit would expose him to the stratagems and devices of a wily and insidious party, and that if, by any accident, an expression should fall from him in all the freedom of convivial enjoyment that could be tortured into even the resemblance of a pledge, he well knew that his friend would deem any sacrifice of personal feeling light in the balance, rather than not adhere to it.

Resolved not to lose a moment, he despatched Sandy to order horses along the line, and having passed the remainder of the day in the preparations for his departure, he left the abbey before midnight. A less determined traveller might have hesitated on setting out in such a night: the long menacing storm had at length burst forth, and the air resounded with a chaos of noise, amid which, the roaring breakers and the crash of falling trees were uppermost; with difficulty the horses were enabled to keep their feet, as the sea washed heavily over the wall, and deluged the road, while at intervals the fallen timber obstructed the way, and delayed his progress. Difficulty was, however, the most enjoyable stimulant to Daly's nature; he loved an obstacle as other men love a pleasure, and, as he grew older, so far from yielding to the indolence of years, his hardy spirit seemed to revel in the thought, that amid dangers and perils his whole life had been passed, yet never had he suffered himself to be a beaten enemy.

The whole of that night, and all the following day, the violence of the storm was unabated; uprooted trees and wrecked villages met his eye as he passed, while, in the larger towns, the houses were strongly barred and shuttered, and scarcely one living thing to be seen through the streets. Nothing short of the united influence of bribery and intimidation could procure horses in such a season, and had any messenger of less sturdy pretensions than honest Sandy been despatched to order them, they would have been flatly refused. Bagenal Daly and his man were, however, too well known in that part of Ireland to make such a course advisable, and though postboys and ostlers condoled together, the signal of Daly's appearance silenced every thought of opposition, and the words "I'm ready!" were an order to dash forward none dared to disobey.

So had it continued until he reached Moate, where he found a message from Sandy, informing him that no horses could be procured, and that he must bring on those from Athlone the entire way to Kilbeggan.

"You hear me," cried Daly to the astonished postboy, who, for the last two miles, had spared neither whip nor spur, in the glad anticipation of a speedy shelter—"you hear me. To Kilbeggan."

"Oh, begorra! that's impossible, yer honour. If it was the month of May, and the road was a bowling-green, the bastes couldn't do it."

"Go on!" cried Daly, shutting up the glass, and throwing himself back in the chaise.

But the postboy only buttoned up the collar of his coat around his face, thrust his whip into his boot, and drawing his sleeves over his hands, sat a perfect picture of fatalism.

"I say, go on!" shouted Daly, as he lowered the front window of the chaise.

A low muttering from the driver, still impassive as before, was all the reply, and at the same instant a sharp report was heard, and a pistol bullet whizzed beside his hat.

"Will you go *now?*" cried Bagenal Daly, as he levelled another weapon n the window: but no second entreaty was necessary, and with his head bent down almost to the mane, and with a mingled cry for mercy and imprecation together, he drove the spurs into his jaded beast, and whipped with all his might through the almost deserted town. With the despairing energy of one who felt his life was in peril, the wretched postboy hurried madly forward, urging the tired animals up the hills, and caring neither for rut nor hollow in his onward course, till at length, blown and exhausted, the animals came to a dead stand, and with heaving flanks and outstretched forelegs, refused to budge a step farther.

"There!" cried the postboy, as dropping from the saddle he fell on his knees upon the road, "shoot, and be d—d to you. I can do no more."

The terrified expression of the fellow's face, as the lamp of the chaise threw its light upon him, seemed to change the current of Daly's thoughts, for he laughed loud and heartily as he looked upon him.

"Come, come," said he, good-humouredly, "is not that Kilbeggan where I see the lights yonder?"

"Sorra bit of it," sighed the other, "it is only Horseleap."

"Well, push on to Horseleap, perhaps they've horses there."

"Begorra! you might as well look for black tay in a bog hole; 'tis a poor shebeen' is the only thing in the village;" and, so saying, he took the idle on his arm, and walked along before the horses, who with drooping heads tottered after at a foot's pace.

About half an hour of such travelling brought Daly in front of a miserable cabin, over the door of which a creaking sign proclaimed accommodation for man and beast. To the partial truth of this statement the bright glare of a fire that shone between the chinks of the shutters bore witness, and disengaging himself from the chaise Daly knocked loudly for admission. There are few less conciliating sounds to the ears of a hot-tempered man than those hesitating whispers which, while exposed to a storm himself, he hears deliberating on the question of his admission. Such were the mutterings Daly now listened to, and to which he was about to reply by forcing his entrance, when the door was opened by a man in the dress of a peasant, who somewhat sulkily demanded what he wanted.

"Horses, if you have them, to reach Kilbeggan," said Daly, "and if you have not, a good fire and shelter until they can be procured;" and, as he spoke, he pushed past the man, and entered the room from which the blazing light proceeded.

With his back to the fire, and hands thrust carelessly into the pockets of his coat, stood a man of eight-and-thirty or forty years of age; in dress, air, and appearance, he might have been taken for a country horse-dealer; and so, indeed, his well-worn top-boots and green coat, cut in jockey fashion, seemed to bespeak him. He was rather under the middle size, but powerfully built, his wide chest, long arms, and bowed legs, all indicating the possession of that strength which is never the accompaniment of more perfect symmetry.

Although Daly's appearance unquestionably proclaimed his class in life, the other exhibited no mark of deference or respect to him as he entered, but maintained his position with the same easy indifference as at first.

"You make yourself at home here, good friend, if one might judge from the way you knocked at the door," said he, addressing Daly with a look whose easy familiarity was itself an impertinence.

"I have yet to learn," said Daly, sternly, "that a gentleman must practise any peculiar ceremony when seeking the shelter of a 'shebeen,' not to speak of the right by which such as you address me as your good friend."

An insolent laugh, that Daly fancied was re-echoed by some one without, was the first reply to this speech; when, after a few minutes, the man added, "I see you're a stranger in these parts."

"If I had not been so, the chance is I should have taught you somewhat better manners before this time. Move aside, sir, and let me see the fire."

But the other never budged in the slightest, standing in the same easy posture as before.

Daly's dark face grew darker, and his heavy brows met in a deep frown, while with a spring that showed no touch of time in his strong frame, he bounded forward, and seized the man by the collar. Few men were Daly's equals in point of strength; but although he with whom he now grapple made no resistance whatever, Daly never stirred him from the spot, to which he seemed fast and firmly rooted.

"Well, that's enough of it!" said the fellow, as with a rough jerk he freed himself from the grasp, and sent Daly several paces back into the room.

"Not so!" cried Daly, whose passion now boiled over, and drawing a pistol from his bosom, he levelled it at him. Quick as the motion was, the other was equally ready, for his hand now presented a similar weapon at Daly's head.

"Move aside, or——"

A coarse, insulting laugh drowned Daly's words, and he pulled the trigger, but the pistol snapped without exploding.

"There it is now," cried the fellow, rudely; "luck's against you, old boy, so you'd better keep yourself cool and easy;" and with these words he uncocked the weapon, and replaced it in his bosom. Daly watched the moment, and with a bound placed himself beside him, when, bringing his leg in front, he caught the man round the middle, and hurled him headlong on the ground.

He fell as if he had been shot; but, rolling over, he leaned upon his elbow and looked up, without the slightest sign of passion, or even excitement, on his features.

"I'd know that trip in a thousand; begad, you're Bagenal Daly, and nobody else!"

Although not a little surprised at the recognition, Daly suffered no sign of astonishment to escape him, but drew his chair to the fire, and stretched out his legs before the blaze. Meanwhile, the other having arisen, leaned over the back of a chair, and stared at him steadfastly.

"I am as glad as a hundred pound note, now, you didn't provoke me to lay a hand on you, Mr. Daly," said he, slowly, and in a voice not devoid of a touch of feeling; "'tisn't often I bear malice, but I'd never forgive my self the longest day I'd live."

Daly turned his eyes towards him, and, for some minutes, they continued to look at each other without speaking.

"I see you don't remember me, sir," said the stranger, at length; "but I've a better memory, and a better reason to have it besides—you saved my life once."

"Saved your life!" repeated Daly, thoughtfully; "I've not the slightest recollection of ever having seen you before."

"It's all true I'm telling, for all that," replied the other; "and although it happened above five-and-twenty years since, I'm not much changed, they tell me, in look or appearance." He paused at these words, as if to give

Daly time to recognise him; but the effort seemed in vain, as, after a long and patient scrutiny, Daly said, "No, I cannot remember you."

"Let me see, then," said the man, "if I can't refresh your memory. Were you in Dublin in the winter of '75 ?"

"Yes; I had a house in Stephen's-green——"

"And used to drive four black thorough-breds without winkers."

"It's clear that *you* know *me*, at least," said Daly; "go on."

"Well, sir, do you remember, it was about a week before Christmas, that Captain Burke Fitzsimon was robbed of a pair of pistols in the guard-room of the Upper Castle Yard, in noonday, ay, and tied with his own sash to the guard-bed ?"

"By Jove! I do. He was regularly laughed out of the regiment."

"Faix, and many that laughed at him mightn't have behaved a deal better than he did," replied the other, with a dogged sternness in his manner. He became silent after these words, and appeared deeply sunk in meditation, when suddenly he drew two splendidly chased pistols from his bosom, and held them out to Daly as he said, "There they are, and as good as they are handsome, true at thirty paces, and never fail."

Daly gazed alternately from the pistols to their owner, but never uttered a word.

"That same day," resumed the man, "you were walking down the quay near the end of Watling-street, when there was a cry of 'Stop thief!—stop him!—a hundred guineas to the man that takes him!' and shortly after a man crossed the quay, pursued closely by several people, one of them, and the foremost, being Tom Lambert the constable, the strongest man, they said, of his day, in Ireland. The fellow that ran could beat them all, and was doing it too, when, just as he gained Bloody-bridge, he saw a child on the pathway all covered with blood, and a bulldog standing over him, worrying him——"

"I have it all," said Daly, interrupting him; "'tis as fresh before me as if it happened yesterday. The robber stopped to save the child, and seizing the bulldog by the throat, hurled him over the wall into the Liffey. Lambert, as you call him, had by this time come close up, and was within two yards of the man, when I, feeling compassion for a fellow that could be generous at such a moment, laid my hand on the constable's arm to stop him; he struck me; but, if he did, he had his reward, for I threw him over the hip on the crown of his head, and he had a brain fever after it that almost brought him to death's door. And where were you all this time, and what were you doing ?"

"I was down Barrack-street, across the Park, and near Knockmaroon-gate, before they could find a door to stretch Tom Lambert on."

"You!" said Daly, staring at him, "why, it was Freney, they told me, performed that exploit for a wager."

"So it was, sir," said the man, standing up and crossing his arms, not without something of pride in his look—"I'm Freney."

Daly arose and gazed at the man with all that curious scrutiny one bestows upon some remarkable object, measuring his strong athletic frame with the eye of a connoisseur, and, as it were, calculating the physical resources of so powerful a figure.

"You see, sir," said the robber, at last, "I was right when I told you that you saved my life; there were thirteen indictments hanging over my head that day, and if I'd been taken they'd have hanged me as round as a turnip."

"You owe it to yourself," said Daly; "had you not stopped for the child, it was just as likely that I'd have tripped you up myself."

"'Tis a feeling I never could get over," said the robber; "'twas a little boy, about the same age as that, that saved the Kells coach the night I stopped it near Dangan. And now, sir, let me ask you what in the world brought you into the village of Horseleap? for I'm sure," added he, with a laugh, "it was never to look after me."

"You are right there, friend; I'm on my way up to town to be present at the debate in Parliament on the Union—a question that has its interest for yourself, too."

"How so, sir," said the other, curiously.

"Plainly enough, man; if they carry the Union, they'll not leave a man worth robbing in the island. You'll have to take to an honest calling, Freney—turn cattle-drover. By the way, they tell me you're a good judge of a horse."

"Except yourself, there's not a better in the island; and if you've no objection, I'll mount and keep you company as far as Maynooth, where you'll easily get horses—and it will be broad daylight by that time—to bring you into Dublin."

"I accept the offer willingly. I'll venture to say we shall not be robbed on the journey."

"Well, sir, the horses won't be here for an hour yet, and if you'll join me in a bit of supper I was going to have when you came in, it will help to pass the time till we are ready to start."

Daly assented, not the less readily that he had not eaten anything since morning, and Freney left the room to hasten the preparations for the meal.

"Come, Freney," said Daly, as the other entered the room a few moments after, "was it the strength of conscious rectitude that made you stand my fire as you did a while ago, or did you think me so bad a marksman at four paces?"

"Neither, sir," replied the robber, laughing; "I saw the pan of the lock half open as you drew it from your pocket, and I knew the priming must have fallen out, but for that——"

"You had probably fired, yourself?"

"Just so," rejoined he, with a short nod. "I could have shot you before you levelled at me. Now, sir, here's something far better than burning powder. I am sure you are too old a traveller not to be able to eat a rasher of bacon."

"And this I take to be as free of any allegiance to the King as yourself," said Daly, as he poured out a wine-glass full of "poteen" from a short black bottle.

"You're right, sir," said Freney, with a laugh. "We're both duty free. Let me help you to an egg."

"I never ate better bacon in my life," said Daly, who seemed to relish his supper with considerable gusto.

"I'm glad you like it, sir. It is a notion of mine that Costy Moore of Kilcock cures a pig better than any man in this part of Ireland; and though his shop is next the police-barracks, I went in there myself to buy this."

Daly stared, with something of admiration in his look, at the man, whose epicurism was indulged at the hazard of his neck, and he pledged the robber with a motion of the head that betokened a high sense of his daring. "I've heard you have had some close escapes, Freney."

"I was never taken but once, sir. A woman hid my shoes when I was asleep. I was at the foot of the Galtee mountains: the ground is hard and full of sharp shingle, and I couldn't run. They brought me into Clonmel, and I was in the heaviest irons in the gaol before two hours were over. That's the strong gaol, Mr. Daly; they've the best walls and the thickest doors there I have ever seen in any gaol in Ireland. For," added he, with a sly laugh, "I went over them all, in a friendly sort of a way."

"A kind of professional tour, Freney?"

"Just so, sir; taking a bird's-eye view of the country from the drop, because, maybe, I wouldn't have time for it at another opportunity."

"You're a hardened villain!" said Daly, looking at him with an expression the robber felt to be a finished compliment.

"That's no lie, Mr. Daly; and if I wasn't, could I go on for twenty years, hunted down like a wild beast, with fellows tracking me all day, and lying in watch for me all night? Where we are sitting now is the only spot in the whole island where I can say I'm safe. This is my brother's cabin."

"Your brother is the same man that opened the door for me?"

Freney nodded, and went on: "He's a poor labouring man, with four acres of wet bog for a farm, and a young woman, in the ague, for a wife, and if it wasn't for myself he'd be starving; and would you believe it, now, he'd not take to the road for one night—just one single night—to be as rich as the Duke of Leinster; and here am I"—and, as he spoke, his chest expanded, and his dark eyes flashed wildly—"here am I, that would rather be on my black mare's back, with my holsters at the saddle, watching the sounds of wheels on a lonely road, than I'd be any gentleman in the land, barring your own self."

"And why me?" said Daly, in a voice whose melancholy cadence made it solemn as a death-bell.

"Just because you're the only man I ever heard tell of that was fond of danger for the fun of it. Didn't I see the leap you took at the Black Lough, just to show the English Lord-Lieutenant how an Irish gentleman rides, with the rein in your mouth, and your hands behind your back. Isn't that true?"

Daly nodded, and muttered, "I have the old horse still."

"By the good day! I'd spend a week in Newgate to see you on his back."

"Well, Freney," said Daly, who seemed not disposed to encourage a conversation so personal in its allusions, "where have you been lately?—in the south?"

"No, sir; I spent the last fortnight watching an old fox that doubled on me at last—old Hickman, of Loughrea, that used to be."

"Old Hickman!—what of him?" cried Daly, whose interest became at once excited by the mention of the name.

"I found out, sir, that he was to be down here at Kildare to receive his rents—for he owns a fine estate here—and that, besides, Tom Gleeson, the great agent from Dublin, was to meet him, as some said, to pay him a large sum of money for the Knight of Gwynne—some heavy debt, I believe, owing for many a year."

"Yes—go on. What then?"

"Well, I knew the reason Hickman wanted the money here: Lord Tyrawley was going to sell him a part of Gore's Wood, for hard cash—d'ye mind, sir, hard cash—down on the nail, for my Lord likes high play at Daly's——"

"D—n Lord Tyrawley!" said Daly, impatiently. "What of Hickman?"

"Well, d—n him too! He's a shabby negur. I stopped him at Ball's-bridge once, and got but three guineas and some shillings for my pains. But to come back to old Hickman: I found he had arrived at the 'Black Dog,' and that Gleeson had come the same evening, and so I disguised myself like an old farmer the next morning, and pretended I wanted his advice about an asthma that I had, just to see the lie of the old premises, and whether he was alone, or had the two bailiffs with him, as usual. There they were, sir, sure enough, and well armed too, and fresh hasps on the door, to lock it inside, all secure as a bank. I saw these things while the old doctor was writing the prescription, for he tore a leaf out of his pocket-book to order me some stuff for the cough—faith, 'tis pills of another kind they'd have given me if they found me out. That was all I got for my guinea in goold, not to speak of the danger;" and so saying, he pulled a crumpled piece of paper from his pocket, and held it out towards Daly. "That's not it, sir; 'tis the other side the writing is on."

But Daly's eyes were fixed upon the paper, which he held firmly between both hands.

"Ay, I see what you are looking at," said Freney; "that was a kind of memorandum the old fellow made of the money Gleeson paid him the day before."

Daly paid no attention to the remark, but muttered half aloud the contents of the document before him: "Cheque on Ball for eighteen thousand, payable at sight—thirty-six thousand eight hundred and ten pounds in notes of the Bank of England—gold, seventeen hundred guineas."

"There was a lob," cried Freney, as he rubbed his hands together. "I was set up for life if I got half of it! And now, Mr. Daly, just tell me one thing—isn't Mr. Darcy there as bad as myself, to take all this money for his vote?"

"How do you mean?" said Daly, sternly.

"I mean that a gentleman born and bred as he is, oughtn't to sell his country for goold; that if a blackguard like myself takes to the road, it's all natural and reasonable, and the world's little worse off when they hang half a dozen of my kind; but for a real born gentleman of the old stock of the land, to go and take money for his vote in Parliament!"

"And who dares to say he did so?" cried Daly, indignantly.

"Faix, that's the story up in Dublin; they say he'd no other way of clearing off the debts on his property. Bad cess to me if I'd do it. Here I am, a robber and a highwayman, I don't deny it, but may I wear hemp for a handkerchief if I'd sell my country. Bad luck to the Union, and all that votes for it," said he, as, filling a bumper of whisky, he tossed it off to this laudable sentiment.

"If you hadn't wronged my friend the Knight of Gwynne, I'm not certain that I wouldn't have pledged your toast myself."

"If he's a friend of yours I say nothing against him; but sure when he——"

"Once for all," said Daly, sternly, "this story is false;" while he added, in a low muttering to himself, "corruption must needs have spread widely when such a calumny was even ventured on. And so, Freney, Hickman escaped you?"

"He did, sir," said Freney, sighing; "he made a lodgment in Kildare next day, and more of the money he carried up to town, guarded all the way by the two fellows I told you. Ah! Mr. Daly, if all the world was as cunning as old Peter, I might give up the road as a bad job. There! do you hear that? Listen, sir."

"What is it?" said Daly, after a moment's silence.

"They're my nags, sir, coming up the road. I'd know their trot if I heard it among a troop of dragoons. 'Tis clippers they are."

As he spoke he arose from the table, and lighting a small lantern he always carried with him, hastened to the door, where already the two horses were standing, a bare-legged "gossoon" holding the bridles.

"Well, Jemmy, what's the news to-night?" said Freney.

"Nothing, sir, at all. I passed the down mail at Seery's Mill, and when the coachman heard the step of the horses, he laid on the wheelers wid all his might, and sat down on the footboard, and the two outside passengers lay flat as a pancake on the top when I passed. I couldn't help giving a screech out of me for fun, and the old guard let fly, and sent a ball through my 'caubeen;'" and, as he said the words, he exhibited his ragged felt hat, which, in addition to its other injuries, now displayed a round bullet hole through either side.

"Serve you right," said Freney, harshly; "I wish he'd levelled three inches lower. That young rascal, sir, keeps the whole road in a state of alarm that stops all business on it:" then he added, in a whisper, "but he never failed me in his life. I've only to say when and where I want the horses, and I'd lay my neck on it he's there."

Daly, who had been for some minutes examining the two horses by the lantern with all the skill of an adept, now turned the light full upon the figure of the boy whose encomium was thus pronounced. The urchin, as if conscious that he was passing an inspection, set his tattered hat jauntily on one side, and with one arm a-kimbo, and a leg advanced, stood the very perfection of ragged self-sufficient rascality. Though at most not above fourteen years of age, and short in size even for that, his features had the shrewd intelligence of manhood; a round, wide head, covered with dark red hair, projected over two eyes set wide apart, whose bad expression was ingeniously improved by a habit of squinting at pleasure, a practice with which he now amused himself, as Mr. Daly continued to stare at him. His nose, which a wound had partly separated from the forehead, was short and wide, leaving an unnatural length to the lower part of the face, where an enormous mouth, garnished with large and regular teeth, was seen, a feature that actually gave a look of ferocity even to a face so young.

"It's plain to see what destiny awaits that young scoundrel," said Daly, as he gazed almost sadly at the assemblage of bad passions so palpably displayed in his countenance. "I'd wager the young devil knows it himself, and can see the gallows even now before him."

A wild burst of frantic laughter broke from the urchin, as, in the exuberance of his merriment, he capered round Daly with gambols the most strange and uncouth, and then, mimicking an air of self-admiration, he strutted past, while he broke into one of the slang ditties of the day:

With beauty and manners to plaze,
I'll seek a rich wife, and I'll find her,
And live like a Lord all my days,
And sing, Tally-high-ho the Grinder!

Freney actually screamed with laughter as he watched the mingled astonishment and horror depicted in Daly's face.

"That fellow's fate will lie heavily on your heart yet," said Daly, in a voice whose solemn tones at once arrested Freney's merriment, while the "gossoon," with increased animation, and in a wilder strain, burst forth,

My Lord cheats at play like a rogue,
And my Lady flings honour behind her,
And why wouldn't I be in vogue,
And sing, Tally-high-ho the Grinder!

"Come," said Daly, turning away, for, amid all his disgust, a sense of the ludicrous was stealing over him, and the temptation to laugh was struggling in him—"come, let us be off; you have nothing to wait for, I suppose?"

"Nothing, sir; I'm ready this instant. Here, Jemmy, take this portmanteau, and meet us outside of Maynooth, under the old castle wall."

"Stay," cried Daly, whose misgivings about the safe arrival of his luggage would have made him prefer any other mode of transmission, "he'll scarcely be in time."

"Not in time! I wish I'd a bet of fifty guineas on it that he would not visit every stable on the road, and know every traveller's name and business, and yet be a good half hour before us. Off with you! Away!"

Diving under the two horses, the "gossoon" appeared at the other side of the road, and then, with a wild spring in the air, and an unearthly shout of laughter, he cleared the fence before him and disappeared, while as he went the strain of his slang song still floated in the air, and the *refrain*, "Tally-high-ho the Grinder," could be heard through the stillness of the night.

"Take the dark horse, sir, you're heavier than me," said Freney, as he held the stirrup.

"A clever hack, faith," said Daly, as he seated himself in the saddle, and gathered up the reins.

"And mounts you well," cried Freney, admiring both horse and rider once more by the light before he extinguished the lantern.

The storm had now considerably abated, and they rode on at a brisk pace, nor did they draw rein till the tall ruined castle of Maynooth could be seen, rearing its dark head against the murky sky.

"We part here," said Daly, who for some time had been lost in thought, "and I have nothing but thanks to offer you for this night's service, Freney; but if the time should come that I can do you a good turn——"

"I'll never ask it, sir," said Freney, interrupting him.

"And why not? Are you too proud?"

"Not too proud to be under any obligation to you," said the robber, stopping him, "but too proud of the honour you did me this night by keeping my company, ever to hurt your fame by letting the world know it. No, Mr. Daly, I knew your courage well, but this was the bravest thing ever you did."

He sprang from his horse as he spoke, and gave a long, shrill whistle. A deep silence followed, and he repeated the signal, and, soon after, the tramp of naked feet was heard on the road, and Jemmy advanced towards them at his ordinary sling trot.

"Take the trunk up to the town."

"No, no," said Daly, "I'll do that myself;" and he relieved the urchin of his burden, taking the opportunity to slip some crown pieces into his willing hand while he did so.

"Good-by, sir," said Freney, taking off his hat with courteous deference.

"Good-by, Freney," said Daly, as he seized the robber's hand and shook it warmly.—"I'll soon be shaking hands with twenty fellows not a whit more honest," said Daly, as he looked after him through the gloom. "Hang me if I don't think he's better company, too;" and with this very flattering reflection on some parties unknown, he plodded along towards the town.

Here, again, new disappointment awaited him—a sudden summons had called the members of both political parties to the capital, and horses were not to be had at any price.

"'Tis the Lord's marciful providence left him only the one arm," said a waiter, as he ushered Daly into a sitting-room, and cast a glance of most meaning terror at the retiring figure of Sandy.

"What do you mean?" asked Daly, hastily.

"It's what he smashed the best chaise in the yard, as if was a taycup, this morning. Mr. Tisdal ordered it to be ready at seven o'clock, to take him up to town, and, when it came to the door, up comes that long fellow with his one arm, and says: 'This will do for my master,' says he. and cool and asy he gets up into the chaise, and sits down, and, when he was once there, by my conscience you might as well try to drain the canal with a cullender as get him out again! We had a fight that lasted nigh an hour, and, sign on it, there's many a black eye in the stable-yard to show for it; but he beat them all off, and kept his ground. 'Never mind,' said Mr. Tisdal, and he whispered a word to the master; and what did they do, sir, but nailed him up fast in the chaise, and unharnessed the horses, put them to a jaunting-car, and started with Mr. Tisdal before you could turn round."

"And Sandy," cried Daly—"what did he do?"

"Sandy?—av it's that you call him—a divil a doubt but he's sandy and stony too—he made a drive at the front panel wid one leg, and away it went, and he smashed open the door with his fist, and put that short stump of an arm through the wood as if it was cheese. 'Tis a holy show, the same chaise now! And when he got out, may I never spread a tablecloth if you'd see a crayture in the street—they ran in every direction, as if it was the Duke's bull was out of the paddock, and it's only a while ago he grew raysonable."

However little satisfactory the exploit was to the innkeeper and his household, it seemed to sharpen Daly's enjoyment of his breakfast, and compensate him for the delay to which he was condemned. The messenger sent to seek for horses returned at last without them, and there was now no alternative but to await, with such patience as he could muster, some chaise for town, and thus reach Dublin before nightfall.

A return chaise from Kilcock was at last secured, and Daly, with his servant on the box, proceeded towards Dublin.

It was dark when they reached the capital, and drove with all the speed they could accomplish to the Knight's house in Henrietta-street. Great was Daly's discomfort to learn that his friend Darcy had just driven from the door.

"Where to?" said he, as he held his watch in his hand, as if considering the chances of still overtaking him.

"To a dinner-party, sir, at Lord Castlereagh's," said the servant.

"At Lord Castlereagh's!" And nothing but the presence of the man repressed the passionate exclamation that quivered on his lip.

"Yes, sir; his Lordship and Mr. Heffernan called here——"

"Mr. Heffernan—Mr. Con Heffernan do you mean?" interrupted he, quickly. "Ah! I have it now—and when was this visit?"

"On Monday last, sir."

"On Monday," said Daly, to himself. "The very day the letter was written to me—there's something in it, after all. Drive to Kildare-place, and as fast as you can," said he, aloud, as he sprang into the chaise.

The steps were up, the door banged to, the horses lashed into a gallop, and the next moment saw the chaise at the end of the street.

Short as the distance was—scarcely a mile to Heffernan's house—Daly's impatient anxiety made him think it an eternity. His object was to reach the house before Heffernan started; for he judged rightly that not only was the Secretary's dinner planned by that astute gentleman, but that its whole conduct and machinery rested on his dexterity.

"I know the fellow well," muttered Daly—ay, and by Heaven! he knows *me*. His mock candour and his counterfeit generosity have but a bad chance with such men as myself, but Darcy's open, unsuspecting temperament is the very metal he can weld and fashion to his liking."

It was in the midst of reflections like these, mingled with passionate bursts of impatience at the pace, which was, notwithstanding, a sharp gallop, that they dashed up to Heffernan's door. To make way for them, a chariot that stood there was obliged to move on.

"Whose carriage is this?" said Daly, as, without waiting for the steps to be lowered, he sprang to the ground.

"Mr. Heffernan's, sir."

"He is at home, then?"

"Yes, sir; but just about to leave for a dinner-party."

"Stand by that chariot, Sandy, and take care that no one enters it till I come back," whispered Daly in his servant's ear. And Sandy took up his post at the door like a sentinel on duty. "Tell your master," said Daly to the servant who stood at the open hall-door, "that a gentleman desires to speak with him."

"He's just going out, sir."

"Give my message," said Daly, sternly.

"With what name, sir?"

"Repeat the words as I have given them to you, and don't dictate to me how I am to announce myself," said he, harshly, as he opened the door and walked into the parlour.

Scarcely had he reached the fireplace when a bustle without proclaimed that Heffernan was passing down stairs, and the confused sound of voices was heard as he and his servant spoke together. "Ah! very well," said Heffernan, aloud, "you may tell the gentleman, John, that I can't see him at present. I've no notion of keeping dinner waiting half an hour." And so saying, he passed out to enter the carriage.

"Na, na," said Sandy, as the footman offered his arm to assist his master to mount the steps; "ye maun wait a wee. I trow ye hae no seen my master yet."

"What means this insolence! Who is this fellow?—push him aside."

"That's na sae easy to do," replied Sandy, gravely; "and though I hae but one arm, ye'll no be proud of yersel 'gin you try the game."

"Who are you? By what right do you stop me here?" said Heffernan, who, contrary to his wont, was already in a passion.

"I am Bagenal Daly's man; and there's himsel in the parlour, and he'll tell you mair, maybe."

The mention of that name seemed to act like a spell upon Heffernan, and, without waiting for another word, he turned back hastily, and re-entered the house. He stopped as he laid his hand on the handle of the door, and his face, when the light fell on it, was pale as death, and although no other sign of agitation was perceptible, the expression of his features was very different from ordinary. The pause, brief as it was, seemed sufficient to rally him, for, opening the door with an appearance of haste, he advanced towards Daly, and with an outstretched hand, exclaimed,

"My dear Mr. Daly, I little knew who it was I declined to see. They gave me no name, and I was just stepping into my carriage when your servant told me you were here. I need not tell you that I would not deny myself to *you*."

"I believe not, sir," said Daly, with a strong emphasis on the words. "I have come a long journey to see and speak with you."

"May I ask it, as a great favour, that you will let our interview be for to-morrow morning? you may name your hour, or as many of them as you like—or, will you dine with me?"

"We'll dine together to-day, sir," said Daly.

"That's impossible," said Heffernan, with a smile, which all his tact could not make an easy one. "I have been engaged for four days to Lord Castlereagh—a party which I had some share in assembling together—and, indeed, already I am five-and-twenty minutes late."

"I regret deeply, sir," said Daly, as, crossing his hands behind his back, he slowly walked up and down the room—"I regret deeply that I must deprive the noble Secretary's dinner-party of so very gifted a guest. I know something of Mr. Heffernan's entertaining powers, and I have heard even more of them, but, for all that, I must be unrelenting, and——"

"The thing is really impossible."

"You will dine with me to-day," was the cool answer of Daly, as, fixing his eyes steadily on him, he uttered the words in a low, determined tone.

"Once for all, sir——" said Heffernan, as he moved towards the door.

"Once for all," repeated Daly, "I will have my way. This is no piece of caprice—no sudden outbreak of that eccentricity which you and others affect to fasten on me. No, Mr. Heffernan: I have come a hundred and fifty miles with an object, and not all the wily dexterity of even you shall balk me. To be plain, sir, there are reports current in the clubs and society generally that you have been the means of securing the Knight of Gwynne to the side of Government. I know—ay, and you know—how many of these rumours originate on the shallow foundation of men being seen together in public, and cultivating an intimacy on purely social grounds. Now, Mr. Heffernan, Darcy's opinions, it is well known, are not those of the Ministry, and the only result of such calumnies will be that he, the head of a family, and a country gentleman of the highest rank, will be drawn into a dangerous altercation with some of those lounging puppies that circulate such slanders. I am his friend, and, as it happens, with no such ties to life and station as he possesses. I will, if possible, place myself in a similar position—and to do so I know no readier road than by keeping your company; I will give the gentlemen every pretext to talk of me as they have done of him; and if I hear a mutter, or if I see a signal that the most suspicious nature can torture into an affront, I will teach the parties that if they let their tongues run glibly they at least shall keep their hair-triggers in order. Now, sir, you'll not only dine with me to-day, but you'll do so in the large room of the Club. I've given you my reasons, and I tell you flatly that I will hear nothing in opposition to them, for I am quite ready to open the ball with Mr. Con Heffernan."

Heffernan's courage had been proved on more than one occasion, but somehow he had his own reasons, it would seem, for declining the gage of battle here. That they were valid ones would appear from the evident struggle compliance cost him, as with a quivering lip and a whisper, he said,

"There may be much force in what you say, Mr. Daly—your motives, at least, are unquestionable. I will offer, therefore, no further opposition." So saying, he opened the door to permit Daly to pass out. "To the Club," said he to the footman, as they both seated themselves in the chariot.

"The Club, sir!" repeated the astonished servant.

"Yes, to Daly's Club," said Bagenal himself. And they drove off.

CHAPTER XVIII.

LORD CASTLEREAGH'S DINNER-PARTY.

The day of Lord Castlereagh's dinner-party had arrived, and the guests, all save Mr. Heffernan, were assembled in the drawing-room. The party was small and select, and his Lordship had gone through the usual routine of introducings, when Hamilton asked if he still expected any one.

"Yes; Mr. Heffernan promised to make one of our twelve; he is generally punctuality itself, and I cannot understand what detains him."

"He said he'd call for me on his way," said Lord Beerhaven, "and I waited some time for him; but as I would not risk spoiling your Lordship's *entrées*, I came away at last."

This speech was made by one who felt no small uneasiness on his own part respecting the cookery, and took the occasion of suggesting his fears, as a hint to order dinner.

"Shall we vote him present, then?" said Lord Castlereagh, who saw the look of dismay the further prospect of waiting threw over the party.

"By all means," said Lord Beerhaven; "Heffernan never eats soup."

"I don't think he cares much for fish, either," said Hamilton.

"I think our friend Con is fond of walnuts," said the Knight, dryly.

"Them's the unwholesomest things he could eat," muttered old Hickman, who, although seated in a corner of the room, and partly masked by his son and grandson, could not be altogether secluded from earshot.

"Are they indeed?" said the Bishop, turning sharply round; for the theme of health was one that engaged all his sympathies, and although his short apron covered a goodly rotundity of form, eating exacted to the full as many pains as it afforded pleasures to the Churchman.

"Yes, my Lord," said Hickman, highly gratified to obtain such exalted notice, "there's an essential oil in them that destroys the mucous membrane——"

"Destroys the mucous membrane!" said the Bishop, interrupting him.

"Mine is pretty much in that way already," said Lord Beerhaven, querulously; "five-and-twenty minutes past six."

"No, no, my dear Darcy," said Lord Drogheda, who, having drawn the Knight aside, was speaking in an earnest, but low tone, "I never was easier in my life, on the score of money; don't let the thing give you any trouble—consult Gleeson about it, he's a clever fellow—and take your own time for the payment."

"Gleeson is a clever fellow, my Lord, but there are straits that prove too much even for his ingenuity."

"Ah! I know what you mean," said Lord Drogheda, secretly; "you've heard of that Spanish-American affair—yes, he made a bad hit there—some say he'll lose fifty thousand by it."

Dinner was at this moment announced, and the Knight was unable to learn further on a subject the little he had heard of which gave him great sorrow. Unfortunately, too, his position at table was opposite, not next, to Lord Drogheda, and he was thus compelled to wait for another opportunity of interrogating him.

Lord Castlereagh has left behind him one reputation, which no political or party animosity has ever availed to detract from, that of being the most perfect host that ever dispensed the honours of a table. Whatever seeming reserve or coldness he maintained at other times, here he was courteous to cordiality; his manner, the happy union of thorough good-breeding and friendly ease. Gifted with a most retentive memory, and well versed on almost every topic that could arise, he possessed that most difficult art, the power of developing the resources and information of others, without ever making any parade of his own acquirements; or, what is still harder, without betraying the effort which, in hands less adroit, becomes that most vulgar of all tricks, called "drawing out."

With all these advantages, and well suited as he was to meet every emergency of a social meeting, he felt on the present occasion far less at ease than was his wont. The party was one of Heffernan's contriving—the elements were such as he himself would never have dreamed of collecting together, and he relied upon his "Ancient" to conduct the plan he had so skilfully laid down. It was, as he muttered to himself, "Heffernan's Bill," and he was not coming forward to explain its provisions, or state its object.

Happily for the success of such meetings in general, the adjuncts contribute almost equally with the intellectual resources of the party; and here Heffernan, although absent, had left a trace of his skill. The dinner was admirable. Lord Castlereagh knew nothing of such matters; the most simple, nay, the most ill-dressed meats would have met equal approval from him with the greatest triumphs of the art; and as to wine, he mixed up his madeira, his claret, and his burgundy together, in a fashion which sadly deteriorated him in the estimation of many of his more cultivated acquaintances.

All the detail of the dinner was perfect, and Lord Beerhaven, his fears on that score allayed, emerged from the cloud of his own dreary anticipations, and became one of the pleasantest of the party. And thus the influence of good cheer and easy converse extended its happy sway until even Mr. Hickman O'Reilly began to suffer less anxiety respecting his father's presence, and felt relieved at the preoccupation the good things of the table exacted from the old "Doctor."

The party was of that magnitude which, while enabling the guests to form into the twos and threes of conversational intimacy, yet affords, from time to time, the opportunity of generalising the subject discussed, and drawing, as it were, into a common centre the social abilities of each. And there Lord Castlereagh shone conspicuously, for at the same time that he called forth all the anecdotic stores of Lord Beerhaven, and the witty repartee for which Hamilton was noted, he shrouded the obtrusive common-places of old Hickman, or gave a character of quaint originality to remarks which, with less flattering introduction, had been deemed low-lived and vulgar.

The wine went freely round, and claret, whose flavour might have found acceptance with the most critical, began to work its influence upon the party, producing that pleasant amalgamation in which individual peculiarities are felt to be the attractive, and not the repelling, properties, of social intercourse.

"What splendid action that horse you drive has, Mr. Beecham O'Reilly," said Lord Loughdooner, who had paid the most marked attention to him during dinner. "That's the style of moving they're so mad after in London —high and fast at the same time."

"I gave three hundred and fifty for him," lisped out the youth, care lessly, "and think him cheap."

"Cheap at three hundred and fifty!" exclaimed old Hickman, who had heard the fact for the first time. "May I never stir from the spot, but you told me forty pounds."

"When you can pick up another at that price let me know, I beg you," said Lord Loughdooner, coming to the rescue, with a smile that seemed to say, How well you quizzed the old gentleman. "I say, Hamilton, who bought your grey?"

"Ecclesmere bought him for his uncle."

"Why, he starts, or shies, or something of that sort, don't he?"

"No, my Lord, he 'comes down,' which is what the uncle does not; and as he stands between Ecclesmere and the Marquisate——"

"That's what I've always maintained," said the Bishop to Lord Castle reagh. "The potato disposes to acidity. I know the poor people correct that by avoiding animal food—a most invaluable fact."

"There are good grounds for your remark," said Lord Castlereagh to the Knight, while he smiled an easy assent to the Bishop without attending to him, "and the social relations of the country will demand the earliest care of the Government whenever measures of immediate importance permit this consideration. We have been unfortunate in not drawing closer to us men who, like yourself, are thoroughly acquainted with the condition of the people generally. It is not too late——"

"Too late for what?" interrupted Lord Drogheda. "Not too late for more claret, I trust; and the decanter has been standing opposite to me these ten minutes."

"A thousand pardons! O'Reilly, will you touch that bell?—Thanks."

The tone of easy familiarity with which he spoke covered Hickman with a flush of ecstatic pleasure.

"They ginger them up so, now-a-days," said Lord Loughdooner to Beecham O'Reilly.

"Ginger!" chimed in Hickman—"the devil a finer thing for the stomach. I ask your pardon, my Lord, for saying his name; but I'll give you a receipt for the windy bile worth a guinea note."

"Take a pinch of snuff, Dr. Hickman," said Lord Castlereagh, who saw the mortification of the two generations at the old man's vulgarity.

"Thank you, my Lord. 'Tis blackguard I like best: them brown snuffs ruins the nose entirely. I was saying about the mixture," said he, addressing the Bishop. "Take a pint of infusion of gentian, and put a pinch of coriander seeds, and the peel of a Chaney orange——"

"I recommend a bumper of that claret, my Lord," said Lord Castlereagh, determined to cut short the prescription, which now was being listened to by the whole board; "and when I add the health of the Primate, I'm sure you'll not refuse me." The toast was drunk with all suitable honours, and the Secretary resumed, in a whisper: "He wants our best wishes on that score, poor fellow, if they could serve him. He's not long to be with us, I fear."

"Indeed, my Lord!" said the Bishop, eagerly.

"Alas! too true," sighed Lord Castlereagh; "he'll be a severe loss, too. I wanted to have some minutes' talk with you on the matter. These are times of no common emergency, and the men we promote are of great consequence at this moment. Say to-morrow, about one."

"I'll be punctual," said the Bishop, taking out his tablets to make a note of what his memory would retain to the end of his life.

Lord Castlereagh caught the Knight's eye at the instant, and they both smiled, without being able to control their emotion.

"And so," said Lord Castlereagh, hastening to conceal his laugh, "my young relation continues to enjoy the hospitalities of your house. I don't doubt in the least that he reckons that wound the luckiest incident of his life."

"My friend Darcy paid even more dearly for it," said Lord Drogheda, overhearing the remark; "but for Heffernan's tidings, I should certainly have lost my wager."

"I assure you, Knight," broke in Hickman O'Reilly, "it was through no fault of mine that the altercation ended so seriously. I visited Captain Forester in his room, and thought I obtained his pledge to take no further notice of the affair."

"And I, too, told him the style of fellow Mac Donough was," said Beecham, affectedly.

"I have heard honourable mention of both facts, gentlemen," said Darcy, dryly; "that nothing could have less contributed to a breach of the peace than Mr. Beecham O'Reilly's conduct, my friend Daly is willing to vouch for."

"I wish his own had been equally prudent and pacific," said Hickman O'Reilly, reddening at the taunt conveyed in the Knight's speech.

"Daly is unquestionably the best friend on the ground——"

"On or off the ground, my Lord Loughdooner," interrupted the Knight, warmly; "he may be, now and then, somewhat hasty or rash; but rich as our country is in men of generous natures, Bagenal Daly is second to none."

"I protest, gentlemen," said the Bishop, gravely, "I wish I could hear a better reason for the panegyric than his skill as a duellist."

"True for you, my Lord," muttered old Hickman, in a whisper; "he's readier with a pistol-bullet than with the interest on his bond."

"He'd favour you with 'a discharge in full,' sir, if he heard the observation," said Hamilton, laughing.

"A letter, my Lord," said a servant, presenting a sealed epistle to the Secretary.

"Heffernan's writing, gentlemen; so I shall, with your permission, read it." He broke the seal, and read aloud: "'My dear Lord, an adventure, which would be laughable if it were not so provoking, prevents my coming to dinner, so I must leave the menagerie——'" Here he dropped his voice, and crumpling up the letter, laughingly remarked, "Oh, we shall hear it all later on, I've no doubt."

"By-the-by, my Lord, there's a House to-night, is there not?"

"No, Bishop; we moved an adjournment for to-morrow evening. You'll come down for the debate, won't you?"

The Bishop nodded significantly, and sipped his wine. There was now a pause. This was the great topic of the day, and yet, up to this moment, not even a chance allusion to politics had been dropped, and all recoiled from adventuring, even by a word, on a theme which might lead to disagreement or discordance. Old Hickman, however, dated his origin in life too far back for such scruples, and leaning across the table, said, with an accent to which wine imparted a tone of peculiar cunning, "I wish you well through it, my Lord; for, by all accounts, it is dirty work."

The roar of laughter that followed the speech actually shook the table, Lord Castlereagh giving way to it with as much zest as the guests themselves. Twice he essayed to speak, but each time a fresh burst of mirth interrupted him, while old Hickman, unable to divine the source of the merriment, stared at each person in turn, and at last muttered his consolatory "Ay," but with a voice that showed he was far from feeling satisfied.

"I wish you'd made that speech in the House, Mr. Hickman," said Lord Drogheda; "I do believe you'd have been the most popular man in Ireland."

"I confess," said Lord Castlereagh, wiping his eyes, "I cannot conceive a more dangerous opponent to the Bill."

"If he held your own bill, with a protest on it," whispered Hamilton, "your opinion would not be easily gainsaid."

"May I ask for a cup of coffee?" said the Bishop, rising, for he saw that although as yet no untoward results had followed, at any moment something unpleasant might occur. The party rose with him and adjourned to the drawing-room.

"Singular old man!" said Lord Castlereagh, in a whisper to the Knight. "Shrewd and cunning, no doubt, but scarcely calculated, as our friend Drogheda thinks, to distinguish himself in the House of Commons."

"Do you think the Upper House would suit him better, my Lord?" said Darcy, slyly.

"I see, Knight," said Lord Castlereagh, laughing, "you have caught up the popular joke of the day."

"I trust, my Lord, it may be no more than a joke."

"Can you doubt it?"

"At the present moment," said the Knight, gravely, "I see no reason for doubting anything merely on the score of its unlikelihood; your Lordship's colleagues have given us some sharp lessons on the subject of credulity, and we should be more unteachable than the savage, if we had not learnt something by this time."

Lord Castlereagh was about to answer, when Lord Drogheda came forward to say "good night." The others were going, too, and in the bustle of leave-taking some moments were passed.

"Your carriage has not come yet, sir," replied a servant to the Knight.

"Shall we take you home, Darcy," said Lord Drogheda; "or are you going to the Club?"

"Let me say no to that offer, Knight," interposed Lord Castlereagh, "and give me the pleasure of your company till the carriage arrives."

Darcy acceded to a request, the courteous mode of making which had already secured its acceptance, and the Knight sat down at the fire *tête-à-tête* with the Secretary.

"I was most anxious for a moment like this," said Lord Castlereagh, with the air of one abandoning himself to the full liberty of sincerity. "It very seldom happens to men placed like myself to have even a few brief minutes' intercourse with any one out of the rank of partisans or opponents. I will not disguise from you how highly I should value the alliance of yourself to our party; I place the greatest price upon such support, but there is something better and more valuable than even a vote in a strong division, and that is, the candid judgment of a man who has enjoyed your opportunities and your powers of forming an opinion. Tell me, now, frankly—for we are here in all freedom of intercourse—what do you object to? What do you fear from this contemplated enactment?"

"Let me rather hear," said the Knight, smiling, "what do you hope from it—how you propose it to become the remedy of our existing evils? Because I shall thereby see whether your Lordship and myself are like minded on the score of the disease, before we begin to discuss the remedy."

"Be it so, then," said the Secretary, gaily; and at once, without hesitation, he commenced a short and most explicit statement of the Government intentions. Arguments that formed the staple of long Parliamentary harangues he condensed into a sentence or two; views that, dilated upon, sufficed to fill the columns of a newspaper, he displayed palpably and boldly, exhibiting powers of clear and rapid eloquence for which so few gave him credit in public life. Not an epithet nor an expression could have been retrenched from a detail which denoted faculties of admirable training, assisted by a memory almost miraculous. Stating in order the various objections to the measure, he answered each in turn, and wherever the reply was not sufficiently ample and conclusive, he adroitly took occasion to undervalue either the opinion, or the source from which it originated, exhibiting, while restraining, considerable powers of sarcasm, and a thorough insight into the character of the public men of the period.

If the Knight was unconvinced by the arguments, he was no less astonished by the abilities of the Secretary. Up to that hour he had been a follower of the popular notion of the Opposition party, which agreed in decrying his talents, and making his displays as a speaker the touchstone of his capacity. Darcy was too clever himself to linger longer in this delusion. He saw the great and varied resources of the youthful statesman tested by a question of no common difficulty, and he could not control the temptation of telling him, as he concluded,

"You have made me a convert to the union——"

"Have I, indeed?" cried the Secretary, in an ecstasy of pleasure.

"Hear me out, my Lord—to the union of great political abilities with the most captivating powers of conversation—yes, my Lord, I am old enough to make such a remark without the hazard of being deemed impertinent or a flatterer—*your* success in life is certain."

"But the Bill!" cried Lord Castlereagh, while his handsome face was flushed between delight and eagerness—"the Bill!"

"Is an admirable Bill for England, my Lord, and were there not two sides to a contract, would be perfect—indeed, until I heard the lucid statement you have just made, I never saw one tenth part of the advantages it must render to your country, nor, consequently—for we move not in parallel lines—the great danger with which it is fraught to mine. Let me now explain more fully."

With these words the Knight entered upon the question of the Union in its relations to Ireland, and while never conceding, nor even extenuating the difficulties attendant upon a double legislature, he proceeded to show the probable train of events that must result on the passing of the measure, strengthening his anticipations by facts derived from deep knowledge of the country.

Far be it from us to endeavour to recapitulate his arguments; some of them, now forgotten, were difficult enough to answer, others, treasured up, have been fashionable fallacies in our own day. Such as they were, they were the reasons why an Irish gentleman demurred to surrendering privileges that gave his own country rank, place, and pre-eminence, without the evidence of any certain or adequate compensation.

"Do not tell me, my Lord, that we shall hold our influence and our station in the Imperial Parliament. There are many reasons against such a belief. We shall be in the minority, a great minority; a minority branded with provincialism as our badge, and accused of prejudice and narrow-sightedness, from the very fact of our nationality. No, no; we shall occupy a very different position in your country; and who will take our places here? That's a point your Lordship has not touched upon, but I'll tell you. The demagogue, the public disturber, the licensed hawker of small grievances, every briefless lawyer of bad fortune and worse language, every mendicant patriot that can minister to the passions of a people deserted by their natural protectors—the day will come, my Lord, when these men will grow ambitious, their aspirings may become troublesome; if you coerce them, they are martyrs—conciliate them, and they are privileged. What will happen then? You will be asked to repeal the Union, you will be charged with all the venality by which you carried your Bill, every injustice with which it is chargeable, and with a hundred other faults and crimes with which it is unconnected. You will be asked, I say, to repeal the Union, and make of this miserable rabble, these dregs and sweepings of party, a Parliament. You shake your head. No, no, it is by no means impossible—nay, I don't think it even remote. I speak as an old man, and age, if it have many deficiencies as regards the past, has, at least, some prophetic foresight for the future. You will be asked to repeal the Union, to give a Parliament to a country which you have drained of its wealth, from which you have seduced the aristocracy; to restore a deliberative body to a land whose resources for self-legislation you have studiously and industriously ruined. Think, then, twice of a measure from which, if it fail, there is no retreat, and the opposition to which may come in a worse form than a vote in the House of Commons. I see you deem my anticipations have more gloom than truthfulness—I hope it may be so."

"The Knight of Gwynne's carriage," cried a servant, throwing wide the door.

"How opportune!" said Darcy, laughing; "it is so satisfactory to have the last shot at the enemy."

"Pray don't go yet—a few moments more."

"Not a second, my Lord; I dare not. The fact is, I have strennously avoided this subject; an old friend of mine, Bagenal Daly, has wearied me of it—he is an Anti-Unionist, but on grounds I scarcely concur in. Your Lordship's defence of the measure I also demur to. I am like poor old Murray, the Chief Justice of the Common Pleas, who, when called on for his opinion in a case where Judge Wallace was in favour of a rule, and Judge Mayne against it, he said, 'I agree with my brother Mayne, for the cogent reasons laid down by my brother Wallace.'"

"So," said the Secretary, laughing heartily, "I have convinced you against myself."

"Exactly, my Lord. I came here this evening intending not to vote on the Bill—indeed, I accepted your Lordship's hospitality without a thought upon a party question—I am equally certain you will acquit me of being a spy in the camp. To-morrow I intend to vote against you."

"I wish I could have the same esteem for my friends that I now pledge for my——"

"Don't say enemy, my Lord; we both aspire to the same end—our country's good. If we take different roads, it is because each thinks his own path the shortest. Good night."

Lord Castlereagh accompanied the Knight to his carriage, and again shook his hand cordially as they parted.

CHAPTER XIX.

A DAY OF EXCITEMENT

GREAT was the Knight's astonishment, and not less his satisfaction, as he entered the breakfast-room the morning after his dinner with the Secretary, to find Bagenal Daly there before him. They met with all the cordial warmth of men whose friendship had continued without interruption for nigh half a century; each well-disposed to prize good faith and integrity at a time when so many lapsed from the path of honour and principle.

"Well, Darcy," cried Daly, the first greetings over, "there is little hope left us; that rascally newspaper already proclaims the triumph—a majority of twenty-eight."

"They calculate on many more; you remember what old Hayes, of the Recruiting Staff, used to say: 'There was no getting fellows to enlist when the bounty was high; make it half-a-crown,' said he, 'and I'll raise a battalion in a fortnight.'"

"Is Castlereagh adopting the policy?"

"Yes, and with infinite success! Some that held out for English Peerages are fain to take Irish Baronetcies, expectant Bishops put up with Deaneries, and an acquaintance of ours, that would take nothing below a separate command, is now satisfied to make his son a clerk in the War Office."

"I'm sorry for it," said Daly, as he arose and paced the room backwards and forwards—"sincerely sorry. I had fostered the hope that if they succeeded in corrupting *our* gentry, they had polluted *their own* Peerage. I wish every fellow had been bought by an Earldom at least. I would like to think that this Judas Peerage might become a jest and a scoff among their order."

"Have no such expectation, Bagenal," said the Knight, reflectively; "their origin will be forgiven before the first generation dies out. To all purposes of worldly respect and esteem, they'll be as high and mighty Lords as the best blood of all the Howards. The penalty will fall upon England in another form."

"How? Where?"

"In the Lower House politics will become a trade to live by, and the Irish party, with such an admirable market for grievances, will be a strong and compact body in Parliament, too numerous to be bought by anything save great concessions. Englishmen will never understand the truth of the condition of the country from these men, nor how little personal importance they possess at home. They will be regarded as the exponents of Irish opinion—they will browbeat, denounce, threaten, fawn, and flatter by turns; and Ireland, instead of being easier to govern, will be rendered ten times more difficult, by all the obscuring influences of falsehood and misrepresentation. But let us quit the theme. How have you left all at the abbey?"

"Well and happy; here are my despatches." And he laid on the table several letters, the first the Knight had received since his arrival, save a few hurried lines from Lady Eleanor. Darcy broke the envelopes, and skimmed the contents of each.

"How good!" cried he, handing Lord Netherby's letter across the table "this is really amusing!"

"I have seen it," said Daly, dryly. "Lady Eleanor asked my opinion as to what answer she should make."

"Insolent old miser!" broke in Darcy, who, without attending to Daly's remark, had been reading Lady Eleanor's account of Dr. Hickman's proposal.—"I say, Bagenal, you'll not believe this? What social earthquakes are we to look for next? Read that." And with a trembling hand he presented the letter to Daly.

If the Knight's passion had been more openly displayed, Daly's indignation seemed to evoke deeper emotion, for his brows met, and his stern lips were clenched, as he perused the lines.

"Darcy," said he, at length, "O'Reilly must apologise for this—he must be made to disavow any share in the old man's impertinence——"

"No, no," interrupted Darcy, "never speak of it again; rest assured Lady Eleanor received the offer suitably. The best thing we can do is to forget it; if," added he, after a pause, "the daring that prompted such a proposition has not a deeper foundation than mere presumption. You know these Hickmans have purchased up my bonds and other securities."

"I heard as much."

"Well, Gleeson is making arrangements for the payment. One large sum, something like 20,000*l.*——"

"Was paid the day before yesterday," said Daly; "here is a memorandum of the moneys."

"How the deuce came you by the information? I have heard nothing of it yet."

"That entails somewhat of a story," said Daly; "but I'll be brief with it." And in a few words he narrated his meeting with the robber Freney, and how he had availed himself of his hospitality and safe convoy as far as Maynooth.

"Ireland for ever!" said the Knight, in a burst of happy laughter; "for every species of incongruity, where was ever its equal? An independent member of the Legislature sups with a highwayman, and takes a loan of his hackney!"

"Ay, faith," said Daly, joining in the laugh; "and had I not been one of the Opposition, I had been worth robbing, and consequently not so civilly treated. By Jove! Darcy, I felt an evening with Freney to be a devilish good preparation for the company I should be keeping up in town."

"I'll wager ten pounds you talked politics together."

"That we did, and he is as stout an Anti-Unionist as the best of us, though he told me he signed a petition in favour of the Bill when confined in Clonmel gaol."

"Is that true, Bagenal; did they hawk a petition for signature among the prisoners of a gaol?"

"He took his oath of it to me, and I intend to declare it in the House."

"What if asked for your authority?"

"I'll give it," said Daly, determinedly. "Ay, faith, and if I catch a sneer or a scoff amongst them, I'll tell them that a highwayman is about as respectable and somewhat more courageous than a bribed representative."

If the Knight enjoyed the absurdity of Daly's supper with the noted Freney, he laughed till the tears came at the account of his dining with Con Heffernan. Darcy could appreciate the dismay of Heffernan, and the cool, imperturbable tyranny of Daly's manner throughout, and would have given largely to have witnessed the *tête-à-tête*.

"I will do him the justice to say," said Daly, "that when he found escape impossible, he behaved as well as any man, his conversation was easy and unaffected, and his manner perfectly well-bred. Freney was more anecdotic, but Heffernan saw deeper into mankind."

"I hope you hinted the comparison?" said Darcy, slyly.

"Yes, I observed upon the superiority practical men possess in all the relations of social intercourse, and quoted Freney and himself as instances!"

"And he took it well?"

"Admirably. Once, and only once, did he show a little disposition to turn restive; it was when I remarked upon their discrepancy in point of destiny, the one being employed to empty, the other to fill, the pockets of his Majesty's lieges. He winced, but it was over in a second. His time was up at ten o'clock, but we sat chatting till near twelve, and we parted with what the French term a 'sense of the most distinguished consideration' on each side."

"By Jove! I envy the fellows who sat at the other tables and saw you."

"They were most discreet in their observations," remarked Daly, significantly. "One young fellow, it is true, coughed twice or thrice as a signal to a friend across the room, but I ordered the waiter to bring me a plate, and taking three or four bullets out of my pocket, sent them over to him with my respectful compliments, as 'admirable pills for a cough.' The cure was miraculous."

"Excellent! Men have taken out a patent for a poorer remedy. And now, Bagenal, for the reason of your journey. What, in the name of everything strange and eccentric, brought you up to town? Don't affect to tell me you came for the debate."

"And why not?" said Daly, who, unwilling to reveal the true cause, preferred to do battle on this pretence. "I admit as freely as ever I did, I'm no lover of Parliament. I have slight respect or esteem for deliberative assemblies split up into factions and parties. A Government, to my thinking, should represent unity as the chief element of strength; but such as it is—bad enough and base enough, in all conscience—yet it is the last remnant of national power left, the frail barrier between us and downright provincialism. But I had another reason for coming up—half a dozen other reasons, for that matter—one of them was, to see your invaluable business man, Gleeson, who, from some caprice or other about a higher rate of interest, has withdrawn my sister's fortune from the funds, to invest it in some confounded mortgage. I suppose it's all right and judicious to boot; but Maria, like every other Daly I ever heard of, has a will of her own, and has commissioned me to have the money restored to its former destination. I verily believe, Darcy, the most troublesome animal on the face of the globe is an old maid with a small funded capital. At one moment, deploring the low rate of interest and dying for a more profitable use of the money; at another, decrying all deposit save the Bank, she inveighs against public theft and private credit, and takes off three-and-a-half per cent. of her happiness in pure fretting."

"Is she quite well?" said the Knight, in an accent which a more shrewd observer than Daly might have perceived was marked by some agitation.

"I never knew her better; as fearless as we both remember her at sixteen; and, save those strange intervals of depression she has laboured under all through her life, the same gay-hearted spirit she was when the flattered heiress and beauty, long, long years ago."

The Knight heaved a sigh. It might have been for the years thus passed, the pleasant days of early youth and manhood so suddenly called up before him; it might have been that other and more tender memories were crowding on his mind; but he turned away and leaned on the chimney-piece, lost in deep thought.

"Poor girl," said Daly, "there is no question of it, Darcy, but she must have formed some unfortunate attachment; she had pride enough always to rescue her from the dangers of an unsuitable marriage, but her heart, I feel convinced, was touched, and yet I never could find a clue to it. I suspected something of the kind when she refused Donington—a handsome fellow, and an old title. I pressed her myself on the subject—it was the only time I did so—and I guessed at once, from a chance phrase she dropped, that there had been an old attachment somewhere. Well, well, what a lesson might be read from both our fortunes! The beauty—and you remember how handsome she was—the beauty with a splendid fortune, a reduced maiden lady; and myself"—he heaved a heavy sigh, and with clasped hands sat back in the chair, as he added—"the shattered wreck of every hope I once set out with."

The two old men's eyes met, and, although undesignedly, exchanged looks of deepest, most affectionate interest. Daly was the first to rally from his brief access of despondency, and he did so with the physical effort he would have used to shake a load from his shoulders.

"Well, Darcy, let us be up and stirring; there's a meeting at Barrington's at two; we must not fail to be there."

"I wish to see Gleeson in the mean while," said the Knight; "I am uneasy to learn what has been done with Hickman, and what day I can leave town."

"Send Sandy out with a note, and tell him to come to dinner here at six."

"Agreed; nothing could be better; we can talk over our business matters comfortably, and be down at the House by nine or ten."

The note was soon written, and Sandy despatched, with orders to wait for Gleeson's return, in case he should be absent when he arrived.

The day for the evening of which was fixed the second reading of the Bill of Union, was a busy one in Dublin. Accounts the most opposite and contradictory were everywhere in circulation; some, asserting that the Ministerial majority was certain; others, equally positive, alleging that many of their supposed supporters had lapsed in their allegiance, and that the most enormous offers had been made, without success, to parties hitherto believed amongst the ranks of the Government. The streets were crowded, not by persons engaged in the usual affairs of trade and traffic, but by groups and knots talking eagerly over the coming event, and discussing every rumour that chance or scandal suggested.

Various meetings were held in different parts of the town; at some, the Government party were canvassing the modes of reaching the House in safety, and how best they might escape the violence of the mob; at others, the Opposition deliberated on the prospects before them, and by what stratagems the debate might be prolonged till the period when, the Wicklow election over, Mr. Grattan might be expected to take his seat in the House, since, by a trick of "the Castle party," the writ had been delayed to that very morning.

Con Heffernan's carriage was seen everywhere, and some avowed that at five o'clock he was driving with the third pair of posters he had that day employed. Bagenal Daly was also a conspicuous character "on town;" on foot and alone, he was at once recognised by the mob, who cheered him as an old but long-lost-sight-of acquaintance. The densest crowd made way for him as he came, and every mark of respect was shown him by those who set a higher price on his eccentricity and daring than even upon his patriotism; and a murmuring commentary on his character followed him as he went.

"By my conscience! it's well for them they haven't to fight for the Union, or they wouldn't like old Bagenal Daly agin them!"

"He looks as fresh and bould as ever he did," said another; "sorra a day oulder than he was twenty-eight years ago, when I seen him tried for his life at Newgate."

"Was you there, Mickey?" cried two or three, in a breath.

"Faix was I, as near as I am to you. 'Twas a coalheaver he kilt, a chap that was called Big Sam; and they say he was bribed by some of the gentlemen at Daly's Club House to come up to Bagenal Daly in the street and insult him about the beard he wears on his upper lip, and sure enough so he did—it was Ash Wednesday more by token—and Sam had a smut on his face just to imitate Mr. Daly's. 'We are a purty pair, ain't we?' says Sam, grinning at him, when they met on Essex-bridge. And wid that he slips his arm inside Mr. Daly's to hook wid his."

"To walk beside him, is't?"

"Just so, divil a less. 'Come round to the other side of me,' says Daly, 'for I want to step into Kertland's shop.' And in they went together, and Daly asks for a pound of strong white soap, and pays down one-and-eightpence for it, and out they comes again quite friendly as before. 'Where to now?' says Sam, for he held a grip of him like a bailiff. 'Across the bridge,' says Daly; and so it was. When they reached the middle arch of the bridge, Daly made a spring and got himself free, and then stooping down, caught Sam by the knees, and, before you could say 'Jack Robinson,' hurled him over the battlements into the Liffey. 'You can wash your face now,' says he, and he threw the soap after him; divil a word more he said, but walked on, as cool as you saw him there."

"And Sam?" said several together.

"Sam was drowned; there came a fresh in the river, and they took him up beyand the North Wall—a corpse."

"Millia murther! what did Daly do?"

"He took his trial for it, and sorra excuse he gave one way or other, but that he 'didn't know the blackguard couldn't swim.'"

"And they let him off?"

"Let him off? Arrah, is it hang a gentleman?"

"True for you," chimed in the bystanders; "them that makes the laws knows better than that!"

Such was one of the narratives his reappearance in Dublin again brought up; and, singular enough, by the respect shown him by the mob, derived much of its source in that same feeling of awe and dread they manifested towards one they believed privileged to do whatever he pleased. Alas, for human nature! the qualities which find favour with the multitude are never the finer and better traits of the heart, but rather the sterner features that emanate from a strong will and firm purpose.

If the voices of the closely-compacted mass which filled the streets and avenues of Dublin on that day could have been taken, it would have been found that Bagenal Daly had an overwhelming majority; while, on a converse scrutiny, it would appear, that not a gentleman of Ireland entertained for that mob sentiments of such thorough contempt as he did. Nor was the sentiment concealed by him. The crowd which, growing as it went, followed him from place to place throughout the city, would break forth at intervals into some spontaneous shout of admiration, and a cheer for Bagenal Daly, commanded by some deep throat, would be answered in a deafening roar of voices. Then would Daly turn, and, as the moving mass fell back, scowl upon their unwashed faces with such a look of scorn, that even they half felt the insult. In such wise was his progress through the streets of Dublin, now moving slowly onward, now turning to confront the mob that in slavish adulation still tracked his steps.

It was at a moment like this, when, standing at bay, he scowled upon the dense throng, Heffernan's carriage drove slowly past, and Con, leaning from the window, called out in a dramatic tone, "Thy friends, Siccius Dentatus, thy friends!"

Daly started, and as his cheek reddened, answered, "Ay, and by my soul, for the turning of a straw, I'd make them your enemies." And as if responsive to the threat, a groan for "the Castle hack, three groans for Con Heffernan!" were shouted out in tones that shook the street. For a second or two Daly's face brightened, and his eyes sparkled with the fire of enterprise, and he gazed on the countless mass with a look of indecision; but suddenly folding his arms, he dropped his head, and muttered, "No, no, it wouldn't do; robbery and pillage would be the whole of it;" and, without raising his eyes again, walked slowly homewards.

The hours wore on, and six o'clock came, but no sign of Gleeson, nor had Sandy returned with any answer.

"And yet I am positive he is not from home," said Darcy. "He pledged himself not to leave this until the whole business was completed. Honest Tom Gleeson is a man to keep to the strictest letter of his word."

"I'd not think that less likely," said Daly, sententiously, "if the world had spared him the epithet. I hate the cant of calling a man by some title that should be common to all men—at least, to all gentlemen."

"I cannot agree with you," said Darcy. "I deem it a proud thing for any one so to have impressed his reputation for honourable dealing on society that the very mention of his name suggests his character."

"Perhaps I am soured by what we have seen around us," said Daly; "but the mention of every virtue latterly has been generally followed by the announcement of the purchase of its possessor. I never hear of a good character that I don't think it is a puffing advertisement of 'a high-priced article to be had cheap for cash.'"

"You'll think better of the world after a glass or two of Madeira," said Darcy, laughing; "and rather than hear you inveigh against mankind, I'll let Gleeson eat his soup cold." And so saying, he rang the bell and ordered dinner.

The two friends dined pleasantly, and although, from time to time, some stray thought of Gleeson's absence would obtrude, they chatted away agreeably till past nine o'clock.

"I begin to suspect that Sandy may have met some acquaintance, and lingered to pledge 'old times' with him," said Darcy, looking at his watch "It is now nearly twenty minutes past nine."

"I'll stake my life on it, Sandy is true to his mission. He'd not turn from the duty entrusted to him to hob-nob with a Prince of the Blood. Here he comes, however; there was a knock at the door."

"But no; it was a few hurried lines in pencil from the House, begging of them to come up at once, as the Ministerial party was mustering in strength, and the Opposition benches filling but slowly. While deliberating on what course to take, a second summons came from one of the leading men of the party. It was brief, but significant: "Come up quickly. They are evidently pushed hard. Toler has sent a message to O'Donnell, and they are gone out, and Harvey says Castlereagh has six of his fellows ready to provoke us.—W. T."

"That looks like business, Darcy," cried Daly, in a transport of delight. "Let us lose no time; there's no knowing how soon so much good valour may ooze out."

"But Gleeson——"

"If he comes, let him follow us to the House. We can walk—there's no use waiting for the carriage." Then added, in a mutter to himself, "I'd give a hundred down to have a shot at the Attorney-General. There, that's Sandy's voice in the hall;" and at the same instant the trusty servant entered.

"Well, have you seen him."

"Is he at home?"

"No, sirs, he's no at hame, that's clear. When I asked for him, they told me he was in bed, asleep, for that he was just arrived after a long journey; and so I waited a bit, and gaed out for a walk into the shrubberies, where I could have a look at his chamber windows, and sure enough they were a' closed. I waited a while longer, but he was still sleeping, and they dared na wake him; and so it came to nigh five o'clock, and then I was fain to send up the bit letter by the flunkie, and ask for the answer; but none came."

"Did you say that the letter was from me?" said the Knight, hastily.

"Na, sir; but I tauld them what most people mind as well, that Mister Bagenal Daly sent me. It's a name few folk are fond to trifle wi'."

"Go on, Sandy," said Daly. "What then?"

"Weel, sir, I sat down on the stair at the foot of the big clock, and said to mysel, 'I'll gie ye ten minutes mair, but not a second after.' And sure enough ye might hear every tick of her through the house, it was so still and silent. Short as the time was, I thought it wad never gae past, for I did no tak my eyes aff o' her face. When the ten minutes was up, I stole gently up the stair, and opened the door. A' was dark inside, so I opened the window, and there was the bed—empty; naebody had lain in it syne it was made. There was a bit ashes in the grate, and some burned paper on the hearth, but na other sign that onybody was there at a', sae I crept back again, and met the flunkie as he was coming up, for he had just missed me, and was in a real fright where I was gone to. I saw by his face that he was found out, and so I laid my hand on his shoulder, and said, 'Ye ha tauld me ane lee; ye maun tak care no to tell me anither. Where is yer maister?' Then came out the truth. Mr. Gleeson was gane awa to England. He sailed for Liverpool in the *Shamrock*."

"Impossible!" said Darcy. "He could not be away from Dublin at this moment."

"It's even sae," replied Sandy, gravely; "for when I heard a' that I could from the flunkie, I put him into the library, and locked the door on him, and then went round to the stable-yard, where the coachman was sitting in the harness-room, smoking. 'And so he's off to England,' said I to him, as if I kenned it a'.

"'Just sae,' said he, wi' the pipe in his mouth.

"'And he's nae to be back for some time,' said I, speerin' at him.

"'On Friday,' said he; and he smoked away, and never a word mai could I get out o' him."

"Why, Sandy," said the Knight, laughing, "they'd make you a prefect o police, if they had you in France."

"I dinna ken, sir," said Sandy, not exactly appreciating what the nature of the appointment might portend.

"I only hope Gleeson may not hear of the perquisition on his return," said the Knight, in a whisper to Daly. "Our friend Sandy pushes his spirit of inquiry somewhat far."

"I don't know that," said Daly, thoughtfully; "he's a shrewd fellow, and rarely makes a mistake of that kind. But come, let us lose no more time."

"I half suspect the reason of this mystery about Gleeson," said the Knight, who stood musing deeply on the event; "a few words Drogheda let fall yesterday, going in to dinner—some unfortunate speculation in South America—this may require his keeping out of the way for a little time. But why not say so, manfully?—I'm sure I'm ready to assist him."

"Come along, Darcy, we must walk; they say no carriage can get through the mob." And, with these words, he took the Knight's arm and sallied forth, while Sandy followed, conveying a large cloth cloak over his arm, which only partially concealed an ominous-looking box of mahogany wood, strapped with brass.

A crowd awaited them as they reached the street, by which they were escorted through the denser mass that thronged the great thoroughfare, the mere mention of their names being sufficient to force a passage even where the mob stood thickest.

The space in front of the Parliament House and before the College was filled with soldiers; while patrols of cavalry traversed every avenue leading to it, for information had reached the Government that violence might be apprehended from a mob whose force and numbers were alluded to by members within the House in terms meant to intimidate, while the presence of the soldiery was retorted by the Opposition, as a measure of tyranny and oppression of the Castle party. Brushing somewhat roughly through the armed line, Daly, with the Knight beside him, entered the space, and was passing onward, when a bustle and a confused uproar behind him arrested his steps. Believing that it might be to Sandy's progress some objection was offered, Daly wheeled round, when he saw two policemen in the act of dragging away a boy, whose loud cries for help from the mob were incessant, while he mingled the name of Mr. Daly through his entreaties.

"What is it?" said Daly. "Does the fellow want me?"

"Never mind him," said Darcy; "the boy has caught up your name, and that's all."

But the urchin struggled and kicked with all his might; and, although overpowered by superior strength, gave battle to the last, screaming at the top of his voice, "One word with Mr. Daly—just one word!"

Bagenal Daly turned back, and, approaching the scene of contest, said, "Have you anything to say to me? I am Mr. Daly."

"If they'd let me go my hands, I've something to give you," said the boy, who, although sorely bruised and beaten, seemed to care less for his own troubles than for the object of his enterprise.

At a word from Daly, the policemen relinquished their hold, and stood guard on either side, while the boy, giving himself a shake, leered up in Daly's face with an expression he could not fail to recognise.

"There's a way to treat a young gentleman at home for the Christmas holidays!" said the imp, with a compassionating glance at his torn and tattered garments, while the words and the tone they were uttered in sent a shout of laughter through the mob.

"What, Jemmy!" said Daly, stooping down and accosting him in a whisper, for it was no other than that reputable youth himself, "you here!"

"Just so, sir. Ain't I in a nice way to appear at the Privy Council?"

The police were growing impatient at the continued insolence of the fellow, and were about to lay hold on him once more, when Daly interposed, and said, in a still lower voice, "Have you anything to tell me?"

"I've a bit of paper for you somewhere, from one you know, if them blackguards the 'polis' has not made me lose it."

"Be quick, then," said Daly, "and see after it." For Darcy was chafed at a delay he could not see any reason for.

"Here it is," said the imp, taking a piece of dirty and crumpled paper from the lining of his hat; "there, you have it now safe and sure. Give my best respects to Alderman Darby," added he to the police; "say I was too hurried to call;" and with that, he dived between the legs of one of them, dashed through the line of soldiers, and was speedily concealed among the dense crowd outside, where shouts of approving laughter welcomed him.

"A rendezvous or a challenge, Bagenal—which?" said the Knight, laughing, as Daly stood endeavouring, by the light of a lamp in the corridor, to decipher the torn scrawl.

The other made no reply, but, holding the paper close to his eyes, stood silent and motionless. At last an expression of impatient anger burst from him: "That imp of h—l has almost effaced the words—I cannot make them out!" Then he added, in a low muttering, "I trust in Heaven I have not read them aright. Come here, Darcy." And so saying, he grasped the Knight's hand, and led him along to one of the many small chambers used as offices of the House.

"Ah! they're looking anxiously out for you, sir," said a young man who stood with his back to the fire reading a paper. "Mr. Ponsonby has just been here."

"Leave us together here for a few minutes," said Daly, "and let there be no interruption." And as he spoke, he motioned to the door with a gesture there was no mistaking. The clerk left the room, and they were alone.

"Maurice Darcy," said Daly, as he turned the key in the lock, "you have a stout heart and a courage I never saw fail, and you need both at this moment."

"What is it, Bagenal?" gasped the Knight, as a deadly pallor covered his face. "Is my wife—are my children——"

"No, no; be calm, Darcy, they are all well."

"Go on, then," cried he, with a firmer voice, "I'll listen to you patiently."

"Read that," said Daly, as he held the paper near the candle; and the Knight read aloud: "'Honoured sir,—I saw the other night you were troubled when I spoke of Gleeson, and I take the occasion of——'"

"'Warning you,' I think the words are," broke in Daly.

"So it is;—'warning you honest Tom is away to America!'" The paper fell from Darcy's hand, and he staggered back into a seat.

"With they say above a hundred thousand pounds, Darcy," continued Daly, taking up the fragment. "If the news be true——"

"If so, I'm ruined; he received the whole loan on Saturday last--he could not delay Hickman's payment beyond Wednesday without suspicion."

"Ah! I see it all, and the American packet does not sail till to-morrow morning from Liverpool."

"But it may all be false," said Darcy. "Who writes you this story?"

"It is signed 'F.,' and Freney is the man; I know the fellow that brought it."

"I'll not believe a word of it, Bagenal," said the Knight, impetuously. "I'll not credit the calumny of a highwayman against the honour of one I have known and respected for years. It is false, depend upon it."

"Yet how it tallies with Sandy's tidings; there is something in it. Hush, Darcy, don't speak, there is some one passing."

The sounds of feet and voices were heard at the same instant without, and among them the clear, distinctive accents of Hickman O'Reilly.

"Yes," said he, "if the news had come a little earlier, Lord Castlereagh would have found some of our patriots less stern in virtue. Gleeson will have carried away half a province with him."

"There!" whispered Daly, "you heard that—the news is about already."

But Darcy was now totally overcome, and, with his head resting on the table, neither spoke nor stirred. "Bagenal," said he, at length, but in a voice faint as a whisper, "I am too ill to face the House, let us turn homewards."

"I'll see for a carriage," said Daly, who issued forth to take the first he could find.

"I say, Hamilton," cried a member, as he alighted from his chariot, "there's the Knight of Gwynne and Bagenal Daly in Castlereagh's carriage."

"Daly said he could drive a coach and six through the Bill," replied the other; "perhaps he's gone to practise with a pair first."

CHAPTER XX.

THE ADJOURNED DEBATE.

Although the debate had commenced at seven o'clock, none of the great speakers on either side arose before eleven. Some fierce skirmishes had, indeed, occurred; personalities and sarcasms the most cutting had been interchanged with a freedom that showed that if shame were in a great measure departed, personal daring and intrepidity were qualities still in repute. The Ministerial party, no longer timid or wavering, took no pains to conceal their sense of coming victory, and even Lord Castlereagh, usually so guarded on every outward observance, entered the House and took his seat with a smile of conscious triumph that did not escape observation from either friends or opponents.

The tactics of the Treasury benches, too, seemed changed: not waiting, as hitherto, to receive and repel the attack of the Opposition, they now became themselves the assailants, and evinced, by the readiness and frequency of their assaults, the perfect organisation they had attained. The Opposition members, who opened the debate, were suffered to proceed without any attempt at reply, an ironical cheer, a well-put question, some homethrust as to former opinions, alone breaking the thread of an argument which, even from its monotony, was becoming less effective.

Sir Henry Parnell, the late Chancellor of the Exchequer, and who had been dismissed from office for his opinions on the Union, was the first speaker; with a moderation, in part the result of his former position with regard to those who had been his colleagues, he limited himself to a strict examination of the measure in its bearings and consequences, and never, even for a moment, digressed into anything like reflection on the motives of its advocates. His speech was able and argumentative, but evidently unsatisfactory to his party, who seemed impatient and uneasy till he concluded, and hailed Ponsonby, who rose after him, with cheers that showed their expectations were now, at least, more likely to be realised.

Whether the occasion alone was the cause, or that catching the excitement of his supporters, Ponsonby deviated from the usually calm and temperate character he was accustomed to assume in the House, and became warm and impassioned. Disdaining to examine the relative merits or demerits of the proposed Bill, he boldly pronounced Parliament incompetent to decide it, and concluded by declaring that, if carried, the measure might endanger, not only the ties of amity between the two nations, but dissolve those of allegiance also. A loud burst of mingled indignation and irony broke from the Treasury benches at this daring flight, when the speaker, at once collecting himself, turned the whole force of his attack on the Secretary. With slow and measured intonation, he depicted the various stages of his political career, recalling to memory the liberal pledges he had once contracted, and the various shades of defection by which he had at last reached the position in which he could "betray Ireland."

None were prepared for the degree of eloquent power Ponsonby displayed on this occasion; and the effect of such a speech from one habitually calm, even to coldness, was overwhelming. It was not Lord Castlereagh's intention to have spoken at this early hour of the debate; but, apologising for occupying the time of the House by a personality, he arose, not self-possessed and at ease, but flushed and excited.

Without adverting for a second to the measure in debate, he launched forth into a most violent invective on his adversary. With a vehement passion, that only his nearest friends knew him to possess, he exposed every act of his political life; taunted him with holding opinions, liberal enough to be a patriot, but sufficiently plastic to be marketable; he accused his very calmness as being an hypocritical affectation of fairness, while, in reality, it was but the tacit admission of his readiness to be bought; and at length pushed his violent sarcasm so far, that a loud cry of "Order!" burst forth from the Opposition, while cheers of defiance were heard along the densely-crowded ranks of the Ministerial party.

From this moment the discussion assumed a most bitter character: assertions and denials, uttered in language the most insulting, were heard at every moment, and no speaker could proceed without some interruption which demanded several minutes to subdue. More than one member was seen to cross the floor, and interchange a few words with an adversary, the import of which, as he returned to his place, no physiognomist need have doubted. It was not debate or discussion, it was the vehement outpouring of personal and political hatred, by men whose passions were no longer restrainable, and many of whom saw in this the last occasion of their ever being able to confront their enemies. Language that could not be uttered with impunity elsewhere, was heard at every moment; open declarations were made that, the Bill once carried, allegiance and loyalty were dissolved; and Sir Neil O'Donnell went so far as to say that he regarded the measure as an act of treason, and would place himself at the head of his regiment to oppose and annul it.

It was in a momentary pause of this bitter conflict that rumour announced the arrival of the Knight of Gwynne and Bagenal Daly at the

House. Never were reinforcements more gladly hailed by a weakened and disabled army; cheers of triumphant delight broke from the Opposition benches, answered by others, not less loud and taunting, from the Ministerial side, and every eye was turned eagerly towards the door by which they were expected to enter.

To such a pitch of violence had partisanship carried the members on both sides, expressions of open defiance and insult were exchanged in the midst of this scene of tumult, nor was the authority of the Speaker able to restore order for several minutes; when at last the doors were thrown open, and Hickman O'Reilly entered, and walked up the body of the House. Shouts of loud laughter now resounded from either side; such an apparition at the moment was the most ludicrous contrast to that expected, and a boisterous gaiety succeeded to the late scene of acrimony and intemperance.

The individual himself seemed somewhat puzzled at these unlooked-for marks of public notice, and stared around him in astonishment, till his eyes rested on the spot where Lord Castlereagh sat whispering with Mr. Corry Brief as was the glance, it seemed to have conveyed some momentous intelligence to the gazer, for he became at first scarlet and then pale as death; he looked again, but the Secretary had turned his head away, and Corry was coolly unfolding the plaits of a white cambric handkerchief, and apparently only occupied with that object. At this moment Hickman was standing with one foot upon the steps which led towards the Treasury benches: he wheeled abruptly round, and walked over to the other side of the House, where he sat down between Egan and Ponsonby.

The cheers of the Opposition now burst forth anew, and with a deafening clamour, while from back and cross benches, and everywhere within reach, hands were eagerly stretched forward to grasp O'Reilly's. Never was support less expected, never an alliance less speculated on, and the cries of exultation were almost maddening. How long the scene of tumultuous excitement might have lasted, it is difficult to say, when Lord Castlereagh rose with a calm dignity of manner that never in the most trying moments forsook him. "He begged to remind the gentlemen opposite, that if these triumphant expressions were not indecorous, they were at least premature; that the momentous occasion on which they were met demanded all the temperate and calm consideration which they could bestow upon it; that the time for the adoption of any course would not be distant, and would sufficiently show to which side, with most propriety, the expression of triumph belonged."

The hint was significant, the foreshadowed victory was too plainly and too palpably predicted to admit of a doubt, and a chilling silence succeeded to the former uproar. The individual whose address this long scene of tumult had interrupted was now suffered to proceed; he was a Law-Serjeant, a man of inferior capacity and small professional repute, whose advocacy of the Government plan had raised him to an unbecoming and dangerous eminence at the Bar. Without the slightest pretensions as a speaker, or one quality that should adorn a statesman, he possessed other gifts scarcely less valuable at that day: he was a ready pistol; he came of a fighting family, not one of whom did not owe some advancement in life to a cool hand and a steady eye; and he occupied his place in the Ministerial van by virtue of this signal accomplishment. As incapable of feeling the keen sarcasm of his opponents as he was of using a similar weapon, he was yet irascible from temperament and overbearing in manner; and was used by his party as men employ a fire-ship—with a strong conviction that it may damage more than the enemy.

To cover the deficiencies of his oratory, as well as to add poignancy to his personalities, it was the invariable custom of his friends to cheer him vociferously at the end of every sentence which contained anything like attack on the Opposition, and to this species of backing he was indebted for the courage that made him assail men incomparably above him in every quality of intellect.

Mr. Plunkett was now the object of his invective, nor was the boldness of such a daring its least recommendation. Few of the Government side of the House would have adventured to cross weapons with this master of sarcasm and irony; none but the Serjeant Nickolls could have done so without a strong fear of consequences. He, however, was unconcerned for the result as it affected himself personally, and as for the withering storm that awaited him, the triple hide of his native dulness was an armour of proof that nothing could penetrate. From Plunkett he passed on to Bushe, from Bushe to Grattan; no game flew too high for his shafts, nor was any invective coarse enough to level at the great leaders of the Opposition. If the overbearing insolence of his harangue delighted his own party, it called down peals of laughter from his opponents, who cheered every figurative absurdity and every illogical conclusion with shouts of ironical admiration.

Lord Castlereagh saw the mischief, and would gladly have cut short the oration; but the speaker was revelling in an imaginary victory, and would listen to no suggestions whatever. Passing from the great names of the Irish party, he launched forth in terms of insult towards the county members, whom he openly accused of holding their opinions under a mistaken hope that they were a marketable commodity; and that as some staunch adherents of the Crown had reaped the honours due to "their loyalty," these quasi Patriots were only waiting for their price. The allusion was so palpable, that every eye was turned to where Hickman O'Reilly sat, and whose confusion was now overwhelming.

"Ay," continued the speaker, now carried beyond all self-restraint by the evident sensation he had caused, "there are gentlemen opposite whose confessions would reveal much of this kind of independence. I have my eye on some of them; men who will be Patriots if they cannot be Peers, ready to put on the cap of liberty for the Mob, if they cannot get the coronet from the Crown. Many, too, are absent from this debate; they stand out, perhaps, for high terms; they have got Peerages for their wives, and now, like a hackney coachman, not content with their fare, they want 'something for themselves.' I heard of two such a while ago; they even came as far as the lobby of this House, where they halted and hesitated; a mitre, or a regiment, a blue ribbon, or a red one, would have turned the scale, perhaps. Why are they not here now? I ask; what has become of them?"

"Name! name!" screamed the Opposition, in a torrent of mad excitement, while the Government party, outrageous at the blundering folly of the whole harangue, endeavoured to pull the speaker back into his seat. Never was such a scene; one party lashed to madness by suspected treachery and open insult; the other indignant at the stupidity of a man who, in his attempts at attack, had raked up every calumny against his own friends. Already more than one hand was laid on his arms to press him down into his seat, when he, with the obstinacy of thorough dulness, shook himself free, and called out, "I'm ready to name."

Again the cries of "Name!" were shouted, mingled with no less vociferous cries of "No, no!" and the struggle now had every appearance of a personal one, when the Speaker, calling to order, asked if it was the sense of the House that the Serjeant should give the names he alluded to.

"I'll soon cut the matter short," called out the Serjeant, in a voice that resounded through every corridor of the House. "I mean the Knight of Gwynne and Bagenal Daly."

A cry of "Order! order!" now arose from all parts of the House, the direct mention of any member by name being a liberty unprecedented.

"I beg to correct myself," said the Serjeant. "I should have said the honourable members for Mayo and Old Castle. I ask again, why are they not here?"

"Better you had never put the question," said a deep, low voice from beneath the gallery; and at the same instant Bagenal Daly advanced along one of the passages, and took his place at the table directly in front of the Serjeant. A tremendous cheer now broke from the Opposition benches, which the Ministerial party in vain essayed to return.

"I perceive, sir," said the Serjeant, with an effort to resume his former ease—"I perceive I have succeeded in conjuring up one at least of these truant spirits, and I cannot do better than leave him to make his explanations to the House."

With this lame, disjointed conclusion the learned Serjeant sat down, and although the greatest exertions were made by his friends to cover this palpable failure, the cries of derision drowned all other sounds, and before they were silenced a shout of "Daly! Daly!—Bagenal Daly!" resounded through the building.

Daly arose slowly, and saluted the Speaker with a most deferential courtesy. It was several minutes before the tumult had sufficiently subsided to make his words audible; but when silence prevailed he was heard to regret, in terms of unaffected ease, that any circumstance might occur which should occupy the time of the House by observations from one so rude and unlettered as himself, nor would he now venture on the trespass were the occasion merely a personal one. From this he proceeded to state that great emergencies were always occurring, in which even the humblest opinions should be made known as evidencing the probable impressions upon others as lowly circumstanced as he who now addressed them.

"Such is the present one," said he, raising his voice, and looking around him with a glance of bold defiance. "You are about to take away the right of self-government from a nation, and every man in the land, not only such as sit here, sir, but every man to whose future ambition a seat in this House may form a goal, every man has a deep interest in your proceedings. It is a grave and weighty question, whose conditions impose the conviction that we are unfit to legislate for ourselves—that we are too weak, or too venal, or too ignorant, or too dishonest. To that conclusion you must come, or no other. Absence from Ireland must suggest enlightenment on her interests; distance must lend knowledge as well as enchantment, or an English Parliament cannot be better than our own. I have listened attentively, but unconvinced, to all arguments on this head; I have heard over and over again the long catalogue of benefits to accrue to this country when the power of realising them herself has been wrested from her, and I have thought of Lear and his daughters! It would seem to me, however, that the social welfare and the commercial prosperity of a people are themes too vulgar for the high consideration of our times. The real question at issue is not whether a Parliament should or should not continue to sit here, but what shall I, and others like me, benefit by voting it away for ever?"

"Order! order!" called out several voices.

But Daly resumed: "I ask pardon. It is more parliamentary to put the case differently, and I shall, under correction, do so. Well, sir, we may benefit largely. I trust I am not disorderly in saying that Peerages, Bishoprics, Regiments, Frigates, Commissionerships, and Heaven knows what more, will reward us, when our utility to the State has met the approval of an Imperial Parliament. I can well credit every promise of such gratitude, and have only to ask in turn, are these the arguments that should sway us now? Is it because we are bungling legislators that they wish for us in London?—is it because we are venal they seek our company, because we are inefficient they ask for our co-operation? Are they so supremely right-minded, honourable, and far-seeing, that they need the alloy of our dulness to make them mortal? And suppose such the case, will it be gratifying to us to become the helots to this people? Will our national pride be flattered because our eloquence is sneered at, our law derided, our political knowledge a scoff, and our very accent a joke? Do not tell me such things are unlikely: we are far weaker on the point than we like to confess. For myself, I can imagine the sense of shame—of deep, heartfelt, abasing shame—I should feel at seeing some of those I see here rise in a British House of Commons to address that body, while the rumour should run, 'He is the member for Meath or for Wicklow.' I can picture to myself such a man: a man of low origin and mean capacity; a man who carves his path in life less from his own keen abilities than that others shirk from his contact, and leave him unopposed in every struggle; a pettifogger at the Bar; a place-hunter at the Parliament; half beggar, half bravo, with a petition for the Minister, and a pistol for the Opposition. Imagine a man like this, and reflect upon the feeling of every gentleman at hearing the rumour announce, 'Ay, that's a learned Serjeant, a leader at the Bar of Ireland.'"

The last words were delivered in a tone of direct personality, as, turning towards where Nickolls sat, Daly threw at him a look of defiance. The whole House arose as if one man, with cheers and counter-cheers, and loud yells of insult, mingled with cries of "Order!" nor was it till after a long and desperate wordy altercation that the clamour was subdued, and decorum at length restored. Then it was remarked that Nickolls had left the House.

The Speaker immediately ordered the Serjeant of the House to place Daly under arrest, a measure which, however dictated by propriety, seemed to call forth a burst of indignation from the Opposition benches.

"I hope, sir," said Daly, rising with an air of most admirably feigned humility—"I hope, sir, you will not execute this threat—the inconvenience to me will be very great—I was about to pair off with the honourable and learned member for Newry."

The mention of the town for which the Serjeant sat in Parliament renewed the laughter which now prevailed on both sides of the House.

"I cannot understand the mirth of the gentlemen opposite," said Daly, with affected simplicity, "without it be from their astonishment that the Government can spare so able and so eloquent an advocate as the honourable and learned gentleman, but let them reassure themselves and look around, and, believe me, they'll find the Treasury benches filled by gentlemen as like him as possible."

The Speaker reissued the order to the Serjeant-at-Arms, and Daly now came forward to the table and begged in all form to know the reason of such severity. "If, sir," said he, in conclusion—"if I could believe it possible that you anticipate any personal collision between myself and any member of this House, I have only to say, that I am bound over in the sum of two thousand pounds to keep the peace within the limits of this kingdom. I take out a license at two pounds fifteen to kill game, it is true, but I'd not pay sixpence for the privilege to shoot a lawyer."

The fact of the heavy recognisances to which Daly alluded was at once confirmed by several members, and after a brief conversation with the Speaker the matter was dropped.

It was, as may be supposed, a considerable time before the debate could assume its due decorum and solemnity after an incident like this; for although hostile collisions were neither few nor unfrequent, an insult of so violent a character had never before been witnessed.

At length, however, order was restored, and another speaker addressed the House. All had assumed its wonted propriety, when a messenger delivered into Daly's hands a small sealed note: he glanced at the contents and rose immediately—Lord Castlereagh's quick eye caught the motion, and he at once called on the Speaker to interfere. "I have myself seen a letter conveyed to the honourable member's hands," said he; "it requires no peculiar gift of divination to guess the object."

"I will satisfy the noble Lord at once," said Daly; "there is the letter I have received—I pledge my word of honour the subject is purely a private one, having no reference whatever to anything that has passed here. He held out the letter as he spoke, but Lord Castlereagh declined to peruse it, and expressed his regret at having made the remark. Daly bowed courteously to him and left the House.

"Well, Sandy," said he, as soon as he reached the corridor, where his faithful follower stood waiting his coming, "what success?"

"No sae bad," said Sandy. "I've got a wherry, ane of them Wicklow craft; she's only half-decked, but she's a stout-looking sea-boat and broad in the beam."

"And the wind—how's that?"

"As it should be, west, or west wi' a point north."

"Is there enough of it?"

"Enough! I trow there is," said Sanders, with a grin; "if there be no a blast too much. Hear till it now." And, as if waiting for the remark, a tremendous gust of wind shook the strong building, while the clanking sound of falling slates and chimney-pots resounded through the street. "There's music for ye," said Sandy; "there came a clap like that when I had a'maist made the bargain, and the carles would no budge without ten guineas mair. I promised them fifty, and the handsel whatever your honour liked after."

"It's all right—quite right," said Daly, wishing to stop details he never listened to with patience.

"It's a' right, I know weel enough," said Sandy, querulously; "but it wad no be a' right av ye went yersel; they'd have a gude penny, forbye what I say."

"And what say the fellows of this wind—is it like to last?"

"It will blow hard from the west for three or four days mair, and then draw round to the north."

"But we shall get to Liverpool before noon to-morrow."

"Maybe," said Sandy, with a low, dry laugh.

"Well, I mean, if we do get there. You told them I'd double the pay if we catch the American ship in the Mersey. I'd triple it, let them know that."

"They canna do mair than they can do; ten pounds is as good as ten hundred."

While this conversation was going forward, they had walked on together, and were now at the entrance door of the House, where a group of four persons stood under the shadow of the portico.

"Mr. Daly, I presume," said one, advancing, and touching his hat in salutation. "We have waited somewhat impatiently for your coming."

"I should regret it, sir, if I was aware you did me the honour to expect me."

"I am the friend of Serjeant Nickolls, sir," said the other, in a voice meant to be eloquently meaning.

"For your sake, the fact is to be deplored," answered Daly, calmly. "But proceed."

With a great effort to subdue his passion, the other resumed: "It does not require your experience in such matters to know that the insult you have passed upon a high-minded and honourable gentleman—the gross and outrageous insult—should be atoned for by a meeting. We are here for this purpose, ready to accompany you as soon as you have provided yourself with a friend to wherever you appoint."

"Are you aware," said Daly, in a whisper, "that I am bound over in heavy recognisances——"

"Ah, indeed!" interrupted the other; "that, perhaps, may explain——"

"Explain what, sir?" said Daly, as he grasped the formidable weapon which, more club than walking-stick, he invariably carried.

"I meant nothing—I would only observe——"

"Never observe, sir, when there's nothing to be remarked. I was informing you that I am bound over to keep the peace in this same kingdom of

Ireland—circumstances compel me to be in England to-morrow morning—circumstances of such moment, that I have myself hired a vessel to convey me thither—and, although the object of my journey is far from agreeable, I shall deem it one of the happiest coincidences of my life if it can accommodate your friend's wishes. Nothing prevents my giving him the satisfaction he desires on English ground. I have sincere pleasure in offering him and every gentleman of his party, a passage over—the tide serves in half an hour. Eh, Sandy?"

"At a quarter to twelve, sir."

"The wind is fair."

"It is a hurricane," replied the other, almost shuddering.

"It blows fresh," was Daly's cool remark.

For a moment or two the stranger returned to his party, with whom he talked eagerly, and the voices of the others were also heard speaking in evident excitement.

"You have the pistols safe, Sandy?" whispered Daly.

"They're a' safe, and in the wherry—but you'll no want them this time, I trow," said Sandy, with a shrug of his shoulders; "yon folk would rather bide where they are the night, than tak a bit o' pleasure in the Channel."

Daly smiled, and turned away to hide it, when the stranger again came forward. "I have consulted with my friends, Mr. Daly, who are also the friends of Serjeant Nickolls; they are of opinion that, under the circumstances of your being bound over, this affair cannot with propriety go further, although it might not, perhaps, be unreasonable to expect that you, feeling the peculiar situation in which you stand, might express some portion of regret at the utterance of this most severe attack."

"You are really misinformed on the whole of the business," said Daly. "In the few words I offered to the House, I was but responding to the question of your friend, who asked, I think somewhat needlessly, 'Where was Bagenal Daly?' I have no regrets to express for any terms I applied to him, though I may feel sorry that the forms of the House prevented my saying more. I am ready to meet him now; or, as he seems to dislike a breeze, when the weather is calmer. Tell him so; but tell him besides, that if he utters one syllable in my absence that the most malevolent gossip of a club-room can construe into an imputation on me, by G—d I'll break every bone in his cowardly carcase! Come, Sandy, lead on. Good evening, sir. I wish you a bolder friend, or better weather." So saying, he moved forward, and was soon hastening towards the North Wall, where the wherry was moored.

"It's unco like the night we were wrecked in the Gulf," said Sandy. "I mind the moon had that same blude colour, and the clouds were a' below, and none above her."

"So it is, Sandy—there's a heavy sea outside, I'm sure. How many men have we?"

"Four, and a bit o' a lad, that's as gude as anither. Lord save us! there was a flash! I wish it wud come to rain, and beat down the sea, we'd have aye wind enough after."

"Where does she lie?"

"Yonder, sir, where you see the light bobbing. By my certie, but the chiels were no far wrang. A bit fighting's hard bought by a trip to sea on such a night as this."

CHAPTER XXI.

TWO OF A TRADE.

When the newspapers announced the division on the adjourned debate, they also proclaimed the flight of the defaulter; and, wide as was the disparity between the two events in point of importance, it would be difficult to say which more engaged the attention of the Dublin public on that morning, the majority for the Minister, or the published perfidy of "Honest Tom Gleeson."

Such is, however, the all-engrossing interest of a local topic, aided, as in the present case, by almost incredulous amazement, the agent's flight was talked of and discussed in circles where the great political event was heard as a matter of course. Where had he fled to? What sum had he carried away with him? Who would be the principal losers? were all the questions eagerly discussed, but none of which excited so much diversity of opinion as the single one, What was the cause of his defalcation? His agencies were numerous and profitable, his mode of life neither extravagant nor ostentatious; how could a man with so few habits of expense have contracted debts of any considerable amount, or what circumstances could induce him to relinquish a station of respectability and competence for a life-long of dishonourable exile?

Such has been our progress of late years in the art of revealing to the world at large the hidden springs of every action and event around us, that a secret is in reality the only thing now impossible. Forty-five years ago, this wonderful exercise of knowledge was in a great measure unknown; the guessers were then a large and respectable class in society, and men were content with what mathematicians call approximation. In our own more accurate days, what between the Newspaper, the Club-room, and "'Change," such mystery is no longer practicable. One day, or two, at furthest would now proclaim every item in a man's schedule, and afford that most sympathetic of all bodies, the world, the fruitful theme of expatiating on his folly or his criminality. In the times we refer to, however, it was only the "Con Heffernans" of society that ventured even to speculate on the secret causes of these events.

Although the debate had lasted from eight o'clock in the evening to past eleven on the following morning, before twelve Mr. Heffernan's carriage was at the door, and the owner, without any trace of fatigue, set off to ascertain so much as might be learned of this strange and unexpected catastrophe. It was no mere passion to know the current gossip of the day, no prying taste for the last piece of scandal in circulation—Con Heffernan was above such weaknesses; but he had a habit, one which some men practise even yet with success, of, whenever the game was safe, taking credit to himself for casualties in which he had no possible connexion, and attributing events in which he had no share to his own direct influence. After all, he was in this only imitating the great navigators of the globe, who have established the rule that discovery gives a right only second to actual creation.

This was, however, a really provoking case; no one knew anything of Gleeson's embarrassments. Several of those for whom he acted as agent were in Dublin, but they were more amazed than all others at his flight; most of them had settled accounts with him very lately, some men owed him small sums. "Darcy, perhaps, knows something about him," was a speech Heffernan heard more than once repeated; but Darcy's house was shut up, and the servant announced "he had left town that morning." Hickman O'Reilly was the next chance; not that he had any direct intercourse with Gleeson, but his general acquaintanceship with moneyed men and matters made him a likely source of information; while a small sealed note addressed to Dr. Hickman was in possession of a banker with whom Gleeson had transacted business the day before his departure. But O'Reilly had left town with his son. "The Doctor, sir, is here still; he does not go before to-morrow," said the servant, who, knowing that Heffernan was a person of some consequence in the Dublin world, thought proper to give this piece of unasked news.

"Will you give Mr. Con Heffernan's compliments, and say he would be glad to have the opportunity of a few minutes' conversation?" The servant returned immediately, and showed him up-stairs into a back drawing-room, where, before a table covered with law papers and parchments, sat the venerable Doctor. He had not as yet performed the usual offices of a toilet, and with unshaven chin and uncombed hair, looked the most melancholy contrast of age, neglect, and misery, with the gorgeous furniture of a most splendid apartment.

He lifted his head as the door opened, and stared fixedly at the new comer, with an expression at once fierce and anxious, so that Heffernan, when speaking of him afterwards, said that, "Dressed as he was, in an old flannel morning-gown, dotted with black tufts, he looked for all the world like a sick tiger making his will."

"Your humble servant, sir," said he, coldly, as Heffernan advanced with an air of cordiality; nor were the words and the accents they were uttered in lost upon the man they were addressed to. He saw how the land lay in a second, and said, eagerly, "He has not left town, I trust, sir. I sincerely hope your son has not gone."

"Yes, sir, he's off—I'm sure I don't know what he'd wait for."

"Too precipitate—too rash by far, Mr. Hickman," said Heffernan, seating himself and wiping his forehead with an air of well-assumed chagrin.

"Maybe so," repeated the old man two or three times over, while he lowered his spectacles to his nose, and began hunting among his papers, as though he had other occupation in hand of more moment than the present topic.

"Are you aware, sir," said Heffernan, drawing his chair close up, and speaking in a most confidential whisper—"are you aware, sir, that your son mistook the signal—that when Mr. Corry took out his handkerchief and opened it on his knee, that it was in token of Lord Castlereagh's acquiescence of Mr. O'Reilly's demand—that, in short, the Peerage was at that moment his own if he wished it?"

The look of dogged incredulity in the old man's face would have silenced a more sensitive advocate than Heffernan; but he went on: "If any one should feel angry at what has occurred, I am the person; I was the guarantee for your son's vote, and I have now to meet Lord Castlereagh without one word of possible explanation."

"Hickman told me," said the old man, with a voice steady and composed, "that if Mr. Corry did not raise the handkerchief to his mouth the terms were not agreed upon—that opening it before him only meant the bargain was not quite off—more delay—more talk, Mr. Heffernan—and I think there was enough of that already."

"A complete mistake, sir—a total misconception on his part."

"Just like Beecham being black-balled at the Club," said the Doctor, with a sarcastic bitterness all his own.

"With that, of course, we cannot be charged," said Heffernan. "Why was he put up without our being apprised of it? the black-balling was Bagenal Daly's doing——"

"So I heard," interrupted the other; "they told me that; and here, look here, here's Daly's bond for four thousand six hundred. Maybe he won't be so ready with his bank-notes as he was with his black ball—ay!"

"But, to go back to the affair of the House——"

"We won't go back to it, sir, if it's the same to you. I'm glad, with all my heart, the folly is over—sorra use I could see in it, except the expense, and there's plenty of that. The old families, as they call them, can't last for ever, no more than old houses and old castles; there's an end of everything in time, and if Hickman waits, maybe his turn will come as others' did before him. Where's the Darcys now, I'd like to know?——" Here he paused and stammered, and at last stopped dead short, an expression of as much confusion as age and wrinkles would permit covering his hard, contracted features.

"You say truly," said Heffernan, finishing what he guessed to be the sentiment—"you say truly, the Darcys have run their race; when men's incumbrances have reached the point that his have, family influence soon decays. Now this business of Gleeson's——" Had he fired a shot close to the old man's ear he could not have startled him more effectually than by the mention of this name.

"What of Gleeson?" said he, drawing in his breath and holding on the chair with both hands.

"You know that he is gone—fled away no one knows where?"

"Gleeson! Honest Tom Gleeson ran away!" exclaimed Hickman; "no, no, that's impossible—I'd never believe that."

"Strange enough, sir, that the paragraphs here have not convinced you," said Heffernan, taking up the newspaper which lay on the table, and where the mark of snuffy fingers denoted the very passage in question.

"Ay! I didn't notice it before," muttered the Doctor, as he took up the paper, affecting to read, but in reality to conceal his own confusion.

"They say the news nearly killed Darcy; he only heard it when going into the House last night, and was seized with an apoplectic fit and carried home insensible." This latter was, it is perhaps needless to say, pure invention of Heffernan, who found it necessary to continue talking as a means of detecting old Hickman's game. "Total ruin to that family of course results. Gleeson had raised immense sums to pay off the debts, and carried all away with him.'

"Ay!" muttered the Doctor, as he seemed greatly occupied in arranging his papers on the table.

"You'll be a loser too, sir, by all accounts," added Heffernan.

"Not much—a mere trifle," said the Doctor, without looking up from the papers. "But maybe he's not gone after all—I won't believe it yet."

"There seems little doubt on that head," said Heffernan; "he changed three thousand pounds in notes for gold at Ball's after the bank was closed on Tuesday, and then went over to Finlay's, where he said he had a lodgment to make. He left his great-coat behind him, and never came back for it. I found that paper—it was the only one—in the breast pocket."

"What is it? what is it?" repeated the old man, clutching eagerly at it.

"Nothing of any consequence," said Heffernan, smiling; and he handed him a printed notice, setting forth that the United States barque, the *Congress*, of five hundred tons burden, would sail for New York on Wednesday, the 16th instant, at an hour before high water. "That looked suspicious, didn't it?" said Heffernan; "and on inquiry I found he had drawn largely out of, not only the banks in town, but from the provincial ones also. Now, that note addressed to yourself, for instance——"

"What note?" said Hickman, starting round as his face became pale as ashes; "give it to me—give it at once!"

But Heffernan held it firmly between his fingers, and merely shook his head, while, with a gentle smile, he said, "The banker who entrusted this letter to my hands was well aware of what importance it might prove in a court of justice, should this disastrous event demand a legal investigation."

The old Doctor listened with breathless interest to every word of this speech, and merely muttered at the close the words, "The note, the note!"

"I have promised to restore the paper to the banker," said Heffernan.

"So you shall—let me read it," cried Hickman, eagerly; and he clutched from Heffernan's fingers the document, before the other had seemingly determined whether he would yield to his demand.

"There it is for you, sir," said the Doctor; "make what you can of it;" and he threw the paper across the table.

The note contained merely the words, "Ten thousand pounds." There was no signature nor any date, but the handwriting was Gleeson's.

"Ten thousand pounds," repeated Heffernan, slowly; "a large sum!"

"So it is," chimed in Hickman, with a grin of self-satisfaction, while a consciousness that the mystery, whatever it might be, was beyond the reach of Heffernan's skill, gave him a look of excessive cunning, which sat strangely on features so old and time-worn.

"Well, Mr. Hickman," said Heffernan, as he arose to take leave, "I have neither the right nor the inclination to pry into any man's secrets. This affair of Gleeson's will be sifted to the bottom one day or other, and that small transaction of the ten thousand pounds as well as the rest. It was not to discuss him or his fortunes I came here. I hoped to have seen Mr. O'Reilly, and explained away a very serious misconception. Lord Castlereagh regrets it, not for the sake of the loss of Mr. O'Reilly's support, valuable as that unquestionably is, but because a wrong interpretation would seem to infer that the conduct of the Treasury bench was disingenuous. You will, I trust, make this explanation for me, and in the name of his Lordship."

"Faith, I won't promise it," said old Hickman, looking up from a long column of figures which he was for some minutes poring over; "I don't un derstand them things at all; if Bob wanted to be a Lord, 'tis more than ever I did—I don't see much pleasure there is in being a gentleman. I know, for my part, I'd rather sit in the back parlour of my little shop in Loughrea, where I could have a chat over a tumbler of punch with a neighbour, than all the grandeur in life."

"These simple, unostentatious tastes do you credit before the world, sir," said Heffernan, with a well put-on look of admiration.

"I don't know whether they do or not," said Hickman, "but I know they help to make a good credit with the bank, and that's better—ay!"

Heffernan affected to relish the joke, and descended the stairs, laughing as he went; but scarcely had he reached his carriage, however, than he muttered a heavy malediction on the sordid old miser, whose iniquities were not less glaring because Con had utterly failed to unravel anything of his mystery.

"To Lord Castlereagh's," said he to the footman, and then lay back to ponder over his late interview.

The noble Secretary was not up when Con arrived, but had left orders that Mr. Heffernan should be shown up to his room whenever he came. It was now about five o'clock in the afternoon, and Lord Castlereagh, wrapped up in a loose morning gown, lay on the bed where he had thrown himself, without undressing, on reaching home. A debate of more than fifteen hours, with all its strong and exciting passages, had completely exhausted his strength, while the short and disturbed sleep had wearied rather than refreshed him. The bed and the table beside it were covered with the morning papers and open letters and despatches, for, tired as he was, he could not refrain from learning the news of the day.

"Well, my Lord," said Heffernan, with his habitual smile, as he stepped noiselessly across the floor, "I believe I may wish you joy at last—the battle is gained now."

"Heigho!" was the reply of the Secretary, while he extended two fingers f his hand in salutation. "What hour is it, Heffernan?"

"It is near five, but really there's not a creature to be seen in the streets, and, except old Killgobbin airing his pocket handkerchief at the fire, not a soul at the Club. Last night's struggle has nearly killed every one."

"Who is this Mr. Gleeson that has run off with so much money—did you know him?"

"Oh yes, we all knew 'honest Tom Gleeson.'"

"Ah! that was his sobriquet, was it?" said the Secretary, smiling.

"Yes, my Lord, such was he—or such, at least, was he believed to be, ti yesterday evening. You know it's the last glass of wine always makes a man tipsy."

"And who is ruined, Heffernan—any of our friends?"

"As yet there's no saying. Drogheda will lose something considerable, I believe, but at the banks the opinion is that Darcy will be the heaviest loser of any."

"The Knight?"

"Yes, the Knight of Gwynne."

"I am sincerely sorry to hear it," said Lord Castlereagh, with an energy of tone he had not displayed before; "if I had met half a dozen such men as he is, I should have had some scruples——" He paused, and at the instant caught sight of a very peculiar smile on Heffernan's features; then suddenly changing the topic, he said, "What of Nickolls—is he shot?"

"No, my Lord, there was no meeting. Bagenal Daly, so goes the story, proposed going over to the Isle of Man in a row-boat."

"What, last night!" said the Secretary, laughing.

"Yes, when it was blowing the roof off the Custom House; he offered him his choice of weapons, from a blunderbuss to a harpoon, and his own distance, over a handkerchief, or fifty yards with a rifle."

"And was Nickolls deaf to all such seductions?"

"Quite so, my Lord; even when Daly said to him, 'I think it a public duty to shoot a fellow like you, for, if you are suffered to live, the Government will make a judge of you one of these days.'"

"What profound solicitude for the purity of the judgment-seat!"

"Daly has reason to think of these things; he has been in the dock already, and perhaps suspects he may be again."

"Poor Darcy," said Lord Castlereagh to himself, in a half whisper, "I wish I knew you were not a sufferer by this fellow's flight. By-the-by, Heffernan, sit down and write a few lines to Forester; say that Lord Cornwallis is greatly displeased at his protracted absence. I am tired of making excuses for him, and as I dine there to-day, I shall be tormented all the evening."

"Darcy's daughter is very good-looking, I hear," said Heffernan, smiling slyly, "and should have a large fortune if matters go right."

"Very possibly, but old Lady Wallincourt is the proudest dowager in England, and looks to the blood-royal for alliances. Forester is entirely dependent on her, and that reminds me of a most solemn pledge I made her to look after her 'dear Dick,' and prevent any entanglement in this barbarous land, as if I had nothing else to think of! Write at once, Heffernan, and order him up; say he'll lose his appointment by any further delay, and that I am much annoyed at his absence."

While Heffernan descended to the library to write, Lord Castlereagh turned once more to sleep until it was time to dress for the Viceroy's dinner,

CHAPTER XXII.

"A WARNING" AND "A PARTING."

If we wanted any evidence of how little avail all worldly wisdom is, we might take it from the fact, that our severest calamities are often impending us at the moments we deem ourselves most secure from misfortune. Thus was it that while the events were happening whose influence was to shadow over all the sunshine of her life, Lady Eleanor Darcy never felt more at ease. That same morning the post had brought her a letter from the Knight —only a few lines, hastily written—but enough to allay all her anxiety. He spoke of law arrangements, then almost completed, by which any immediate pressure regarding money might be at once obviated, and promised, for the very first time in his life, to submit to any plan of retrenchment she desired to adopt. Had it been in her power, she could not have dictated lines more full of pleasant anticipation. The only drawback on the happiness of her lot in life was the wasteful extravagance of a mode of living which savoured far more of feudal barbarism than of modern luxury.

Partly from long habit and association, partly from indolence of character, but more than either from a compassionate consideration of those whose livelihood might be impaired by any change in his establishment, the Knight had resisted all suggestion of alteration. He viewed the very peculations around him as vested rights, and the most he could pledge himself to was, that when the present race died out he would not appoint any successors.

The same post that brought this pleasant letter, conveyed one of far less grateful import to Forester. It was a long epistle from his mother, carefully worded, and so characteristic withal, that if it were any part of our object to introduce that lady to our readers, we could not more easily do so than through her own letter. Such is not, however, our intention; enough if we say that it was a species of domestic homily, where moral principles and worldly wisdom found themselves so inextricably interwoven, no mean skill could have disentangled them. She had learned, as careful mothers somehow always contrive to learn, that her son was domesticated in the house with a very charming and beautiful girl, and the occasion seemed suitable to enforce some of those excellent precepts, which hitherto had been deficient in force for want of a practical example.

Had Lady Wallincourt limited herself to cautious counsels about falling in love with some rustic beauty in a remote region, Forester might have treated the advice as one of those matter-of-course events, which cause no more surprise than the receipt of a printed circular; but she went further. She deemed this a fitting occasion to instruct her son into the mystery of that craft which, in her own experience of life, she had seen make more than one man's fortune, and by being adepts in which many of her own family had attained to high and lasting honours. This science was neither more nor less than success in female society. "I will not insult either your good taste or your understanding," wrote she, "by any warning against falling in love in Ireland. Beauty is—France excepted—pretty equally distributed through the world; neither is there any nationality in good looks, for, now-a-days, admixture of race has obliterated every peculiarity of origin. In all then that concerns manner, tone, and breeding, your own country possesses the true standard; every deviation from this is a fault. What is conventional must be right, because it is the exponent of general opinion on those topics for which each feels interested. Now the Irish, my dear boy, the Irish are never conventional; they are clannish, provincial, peculiar, but never conventional. Their pride would seem to be rather to ruffle than fall in with the general sympathies of society. They forget that the social world is a great compact, and they are always striving for individual successes by personal distinction: this is the very acme of vulgarity.

"If they, however, are very indifferent models for imitation, they afford an excellent school for your own training; they are a shrewd, quick-sighted race, with a strong sense of the ludicrous, and are what the French call *malin* to a degree. To win favour among them without any subservient imitation of their own habits, which would be contemptible, is not over easy.

"If I am rightly informed, you are at present well circumstanced to profit by my counsels. I am told of a very agreeable and very pretty girl with whom you ride and walk out constantly, and far from feeling any maternal uneasiness—for I trust I know my son—I am rejoiced at the circumstance. Make the most of such an advantage by exercising your own abilities and powers of pleasing, give yourself the habit of talking your very best on every topic, without pedantry or any sign of premeditation. Practise that blending of courteous deference to a woman's opinions with a subdued consciousness of your own powers, which I have so often spoken to you of in your dear father's character. Seldom venture on an axiom, never tell an anecdote—be most guarded in any indulgence of humour; a laugh is the most dangerous of all triumphs. It is the habit to reproach us with our frigidity—I believe not without reason—cultivate, then, a certain amount of warmth which may suggest the idea of earnestness, apart from all sussion of enthusiasm, which I have often told you is low-lived. Watch carefully by what qualities your success is more advanced; examine yourself as to what defects you experience in your own character; make yourself esteemed as a means of being estimable; win regard, and the habit of pleasing will give a charm to your manner, even when you are not desirous to secure affection. Your poor dear father often confessed the inestimable advantages of his first affairs of the heart, and used to say, whenever by any adroit exercise of his captivation he had gained over an adverse Maid of Honour, I owe that to Louisa, for such was the name of the young lady—I forget now who she was. The mechanism of the heart is alike in all lands; the means of success in Ireland will win victory where the prize is higher. In all this, remember I by no means advise you to sport with any young lady's feelings, nor to win more of her affection than may assure you that the entire could also become yours—a polite chess-player will rest satisfied to say 'check,' without pushing the adversary to 'mate.'

"It will soon be time you should leave the army, and I hope to find you have acquired some other education by the pursuit than mere knowledge of dress."

This is a short specimen of the maternal Machiavelism by which "the most fascinating woman of her set" hoped to instruct her son, and teach him the road to fortune.

Such is the fatal depravity of every human heart, that any subtle appeal to selfishness, if it fail to flex the victim to the will, at least shakes the strong sense of conscious rectitude, and makes our very worthiness seem weakness.

Forester's first impression was almost anger as he read these lines, the second time he perused them he was far less shocked, and at last was puzzled whether more to wonder at the keen worldly knowledge they betrayed, or the solicitude of that affection which consented to unveil so much of life for his guidance. The result of all these conflicting emotions was depression of spirits, and a discontent with himself and all the world; nor could the fascinations of that little circle in which he lived so intimately, subdue the feeling.

Lady Eleanor saw this, and exerted herself with all her wonted powers to amuse and interest him; Helen too, delighted at the favourable change in her mother's spirits, contributed to sustain the tone of light-hearted pleasantry, while she could not restrain a jest upon Forester's unusual gloominess.

The manner, whose fascinations had hitherto so many charms, now almost irritated him; the poison of suspicion had been imbibed, and he continually asked himself, what if the very subtlety his mother's letter spoke of was now practised by her? If all the varied hues of captivation her changing humour wore were but the deep practised lures of coquetry? His self-love was piqued by the thought, as well as his perceptive shrewdness, and he set himself, as he believed, to decipher her real nature; but, such is the blindness of mere egotism, in reality to misunderstand and mistake her.

How often it happens in life that the moment a doubt prevails as to some trait or feature of our character, we should exactly seize upon that very instant to indulge in some weakness or passing levity that may strengthen a mere suspicion or make it certainty.

Helen never seemed gayer than on this evening, scarcely noticing Forester, save when to jest upon his morose and silent mood; she talked, and laughed, and sang in all the free joyousness of a happy heart, unconsciously displaying powers of mind and feeling which, in calmer moments, lay dormant and concealed.

The evening wore on, and Helen had just risen from her harp—where she was playing one of those wild, half-sad, half-playful melodies of her country—when a gentle tap came to the door, and, without waiting for leave to enter, old Tate appeared.

The old man was pale, and his features wore an expression of extreme terror; but he was doing his very utmost, as it seemed, to struggle against some inward fear, as, with a smile of far more melancholy than mirth, he said, "Did ye hear it, my Lady? I'm sure ye heerd it."

"Heard what, Tate?" said Lady Eleanor.

"The——but I see Miss Helen's laughing at me. Ah! don't then Miss, darlin—don't laugh."

"What was it, Tate? Tell us what you heard."

"The Banshee, my Lady! Ay, there's the way—I knew how 'twould be, you'd only laugh when I tould you."

"Where was it you heard it?" said Lady Eleanor, affecting seriousness to gratify the old man's superstition.

"Under the east window, my Lady; then it moved across the flower-garden, and down to the shore beneath the big rocks."

"What was it like, Tate?"

"'Twas like a funeral 'coyne' first, Miss, when ye heerd it far away in the mountain; and then it rose, and swelled fuller and stronger, till it swam all round me, and at last died away to the light, soft cry of an infant."

"Exactly, Tate; it was Captain Forester sighing. I never heard a better description in my life."

"Ah! don't laugh, my Lady—don't now, Miss Helen, dear. I never knew luck nor grace come of laughing when the warnin' was come. 'Tis the Captain, there, looks sad and thoughtful—the Heavens bless him for it. He knows 'tis no time for laughing."

Forester might have accepted the eulogy in better part, perhaps, had he understood it; but as it was, he turned abruptly about, and asked Lady Eleanor for an explanation of the whole mystery.

"Tate thinks he has heard——"

"Thinks!" interrupted the old man, with a sorrowful gesture of both hands. "Musha! I'd take the Gospel on it; I heerd it as plain as I hear your Ladyship now."

Lady Eleanor smiled, and went on—"the cry of the Banshee, that dreadful warning which, in the superstition of the country, always betokens death, or, at least, some great calamity, to the house it is heard to wail over."

"A polite attention, to say the least," said Forester, smiling sarcastically, "of the witch, or fairy, or whatever it is, to announce to people an approaching misfortune. And has every cabin got its own Ban——what do you call it?"

"The cabins has none," said Tate, with a look of severe reproach the most remote possible from his habitual air of deference; "'tis only the ouldest and most ancient families, like his honour the Knight's, has a Banshee. But it's no use talking; I see nobody believes me."

"Yes, Tate, I do," cried Helen, with an earnestness of manner, either really felt, or assumed to gratify the poor old man's superstitious veneration; "just tell me how you heard it first."

"Like that!" whispered Tate, as he held up his hand to enforce silence; and at the same instant a low, plaintive cry was heard, as if beneath the very window. The accent was not of pain or suffering, but of melancholy so soft, so touching, and yet so intense, that it stilled every voice within the room, where now each long-drawn breath was audible.

There is a lurking trait of superstition in every human heart, which will resist, at some one moment or other, every effort of reason and every scoff of irony. An instant before, and Forester was ready to jest with the old man's terrors, and now his own spirit was not all devoid of them. The feeling was, however, but of a moment's duration; suspicion again assumed its sway, and, seizing his hat, he rushed from the room, to search the flower-garden and examine every spot where any one might lie concealed.

"There he goes now, as if he could see *her;* and maybe 'twould be as well for him he didn't," said Tate, as, in contempt of the English incredulity, he gazed after the eager youth. "Is his honour well, my Lady?—when did you hear from him?"

"We heard this very day, Tate; he is perfectly well."

"And Master Lionel—the Captain, I mane—but I only can think he's a child still."

"Quite well, too," said Helen. "Don't alarm yourself, Tate; you know how sadly the wind can sigh through these old walls at times, and under the yew-trees, too, it sounds drearily; I've shuddered to myself often, as I've heard it."

"God grant it!" said old Tate, piously; but the shake of his head and the muttering sounds between his teeth, attested that he laid no such flattering unction to his heart as mere disbelief might offer. "'Tisn't a death-cry, anyhow, Miss Helen," whispered he to Miss Darcy, as he moved towards the door; "for I went down to the back of the abbey, were Sir Everard was buried, and all was still there."

"Well, go to bed now, Tate, and don't think more about it; if the wind——"

"Ah! the wind! the wind!" said he, querulously; "that's the way it always is, as if God Almighty had no other way of talking to our hearts than the cry of the night-wind."

"Well, Captain Forester, what success? Have you confronted the spectre?" said Lady Eleanor, as he re-entered the apartment.

"Except having fallen into a holly-bush, where I rivalled the complaining accents of the old witch, I have no adventure to recount; all is perfectly still and tranquil without."

"You have got your cheek scratched for following the Syren," said Lady Eleanor, laughing; "pray put another log on the fire, it is fearfully chilly here."

Old Tate withdrew slowly and unwillingly; he saw that his intelligence had failed to produce a proper sense of terror on their minds; and his own load of anxiety was heavier, from want of participation.

The conversation, by that strange instinct which influences the least as well as the most credulous people, now turned on the superstitions of the peasantry, and many a legend and story were remembered by Lady Eleanor and her daughter, in which these popular beliefs formed a chief feature.

"It is unfair and unwise," said Lady Eleanor, at the conclusion of one of these stories, "to undervalue such influences; the sailor, who passes his life in dangers, watches the elements with an eye and an ear that training have rendered almost preternaturally observant, and he sees the sign of storm where others would but mark the glow of a red sunset; so among a primitive people communing much with their own hearts in solitary, unfrequented places, imagination becomes developed in undue proportion, and the mind seeks relief in creative efforts from the wearying sense of loneliness; but even these are less idle fancies than conclusions come to from long and deep thought. Some strange process of analogy would seem the parent of superstitions which we know to be common to all lands."

"Which means, that you half believe in a Banshee!" said Forester smiling.

"Not so; but that I cannot consent to despise the frame of mind which suggests these beliefs, although I have no faith in the apparitions. Poor Tate there had never dreamed of hearing the Banshee cry if some painful thought of impending misfortune had not suggested her presence; his fears may not be unfounded, although the form they take be preternatural."

"I protest against all such plausibilities," said Helen. "I'm for the Banshee, as the Republicans say in France, 'one and indivisible.' I'll not accept of natural explanations. Mr. Bagenal Daly says we may well believe in spirits, when we put faith in the mere ghost of a Parliament."

"Helen is throwing out a bait for a political discussion," said Lady Eleanor, laughing, "and so I'll even say good night. Good night, Captain Forester, and pleasant dreams of the Banshee."

Forester rose and took his leave, which, somehow, was colder than usual. His mother's counsels had got possession of his mind, and distrust perverted every former source of pleasure.

"Her manner is all coquetry," said he, angrily, to himself, as he walked towards his room.

Poor fellow! and what if it were? Coquetry is but gilding, to be sure; but it can never be well laid on if the substance beneath is not a precious metal.

There was, at the place where the river opened into the sea, a small inlet of the bay guarded by two bold and rocky headlands, between which the tide swept with uncommon violence, accumulating in time a kind of bar, over which, even in calm weather, the waves were lashed into breakers, while the waters within were still as a mountain lake. The ancient ruin we have already alluded to passingly, stood on a little eminence fronting this small creek, and although unmarked by any architectural beauty, or any pretensions, save the humble possession of four rude walls pierced by narrow windows, and a low doorway formed of three large stones, was yet, in the eyes of the country people, endowed with some superior holiness—so it is certain the little churchyard around bespoke. It was crowded with graves, whose humble monuments consisted in wooden crosses, decorated in recent cases with little garlands of paper or wild flowers, as piety or affection suggested. The fragments of ship-timber around showed that they who slept beneath had been mostly fishermen, for the chapel was peculiarly esteemed by them; and at the opening of the fishing season a mass was invariably offered here for the success of the herring-fishery, by a priest from a neighbouring parish, whose expenses were willingly and liberally rewarded by the fishermen.

In exact proportion with the reverence in which this spot was regarded by day was the fear and dread entertained of it by night. Stories of ghosts and evil spirits were rife far and near of that lonely ruin, and the hardiest seamen who would brave the wild waves of the Atlantic would not venture alone within these deserted walls after dark. Helen remembered, as a child, having been once there after sunset, induced by an intense curiosity to hear or see something of those sounds and shapes her nurse had told of, and what alarm her absence created among the household increased when it was discovered where she had been.

The same strange desire to hear if it might be that sad and wailing voice which all had so distinctly heard in the drawing-room, led her, when she had wished her mother good night, to leave her chamber, and crossing the flower-garden, to descend to the beach by a small door which opened on a little pathway down to the sea. When the superstitions whose terrors have affrighted childhood are either conquered by reason or uprooted by worldly influence, they still leave behind them a strange passion for the marvellous, which in imaginative temperaments is frequently greatly developed, and becomes a great source of enjoyment or suffering to its possessor. Helen Darcy's nature was of this kind, and she would gladly have accepted all the tremors and terrors of her nursery days to feel once again that intense awe, that anxious heart-beating expectancy, a ghost story used to create within her.

The night was calm and starlit, the sea was tranquil and unruffled, except where the bar broke the flow of the tide, and marked by a long line of foam the struggling breakers, whose hoarse plash was heard above the rippling on the strand. Even in the rocky caves all was still, not an echo resounded within those dreary caverns where at times the thunder's self was not louder. Helen reached the little churchyard; she knew every path and foot-track through it, and at last, strolling leisurely onward, entered the ruin and sat down within the deep window that looked over the sea.

For some time her attention was directed seaward, watching the waves as they reflected back the spangled heaven, or sank again in dark shadow, when suddenly she perceived the figure of a man, who appeared slowly pacing the beach immediately beneath where she sat.

What could have brought any one there at such an hour she could not imagine; and however few her terrors of the world of spirits, she would gladly at this moment have been safe within the abbey. While she debated with herself how to act—whether to remain in her present concealment, or venture on a sudden flight—the figure halted exactly under the window. Her doubts and fears were now speedily resolved, for she perceived it was Forester, who, induced by the beauty of the night, had thus strolled out upon the shore. "What if I should put his courageous incredulity to the test?" thought Helen; "the moment is propitious now. I could easily imitate the cry of the Banshee!" The temptation was too strong to be resisted, and without further thought she uttered a low thrilling wail, in an accent of most touching sorrow. Forester started and looked up, but the dark walls were in deep shadow: whatever his real feeling at the moment, he lost no time in clambering up the bank on which the ruin stood, and from which he rightly judged the sound proceeded. Helen was yet uncertain whether to attribute this step to terror or the opposite, when she heard his foot as he traversed the thickly-studded graveyard—a moment more and he would be in the church itself, where he could not fail to discover her by her white dress. But one chance offered of escape, which was to leap from the window down upon the strand—it was deeper than she fancied, nearly twice her own height, but then detection, for more than one good reason, was not to be thought of.

Helen was not one of those who long hesitate when their minds are to be made up; she slipped noiselessly between the stone mullion and the side of the window, and sprang out; unfortunately one foot turned on a small stone, and she fell on the sand, while a slight accent of pain unconsciously broke from her. Before she could rise, Forester was beside her; with one arm round her waist, he half pressed, as he assisted her to recover her feet.

"So, fair spirit," said he, jocularly, "I have tracked you, it would seem;" then, for the first time discovering it was Helen, he muttered in a different tone, "I ask pardon, Miss Darcy—I really did not know——"

"I am sure of that, Captain Forester," said she, disengaging herself from his aid. "I certainly deserve a lesson for my silly attempt to frighten you, and I believe I have sprained my ankle. Will you kindly send Florence to me?"

"I cannot leave you here alone, Miss Darcy; pray take my arm and let me assist you back to the abbey."

The tone of deference he now spoke in, and the increasing pain, concurred to persuade her, and she accepted the proffered assistance.

"The absurdity of this adventure is not repaid by the pleasure of having frightened you," said she, laughing; "if I could only say how terrified you were——"

"You might indeed have said so," interrupted Forester, "had I guessed the figure I saw leap out was yours."

"It was even higher than I thought," said she, avoiding to remark the fervent accents in which these words were spoken.

Forester was silent; his heart was full to bursting; the passion so lately dashed by doubts and suspicions returned with tenfold force now that he felt her arm within his own, as step by step they moved along.

"You are in great pain, I fear," said he, tremulously.

"No, not now. I am so much more ashamed of my folly than a sufferer from it, that I could forgive the sprain, if I could the silly notion that caused it. 'Twas an unlucky fancy, to say the least of it."

Again there was a pause, and although they walked but slowly, they were fast approaching the little gate that opened into the flower-garden. Forester was silent. Was it from this cause, or by some secret freemasonry of the female heart, that she suspected what was passing in his mind, and exerted herself to move on more rapidly?

"Take time, Miss Darcy; not so fast; if not for your sake, for mine at least."

The last few words were scarcely above a whisper, but every one of them reached her to whom they were addressed; whether affecting not to hear them, or preferring to mistake their meaning, Helen made no answer.

"I said for *my* sake," resumed he, with a courage that demanded all his energy, "because on these few moments the whole fortune of my future life is placed. I love you."

"Nay, Captain Forester," said she, smiling, "this is not quite fair, I failed in my attempt to terrify you, and have paid the penalty; let there not be a further one of my listening to what I should not hear."

"And why not hear it, Helen? Is the devotion of one, even humble as I am, a thing to offend? Is it the less sincere that I feel how much you are above me in every way? Will not my very presumption prove how fervent is the passion that has made me forget all save itself—all, save you?"

Truth has its own accents, however weak the words it syllables. Helen laughed not now, but walked on with quicker steps; while the youth, the barrier once passed, poured forth with heartfelt eloquence his tale of love, recalling to her mind by many a slight, unnoticed trait, his long-pledged devotion; how he had watched and worshipped her, seeking to win favour in her eyes, and seem not all unworthy of her heart.

"It is true," said he, "I cannot, dare not ask in return for an affection which should repay my own; but let me hope that what I now speak, the devotion I pledge, is no rejected offering; that although you care not for me, you will not crush for ever one who lives but in your smile, that you will give me time to show myself more worthy of the prize I strive for There is no trial I would not dare——"

"I must interrupt you, Captain Forester," said Helen, with a voice that all her efforts had not rendered quite steady; "it would be an ungenerous requital for the sentiments you say you feel——"

"Say!—nay, Helen, I swear it, by every hope that now thrills within me——"

"It would be," resumed she, tremulously, "an ungenerous requital for this, were I to practise any deception on you. I am sincerely, deeply sorry to hear you speak as you have done. I had long since learned to regard you as the friend of Lionel, almost like a brother. The pleasure your society afforded one I am most attached to increased the feeling; and as intimacy increased between us, I thought how happy were it if the ambitions of life did not withdraw from home the sons whose kindness can be as thoughtful and as tender as that of the daughters of the house. Shall I confess it? I almost wished my brother like you—but yet all this was not love—nay, for I will be frank, at whatever cost—I had never felt this towards you, if I suspected your sentiments towards me——"

"But, dearest Helen——"

"Hear me out. There is but one way in which the impropriety of such a meeting as this can be obviated, chance though it be, and that is, by perfect candour. I have told you the simple truth, not with any undervaluing sense of the affection you proffer, still less with any coquetry of reserve. I should be unworthy of the heart you offer me, since I could not give my own in exchange."

"Do you deny me all hope?" said he, in an accent almost bursting with grief.

"I am not arrogant enough to say I shall never change; but I am honest enough to tell you that I do not expect it."

"Farewell, then, Helen! I do not love you less that you have taught me to think more humbly of myself. Good-by—for ever!"

"It is better it should come to this," said Helen, faintly; and she held out her hand towards him. "Good-by, Forester!"

He pressed one long and burning kiss upon her hand, and turned away while she, pushing open the door, entered the little garden. Scarcely, however, was the door closed behind her, when the calm courage in which she spoke forsook her, and she burst into tears.

So is it, the heart can be moved, even its most tender chords, when the touch that stirs it is less of love than sorrow.

CHAPTER XXIII.

SOME SAD REVELATIONS.

It was on the fourth day after the memorable debate we have briefly alluded to, that the Knight of Gwynne was sitting alone in one of the large rooms of his Dublin mansion. Although his servants had strict orders to say he had left town, he had not quitted the capital, but passed each day, from sunrise till late at night, in examining his various accounts, and endeavouring, with what slight business knowledge he possessed, to ascertain the situation in which he stood, and how far Gleeson's flight had compromised him. There is no such chaotic confusion to the unaccustomed mind as the entangled web of long-standing moneyed embarrassments, and so Darcy found it. Bills for large sums had been passed, to provide for which, renewals had been granted, and this for a succession of years, until the debt accumulating had been met by a mortgage or a bond: many of these bills were missing—where were they? was the question, and what liability might yet attach to them?

Again, loans had been raised more than once to pay off these encumbrances, the interest on which was duly charged in his account, and yet there was no evidence of these payments having been made; nor among the very last sent papers from Gleeson was there any trace of that bond, to release which the enormous sum of seventy thousand pounds had been raised. That the money was handed to Hickman, Bagenal Daly was convinced; the memorandum given him by Freney was a corroboration of the probability at least, but still there was no evidence of the transaction here. Even this was not the worst, for the Knight now discovered that the rental charged in his accounts was more than double the reality, Gleeson having for many years back practised the fraud of granting leases at a low, sometimes a merely nominal rent, while he accepted renewal fines from the tenants, which he applied to his own purposes. In fact, it at length became manifest to Darcy's reluctant belief that his trusted agent had for years long pursued a systematic course of perfidy, merely providing money sufficient for the exigencies of the time, while he was, in reality, selling every acre of his estate.

The Knight's last hope was in the entail. "I am ruined—I am a beggar, it is true!" muttered he, as each new discovery broke upon him, "but my boy, my dear Lionel, at my death will have his own again." This cherished dream was not of long duration, for to his horror he discovered a sale of a considerable part of the estate in which Lionel's name was signed as a concurring party. This was the crowning point of his affliction; the ruin was now utter, without one gleam of hope remaining.

The property thus sold was that in the possession of the O'Reillys, and the sale was dated the very day Lionel came of age. Darcy remembered well having signed his name to several papers on that morning. Gleeson had followed him from place to place, through the crowds of happy and rejoicing people assembled by the event, and at last, half vexed at the importunity, he actually put his name to several papers as he sat on horseback on the lawn: this very identical deed was thus signed; the writing was straggling and irregular as the motion of the horse shook his hand. So much for his own inconsiderate rashness; but how, or by what artifice, was Lionel's signature obtained?

Never had Lionel Darcy practised the slightest deception on his father; never concealed from him any difficulty or any embarrassment, but frankly confided to him his cares, as he would to one of his own age. How, then, had he been drawn into a step of this magnitude without apprising him? There was one explanation, and this was, that Gleeson persuaded the young man, that by thus sacrificing his own future rights he would be assisting his father, who, from motives of delicacy, could not admit of any negotiation in the matter, and that by ceding so much of his own property, he should relieve his father from present embarrassment.

Through all the revelation of the agent's guilt now opening before him, not one word of anger, one expression of passion, escaped the Knight till his eyes fell upon this paper; but then, grasping it in both hands, he shook in every limb with indignant rage, and in accents of bitterest hate invoked a curse upon his betrayer. The very sound of his own voice in that silent chamber startled him, while a sick tremor crept through his frame at the unhallowed wish he uttered. "No, no," said he, with clasped hands, "it is not for one like me, whose sensual carelessness has brought my own to ruin, to speak thus of another; may Heaven assist me, and pardon him that injured me."

The stunning effects of heavy calamity are destined in all likelihood to give time to rally against the blow—to permit exhausted Nature to fortify herself by even a brief repose against the harassing influences of deep sorrow. One who saw far into the human heart tells us, that it is not the strongest natures are the first to recover from the shock of great misfortunes, but that "light and frivolous spirits regain their elasticity sooner than those of loftier character."

The whole extent of his ruin unfolded itself gradually before Darcy's eyes, until at length the accumulated load became too great to bear, and he sat in almost total unconsciousness gazing at the mass of law papers and accounts before him, only remembering at intervals, and then faintly, the nature of the investigation he was engaged in, and by an effort recalling himself again to the task: in this way passed the entire day we speak of. Brief struggles to exert himself in examining the various papers and letters on the table were succeeded by long pauses of apparent apathy, until, as evening drew near, these intervals of indifference grew longer, and he sat for hours in this scarce-waking condition.

It was long pastmid night as a loud knocking was heard at the street door, and ere Darcy could sufficiently recal his wandering faculties from their reverie, he felt a hand grasp his own—he looked up and saw Bagenal Daly

"Well, Darcy," said he, in a low whisper, "how stand matters here?"

"Ruined!" said he, in an accent hardly audible, but with a look that thrilled through the stern heart of Daly.

"Come, come, there must be a long space between *your* fortune and ruin yet. Have you seen any legal adviser?"

"What of Gleeson, Bagenal, has he been heard of?" said the Knight, not attending to Daly's question.

"He has had the fitting end of a scoundrel. He leaped overboard in the Channel——"

"Poor fellow!" said Darcy, while he passed his hand across his eyes; "his spirit was not all corrupted, Bagenal; he dared not to face the world."

"Face the world! the villain, it was the gallows he had not courage to face. Don't speak one word of compassion about a wretch like him, or you'll drive me mad. There's no iniquity in the greatest crimes to compare with the slow, dastardly scoundrelism of your fair-faced swindler. It seems so at least. The sailors told us that he went below immediately on their leaving the river, and having locked the cabin door, spent his time in writing till they were in sight of the Holyhead light, when a sudden splash was heard, and a cry of 'A man overboard!' called every one to the deck; then it was discovered that the fellow had opened one of the stern-windows and thrown himself into the sea. They brought me this open letter, the last, it is said, he ever wrote, and, though unaddressed, evidently meant for you. You need not read it; it contains nothing but the whining excuses of a scoundrel, who bases his virtue on the fact that he was more coward than cheat. Strangest thing of all, he had no property with him beyond some few clothes, a watch, and about three hundred guineas in a purse. These were deposited by the skipper with the authorities in Liverpool—not a paper, not a document of any kind. Don't read that puling scrawl, Darcy; I have no patience with your pity!"

"I wish he had escaped with life, Bagenal," said Darcy, feelingly; "it is a sad aggravation of all my sorrow to think of this man's suicide."

"And so he might, had he had the courage to take his chance. The *Congress* passed us as we went up the river; she had her studding-sails set, and, with the strong tide in her favour, was cutting through the water as fast as ever a runaway scoundrel could wish or ask for. Gleeson's servant contrived to reach her in time, and got away safe, not improbably with a heavy booty, if the truth were known."

Daly continued to dwell on the theme, repeating circumstantially the whole of the examination before the Liverpool justices, where the depositions of the case were taken, and the investigation conducted with strict accuracy; but Darcy paid little attention. The sad end of one for whom through years long he had entertained feelings of respect and friendship, seemed to obliterate all memory of his crime, and he had no other feelings in his heart than those of sincere grief for the suicide.

"There is but one circumstance in the whole I cannot understand," said Daly, "and that is why Gleeson paid off Hickman's bond last week, when he had evidently made up his mind to fly—seventy thousand was such a sum to carry away with him, all sound and safe as he had it."

"But where's the evidence of such a payment?" said Darcy, sorrowfully; "the bond is not to be found, nor is it among the papers discovered at Gleeson's house."

"It may be found yet," said Daly, confidently. "That the money was paid I have not a particle of doubt on my mind; Freney's information, and the memorandum I showed you, are strong in corroborating the fact; old Hickman dared not deny it, if the bond never were to turn up."

"Heaven grant it!" said Darcy, fervently; "that will at least save the abbey, and rescue our old house from the pollution I dreaded."

"All that, however, does not explain the difficulty," said Daly, thoughtfully; "I wish some shrewder head than mine had the matter before him. But now that I have told you so much, let me have some supper, Darcy, for we forgot to victual our sloop, and had no sea-store but whisky on either voyage."

Though this was perfectly true, Daly's proposition was made rather to induce the Knight to take some refreshment, which it was so evident he needed, than from any personal motive.

"They carried the second reading by a large majority; I read it in Liverpool," said Daly, as the servant laid the table for supper.

The Knight nodded an assent, and Daly resumed: "I saw also that an address was voted by the patriotic members of Daly's to Hickman O'Reilly, Esquire, M.P., for his manly and independent conduct in the debate, when he taunted the Government with their ineffectual attempts at corruption, and spurned indignantly every offer of their patronage."

"Is that the case?" said the Knight, smiling faintly.

"All fact; while the mob drew his carriage home, and nearly smoked the entire of Merrion-square into blackness with burning tar-barrels."

"He has improved on Johnson's definition, Bagenal, and made patriotism the first as well as the last refuge of a scoundrel."

"I looked out in the House that evening, but could not see him, for I wanted him to second a motion for me."

"Indeed! of what nature?"

"A most patriotic one, to this effect: that all bribes to members of either House should be in money, that we might have at least the benefit of introducing so much capital into Ireland."

"You forget, Bagenal, how it would spoil old Hickman's market; loans would then be had for less than ten per cent."

"So it would, by Jove! That shows the difficulty of legislating for conflicting interests."

This conversation was destined only to occupy the time the servant was engaged about the table, but when he had withdrawn, the Knight and his friend at once returned to the eventful theme that engaged all their anxieties, and where the altered tone of their voices and eager looks betokened the deepest interest.

It would have been difficult to find two men more generally well informed, and less capable of comprehending or unravelling the complicated tissue of a business matter. At the same time, by dint of much mutual inquiry and discussion, they attained to that first and greatest of discoveries, namely, their own insufficiency to conduct the investigation, and the urgent necessity of employing some able man of law to go through all Gleeson's accounts, and ascertain the real condition of Darcy's fortune. With this prudent resolve, they parted; Darcy to his room, where he sat with unclosed eyes till morning; while Daly, who had disciplined his temperament more rigidly soon fell fast asleep, and never awoke till roused by the voice of his servant Sandy.

"You must find out the fellow that brought the note from Freney," said Daly, the moment he opened his eyes.

"I was thinking so," said Sandy, sententiously.

"You'd know him again?"

"I'd ken his twa eyes amang a thousand."

"Very well, then, set off after breakfast and search for him; you used to know where devils of this kind were to be found."

"Maybe I havna quite forget it yet," replied he, dryly; "but it winna do to gae there before nightfall."

"Lose no more time than you can help about it," said Daly; "bring him here if you can find him."

We have not the necessity, and more certainly it is far from our inclination, to dwell upon the accumulated calamities of the Knight, nor recount more particularly the sad disclosures which the few succeeding days made regarding his fortunes. His own words were correct; he was utterly ruined. Every species of iniquity which perfidy could practise upon unbounded confidence had been effected. His property subdivided and leased at nominal rents, debts long supposed to have been paid yet outstanding; mortgages alleged to have been redeemed still impending; while of the large ums raised to meet these encumbrances, not one shilling had been paid by Gleeson, save perhaps the bond for seventy thousand; but even of this there was no evidence, except the vague assertion of one whose testimony the law would reject.

Such, in brief, were the sad results of that investigation to which the Knight's affairs were submitted, nor could all the practised subtlety of the lawyer suggest one reasonable chance of extrication from the difficulty.

"Your friend is a ruined man, sir," said he to Daly, as they both arose after a seven hours' examination of the various documents; "there is a strong presumption that many of these signatures are forged, and that the Knight of Gwynne never even saw the papers; but he appears to have written his name so carelessly, and in so many ways, as to have no clear recollection of what he did sign, and what he did not. It would be very difficult to submit a good case for a jury."

That the payment of the seventy thousand had been made he regarded as more than doubtful, coupling the fact of Gleeson's immediate flight with the temptation of so large a sum, while nothing could be less accurate than the robber's testimony. "We must watch the enemy closely on this point," said he; "we must exhibit not the slightest apparent doubt upon it. They must not be led to suspect that we have not the bond in our possession. This question will admit of a long contest, and does not press like the others. As to young Darcy's concurrence in the sale——"

"Ay, that is the great matter in my friend's eyes."

"He must be written to at once—let him come over here without loss of time, and if it can be shown that this signature is a forgery, we might make it the ground of a compromise with the O'Reillys, who, to obtain a good title, would be glad to admit us to liberal terms."

"Darcy will never listen to that, depend upon it," said Daly; "his greatest affliction is for his son's ruin."

"We'll see, we'll see—the game shall open its own combinations as we go on; for the present all the task of your friend, the Knight, is to carry a bold face to the world, let no rumour get abroad that matters are in their real condition. Our chance of extrication lies in the front we can show to the enemy."

"You are making a heavier demand than you are aware of—Darcy detests anything like concealment. I don't believe he would practise the slightest mystery that would involve insincerity for twelve hours to free the whole estate."

"Very honourable, indeed; but at this moment we must waive a punctilio."

"Don't give it that name to him—that's all," said Daly, sternly. "I am as little for subterfuge as any man, and yet I did my best to prevent him resigning his seat in the House; this morning he would send a request to

Lord Castlereagh, begging he might be permitted to accept an escheatorship; I need not say how willingly the proposal was accepted, and his name will appear in the *Gazette* to-morrow morning."

"This conduct, if persisted in, will ruin our case," said the lawyer, despondingly. "I cannot comprehend his reasons for it."

"They are simple enough—his own words were, 'I can never continue to be a member of the Legislature, when the only privilege it could confer is freedom from arrest.'"

"A very valuable one at this crisis, if he knew but all," muttered the other. "You will write to young Darcy at once."

"That he has done already, and to Lady Eleanor also; and as he expects me at seven, I'll take my leave of you till to-morrow."

"Well, Daly," said the Knight, as his friend entered the drawing-room before dinner, "how do you like the lawyer?"

"He's a shrewd fellow, and I suppose, for his calling, an honest one; but the habit of making the wrong seem right leads to a very great inclination to reverse the theorem, and make the right seem wrong."

"He thinks badly of our case, isn't that so?"

"He'd think much better of it, and of us too, I believe, if both were worse."

"I am just as well pleased that it is not so," said Darcy, smiling; "a bad case is far more endurable than a bad conscience. But here comes dinner, and I have got my appetite back again."

CHAPTER XXIV.

A GLANCE AT "THE FULL MOON."

To rescue our friend Bagenal Daly from any imputation the circumstance might suggest, it is as well to observe here, that when he issued the order to his servant to seek out the boy who brought the intelligence of Gleeson's flight, he was merely relying on that knowledge of the obscure recesses of Old Dublin which Sandy possessed, and not by any means upon a distinct acquaintance with gentlemen of the same rank and station as Jemmy.

When Daly first took up his residence in the capital, many, many years before, he was an object of mob worship. He had every quality necessary for such. He was immensely rich, profusely spendthrift, and eccentric to an extent that some characterised as insanity. His dress, his equipage, his liveries, his whole retinue and style of living were strange and unlike other men's, while his habits of life bid utter defiance to every ordinance of society.

In the course of several years' foreign travel he had made acquaintances the most extraordinary and dissimilar, and many of these were led to visit him in his own country. Dublin being less resorted to by strangers than most cities, the surprise of its inhabitants was proportionably great as they beheld not only Hungarian and Russian nobles, with gorgeous equipages and splendid retinues, driving through the streets, but Turks, Armenians, and Greeks, in full costume; and, on one occasion, Daly's companion on a public promenade was no less remarkable a person than a North American chief, in all the barbaric magnificence of his native dress. To obviate the inconvenience of that mob accompaniment such spectacles would naturally attract, Daly entered into a compact with the leaders of the various sets or parties of low Dublin, by which, on payment of a certain sum, he was guaranteed in the enjoyment of appearing in public without a following of several hundred ragged wretches in full cry after him. Nothing could be more honourable and fair than the conduct of both parties in this singular treaty; the subsidy was regularly paid through the hands of Sandy M'Grane, while the subsidised literally observed every article of the contract, and not only avoided any molestation on their own parts, but were a formidable protective force in the event of any annoyance from others of a superior rank in society.

The hawkers of the various newspapers were the deputies with whom Sandy negotiated this treaty, they being recognised as the legitimate interpreters of mob opinion through the capital; men who combined an insight into local grievances with a corresponding knowledge of general politics; and certain it is, their sway must have been both respected and well protected, for a single transgression of the compact with Daly never occurred.

Bagenal Daly troubled his head very little in the matter, it is true; for his own sake he would never have thought of such a bargain, but he detested the thought of foreigners carrying away with them from Ireland any unpleasant memories of mob outrage or insult; and desired that the only remembrance they should preserve of his native country should be of its cordial and hospitable reception. A great many years had now elapsed since these pleasant times, and Daly's name was scarcely more than a tradition among those who now lounged in rags and idleness through the capital. A fact of which he could have had little doubt himself, if he had reflected on that crowd which followed his own steps but a few days before. Of this circumstance, however, he took little or no notice, and gave his orders to Sandy with the same conscious power he had wielded nearly fifty years back.

A small public-house, called the Moon, in Duck-alley, a narrow lane off the Cross Poddle, was the resort of this Rump Parliament, and thither

Sandy betook himself o.. a Saturday evening, the usual night of meeting, as there being no issue of newspapers the next morning, nothing interfered with a prolonged conviviality. Often and often had he taken the same journey at the same hour; but now, such is the effect of a long interval of years, the way seemed narrower and more crooked than ever, while as he went not one familiar face welcomed him as he passed; nor could he recognise, as of yore, his acquaintances amid the various disguises of black eyes and smashed noses, which were frequent on every side. It was the hour when crime and guilt, drunken rage and grief, mingled together their fearful agencies; and every street and alley was crowded by half-naked wretches quarrelling and singing; some screaming in accents of heart-broken anguish; others shouting their blasphemies with voices hoarse from passion; age and infancy, manhood in its prime, the mother and the young girl, were all there reeling from drunkenness, or faint from famine; some struggling in deadly conflict, others bathing the lips and temples of ebbing life.

Through this human hell Sandy wended his way, occasionally followed by the taunting ribaldry of such as remarked him; such testimonies were very unlike his former welcomes in these regions; but for this honest Sandy cared little; his real regret was to see so much more evidence of depravity and misery than before. Drunkenness and its attendant vices were no new evils, it is true, but he thought all these were fearfully aggravated by what he now witnessed; loud and violent denunciations against every rank above their own, imprecations on the Parliament and the Gentry that "sowld Ireland;" as if any political perfidy could be the origin of their own degraded and revolting condition! Such is, however, the very essence of that spirit that germinates amid destitution and crime, and it is a dangerous social crisis when the masses begin to attribute their own demoralisation to the vices of their betters. It well behoves those in high places to make their actions and opinions conform to their great destinies.

Sandy's northern blood revolted at these brutal excesses, and the savage menaces he heard on every side; but perhaps his susceptibilities were more outraged by one trait of popular injustice than all the rest, and that was to hear Hickman O'Reilly extolled by the mob for his patriotic rejection of bribery, while the Knight of Gwynne was held up to execration by every epithet of infamy; ribald jests and low ballads conveying the theme of attack upon his spotless character.

The street lyrics of the day were divided in interest between the late rebellion and the act of Union; the former being, however, the favourite theme, from a species of irony peculiar to this class of poetry, in which certain living characters were held up to derision or execration. The chief chorist appeared to be a fiend-like old woman, with one eye, and a voice like a cracked bassoon; she was dressed in a cast-off soldier's coat and a man's hat, and neither from face nor costume had few feminine traits. This fair personage, known by the name of Rhoudlum, was, on her appearing, closely followed by a mob of admiring amateurs, who seemed to form both her body-guard and her chorus. When Sandy found himself fast wedged up in this procession, the enthusiasm was at its height, in honour of an elegant new ballad called "The two Majors," the air, should our reader be musically given, was the well-known one, "There was a miller had three sons:"

> Says Major Sirr to Major Swan,
> You have two rebels, give me one,
> They pay the same for one as two,
> I'll get five pounds, and I'll share with you.
> Tol! lol! lol! lay.

"That's the way the blackguards sowld yer blood, boys!" said the hag, in recitative; "pitch caps, the ridin' house, and the gallows was iligant tratement for wearin' the green."

"Go on, Rhoudlum, go on wid the song," chimed in her followers, who cared more for the original text than prose vulgate.

"Arn't I goin' on wid it?" said the hag, as fire flashed in her eyes; "is it the likes of you is to tache me how to modulate a strain?" And she resumed:

> Says Major Swan to Major Sirr,
> One man's a woman! ye may take her.
> 'Tis little we gets for them at all—
> Oh! the curse of Cromwell be an ye all!
> Tol! lol! lol! lay

The grand Demosthenic abruptness of the last line was the signal for an applauding burst of voices, whose sincerity it would be unfair to question.

"Where are you pushin' to! bad scran to ye! ye ugly varmint!" said the lady, as Sandy endeavoured to force his passage through the crowd. "Hurroo! by the mortial, it's Daly's man!" screamed she, in transport, as the accidental light of a window showed Sandy's features.

Few, if any, of those around had ever seen him; but his name and his master's were among the favoured traditions of the place, and however unwilling to acknowledge the acquaintance, Sandy had no help for it but to exchange greetings and ask the way to "the Moon," which he found he had forgotten.

"There it is forninst ye, Mr. M'Granes," said the lady, in the most dulcet tones; 'and if it's thinking of trating me ye are, 'tis a 'crapper' in a pint of porter I'd take; nothing stronger would sit on my heart now."

"Ye shall hae it," said Sandy; "but come into the house."

"I darn't do it, sir; the committee is sittin'—don't ye see, besides, the moon lookin' at you?" And she pointed to a rude representation of a crescent moon, formed by a kind of transparency in the middle of a large window, a signal which Sandy well knew portended that the council were assembled within.

"Wha's the man, noo?" said Sandy, with one foot on the threshold.

"The ould stock still, darlint," said Rhoudlum—"don't ye know his voice?"

"That's Paul Donellan—I ken him noo."

"Be my conscience! there's no mistake. Ye can hear his screech from the Poddle to the Pigeon House when the wind's fair."

Sandy put a shilling into the hag's hand, and without waiting for further parley, entered the little dark hall, and turning a corner he well remembered, pressed a button and opened the door into the room where the party were assembled.

"Who the blazes are you? What brings you here?" burst from a score of rude voices together, while every hand grasped some projectile to hurl at the devoted intruder.

"Ask Paul Donellan who I am, and he'll tell ye," said Sandy, sternly, while, with a bold contempt for the hostile demonstrations, he walked straight up to the head of the room.

The recognition on which he reckoned so confidently was not forthcoming, for the old decrepid creature who, cowering beneath the wig of some defunct chancellor, presided, stared at him with eyes bleared with age and intemperance, but seemed unable to detect him as an acquaintance.

"Holy Paul doesn't know him!" said half a dozen together, as in passionate indignation they arose to resent the intrusion.

"He may remember this better," said Sandy, as seizing a full bumper of whisky from the board, he threw it into the lamp beneath the transparency, and in a moment the moon flashed forth and displayed its face at the full. The spell was magical, and a burst of savage welcome broke from every mouth, while Donellan, as if recalled to consciousness, put his hand trumpet-fashion to his lips, and gave a shout that made the very glasses ring upon the board. Place was now made for Sandy at the table, and a wooden vessel called "a noggin" set before him, whose contents he speedily tested by a long draught.

"I may as weel tell you," said Sandy, "that I am Bagenal Daly's man. I mind the time it wad na hae been needful to say so much—my master's picture used to hang upon that wall."

Had Sandy proclaimed himself the Prince of Wales the announcement could not have met with more honour, and many a coarse and rugged grasp of the hand attested the pleasure his presence there afforded.

"We have the picture still," said a young fellow, whose frank, good-humoured face contrasted strongly with many of those around him; "but that old divil, Paul, always told us it was a likeness of himself when he was young."

"Confound the scoundrel!" said Sandy, indignantly, "he was no mair like my maister than a Dutch skipper is like a chief of the Delawares. Has the creature lost his senses a'togither?"

"By no manner of manes. He wakes up every now and then wid a speech, or a bit of poethry, or a sentiment."

"Ay," said another, "or if a couple came in to be married, see how the old chap's eyes would brighten, and how he would turn the other side of his wig round, before you could say 'Jack Robinson.'"

This was literally correct, and was the simple manœuvre by which Holy Paul converted himself into a clerical character, the back of his wig being cut in horse-shoe fashion, in rude imitation of that worn by several of the bishops.

"Watch him now—watch him now!" said one in Sandy's ear; and the old fellow passed his hand across his eyes as if to dispel some painful thought, while his careworn features were lit up with a momentary flash of sardonic drollery.

"Your health, sir," said he to Sandy; "or, as Terence has it, 'Hic tibi, Dave'—here's to you, Davy."

"A toast, Paul! a toast! Something agin the Union—something agin old Darcy."

"Fill up, gentlemen," said Paul, in a clear and distinct voice. "I beg to propose a sentiment which you will drink with a bumper. Are you ready?"

"Ready!" screamed all together.

"Here, then—repeat after me

Whether he's out or whether he's in,
It doesn't signify one pin;
Here's every curse of every sin
On Maurice Darcy, Knight of Gwynne."

"Hold!" shouted Sandy, as he drew a double-barrelled pistol from his bosom. "By the saul o' my body the man that drinks that toast shall hae mair in his waim than hot water and whisky. Maurice Darcy is my maister's friend, and a better gentleman never stepped in leather—wha dar say no?"

"Are we to drink it, Paul?"

"As I live by drink," cried Paul, stretching out both hands, "this is my *alter ego*, my duplicate self, Sanders M'Granes, 'revisiting the glimpses of the moon,' *post totidem annos!*" And a cordial embrace now followed which at once dispelled the threatened storm.

"Mr. M'Grane's health in three times three, gentlemen;" and, rising Paul gave the signal for each cheer as he alone could give it.

Sandy had now time to throw a glance around the table, where, however, not one familiar face met his own; that they were of the same calling and order as his quondam associates in the same place he could have little doubt, even had that fact not been proclaimed by the names of various popular journals affixed to their hats, and by whose titles they were themselves addressed. The conversation, too, had the same sprinkling of politics, town gossip, and late calamities he well remembered of yore, interspersed with lively commentaries on public men, which, if printed, would have been suggestive of libel.

The new guest soon made himself free of the guild by a proposal to treat the company, on the condition that he might be permitted to have five minutes' conversation with their president in an adjoining room. He might have asked much more in requital for his liberality, and without a moment's delay, or even apprising Paul of what was intended, the *Dublin Journal* and the *Free Press* took him boldly between them and carried him into a closet off the room where the carouse was held.

"I know what you are at," said Paul, as soon as the door closed. "Daly wants a rising of the Liberty boys for the next debate—don't deny it, it's no use. Well, now listen, and don't interrupt me. Tom Conolly came down from the Castle yesterday and offered me five pounds for a good mob to rack a house, and two ten if they'd draw Lord Clare home; but I refused—I did, on the virtue of my oath. There's patriotism for ye!—yer soul, where's the man wid only one shirt and a supplement to his back would do the same?"

"You're wrang—we dinna want them devils at a'; it's a sma' matter of inquiry I cam about. Ye ken Freney?"

"Is it the Captain? Whew!" said Paul, with a long whistle.

"It's no him," resumed Sandy, "but a wee bit of a callant they ca' Jamie."

"Jemmy the diver—the divil's own grandson, that he is."

"Where can I find him?" said Sandy, impatiently.

"Wait a bit, and you'll be sure to see him at home in his lodgings in Newgate."

"I must find him out at once; put me on his track, and I'll gie a goold guinea in yer hand, mon. I mean the young rascal no harm; it's a question I want him to answer me, that's all."

"Well, I'll do my best to find him for you, but I must send down to the country. I'll have to get a man to go beyond Kilcullen."

"We'll pay any expense."

"Sure I know that." And here Paul began a calculation to himself of distances and charges only audible to Sandy's ears at intervals. "Two and four, and six, with a glass of punch at Naas—half an hour at Tims'—the coach at Athy—ay, that will do it. Have ye the likes of a pair of ould boots or shoes? I've nothing but them, and the soles is made of two pamphlets of Roger Connor's, and them's the driest things I could get."

"I'll gie ye a new pair."

"You're the son of Fingal of the Hills, divil a less. And now if ye had a cast-off waistcoat—I don't care for the colour—orange or green, blue or yellow, *Tros Tyriusve mihi*, as we said in Trinity."

"Ye shall hae a coat to cover your old bones. But let us hae nae mair o' this—when may I expect to see the boy?"

"The evening after next, at eight o'clock, at the corner of Essex-bridge, Capel-street—'on the Rialto'—eh? that's the cue. And now let us join the revellers—*per Jove*, but I'm dry." And so saying, the miserable old creature broke from Sandy, and, assisted by the wall, tottered back to the room to his drunken companions, where his voice was soon heard high above the discord and din around him.

And yet this man, so debased and degraded, had been once a scholar of the University, and carried off its prizes from men whose names stood high among the great and valued of the land.

CHAPTER XXV.

BAGENAL DALY'S COUNSELS.

Every hour seemed to complicate the Knight of Gwynne's difficulties, and to increase that intricacy by which he already was so much embarrassed. The forms of law, never grateful to him, became now perfectly odious, obscuring instead of explaining the questions on which he desired information. He hated, besides, the small and narrow expedients so constantly suggested in cases where his own sense of right convinced him of the justice of his cause, nor could he listen with common patience to the detail of all those legal subtleties by which an adverse claim might be, if not resisted, at least protracted indefinitely.

His presence, far from affording any assistance, was, therefore, only an embarrassment both to Daly and the lawyer, and they heard with unmixed satisfaction of his determination to hasten down to the west, and communicate more freely with his family, for as yet his letter to Lady Eleanor, far from disclosing the impending ruin, merely mentioned Gleeson's flight as a disastrous event in the life of a man esteemed and respected, and adverting but slightly to his own difficulties in consequence.

"We must leave the abbey, Bagenal, I foresee that," said Darcy, as he took his friend aside a few minutes before starting.

Daly made no reply, for already his own convictions pointed the same way.

"I could not live there with crippled means and broken fortune; 'twould kill me in a month, by Jove, to see the poor fellows wandering about idle and unemployed, the stables nailed up, the avenue grass-grown, and not hear the cry of a hound when I crossed the court-yard. But what is to be done? Humbled as I am I cannot think of letting it to some Hickman O'Reilly or other, some vulgar upstart, feasting his low companions in those old halls, or plotting our utter ruin at our own hearth-stone; could we not make some other arrangement?"

"I have thought of one," said Daly, calmly; "my only fear is, how to ask for Lady Eleanor's concurrence to a plan which must necessarily press most heavily on her."

"What is it?" said Darcy, hastily.

"Of course, your inclination would be, for a time at least, perfect seclusion."

"That, above all and everything."

"Well, then, what say you to taking up your abode in a little cottage of mine on the Antrim coast? it is a wild and lonely spot, it's true, but you may live there without attracting notice or observation. I see you are surprised at my having such a possession. I believe I never told you, Darcy, that I bought Sandy's cabin from him the day he entered my service, and fitted it up, intending it as an asylum for the poor fellow if he should grow weary of my fortunes, or happily survive me. By degrees, I have added a room here and a closet there, till it has grown into a dwelling that any one, as fond of salmon fishing as you and I were, would not despise; come, will you have it?" Darcy grasped his friend's hand without speaking, and Daly went on: "That's right; I'll give orders to have everything in readiness at once; I'll go down, too, and induct you. Ay, Darcy, and if the fellows could take a peep at us over our lobster and a glass of Isla whisky, they'd stare to think those two jovial old fellows, so merry and contented, started, the day they came of age, with the two best estates in Ireland."

"If I had not brought ruin on others, Bagenal——"

"No more of that, Darcy; the most scandal-loving gossip of the Club will never impute, for he dare not, more than carelessness to your conduct, and I promise you, if you'll only fall back on a good conscience, you'll not be unhappy under the thatched roof of my poor shealing. My sincerest regards to Lady Eleanor and Helen. I see there is a crowd collecting at the sight of the four posters, so don't delay."

Darcy could do no more than squeeze the cordial hand that held his own, and passing hastily out, he stepped into the travelling carriage at the door, not unobserved, indeed, for about a hundred ragged creatures had now assembled, who saluted his appearance with groans and hisses, accompanied with ruffianly taunts about bribery and corruption; while one, more daring than the rest, mounted on the step, and with his face to the window, cried out: "My Lord, my Lord, won't you give us a trifle to drown your new coronet?"

The words were scarcely out, when, seizing him by the neck with one hand, and taking a leg in the other, Daly hurled the fellow into the middle of the mob, who, such is their consistency, laughed loud and heartily at the fellow's misfortunes; meanwhile, the postilions plied whip and spur, and ere the laughter had subsided the carriage was out of sight.

"There is a gentleman in the drawing-room wishes to speak to you, sir," said a servant to Daly, who had just sat down to a conference with the lawyer.

"Present my respectful compliments, and say that I am engaged on most important and pressing business."

"Had you not better ask his name?" said the lawyer.

"No, no, there is nothing but interruptions here; at one moment it is Heffernan, with a polite message from Lord Castlereagh; then some one from the Club, to know if I have any objection to waive a standing order, and have that young O'Reilly balloted for once more; and here was George Falkner himself a while ago, asking if the Knight had really taken office, with a seat in the Cabinet. I said it was perfectly correct; that he was at liberty to state it in his paper."

"You did!"

"Yes; and that he might add that I myself had refused the see of Llandaff, preferring the command of the West India Squadron. But, what's this? What do you want now, Richard?"

"The gentleman up-stairs, sir, insists on my presenting his card."

"Oh, indeed!—Captain Forester!—I'll see him at once." And so saying, Daly hastened up-stairs to the drawing-room, where the young officer awaited him.

Daly was not in a mood to scrutinise very closely the appearance of his visitor, but he could not fail to feel struck at the alteration in his looks since last they met; his features were paler and marked by sorrow, so much so, that Daly's first question was, "Have you been ill?" and as Forester answered in the negative, the old man fixed his eyes steadily on him, and said, "You have heard of our misfortune, then?"

"Misfortune! no. What do you mean?"

Daly hesitated, uncertain how to reply, whether leaving to time and some other channel to announce the Knight's ruin, or at once communicate it with his own lips.

"Yes, it is the better way," said he, half aloud, while taking Forester's hand he led him over to a sofa, and pressed him down beside him. "I seldom have made an error in guessing a man's character, throughout a long and somewhat remarkable life. I think I am safe in saying that you feel a warm interest in my friend Darcy's family?"

"You do me but justice; gratitude alone, if I had no stronger motive, secures them every good wish of mine."

"But you have stronger motives, young man," said Daly, looking at him with a piercing glance; "if you had not, I'd think but meanly of you, nor did I want that blush to tell me so."

Forester looked down in confusion. The abruptness of the address so completely unmanned him that he could make no answer. While Daly went on: "I force no confidences, young man, nor have I any right to ask them; enough for my present purpose that I know you care deeply for this family; now, sir, but a week back the ambition to be allied with them had satisfied the proudest wish of the proudest house—to-day they are ruined."

Overwhelmed with surprise and sorrow, Forester sat silently, while Daly rapidly, but circumstantially, narrated the story of the Knight's calamity, and the total wreck of his once princely fortune.

"Yes," said Daly, as with flashing eyes he arose and uttered aloud—"yes, the broad acres won by many a valiant deed, the lands which his ancestors watered with their blood, lost for ever; not by great crimes, not forfeited by any bold but luckless venture, for there is something glorious in that—but stolen, filched away by theft. By Heaven! our laws and liberties do but hedge round crime with so many defences, that honesty has nothing left but to stand shivering outside. Better were the days when the strong hand avenged the deep wrong, or if the courage were weak, there was the Throne to appeal to against oppression. Forester, I see how this news afflicts you; I judged you too well to think that your own dashed hopes entered into your sorrow. No, no, I know you better. But come, we have other duties than to mourn over the past. Has Lord Castlereagh received Darcy's note, resigning his seat in Parliament?"

"He has; a new writ is preparing for Mayo."

"Sharp practice; I think I can detect the fair round hand of Mr. Heffernan there—no matter, a few days more, and the world will know all; ay, the world, so full of honourable sentiments and noble aspirations, will smile and jest on Darcy's ruin, that they may with better grace taunt the vulgar assumption of Hickman O'Reilly. I know it well—some would say I bought the knowledge dearly. When I set out in life, my fortune was nearly equal to the

Knight's, my ideas of living and expenditure based on the same views as his own, that same barbaric taste for profusion, which has been transmitted to us from father to son. Ay, we retained everything of feudalism save its chivalry! Well, I never knew a day nor an hour of independence till the last acre of that great estate was sold and gone from me for ever. Fawning flattery, intrigue, and trickery beset me wherever I went; ruined gamblers, match-making mothers, bankrupt speculators, plotting political adventurers dogged me at every step; nor could I break through the trammels by which they fettered me, except at the price of my ruin; when there was no longer a stake to play for, they left the table. Poor Darcy, however, is not a lonely stem like me, riven and lightning-struck; he has a wife and children; but for that, I would not fear to grasp his stout hand, and say, 'Come on to fortune.' Poor Maurice, whose heart could never stand the slightest wrong done the humblest cottier on his land, how will he bear up now? Forester, you can do me a great service. Could you obtain leave for a day or two?"

"Command me how and in what way you please," said the youth, eagerly.

"I understand that proffer, and accept it as freely as it is given."

"Nay, you are mistaken," said Forester, faltering. "I will be candid with you; you have a right to all my confidence, for you have trusted in me. Your suspicions are only correct in part—my affection is indeed engaged, but I have received none in return—Miss Darcy has rejected me."

"But not without hope?"

"Without the slightest hope."

"By Heaven, it is the only gleam of light in all the gloomy business," said Daly, energetically; "had Helen's love been yours, this calamity had been ten thousand times worse. Nay, nay, this is not the sentiment of cold and selfish old age; you wrong me, Forester, but the hour is come when every feeling within that noble girl's heart is due to those who have loved and cherished her from childhood. Now is the time to repay the watchful care of infancy, and recompense the anxious fears that spring from parental affection; not a sentiment, not a thought should be turned from that channel now. It would be treason to win one smile, one passing look of kind meaning from those eyes, every beam of which is claimed by 'Home.' Helen is equal to her destiny, that I know well, and you, if you would strive to be worthy of her, do not endeavour to make her falter in her duty. Trust me there is but one road to a heart like hers—the path of high and honourable ambition."

"You are right," said Forester, in a sad and humble voice—"you are right; I offered her a heart before it was worthy of her acceptance."

"That avowal is the first step towards rendering it such one day," said

Daly, grasping his hand in both his own. "Now to my request; you can obtain this leave, can you?"

"Yes, yes: how can I make it of any service to you?"

"Simply thus: I have offered, and Darcy has accepted, an humble cottage on the northern coast, as a present asylum for the family. The remote and secluded nature of the place will at least withdraw them from the impertinence of curiosity, or the greater impertinence of vulgar sympathy. A maiden sister of mine is the present occupant, and I wish to communicate the intelligence to her, that she may make any preparations which may be necessary for their coming, and also provide herself with some other shelter. Maria is as great a Bedouin as myself, and with as strong a taste for vagabondage; she'll have no difficulty in housing herself, that's certain. The only puzzle is how to apprise her of the intended change; there is not a post-office within eight or ten miles of the place, nor if there were, would she think of sending to look for a letter: there's nothing for it but a special envoy; will you be the man?"

"Most willingly, only give me the route, and my instructions."

"You shall have both. Come and dine with me here at five—order horses to your carriage for eight o'clock, and I'll take care of the rest."

"Agreed," said Forester; "I'll lose no time in getting ready for the road—the first thing is my leave."

"Is there a difficulty there?"

"There shall be none," said Forester, hurriedly, as he seized his hat; and, bidding Daly "good-by," hastened down stairs and into the street. "They'll refuse me, I know that," muttered he, as he went along; "and if they do, I'll pitch up the appointment on the spot; this slight service over, I'm ready to join my regiment." And so saying, he turned his steps towards the Castle, resolved on the course to follow.

Meanwhile Daly, after a brief consultation with the lawyer, sat down to write to his sister. Simple and easy as the act is to many—far too much so, as most men's correspondence would testify—letter-writing, to some people, is an affair of no common difficulty. Perhaps every one in this world has some stumbling-block of this kind ever before him; some men cannot learn chess, some never can be taught to ride, others, if they were to get the world for it, could not carve a hare. It would be unfair to quote newly-introduced difficulties, such as how to bray in the House of Commons, the back step in the Polka, and so on—the original evils are enough for our illustration.

Bagenal Daly's literary difficulties were manifold; he was a discursive thinker, passionate and vehement whenever the occasion prompted, and as unable to control such influences when writing as speaking; and with very liberal ideas on the score of spelling, he wrote a hand which, if only examined upside down, might have passed for Hebrew, with an unduo proportion of points; beside these defects, he entertained a thorough contempt for all writing as an exponent of men's sentiments. His opinion was, that speech was the great prerogative of living men, all other modes of expression being feeble and miserable expedients; and to do him justice, he conformed, as far as in him lay, to his own theory, and made his writing as like his speaking as could be. Brevity was the great quality he studied, and for this reason we venture to present the epistle to our readers:

"DEAR MOLLY,—

"The bill is carried—or, what comes to the same, the third reading comes on next Tuesday, and they'll have a majority—d——n their majority, I forget the number. I was told that bribes were plenty as blackberries. I wish they'd leave as many stains after them. They offered me nothing—they were right there. There is a kind of bottle-nosed whale the Indians never harpoon; they call him 'Hik-na-cntchka,'—more bone than blubber. Darcy might have been an Earl, or a Marquis, or a Duke, perhaps; they wanted one gentleman so much, they'd have bid high for him. Poor fellow, he is ruined now! that scoundrel Gleeson has run away with everything, forged, falsified, and thieved to any extent. Your unlucky four thousand, of course, is gone to the devil with the rest. I'm sick of cant. People talk of badgers and such like, and yet no one says a word about exterminating attorneys! The rascal jumped over in the Channel, and was drowned—the shark got a bitter pill that swallowed him. I have told Darcy he might have 'the Corvy;' you can easily find a wigwam down the coast. Forester, who brings this, knows all. We must all economise, I suppose. I've given up Maccabaw already, and taken to Blackguard, in compliment to the Secretary. I must sell or shoot old Drummer at last, he can't draw his breath, and won't draw the gig. I only remain here till the House is up, when I must be up too, and stirring—there is a confounded bond—no matter, more at another time.

"Yours ever,

"BAGENAL DALY.

"St. George is to be the Chief Baron—an improvement of the allegory, 'Justice will be deaf as well as blind.' Devil take them all."

The chorus of a Greek play, so seemingly abstruse and incoherent to our present thinking, was, we are told, made easily comprehensible by the aid of gesture and pantomime; and in the same way, by supplying the fancied accompaniment of her brother's voice and action, Miss Daly was enabled to read and understand this strange epistle. Bagenal gave himself little trouble in examining how far it conveyed his meaning; but like a careless traveller who huddles his clothes into his portmanteau, and is only anxious to make the lock meet, his greatest care was to fold up the document and enclose it within an envelope—that done, he hoped it was all right—in any case, his functions were concluded regarding it, for, as he muttered to himself, he only contracted to write, not to read his own letter.

Forester was punctual to the hour appointed; and if not really less depressed than before, the stimulating sense of having a service to perform made him seem less so. His self-esteem was flattered, too, by his own bold line of acting, for he had just resigned his appointment on the Staff, his application for leave having been unsuccessful. The fact that his rash conduct might involve him in trouble or difficulty was not without its own sense of pleasure, for, so is it in all rebellion, the great prompter is personal pride. He would gladly have told Daly what had happened, but a delicate fear of increasing the apparent load of obligation prevented him, and he consequently confined his remarks on the matter to his being free, and at liberty to go wherever his friend pleased.

"Here, then," said Daly, leading him across the room to a table, on which a large map of Ireland lay open, "I have marked your route the entire way; follow that dark line with your eye northwards to Coleraine, so far you can travel with your carriage and post horses—how to cross this bit of desert here I must leave to yourself; there may be a road for a wheeled carriage or not, in my day there was none; that is, however, a good many years back; the point to strive for should be somewhere hereabouts. This is Dunluce Castle—well, if I remember aright, the spot is here—you must ask for 'the Corvy,' the fishermen all know the cabin by that name; it was originally built out of the wreck of a French vessel that was lost there, and the word Corvy is a northern version of Corvette. Once there—and I know you'll not find any difficulty in reaching it—my sister will be glad to receive you; I need not say the accommodation does not rival Gwynne Abbey, no more than poor Molly does Helen Darcy; you will be right welcome, however, so much I can pledge myself, not the less so that your journey was undertaken from a motive of true kindness. I don't well know how much or how little I have said in that letter; you can explain all I may have omitted—the chief thing is to get the cabin ready for the Darcys as soon as may be. Give her this pocket-book, I was too much hurried to-day to transact business at the bank, but the north road is a safe one, and you'll not incur any risk. And now one glass to the success of the enterprise, and I'll not detain you longer; I'll give you old Martin's toast—

May better days soon be our lot,
Or better courage, if we have them not."

Forester pledged the sentiment in a bumper, and they parted.

"Good stuff in that young fellow," muttered Daly, as he looked after him; "I wish he had some Irish blood though; these Saxons require a deal of the hammer to warm them, and never come to a white heat after all."

CHAPTER XXVI.

"THE CORVY."

If the painter's licence enables him to arrange the elements of scenery into new combinations, disposing and grouping anew, as taste or fancy may dictate, the novelist enjoys the lesser privilege of conveying his reader at will from place to place, and thus, by varying the point of view, procuring new aspects to his picture; less in virtue of this privilege than from sheer necessity, we will now ask of our readers to accompany us on our journey northward.

Whether it be the necessary condition of that profusion of nature's gifts, so evident in certain places, or a mere accident, certain it is there is scarcely any one spot remarkable for great picturesque beauty to arrive at which some bleak and uninteresting tract must not be traversed. To this rule, if it be such, the northern coast of Ireland offers no exception.

The country, as you approach "the Causeway," has an aspect of dreary desolation, that only needs the leaden sky and the drifting storm of winter to make it the most melancholy of all landscapes. A slightly undulating surface extends for miles on every side, scarcely a house is to be seen, and save where the dip of the ground affords shelter, not a tree of any kind. A small isolated spot of oats, green even in the late autumn, is here or there to be descried, or a flock of black sheep wandering half wild o'er these savage wastes; vast masses of cloud, dark and lowering as rain and thunder can make them, hang gloomily overhead, for the table-land is still a lofty one, and the horizon is formed by the edge of those giant cliffs that stand the barriers of the western ocean, and against whose rocky sides the waves beat with the booming of distant artillery.

It was in one of those natural hollows of the soil, whose frequency seems to acknowledge a diluvian origin, that the little cottage which Sandy once owned, stood. Sheltered on the south and east by rising banks, it was open on the other sides, and afforded a view seaward, which extended from the rocky promontory of Port Rush to the great bluff of Fairhead, whose summit is nigh one thousand seven hundred feet above the sea.

Perhaps, in all the sea-board of the empire, nothing of the same extent can vie in awful sublimity with this iron-bound coast. Gigantic cliffs of four and five hundred feet, straight as a wall, are seen perforated beneath by lofty tunnels, through which the wild waters plunge madly. Fragments of basalt, large enough to be called islands, are studded along the shore, the outlines fanciful and strange as beating waves and winds can make them, while, here and there, in some deep-creviced bay, the water flows in with long and measured sweep, and at each moment retiring, leaves a trace upon the strand, fleeting as the blush upon the cheek of beauty; and here a little group of fisher children may be seen at play, while the nets are drying on the beach, the only sight or sound of human life, save that dark moving speck, alternately seen as the great waves roll on, be such, and, while tossing to and fro, seems by some charmed influence fettered to the spot. Yes, it is a fishing boat, that has ventured out at the half ebb, with the wind off shore—hazardous exploit, that only poverty suggests the courage to encounter!

In front of one of these little natural bays stood "the Corvy;" and the situation might have been chosen by a painter, for while combining every grand feature of the nearer landscape, the Scottish coast, and even Staffa, might be seen of a clear evening; while westward, the rich sunsets were descried in all their golden glory, tipping the rolling waves with freckled lustre, and throwing a haze of violet-coloured light over the white rocks. And who is to say, that while the great gifts of the artist are not his who dwells in some rude cot like this, yet the heart is not sensitively alive to all the influences of such a scene—its lonely grandeur, its tranquil beauty, or its fearful sublimity; and that the peasant, whose associations from infancy to age are linked with every barren rock and fissured crag around, has not created for himself his own store of fancied images, whose power is not less deeply felt that it has asked for no voice to tell its workings.

"The Corvy" was a strange specimen of architecture, and scarcely capable of being classified in any of the existing orders. Originally, the hut was formed of the stern of the corvette, which, built of timbers of great size and strength, alone of all the vessel resisted the waves. This being placed keel uppermost, as most consisting with terrestrial notions of building, and accommodated with a door and two windows, the latter being filled with two ship lenses, comprised the entire edifice. Rude and uncouth as it unquestionably was, it was regarded with mingled feelings of envy and admiration by all the fishermen for miles round, for while they had contributed their tackle and their personal aid to place the mass where it stood, they never contemplated its becoming the comfortable dwelling they soon beheld, nor were these jealous murmurings allayed by the assumption of a lofty flag staff, which, in the pride of conquest, old M'Grane displayed above his castle, little wotting that the banner that floated overhead waved with the lilies of France, and not the Union Jack of England.

Sandy's father, however, possessed those traits of character which confer ascendancy, whether a man's lot be cast among the great or the humble, and he soon not only subdued those ungenerous sentiments, but even induced his neighbours to assist him in placing a small brass carronade on the keel, or, as he now termed it, the ridge of his dwelling, where, however little serviceable for warlike purposes, it made a very specious and imposing ornament.

Such was the inheritance to which Sandy succeeded, and such the possession he ceded for a consideration to Bagenal Daly, on that eventful morning their acquaintance began. In course of time, however, it fell to ruin, and lay untenanted and uncared for, when Miss Daly, in one of her rambling excursions, chanced to hear of it, and, being struck by the beauty of the situation, resolved to refit it as a summer residence. Her first intentions on this head were humble enough; two small chambers at either side of the original edifice—now converted into a species of hall and a kitchen—comprised the whole, and thither she betook herself, with that strange secret pleasure a life of perfect solitude possesses for certain minds. For a year she endured the inconveniences of her narrow dwelling tolerably well; but, as she grew more attached to the spot, she determined on making it more comfortable; and, communicating the resolve to her brother, he not only concurred in the notion, but half anticipated his assent by despatching an architect to the spot, under whose direction a cottage containing several comfortable rooms was added, and with such attention to the circumstances of the ground, and such regard for the ancient character of the building, that the traces of its origin could still be discovered, and its old name of "The Corvy" be, even yet, not altogether inapplicable. The rude hulk was now, however, the centre of a long cottage, the timbers, partly covered by the small-leaved ivy, partly concealed by a rustic porch, displaying overhead the great keel and the flag-staff, an ornament which no remonstrance of the unhappy architect could succeed in removing. As a sort of compromise, indeed, the carronade was dismounted, and placed beside the hall door. This was the extreme stretch of compliance to which Daly assented.

The hall, which was spacious and lofty in proportion with other parts of the building, was fitted with weapons of war and the chase, brought from many a far-off land, and assembled with an incongruity that was no mean type of the owner. Turkish scimitars and lances, yataghans, and Malay creeses were grouped with Indian bows, tomahawks, and whale harpoons while richly embroidered pelisses hung beside coats of Esquimaux seal, or boots made from the dried skin of the sun-fish. A long Swiss rifle was suspended by a blue silk scarf from one wall, and, over it, a damp, discoloured parchment bore testimony to its being won as the prize in the great shooting-match of the Oberland, nearly forty years before. Beneath these, and stretching away into a nook contrived for the purpose, was the bark canoe in which Daly and Sandy made their escape from the tribe of the Sioux, by whom they were held in captivity for six years. Two very unprepossessing figures, costumed as savages, sat in this frail bark, paddle in hand, and to all seeming resolutely intent on their purpose of evasion. It would have been pardonable, however, for the observer not to have identified in these tattooed and wild-looking personages a member of Parliament and his valet, even though assisted to the discovery by their Indian names, which, with a laudable care for public convenience, had been written on a card, and suspended round the neck of each. Opposite to them, and in a corner of the hall, stood a large black bear, with fiery eyeballs and snow-white teeth, so admirably counterfeiting life as almost to startle the beholder; while over his head was a fearful, misshapen figure, whose malignant look and distorted proportions at once proclaimed it an Indian idol. But why enumerate the strange and curious objects which, notwithstanding their seeming incongruity, were yet all connected with Daly's history, and formed, in fact, a kind of pictorial narrative of his life? Here stood the cup—a splendid specimen of Benvenuto's chisel, given him by the Doge of Venice—and there was the embossed dagger presented by a King of Spain, with a patent of Grandee of the first class; while in a small glass case, covered with dust, and scarce noticeable, was a small and beautifully shaped satin slipper, with a rosette of, now, faded silver. But of this only one knew the story, and *he* never revealed it.

If we have taken an unwarrantable liberty with our reader by this too prolix description, our excuse is, that we might have been far more tiresome had we been so disposed, leaving, as we have, the greater part of this singular chamber unnoticed; while our *amende* is ready, and we will spare any further detail of the rest of the cottage, merely observing that it was both commodious and well arranged, and furnished not only with taste, but even elegance. And now to resume our long-neglected story.

It was about eight o'clock of a cold, raw February night, with occasional showers of sleet, and sudden gusts of fitful wind—that happy combination which makes up the climate of the north of Ireland, and, with a trifling abatement of severity, constitutes its summer as well as its winter—that Miss Daly sat reading in that strange apartment we have just mentioned, and which, from motives of economy, she occupied frequently during the rainy season, as the necessity of keeping it aired required constant fires, not so necessary in the other chambers.

A large hearth displayed the cheerful blaze of burning bog-deal, and an old Roman lamp, an ancient patera, threw its lustre on the many curious and uncouth objects on every side. If the flashing jets of light that broke from the dry wood gave at times a false air of vitality to the stuffed figures around, in compensation, it made the only living thing there seem as unreal as the rest.

Wrapped up in the great folds of a wide Greek capote she had taken from the wall, and the hood of which she had drawn over her head, Miss Daly bent over the yellow pages of an old quarto volume. Of her figure no trace could be marked, nor any guess concerning it, save that she was extremely tall. Her features were bold and commanding, and in youth must have been eminently handsome. The eyebrows were large and arched, the eyes dark and piercing, and the whole contour of the face had that character of thoughtful beauty so often seen in the Jewish race. Age and solitude, perhaps, had deepened the lines around the angles of the mouth, and brought down the brows, so as to give a look of severity to features which, from this cause, became strikingly resembling her brother's. If time had made its sad inroad on those lineaments once so lovely, it seemed to spare even the slightest touch to that small white hand which, escaping from the folds of her mantle, was laid upon the volume before her. The taper fingers were covered with rings, and more than one bracelet of great price glittered upon her wrist; nor did this taste seem limited to these displays, for in the gold combs that fastened, on either temple, her masses of grey hair, rich gems were set profusely, forming the strangest contrast to the coarse folds of that red-brown cloak in which she was enveloped.

However disposed to profit by her studies, Miss Daly was occasionally broken in upon by the sound of voices from the kitchen, which, by an unlucky arrangement of the architect, was merely separated from the hall by a narrow corridor. Sometimes the sound was of laughter and merriment, far oftener, however, the noises betokened strife, for so it is, in the very smallest household—there were but two in the present case—unanimity will not always prevail. The contention was no less a one than that great national dispute, which has separated the island into two wide and opposing parties, Miss Daly's butler, or man of all work, being a stout representative of southern Ireland; her cook, an equally rigid upholder of the northern province. If little Dan Nelligan had the broader cause, he was the smaller advocate, being scarcely four feet in height, while Mrs. M'Kerrigan was fifteen stone of honest weight, and with a *torso* to rival the Farnese Hercules. Their altercations were daily, almost hourly, for, living in a remote, unvisited spot, they seemed to console themselves for want of collision with the world by mutual disputes and disagreements.

To these family jars habit had so reconciled Miss Daly, that she seldom noticed them; indeed, the probability is, that like the miller who wakes up when the mill ceases its clamours, she might have felt a kind of shock had matters taken a quieter course. People who employ precisely the same weapons cannot long continue a warfare without the superiority of one or the other being sure to evince itself. The diversity of the forces, on the contrary, suggests new combinations, and with dissimilar armour the combat may be prolonged to any extent. Thus was it here; Dan's forte was aggravation, that peculiarly Irish talent which makes much out of little, and, when cultivated with the advantages of natural gifts, enables a man to assume that proud political position of an Agitator, and in time a Liberator.

Mrs. M'Kerrigan, slow of thought, and slower of speech, was ill-suited to repel the assaults of so wily and constant a foe; she consequently fell back on the prerogatives of her office in the household, and repaid all Dan's declamation by changes in his diet. A species of retribution the heaviest she could have hit upon.

Such was the present cause of disturbance, and such the reason for Dan's loud denunciations on the "black north," uttered with a volubility and vehemence that pertain to a very different portion of the empire. Twice had Miss Daly rung the little hand-bell that stood beside her, to enforce order, but it was unnoticed in the clamour of the fray, while louder and louder grew the angry voice of Dan Nelligan, which at length was plainly audible in the hall.

"Look now, see then, may the divil howld a looking-glass to your sins, but I'll show it to the mistress. I may, may I? That's what you're grumbling, ye ould black-mouthed Prasbytarien! 'Tis the fine supper to put before a crayture wet to the skin!"

"Dinna ye hear the bell, Nelly?" This was an epithet of insult the little man could not endure. "Ye'd ken the tinkle o' that, av ye heard it at the mass."

"Oh, listen to the ould heretic! Oh, holy Joseph! there's the way to talk of the blessed ould ancient religion! Give me the dish; I'll bring it into the parlour this minit, I will. I'll lave the place—my time's up in March. I wouldn't live in the house wid you for a mine of goold!"

"Are ye no goin' to show the fish to the leddy?" growled out the cook, in her quiet barytone.

At this moment Miss Daly's bell announced that endurance had reached its limit, and Dan, without waiting to return the fire, hastened to the hall, muttering as he went, loud enough to be heard: "There, now, that's the mistress ringing, I'm sure; but sorra bit one can hear wid your noise and ballyragging!"

"What is the meaning of this uproar?" said Miss Daly, as the little man entered, with a very different aspect from what he wore in the kitchen.

"'Tis Mrs. M'Kerrigan, my Lady; she was abusin' the ould families in the county Mayo, and I couldn't bear it, and because I wouldn't hear the master trated that way, she gives me nothing but fish the day after a black fast, though she does be ating beef under my nose when I darn't touch meat, and it's what, she put an ould baste of a cod before me this evening for my supper, and here's Lent will be on us in a few days more."

"How often have I told you," said Miss Daly, sternly, "that I'll not suffer these petty, miserable squabbles to reach me? Go back to the kitchen, and, mark me, if I hear a whisper, or muttering ever so low in your voice, I'll put you to spend the night upon the rocks."

Dan skulked from the room like a culprit remanded to gaol, but no sooner had he reached the kitchen, than, assuming a martial air and bearing, he strutted up to the fire and turned his back to it.

"Ay," said he, in a stage soliloquy, "it was what it must come to sooner or later, and now she may go on her knees, and divil a foot I'll stay! It's not like the last time, sorra bit! I know what she's at—' 'Tis my way, Danny, you must have a pound at Ayster'—bother! I'm used to that now."

"There's the bell again, ye auld blethering deevil."

But Mrs. M'Kerrigan ran no risk of a reply now, for at the first tinkle Dan was back in the hall.

"There is some one knocking at the wicket without, see who it may be at this late hour of the night," said Miss Daly, without raising her head from the book, for strange as were such sounds in that solitary place, her attention was too deeply fixed on the page before her to admit of even a momentary distraction of thought. Dan left the room with becoming alacrity, but in reality bent on anything rather than the performance of his errand. Of all the traits of his southern origin, none had the same predominance in his nature as a superstitious fear of spirits and goblins, a circumstance not likely to be mitigated by his present lonely abode, independently of the fact that more than one popular belief attributed certain unearthly sights and sounds to the old timbers of "the Corvy," whose wreck was associated with tales of horror sufficient to shake stouter nerves than "Danny's."

When he received this order from his mistress, he heard it pretty much as a command to lead a forlorn hope, and sat himself down at the outside of the door, to consider what course to take. While he was thus meditating, the sounds became plainly audible, a loud and distinct knocking was heard high above the whistling wind and drifting rain, accompanied from time to time by a kind of shout, or, as it seemed to Dan's ears, a scream like the cry of a drowning man.

"Dinna ye hear that, ye auld daft body?" said Nancy, as, pale with fear, and trembling in every limb, Dan entered the kitchen.

"I do, indeed, Mrs. Mac"—this was the peace appellation he always conferred on Nancy—"I hear it, and my heart's beatin' for every stroke I listen to; 'tisn't afeard I am, but a kind of a notion I have, like a dhrame, you know"—(here he gave a sort of hysterical giggle)—" as if the ould French Captain was coming to look after his hand, that was chopped off with the hatchet when he grasped hold of the rock."

"He canna hae muckle use for it noo," responded Nancy, dryly, as she smoked away as unconcerned as possible.

"Or the mate!" said Dan, giving full vent to his store of horrors; "they say, when he got hold of the rope, that they gave it out as fast as he hauled on it, till he grew faint, and sank under the waves."

"He's no likely to want a piece of spunyarn at this time o' day," rejoined Nancy again. "He's knocking brawly whoever he be; had ye no better do the leddy's bidding, and see who's there?"

"Would it be plazing to you, Mrs. Mac," said Dan, in his most melting accents, "to come as far as the little grass-plot, just out of curiosity ye know, to say ye seen it?"

"Na, na, my bra' wee mon, ye maun een gae by yoursel; I dinna ken mickle about sperits and ghaists, but I hae a gude knowledge of the rheumatiz without seekin' it on a night like this; there's the leddy's bell again, she's no pleased wi' yer delay."

"Say I was puttin' on my shoes, Nancy," said Dan, as his teeth chattered with fear, while he took down an old blunderbuss from its place above the fire, and which had never been stirred for years past.

"Lay her back agen where ye found her," said Nancy, dryly; "'tis na every fule kens the like o' them! Take your mass-book, and the gimcracks ye hae ower your bed, but dinna try mortal weapons with them creatures."

Ironical as the tone of this counsel unquestionably was, Dan was in no mood to reject it altogether, and he slipped from its place within his breast to a more ostensible position a small blessed token, or "gospel," as it is called, which he always wore round his neck. By this time the clank of the bell kept pace with the knocking sounds without, and poor Dan was fairly at his wits' end which enemy to face. Some vague philosophy about the "devil you know, and the devil you don't," seemed to decide his course, for he rushed from the kitchen in a state of frenzied desperation, and, with the blunderbuss at full cock, took the way towards the gate.

The wicket, as it was termed, was in reality a strong oak gate, garnished at top with a row of very formidable iron spikes, and as it was hung between two jagged and abrupt masses of rock, formed a very sufficient outwork, though a very needless one, since the slightest turn to either side would have led to the cottage without any intervening barrier to pass. This fact it was which now increased Dan Nelligan's terrors, as he reasoned that no body but a ghost or evil spirit would be bothering himself at the wicket, when there was a neat footpath close by.

"Who's there?" cried Dan, with a voice that all his efforts could not render steady.

"Come out and open the gate," shouted a deep voice, in return.

"Not till you tell me where you come from, and who you are, if you are 'lucky?'"

"That I'm not," cried the other, with something very like a deep groan; "if I were, I'd scarce be here now."

"That's honest, anyhow," muttered Dan, who interpreted the phrase in its popular acceptation among the southern peasantry. "And what are you come back for, alanah!" continued he, in a most conciliating tone.

"Open the gate, and don't keep me here answering your stupid questions."

Though these words were uttered with a round, strong intonation that sounded very like the present world, Dan made no other reply than an endeavour to repeat a Latin prayer against evil spirits, when suddenly, and with a loud malediction on his obstinacy, Dan saw "the thing," as he afterwards described it, take a flying leap over the gate, at least ten feet high, and come with a bang on the grass, not far from where he stood. To fire off his blunderbuss straight at the drifting clouds over his head and take to flight was Dan's only impulse, screaming out, "The Captain's come! he's come!" at the very top of his lungs. The little strength he possessed only carried him to the kitchen door, where, completely overcome with terror, he dropped senseless on the ground.

While this was occurring, Miss Daly, alarmed by the report of fire-arms, but without any personal fears of danger, threw open the hall door, and called out, "Who is there?" and as the dark shadow of a figure came nearer, "Who are you, sir?"

"My name is Forester, madam—a friend of your brother's, for I perceive I have the honour to address Miss Daly."

By this time the stranger had advanced into the full light of the lamp within, where his appearance, tired and travel-stained as he was, corroborated his words.

"You have had a very uncourteous welcome, sir," said Miss Daly, extending her hand and leading him within the cottage.

"The reception was near being a warm one, I fear," said Forester, smiling; "for as I unfortunately, growing rather impatient, threw my carpet-bag over the gate, intending to climb it afterwards, some one fired at me, not with a good aim, however, for I heard the slugs rattling on a high cliff behind me."

"Old Dan, I am certain, mistook you for a ghost or a goblin," said Miss Daly, laughing, as if the affair were an excellent joke devoid of all hazard; "we have few visitors down here from either world."

"Really, madam, I will confess it—if the roads are only as impassable for ghosts as for men of mortal mould, I'm not surprised at it. I left Coleraine at three o'clock to-day, where I was obliged to exchange my travelling carriage for a car, and I have been travelling ever since, sometimes on what seemed a highway, far oftener, however, across fields, with now and then an intervening wall to throw down, which we did, I own, unceremoniously; while lifting the horse twice out of deep holes, mending a shaft, and splicing the traces, lost some time. The driver, too, was once missing, a fact I only discovered after leaving him half a mile behind. In fact, the whole journey was full of small adventures up to the moment when we came to a dead stand at the foot of a high cliff, where the driver told me the road stopped, and that the rest of my way must be accomplished on foot; and on my asking what direction to take, he brought me some distance off to the top of a rock, whence I could perceive the twinkling of a light, and said, 'That's the Corvy.' I did my best to secure his services as a guide, but no offer of money nor persuasions could induce him to leave his horse and come any further; and now, perhaps, I can guess the reason—there is some superstition about the place at nightfall."

"No, no, you're mistaken there, sir; few of these people, however they may credit such tales, are terrified by them. It was the northern spirit dictated the refusal; his contract was to go so far, it would have 'put him out of his way' to go further, and his calculation was that all the profit he could fairly derive—and he never speculated on anything unfair—would not repay him. Such are the people of this province."

"The trait is honest, I've no doubt, but it can scarcely be the source of many amiable ones," said Forester, smarting under the recent inconvenience.

"We'll talk of that after supper," said Miss Daly, rising, "and I leave you to make a good fire while I go to give some orders."

"May I not have the honour to present my credentials first?" said Forester, handing Bagenal Daly's letter to her.

"My brother is quite well, is he not?"

"In excellent health—I left him but two days since."

"The despatch will keep, then," said she, thrusting it into a letter rack over the chimney-piece, while she left the room to make the arrangement she spoke of.

Miss Daly's absence was not of long duration, but, brief as it was, it afforded Forester time enough to look around at the many strange and incongruous decorations of the apartment, nor had he ceased his wonderment when Dan, pale and trembling in every limb, entered, tray in hand, to lay the supper table.

With many a sidelong, stealthy look, Dan performed his duties, and it was easy to see, that however disposed to regard the individual before him as of this world's company, "the thing that jumped out of the sky," as he called it, was yet an unexplained phenomenon.

"I see you are surprised by the motley companionship that surrounds me," said Miss Daly; "but as a friend of Bagenal's, and acquainted, doubtless, with his eccentric habits, they will astonish you less. Come, let me hear about him—is he going to pay me a visit down here?"

"I fear not, at this moment," said Forester, with an accent of melancholy; "his friendship is heavily taxed at the present juncture. You have heard, perhaps, of the unhappy event which has spread such dismay in Dublin?"

"No! what is it? I hear of nothing, and see nobody here."

"A certain Mr. Gleeson, the trusted agent of many country gentlemen, has suddenly fled——"

Before Forester could continue, Miss Daly arose and tore open her brother's letter. For a few seconds Forester was struck with the wonderful resemblance to her brother, as, with indrawn breath and compressed lips, she read; but gradually her colour faded away, her hands trembled, and the paper fell from them, while, with a voice scarcely audible, she whispered—"And it has come to this!" Covering her face with the folds of her cloak, she sat for some minutes buried in deep sorrow, and when she again looked up, years seemed to have passed over, and left their trace upon her countenance; it was pale and haggard, and a braid of grey hair, escaping beneath her cap, had fallen across her cheek, and increased the sad expression.

"So is it," said she aloud, but speaking as though to herself—"so is it: the heavy hand is laid on all in turn; happier they who meet misfortune early in life, when the courage is high and the heart unshrinking; if the struggle be life-long, the victory is certain, but after years of all the world can give of enjoyment——You know Maurice?—you know the Knight, sir?"

"Yes, madam, slightly; but with Lady Eleanor and her daughter I have the honour of intimate acquaintance."

"I will not ask how he bears up against a blow like this. If his own fate only hung in the balance, I could tell that myself; but for his wife, to whom they say he is so devotedly attached—you know it was a love match, so they called it in England, because the daughter of an Earl married the first Commoner in Ireland. And Bagenal advises their coming here! Well, perhaps he is right; they will at least escape the insolence of pity in this lonely spot. Oh! sir, believe me, there is a weighty load of responsibility on those who rule us; these things are less the faults of individuals than of a system. You began here by confiscation, you would finish by corruption.

Stimulating to excesses of every kind a people ten times more excitable than your own—now flattering, now goading—teaching them to vie with you in display while you mocked the recklessness of their living, you chafed them into excesses of alternate loyalty or rebellion."

However satisfied of its injustice, Forester made no reply to this burst of passion, but sat without speaking as she resumed:

"You will say there are knaves in every country, and that this Gleeson was of our rearing; but I deny it, sir. I tell you he was a base counterfeit we have borrowed from yourselves. That meek, submissive manner, that patient drudgery of office, that painstaking, petty rectitude, make up 'your respectable men;' and in this garb of character the business of life goes on with you. And why? Because you take it at its worth. But here, in Ireland, we go faster; trust means full confidence, confidence without limit or bound, and then, too often, ruin without redemption. Forgive me, sir; age and sorrow both have privileges, and I, perhaps, have more cause than most others to speak warmly on this theme. Now, let me escape my egotism by asking you to eat, for I see we have forgotten our supper all this time."

From that moment Miss Daly never adverted further to the burden of her brother's letter, but led Forester to converse about his journey and the people whom, even in his brief experience, he perceived to be so unlike the peasantry of the west.

"Yes," said she, in reply to an observation of his, "these diversities of character observable in different places, are doubtless intended, like the interminable varieties of natural productions, to increase our interest in life, and, while extending the sphere of speculation, to contribute to our own advancement. Few people, perhaps not any, are to be found without some traits of amiability; here there is much to be respected, and, when habit has dulled the susceptibility of first impressions, much also to be liked. But shall I not have the pleasure of showing you my neighbours and my neighbourhood?"

"My visit must be of the shortest; I rather took than obtained my leave of absence."

"Well, even a brief visit will do something; for my neighbours all dwell in cottages, and my neighbourhood comprises the narrow strip of coast between this hut and the sea, whose plash you hear this minute. To-morrow you will be rested from your journey, and if the day permits we'll try the Causeway."

Forester accepted the invitation so frankly proffered, and went to his room, not sorry to lay his head upon a pillow after two weary nights upon the road.

Forester was almost shocked as he entered the breakfast-room on the following morning to see the alteration in Miss Daly's appearance. She had evidently passed a night of great sorrow, and seemed with difficulty to bear up against the calamitous tidings of which he was the bearer. She endeavoured, it is true, to converse on matters of indifference—the road he had travelled, the objects he had seen, and so on—but the effort was ever interrupted by broken snatches of reflection that would vent themselves in words, and all of which bore on the Knight and his fortunes.

To Forester's account of her brother Bagenal's devotion to his friend she listened with eager interest, asking again and again what part he had taken, whether his counsels were deemed wise ones, and if he still enjoyed to the fullest extent the confidence of his old friend.

"It is no friendship of yesterday, sir," said she, with a heightened colour and a flashing eye; "they knew each other as boys, they walked the mountains together as young men, speculating on the future paths fate might open before them, and the various ambitions which, even then, stirred within them. Bagenal was ever rash, headstrong, and impetuous, rarely firm in purpose till some obstacle seemed to defy its accomplishment. Maurice—the Knight I mean—was not less resolute when roused, but more often so much disposed to concede to others, that he would postpone his wishes to their own; and once believing himself in any way pledged to a course, would forget all, save the fulfilment of the implied promise. Such were the two dispositions, which, acting and reacting on each other, effected the ruin of both: the one wasted in eccentricity what the other squandered in listless indifference; and with abilities enough to have won distinction for humble men, they have earned no other reputation than that of singularity or convivialism.

"As for Bagenal," she said, after a pause, "wealth was never but an encumbrance to him; he was one of those persons who never saw any use for money, save in the indulgence of mere caprice; he treated his great fortune as a spoiled child will do a toy, and never rested till he had pulled it to pieces, and perhaps derived the same moral lesson too—astonishment at the mere trifle which once amused him. But Maurice Darcy—whose tastes were ever costly and cultivated, who regarded splendour not as the means of vulgar display, but as the fitting accompaniment of a house illustrious by descent and deeds, and deemed that all about and around him should bear the impress of himself, generous and liberal as he was—how is he to bear this reverse? Tell me of Lady Eleanor; and Miss Darcy, is she like the Knight, or has her English blood given the character to her beauty?"

"She is very like her father," said Forester; "but more so even in disposition than in features."

"How happy I am to hear it," said Miss Daly, hastily; "and she is, then, high-spirited and buoyant? What gifts in an hour like this!"

"You say truly, madam, she will not sink beneath the stroke, believe me."

"Well, this news has reconciled me to much of your gloomier tidings," said Miss Daly; "and now let us wander out upon the hills; I feel as if we could talk more freely as we stroll along the beach."

Miss Daly arose as she spoke, and led the way through the little garden wicket, which opened on a steep pathway down to the shore.

"This will be a favourite walk with Helen, I'm certain," said she; "the caves are all accessible at low water, and the view of Fairhead finer than from any other point. I must instruct you to be a good and a safe guide. I must teach you all the art and mystery of the science, make you learned in the chronicles of Dunluce, and rake up for you legends of ghostcraft and shipwreck enough to make the fortunes of a romancer."

"I thank you heartily," said Forester; "but I cannot remain here to meet my friends."

"Oh, I understand you," said Miss Daly, who in reality put a wrong interpretation on his words; "but you shall be my guest. There is a little village about four miles from this, where I intend to take up my abode. I hope you will not decline hospitality which, if humble, is at least freely proffered."

"I regret deeply," said Forester, and he spoke in a tone of sorrow, "that I cannot accept your kindness. I stand in a position of no common difficulty at this moment." He hesitated, as if doubting whether to proceed or not, and then, in a more hurried voice, resumed: "There is no reason why I should obtrude my own petty cares and trials where greater misfortunes are impending; but I cannot help telling you that I have been rash enough, in a moment of impatience, to throw up an appointment I held on the Viceroy's Staff, and I know not how far the step may yet involve me with my relatives."

"Tell me how came you first acquainted with the Darcys?" said Miss Daly, as if following out in her own mind a train of thought.

"I will be frank with you," said Forester, "for I cannot help being so; there are cases where confidence is not a virtue but a necessity. Every word you speak, every tone of your voice is so much your brother's, that I feel as if I were confiding to him in another form. I learned to know the Knight of Gwynne in a manner which you may deem, perhaps, little creditable to myself, though I trust you will see that I neither abused the knowledge, nor perverted the honour of the acquaintanceship. It was in this wise."

Briefly, but without reserve, Forester narrated the origin of his first journey to the west, and without implicating the honour of his relative, Lord Castlereagh, explained the nature of his mission, to ascertain the sentiments of the Knight, and the possibility of winning him to the side of the Government. His own personal adventures could not, of course, be omitted in such a narrative, but he touched on the theme as slightly as he could, and only dwelt on the kindness he had experienced in his long and dangerous illness, and the long debt of gratitude which bound him to the family.

Of the intimacy that succeeded he could not help speaking, and whether from his studied avoidance of her name, or that, when replying to any question of Miss Daly's concerning Helen Darcy, his manner betrayed agitation, certain it is, that when he concluded, Miss Daly's eyes were turned towards him with an expression of deep significance that called the colour to his cheek.

"And so, sir," said she, in a slow and measured voice, "you went down to play the tempter, and were captured yourself. Come, come, I know your secret; you have told it by signs less treacherous than words; and Helen—for I tell you freely my interest is stronger for her—how is she disposed towards you?"

Forester never spoke, but hung his head abashed and dejected.

"Yes, yes, I see it all," said Miss Daly, hurriedly; "you would win the affection of a generous and high-souled girl by the arts which find favour in your more polished world, and you have found that the fascinations of manner, and the glittering *éclat* of an aide-de-camp, have failed. Now, take my counsel. But first let me ask, is this affection the mere prompting of an idle or capricious moment, or do you love her with a passion round which the other objects of your life are to revolve and depend? I understand that pressure of the hand; it is enough. My advice is simple. You belong to a profession second to none in its high and great rewards, do not waste its glorious opportunities by the life of a courtier—be a soldier in feeling as well as in garb; let her whose heart you would win, feel, that in loving you, she is paying the tribute to qualities that make men esteem and respect you—that she is not bestowing her hand upon the mere favourite of a Court, but on one, whose ambitions are high, and whose darings are generous. Oh! leave nothing, or as little as you may, to mere influence—let your boast be, and it will be a proud one, that with high blood and a noble name you have started fairly in the race, and distanced your competitors. This is my counsel. What think you of it?"

"I will follow it," said Forester, firmly; "I will follow it, though I own to you, it suggests no hope, where hope would be happiness."

"Well, then," said Miss Daly, "you shall spend this day with me, and I will not keep you another; you have made me your friend by this confidence, and I will use the trust with delicacy and with fidelity."

"May I write to you?" said Forester, "and will you let me hear from you again?"

"With pleasure; I should have asked it myself had you not done so. Now, let us talk of the first steps to be taken in this affair, and here is a bench where we can rest ourselves while we chat."

Forester sat down beside her, and in the freedom of one to whom fortune had so unexpectedly presented a confidant, opened all the secret store of his cares, and hopes, and fears. It was late when they turned again towards "the Corvy," but the youth's step was lighter, and his brow more open, while his heart was higher than many a previous day had found him.

CHAPTER XXVII.

THE KNIGHT'S RETURN.

We must now, for a brief space, return to the Knight, as with a heavy heart he journeyed homeward. Never did the long miles seem so wearisome before, often and often as he had travelled them. The little accidental delays, which once he had met with a ready jest, and in a spirit of kindly indulgence, he now resented as so many intentional insults upon his changed and ruined fortune. The gossiping landlords, to whom he had ever extended so much of freedom, he either acknowledged coldly, or repelled with distance; their liberties were now construed into want of deference and respect; the very jestings of the postboys to each other seemed so many covert impertinences, and equivocal allusions to himself, for even so much will the stroke of sudden misfortune change the nature, and convert the contented and happy spirit into a temperament of gloomy sorrow and suspicion.

Unconscious of his own altered feelings, and looking at every object through the dim light of his own calamity, he hurried along not as of old, recognising each well-known face, saluting this one, inquiring after that; he sat back in his carriage, and with his hat drawn almost over his eyes, neither noticed the way nor the wayfarers.

In this mood it was he entered Castlebar. The sight of his well-remembered carriage drew crowds of beggars to the door of the inn, every one of whom had some special prayer for aid, or some narrative of sickness for his hearing. By the time the horses drew up, the crowd numbered some hundreds of every variety, not only in age, but in raggedness, all eagerly calling on him by name, and imploring his protection on grounds the most strange and dissimilar.

"I knew the sound of the wheels; ax Biddy if I didn't say it was his honour was coming!" cried one, in a sort of aside intended for the Knight himself.

"Ye're welcome home, sir; long may you reign over us," said an old fellow with a beard like a pilgrim. "I dreamed I seen you last night standing at the door there, wid a half-crown in your fingers. 'Ould Luke,' says you, 'come here!——' "

A burst of rude laughter drowned this sage parable, while a good-looking young woman, with an expression of softness in features degraded by poverty and its consequences, curtseyed low, and tried to attract his notice, as she held up a miserable-looking infant to the carriage window. "Clap them, acushla! 'tis proud he is to see you back again, sir; he never forgets the goold guinea ye gave him on New Year's-day! Don't be pushin' that way, you rude craytures; you want to hurt the child, and it's the image of his honour."

"Many returns of the blessed sayson to you," growled out a creature in a bonnet, but in face and figure far more like a man than a woman; "throw us out a fippenny to buy two ounces of tay. Asy, asy, don't be drivin' me under the wheels—ugh! it's no place for a faymale, among such rapscallions."

"What did they give you, Maurice? how much did you get, honey?" cried a tall and almost naked fellow, that leaned over the heads of several others, and put his face close to the glass of the carriage, which, for safety's sake, the Knight now let down, while he called aloud to the postboys to make haste and bring out the horses.

"Tell us all about it, Maurice, my boy—are you a Lord, or a Bishop?" cried the tall fellow, with an eagerness of face that told his own sad bereavement, for he was deranged in intellect, from a fall from one of the cliffs on the coast. "By my conscience, I think I must change my politics myself soon; my best pantaloons is like Nat Fitzgibbon—it has resigned its sate! Out with a bit of silver here!—quick, I didn't kiss the King's face this ten days."

To all these entreaties Darcy seemed perfectly deaf; if his eyes wandered over the crowd, they noticed nothing there, nor did he appear to listen to a word around him, while he again asked why the horses were not coming.

"We're doing our best, your honour," cried a postboy, "but it's mighty hard to get through these divils; they won't stir till the beasts is trampling them down."

"Drive on, then, and let them take care of themselves," said the Knight sternly.

"Oh, blessed Father! there's a way to talk of the poor! Oh, heavenly Vargin! but you are come back cruel to us, after all!"

"Drive on!" shouted out Darcy, in a voice of angry impatience.

The postboys sprang into their saddles, cracked their whips, and dashed forward, while the mob, rent in a hundred channels, fled on every side, with cries of terror and shouts of laughter, according as the distance suggested danger or security. All escaped safely, except the poor idiot, Flury, who, having one foot on the step when the carriage started, was thrown backward, when, to save himself, he grasped the spring, and was thus half dragged, half carried along to the end of the street, and there, failing strength and fear combining, he relinquished his hold and fell senseless to the ground, where the wheel grazed but did not injure him as he lay.

With a cry of terror the Knight called out "Stop!" and flinging wide the door, sprang out. To lift the poor fellow up to a sitting posture was the work of a second, while he asked, in accents the very kindest, if he were hurt.

"Sorra bit, Maurice," said the fellow, whose faculties sooner rallied than if they were habitually under better control. "I was on the wrong side of the coach, that's all; 'tis safer to be within. The clothes is not the better of it," said he, looking at his sleeve, now hanging in stripes.

"Never mind that, Flury; we'll soon repair that misfortune; it does not signify much."

"Doesn't it, faith?" said the other, shaking his head dubiously; "'tis asy talking, but I can't turn my coat without showing the hole in it. 'Tis only the rich can do that."

The Knight bit his lip, for even from the fool's sarcasm he could gather the imputations already rife upon his conduct. Another and a very different thought succeeded to this, and he blushed with shame to think how far his sense of his own misfortune had rendered him indifferent, not only to the kindly feelings, but the actual misery of others. The right impulses of high-minded men are generally rapid in their action, like the spring of the bent bow when the cord is cut asunder. It did not cost Darcy many minutes to be again the warm-hearted, generous soul nature had made him.

"Come, Flury," said he to the poor fellow, as he stood ruefully surveying his damaged drapery, "give that among the people there in the town, and keep this for yourself."

"This is goold, Maurice—yellow goold!"

"So it is; but you're not the less welcome to it; tell them, too, that I have had troubles of my own lately, and that's the reason I hurried on without exchanging a word with them."

"How do you know, Maurice, but I'll keep it all to myself?"

"I'd trust you with a heavier sum," said the Knight, smiling.

"I know why—I know why, well enough—because I'm a fool. Never mind, there's greater fools nor me going. What did they give you up there for your vote, Maurice—tell me, how much was it?"

The Knight shook his head, and Flury resumed: "Didn't I say it? Wasn't I right? By my ould hat! there's two fools in the country now—Maurice Darcy and Red Flury, and Maurice the biggest of the two! Whoop, the more the merrier, there's room for us all!" And with this wise reflection, Flury gave a very wild caper and a wilder shout, and set off at the speed of a hare towards Castlebar.

The Knight resumed his journey, and in a more contented mood. The little incident had called on him for an exertion, and his faculties only needed the demand to respond to the call. He summoned to his aid, besides, every comforting reflection in his power; he persuaded himself that there were some hopes remaining still, and tried to believe the evil not beyond remedy. "After all," thought he, "we are together; it is not death has been dealing with us, nor is there any stain upon our fair fame; and save these, all ills are light, and can be borne."

From thoughts like these he was aroused by the heavy clank of the iron gate, as it fell back to admit the carriage within the park, while a thousand welcomes saluted him.

"Thank you, Darby!—thank you, Mary! All well up at the abbey?"

But the carriage dashed past at full speed, and the answer was drowned in the tumult. The postboys, true to the etiquette of their calling, had reserved their best pace for the finish, and it was at the stride of a hunting gallop they now tore along.

It was a calm night, with a young faint moon and a starry sky, which, without displaying in bright light the details of the scenery, yet exhibited them in strong bold masses, making all seem even more imposing and grander than in reality; the lofty mountain appeared higher, the dark woods vaster, and the wide-spreading lawn seemed to stretch away into immense plains. Darcy's heart swelled with pride as he looked, while a pang shot through him as he thought, if even at that hour, he could call them his own.

They had now reached a little glen, where the postboys were obliged to walk their blown cattle; emerging from this, they passed a thick grove of beech, and at once came in sight of the abbey. Darcy leaned anxiously from the window to catch the first sight of home, when, what was his amazement, to perceive that the whole was lighted up from end to end. The great suite of state rooms were a blaze of lustres, which even at that distance glittered in their starry brilliancy, and showed the shadows of figures moving within. He well knew that Lady Eleanor never saw company in his absence—what could this mean? Tortured with doubts that in his then state of mind took every painful form, he ordered the postilions to get on faster, and at the very top of their speed they tore along, over the wide lawn, across the terrace drive, up the steep ascent to the gate tower into the court-yard.

This was also brilliantly lighted by lamps from the walls, and also by the lights of numerous carriage lamps which crowded the ample space.

"What is this? Can no one tell me?" muttered the Knight, as he leaped from the carriage, and seizing a livery servant who was passing, said, "What is going on here? What company has the abbey?"

"Full of company," said the man, in an English accent; "there's my Lord——"

"Who do you mean?"

"The Earl of Netherby, sir, and Sir Harry Beauclerk, and Colonel Crofton, and——"

"When did they arrive?" said the Knight, interrupting a catalogue, every name of which, although unknown, sent a feeling like a stab through his heart.

"They came the evening before last, sir; Mr. Lionel Darcy, who arrived the same morning——"

"Is he here?" cried the Knight; and without waiting for more, hastened forward.

The servants, of whom there seemed a great number about, were in strange liveries, and unknown to the Knight; nor was it without undergoing a very cool scrutiny from them, that Darcy succeeded in gaining admittance to his own house. At last he reacned the foot of the great stair, whence the sounds of music and the din of voices filled the air; servants hurried along with refreshments, or carried orders to others in waiting; all was bustle and excitement, in the midst of which Darcy stood only half conscious of the reality of what he saw, and endeavouring to reason himself into a conviction of what he heard. It was at this moment that several officers of a newly-quartered regiment passed up, admiring, as they went, the splendour of the house, and the magnificent preparations they witnessed on every side.

"I say, Dallas," cried one, "you're always talking of your uncle Beverley, does he do the thing in this style, eh?"

"By Jove!" interposed a short, thick-set Major, with a bushy beard and eyebrows, "this is what I call going the pace; do they give dinners here?"

"Yes, that they do," said a white-faced, ghostly-looking Ensign; "I heard all about this place from Giles, of the 40th; he was quartered six months in this county, and used to grub here half the week. The old fellow isn't at home now, but they say he's a trump."

"Let's drink his health, Watkins," cried the first speaker, "here's champagne going up;" and so saying, the party gathered around two servants, one of whom carried an ice-pail with some bottles, and the other a tray of glasses.

"Does any one know his name, though?" said the Major, as he held his glass to be filled.

"Yes, it's something like——Oh, you know that fellow that joined us at Coventry?"

"Brereton, is it?"

"No, hang it! I mean the fellow that had the crop-eared cob with the white legs. Never mind, here he goes, anyhow."

"Oh, I know who you mean—it was Jack Quin."

"That's the name; and our friend here is called 'Gwynne,' I think. Here, gentlemen, I give you Gwynne's health, and all the honours; may he live a few centuries more——"

"With a warm heart and a cool cellar," added one.

"Pink champagne and red coats to drink it," chimed in the Ensign.

"May I join you in that pleasant sentiment, gentlemen?" said the Knight, bowing courteously, as he took a glass from the tray and held it towards the servant.

"Make no apology, sir," said the Major, eyeing him rather superciliously, for the travelling dress concealed the Knight's appearance, and distinguished him but slightly from many of those lounging around the doors.

"Capital ginger beer that! eh?" said the Ensign, as winking at his companions he proceeded to quiz the stranger.

"I have certainly drunk worse," said the Knight, gravely—"at an infantry mess."

There was a pause before he uttered the last few words, which gave them a more direct application; a stare, half stupid, half impertinent, was, however, all they elicited, and the group moved on, while the Knight, disencumbering himself of his travelling gear, slowly followed them.

"Grim old gentlemen these, ain't they?" said the Major, gazing at the long line of family portraits that covered the walls; "that fellow with the truncheon does not seem to like the look of us."

"Here's a Bishop, I take it, with the great wig."

"That's a Chancellor, man, don't you see the mace, but he's not a whit more civil-looking than the other. Commend me to the shepherdess yonder in blue satin; but come on, we're losing time, I hear the flourish of a new dance. I say," said he, in a whisper, "do you see who we've got behind us?" And they turned and saw the Knight as he mounted the stairs behind them.

"A friend of the family, sir?" asked the Major, in a voice that might bear the equivocal meaning of either impertinence or mere inquiry.

The Knight seemed to prefer taking it in the latter acceptation, as he answered mildly, "I have that honour."

"Ah! indeed; well, we've the misfortune to be strangers in these parts; only arrived in the neighbourhood last week, and were invited here through our Colonel. Would you have any objection to present us?—Major Hopecot of the 5th, Captain Mills, Mr. Dallas, Mr. Fothergill, Mr. Watkins."

"How the Major *is* going it," lisped the Ensign, while his goggle eyes rolled fearfully, and the others seemed struggling to control their enjoyment of such drollery.

"It will afford me much pleasure, sir, to do your bidding," said the Knight, calmly.

"Take the head of the column, then," resumed the Major, making way for him to pass; and the Knight entered, with the others after him.

"My father, my dearest father!" cried a voice at the moment, and, escaping from her partner, Helen was in a moment in his arms. The next instant Lionel was also at his side.

"My dear children!—my sweet Helen—and Lionel, how well you're looking, boy. Ah! Eleanor, what a pleasant surprise you have managed for me."

"Then perhaps you never got our letter," said Lady Eleanor, as she took his arm and walked forward. 'I wrote the moment I heard from Lionel."

"And I, too, wrote you a long letter from London," said Lionel.

"Neither reached me; but the last few days I have been so busy, and so much occupied. How are you, Conolly? Delighted to see you, Martin. And Lady Julia, is she here? I must take a tour and see all my friends. First of all, I have a duty to perform; let me introduce these gentlemen. But where are they? Oh, I see them yonder." And, as he spoke, he led Lady Eleanor across the room to the group of officers, who, overwhelmed with shame at their discovery, stood uncertain whether they should remain or retire.

"Let me introduce Major Hopecot and the officers of the 5th," said he, bowing courteously. "These gentlemen are strangers, Lady Eleanor; will you take care that they find partners."

While the abashed subalterns left their Major to make his speeches to Lady Eleanor, the Knight moved round the room with Helen still leaning on his arm. By this time Darcy's arrival was generally known, and all his old friends came pressing forward to see and speak to him.

"Lord Netherby," whispered Helen in the Knight's ear, as a tall and very thin old man, with an excessive affectation of youthfulness, tripped forward to meet him.

"My dear Lord," exclaimed Darcy, "what a pleasure, and what an honour to see you here."

"You would not come to *me*, Knight, so there was nothing else for it," replied the other, laughing, as he shook hands with a great display of cordiality. "And you were quite right," continued he; "I could not have received you like this. There's not so splendid a place in England, nor has it ever been my fortune to witness so much beauty." A half bow accompanied the last words, as he turned towards Helen.

"Take care, my Lord," said the Knight, smiling; "the flatteries of a courtier are very dangerous things, when heard out of the atmosphere that makes them common-place. We may take you literally, and have our heads turned by them."

At this moment Lionel joined them, to introduce several of his friends and brother officers who accompanied him from England, all of whom were received by the Knight with that winning courtesy of manner of which he was a perfect master, for, not affecting either the vices or frivolities ot youth as a claim to the consideration of younger men, the Knight possessed the happy temper that can concede indulgence without asking to partake of it, and, while losing nothing of the relish for wit and humour, chasten both by the fruits of a life's experience.

"Now, Helen, you must go back to your partner; that young Guardsman looks very sulkily at me for having taken you off—yes, I insist on it. Lionel, look to your friends, and I'll join Lord Netherby's whist-table, and talk whenever permitted. Where's poor Tate?" whispered he in Lady Eleanor's ear, as she just came up.

"Poor fellow! he has been ill for some days back; you know what a superstitious creature he is; and about a week since he got a fright—some warning of a Banshee, I think—but it shook his nerves greatly, and he has kept his bed almost ever since. Lionel brought over some of these servants with him, but Lord Netherby's people are Legion, and the servants' hall now numbers something like seventy, I hear."

The Knight heaved a sigh, but, catching himself, tried to conceal it by a cough. Lady Eleanor had heard it, however, and stole a quick glance towards him, to evade which he turned abruptly round and spoke to some one near.

"Seventy, my dear Eleanor!" said he, after a pause, and as if he had been reflecting over his last observation; "and what a Babel, too, it must be! I heard French, German, and Italian in the hall; I think we can promise Irish ourselves."

"Yes," said Lionel, "it is the most amusing scene in the world. They had a ball last night in the lower gallery, where boleros and jigs succeeded each other, while the refreshments ranged from iced lemonade to burnt whisky."

"And what did our worthy folk think of their visitors?" said Darcy, smiling.

"Not over much. Paddy Lennan looked with great contempt at the men sipping *orgeat*, and when he saw the waltzing, merely remarked, 'We're a betther way of getting round the girls in Ireland;' while old Pierre Duange, Netherby's valet, persists in addressing the native company as Messieurs les Sauvages.'"

"I hope, for the sake of the public peace, they've not got an interpreter among them."

"No, no, all's safe on that score, and freedom of speech has suggested the most perfect code of good manners; for it would seem, as they can indulge themselves in the most liberal reflections on each other, they have no necessity of proceeding to overt acts."

"Now," said the Knight, "let me not interrupt the revelry longer. To your place, Lionel, and leave me to pay my devoirs to my friends and kind neighbours."

The Knight's presence seemed alone wanting to fill up the measure of enjoyment. Most of those present were his old familiar friends, glad to see once more amongst them the great promoter of kind feeling and hospitality, while from such as were strangers he easily won golden opinions, the charm of courtesy being with him like a well-fitting garment, which graced, but did not impede the wearer's motions.

He had a hundred questions to ask and to answer. The news of the capital travelled in those days by slow and easy stages, and the moment was sufficiently eventful to warrant curiosity, and so, as he passed from group to group, he gave the current gossip of the time as each in turn asked after this circumstance or that.

At length he took his place beside Lord Netherby, as he sat engaged at a whist-table, where the gathering crowd that gradually collected soon converted the game into a social circle of eager talkers.

Who could have suspected that easy, unconstrained manner, that winning smile, that ready laugh, the ever-present jest, to cover the working of a heart so nigh to breaking? And yet he talked pleasantly and freely, narrating with all his accustomed humour the chit-chat of the time; and while, of course, the great question of the hour occupied every tongue and ear, all Lord Netherby's practised shrewdness could not enable him to detect the exact part the Knight himself had taken.

"And so they have carried the bill," said Conolly, with a sigh, as he listened to Darcy's account of the second reading. "Well, though I never was a Parliament man, nor expected to be one, I'm sorry for it. You think that strange, my Lord?"

"By no means, sir. A man may love monarchy without being the heir apparent."

"Quite true," chimed in the Knight. "I would even go further, and say that, without any warm devotion to a king, a man may hate a regicide."

Lord Netherby's eyes met Darcy's, and the wily Peer smiled with a significance that seemed to say, "I know you, *now*."

CHAPTER XXVIII.

THE HUNT-BREAKFAST.

THE ball lasted till nigh daybreak, and while the greater number of the guests departed, some few remained by special invitation at the abbey, to join a hunting party on the following day. For this Lionel had made every possible preparation, desiring to let his English friends witness a favourable specimen of Irish sport and horsemanship. The stud and kennel were both in high condition, the weather favourable, and, as the old huntsman said, "'Twould be hard if a fox wouldn't be agreeable enough to give the strange gentlemen a run."

In high anticipation of the coming morning, and with many a prayer against a frost, they separated for the night. All within the abbey were soon sound asleep, all save the Knight himself, who, the restraint of an assumed part withdrawn, threw himself on a sofa in his dressing-room, worn out and exhausted by his struggle. Ruin was inevitable, that he well knew; but as yet the world knew it not, and for Lionel's sake he resolved to keep his own secret a few days longer. The visit was to last but eight days; two were already over; for the remaining six, then, he determined—whatever it might cost him—to preserve all the appearances of his former estate, to wear the garb and seeming of prosperity, and do the princely honours of a house that was never again to be his home.

"Poor Lionel!" thought he, "'twould break the boy's heart if such a disclosure should be made now; the high and daring promptings of his bold spirit would not quail before misfortune, although his courage might not sustain him in the very moment of the reverse. I will not risk the whole fortune of his future happiness in such a trial; he shall know nothing till they are gone; one week of triumphant pleasure he shall have, and then let him brace himself to the struggle, and breast the current manfully."

While endeavouring to persuade himself that Lionel's lot was uppermost in his mind, his heart would force the truth upon him that Lady Eleanor and Helen's fate was, in reality, a heavier stroke of fortune. Lionel was a soldier, ardent and daring, fond of his profession, and far more ambitious of distinction than attached to the life of pleasure a Court and a great capital suggested; but they, who had never known the want of every luxury that can embellish life, whose whole existence had been like some fairy dream of pleasure, how were they to bear up against the dreadful shock? Lady Eleanor's health was frail and delicate in the extreme; Helen's attachment to her mother such that any impression on her would invariably recoil upon herself. What might be the consequences of the disclosure to them Darcy could not, dared not contemplate.

As he revolved all these things in his mind, and thought upon the difficulties that beset him, he was at a loss whether to deplore the necessity of wearing a false face of pleasure a few days longer, or rejoice at the occasion of even this brief reprieve from ruin. Thus passed the weary hours that preceded daybreak, and while others slept soundly, or reviewed in their dreams the pleasures of the past night, Darcy's gloomy thoughts were fixed upon the inevitable calamity of his fate, and the years, few but sad, that in all likelihood were now before him.

The stir and bustle of the servants preparing breakfast for the hunting party broke in upon his dreary reverie, and he suddenly bethought him of the part he had assigned himself to play. He dreaded the possibility of an interview with Lady Eleanor, in which she would inevitably advert to Gleeson, and the circumstances of his flight; this could not be avoided, however, were he to pass the day at home, and so he resolved to join the hunting-field, where perhaps, some lingering trace of his old enthusiasm for the sport might lead him to hope for a momentary relief of mind.

"Lionel, too, will be glad to see me in the saddle—it's some years since I crossed the sward at a gallop—and I am curious to know if a man's nerve is stouter when the world looks fair before him, or when the night of calamity is louring above his head." Muttering these words to himself, he passed out into the hall, and, crossing which, entered the court-yard, and took his way towards the stables. It was still dark, but many lights were moving to and fro, and the groom population were all about and stirring. Darcy opened the door and looked down the long range of stalls, where above twenty saddle-horses were now standing, the greater number of them highly bred and valuable animals, and all in the highest possible condition. Great was the astonishment of the stablemen as the Knight moved along, throwing a glance as he went at each stall, while a muttered "Welcome home to yer honour," ran from mouth to mouth.

"The bastes is looking finely, sir," said Bob Carney, who, as stud-groom and huntsman, had long presided over his department.

"So they are, Bob, but I don't know half of them; where did this strong brown horse come from?"

"That's Clipper, yer honour; I knew you wouldn't know him. He took up finely after his run last winter."

"And the fore leg, is it strong again?"

"As stout as a bar of iron; one of the boys had him out two days ago and he took the yellow ditch flying—we measured nineteen feet between the mark of his hoofs."

"He ought to be strong enough to carry me, Bob."

"Don't ride him, sir, he's an uncertain divil; and though he'll go straight over everything for maybe twenty minutes or half an hour, he'll stop short at a drain not wider than a potato furrow, and the power of man wouldn't get him over it."

"That's a smart grey, yonder—what is she?"

"She's the one we tried as a leader one day; yer honour remembers you bid me shoot her, or get rid of her, for she kicked the traces, and nearly the wheel-horse all to smash; and now she's the sweetest thing to ride, for eleven stone, in the whole county. There's an English Colonel to try her to-day; my only advice to him is, let her have her own way of it, for, if he begins pulling at her, 'tis maybe in Donegal he'll be before evening."

"And what have you for me?" said the Knight, "for I scarcely know any of my old friends here."

"There's the mouse-coloured cob——"

"No, no," said the Knight, laughing; "I want to keep my place, Bob. You must give me something better than that."

"Faith, an' your honour might have worse; but if it's for riding you are, take Black Peter, and you'll never find the fence too big, or the ground too heavy for him. I was going to give him to the English Lord; I suppose, after all, he'll be better pleased with the cob."

"Well, then, Peter for me. And now let's see what Mr. Lionel has to ride."

"There she is, and a beauty!" said Bob, as, with a dexterous jerk, he chucked a sheet off her haunches, and displayed the shining flanks and splendid proportions of a thorough-bred mare. "That's Cushleen," said he, as he fixed his eyes on the Knight's face to enjoy the reflection of his own delight. "That's the darlin' can do it!—a child can hould her, but it takes a man to sit on her back—racing speed over a flat, and a jump!—'tis more like the bound of a football than anything else."

"She has the eye of a hot one, Bob."

"And why wouldn't she? But she knows when to be so. Let her take her place at the head of the whole field, with a light finger to guide, and a stout heart to direct her, and she's a kitten; but the divil a tiger was ever as fierce if another passes her, or a cowardly hand would try to hold her back. And there's a nate tool, that black horse—that's for another of the English gentlemen. Master Lionel calls him Sir Harry. They tell me he's a fine rider, and has a pack of hounds himself in his own place, and I am mistaken if he has the baste in his stable will give him a betther day's sport. The chesnut here is for Miss Helen, for she's coming to see them throw off, and it'll be a fine sight; we'll be thirty-six out of your honour's stables, Mr. Conolly is bringing nine more, and all the Martins, and the Lynches, and Dalys, and Mr. Hickman O'Reilly and his son, though, to be sure, *they* won't do much for the honour of ould Ireland."

The Knight turned away laughing, and re-entered the house.

Early as it yet was, the inmates of the abbey were stirring, and a great breakfast, laid for above thirty, was prepared in the library, for the supper-tables occupied the dining-rooms, and the *débris* of the magnificent entertainment of the night before still lingered there. Two cheerful fires blazed on the ample hearths, and threw a mellow lustre over that spacious room, where old Tate now busied himself in those little harmless duties he fancied indispensable to the Knight's comfort, for the poor fellow, on hearing of his master's return, had once more resumed his office.

The Knight's meeting with him was one of true friendship; difference of station interposed no barrier to affection, and Darcy shook the old man's hand as cordially as though they were brothers. Yet each was sad with a secret sorrow, which all their efforts could scarce conceal from the other. In vain the Knight endeavoured to turn away old Tate's attention by inquiries after his health, questions about home, or little flatteries about his preparations, Tate's filmy eyes were fixed upon his master with a keenness that age could not dim.

"'Tis maybe tired your honour is," said he, in a voice half meant as inquiry, half insinuation; "the Parliament, they tell me, destroys the health entirely."

"Very true, Tate; late hours, heated rooms, and some fatigue, will not serve a man of my age; but I am tolerably well, for all that."

"God be praised for it!" said Tate, piously, but in a voice that showed it was rather a wish he expressed than a conviction, when, suspecting that he had suffered some portion of his fears to escape, he added more cheerfully, "And isn't Master Lionel grown an iligant, fine young man! When I seen him comin' up the stairs, it was just as if the forty-eight years that's gone over was only a dhrame, and I was looking at your honour the day you came home from college; he has the same way with his arms, and carries his head like you, and the same light step. Musha!" muttered he, below his breath, "the ould families never die out, but keep their looks to the last."

"He's a fine fellow, Tate!" said the Knight, turning towards the window, for while flattered by the old man's praises of his son, a deep pang shot through his heart at the wide disparity of fortune with which life opened for both of them. At the instant an arm was drawn round him, and Helen stood at his side: she was in her riding-habit, and looking in perfect beauty. Darcy gazed at her for a few seconds, and with such evident admiration, that she, as if accepting the compliment, drew herself up, and, smiling, said, "Yes, nothing short of conquest. Lionel told his friends to expect a very unformed country girl; they shall see, at least, she can ride."

"No hare-brained risks, Helen, dearest. I'm to take the field to-day, and you mustn't shake my nerve, for I want to bring no disgrace on my county."

"I was but jesting, my own dear papa," said she, drawing closer to him "but I really felt so curious to see these English horsemen's performance, that I asked Lionel to train Alice for me."

"And Lionel, of course, but too happy to show his pretty sister——"

"Nay, nay, if you will quiz, I must only confess that my head is quite turned already; our noble cousin overwhelms me with flatteries, which, upon the principle the Indian accepts glass beads and spangles as gems and gold, I take as real value. But here he comes."

And Lord Netherby, attired for the field in all the accuracy of costume. slipped towards them. After came Colonel Crofton, a well-known fashionable of the Clubs and a hanger-on of the Peer; then Sir Harry Beauclerk, a young Baronet of vast fortune, gay, good-tempered, and extravagant; while several others of lesser note, brother officers of Lionel's, and men about town, brought up the rear, one only deserving remark, a certain Captain, or, as he was better known, Tom Nolan—a strange, ambiguous kind of fellow, always seen in the world, constantly met at the best houses, and yet nobody being able to explain why he was asked, nor—as it very often happened—who asked him.

Lady Eleanor never appeared early in the day, but there was a sprinkling of lady-visitors through the room, guests at the abbey; a very pretty, but not over-afflicted widow, a Mrs. Somerville, with several Mrs. and Miss Lynches, Brownes, and Martins, comprising the beauties of the neighbourhood. Lionel was the last to make his appearance, so many directions had he to give about earth-stoppers, and cover-hacks, drags, phaetons, fresh horses, and all the contingent requirements of a day's sport. Besides, he had pledged himself most faithfully to give Mrs. Somerville's horse, a very magnificent barb, a training canter himself, with a horse sheet round his legs, for she was a timid rider—on some occasions—though certain calumnious people averred that, when alone, she would take any fence in the whole barony.

At length they were seated, and such a merry, happy party! There was but one sad heart in the company, and that none could guess at. And what a running fire of pleasant raillery rattled round the table! How brimful of wit and good-humour were they all! How ready each to take the jest against himself, and even heighten its flavour by some new touch of drollery. Harmless wagers especting the places they would occupy at the finish, gentle quizzings about safe riding through the gaps, and joking counsels as to the peculiar difficulties of an Irish country, were heard on all sides; while the Knight recounted the Galway anecdote of Dick Perse taking an immense leap and disappearing afterwards. "'Call the ground, Dick!' cried Lord Clanricarde, who was charging up at top speed—'call the ground! What's at the other side?'

"'I *am*, thank God!' was the short reply, and the words came from the depth of a gravel-pit."

At last, venison pasties and steaks, rolls and coffee, with their due accompaniment of liqueurs, came to an end, and a very sufficient uproar without, of men, dogs, and horses, commingled, bespoke the activity of preparation there, while old Bob Carney's voice topped every other, as he swore at or commended men and beasts indiscriminately.

"What a glorious morning for our sport!" said the Knight, as he threw open the sash, and let into the room the heavy perfume of the earth, borne on a southerly wind. The sea was calm as an inland lake, and the dark clouds over it were equally motionless. "We shall be unlucky, my Lord, if we do not show you some sport on such a day. Ah, there go the dogs!" And, as he spoke, the hounds issued from beneath the deep arch of the gateway, and with Bob and the Whipper-in at their head, took their way across the lawn.

"To horse! to horse!" shouted Lionel, gaily, from the court-yard, for the riding party were not to proceed to the cover by the short path the hounds were gone, but to follow by a more picturesque and circuitous route.

"I hope sincerely that beast is not intended for me," said Lord Netherby, as a powerful black horse crossed the court-yard in a series of bounds, and finished by landing the groom over his head.

"Never fear, my Lord," said Lionel, laughing; "Billy Pitt is meant for Beauclerk."

"You surely never named that animal after the Minister, Knight?" said his Lordship.

"Yes, my Lord," said Darcy, with a smile; "it's just as unsafe to back one as the other. But here comes the heavy brigade. Which is your choice—Black Peter or Mouse?"

"If I may choose, I will confess this is more to my liking than anything I have seen yet. You know that I don't mean to take any part in the debate, so I may as well secure a quiet seat under the gallery. But, my dear Miss Darcy, what a mettlesome thing you've got there!"

"She's only fidgety; if I can hold her when they throw off, I'll have no trouble afterwards." And the graceful girl sat back easily in her saddle, as the animal bounded and swerved with every stroke of her long riding-habit.

"There goes Beauclerk!" cried Lionel, as the young Baronet shot like an arrow through the archway on the back of Billy Pitt; for no sooner had he touched the saddle, than the unmanageable animal broke away from the groom's hands, and set off at full speed down the lawn.

"I say, Darcy," cried Colonel Crofton, "isn't Beauclerk a step over you in the 'Army List?'"

But Lionel never heard the question, for he was most busily occupied about Mrs. Somerville and her horse.

"Who drives the phaeton?—where's a safe whip to be found for Mrs. Martin?" said the Knight; and seizing on a young Guardsman, he promoted him to the box, with a very pretty girl beside him. A drag, with four greys, was filling at the same instant, with a mixed population of horsemen and spectators, among whom Captain Nolan seemed the presiding spirit, as, seated beside a brother officer of Lionel's on the box, he introduced the several parties to each other, and did "the honours" of the conveyance.

Troops of horses, sheeted and hooded, now passed out, with a number of grooms and stable-boys, on their way to cover; and at last the great cavalcade moved forward, the Knight, his daughter, and Lord Netherby gaily cantering on the grass, to permit the carriages to take the road. The drag came last; and although but newly met, the company were already in the full enjoyment of that intimacy which high spirits and pleasure beget, while Tom Nolan contributed his utmost to the merriment by jests, which lost nothing of their poignancy from any scruples of their maker.

"There they go at last," said he, as Lionel and Mrs. Somerville cantered forth, followed by two grooms. "I never heard of a stirrup so hard to arrange as that, in all my life!"

CHAPTER XXIX.

THE HUNT.

The cover lay in a small valley, almost deep enough to be called a glen, watered by a stream, which in winter and summer took the alternate character of torrent or rivulet: gently sloping hills rose on either side, their banks clad with low furze and fern, and behind them a wide plain extended to the foot of the great mountains of Connemara.

Both sides of the little glen were now occupied by groups on foot or horseback, as each calculated on the likelihood of the fox taking this direction or that. On the narrow road which led along the crest of the lower hill were many equipages to be seen, some of which were filled with ladies, whose waving feathers and gay colours served to heighten the effect of the landscape. The horsemen were dotted about, some, on the ridge of the rising ground, some, lower down on the sloping sides, and others walked their horses through the dense cover, watching as the dogs sprang and bounded from copse to copse, and made the air vibrate with their deep voices.

The arrival of the Knight's party created no slight sensation, as carriages and horsemen came dashing up the hill, and took their station on an eminence, from whence all who were not mounted might have a view of the field. No sooner was he recognised, than such as had the honour of personal acquaintance moved forward to pay their respects, and welcome him home again; among whom Beecham O'Reilly appeared, but with such evident diffidence of manner and reserve, that Darcy, from motives of delicacy, was forced to take a more than ordinary notice of him.

"We were sorry not to have your company at the abbey last night; you've had a cold, I hear," said the Knight.

"Yes, sir; this is the first day I've ventured out."

"Let me introduce you to Lord Netherby. One of our foremost riders, my Lord, Mr. Beecham O'Reilly. You may see that the merit is not altogether his own—splendid horse you have there."

"He's very powerful," said the young man, accepting the praise with an air of easy indifference.

"In my country," interposed Lord Netherby, "we should value him at three hundred guineas, if his performance equal his appearance."

"I say, Lionel, come here a moment," cried the Knight. "What do you think of that horse?—but don't you know your old playfellow, Beecham? Have you both forgotten each other?"

"How are you, Beecham? I'd never have guessed you. To be sure, it is six years since we met. You were in Dublin, I think, when I was over on leave last?"

"No, at Oxford," said Beecham, with a slight flush as he spoke; for although he accepted the warm shake-hands Lionel proffered, his manner was one of constraint all through. Young Darcy was, however, too much occupied in admiring the horse to bestow much attention on the rider.

"He'd carry you well," said Beecham, as if interpreting what was passing in his mind, "and as I have no fancy for him—a worse horse will carry my weight as well—I'd sell him."

"At what price?"

"Lord Netherby has valued him at three hundred," said the young man "I gave nearly as much myself."

The Knight, who heard this conversation, without being able to interrupt it, was in perfect misery. The full measure of his ruin rushed suddenly on his mind, and the thought that, at the very moment his son was meditating this piece of extravagance, he was himself actually a beggar, sickened him to the heart. Meanwhile, Lionel walked his horse slowly round, the better to observe the animal he coveted, and then cantered back to his place at Mrs. Somerville's side.

Beecham seemed to hesitate for a second or two, then riding forward, he approached Lionel: "Perhaps you would try him to-day, Captain Darcy?" The words came hesitatingly and with difficulty.

"Oh, no! he's beyond my reach," said Lionel, laughing.

"I'd really take it as a favour if you would ride him; I'm not strong enough to hold him, consequently cannot do him justice."

"Take the offer, Darcy," said Lord Netherby, in a whisper, as he rode up to his side; "I have a great liking for that horse myself, and will buy him if you report favourably."

"In that case, my Lord, I'll do it with pleasure. I accept your kind proposal, and will change nags if you agree."

Beecham at once dismounted, and, beckoning to his servant, ordered him to change the saddles.

While this little scene was enacting, old Conolly rode up to the Knight, with a warning to keep the ladies in the road. "The fox will take the country towards Burnadarig," said he; "the start's with the wind; and as the fences are large and the ground heavy, they had better not attempt to follow the run."

"We will take your advice, Tom," said the Knight. "Come here, Helen—Colonel Crofton, will you kindly bring Mrs. Somerville up here, and tell Lord Netherby to join us?—the day will be for the fast ones only. There they go—are they off?"

"Not yet, not yet," said Conolly, as, standing in his stirrups, he looked down into the glen; "they're hunting him through that furze cover this half hour. I know that fox well; he never breaks till the dogs are actually on him."

By this time the scene in the valley was becoming highly exciting; the hounds, yelping and barking, bounded hither and thither, some, with uplifted throats, bayed deeply a long protracted note; others, with noses to the earth, ran swiftly along, and then stopping, burst into a sharp cry, as if of pain, while old Bob Carney's voice, encouraging this one, and cursing that, was high above the tumult.

"Tiresome work, this is," said Sir Harry Beauclerk; for his horse, mad with impatience, was white with sweat, and trembled in every limb.

"You'll have it very soon, sir," said old Conolly; "the dogs are together now. I wish that young gentleman there would move a little up the hill." This was said of a young officer, who took his station at the exit of the cover. "There they go, now! Tally-ho!" cried he, in ecstasy, and the shout re-echoed from a hundred voices, as the hounds, in full cry, burst from the cover, and were seen, in one compact mass, rising the opposite hill.

In a second every horse was away, save that little group around the Knight, and which, notwithstanding all the efforts of the servants, bounded and plunged in mad impatience. Beauclerk was the first down the hill, and over the brook, which he cleared gallantly. Conolly followed close; and then came Crofton in a group of others, among whom rode O'Reilly, all riding well and safely; and last of all was Lionel, mounted on the brown thorough-bred, and holding him together, in spite of all his eagerness to get on.

The Knight forgot everything that lay heavily on his heart as he watched his son nearing the brook, which he took flying. "He knows his horse; now! see!" cried Darcy, as his whole face beamed with enthusiastic delight; "look a little this way, my dear Mrs. Somerville, Lionel's gaining on them!"

Mrs. Somerville scarcely needed the direction, for, notwithstanding her horse's plunging, she had never taken her glass from her eye.

"Is that a wall on the side of the hill? I really believe it is!" said Lord Netherby, with an accent of amazement and horror.

"A stone wall, and a stout one. I know it well," said Darcy. "There goes Sir Harry Beauclerk at it. Too fast, sir! too fast!" screamed out the Knight, as if his advice could be heard and followed at that distance.

"He's down! he's down!" cried several voices together, as horse and rider balanced for a second on the top, and rolled headlong on the opposite side, while Helen grasped her father's arm, but never uttered a word.

"His horse is away—there he goes!—but the young man is on his legs again!" called out the Knight; "see how the rest are scattering now—they've no fancy for it;" for so it was, Beauclerk's catastrophe, mounted, as they knew him to be, on one of the most perfect of hunters, had terrified the field, and they broke up into different groups, searching an exit where they could.

"There he goes—that's the way to take it!" cried Darcy, as Lionel, emerging from the little valley, was seen ascending the hill in a sharp canter; "see, my Lord! Do you mark how he holds his horse together? the hind legs are well forward—beautifully done!"

"Oh, beautifully done!" re-echoed Mrs. Somerville, as the young man, with one cut of his whip, rose the horse to the wall, topped, poised for an instant on its summit, and bounded down with the seeming lightness of a bird.

"They're all together again," said Helen. "Mr. Conolly has found a gap, and there they go."

For a few moments the whole field were in sight, as they rode in a waving line, only a few stragglers in their rear; but the gradual dip of the ground soon hid them from view, and nothing remained save the occasional glance of a red coat, as some rider, "thrown out" for a moment, sought to recover his place by an adroit "cast."

"I suppose we are not destined to see much more of the day's sport?" said Mrs. Somerville, with a pouting look; for she would infinitely rather have braved all the hazards of the field, than have remained behind with the spectators.

"I trust we shall have another peep at them," said the Knight. "By following this by-road to Burris-hill, the chances are that we see them winding along at our feet; the fox generally runs from this cover to the scrub beneath Nephin. We may go slowly, for, if I be right in my calculation, they have a wide circuit to make yet."

The Knight, after a few words to the parties in the carriage, took the lead with Lord Netherby, while Mrs. Somerville and Helen followed, an indiscriminate crowd of carriages and horsemen bringing up the rear.

This was an arrangement artfully accomplished by the Earl, who had been most impatiently awaiting some opportunity of conferring with the Knight on the question of politics, and ascertaining how far he himself might adventure on claiming the merit of converting him, when he returned to England. He had already remarked that Darcy's name did not appear in the division on the second reading of the Bill of Union, and the fact seemed so far indicative of a disposition not to oppose the Government. The subject was one to be approached with skill, and it was at last by an adroit congratulation on the pleasant contrast of a country life with the fatigues of Parliament, that he opened the discussion.

"I believe, my Lord," said the Knight, laughing, "that Irish gentlemen are very likely to enjoy in future a fair proportion of that agreeable retirement you have so justly lauded. The wisdom of our rulers has thought fit to relieve us of the burden of self-government in Parliament, and left us, if we can succeed in effecting it, to govern ourselves at home."

"That will be unquestionably the lot of many, Knight. I am quite aware that men of second-rate importanae will no longer possess any at all; but estated gentlemen, of high position and liberal fortunes, like yourself for instance, will not lose their influence by the greater extent of the field in which it is exercised."

Darcy sighed, but made no reply; the thought of his utter ruin came too painfully across him to permit of an answer. Lord Netherby interpreted his silence as doubt, and continued: "You are unjust, not only to yourself but to us, by any discredit of this point. Men of real knowledge about Ireland and her interests will have a greater position than ever they enjoyed before; no longer buried and lost among the impracticable horde of theorists and false patriots of a Dublin Parliament, they will be known and appreciated by a deliberative assembly, where the greatest men of the empire hold council."

"I am forced to differ with you on every point, my Lord," said the Knight, calmly; "we are united to England, not that we may make an integral portion of your empire, but simply, that we may be more easily governed. Up to this hour, you have ruled this country through the instrumentality of certain deputed individuals here amongst us; your system has had but indifferent success. You are now about to try another method, and govern us through the means of Party. Into the subdivisions of these parties Irishmen will fall—with such success, personally, as their abilities and weight may obtain for them—but Party, I assert, will now rule Ireland, not with any regard to Irish interests or objects, but simply to put this man into power, and to put that man out. Now I, my Lord, humble as my station is, have no fancy for such contests as these—contests in which the advantages of my country will always be subordinate to some Cabinet intrigue or Ministerial stratagem. To-day, the Government may find it suit their views to administer the affairs of Ireland ably, justly, and fearlessly—to-morrow, a powerful faction may spring up here, who, by intimidation without, and by votes within the House, shall be able to thwart the Administration in their Home measures. What will happen then? This faction will be bought off. By concessions to them *in Ireland*, they will obtain all their demands, for the sake of pliancy about interests of which they care little, and know nothing. This will succeed for a time; the 'King's Government' will go well and flippantly on; you may tax the people, promote your followers, and bully your opponents to your heart's content, but, meanwhile, Ireland will be gaining on you; your allies, grown exacting by triumph, will ask more than you dare, or even have to give; and the question will then arise, that the party who aspires to power must bid for it by further concession, and who is to vouch for the moderation of such demands, or what limit will there be to them? I see a train of such evils in the vista; and although I neither pretend to think our domestic legislature safe nor faultless, I think the dangers we have before us are even greater than such as would spring from an Irish Parliament."

Lord Netherby listened with great impatience—as perhaps the reader may have done also—to this declaration of the Knight's views, and was about to reply, when suddenly a cheer from some country people, stationed on a rocky height at a short distance, drew all eyes towards the valley, where now the hounds were seen in full cry, three horsemen alone following. One of these was the huntsman, Lionel another, the third was in plain clothes, and not known to any of the party. He was mounted on a powerful horse, and, even at that distance, could be seen to manage him with the address of a perfect rider. The rest of the field were far behind, some still standing on the verge of a mountain torrent, which appeared to have formed the obstacle to the run, and into which more than one seemed to have fallen.

Groups were gathered here and there along the bank, and dismounted horses galloped wildly to and fro, showing that the catastrophes had been numerous. While Lord Netherby looked with some alarm at the fearful chasm which had arrested all but three out of the entire field, the Knight followed Lionel with anxious eyes, as he led over the most desperate line of country in the west.

"I never knew a fox take that line but once," said Darcy, pointing to a wide expanse of bleak country, which stretched away to the base of the great mountain of Nephin. "I was a child at the time, but I remember the occurrence well: horse, men, and hounds tailed off one by one, some sorely injured, others dead beat, for the fellow was a most powerful dog-fox, and ran straight ahead for thirty-four miles of a desperate country. The following morning, at a little after daybreak, the fox was seen in a half trot near Ballycroy, still followed by two of the dogs, and he lived many years afterwards as a pensioner at the abbey; the dogs were never worth anything from that day."

While the Knight related this anecdote, the hounds and the hunters were gradually receding from view; and although, at intervals, some thought they could catch glimpses of them, at last they disappeared altogether.

"I am sorry, Helen," said the Knight, "that our visitors should hav been so unfortunate in their sport."

"I am more grieved to think that Lionel should follow over such a country," said Lord Netherby.

"He's well mounted, my Lord; and though many would call him a reckless rider, he has as much judgment as he has daring. I am tolerably easy about him."

Helen did not seem so confident as her father; and as for Mrs. Somerville, she was considerably paler than usual, and managed her mettlesome horse with far less than her customary address.

As well to meet their friends who were thrown out, as to show some of the scenery of the coast, the Knight proposed they should retrace their steps for a short distance, and take a view of the bay on their way back to the abbey. Leaving them, therefore, to follow their route, and not delaying our reader by an account of the various excuses of the dicomfited, or the banterings of Tom Nolan, we will turn to the wide plain, where, still in full cry, the dogs pursued their game.

The Knight had not exaggerated when calling it a dreadful country to ride over; yawning trenches, deep enough to engulph horse and rider, were cut in the bog, and frequently so close together, that, in clearing one, a few strides more presented another; the ground itself, only in part reclaimed, was deep and heavy, demanding great strength both of horse and horseman. Through this dangerous and intricate track the fox serpentined and wound his way with practised cunning, while at every turning some unlucky hound would miss his spring, or lose his footing in the slippery soil, and their cries could be heard far over the plain, as they struggled in vain to escape from a deep trench. It was in such an endeavour that a hound was catching at the bank with his fore-legs, as the huntsman dashed forward to take the leap; the horse suddenly taking fright, swerved, and, before he could recover, the frail ground gave way, and the animal plunged headlong down, fortunately flinging his rider over the head on the opposite bank.

"All safe, Bob!" cried Lionel, as he turned in his saddle. But he had no time for more, for the strange rider was fast nearing on him, and the chase had now become a trial of speed and skill. By degrees they emerged from this unsafe tract and gained the grass country, where high ditches and stone walls presented a more fair, but scarcely less dangerous kind of fencing. Here the stranger made an effort to pass Lionel and take the lead, and more than once they took their leaps exactly side by side.

As they rode along close to each other, Lionel from time to time caught glimpses of his companion, who was a strong-built man of five-and-thirty, frank and fresh-looking, but clearly not of the rank of gentleman. His horse was a powerful thorough-bred, with more bone than is usually found in Irish breeding, and trained to perfection.

"Now, sir," said the stranger, "we're coming near the Crumpawn river; that line of mist yonder is over the torrent. I warn you, the leap is a big one."

Lionel turned a haughty glance towards the man, for there was a tone of assumed superiority in the words he could ill brook. That instant, however, his eyes were directed to the front, where the roaring of a mountain stream mingled with the sharp cry of the hounds, as they struggled in the torrent, or fell back in their efforts to climb the steep bank.

"Ride him fairly at it—no flinching—and d—me if I care what your father was, I'll say you're a gentleman."

Lionel bit his lip almost through with passion; and had the occasion permitted, the heavy stroke of his whip had fallen on a very different quarter from his horse's flank, but he never uttered a word.

"Badly done! Never punish your horse at the stride!" said the fellow, who seemed bent on provoking him.

Lionel bounded in his saddle at this taunt on his riding; but there was no time for bandying words of anger; the roar of rushing water, and the misty foam, proclaimed the torrent near.

"The best man is first over!" shouted the stranger, as he rushed at the terrific chasm. Lionel dashed forward; so close were they they could have touched; when, with a wild cheer, the stranger gave his horse a tremendous cut, and the animal bounded from the earth like a stag, and, soaring over the mad torrent, descended lightly on the sward beyond.

Lionel had lifted his horse at the very same instant, but the treacherous bank gave way beneath the animal's fore-legs; he struggled dreadfully to regain his footing, and, half rearing and half backing, tried to retire, but the effort was in vain, the slippery earth carried him with it, and down both horse and rider came into the stream.

"Keep his head to the current, and sit steady!" shouted the stranger, who now watched the struggle with breathless eagerness. "Well done! well done!—don't press him, he'll do it himself."

The counsel was wise, for the noble animal needed neither spur nor whip, but breasted the white torrent with vigorous effort, sometimes plunging madly above, and again sinking, all save the head, beneath the flood. At last they reached the side, and the strong beast, with one bold spring, placed his fore-legs on the high bank. This was the most dangerous moment, for, unable to follow with his hind-legs, he stood opposed to the whole force of the current, that threatened every instant to engulph him. Lionel's efforts were tremendous: he lifted, he spurred, he strained, he shouted, but all in vain; the animal, worn out by exertion, faltered, and would have fallen back, when the stranger, springing from his saddle, leaned over the bank, and, seizing Lionel by the collar, jerked him from his horse. The beast, relieved of the weight, at once rallied and bounded up the bank, where Lionel now found himself, stunned, but not senseless.

"Let them say what they like," muttered the stranger, as he stood over him, "your're a devilish fine young fellow! D—me if I'll ever think so much about good blood again!"

Lionel was too weak and too much exhausted to reply, and even his fingers could scarcely close upon the whip he tried to grasp yet, for all that, the stranger's insolence sickened him to the very heart. Pride of race was the strongest feeling of his nature, and this fellow seemed determined to outrage it at every turn.

"Here, take a pull at this; you'll be all right presently," said the man, as he presented a little leather flask to the youth's lips. But Lionel repulsed the offer rudely, and turned his head away. "The more fool you!" said he, coarsely; "your grandfather mixed many a worse-flavoured one, and charged more for it;" and, so saying, he emptied the measure at a draught.

Lionel pondered on the words for some seconds, and suddenly the thought occurred to him that the stranger had mistaken him for another. "Ah! I see it all now!" thought he, and he turned his head to undeceive him, when, what was his surprise, as he looked up, to see that the fellow was gone. Mounted on his own horse, he was leading Lionel's by the bridle, and, at a smart trot, moving down the glen.

The young man sprang to his feet and shouted aloud; he even tried to follow him, but both efforts were fruitless. At the turn of the road the man halted, and, looking round, waved his hat as in sign of adieu; then, moving forward, disappeared, while Lionel, his passion giving way to his sense of the absurdity of the whole adventure, burst into a fit of hearty laughter.

"I'll be laughed at to the day of my death about this," thought he, as he turned his steps to seek the path homeward on foot.

It was late in the evening when Lionel reached the abbey. The guests had for the most part left the dinner-room, and were dropping by twos and threes into the drawing-room, when he made his appearance in the midst of them, splashed and travel-stained from head to foot.

A burst of merry laughter rang out as they beheld his torn habiliments and mud-coloured dress, in which none joined more heartily than the Knight himself, as he called aloud, "Well, Lionel, did you kill him boy, or run him to earth below Nephin?"

"By Jove, sir! if old Carney is safe, I think nobody has been killed to-day."

"Well, Bob is all right, he came back three hours ago; he has lamed Scaltheen, but she'll get over it."

"But your own adventures," interposed Lord Netherby, "for so they ought to be, judging from the state of your toilet. Let us hear them."

"Yes, by all means," added Beauclerk; "the huntsman says that the last he saw of you was riding by the side of some one in green, with three of the pack in front, the rest tailed off, and himself in a bog-hole."

"But there was no one in green in the field," said Crofton, "at least I did not see any one riding except the red-coats."

"Let us not be too critical about the colour of the dress," said Lord Netherby; "I am sure it would puzzle any of us to pronounce on the exact hue of Lionel's at this moment."

"Well, Lionel, will you decide it?" said the Knight; "is the green man apocryphal, or not?"

"I'll decide nothing," said Lionel, "till I get something to eat. Any one that wishes to hear my exploits must come into the dinner-room;" and, so saying, he arose and walked into the parlour, where, under Tate's superintendence, a little table was already spread for him beside the fire. To the tempting fare before him the young man devoted all the energy of a hunter's appetite, regardless of the crowd who had followed him from the drawing-room, and stood in a circle around him.

Many were the jests, and sharp the raillery, on his singular appearance, and certainly it presented a most ludicrous contrast with the massive decorations of the table at which he sat, and the full dress of the party around him.

"I remember," said Lord Netherby, "seeing the King of France—when such a functionary existed—eat his dinner in public on the terrace of Versailles, but I confess, great as was my admiration of the monarch's powers, I think Lionel exceeds them."

"Another leg?" said Beauclerk, who, with knife and fork in hand, performed the duty of carver.

"Why don't you say another turkey?" said Nolan; then turning to Mrs. Somerville, he added, "I am sure that negus is perfect."

The pretty widow, who had been contributing, as she thought unobserved, to Lionel's comfort, blushed deeply, and Lionel, at last roused from his apathy, said, "I am ready now, ladies and gentlemen all, to satisfy every reasonable demand upon your curiosity. But first, where is Mr. Beecham O'Reilly?"

"He went home," said the Knight; "he resisted all my efforts to detain him to dinner."

"Perhaps he only came over to sell that horse," said Nolan, in a half whisper.

"I wish I had bought him, with all my heart," said Lionel.

"Do you like him so much," said the Knight, with a meaning smile.

"I sincerely hope you do," said Lord Netherby, "for he is yours already—at least, if you will do me the honour to accept him; I often hoped to have mounted you one day——"

"I accept him, my Lord," interposed Lionel, "most willingly and most gratefully. You have, literally speaking, mounted me 'one day,' and I very much doubt if I ever mount the same animal another."

"What! is he lame?—or staked?—did he break down?—is he a devil to ride?" broke from several of the party.

"Not one of all these; but if you'll bestow five minutes' patience on me I'll perhaps inform you of a mode of being unhorsed, novel, at least, to most fox-hunters." With this, Lionel narrated the conclusion of the run, the leap of the Crumpawn river, and the singular departure of his companion at the end.

"Is this a practical joke, Knight?" said Lord Netherby.

"I think so, my Lord; one of those admirable jests which the statutes record among their own Joe Millers."

"Then you suspect he was a robber?"

"I confess it looks very like it."

"I read the riddle otherwise," said Lionel; "the fellow, whoever he was, mistook me for somebody else, and there was evidently something more like a reprisal than a theft in the whole transaction."

"But you have really lost him?" said Beauclerk.

"When I assure you that I came home on foot, I hope that question is answered."

"By Jove! you have most singular ways of doing matters in this country," cried the Colonel; "but I suppose when a man is used to Ireland, he gets pretty much accustomed to hear of his horse being stolen away as well as the fox."

"Oh! we'll chance upon him one of these days yet," said the Knight; "I am half of Lionel's mind myself now—the thing does not look like a robbery."

"There's no end of the eccentricity of these people," muttered Lord Netherby to himself, "they can get into a towering passion, and become half mad about trifles, but they take a serious loss as coolly as possible." And with this reflection on national character he moved into the drawing-room, where soon afterwards the party repaired to talk over Lionel's adventure, with every turn that fancy or raillery could give it.

CHAPTER XXX.

BAGENAL DALY'S VISITORS.

It was at a late hour of a night, some days after this event occurred, that Bagenal Daly sat closeted with Darcy's lawyer, endeavouring, by deep and long thought, to rescue him from some at least of the perils that threatened him. Each day, since the Knight's departure, had added to the evil tidings of his fortune. While Gleeson had employed his powers of attorney to withdraw large sums from the banker's hands, no information could be had concerning the great loan he had raised from the London Company, nor was there to be found among the papers left behind him the bond passed to Hickman, and which he should have received had the money been paid. That such was the case Bagenal Daly firmly believed; the memorandum given him by Freney was corroborated by the testimony of the clerks in two separate banking-houses, who both declared that Gleeson drew these sums on the morning before he started for Kildare, and to one of Daly's rapid habits of judgment such evidence was quite conclusive. This view of the subject was, unhappily, not destined to continue undisturbed, for, on the very morning after the Knight's departure from Dublin came a formal letter from Hickman's solicitor, demanding payment of the interest on the sum of seventy-four thousand eight hundred and twenty pounds, odd shillings, at five per cent., owing by seven weeks, and accompanying which was a notice of foreclosure of the mortgage on the ensuing 17th of March, in case the full sum aforesaid were not duly paid.

To meet these demands Daly well knew Darcy had no disposable property; the large sums raised by Hickman, at a lower rate of interest, were intended for that purpose; and although he persisted in believing that this debt, at least, was satisfied, the lawyer's opinion was strongly opposed to that notion.

Mr. Bicknell was a shrewd man, deep not only in the lore of his professional knowledge, but a keen scrutiniser of motives, and a far-seeing observer of the world. He argued thus: Gleeson would never have parted with such a sum on the eve of his own flight; a day was of no consequence, he could easily have put off the payment to Hickman to the time of the American ship's sailing—why, then, hand over so large an amount, all in his possession? It was strange, of course, what had become of the money; but then they heard that his servant had made his escape. Why might not he have possessed himself of it after his master's suicide? Who was to interfere or prevent it? Besides, if he had paid Hickman, the bond would, in all likelihood, be forthcoming; to retain possession of it could have been no object with Gleeson; he had met with nothing but kind and friendly treatment from Darcy, and was not likely to repay him by an act of useless, gratuitous cruelty.

As to the testimony of the bank clerks, it was as applicable to one view of the case as the other. Gleeson would, of course, draw out everything at his disposal; and although the sums tallied with those in the memorandum, that signified little, as they were the full amount in each banker's hands to the Knight's credit. Lastly, as to the memorandum, it was the only real difficulty in the case; but that paper might have been in Gleeson's possession, and in the course of business discussion either might have been dropped inadvertently, or have been given to Hickman as explaining the moneys already prepared for his acceptance.

Mr. Bicknell's reasonings were confirmed by the application of Hickman's solicitors, who were men of considerable skill and great reputed caution. "Harris and Long make no such mistakes as this, depend upon that, sir; they see their case very clearly, or would never adventure on such an application."

"D—n their caution! The question is not of their shrewdness."

"Yes, but it is, though; we are weighing probabilities, let us see to which side the balance inclines. Would they serve notice of foreclosure, not knowing whether or not we had the receipt in our possession? That is the whole matter."

"I don't pretend to say what they would do, but I know well what I should."

"And pray what may that be?"

"Hold possession of the abbey, stand fast by the old walls—call in the tenantry—and they are ready to answer such a call at a moment, if need be—and while I proclaimed to the wide world by what right I resisted, I'd keep the place against any force they dared to bring. These are ticklish times, Bicknell; the Government have just cheated this country—they'd scarcely risk the hazard of a civil war for an old usurer—old Hickman would be left to his remedies in Banco or Equity, and who knows what might turn up one day or other to strengthen the honest cause?"

"I scarcely concur in your suggestion, sir."

"How the devil should you? There are neither declarations to draw, nor affidavits to swear, no motions, nor rules, nor replies, no declarations, no special juries! No, Bicknell, I never suspected your approval of my plan. It would not cost a single skin of parchment."

Though Daly spoke this sarcasm bitterly, it produced no semblance of irritation in the man of law, who was composedly occupied in perusing a document before him.

"I have made memoranda," said Bicknell, "of certain points for counsel's opinion, and as soon as we can obtain some information as to the authenticity of young Darcy's signature, we shall see our way more clearly. The case is not only a complicated but a gloomy one; our antagonists are acute and wealthy, and I own to you the prospect is far from good."

"The better counsel mine," said Daly, sternly; "I have little faith in the justice that hangs upon the intelligence of what you facetiously call twelve honest men; methinks the world is scarcely so well supplied with the commodity that they are sure to answer the call of the sheriff. It is probable, however, nay, it is more than probable, Darcy will be of your mind, and reject my advice; if so, there is nothing for it but the judge and jury, and he will be despoiled of his property by the law of the land."

Bicknell knew too well the eccentric nature of Daly's character, in which no feature was more prominent than his hatred of everything like the recognised administration of the law, to offer him any opposition, and merely repeating his previous determination to seek the advice of able counsel, he took his leave.

"There is some deep mystery in this business," said Daly to himself, as he paced the room alone; "Bicknell is right in saying that Gleeson would not have committed an act of unnecessary cruelty, nor, if he had paid the money, would he have failed to leave the bond among his papers. Every circumstance of this fellow's flight is enveloped in doubt, and Freney, the only man who appears to have suspected his intention, by some mischance is not now to be found—Sandy has not succeeded in meeting with the boy, notwithstanding all his efforts. What can this be owing to? What machinery is at work here? Have the Hickmans their share in this?" Such were the broken sentences he muttered, as, in turn, suspicions tracked each other in his mind.

Daly was far too rash, and too impetuous in temper, to be well qualified for an investigation of so much difficulty. Unable to weigh probabilities with calmness, he was always the victim of his own prejudices in favour of certain things and people, and to escape from the chaotic trouble of his own harassed thoughts, he was ever ready to adopt some headlong and desperate expedient, in preference to the quieter policy of more patient minds.

"Yes, faith," said he, "my plan is the best after all, and who knows but by showing the bold front we may reduce old Hickman's pretensions, or at least make a compromise with him. There are plenty of arms and ammunition—eight stout fellows would hold the inner gate tower against a battalion—we could raise the country from Murrisk to Killery Harbour, and one gun fired from the Boat Quay would bring the fishermen from Clare Island and Achill to the rescue—we'd soon make a signal they'd recognise, old Hickman's house, with all its porticoes and verandahs, would burn like tinder. If they are for law, let them begin then."

The door opened as he spoke these words, and Sandy entered cautiously. "There is a countryman without wha says he's come a long way to see your honour, and maun see you this night."

"Where from?"

"Fra' the west, I think, for he said the roads were heavy down in them parts."

"Let him come in," said Daly; and, with his hands crossed behind his back, he continued to walk the room. "Some poor fellow for a renewal of his lease, or an abatement, or something of that kind—they'll never learn that I'm no longer the owner of that estate that still bears my name, and they cling to me as though I had the power to assist them, when I'm defenceless for myself. Well, what is it? Speak out, man—what do you want with me?"

The individual to whom this question was addressed stood with his back to the door, which he had cautiously shut close on entering, but, instead of returning an answer to the question, he cast a long and searching glance around the room, as if to ascertain whether any other person was in it. The apartment was large, and being dimly lighted, it took some time to assure him that they were alone, but when he had so satisfied himself, he walked slowly forward into the light, and throwing open his loose coat of grey frieze, exhibited the well-known figure of Freney the robber.

"What, Freney!—the man of all Ireland I wish to see."

"I thought so, sir," said the other, wiping his forehead with his hand, for he was flushed and heated, and seemed to have come off a long journey. "I know you sent for me, but I was unable to meet your messenger, and I can seldom venture to send that young villain Jemmy into the capital—the police are beginning to know him, and he'll be caught one of these days."

"You weren't in Kildare, then?" said Daly.

"No, sir, I was in the far west, down in Mayo; I had a little business in Ballina a short time back, and some fellow who knew me, and thought the game a safe one, stole my brown horse out of the inn-stable, in the broad noonday, and sold him at the fair green at Ballinasloe. When I tell you that he was the best animal I ever crossed, I needn't say what the loss was to me—the nags you saw were broken-down hackneys in comparison—he was strong in bone and untiring, and I kept him for the heavy country around Boyle and down by Longford. It is not once, nor twice, but a dozen times, Matchlock has saved me from a loop and a leap in the air, but the rascal that took him well knew the theft was safe—Freney, the highway man, could scarcely lodge informations with a magistrate."

"And you never could hear traces of him?"

"Yes, that I did, but it cost me time and trouble too. I found that he was twice sold within one week. Dean Harris bought him, and sold him the day after." Here Freney gave a low cunning laugh, while his eyes twinkled with malignant drollery.

"He didn't think as highly of him as you did, Freney?"

"Perhaps he hadn't as good reason," said the robber, laughing. "He was riding home from an early dinner with the Bishop, and as he was cantering along the side of the road, a chaise with four horses came tearing past; Matchlock, true to his old instinct, but not knowing who was on his back, broke into a gallop, and in half a dozen strides brought the Dean close up to the chaise window, when the traveller inside sent a bullet past his ear, that very nearly made a vacancy in the best living of the diocese. As I said, sir, the Dean had had enough of him; he sold him the next morning, and that day week he was bought by a young fellow in the west, whom I found out to be a grandson of old Hickman."

"Was he able to ride a horse like this?" said Daly, doubtfully.

"Ride him?—ay; and never a man in the province brought a beast to a leap with a lighter hand, and a closer seat in the saddle. We were side by side for three miles of a stiff country, and I don't believe I'm much of a coward at any rate, I set very little value on my neck; but I'll tell you what, sir, he pushed me hard."

"How was this, then? Had you a race together?"

"It was something very like it, sir," said Freney, laughing; "for when I reached Westport, I heard that young O'Reilly was to ride a new brown horse that day with the hounds, and a great hunt was expected, to show some English gentlemen who were staying at Gwynne Abbey. So I went off early to Hooley's Forge, near the cross-roads, to see the meet, and look out for my man. I didn't want any one to tell me which he was, for I'd know Matchlock at half a mile distance. There he was, in splendid condition too, and looking as I never saw him look before; by my conscience, Mr. Daly, there's a wide difference between the life of a beast in the stables of a county member, and one that has to stretch his bones in the shealing of such as myself. My plan was to go down to the cover, and the moment the fox broke away, to drive a bullet through my horse's head, and be off as hard as I could; for, to tell you the truth, it was spite more than the value of him was grieving me; so I took my own horse by the bridle, and walked down to where they were all gathered. I was scarcely there when the dogs gave tongue, and away they went—a grand sight it was, more than a hundred red coats, and riding close every man of them. Just then, up comes Matchlock, and takes the fence into the field where I was standing, a stone wall and a ditch, his rider handling him elegantly, and with an easy smile, sitting down in his saddle as if it was child's play. Faith, I couldn't bring myself to fire the shot, partly for the sake of the horse, more too, maybe, for the sake of the rider. 'I'll go a bit beside him,' said I to myself, for it was a real pleasure to me to watch the way how both knew their business well. I'm making a long story of it, but the end of it was this: I took the Crumpawn river just to dare him, and divil a bit but he fell in—no fault of his, but the bank was rotten—and down they went; the young fellow had a narrow escape of it, but he got through it at last, and, as he lay on the grass more dead than alive, I saw Matchlock grazing just close to me—temptations are bad things, Mr. Daly, particularly when a man has never trained himself off them—so I slipped the bridle over his head, and rode away with him beside me."

"Carried him off?"

"Clean and clever; he's at the hall-door this minute, and by the same token, sixty-four miles he has covered this day."

"There's only one part of the whole story surprises me; it is that this fellow should have ridden so boldly and so well. I know such courage is often no more than habit; yet even that lower quality of daring I never should have given him credit for. Was he hurt by his fall?"

"Stunned, perhaps, but nothing the worse."

"Well, well, enough of him. I wanted to see you, Freney, to learn anything you may know of this fellow Gleeson's flight. It's a sad affair for my friend, the Knight of Gwynne."

"So I've heard, sir. It's bad enough for myself, too."

"For you! He was not your man of business, was he?" said Daly, with a sly laugh.

"No, sir, I generally manage my money matters myself; but he happened to have a butler, one Garrett by name, who betted smartly on the turf, and played a little with the bones besides. He was a steady going chap, that knew a thing or two, but honest enough in booking up when he lost; he borrowed two hundred from me on the very day they started; he owed me nearly three besides, and I never saw him since. They say that when his master jumped overboard, Jack Garrett laid hands on all his property, and sailed for America, but I don't believe it, sir."

"Well, but, Freney, you may believe it, for I was the means of an investigation at Liverpool, in which the fact transpired; and the name of John Garrett was entered in the ship-agent's books. I read it there myself."

"No matter for that, he dared not venture into the States. I know something of Jack's doings among the Yankees, and depend upon it, Mr. Daly, he's not gone; it's only a blind to stop pursuit."

Daly shook his head dubiously, for having satisfied himself of Garrett's escape when at Liverpool, he felt annoyed at any discredit attaching to what he deemed his own discovery.

"Take my word for it, Mr. Daly, I'm right this time; you cannot think what an advantage a man like me possesses in guessing at the way another rogue would play his game. Why, sir, I know every turn and double such a fellow as Garrett would make. Now, I'd wager Matchlock against a car-horse, that he has not left England, and I'd take an even bet he'll be at the Spring Meeting at Doncaster."

"This may be all as you say, Freney," said Daly, after a pause, "and yet I see no reason to suppose it can interest me or my friend either. He might know something of Gleeson's affairs, he might, perhaps, be able to tell something of the payment of that sum at Kildare—if so——"

"If so," interrupted Freney, "money would buy the secret; at all events, I'm determined he shall not escape me so easily. I'll follow the fellow to the very threshold of Newgate but I'll have my own—it is for that purpose I'm on my way now. A fishing-boat will sail from Howth by to-morrow's tide, and land me somewhere on the Welsh coast, and, if I can serve you, why, it's only doing two jobs at the same time. What are the points you are anxious to discover?"

Daly reflected for a few moments, and then with distinctness detailed the several matters on which he desired information, not only regarding the reasons of Gleeson's embarrassments, but the nature of his intimacy with old Hickman, of which he entertained deep suspicions.

"I see it all," said Freney. "You think that Gleeson was in league with the Doctor?"

Daly nodded.

"That was my own notion, too. Ah, sir, if I'd only the King's pardon in my pocket this night, and the power of an honest man for one month, I'd stake my head on it, but I would have the whole mystery as clear as water."

"You'll want some money, Freney," said Daly, as he turned to the table, and, taking up a key, unlocked the writing-case. "I'm not as rich just now as a Member of Parliament might be after such a Bill as the Union, but I hope this may be of some service;" and he took a fifty-pound note from the desk to hand it to him, but Freney was gone. He had slipped noiselessly from the room; the bang of the hall-door was heard at the instant, and immediately after the tramp of a horse, as he trotted down the street.

"The world all over!" said Daly to himself. "If the man of honour and integrity has his flaws and defects, even fellows like that have their notions of principle and delicacy too. Confound it! mankind will never let me love or hate them."

CHAPTER XXXI.

"A LEAVE-TAKING."

At Gwynne Abbey, time sped fast and pleasantly; each day brought its own enjoyments, and of the Knight's guests there was not one who did not in his heart believe that Maurice Darcy was the very happiest man in the kingdom.

Lord Netherby, the frigid courtier, felt, for the first time, perhaps, in his life, how much cordiality can heighten the pleasures of social intercourse, and how the courtesy of kind feeling can add to the enjoyments of refined and cultivated tastes. Lady Eleanor had lost nothing of the powers of fascination for which her youth had been celebrated, and there was, in the very seclusion of her life, that which gave the charm of novelty to her remarks on people and events. The Knight himself, abounding in resources of every kind, was a companion the most fastidious or exacting could not weary of, and as for Helen, her captivations were acknowledged by those who, but a week before, would not have admitted the possibility of any excellence that had not received the stamp of London approval.

Crofton could never expatiate sufficiently on the delights of an establishment which, with the best cook, the best cellar, and the best stable, called not upon him for the exercise of the small talents and petty attentions by which his invitations to great houses were usually purchased; while the younger men of the party agreed in regarding their friend Lionel as the most to be envied of all their acquaintance.

Happiness, perhaps, shines more brightly by reflected light; certainly Lionel Darcy never felt more disposed to be content with the world, and, although not devoid of a natural pride at exhibiting to his English friends the style of his father's house and habits, yet was he far more delighted at the praises he heard on every side of the Knight himself. Maurice Darcy possessed that rarest of all gifts, the power of being a delightful companion to younger men, without ever detracting in the slightest degree from the most rigid tone of good taste and good principle. The observation may seem an illiberal one, but it is unhappily too true, that even among those who from right feeling would be incapable of anything mean or sordid, there often prevails a laxity in expression, and a libertinism of sentiment very far remote from their real opinions, and, consequently, such as flatter this tendency are frequently the greatest favourites among them. The Knight, not less from high principle than pride, rejected every such claim; his manly joyous temperament needed no aids to its powers of interesting and amusing; his sympathies went with young men in all their enthusiasm for sport; he gloried in the exuberance of their high spirits, and felt his own youth come back in the eager pleasure with which he listened to their plans of amusement.

It may well be believed with what sorrow to each the morning dawned that was to be the last of their visit. These last times are sad things! They are the deaths of our affections and attachments, for assuredly the memory we retain of past pleasures is only the unreal spirit of a world we are to know of no more. Not alone the records of friends lost or dead, but of ourselves, such as we once were, and can never again be: of a time when hope was fed by credulity, and could not be exhausted by disappointment. They must have had but a brief experience of life who do not see in every separation from friends the many chances against their meeting again, least of all, of meeting unchanged with all around them as they parted.

These thoughts, and others like them, weighed heavily on the hearts of those who now assembled for the last time beneath the roof of Gwynne Abbey.

It was in vain that Lionel suggested various schemes of pleasure for the day, the remembrance that it was the last was ever present, and while every moment seemed precious, there was a fidgety impatience to be about and stirring, mingled with a desire to loiter and linger over the spot so associated with pleasant memories.

A boating party to Clare Island, long planned and talked over, could find now no advocates. All Lionel's descriptions of the shooting along the rocky shores of the bay were heard unheeded; every one clung to the abbey, as if to enjoy to the very last the sense of home happiness they had known there. Even those less likely to indulge feelings of attachment were not free from the depressing influence of a last day. Nor were these sentiments confined to the visitors only. Lady Eleanor experienced a return of her former spirits in her intercourse with those whose habits and opinions all reminded her of the past, and would gladly have prolonged a visit so full of pleasant recollections. The request was, however, in vain; the Earl was to be in Waiting early in the following week, Lionel's leave was only regimental, and equally limited, and each of the others had engagements and projects no less fixed and immutable.

In little knots of two and three they spent the day, wandering about from place to place, to take a last look of the great cliff, to visit for the last time the little wood path, whose every turning presented some new aspect of the bay and the shore. Lord Netherby attached himself to the Knight, devoting himself with a most laudable martyrdom to a morning in the farm-yard and the stable, where, notwithstanding all his efforts, his blunders betrayed how ill-suited were his habits to country life and its interests. He bore all, however, well and heroically, for he had an object in view, and that, with him, was always sufficient to induce any degree of endurance. Up to this moment he had scarcely enjoyed an opportunity of conversing with the Knight on the subject of politics. The few words they had exchanged at the cover side, were all that passed between them, and although they conveyed sentiments very remote from his own, he did not entirely despair of gaining over one who evidently was less actuated by party motives than impressed by the force of strong personal convictions.

"Such a man will, of course," thought the Earl, "be in the Imperial Parliament, and carry with him great influence on every question connected with Ireland: his support of the Ministry will be all the more valuable that his reputation is intact from every stain of corruption. To withdraw him from his own country by the seductions of London life, would not be easy but he may be attached to England by ties still more binding." Such were some of the reasonings which the wily Peer revolved in his mind, and to whose aid a fortunate accident had in some measure contributed.

"I believe I have never shown you our garden, my Lord," said the Knight, who, at last taking compassion on the suffering complaisance of the Earl, proposed this change. "The season is scarcely the most flattering but we are early in this part of Ireland. What say you if we walk thither?"

The plan was at once approved of, and after a short circuit through a shrubbery, they crossed a large orchard, and ascending a gentle slope, they entered the garden, which rose in successive terraces behind the abbey, and commanded a wide prospect over the bay and the sea beyond it. Lord Netherby's admiration was not feigned, as he turned his eyes around and beheld the extent and beauty of that cultivated scene, which, in the brightness of a spring morning, glittered like a gem on the mountain's side. The taste alone was not the engrossing thought of his mind, but he reflected on the immense expenditure such a caprice must have cost, terraced as the ground was into the very granite rock, and the earth all supplied artificially. The very keeping these parterres in order was a thing of no mean cost. Not all the terrors of his own approaching fate could deprive Darcy of a sense of pride as he watched the expression of the Earl's features, surprise and wonder depicted in every lineament.

"How extensive the park is," said the courtier at length, half ashamed, as it seemed, of giving way to his amazement; "are those trees yonder within your grounds?"

"Yes, my Lord; the wood at that point where you see the foam splashing up is our limit in that direction, on this side we stretch away somewhat further."

"Whose property, then, have we yonder, where I see the village?"

"It is all the Gwynne estate," said the Knight, with difficulty repressing the sigh that rose as he spoke.

"And the town?"

"The town also. The worthy monks took a wide circuit, and, by all accounts, did not misuse their wealth. I sadly fear, my Lord, their successors were not as blameless."

"A noble possession, indeed!" said the Earl, half aloud, and not attending to Darcy's remark. "Are you certain, my dear Knight, that you have made your political influence at all commensurate with the amount of either your property or your talents? An English gentleman with an estate like this, and ability such as yours, might command any position he pleased."

"In other words, my Lord, he might barter his independence for the exercise of a precarious power, and, in ceasing to dispense the duties of a landed proprietor, he might become a very considerable ingredient in a party."

"I hope you do not deem the devoir of a country gentleman incompatible with the duties of a statesman?"

"By no means; but I greatly regret the gradual desertion of social influence in the search after political ascendancy. I am not for the working of a system that spoils the gentry, and yet does not make them statesmen?"

"And yet the very essence of our Constitution is to connect the power of Government with the possession of landed property."

"And justly so, too; none other offers so little in return as a mere speculation. None is so little exposed to the casualties which affect every other kind of wealth. The legitimate influence of the landed gentry is the safeguard of the State; but if, by the attractions of power, the flatteries of a Court, or the seductions of Party, you withdraw them from the rightful sphere of its exercise, you reduce them to the level of the Borough members, without, perhaps, their technical knowledge or professional acquirements. I am for giving them a higher position—the heritage of the bold Barons, from whom they are descended; but to maintain this, they must live on their own estates, dispense the influences of their wealth and their morals in their own native districts, be the friend of the poor man, the counsellor of the misguided, the encourager of the weak; know and be known to all around, not as the corrupt dispensers of Government patronage, but the guardians of those whose rights are in their keeping for defence and protection. I would have them with their rightful influence in the Senate; an influence which should preponderate in both Houses. Their rank and education would be the best guarantee for the safety and wisdom of their counsels, their property the best surety for the permanence of the institutions of the State. Suddenly acquired wealth can scarcely be entrusted with political power; it lacks the element of prudent caution, by which property is maintained as well as accumulated; it wants also the prestige of antiquity as a claim to respect; and, legislate as you will, men will look back as well as forward."

Lord Netherby made no reply; he thought the Knight, perhaps, was venting his own regrets at the downfal of a political ascendancy he wished to see vested in men of his own station; a position they had long enjoyed, and which, in some respects, had placed them above the law.

"You lay more store by such ties, Knight," said the Earl, in a low, insinuating voice, "than we are accustomed to do. Blood and birth have suffered less admixture with mere wealth here, than with us."

"Perhaps we do, my Lord," said Darcy, smiling; "it is the compensation for our poverty. Unmixed descent is the boast of many who have retained nothing of their ancestors save the name."

"But you yourself can scarcely be an advocate for the maintenance of these opinions: this spirit of clan and chieftainship is opposed not only to progress, but to liberty."

"I have given the best proof of the contrary," said Darcy, laughing, ' by marrying an Englishwoman; a dereliction, I assure you, that cost me many a warm supporter in this very country."

"Indeed! By the way, I am reminded of a subject I wished to speak of to you, and which I have been hesitating whether I should open with my cousin Eleanor or yourself: the moment seems, however, propitious; may I broach it?"

Darcy bowed courteously, and the other resumed:

"I will be brief, then. Young Beauclerk, a friend of your son Lionel, has been, as every one young and older than himself must be, greatly taken by the charms of Miss Darcy. Brief as the acquaintance here has been, the poor fellow is desperately in love, and, while feeling how such an acknowledgment might prejudice his chance of success on so short an intimacy, he cannot leave this without the effort to secure for his pretensions a favourable hearing hereafter. In fact, my dear Knight, he has asked of me to be his intercessor with you—not to receive him as a son-in-law, but to permit him to pay such attentions as, in the event of your daughter's acceptance may enable him to make the offer of his hand and fortune. I need not tell you that in point of position and means he is unexceptionable: a very old Baronetcy—not one of these yesterday creations made up of State Physicians and Surgeons in Ordinary—an estate of above twelve thousand a year. Such are claims to look high with; but I confess I think he could not lay them at the feet of one more captivating than my fair Helen."

Darcy made no reply for several minutes; he pressed his hand across his eyes, and turned his head away, as if to escape observation; then, with an effort that seemed to demand all his strength, he said,

"This is impossible, my Lord. There are reasons—there are circumstances why I cannot entertain this proposition. I am not able to explain them—a few days more, and I need not trouble myself on that subject."

The evident agitation of manner the Knight displayed astonished his companion, who, while he forbore to ask more directly for its reason, yet gently hinted that the obstacles alluded to might be less stringent than Darcy deemed them.

Darcy shook his head mournfully, and Lord Netherby, though most anxious to divine the secret of his thoughts, had too much breeding to continue the subject.

Without any abruptness, which might have left an unpleasant impression after it, the polished courtier once more adverted to Beauclerk, but rather in a tone of regret for the youth's own sake than with any reference to the Knight's refusal.

"There was a kind of selfishness in my advocacy, Knight," said he, smiling. "I was—I am—very much depressed at quitting a spot where I have tasted more true happiness than it has been my fortune for many years to know, and I wish to carry away with me the reflection that I had left the germ of even greater happiness behind me; if Helen, however——"

"Hush!" said Darcy; "here she comes, with her mother."

"My dear Lady Eleanor," said Lord Netherby, "you have come to see me forget all the worldliness it has cost me a life to learn, and actually confess that I cannot tear myself away from the abbey."

"Well, my Lord," interposed Tom Nolan, who had just come up with a large walking party, "I suppose it's only ordering away the posters, and saying another day."

"No, no, by Jove!" cried Crofton; "my Lord is in Waiting, and I'm on duty."

While the groups now gathered together from different parts of the garden, Lord Netherby joined Beauclerk, who awaited him in a distant alley, and soon after the youth was seen returning alone to the abbey.

The time of bustle and leave-taking—that moment when many a false smile and merry speech ill conceals the secret sorrow—was come, and each after each spoke his farewell; and Lord Netherby kindly pledging himself to make Lionel's peace at the Horse Guards for an extended absence of some days, thus conferred upon Lady Eleanor the very greatest of favours.

"Our next meeting is to be in London, remember," said the Peer, in his blandest accents. "I stand pledged to show my countrymen that I have nothing extenuated in speaking of Irish beauty;—nay, Helen, it is my last time, forgive it."

"There they go," said Darcy, as he looked after the retiring equipages. "Now, Eleanor, and my dear children, come along with me into the library. I have long been struggling against a secret sorrow; another moment would be more than I could bear."

They turned silently towards the abbey, none daring, even by a look, to interrogate him whose sad accents foreboded so much of evil; yet as they walked they drew closer around him, and seemed even by that gesture to show that, come what might, they would meet their fortune boldly.

Darcy moved on for some minutes sunk in thought, but, as he ascended the wide steps of the terrace, appearing to read the motives of those who clung so closely to his side, he smiled sadly, and said, "Ay! I knew it well —in weal or woe—together!"

CHAPTER XXXII.

"SAD DISCLOSURES."

The vicissitudes of life are never more palpably displayed before us than when the space of a few brief hours has converted the scene of festivity and pleasure into one of gloom and sorrow, when the same silent witnesses of our joy should be present at our affliction. Thus was it now in the richly-adorned chambers of Gwynne Abbey, so lately filled with happy faces and resounding with pleasant voices—all was silent. In the court-yard, but a day before crowded with brilliant equipages and gay horsemen, the long shadows lay dark and unbroken, and the plash of the fountain was the only sound in the stillness. Over that wide lawn no groups on foot or horseback were to be seen; the landscape was fair and soft to look upon, the mild radiance of a spring morning beamed on the water and the shore, the fresh budding trees, and the tall towers; and the passing traveller who might have stopped to gaze upon that princely dwelling and its swelling woods, might have thought it an earthly paradise, and that they who owned it must needs be above worldly cares and afflictions.

The scene within the walls was very unlike this impression. In a darkened room, where the close-drawn curtains excluded every ray of sunshine, sat Helen Darcy by the bedside of her mother. Lady Eleanor had fallen asleep after a night of intense suffering, both of mind and body, and her repose even yet exhibited, in short and fitful starts, the terrible traces of an agony not yet subdued. Helen was pale as death, two dark circles of almost purple hue surrounded her eyes, and her cheeks seemed wasted—yet she had not wept. The overwhelming amount of misfortune had stunned her for a moment or two, but, recalled to active exertion by her mother's illness, she addressed herself to her task, and seemed to have no thought or care save to watch and tend her. It was only at last, when, wearied out by suffering, Lady Eleanor fell into a slumber, that Helen's feelings found their vent, and the tears rolled heavily along her cheek, and dropped one by one upon her neck.

Her sorrow was indeed great, for it was unalloyed by one selfish feeling; her grief was for those a thousand times more dear to her than herself, nor through all her affliction did a single thought intrude of how this ruin was also her own.

The Knight was in the library, where he had passed the night, lying down at short intervals to catch some moments' rest, and again rising to walk the room and reflect upon the coming stroke of fortune. Lionel had parted from him at a late hour, promising to go to bed, but unable to endure the gloom of his own thoughts in his chamber, he wandered out into the woods, and strolled on without knowing or caring whither, till day broke. The bodily exertion at length induced sleep, and after a few hours' deep repose he joined his father, with few traces of weariness or even sorrow.

It was not without a struggle on either side that they met on that morning, and as Darcy grasped his son's hand in both his own, his lip trembled, and his strong frame shook with agitation. Lionel's ruddy cheek and clear blue eye seemed to reassure the old man's courage, and after gazing on him steadfastly with a look where fatherly love and pride were blended, he said, "I see, my boy, the old blood of a Darcy has not degenerated—you are well to-day?"

"Never was better in my life," said Lionel, boldly; "and if I could only think that you, my mother, and Helen had no cause for sorrow, I'd almost say I never felt my spirits higher."

"My own brave-hearted boy," said Darcy, throwing his arms around the youth's neck, while the tears gushed from his eyes and a choking stopped his utterance.

"I see your letters have come," said Lionel, gently disengaging himself, and affecting a degree of calmness his heart was very far from feeling. "Do they bring us any news?"

"Nothing to hope from," said Darcy, sorrowfully. "Daly has seen Hickman's solicitors, and the matter is as I expected: Gleeson did not pay the bond debt; his journey to Kildare was, probably, undertaken to gain time until the moment of the American ship's sailing. He must have meditated this step for a considerable time, for it now appears that his losses in South America occurred several years back, though carefully screened from public knowledge. The man was a cold, calculating scoundrel, who practised peculation systematically and slowly; his resolve to escape was not a sudden notion—these are Bagenal Daly's impressions at least, and I begin to feel their force myself."

"Does Daly offer any suggestion for our guidance, or say how we should act?" said Lionel, far more eager to meet the present than speculate on either the past or the future.

"Yes; he gives us a choice of counsels, honestly confessing that his own advice meets little support or sympathy with the lawyers. It is to hold forcible possession of the abbey, to leave Hickman to his remedy by law, and to defy him when he has even got a verdict; he enumerates very circumstantially all our means of defence, and exhibits a very hopeful array of lawless probabilities in our favour. But this is a counsel I would never follow; it would not become one who has in a long life endeavoured to set the example among the people of obedience and observance to law to obliterate by one act of rashness and folly the whole force of his teaching. No, Lionel, we are clean-handed on this score, and if the lesson be a heavy one for ourselves, let it not be profitless for our poor neighbours. This is your own feeling too, my boy, I'm certain."

Lionel bit his lip, and his cheek grew scarlet; when, after a pause, he said, "And the other plan, what is that?"

"The renewed offer of his cottage on the northern coast, a lonely and secluded spot, where we can remain at least until we determine on something better."

"Perhaps that may be the wiser course," muttered the youth, half aloud; "my mother and Helen are to be thought of first. And yet, father, I cannot help thinking Daly's first counsel has something in it."

"Something in it! ay, Lionel, that it has—the whole story of our country's misery and degradation. The owner of the soil has diffused little else among the people than the licentious terror of his own unbridled passion; he has taught lawless outrage, when he should have inculcated obedience and submission. The corruption of our people has come from above downwards; the heavy retribution will come one day; and when the vices of the peasant shall ascend to the master the social ruin will be complete. To this dreadful consummation let us lend no aid. No, no, Lionel, sorrow may be lessened by time, but remorse is undying and eternal."

"I must leave the Guards at once," said the young man, pacing the room slowly, and endeavouring to speak with an air of calm composure, while every feature of his face betrayed the agitation he suffered; "an exchange will not be difficult to manage."

"You have some debts, too, in London; they must be cared for immediately."

"Nothing of any large amount; my horses and carriages when sold will more than meet all I owe. Have you formed any guess as to what income will be left you to live on?" said he, in a voice which anxiety made weak and tremulous.

"Without Daly's assistance I cannot answer that point; the extent of this fellow Gleeson's iniquity seems but half explored. The likelihood is, that your mother's jointure will be the utmost we can save from the wreck. Even that, however, will be enough for all we need, although from motives of delicacy on her part it was originally set down at a very small sum—not more than a thousand per annum."

A long silence now ensued. The Knight, buried in thought, sat with his arms crossed and his eyes bent upon the ground. Lionel leaned on the window-frame and looked out upon the lawn; nothing stirred, no sound was heard save the sharp ticking of the clock upon the mantelpiece, which marked with distinctness every second, as if reminding them of the fleeting moments that were to be their last beneath that roof.

"This is the 24th, if I remember aright," said Darcy, looking up at the dial; "at noon, to-day, we are no longer masters here."

"The Hickmans will scarcely venture to push matters to such extremities; an assurance that we are willing to surrender peaceable possession will, I trust, be sufficient to prevent the indecency of a rapid flight from our own house and home."

"There are legal forms of possession to be gone through, I believe," said the Knight, sorrowfully; "certain observances the law exacts, which would be no less painful for us to witness than the actual presence of our successors."

"Who can this be? I saw a carriage disappear behind the copse yonder. There it is again, coming along by the lake."

"Daly—Bagenal Daly, I hope and trust!" exclaimed Darcy, as he stood straining his eyes to catch the moving object.

"I think not; the horses do not look like posters. Heaven grant we have no visitors at such a time as this!"

The carriage, although clearly visible the moment before, was now concealed from view by an angle of the wood, nor would it again be in sight before reaching the abbey.

"Your mother's indisposition is reason sufficient not to receive them," said Darcy, almost sternly. "I would not continue the part I have played during the last week, no, not for an hour longer, to be assured of rescue from every difficulty. The duplicity went nigh to break my heart; ay, and it would have done so, or driven me mad, had the effort been sustained any further."

"You did not expect any one, did you?" asked Lionel, eagerly.

"Not one: there are a mass of letters with invitations and civil messages there on the table, but no proffered visits among them."

Lionel walked to the table and turned over the various notes which lay along with newspapers and pamphlets scattered about.

"Ay," muttered the Knight, in a low tone, "they read strangely now, these plans of pleasure and festivity, when ruin is so near us; the kind pressings to spend a week here, and a fortnight there. It reminds me, Lionel"—and here a smile of sad but sweet melancholy passed across his features—"it reminds me of the old story they tell of my grand-uncle Robert. He commanded the *Dreadnought*, under Drake, at Cape St. Vincent, and at the close of a very sharp action was signalled to come on board the Admiral's vessel to dinner. The poor *Dreadnought* was like a sieve, the sea running in and out through her shot holes, and her sails hanging like rags around her, her deck covered with wounded, and slippery with gore. Captain Darcy, however, hastened to obey the command of his superior, changed his dress, and ordered his boat to be manned; but this was no easy matter, there was scarcely a boat's crew to be had without taking away the men necessary to work the ship. The difficulty soon became more pressing, for a plank had suddenly sprung from a double-headed shot, and all the efforts of the pumps could not keep the vessel afloat, with a heavy sea rolling at the same time.

" 'The Admiral's signal is repeated, sir,' said the Lieutenant on duty.

" 'Very well, Mr. Hay; keep her before the wind,' was the answer.

" 'The ship is settling fast, sir,' said the master; 'no boat could live in that sea; they're all damaged by shot.'

" 'Signal the flag-ship,' cried out Darcy; 'signal the Admiral that I am ready to obey him, but we're sinking.'

" The bunting floated at the mast-head for a moment or two, but the waves were soon many fathoms over it, and the *Dreadnought* was never seen more."

" So it would seem," said Lionel, with a half bitter laugh, "we are not the first of the family who went down headforemost. But I hear a voice without. Surely old Tate is not fool enough to admit any one."

" Is it possible——" But before the Knight could finish, the old butler entered to announce Mr. Hickman O'Reilly. Advancing towards the Knight with a most cordial air, he seemed bent on anticipating any possible expression of displeasure at his unexpected appearance.

"I am aware, Knight," said he, in an accent the most soft and conciliating, 'how indelicate a visit from me at such a moment may seem, but if you accord me a few moments of private interview, I hope to dispel the unpleasant impression." He looked towards Lionel as he spoke, and though he smiled his blandest of all smiles, evidently hinted at the possibility of his leaving them alone together.

" I have no confidences apart from my son, sir," said Darcy, coldly.

" Oh, of course not—perfectly natural at Captain Darcy's age—such a thought would be absurd; still, there are circumstances which might possibly excuse my request—I mean——"

Lionel did not suffer him to finish the sentence, but turning abruptly round left the room, saying, as he went, " I have some orders to give in the stable, but I'll not go further away if you want me."

" Now, sir," said the Knight, haughtily, " we are alone, and not likely to be interrupted; may I ask as a great favour, that in any communication you may have to make, you will be as brief as consists with your object; for, to my truth, I have many things on my mind, and many important calls to attend to."

"In the first place, then," said Hickman, assuming a manner intended to convey the impression of perfect frankness and candour, "let me make a confession, which however humiliating to avow, would be still more injurious to hold in reserve. I have neither act nor part in the proceedings my father has lately taken respecting your mutual dealings. Not only that he has not consulted me, but every attempt on my part to ascertain the course of events, or mitigate their rigour, has been met by a direct, not unfrequently a rude, repulse." He waited at this pause for the Knight to speak, but a cold and dignified bow was all the acknowledgment returned. "This may appear strange and inexplicable in your eyes," said O'Reilly, who mistook the Knight's indifference for incredulity, "but perhaps I can explain."

"There is not the slightest necessity to do so, Mr. O'Reilly; I have no reason to doubt one word you have stated; for not only am I ignorant of what the nature and extent of the proceedings you allude to may be, but I am equally indifferent as to the spirit that dictates, or the number of advisers that suggest them; pardon me if I seem rude or uncourteous, but there are circumstances in life in which not to be selfish would be to become insensible; my present condition is, perhaps, one of them. A breach of trust on the part of one who possessed my fullest confidence has involved all, or nearly all, I had in the world. The steps by which I am to be deprived of what was once my own are, as regards myself, matters of comparative indifference; with respect to others"—here he almost faltered—"I hope they may be dictated by proper feeling and consideration."

"Be assured they shall, sir," said Mr. O'Reilly; and then, as if correcting a too hasty avowal, added, "but I have the strongest hopes that matters are not yet in such an extremity as you speak of. It is true, sir, I will not conceal from you, my father is not free from the faults of age; his passion for money-getting has absorbed his whole heart to the exclusion of many amiable and estimable traits; to enforce a legal right with him seems a duty, and not an option; and, I may mention here, that your friend, Mr. Daly, has not taken any particular pains towards conciliating him; indeed, he has scarcely acted a prudent part as regards you, by the unceasing rancour he has exhibited towards our family."

"I must interrupt you, sir," said the Knight, "and assure you that, while there are unfortunately but too many topics which could pain me at this moment, there is not one more certain to offend me than any reflection, even the slightest, on the oldest friend I have in the world."

Mr. O'Reilly denied the most remote intention of giving pain, and proceeded: "I was speaking of my father," said he, "and however unpleasant the confession from a son's lips, I must say that the legality of his acts is the extent to which they claim his observance. When his solicitors informed him that the interest was unpaid on your bond, he directed the steps to enforce the payment, and subsequently to foreclose the deed. These are, after all, mere preliminary proceedings, and in no way preclude an arrangement for a renewal."

"Such a proposition—let me interrupt you—such a proposition is wholly out of the question; the ruin that has cost us our house and home has spared nothing. I have no means by which I could anticipate the payment of so large a sum, nor is it either my intention or my wish to reside longer beneath this roof."

"I hope, sir, your determination is not unalterable; it would be the greatest affliction of my life to think that the loss to this county of its oldest family was even in the remotest degree ascribed to us. The Darcys have been the boast and pride of Western Ireland for centuries; our county would be robbed of its fairest ornament by the departure of those who hold a princely state, and derive a more than princely devotion among us."

"If our claims had no other foundation, Mr. O'Reilly, our altered circumstances would now obliterate them. To live here with diminished fortune——But I ask pardon for being led away in this manner—may I beg that you will now inform me to what peculiar circumstances I owe the honour of your visit?"

"I thought," said O'Reilly, insinuatingly, "that I had mentioned the difference of feeling entertained by my father and myself respecting certain proceedings at law."

"You are quite correct, you did so; but I may observe, without incivility, that however complimentary to your own sense of delicacy such a difference is, for me the matter has no immediate interest."

"Perhaps, with your kind permission, I can give it some," replied O'Reilly, drawing his chair close, and speaking in a low and confidential voice; "but, in order to let my communication have the value I would wish it, may I bespeak for myself a favourable hearing, and a kind construction on what I shall say? If by an error of judgment——"

"Ah!" said Darcy, sighing, while a sad smile dimpled his mouth—"ah! no man should be more lenient to such than myself."

As if reassured by the kindly tone of these few words, O'Reilly resumed: "Some weeks ago my father waited upon Lady Eleanor Darcy with a proposition, which, whether on its own merits, or from want of proper tact in his advocacy of it, met with a most unfavourable reception. It it not because circumstances have greatly altered in that brief interval—which I deeply regret to say is the case—that I dare to augur a more propitious hearing, but simply because I hope to show that in making it we were actuated by a spirit of honourable, if not of laudable ambition. The rank and position my son will enjoy in this county, his fortune and estate are such as to make any alliance, save with your family, a question of no possible pretension. I am well aware, sir, of the great disparity between a new house and one ennobled by centuries of descent. I have thought long and deeply on the interval that separates the rank of the mere country gentleman from the position of him who claims even higher station than nobility itself, but we live in changeful times; the Peerage has its daily accessions of rank, as humble as my own; its new creations are the conscripts drawn from wealth as well as distinction in arms or learning, and in every case the new generation obliterates the memory of its immediate origin. I see you agree with me; I rejoice to find it."

"Your observations are quite just," said Darcy, calmly, and O'Reilly went on:

"Now, sir, I would not only reiterate my father's proposal, but I would add to it what I hope and trust will be deemed no ungenerous offer, which is, that the young lady's fortune should be this estate of Gwynne Abbey, not to be endowed by her future husband, but settled on her by her father as her marriage portion. I see your meaning—it is no longer his to give, but we are ready to make it so; the bond we hold shall be thrown into the fire the moment your consent is uttered. We prefer a thousand times it should be thus, than that the ancient acres of this noble heritage should even for a moment cease to be the property of your house. Let me recapitulate a little——"

"I think that is unnecessary," said Darcy, calmly; "I have bestowed the most patient attention to your remarks, and have no difficulty in comprehending them. Have you anything to add?"

"Nothing of much consequence," said O'Reilly, not a little pleased by the favourable tone of the Knight's manner; "what I should suggest in addition is that my son should assume the name and arms of Darcy——"

The noise of footsteps and voices without at this moment interrupted the speaker, the door suddenly opened, and Bagenal Daly entered. He was splashed from head to foot, his high riding-boots stained with the saddle and the road, and his appearance vouching for a long and wearisome journey.

"Good morrow, Darcy," said he, grasping the Knight's hand with the grip of his iron fingers.—"Your servant, sir; I scarcely expected to see you here *so soon*."

The emphasis with which he spoke the last words brought the colour to O'Reilly's cheek, who seemed very miserable at the interruption.

"You came to take possession," continued Daly, fixing his eyes on him with a steadfast stare.

"You mistake, Bagenal," said the Knight, gently; "Mr. O'Reilly come with a very different object—one which I trust he will deem no breach of confidence or propriety in me if I mention it to you."

"I regret to say, sir," said O'Reilly, hastily, "that I cannot give my permission in this instance. Whatever the fate of the proposal I have made to you, I beg it to be understood as made under the seal of honourable secrecy."

Darcy bowed deeply, but made no reply.

"Confound me," cried Daly, "if I understand any compact between two such men as you as to require all this privacy, unless you were hardy enough to renew your old father's proposal for my friend's daughter, and now had modesty enough to feel ashamed of your own impudence."

"I am no stranger, sir, to the indecent liberties you permit your tongue to take," said Hickman, moving towards the door, "but this is neither the time nor place to notice them."

"So then I was right," cried Daly; "I guessed well the game you would play——"

"Bagenal," interposed the Knight, "I must stop this. Mr. Hickman is now beneath my roof——"

"Is he, faith?—not in his own estimation then. Why, his fellows are taking an inventory of the furniture at this very moment."

"Is this true, sir?" said Darcy, turning a fierce look towards O'Reilly, whose face became suddenly of an ashy paleness.

"If so," muttered he, "I can only assure you that it is without any orders of mine."

"How good," said Daly, bursting into an insolent laugh; "why, Darcy, when you meet with a fellow in your plantations with a gun in his hand and a lurcher at his heels, are you disposed to regard him as one in search of the picturesque or a poacher? So, when a gentleman travels about the country with a sub-sheriff in his carriage and two bailiffs in the rumble, does it seem exactly the guise of one paying morning calls to his neighbours?"

"Mr. O'Reilly, I ask you to explain this proceeding."

"I confess, sir," stammered out the other, "I came accompanied by certain persons in authority, but who have acted in this matter entirely without my permission. The proposal I have made this day was the cause of my visit."

"It is a subject on which I can no longer hold any secrecy," said the Knight, haughtily. "Bagenal, you were quite correct in your surmise. Mr. O'Reilly not only intended us the honour of an alliance, but offered to merge the ancient glories of his house by assuming the more humble name and shield of Darcy."

"What! eh! did I hear aright?" said Daly, with a broken voice; while walking to the window, he looked down into the lawn beneath, as if calculating the height from the ground. "By Heaven, Darcy, you're the best-tempered fellow in Europe—that's all," muttered he, as he walked away.

The door opened at this moment, and the shock bullet head of a bailiff appeared.

"That's Mr. Daly! there he is!" cried out O'Reilly, who, pale with passion and trembling all over, supported himself against the back of a chair with one hand, while with the other he pointed to where Daly stood.

"In that case," said the fellow, entering, while he drew a slip of paper from his breast, "I'll take the opportunity of sarvin' him where he stands."

"One step nearer! one step!" said Daly, as he took a pistol from the pocket of his coat.

The man hesitated and looked at O'Reilly, as if for advice or encouragement, but terror and rage had now deprived him of all self-possession, and he neither spoke nor signed to him.

"Leave the room, sir," said the Knight, with a motion of his hand to the bailiff; and the ruffian, whose office had familiarised him long with scenes of outrage and violence, shrank back ashamed and abashed, and slipped from the room without a word.

"I believe, Mr. O'Reilly," continued Darcy, with an accent calm and unmoved—"I believe our conference is now concluded. I will not insult your own acuteness by saying how unnecessary I feel any reply to your demand."

"In that case," said O'Reilly, "may I presume that there is no objection to proceed with those legal formalities which, although begun without my knowledge, may be effected now as well as at any other period?"

"Darcy, there is but one way of dealing with that gentleman——"

"Bagenal, I must insist upon your leaving this matter solely with me."

"Depend upon it, sir, your interests will not gain by your friend's counsels," said O'Reilly, with an insolent sneer.

"Such another remark from your lips," said Darcy, sternly, "would make me follow them, if they went so far as——"

"Throwing him neck and heels out of that window," broke in Daly, "for I own to you it's the course I'd have taken half an hour ago."

"I wish you good morning, Mr. Darcy," said O'Reilly, addressing him for the first time by the name of his family instead of his usual designation; and without vouchsafing a word to Daly, he retired from the room.

It was not until O'Reilly's carriage drove past the window that either Darcy or his friend uttered a syllable; they stood apparently lost in thought up to that moment, when the noise of wheels and the tramp of horses aroused them.

"We must lose no time, Bagenal," said the Knight, hastily; "I cannot count very far on that gentleman's delicacy or forbearance. Lady Eleanor must not be exposed to the indignities the law will permit him to practise towards us; we must, if possible, leave this to-night." And so saying, he left the room to make arrangements in accordance with his resolve.

Bagenal Daly looked after him for a moment. "Poor fellow!" muttered he, "how manfully he bears it!" When a sudden flush that covered his cheek bespoke a rapid change of sentiment, and at the same instant he left the room, and, crossing the hall and the court-yard, walked hastily towards the stables.

"Saddle a horse for me, Carney, and as fast as may be."

"Here's a mare ready this minute, sir; she was going out to take her gallop."

"I'll give it, then," said Daly, as he buttoned up his coat; and then, breaking off a branch of the old willow that hung over the fountain, sprang in the saddle with an alertness that would not have disgraced a youth of twenty.

"There he goes," muttered the old huntsman, as he looked after him "and there isn't the man between this and Killybegs can take as much out of a baste as himself. 'Tis quiet enough the mare will be when he turns her head into this yard again."

Whatever Daly's purpose, it seemed one which brooked little delay, for no sooner was he on the sward, than he pushed the mare to a fast gallop, and was seen sweeping along the lawn at a tremendous pace. In less than ten minutes he saw O'Reilly's carriage, as, in a rapid trot, the horses advanced along the level avenue, and almost the moment after he had stationed himself in the road, so as to prevent their proceeding further. The coachman, who knew him well, came to a stop at his signal, and, before his master could ask the reason, Daly was beside the window of the chariot.

"I would wish a word with you, Mr. O'Reilly," said he, in a low, subdued voice, so as to be inaudible to the sub-sheriff, who was seated beside him. "You made use of an expression a few moments ago, which, if I understood aright, convinces me I have unwittingly done you great injustice."

O'Reilly, whose ashy cheek and affrighted air bespoke a heart but ill at ease, made no reply, and Daly went on:

"You said, sir, that neither the time nor place suited the notice you felt called upon to take of my remarks on your conduct. May I ask, as a very great favour, what time and what place will be more convenient to you? And I cannot better express my own sense of regret for a hasty expression, than by assuring you that I shall hold myself bound to be at your service in both respects."

"A hostile meeting, sir, is that your proposition?" said O'Reilly, aloud.

"How admirably you read a riddle," said Daly, laughing.

"There, Mr. Jones!" cried O'Reilly, turning to his companion, "I call on you to witness the words—a provocation to a duel offered by this gentleman."

"Not at all," rejoined Daly; "the provocation came from yourself; at least, you used a phrase which men with blood in their veins understand but one way. My error—and I'll not forgive myself in haste for it—was the belief that an upstart need not of necessity be a poltroon. Drive on," cried he to the coachman, with a sneering laugh; "your master is looking pale." And, with these words, he turned his horse's head, and cantered slowly back towards the abbey.

CHAPTER XXXIII.

TATE SULLIVAN'S FAREWELL.

THE sorrows and sufferings of noble minds are melancholy themes to dwell upon; they may "point a moral," but they scarcely "adorn a tale," least of all such a tale as ours is intended to be. While, therefore, we would spare our readers and ourselves the pain of this narration, we cannot leave that old abbey, which we remember so full of happiness, without one parting look at it, in company with those about to quit it for ever.

From the time of Mr. O'Reilly's leave-taking, the day, notwithstanding its gloomy presage, went over rapidly. The Knight busied himself with internal arrangements, while Lionel took into his charge all the preparations for their departure on the morrow, Bagenal Daly assisting each in turn, and displaying an amount of calm foresight and circumspection in details which few would have given him credit for. Meanwhile, Lady Eleanor slept long and heavily, and awoke, not only refreshed in body, but with an appearance of quiet energy and determination she had not shown for years past. Great indeed was the Knight's astonishment on hearing that she intended joining them at dinner; in her usual habit she dined early, and with Helen alone for her companion, so that her present resolve created the more surprise.

Dinner was ordered in the library, and poor old Tate, by some strange motive of sympathy, took a more than common pains in all the decorations of the table. The flowers which Lady Eleanor was fondest of decked the centre—alas! there was no need to husband them now! on the morrow who was to care for them?—a little bouquet of fresh violets marked her place at the table, and more than a dozen times did the old man hesitate how the light should fall through the large window, and whether it would be more soothing to his mistress to look abroad upon that fair and swelling landscape so dear to her, or more painful to gaze upon the scenes she should never see more.

"If it was myself," muttered old Tate, "I'd like to be looking at it as long as I could, and make it follow me in my dhrames after; but sure there's no knowing how great people feels! they say they never has the same kind of thought as us!"

Poor fellow, he little knew how levelling is misfortune, and that the calamities of life evoke the same sufferings in the breast of the king and the peasant. With a delicacy one more highly born might have been proud of, the old butler alone waited at dinner, well judging that his familiar face would be less irksome to them than the prying looks of the other servants.

If there are people who can expend much eloquent indignation on those social usages which exact a certain amount of decorous observance in all the trials and crosses of life, there is a great deal to be said in favour of that system of conventional good breeding whose aim is to repress selfish indulgence, and make the individual feel that whatever his own griefs, the claims of the world demand a fortitude and a bearing that shall not obtrude his sorrows on his neighbours. That the code may be abused, and become occasionally hypocritical in practice, is no argument against it: we would merely speak in praise of that well-bred forbearance which always merges private afflictions in the desire to make others happy. To instance our meaning, we would speak of those who now met at dinner in the old library of Gwynne Abbey.

It would be greatly to mistake us to suppose that we uphold any show or counterfeit of kindliness where there is no substance of the feeling behind it; we merely maintain that the very highest and most acute sympathy is not inconsistent with a bearing of easy, nay, almost cheerful character. So truly was it the case here, that old Tate Sullivan more than once stood still in amazement at the tranquil faces and familiar quietude of those who, in his own condition of life could have found no accents loud or piercing enough to bewail their sorrow, and whom, even with his long knowledge of them, he could scarcely acquit of insensibility.

There is a contagion in an effort of this kind most remarkable. The light and gentle attempts made by Lady Eleanor to sustain the spirits of the party, were met by sallies of manly good-humour by the Knight himself, in which Lionel and Helen were not slow to join, while Bagenal Daly could scarcely repress his enthusiastic delight at the noble and high-souled courage that sustained them one and all.

While by a tacit understanding they avoided any allusion to the painful circumstances of their late misfortune, the Knight adroitly turned the conversation to their approaching journey northwards, and drew from Daly a description of "the Corvy" that actually evoked a burst of downright laughter. From this he passed on to speak of the peasantry, so unlike in every trait those of the south and west; the calm, reflective character of their minds, uninfluenced by passion and unmarked by enthusiasm, were a strong contrast to the headlong impulse and ardent temperament of the "real Irish."

"You'll scarcely like them at first, my dear Helen——"

"Still less on a longer acquaintance," broke in Helen. "I'll not quarrel with the caution and reserve of the Scotchman—the very mists of his native mountains may teach him doubt and uncertainty of purpose; but here at home, what have such frames of mind and thought in common with our less calculating natures?"

"It were far better had they met oftener," said the Knight, thoughtfully; "impulse is only noble when well directed; the passionate pilots are more frequently the cause of shipwreck than of safety."

"Nothing so wearisome as the trade-winds," said Helen, with a saucy toss of the head; "eh, Lionel, you are of my mind?"

"They do push one's temper very hard now and then," said Daly, with a stern frown; "that impassive habit they have of taking everything as in the common order of events, is, I own, somewhat difficult to bear with. I remember being run away with on a blood mare from a little village called Ballintray. The beast was in high condition, and I turned her, without knowing the country, at the first hill I could see; she breasted it boldly, and, though full a quarter of a mile in length, never shortened stride to the very summit. What was my surprise, when I gained the top, to see that we were exactly over the sea. It was a cliff, which, projecting for some distance out, was fissured by an immense chasm, through which the waves passed; not very wide, but deep enough to make it a very awful leap. Over it she went, and then, when I expected her to dash onwards, and was already preparing to fling myself from the saddle, she stood stock still, trembling all over, and snorting with fear at the danger around her. At the same instant, a hard-featured old fellow popped his head up from amid the tall fern which he had been cutting for thatch for his cabin, and looked at me, not the slightest sign of astonishment in his cold, rigid countenance.

"'Ye'll no get back so easy, my bonnie mon,' said he, with the slightest possible approach to a smile.

"'Get back! no, faith, I'll not try it,' said I, looking at the yawning gulf, through which the wild waves boiled, and the opposite bank several feet higher than the ground I stood upon.

"'I thought sae,' was the rejoinder; when, rising slowly, he leisurely walked round the mare, as she stood riveted by fear to the one spot.

I'll gie ye sax shilling for the hide o' her forbye the shoes,' added he, with a voice as imperturbable as though he were pricing the commonest commodity of a market.

"I confess it was fortunate that the ludicrous was stronger in me at the moment than indignation, for if I had not laughed at him I might have done worse."

"I could not endure such a peasantry," said Helen, as soon as the mirth the anecdote called forth had subsided.

"It's quite true," said Daly, "they have burlesqued Scotch prudence in the same way that the Anglo-Hibernian has travestied the Irish temperament. It is the danger of all imitators, they always transgress the limits of their model."

"It is fortunate," broke in the Knight, "that traits which conciliate so little the stranger should win their way on nearer intimacy; and such I believe to be the case with the Ulster peasant."

"You are right," said Daly; "no man can detest more cordially than I do the rudeness that is assumed to heighten a contrast with any good quality behind it. In most instances the kernel is not worth the trouble of breaking off the husk; but with the Northern this is not the case; in his independence he neither apes the equality of the Frenchman, nor the licence of the Yankee. That he suffices for himself, and seeks neither patron nor protector, is the source of honest pride, and if this sometimes takes the guise of stubbornness, let us remember that the virtue was reared in poverty, without encouragement or example."

"And the gentry," said Lady Eleanor, "have they any trace of these peculiarities observable among the people?"

"Gentry!" said Daly, impetuously; "I know of none. There are some thrifty families, who, by some generations of hard saving, have risen to affluence and wealth. They are keen fellows, given to money-getting—millers some of them, bleachers most, with a tenantry of weavers, and estates like the grass-plot of a laundry. They are as crafty and as calculating as the peasant, shrewd as stockbrokers at a bargain, and as pretentious as a Prince Palatine with a territory the size of Merrion-square Gentry! they have neither ancestry nor tradition; they hold their estates from certain Guilds, whose very titles are a parody upon gentle breeding—fishmongers and clothworkers!"

"I will not be their champion against you, Bagenal, but I cannot help feeling how heavily they might retort upon us. These same prudent and prosaic landlords have not spent their fortunes in wasteful extravagance and absurd display; they have not rackrented their tenantry that they might rival a neighbour."

"I am sincerely rejoiced," interposed Lady Eleanor, smiling, "that my

English relative, Lord Netherby, was not a witness to this discussion, lest he should fancy that, between the wastefulness of the south and the thrift of the north, this poor island was but ill provided with a gentry. Pray, Mr. Daly, how does your sister like the north? She is our neighbour, is she not?"

"Yes—that is to say, a few miles distant," said Daly, confusedly, for he had never acknowledged that "the Corvy" had been Miss Daly's residence; "of the neighbourhood she knows nothing; she is not free from my own prejudices, and lives a very secluded life."

The conversation now became broken and unconnected, and the party soon after retired to the drawing-room, where, while Lady Eleanor and Helen sat together, the Knight, Daly, and Lionel gathered in a little knot, and discussed, in a low tone, the various steps for the coming journey, and the probable events of the morrow.

It was agreed upon that Daly should accompany the Darcys to the north, whither Sandy was already despatched, but that Lionel should remain at the abbey for some days longer, to complete the arrangements necessary for the removal of certain family papers and the due surrender of the property to its new owner; after which he should repair to London, and procure his exchange into some regiment of the line, and, if possible, one on some foreign station—the meeting with friends and acquaintances, under his now altered fortunes, being judged as a trial too painful and too difficult to undergo.

Again they all met around the tea-table, and once more they talked in the same vein of mutual confidence; each, conscious of the effort by which he sustained his part, and wondering how the others summoned courage to do what cost himself so much. They chatted away till near midnight, and when they shook hands at separating, it was with feelings of affection to which sorrow had only added fresh and stronger ties.

Daly stood for some time alone in the library, wondering within himself at the noble fortitude with which they severally sustained their dreadful reverse. It is only the man of stout heart can truly estimate the higher attributes of courage, but even to him these efforts seemed surprising. "Ay," muttered he, "each nobly upholds the other; it is opposing a hollow square to fortune; so long as they stand firm and together, well! let one but quail and falter, let the line be broken, and they would be swept away at once and for ever." Taking a candle from the table, he left the room, and ascended the wide staircase towards his chamber. All was still and noiseless, and, to prevent his footsteps being heard, he entered the little corridor which opened on the gallery of the refectory, the same from which Forester first caught sight of the party at the dinner-table.

He had scarcely, with careful hand, closed the door behind him, when, looking over the balustrades of the gallery, he beheld a figure moving slowly along in the great apartment beneath, guided by a small lamp, which threw its uncertain light rather on the wall than on the form of him who carried it. Suddenly stopping before one of the large portraits which in a long succession graced the chamber, the light was turned fully round, so as to display the broad and massive features of old Tate Sullivan. Curious to ascertain what the old man might be about in such a place at such an hour, Daly extinguished the candle to watch him unobserved. Tate was dressed in his most accurate costume: his long cravat, edged with deep lace, descended in front of his capacious white waistcoat, silver buckles, of a size that showed there was no parsimony of the precious metal, shone in his shoes, and his newly-powdered wig displayed an almost snowy lustre; his gestures were in accordance with the careful observances of his toilet; he moved along the floor with a slow, sliding step, bowing deeply and reverentially as he went, and with all the courtesy he would have displayed if ushering a goodly company into the state drawing-room.

Bagenal Daly was not left long to speculate on honest Tate's intentions; and, although to a stranger's eyes the motives might have seemed strange and dubious, the mystery was easily solved to him who knew the old man well and thoroughly. He was there to take a last look, and bid farewell to those venerable portraits, who for more than half a century were enshrined in his memory like saints. Around them were associated all the little incidents of his peaceful life; they were the chroniclers of his impressions in boyhood, in manhood, and in age; he could call to mind the first moments he gazed on them in awe-struck veneration; he could remember the proud period when the duty first devolved upon him of describing them to the strangers who came to see the abbey; of the history of all and each of them he was well read, versed in their noble achievements, their triumphs in camp or cabinet. To his eyes they formed a long line of heroic characters, of which the world had produced no equal; they realised in his conception the proud eulogy of the Bayards, "where all the men were brave, and all the women virtuous;" and it is not improbable that his devotion to his master was in a great measure ascribable to that awe-struck admiration with which he regarded his glorious ancestors.

The old man stood, and holding the lamp above his head, gazed in respectful admiration at the grim figure of a knight in armour. There might have been little to charm the lover of painting in the execution of the picture, and the mere castle-builder could scarcely have indulged his fancy in weaving a story from the countenance of the portrait, for the vizor was down, and he stood in all the unmoved sternness of his iron prison, with his glaived hands clasped upon the cross of a long straight sword. Tate gazed on him for some moments. Heaven knows with what qualities of mind or person the old man had endowed him, for while to others he was only Sir Gavin Darcy, first Knight of Gwynne, Tate in all likelihood had invested him with traits of character and appearance, of which that external shell was the mere envelope.

"We're going, Sir Gavin," muttered the old man, as if addressing the portrait; "'tis the ould stock is laving the place, never to see it more; 'tis your own proud heart will be sorry to-day to look down upon us. Ah, ah!" muttered he, "the world is changed; there was times when a Darcy wouldn't quit the house of his fathers without a blow for it—and they say we are better now!" With a heavy sigh he passed on, and stood before the next picture. "Yes, my lady," said he, "ye may well cry that lost the two beautiful boys the same morning, fighting side by side; but there's heavier grief here now; the brave youths sleep in peace and in honour, but we have no home to shelter us!"

With a slow step, and bent-down head, he tottered on, and placing the lamp upon the floor, crossed his arms upon his breast. "'Tis you that can help us now," said he, as he cast a timid and imploring glance at the goodly countenance and rotund figure of Bernhard Emmeric, fourth Abbot of Gwynne; "'tis your reverence can offer a prayer for your own blood that's in sore trouble and distress. Do it, my Lord; do it in the name of the Vargin. Smiling and happy you look, but it's sorrowful your heart is in you, to see what's going on here. Them, them was the happy days, when it wasn't the cry of grief was heard beneath this roof, but the heavenly chants of holy men, and the prayers of the blessed mass." He knelt down as he said this, and with trembling lips and tearful eyes recited some verses from his breviary.

This done, he arose, and, as if with renovated courage, proceeded on his way:

"Reginald Herbert de Guyon! ah! second Baron of Gwynne, Lord Protector of Munster, Knight of Malta, Chevalier of St. John of Jerusalem, Standard-Bearer to the Queen! and well you desarve it all! 'Tis yourself sits your horse like a proud nobleman!" He stood with eyes riveted upon the picture, while his face glowed with intense enthusiasm, and at last, as a bitter sneer passed across his lips, he added, "Ay, faith! and them that comes after us won't like the look of you. 'Tis you that'll never disguise from them your real mind, and every day they'll dine in the hall, that same frown will darken, and that same hand will threaten them."

He moved on now, and passed several portraits without stopping, muttering as he went, "'Tis more English than Irish blood is in your veins, and you won't feel as much for us as the rest;" then, halting suddenly, he stood before a tall figure, dressed in black velvet, with a deep collar of point lace. A connoisseur of higher pretensions than poor Tate might have gazed with even greater rapture at that splendid canvas, for it was from the hand of Vandyke, and in his very best manner. The picture represented the person of Sir Everard Darcy, Lord Privy Seal to Charles I. It was a specimen of manly beauty and high blood, such as the great Fleming loved to paint, and even yet the proud and lofty forehead, the deep-set brown eyes, the thin compressed lip, the long and somewhat projecting chin, seemed to address themselves to the beholder with traits of character more than mere painting is able to convey. Tate approached the spot with an almost trembling veneration, and bowed deeply before the haughty figure. "There was a time, Sir Everard, when your word could make a duke or a marquis—when your whisper in the King's ear could bring grief or joy to any heart in the empire. Could you do nothing for us now? They say you never were at a loss, no matter what came to pass—that you were always ready-witted to save your master from trouble—and oh! if the power hasn't left you, stand by us now. It is not because your eyes are so bright, and that quiet smile is on your lips, that your heart does not feel, for I know well that the day you were beheaded you had the same look on you as you have now. I think I see you this minute, as you lifted your head off the block to settle the lace collar that the villain the executioner rumpled with his bloody fingers; I think I hear the words you spoke: Honest Martin, for all your practice, you are but a clumsy valet.' Well, well! 'tis a happier and a prouder day that same than to-morrow's dawn will bring to ourselves. Yes, yes, my darlings," said Tate, with a benevolent smile, as he waved his hand towards a picture where two beautiful children were represented, sitting on the grass, and playing with flowers, "be happy and amuse yourselves, in God's name; 'tis the only time for happiness your lives ever gave you. Ah! and here's your father, with a smile on his face and a cheerful brow, for he had both till the day misfortune robbed him of his children;" and he stood in front of a portrait of an officer in an admiral's uniform. He was a distinguished member of the Darcy family; but from the nature of his services, which were all maritime, and the great number of years he had spent away from Ireland, possessed less of Tate's sympathy than most of the others.

"They say you didn't like Ireland; but I don't believe them. There never was a Darcy didn't love the ould island; but I know well whose fault it was if you didn't—it was that dark villain that's standing at your side, ould Harry Inchiquin, the renegade, that turned many a man against his country. Ye may frown and scowl at me; but if you were alive this minute, I'd say it to your face. It was you that first brought gambling and dicing under this blessed roof; it was you that sent the ould acres to the hammer; 'twas you that loved rioting, and duelling, and every wickedness, just like old Bagenal Daly himself, that never could sleep in his bed if he hadn't a fight on hand."

"What ho! you old reprobate!" called out Daly, in a voice which, echoing under the arched roof, seemed rather to float through the atmosphere than issue from any particular quarter.

"Oh! marciful Father!" cried Tate, as, falling on his knees, the lamp dropped from his fingers, and became extinguished—"oh! marciful Father! sure I didn't mane it; 'tis what the lying books said of you—bad luck to the villains that wrote them! Oh, God! pardon me; I never thought you'd hear me; and if it's in trouble you are, I'll say a mass for you every day till Aaster, and one every Friday as long as I live."

A hoarse burst of laughter broke from Daly, while pacing the gallery with heavy tread he went forth, banging the door behind him. The terror was too great for poor Tate's endurance, and, with a faint cry for mercy, he rolled down upon the floor almost insensible.

When morning broke, he was found seated in the refectory, pale and careworn; but no entreaty, nor no pressing, could elicit from him one word of a secret in which he believed were equally involved the honour of the dead and the safety of himself

---

CHAPTER XXXIV.

A GLANCE AT PUBLIC OPINION IN THE YEAR 1800.

Among the arrangements for the departure of the family from the abbey, all of which were confided to Bagenal Daly, was one which he pressed with a more than ordinary zeal and anxiety; this was, that they should set out at a very early hour of the morning—at dawn of day, if possible. Lady Eleanor's habits made such a plan objectionable, and it was only by representing the great sacrifice of feeling a later departure would exact, when crowds of country people would assemble to take their farewells of them for ever, that she consented. While Daly depicted the unnecessary sorrow to which they would expose themselves by the sight of their old and attached tenantry, he strenuously preserved silence on the real reason which actuated him, and to explain which a brief glance at the state of public feeling at the period is necessary.

To such a pitch of acrimony and animosity were parties borne by the agitation which preceded the carrying of the "Union," that all previous character and conduct of those who voted on the question were deemed as nothing in comparison with the line they adopted on the one absorbing subject. If none who advocated the Ministerial plan escaped the foulest animadversions, all who espoused the opposite side were exalted to the dignity of patriots; argument and reason went for little, principle for still less; a vote was deemed the touchstone of honesty. Such rash and hasty judgments suited the temper of the times, and it may be said, in extenuation, were not altogether without some show of reason. Each day revealed some desertion from the popular party of men who, up to that moment, had rejected all the seductions of the Crown; country gentlemen, hitherto supposed inaccessible to all the temptations of bribery, were found suddenly addressing speculative letters to their constituencies, wherein they ingeniously discussed all the contingencies of a measure they had once opposed without qualification. Noblemen of high rank and fortune were seen to pay long visits at the Castle, and, by a strange fatality, were found to have modified their opinions exactly at the period selected by the Crown to bestow on them designations of honour or situations of trust and dignity. Lawyers in high practice at the bar, men esteemed by their profession, and held in honour by the public, were seen to abandon their position of proud independence, and accept Government appointments, in many cases inferior both in profit and rank to what they had surrendered.

There seemed a kind of panic abroad. Men feared to walk without the protective mantle of the Crown being extended over them; the barriers of shame were broken down by the extent to which corruption had spread. The examples of infamy were many, and several were reconciled to the ignominy of their degradation by their associates in disgrace. That in such general corruption the judgments of the public should have been equally wholesale, is little to be wondered at; the regret is rather that they were so rarely unjust and ill-bestowed.

Public confidence was utterly uprooted; there was a national bankruptcy of honour, and none were trusted; all the guarantees for high principle and rectitude a lifetime had given, all the hostages to good faith years of unimpeached honour bestowed, were forgotten in a moment, and such as opposed the Government measure with less of acrimony or activity than their neighbours, were set down "as waiting for or soliciting the bribery of the Crown."

To this indiscriminating censure the Knight of Gwynne was a victim. It may be remarked that in times of popular excitement, when passions are rife and the rude enthusiasm of the mass has beaten down the more calmly weighed opinion of the few, that there is a strange pleasure felt in the detection of any real or supposed lapse of one once esteemed. It were well if this malignant delight were limited to the mere mob, but it is not so; men of education and position are not exempt from its taint. It would seem as if society were so thoroughly disorganised that every feeling was perverted, and all the esteem for what is good and great had degenerated into a general cry of exultation over each new instance of tarnished honour.

Accustomed as we now are to the most free and unfettered criticisms of all public men and their acts, it would yet astonish any one not conversant with that period to look back to the newspapers of the time, and see the amount of violence and personality with which every man obnoxious to a party was visited; coarse invective stood the place of argument, a species of low humour had replaced the light brilliancy of wit. The public mind, fed on grosser materials, had lost all appetite for the piquancy of more highly flavoured food, and the purveyors were not sorry to find a market for a commodity which cost them so little to procure. In this spirit was it that one of the most popular of the Opposition journals announced for the amusement of its readers a series of sketches under the title of "The Gallery o. Traitors,"—a supposed collection of portraits to be painted for the Viceroy, and destined to decorate one of the chambers of the Castle.

Not satisfied with aspersing the reputation, and mistaking the views of any who sided with the Minister, the attack went further, and actually ascribed the casualties which occurred to such persons or their families as instances of Divine vengeance. In this diabolical temper the Knight of Gwynne was held up to reprobation; it was a bold thought to venture on calumniating a man every action of whose life had placed him above even slander, but its boldness was the warranty of success. The whole story of his arrival in Dublin, his dinner with the Secretary, his intimacy with Heffernan, was related circumstantially. The night on which Heffernan entrapped him by the trick already mentioned, was quoted as the eventful moment of his change. Then came the history of his appearance in the House on the evening of the second reading, his hesitation to enter, his doubts and waverings were all described, ending with a minute detail of his compact with Lord Castlereagh, by which his voting was dispensed with, and his absence from the division deemed enough.

Gleeson's flight and its consequences were soon known. The ruin of Darcy's large fortune was a circumstance not likely to lose by public discussion, particularly when the daily columns of a newspaper devoted a considerable space to the most minute details of that catastrophe. It was asserted that the Knight had sold himself for a Marquisate and a seat in the English Peerage. That his vote was deemed so great a prize by the Minister that he might have made even higher terms, but in the confidence of possessing a large fortune he had only bargained for rank, and rejected every offer of mere emolument, and now came the dreadful retribution on his treachery the downfal of his fortune by the villany of his agent. To assume a title when the very expense of the patent could not be borne was an absurdity and this explained why Maurice Darcy remained ungazetted. Such was the plausible calumny generally circulated, and, alas! for the sake of charity, scarcely less generally believed.

There are epidemics of credulity as of infidelity, and such a plague raged at this period. Anything was believed, were it only bad enough. While men, therefore, went about deploring, with all the sanctity of self-esteem, the fall of Maurice Darcy, public favour, by one of those caprices all its own, adopted the cause of his colleague, Hickman O'Reilly. His noble refusal of every offer (and what a catalogue of seductions did they not enumerate!) was given in the largest type. They recounted, with all the eloquence of their calling, the glittering coronets rejected, the places of honour and profit declined, the dignities proffered in vain, preferring as he did the untitled rank of a country gentleman, and the unpurchasable station of a true friend to Ireland.

He was eulogised in capital letters, and canonised among the martyrs of patriotism; public orators belaboured him with praises, and ballad-singers chanted his virtues through the streets. Nor was this turn of feeling a thing to be neglected by one so shrewd in worldly matters. His sudden accession to increased fortune and the position attendant on it, would, he well knew, draw down upon him many a sneer upon his origin, and some unpleasant allusions to the means by which the wealth was amassed. To anticipate such an ungrateful inquiry he seized the lucky accident of his popularity, and turned it to the best account.

Whole "leaders" were devoted to the laudation of his character: the provincial journals, less scrupulous than the metropolitan, boldly asserted their knowledge of the various bribes tendered to him, and threw out dark hints of certain disclosures which, although at present refrained from out of motives of delicacy, should Mr. O'Reilly ultimately be persuaded to make, the public would be horrified at the extent to which corruption had been carried.

The O'Reilly liveries, hitherto a modest snuff colour, were now changed to an emerald green; an Irish motto ornamented the garter of the family crest; while the very first act of his return to the west was a splendid donation to the chapel of Ballyraggan, or, as it was subsequently and more politely named, the Church of St. Barnabas of Trèves; all measures dictated by a high-spirited independence, and a mind above the vulgar bigotry of party.

Had O'Reilly stopped here—had he contented himself with the preliminary arrangements for being a patriot, it is probable that Bagenal Daly had never noticed them, or done so merely with some passing sarcasm; but the fact was otherwise. Daly discovered, in the course of his journey westward, that the rumours of the Knight's betrayal of his party were generally disseminated in exact proportion with the new-born popularity of O'Reilly; that the very town of Westport, where Darcy's name was once adored, was actually placarded with insulting notices of the Knight's conduct, and scandalous aspersions on his character: jeering allusions to his altered fortunes were sung in the villages as he passed along, and it was plain that the whole current of popular opinion had set strong against him.

To spare his friend Darcy a mortification which Daly well knew would be one of the greatest to his feelings, the early departure was planned and decided on. It must not be inferred that because the Knight would have felt deeply the unjust censure of the masses, he was a man to care or bend beneath the angry menace of a mob; far from it. The ingratitude towards himself would have called forth the least of his regrets; it was rather a heartfelt sorrow at the hopeless ignorance and degradation of those who could be so easily deceived—at that populace whose fickleness preferred the tinsel and trappings of patriotism to the acts and opinions of one they had known and respected for years.

Long before day broke, Daly was stirring and busied with all the preparations of the journey; the travelling carriage, covered with its various boxes and imperials, stood before the door in the court-yard, the horses were harnessed and bridled in the stables; everything was in readiness for a start; and yet, save himself and the stable-men, all within the abbey seemed buried in slumber.

Although it was scarcely more than five o'clock, Daly's impatience at the continued quietude around him began to manifest itself: he walked hastily to and fro, endeavouring to occupy his thoughts by a hundred little details, till at last he found himself returning to the same places and with the self-same objects again and again, while he muttered broken sentences of angry comments on people who could sleep so soundly at such a time.

It was in one of these fretful moods he had approached the little flower-garden of the Sub-Prior's house, when the twinkling of a light attracted him; it came from the window of Lady Eleanor's favourite drawing-room, and glittered like a star in the gloom of the morning. Curious to see who was stirring in that part of the house, he drew near, and opening the wicket, noiselessly approached the window. He there beheld Lady Eleanor, who, supported on Helen's arm, moved slowly along the room, stopping at intervals, and again proceeding; she seemed to be taking a last farewell of the various well-known objects endeared to her by years of companionship; her handkerchief was often raised to her eyes as she went, but neither uttered a syllable. Ashamed to have obtruded even thus upon a scene of private sorrow, Daly turned back again to the court-yard, where now the loud voice of the Knight was heard giving his orders to the servants.

The first greetings over, the Knight took Daly's arm and walked beside him.

"I have been thinking over the matter in the night, Bagenal," said he, "and am convinced it were far better that you should remain with Lionel; we can easily make our journey alone—the road is open, and no difficulty in following it—but that poor boy will need advice and counsel. You will probably receive letters from Dublin by the post, with some instructions how to act; in any case my heart fails me at leaving Lionel to himself."

"I'll remain, then," replied Daly; "I'll see you the first stage out of Westport, and then return here. It is, perhaps, better as you say."

"There is another point," said Darcy, after a pause, and with evident hesitation in his manner, "it is perfectly impossible for me to walk through this labyrinth without your guidance, Bagenal—I have neither head nor heart for it—you must be the pilot, and if you quit the helm for a moment——"

"Trust me, Maurice, I'll not do it," said Daly, grasping his hand with a firm grip.

"I know that well," said the Knight, as his voice trembled with agitation; "I never doubted the will, Bagenal, it was the power only I suspected. I see you will not understand me. Confound it! why should old friends, such as we are, keep beating about the bush, or fencing like a pair of diplomatists? I wanted to speak to you about that bond of yours: there is something like seven thousand pounds lying to my credit at Henshaw's; take what is necessary, and get rid of that scoundrel Hickman's claim. If they should arrest you——"

"I wish he had done so yesterday—my infernal temper, that never will let matters take due course, stopped the fellow; you can't see why, but I'll tell you. I paid the money to Hickman's law-agent, in Dublin, the morning I started from town, and they had not time to stop the execution of the writ down here. Yes, Darcy, there was one drop more in the stoup, and I drained it! The last few acres I possessed in the world, the old estate of Hardress Daly, is now in the ownership of one Samuel Kerney, grocer, of Bride-street. I paid off Hickman, however, and found something like one hundred and twenty-eight pounds afterwards in my pocket——But let us talk of something else—you must not yield to these people without a struggle; Bicknell says there are abundant grounds for a trial at bar in the affair. If collusion between Hickman and Gleeson should be proved—that many of the leases were granted with false signatures annexed——"

"I'll do whatever men of credit and character counsel me," said the Knight; "if there be any question of right, I'll neither compromise nor surrender it—I can promise no more. But here comes Lionel—to announce breakfast, perhaps."

And so it was; the young man came towards them with an easy smile, presenting a hand to each. If sorrow had sunk deeply into his heart, few traces of grief were apparent in his manly, handsome countenance.

Notwithstanding the efforts of the party, the breakfast did not pass over as lightly as the dinner of the previous day; the eventful moment of parting was now too near not to exclude every other subject, and even when by an exertion some allusion to a different topic would be made, a chance question, the entrance of a servant for orders, or the tramp of horses in the court-yard, would suddenly bring back the errant thoughts, and place the sad reality in all its force before them.

Breakfast was over, and yet no one stirred; a heavy, dreary reverie seemed to have settled on all except Daly—and he, from delicacy, restrained the impatience that was working within him. In vain he sought to catch Darcy's eye, and then Lionel's—both were bent downwards. Lady Eleanor at last looked up, and at once seemed to read what was passing in his mind.

"I am ready," said she, in a low, gentle voice, "and I see Mr. Daly is not sorry at it. Helen, dearest, fetch me my gloves."

She arose, and the others with her. The calmness in which she spoke on the theme that none dared approach, seemed almost to electrify them, when suddenly a low sob was heard, and the mother fell, in a burst of anguish, into the arms of her son.

"Eleanor, my dearest Eleanor!" said Darcy, as his pale cheek shook and his lip trembled. As if recalled to herself by the words, she raised her head, and, with a smile of deep-meaning sorrow, said,

"It's the first tear I have yet shed; it shall be the last." Then, taking Daly's arm, she walked steadily forward.

"I have often wondered," said she, "at the prayer of a condemned felon for a few hours longer of life, but I can understand it now. I feel as if I could give life itself for another day within these walls, where often I have pined with *ennui*. You will watch over Lionel for me, Mr. Daly. When the world went fairly with us, calamities came softened—as the summer rain falls lighter in sunshine—but now, now that we have lost so much, we cannot afford more."

Daly's stern features grew sterner and darker; his lips were compressed more firmly; he tried to say a few words, but a low, indistinct muttering was all that came.

The next moment the carriage door was closed on the party—they were gone.

Lionel stood gazing after them till they disappeared; and then, with a slow step, re-entered the abbey.

CHAPTER XXXV.

BAGENAL DALY'S RETURN.

LIONEL DARCY bore up manfully against his altered fortunes so long as others were around him, and that the necessity for exertion existed; but once more alone within that silent and deserted house, all his courage failed him at once, and he threw himself upon a seat, and gave way to grief. Never were the brighter prospects of opening life more cruelly dashed, and yet his sorrow was for others. Every object about brought up thoughts of that dear mother and sister, to whom the refinements of life were less luxuries than wants. How were they to engage in the stern conflict with daily poverty—to see themselves bereft of all the appliances which filled up the hours of each day? Could his mother, frail and delicate as she was, much longer sustain the effort by which she first met the stroke of fortune? Would not the reaction, whenever it came, be too terrible to be borne? And Helen, too—his sweet and lovely sister—she whom he had loved to think of as the admired of a splendid Court; on whose appearance in the world he had so often speculated, castle-building over the sensations her beauty and her gracefulness would excite—what was to be her lot? Deep and heartfelt as his sorrow was for them, it was only when he thought of his father that Lionel's anguish burst its bounds, and he broke into a torrent of tears. From very boyhood he had loved and admired him, but never had the high features of his character so impressed Lionel Darcy, as when the reverse of fortune called up that noble spirit whose courage displayed itself in manly submission and the generous effort to support the hearts of others. How cruel did the decrees of fate seem to him, that such a man should be visited so heavily, while vice and meanness prospered on every side. He knew not that virtue has no nobler attribute than its power of sustaining unmerited affliction, and that the destiny of the good man is never more nobly carried out than when he points the example of patience in suffering.

Immersed in such gloomy thoughts, he wandered on from room to room, feeding, as it were, the appetite for sorrow, by the sight of every object that could remind him of past happiness; nor were they few. There, was the window-seat he loved to sit in as a boy, when all the charm of some high-wrought story could not keep his eyes from wandering at intervals over the green hills where the lambs were playing, or adown by that dark stream, where circling eddies marked the leaping trout. Here, was Helen's favourite room, a little octagon boudoir, from every window of which a different prospect opened: it seemed to breathe of her sweet presence even yet; the open desk, from which she had taken some letter, lay there upon the table, the pen she had last touched, the chair she sat upon, all, even to the little nosegay of scarce faded flowers, the last she had plucked, teemed with her memory. He walked on with bent-down head and tardy step, and entered the little room which, opening on the lawn, was used by the Knight to receive such of the tenantry as came to him for assistance or advice; many an hour had he sat there beside his father, and, while listening with the eager curiosity of youth to the little stories of the poor man's life, his trials and his difficulties, imbibed lessons of charity and benevolence never to be forgotten.

The great square volume in which the Knight used to record his notes of the neighbouring poor, lay on the table; his chair was placed near it; all was in readiness for his coming who was to come there no more! As Lionel stood in silent sorrow, surveying these objects, the shadow of a man darkened the window. He turned suddenly, and saw the tall, scarecrow figure of Flury, the madman. A large placard decorated the front of his hat, on which the words "Down with the Darcys!" were written in capital letters, and he carried in his hand a bundle of papers, like handbills, which he shook with a menacing air at Lionel.

"What is this, Flury?" said the youth, opening the window, and at the same time snatching one of the papers from his hand.

"It's the full account of the grand auction of Government hacks," said Flury, with the sing-song intonation of a street-crier, "no longer needed for the service of the Crown, and to be sowld without resarve."

"And who sent you here with this?" said the young man, moderating his tone to avoid startling the other.

"Connor Egan, Hickman's man, gave me a pint and a noggin of spirits to cry the auction, and tould me to come up here, for maybe you'd like to hear of it ye'rselves."

Lionel threw his eyes over the offensive lines, where, in coarse ribaldr names the most venerable were held up to scorn and derision. If it was some satisfaction to find that his father was linked in the ruffianly attack with men of honour as unblemished as his own, he was not less outraged at the vindictive cowardice that had suggested this insult.

"There'll be a fine sight of people there, by all accounts," said Flury, gravely, "for the auction-bills is far and near over the country, and the Castlebar coach has one on each door."

"Is popular feeling always as corrupt a thing as this?" muttered Lionel, with a bitter sneer, while at the same time the door of the room was opened, and Daly entered. His face was marked by a severe cut on one cheek, from which the blood had flowed freely; a dark blue stain, as of a blow, was on his chin, and one hand he carried enveloped in his handkerchief; his clothes were torn besides in many places, and bore traces of a severe personal conflict.

"What has happened!" said Lionel, as he looked in alarm at the swollen and blood-stained features. "Did you fall?"

"Fall! no such thing, boy," replied Daly, sternly; "but some worthy folk in Castlebar planned a little surprise for me this morning. They heard, it seems, that we passed through the town by daybreak, but that I was to return before noon; and so they placed some cars and turf creels in the main street, opposite the inn, in such a way that, while seeming merely accident, would effectually stop a horseman from proceeding. When I arrived at the spot, I halted, and called out to the fellows to move on, and let me pass. They took no heed of my words, and then I saw in a moment what was intended. I had no arms; I purposely left my pistols behind me, for I feared something might provoke me, though not anticipating such as this. So I got down and drew this wattle from the side of a turf creel—you see it is a strong blackthorn, and good stuff, too. Before I was in the saddle the word was passed, and the whole street was full of people, and I now perceived that, by the same manœuvre as they employed in front, they had also closed the rear upon me, and cut off my retreat. 'Now for it! now for it!' they shouted. 'Where's Bully Dodd?—where's the Bully?' I suppose you know the fellow?"

"The man that was transported?"

"The same. The greatest ruffian the country was cursed with. He came at the call, without coat or waistcoat, his shirt-sleeves tucked up to his shoulders, and a handkerchief round his waist, ready for a fight. There was an old quarrel between us, for it was I captured the fellow the day after he burnt down Dawson's house. He came towards me, the mob opening a way for him, with a pewter pot of porter in his hand.

"'We want you to dhrink a toast for us, Mr. Daly,' said he, with a marked courtesy, and a grin that amused the fellows around him. 'You were always a Patriot, and won't make any objections to it.'

"'What is the liquor?' said I.

"'Good porter—divil a less,' cried the mob; 'Mol Heavyside's best. And so I took the vessel in my hands, and before they could say a syllable, drained it to the bottom, for I was very thirsty with the ride, and in want of something to refresh myself.

"'But you didn't dhrink the toast,' said Dodd, savagely.

"'Where was the toast? He didn't say the words,' shouted the mob.

"'Off with his hat, and make him drink it,' cried out several others from a distance. They saved me one part of the trouble, for they knocked off my hat with a stone.

"'Here's health and long life to Hickman O'Reilly!' cried out Dodd, 'that's the toast.'

"'And what have I to wish him either?' said I, while at the same time I tore open the pewter measure, and then with one strong dash of my hand drove it down on the ruffian's head, down to the very brows. I lost no time afterwards, but striking right and left, plunged forwards; the mob fled as I followed, and by good luck, the car-horses getting frightened, sprang forward also, and so I rode on with a few slight cuts a stone or two struck me, nothing more; but they'll need a plumber to rid my friend Dodd of his helmet."

"And we used to call this town our own," said Lionel, bitterly.

"Nothing is a man's own but his honour, sir. That base cowardice yonder believes itself honest and independent, as if a single right feeling, a single good or virtuous thought, could consort with habits like theirs; but they are less base than those who instigate them. The real scoundrels are the Hickmans of this world, the men who compensate for low birth and plebeian origin by calumniating the well-born and the noble. What is Flury wanting here?" said he, as, attracted by Daly's narrative, the poor fellow had drawn near to listen.

"I am glad you put the pewter pot on the Bully's head, he's a disgrace to the town," said Flury, with a laugh; and he turned away as if enjoying the downfal of an enemy.

"Oh! I see," said Daly, taking up one of the papers that had fallen to the ground, "this is the first act of the drama; come along, Lionel, let us talk of matters nearer to our hearts."

They walked along together to the library, each silently following his own train of thought, and for some time neither seemed disposed to speak. Lionel at length broke silence, as he said,

"I have been thinking over it, and am convinced my father will never be able to endure this life of inactivity before him."

"That is exactly the fear I entertain myself for him; altered fortunes will impress themselves more in the diminished sphere to which his influence and utility will be reduced, than in anything else; but how to remedy this?"

"I have been considering that also, but you must advise me if the plan be a likely one. He held the rank of colonel once——"

"To be sure he did, and with good right, he raised the regiment himself

Darcy's Light Horse were as handsome a set of fellows as the service could boast of."

"Well, then, my notion is, that although the Government did not buy his vote on the Union, there would be no just reason why they should not appoint him to some one of those hundred situations which the service includes. His former rank, his connexion and position, his unmerited misfortunes, are, in some sense, claims. I can scarcely suppose his opposition in Parliament would be remembered against him at such a moment."

"I hardly think it would," said Daly, musingly; "there is much in what you propose. Would Lord Netherby support such a request if it were made?"

"He could not well decline it; almost the last thing he said at parting was, that whatever favour he enjoyed should be gladly employed in our behalf. Besides, we really seek nothing to which we may not lay fair and honest claim. My intention would be to write at once to Lord Netherby, acquainting him briefly with our altered fortunes."

"The more briefly on that topic the better," said Daly, dryly.

"To mention my father's military rank and services, to state that having raised and equipped a company at his own expense, without accepting the slightest aid from the Government, now, in his present change of condition, he would be proud of any recognition of those services which once he was but too happy to render unrewarded to the Crown. There are many positions, more or less lucrative, which would well become him, and which no right-minded gentleman could say were ill bestowed on such a man."

"All true," said Daly, whose eye brightened as he gazed on the youth, whose character seemed already about to develop itself under the pressure of misfortune with traits of more thoughtful meaning than yet appeared in him.

"Then I will write to Lord Netherby at once," resumed Lionel; "there can be no indelicacy in making such a request; he is our relative, the nearest my mother has."

"He is far better, he's a Lord in Waiting, and a very subtle courtier," said Daly. "Write this day, and, if you like it, I'll dictate the letter."

Lionel accepted the offer with all the pleasure possible. He had been from boyhood a firm believer in the resources and skill of Daly in every possible contingency of life, and looked on him as one of those persons who invariably succeed when everybody else fails.

There is a species of promptitude in action, the fruit generally of a strong will and a quick imagination, which young men mistake for a much higher gift, and estimate at a price very far above its value. Bagenal Daly had, however, other qualities than these, but truth compels us to own, that in Lionel's eyes his supremacy on such grounds was no small merit. He had ever found him ready for every emergency, prompt to decide, no less quick to act, and without stopping to inquire how far success followed such rapid resolves, this very energy charmed him. It was, then, in perfect confidence on the skill and address of his adviser that Lionel sat down, pen in hand, to write at his dictation.

CHAPTER XXXVI.

THE LAW AND ITS CHANCES.

We left Mr. Daly at the conclusion of our last chapter in the exercise of —what to him was always a critical matter—the functions of a polite letter-writer. His faults, it is but justice to say, were much less those of style than of the individual himself; for if he rarely failed to convey a clear notion of his views and intentions, he still more rarely omitted to impart considerable insight into his own character.

His abrupt and broken sentences, his sudden outbreaks of intelligence or passion, were not inaptly conveyed by the character of a handwriting, which was bold, careless, and hurried. Indifferent to everything like neatness or accuracy, generally blotted, and never very legible, these defects, if they did not palliate, they might, in a measure, explain something of his habits of thought and action, but now, when about to dictate to another, the case was different, and those interruptions which Daly would have set down by a dash of his pen, were to be conveyed by the less significant medium of mere blanks.

"I'm ready," said Lionel, at length, as he sat for some time in silent expectation of Daly's commencement. But that gentleman was walking up and down the room with his hands behind his back, occasionally stopping to look out upon the lawn.

"Very well, begin—'My dear Lord Netnerby,' or 'My dear Lord'—it doesn't signify which, though I suppose he would be of another mind, and find a whole world of difference between the two. Have you that?—very well. Then go on to mention, in such terms as you like yourself, the sudden change of fortune that has befallen your family, briefly, but decisively."

"Dictate it, I'll follow you," said Lionel, somewhat put out by this mode of composition.

"Oh! it doesn't matter exactly what the words are—say, that a d—d scoundrel, Gleeson—Honest Tom we always called him—has cut and run with something like a hundred thousand pounds, after forging and falsifying every signature to our leases for the last ten or fifteen years; we are, in consequence, ruined—obliged to leave the abbey, take to a cottage—a devilish poor one, too."

"Don't go so fast—'we are, in consequence——'"

"Utterly smashed—broken up—no home, and devilish little to live upon—my mother's jointure being barely sufficient for herself and Helen. I want, therefore, to remind you—your Lordship, that is—to remind your Lordship of the kind pledge which you so lately made us, at a time when we little anticipated the early necessity we should have to recal it. My father, some forty-five or six years back, raised the Darcy Light Horse, equipped, armed, and mounted six hundred men at his own expense. This regiment, of which he took the head, did good service in the Low Countries, and, although distinguished in many actions, he received nothing but thanks—happily not wanting more, if so much. Times are changed now with him, and it would be a seasonable act of kindness, and a suitable reward to an old officer—highly esteemed as he is, and has been through life—to make up for past neglect by some appointment—the service has many such—— Confound them! the pension-list shows what fellows there are—'Governors and Deputy-Governors,' 'Acting Adjutants' of this, and 'Deputy-Assistant Commissaries' of that."

"I'm not to write that, I suppose?"

"No, you needn't—it would do no harm, though, to give them a hint on the subject—but never mind it now. 'As for myself, I'll leave the Guards, and take service in the Line. I am only anxious for a regiment on a foreign station, and if in India, so much the better.' Is that down? Well—eh that will do, I think. You may just say, that the matter ought to be arranged without any communication with your father, inasmuch as, from motives of delicacy, he might feel bound to decline what was tendered as an offer, though he would hold himself pledged to accept what was called by the name of duty. Yes, Lionel, that's the way to put the case—active service, by all means, active service—no guard-mounting at Windsor or Carlton House—no Hounslow Heath engagements."

Lionel followed, as well as he was able, the suggestions, to which sundry short interjections and broken "hems!" and ha's!" gave no small confusion, and at last finished a letter, which, if it conveyed some part of the intention, was even a stronger exponent of the character of him who dictated it.

"Shall I read it over to you?"

"Heaven forbid! If you did, I'd alter every word of it. I never reconsidered a note that I did not change my mind about it, and I don't believe I ever counted a sum of money over more than once without making the tot vary each time. Send it off as it is—'Yours truly, Lionel Darcy.'"

It was about ten days after the events we have just related, that Bagenal Daly sat in consultation with Darcy's lawyer in the back parlour of the Knight's Dublin residence. Lionel, who had been in conclave with them for several hours, had just left the room, and they now remained in thoughtful silence, pondering over their late discussion.

"That young man," said Bicknell, at length, "is very far from being deficient in ability, but he is wayward and reckless as the rest of the family, he seems to have signed his name everywhere they told him, and to anything. Here are leases for ever at nominal rents—no fines in renewal—rights of fishery disposed of—oak timber—marble quarries—property of every kind made away with. Never was there such wasteful, ruinous expenditure coupled with peculation and actual robbery at the same time."

"What's to be done?" said Daly, interrupting a catalogue of disasters he could scarcely listen to with patience; "have you anything to propose?"

"We must move in Equity for an inquiry into the validity of these documents; many of the signatures are probably false; we can lay a case for a jury——"

"Well, I don't want to hear the details—you mean to go to law; now, has Darcy wherewithal to sustain a suit? These Hickmans are rich."

"Very wealthy people, indeed," said Bicknell, dryly. "The Knight cannot engage in a legal contest with them without adequate means.—I am not sufficiently in possession of Mr. Darcy's resources to pronounce on the safety of such a step."

"I can tell you, then; they have nothing left to live upon save his wife's jointure. Lady Eleanor has something like a thousand a year in settlement—certainly not more."

"If they can contrive to live on half this sum," said the lawyer, cautiously, "we may, perhaps, find the remainder enough for our purposes. The first expenses will be, of course, very heavy; drafts to prepare, searches to make, witnesses to examine, with opinion of high counsel, will all demand considerable outlay."

"This is a point I can give no opinion upon," said Daly; "they have been accustomed to live surrounded with luxuries of every kind: whether they can at once descend to actual poverty, or would rather cling to the remnant of their former comforts, is not in my power to tell."

"The very bond under which they have foreclosed," said Bicknell, "admits of great question. Unfortunately, that fellow Gleeson destroyed all the papers before his suicide, or we could ascertain if a clause of redemption were not inserted; there was no registry of the judgment, and we are consequently in the hands of the enemy."

"I cannot help saying," said Daly, sternly, "that if it were not for the confounded subtleties of your craft, roguery would have a less profitable sphere of employment: so many hitches, so many small crotchety conjunctures influence the mere question of right and wrong, that a man is led at last to think less of justice itself than of the petty artifices to secure a superiority."

"I must assure you that you are in a great error," said Bicknell, calmly; "the complication of a suit is the necessary security the law has recourse to against the wiles and stratagems of designing men. What you call its hitches and subtleties, are the provisions against craft by which mere honesty is protected: that they are sometimes employed to defeat justice, is saying no more than that they are only human contrivances, for what good institution cannot be so perverted?"

"So much the better if you can think so. Now, what are Darcy's chances of success?—never mind recapitulating details, which remind me a great deal too much of my own misfortunes, but say, in one word, is the prospect good or bad, or has it a tinge of both?"

"It may be any of the three, according to the way in which the claim is prosecuted; if there be sufficient means——"

"Is that the great question?"

"Undoubtedly; large fees to the leading counsel, retainers, if a record be kept for trial at the Assizes, and payment to special Juries, all are expensive, and all necessary."

"I'll write to Darcy to-night, then—or, better still, I'll write to Lady Eleanor, repeating what you have told me, and asking her advice and opinion; meanwhile, lose no time in consulting Mr. Boyle—you prefer him?"

"Certainly, in a case like this he cannot be surpassed; besides, he is already well acquainted with all the leading facts, and has taken a deep interest in the affair. There are classes and gradations of ability at the bar irrespective of degrees of actual capacity; we have the heavy artillery of the Equity Court, the light field pieces of the King's Bench, and the Congreve rockets of Assize display: to misplace or confound them would be a grave error."

"I know where I'd put them all, if *my* pleasure were to be consulted," muttered Daly, in an under growl.

"Now, if we have a case for a Jury, we must secure Mr. O'Halloran——"

"He who made a speech to the mob in Smithfield the other day?"

"The same; I perceive you scarcely approve of my suggestion, but his success at the bar is very considerable; he knows a good deal of law, and a great deal more about mankind. A rising man, sir, I assure you."

"It must be in a falling state of society, then," said Daly, bitterly; "time was when the first requisite of a barrister was to be a Gentleman. An habitual respect for the decorous observances of polite life was deemed an essential in one whose opinions were as often to be listened to in questions of right feeling as of right doing. His birth, his social position, and his acquirements, were the guarantees he gave the world that, while discussing subtleties, he would not be seduced into anything low or unworthy. I am sorry that notion has become antiquated."

"You would not surely exclude men of high talents from a career because their origin was humble?" said Bicknell.

"And why not, sir? Upon what principle was the body-guard of noble persons selected to surround the person of the Sovereign, save that blood was deemed the best security for allegiance? and why should not the law, only second in sacred respect to the person of the monarch, be as rigidly protected? The Church excludes from her ministry all who even by physical defect may suggest matter of ridicule or sarcasm to the laity; for the same reason I would reject from all concern with the administration of justice those coarser minds whose habits familiarise them with vulgar tastes and low standards of opinion."

"I confess this seems to me very questionable doctrine, not to speak of the instances which the law exhibits of her brightest ornaments derived from the very humblest walks in life."

"Such cases are, probably, esteemed the more because of that very reason," said Daly, haughtily; "they are like the pearl in the oyster-shell, not very remarkable in itself, but one must go so low down to seek for it. I have an excuse for warmth; I have lost the greater part of a large fortune in contesting a right pronounced by high authority to be incontrovertible. Besides," added he, with a courteous smile, "if Mr. Bicknell may oppose my opinion, he has the undoubted superiority that attaches to liberality, his own family claiming alliance with the best in the land."

This happy turn seemed to divert the course of a conversation which half threatened angrily. Again the business topic was resumed, and after a short discussion, Bicknell took his leave, while Daly prepared to write his letter to Lady Eleanor.

He had not proceeded far in his task when Lionel entered with a newspaper in his hand.

"Have you heard the news of the notorious robber being taken?" said he.

"Who do you mean? Barrington, is it?"

"No; Freney."

"Freney! taken?—when—now—where?"

"It's curious enough," said Lionel, coolly, seating himself to read the paragraph, without noticing the eagerness of Daly's manner; "the fellow seems to have had a taste for sporting matters, which no personal fear could eradicate. His capture took place this wise. He went over to Doncaster, to be present at the Spring Meeting, where he betted freely, and won largely. There happened, however, to come a reverse to his fortune, and on the last day of the running he lost everything, and was obliged to apply for assistance to a former companion, who, it would seem, was some hundred pounds in his debt; this worthy, having no desire to refund threatened the police; Freney became exasperated, knocked him down on the spot, and then, turning smartly round, chucked one of the jockeys from his saddle, sprang on the horse's back, and made off like lightning. The other, only stunned for a moment, was soon on his legs again, and the cry of 'Freney! it was Freney, the robber!' resounded throughout the race-course. The scene must then have been a most exciting one, for the whole mounted population, with one accord, gave chase. Noblemen and country gentlemen, fox-hunters, farmers, and blacklegs, away they went, Freney about a quarter of a mile in front, and riding splendidly."

"That I'm sure of," said Daly, earnestly. "Go on!"

"Mellington took the lead of every one, mounted on that great steeple-chase horse he is so proud of—no fences too large for him, they say; but the robber—and what a good judge of country the fellow must be—left the heavy ground, and preferred even breasting a long hill of grass-land, with several high rails, to the open country below, where the clay soil distressed his horse. By this manœuvre, says the newspaper, he was obliged to make a circuit which again brought the great body of his pursuers close up with him; and now his dexterity as a horseman became apparent, for while riding at top speed, and handling his horse with the most perfect judgment he actually contrived to divest himself of his heavy great-coat. He had but just accomplished this very difficult task, when Lord Mellington once more came up. There was a heavy dyke in front, with a double post and rail, and at this they rushed desperately, each, apparently, calculating on the other being thrown, or at least checked.

"Freney, now only a dozen strides in advance, turned in his saddle, and drawing a pistol from his breast, took an aim—as steadily, too, as if firing at a mark. Lord Mellington saw the dreadful purpose of the robber; he shouted aloud, and pulling up with all his might, he bent down to the very mane of his horse. Freney pulled the trigger, and with one mad plunge Lord Mellington's horse came head-foremost to the ground with his rider under him Freney was not long the victor; the racer he bestrode breasted the high rail, and, unable to clear it, fell heavily forward, smashing the frail timbers before him, and pitching the rider on his head. He was up in a second and away; for about twenty yards his speed was immense, then reeling, he staggered forwards and fell senseless; before he rallied he was taken, and in handcuffs. There is a description of the fellow," said Lionel, "and, by Jove! one would think they were describing some wild denizen of the woods, or some strange animal of savage life, so eloquent is the paragraph about his appearance and personal strength."

"A well-knit fellow, no doubt, and more than a match for most in single combat," said Daly, musing.

"You have seen him, then?"

"Ay, that I have, and must see him again. Where is he confined?"

"In Newgate."

"That is so far fortunate, because the gaoler is an old acquaintance of mine."

"I have a great curiosity to see this Freney."

"Come along with me, then," said Daly, as he arose and rang the bell to order a carriage; "you shall gratify your curiosity, but I must ask you to leave us alone together afterwards, for, strange as it may seem, we have a little affair of confidence between us."

It did, indeed, appear not a little strange that any secret negotiation or understanding should exist between two such men, but Lionel did not venture to ask any explanation of the difficulty, but silently prepared to accompany him. As they went along towards Newgate, Daly related several anecdotes of Freney, all of which tended to show that the fellow had all his life felt that strange passion for danger so attractive to certain minds, and that his lawless career was more probably adopted from this tendency than any mere desire of money-getting. Many of his robberies resembled feats of daring rather than cautious schemes to obtain property. "Society," added Daly, "is truly not much benefited because the highwayman is capricious, but still, one cannot divest oneself of a certain interest for a rascal who has always shown himself ready to risk his neck, and who has never been charged with any distinct act of cruelty. When I say this much, I must caution you against indulging a sympathy for a law-breaker because he is not a perfect monster of iniquity; such fellows are very rare, and we are always too well inclined to admire the few good qualities of a bad man, just as we are astonished at a few words spoken plain by a parrot.

> The things themselves are neither strange nor rare,
> We wonder how the devil they came there."

While Daly wisely cautioned his young companion against the indulgence of a false and mawkish sympathy for the criminal, he, in his own heart, could not help feeling the strongest interest for any misfortune of a spirit so wild and so reckless.

Daly's card, passed through the iron grating of the strong door, soon procured them admission, and they were conducted into a small and neatly furnished room, where a mild-looking, middle-aged man was seated, reading He rose as they entered, and saluted them respectfully.

"Good evening, Dunn, I hope I see you well. My friend, Captain Darcy—Mr. Dunn. We have just heard that the noted Freney has taken up his lodgings here, and are curious to see him."

"I'm afraid I must refuse your request, Mr. Daly; my orders are most positive about the admission of any one to the prisoner: there have been I can't say how many people here on the same errand since four o'clock, when he arrived."

"I think I ought to be free of the house," said Daly, laughing; "I matriculated here at least, if I didn't take out a high degree."

"So you did, sir," said Dunn, joining in the laugh. "Freney is in the very same cell you occupied for four months."

"Come, come, then, you can't refuse me paying a visit to my old quarters."

"There is another objection, and a stronger one—Freney himself declines seeing any one, and asked a special leave of the Sheriff to refuse all comers admission to him."

"This surprises me," said Daly; "why, the fellow has a prodigious deal of personal vanity, and I cannot conceive his having adopted such a resolution."

"Perhaps I can guess his meaning," said the gaoler, shrewdly; "the greater number of those who came here, and also who tried to see him in Liverpool, were artists of one kind or other, wanting to take busts or profiles of him. Now, my surmise is, Freney would not dislike the notoriety, if it were not that it might be inconvenient one of these days. To be plain, sir, though he is doubly ironed, and in the strongest part of the strongest gaol in Ireland, he is at this moment meditating on an escape, in the event of which he calculates all the trouble and annoyance it would give him to have his picture or his cast stuck up in every town and village of the kingdom. This, at least, is my reading of the mystery, but I think it is not without some show of probability."

"Well, the objection could scarcely apply to me," said Daly; "if his portrait be not taken by a more skilful artist than I am, he may be very easy on the score of recognition. Pray let me send in my name to him, and if he refuses to see me, I'll not press the matter further."

Partly from an old feeling of kindness towards Daly, Dunn gave no further opposition, but in reality he was certain that Freney's refusal would set the matter at rest. His surprise was consequently great when the turnkey returned with a civil message from Freney that he would be very glad to see Mr. Daly.

"Your friend can remain here," said Dunn, in a voice that plainly showed he was not quite easy in his mind as to the propriety of the interview; and Daly, to alleviate suspicions natural enough in one so circumstanced, assented, and walked on after the turnkey, alone.

"That's the way he spends his time; listen to him now," whispered the turnkey, as they stopped at the door of the cell, from within which the deep tones of a man's voice were heard singing to himself, as he slowly paced the narrow chamber, his heavy fetters keeping a melancholy time to the melody:

'Twas afther two when he quitted Naas,
But he gave the spur and he went the pace,
"As many as like may now give chase,"
  Says he, "I give you warning.
You may raise the country far and near,
From Malin Head down to Cape Clear,
But the divil a man of ye all I fear,
  I'll be far away before morning."

By break of day he reach'd Kildare,
The black horse never turn'd a hair;
Says Freney, "We've some time to spare,
  This stage we've rather hasten'd."
So he eat four eggs and a penny rowl,
And he mix'd of whisky such a bowl!
The drink he shared with the beast, by my soul
  For Jack was always dacent.

"You might tighten the girths," Jack Freney cried,
"For I've soon a heavy road to ride."
'Twas the truth he tould, for he never lied,
  The way was dark and rainy.
"Good by," says he, "I'll soon be far,
And many a mile from Mullingar."
So he kiss'd the girl behind the bar,
  'Tis the divil you wor, Jack Freney!

"Sorra lie in that, any way," said the robber, as he repeated the last line over once more, with evident self-satisfaction.

"Who comes there?" cried he, sternly, as the heavy bolts were shot back, and the massive door opened.

"Why don't you say, 'Stand and deliver!'" said the turnkey, with a laugh as harsh and grating as the creak of the rusty hinges.

"And many a time I did to a better man," said Freney.

"You may leave us now," said Daly, to the turnkey.

"Mr. Daly, your sarvant," said the robber, saluting him; "you're the only man in Ireland I wanted to see."

"I wish our meeting had been anywhere else," said Daly, sorrowfully, as he took his seat on a stool opposite the bed where Freney sat.

"Well, well, so it is, sir; it's just what every one prophesied this many a day; as if there was much cunning in saying that I'd be hanged some time or other; why, if they wanted to surprise me, they'd have tould me I'd never be taken. You heard how it was, I suppose?"

Daly nodded, and Freney went on:

"The English horse wouldn't rise to the rail; if I was on the chesnut mare or Black Billy, I wouldn't be where I am now."

"I have several things to ask you about, Freney; but first, how can I serve you? You must have counsel in this business."

"No, sir, I thank you; it's only throwing good money after bad; I'll plead guilty, it will save time with us all."

"But you give yourself no chance, man."

"Faix, I spoiled my chance long ago, Mr. Daly. Do you know, sir"—here he spoke in a low, determined tone—"there's not a mail in Ireland I didn't stop at one time or other. There's few country gentlemen I haven't lightened of their guineas; the Court wouldn't hold the witnesses against me if I were to stand my trial."

"With all that, you must still employ a lawyer; these fellows are as crafty in *their* walk as ever you were in *yours*. Who will you have? Name the man, and leave the rest to me."

Freney seemed to deliberate for a few moments, and he threw his eyes down at the heavy irons on his legs, and he gazed at the strong stanchions of the windows, and then said, in a low voice,

"There's a chap called Hosey M'Garry, in a cellar in Charles-street he's an ould man with one eye, and not a tooth in his head, but he's the only man that could sarve me now."

"Hosey M'Garry," repeated Daly, "Charles-street," as he wrote down the address with his pencil; "a strange name and residence for a lawyer."

'I didn't say he was, sir," said Freney, laughing.

"And who and what is he, then?"

"The only man, now alive, that can make a cowld chisel to cut iron without noise."

"Ah! that's what you're thinking of; you'd rather trust to the flaws of the iron than of the indictment. Perhaps you are not far wrong, after all."

"If I was in the court below without the fetters," said Freney, eagerly, "I could climb the wall with a holdfast and a chisel, and get down the same way on the other side; once there, Mr. Daly, I'd sing the ould ballad,

For the divil a man of ye all I fear,
I'll be far away before morning."

"And how are these tools to reach you here? If they admit any of your friends, won't they search them first?"

"So they will, barrin' it was a gentleman," replied Freney, while his eyes twinkled with a peculiarly cunning lustre.

"So, then, you rely on *me* for this piece of service?" said Daly, after a pause.

"Troth, you're the only gentleman of my acquaintance," said Freney, quaintly.

"Well, I suppose I must not give you a bad impression of the order; I'll do it."

"I knew you would," rejoined Freney, calmly; "you might bring two files at the same time, and a phial of sweet oil to keep down the noise. Hush! here's Gavin coming to turn you out—he said ten minutes."

"Well, then, you shall see me to-morrow, Freney, and I'll endeavour to see your friend in the mean time." This was said as the turnkey stood at the open door

"This gentleman wants to have a look at you, Freney," said the gaoler, "as if he couldn't see you for nothing, some Saturday morning soon."

"Maybe he'd not know me in a nightcap," replied Freney, laughing, while he turned the lamplight full on Lionel Darcy's features.

"The very fellow that rode off with the horse!" exclaimed Lionel, as he saw him.

"Young O'Reilly!" said Freney. "What signifies that charge now Won't it satisfy you if they hang me for something else?"

"That's Captain Darcy, man," broke in Daly. "Is all your knowledge of mankind of so little use to you that you cannot distinguish between a born gentleman and an upstart?"

"By my oath," said the robber, aloud, "I'm as glad as a ten-pound note to know that it wasn't a half-bred one that showed the spirit you did! Hurrah! there's hopes for ould Ireland yet, when the blood and bone is still left in her! And wasn't it real luck that I saw you this night? If I didn't, I'd have done you a bad turn. One word, Mr. Daly, one word in your ear."

The robber drew Daly towards him, and whispered eagerly for some seconds.

A violent exclamation burst from Daly as he listened, and then he cried out, "What! are you sure of this? Don't deceive me, man!"

"May I never, but it's true."

"Why, then, not have told it before?"

"Because"—here he faltered—"because—faix, I'll tell the truth—I thought that young gentleman was Hickman's grandson, and I couldn't bring myself to do him a spite after what I had seen."

"The time is up, gentlemen," said the turnkey, who, out of the delicacy of his official feeling, was slowly pacing the corridor up and down while they talked together.

"If this be but true," muttered Daly to himself, "there's another cast of the dice for it yet."

"I am sorry for that fellow," said Lionel, aloud; "he did me a good turn once; I might have gone down the torrent were it not for his aid."

"So you might, man," said Daly, speaking in a half-soliloquy; "he gives the only chance of victory I've seen yet."

These words, so evidently inapplicable to Lionel's observations, were a perfect enigma, but he did not dare to ask for any explanation, and walked on in silence beside him.

CHAPTER XXXVII.

A SCENE OF HOME.

If the climate of northern Ireland be habitually one of storm and severity, it must be confessed that, in the rare but happy intervals of better weather, the beauty of the coast scenery is unsurpassed. Indented with little bays, whose sides are formed of immense cliffs of chalk, or the more stately grandeur of that columnar basalt which extends for miles on either side of the Causeway, the most vivid colouring unites with forms the wildest and most fantastic; crag and precipice, sandy beach and rocky shore, alternate in endless variety; while islands are there, some, green and sheep-clad, others dark and frowning, form the home of nothing but the sea-gull.

It was on such an evening of calm as displayed the scene to its greatest advantage, when a long column of burnished golden light floated over the sea, tipping each crested wave, and darkened into deeper beauty between them, that the Knight, Lady Eleanor, and Helen, sat under the little porch of their cottage and gazed upon the fair and gorgeous picture.

If the leafy grove, or the dark wood, seem sweeter to our senses when the thrilling notes of the blackbird or the thrush sing in their solitude, so the deepest silence, the most unbroken stillness, has a wonderful effect of soothing to the mind beside the sea shore we have so often seen terrible in the fury of the storm. A gentle calm steals over us as we listen to the long sweeping of the waves, heaving and breaking in measured melody, and our thoughts, enticed by some dreaming ecstasy, wander away over the boundless ocean, not to the far-off lands of other climes alone, but into worlds of brighter and more beauteous mould.

They sat in silence, at first only occupied by the lovely scene that stretched away before them, but at last each deeply immersed in his own thoughts—thoughts which, unconnected with the objects around, yet by some strange mystery were tinctured by all their calm and tranquil beauty. A fisherman was mending his net upon the little beach below, and his children were playing around him, now running merrily along the strand, now dabbling in the white foam left by the retreating waves; the father looked up from time to time to watch them, but without interrupting the low monotonous chant by which he lightened his labour.

Towards the little group at length their eyes were turned. "Yes," said the Knight, as if interpreting what was passing in the minds of those at his side, "that is about as near to human happiness as life affords. I believe there would be very few abortive ambitions if men were content to see their children occupy the same station as themselves; and yet, when the time of one's own reverses arrives, how very little of true happiness is lost by the change of fortune."

"My dearest father!" said Helen, as in a transport of delight she threw her arms around him, "how happy your words make me! You are then contented?"

"Do I not look so, my sweet Helen? And your mother, too, when have you seen her so well?—when do you remember her walking, as she did to-day, to the top of the great cliff of Dunluce?"

"With no other ill consequence," said Lady Eleanor, smiling, "than a most acute attack of vanity, for I begin to fancy myself quite young again."

"Well, mamma, don't forget we have a visit to pay some of these days to Ballintray—that's the name of the place, I think, Miss Daly resides at."

"Yes, we really must not neglect it. There was a delicacy in her note of welcome to us here, judging that we might not be prepared for a personal visit, which prepossesses me in her favour. You promised to make our acknowledgments, but I believe you forgot all about it."

"No, not that," said the Knight, hesitatingly; "but in the midst of so many things to do and think about, I deferred it from day to day."

"Shall we go to-morrow, then?" cried Helen, eagerly.

"I think it were better if your father went first, lest the way should prove too long for us. I am so proud of my pedestrianism, Helen, I'll not risk any failure."

"Be it so," said the Knight, quietly. "And now of this other matter Bagenal presses so strongly upon us, I feel the greatest repugnance to assume any name but that I have always borne, and, I hope, not disgraced; he says we shall be objects of impertinent curiosity here to the neighbourhood."

"Ruins to dispute the honours of lionship with Dunluce," said Lady Eleanor, smiling faintly

"Just so; that might, however, be borne patiently; they will soon leave off talking of us when we give them little matter for speculative gossip. Besides, we are so far away from anything that could be called neighbourhood."

"But he suggests some other reasons, if I mistake not," said Lady Eleanor.

"He does, but so darkly and mysteriously, that I cannot even guess his drift. Here is his letter." And the Knight took several papers from his pocket, from among which he selected one, whose large and blotted writing unmistakably pronounced it Bagenal Daly's. "Yes, here it is: 'Bicknell says that Hickman's people are fully persuaded that you have left Ireland with the intention of never returning; that this impression should be maintained, because it will induce them to be less guarded than if they believed you were still here, directing any legal proceeding. The only case, therefore, he will prepare for trial, will be one respecting the leases falsely signed. The bond and its details must be unravelled by time; here also your incognito is all-essential—it need only be for a short time, and on scruples of delicacy so easily got over: your grandfather called himself Gwynne, and wrote it also.' That is quite true, Eleanor, so he did; his letters are signed Matthew Gwynne, Knight of ——. I remember the signature well."

"I think with Mr. Daly," said Lady Eleanor, "it will save us a world of observant impertinence; this place is tranquil and solitary enough just now, but in summer the coast and the Causeway have many visitors, and although the 'Corvy' is out of the common track, if our names be bruited about, we shall not escape that least graceful of all attentions, the tender commiseration of mere acquaintances."

"Mamma is right," said Helen; "we should be hunted out by every tourist to report on how we bore our reverses, and tormented with anonymous condolences in prose, and short stanzas on the beauty of resignation."

"Well, and, my dear Helen, perhaps the lessons might not be so very inapplicable," said the Knight, smiling affectionately.

"But very inefficient, sir," replied Helen, with a toss of her head; "I'm not a bit resigned."

"Helen, dearest," interposed Lady Eleanor, rebukingly.

"Not a bit, mamma; I am happy, happier than I ever knew myself before, if you like that phrase better, because we are together, because this life realises to me all I ever dreamed of, that quiet and tranquil pleasure people might, but somehow never please to taste of—but, if you ask me am I resigned to see you and my dear father in a station so much beneath your expectations and your habits, I cannot say that I am."

"Then, my dear girl, you accuse us of bearing our misfortunes badly, if we cannot partake of your enjoyments on account of our own vain regrets?"

"No, no, papa, don't mistake me; if I grieve over the altered fortunes that limit your sphere of usefulness as well as of pleasure, it is because I know how well you understood the privileges and demands of your high station, and how little a life, so humble as this is, can exact of qualities that were not given to be wasted in obscurity."

"My sweet child," said the Knight, fondly, "it is a very dangerous practice to blend up affection with principle; depend upon it, the former will always coerce the latter, and bend it to its will; and as for those good gifts you speak of, had I really as many of them as your fond heart would endow me with, believe me there is no station so humble as not to admit of their exercise. There never yet was a walk in life without its sphere of duties; now I intend that not only are we to be happy here, but that we should contribute to the well-being of those about us."

There was a pause after the Knight had done speaking, during which he busied himself in turning over some letters, the seals of which were still unbroken; he knew the handwriting on most of them, and yet hesitated about inflicting on himself the pain of reading allusions to that condition he had once occupied. "Yes," muttered he to himself, "we are always flattering ourselves of how essential we are to our friends, our party, and so forth, and yet, when any events occur which despoil us of our brief importance, we see the whole business of the world go on as currently as ever. What a foretaste this gives one of death! So it is, the stream of life flows on, whether the bubble on its surface float or burst."

"That's Lord Netherby's hand, is it not?" said Lady Eleanor, as she lifted a letter which had fallen to the ground.

"Yes," said Darcy, carelessly; "written probably soon after his return to England; I have no doubt it contains a most courtly acknowledgment of our poor hospitality, and an assurance of undying regard."

"If it be of that tenor, I have no curiosity to read it," said Lady Eleanor, handing the letter to the Knight.

"Helen would like to study so great a master of epistolary flatteries," said the Knight, smiling, "and provided she will keep the whole for her private reading, I am willing to indulge her."

"I accept the favour with thanks," said Helen, receiving the letter; "you know I plead guilty to liking our noble relative. I'm not skilled enough to distinguish between an article trebly gilded and one of pure gold, and his Lordship, to my eyes, looked as like the true metal as possible: he said so many pretty things to mamma, and so many fine things of you and Lionel——"

"And paid so many compliments to the fair Helen herself," interposed the Knight.

"With so much of good tact——"

"And good taste, Helen," added Lady Eleanor, smiling; "why not say that?"

"Well, I see I shall have to defend myself as well as my champion, so, I'll even go and read my letter."

And so saying, she arose, and sauntered down to the shore; under the shelter of a tall rock, from whence the view extended for miles along, she sat down. "What a contrast!" said she, as she broke the seal, "a courtier's letter in such a scene as this!"

Lord Netherby's letter was, as the Knight suspected, written soon after his return to England, expressing, in his own most courtly phrase, the delightful memory he retained of his visit to Ireland. Gracefully contrasting the brilliant excitement of that brief period with the more staid quietude of the life to which he returned, he lightly suggested that none other than one native to the soil could support an existence so overflowing with pleasurable emotions. With all the artifice of a courtier, he recalled certain little incidents, too small, as mere matters of memory, to find a resting-place in the mind, but all of them indicative of the deep impression made upon him who remarked them.

He spoke also of the delight with which his Royal Highness the Prince listened to his narrative of life in Ireland. "In truth," wrote his Lordship, "I do not believe that the exigencies of his station ever cost him more, than when he reflected on the impossibility of his witnessing such perfection in the life of a country-house as I feebly endeavoured to convey to him. Again and again has he asked me to repeat the tale of the hunt—the brilliant ball the night of your arrival—and I have earned a character for story-telling of which Kelly and Sheridan are beginning to feel jealous, by the mere retail of your anecdotes. Lionel's return is anxiously looked for by all here; and the Prince has more than once expressed himself impatient to see him back again. My sweet favourite Helen, too—when is she to be presented? There will be a Court in the early part of next month, of which I shall not fail to apprise you, most earnestly entreating that my cousin Eleanor will not think the journey too far which shall bring her once again among those scenes she so gracefully adorned, and where her triumphs will be renewed in the admiration of her lovely daughter. I need not tell you that my house in town is entirely at her disposal, either as *my* guests, or, if you prefer it, I shall be *theirs*, whenever I am not in Waiting."

Here the writer detailed, with an eloquence all his own, the advantage to Helen of making her *entrée* into life under circumstances so favourable, remarking, with that conventional philosophy just then the popular cant of the day, that the enthusiasm of the world was never long-lived, and that even his beautiful cousin Helen should not be above profiting by the favourable reception the kindly disposition of the Court was sure to procure for ner. This was said in a tone of half-serious banter, but at the same time the invitation was reiterated with an evident desire for its acceptance.

As the letter drew near its conclusion, the lines became more closely written, as though some circumstances hitherto forgotten had suddenly occurred to the writer; and so it proved.

"I was about, my dear Knight, to write myself, with what truth I will not say, your 'most affectionate friend, Netherby,' when I received a letter which requires some mention at my hands. It is, indeed, one of the most extraordinary documents I have ever perused; nothing very wonderful in that, when I tell you from whom it comes—your old sweetheart, Julia Wallincourt, or, as you will better remember her, Julia D'Esterre; she is still very beautiful, and just as capricious, just as *maligne* as when she endeavoured, by every artifice of her coquetry, to make you jilt my cousin Eleanor. There's no doubt of it, Darcy, this woman loved you! at least, as much as she could love anything, except the pleasure of torturing her fellow-creatures. Well, it would seem that a younger son of hers, popularly known as Dick Forester, paid you a visit in Ireland, and, no very unnatural occurrence, fell desperately in love with your daughter—not so Helen with him. She probably regarded him as one of that class upon which London has so stamped its impress of habit and manner, that all individualism is lost in the quiet observance of certain proprieties. He must have been a rare contrast to the high-souled enthusiasm and waywardness of her own brother! Certain it is she refused him; and he, taking the thing much more to heart than a young Guardsman usually does a similar catastrophe, hastened home, and endeavoured to interest his mother in his suit. Lady Julia had an old vengeance to exact, and, like a true woman, could not forego it; she not only positively refused all intercession on her part, but went what you and I will probably feel to be a very unnecessary length, and actually declared she never would consent to such an alliance. We used to remember (some years ago), at Eton, of a certain Dido, who never forgave, and we are told how, for many years after, the *lethalis arundo lateri adhæsit*, but assuredly the poet was speaking less of the woes of an individual than of the sorrows of fine ladies in all ages. Unfortunately, the similitude between her Ladyship and Dido ends here; the classic fair one exhibited, as we are told, the most delicate fondness for the son of her lover. But, to grow serious: Lady Wallincourt's conduct must have been peremptory and harsh; she actually went the length of writing to the Duke of York, to request an exchange for her son into a regiment serving in India: whether Forester obtained some clue to this manœuvre or not, he anticipated the stroke by selling out and leaving the army altogether; whither he is gone, or what has become of him since, no one can tell. Such, my dear Knight, is the emergency in which Lady Wallincourt addresses her letter to me—a letter so peculiarly her own, so full of reproaches against you, and vindication of herself, that I actually scruple to transmit to you this palpable evidence of still-enduring affection.

"Were you both thirty years younger, I should claim great credit to my morality for the forbearance. Let that pass, however, and let me rather ask you, if you know, or have heard anything of this wayward boy? Personally, I am unacquainted with him; but his friends agree in saying that he is high-spirited, honourable, and brave; and it would be a great pity that his affection for a young lady, and his anger with an old one, should mar all the prospects of his life. Could you, by any means, find a clue to him? I do not, of course, ask you to interfere in person, lest it might seem that you encouraged an attachment which you have far more reason to discountenance for your daughter than has Lady Wallincourt for her son; however, your doing so would go far to reconcile the young man to his mother, by showing that, if there was a difficulty on one side, a still greater obstacle existed on the other."

Requesting a speedy answer, and begging that the whole might be in strict confidence between them, the letter concluded:

"I do not doubt, my dear Knight," said the postscript, "that you will see in all this a reason the more for coming up to town. Helen's appearance at the Drawing Room would be the best, if not the only, rebuke Lady Wallincourt's insolence could receive. By all means, come.

"Another complication! Lady W., on first hearing of her son's duel, and the kind treatment he met with after being wounded, wrote a letter of grateful acknowledgments, which she enclosed to her son, neither knowing nor caring for the address of her benefactor. When she did hear it at length, she was excessively angry that she had been, as she terms it, 'the first to make advances.' Ainsi, telles sont les femmes du monde!"

Such was Lord Netherby's letter. With what a succession of emotions Helen read it we confess ourselves unable to depict. If she sometimes hesitated to read on, an influence, too powerful to control, impelled her to continue, while a secret interest in Forester's fortunes—a feeling she had never known till now—induced her to learn his fate. More than once, in the alteration of her condition, had she recalled the proffer of affection she had with such determination rejected, and with what gratitude did she remember the firmness of her decision!

"Poor fellow!" thought she, "I deemed it the mere caprice of one whose gratitude for kindness had outrun his calmer convictions. And so he really loved me!"

We must avow the fact: Helen's indifference to Forester had, in the main, proceeded from a false estimate of his character; she saw in him nothing but a well-bred, good-looking youth, who, with high connexions and moderate abilities, had formed certain ambitious views, to be realised rather by the adventitious aid of fortune than his own merits. He was, in her eyes, a young politician, cautious and watchful, trained up to regard Lord Castlereagh as the model of statesmen, and political intrigue as the very climax of intellectual display. To know that she had wronged him was to make a great revolution in her feelings towards him; to see that this reserved and calmly-minded youth should have sacrificed everything—position, prospects, all—rather than resign his hope, faint as it was, of one day winning her affection!

If these were her first thoughts on reading that letter, those that followed were far less pleasurable. How should she ever be able to show it to her father? The circumstances alluded to were of a nature he never could be cognisant of without causing the greatest pain both to him and herself. To ask Lady Eleanor's counsel would be even more difficult. Helen witnessed the emotion the sight of Lady Wallincourt's name had occasioned her mother the day Forester first visited them; the old rivalry had, then, left its trace on her mind as well as on that of Lady Julia! What embarrassment on every hand! Where could she seek counsel, and in whom? Bagenal Daly, the only one she could have opened her heart to, was away; and was it quite certain she would have ventured to disclose, even to him, the story of that affection, which already appeared so different from at first? Forester was not now in her eyes the fashionable Guardsman, indulging a passing predilection, or whiling away the tedious hours of a country-house by a flirtation, in which he felt interested because repulsed; he was elevated in her esteem by his misfortunes, and the very uncertainty of his fate augmented her concern. And yet, she must forego the hope of saving him, or else, by showing the letter to her father, acknowledge her acquaintance with events she should never have known, or knowing, should never reveal.

There was no help for it, the letter could not be shown. In all likelihood neither the Knight nor Lady Eleanor would ever think more about it; and if they did, there was still enough to speak of in the courteous sentiments of the writer, and the polite attention of his invitation, a civility which even Helen's knowledge of life informed her was rather proffered in discharge of a debt, than as emanating from any real desire to play their host in London.

Thus satisfying herself that no better course offered for the present, she turned homewards, but with a heavier heart and more troubled mind than had ever been her fortune in life to have suffered.

CHAPTER XXXVIII.

SOME CHARACTERS NEW TO THE KNIGHT AND THE READER.

Soon after breakfast the following morning the Knight set out to pay his promised visit to Miss Daly, who had taken up her abode at a little village on the coast, about three miles distant. Had Darcy known that her removal thither had been in consequence of his own arrival at "the Corvy," the fact would have greatly added to an embarrassment sufficiently great on other grounds; of this, however, he was not aware; her brother Bagenal accounting for her not inhabiting "the Corvy" as being lonely and desolate, whereas the village of Ballintray was, after its fashion, a little watering-place much frequented in the season by visitors from Coleraine, and other towns still more inland.

Thither now the Knight bent his steps by a little footpath across the fields, which, from time to time, approached the sea-side, and wound again through the gently undulating surface of that ever-changing tract.

Not a human habitation was in sight; not a living thing was seen to move over that wide expanse; it was solitude the very deepest, and well suited the habit of his mind who now wandered there alone. Deeply lost in thought he moved onward, his arms folded on his breast, and his eyes downcast; he neither bestowed a glance upon the gloomy desolation of the land prospect, nor one look of admiring wonder at the giant cliffs, which, straight as a wall, formed the barriers against the ocean.

"What a strange turn of fortune," said he, at length, as relieving his overburdened brain by speech. "I remember well the last day I ever saw her, it was just before my departure from England for my marriage. I remember well driving over to Castle Daly to say good-by; perhaps, too, I had some lurking vanity in exhibiting that splendid team of four greys, with two outriders; how perfect it all was! and a proud fellow I was that day! Maria was looking very handsome; she was dressed for riding, but ordered the horses back as I drove up. What spirits she had!—with what zest she seized upon the enjoyments her youth, her beauty, and her fortune gave her!—how ardently she indulged every costly caprice, and every whim, as if revelling in the pleasure of extravagance even for its own sake! Fearless in everything, she did indeed seem like a native princess, surrounded by all that barbaric splendour of her father's house, the troops of servants, the equipages without number, the guests that came and went unceasingly, all rendering homage to her beauty. 'Twas a gorgeous dream of life! and well she understood how to realise all its enchantment. We scarcely parted good friends on that same last day," said he, after a pause; "her manner was almost mordant. I can recal the cutting sarcasms she dealt around her —strange exuberance of high spirits carried away to the wildest flights of fancy—and after all, when, having dropped my glove, I returned to the luncheon-room to seek it, I saw her in a window, bathed in tears; she did not perceive me, and we never met after! Poor girl! were those outpourings of sorrow the compensation nature exacted for the exercise of such brilliant powers of wit and imagination? or had she really, as some believed, a secret attachment somewhere? Who knows? And now we are to meet again, after years of absence—so fallen, too! If it were not for these grey hairs and this wrinkled brow, I could believe it all a dream;—and what is it but a dream, if we are not fashioned to act differently because of our calamities? Events are but shadows if they move us not."

From thoughts like these he passed on to others—as to how he should be received, and what changes time might have wrought in her.

"She was so lovely, and might have been so much more so, had she but curbed that ever-rising spirit of mockery that made the sparkling lustre of her eyes seem like the scathing flash of lightning rather than the soft beam of tranquil beauty. How we quarrelled and made up again! what everlasting treaties ratified and broken! and now to look back on this with a heart and a spirit weary, how sad it seems! Poor Maria! her destiny has been less happy than mine! She is alone in the world; I have affectionate hearts around me to make a home beneath the humble roof of a cabin."

The Knight was aroused from his musings by suddenly finding himself on the brow of a hill, from which the gorge descended abruptly into a little cove, around which the village of Ballintray was built. A row of whitewashed cottages, in winter inhabited by the fishermen and their families, became, in the summer season, the residence of the visitors, many of whom deserted spacious and well-furnished mansions to pass their days in the squalid discomfort of a cabin. If beauty of situation and picturesque charms of scenery could ever atone for so many inconveniences incurred, this little village might certainly have done so. Land-locked by two jutting promontories, the bay was sheltered both east and westward, while the rising ground behind defended it from the sweeping storms which the south brings in its seasons of rain; in front the distant island of Isla could be seen, and the Scottish coast was always discernible in the clear atmosphere of the evening.

While Darcy stood admiring the well-chosen spot, his eye rested upon a semicircular panel of wood, which, covering over a short and gravelled avenue, displayed in very striking capitals the words "Fumbally's Boarding

House." The edifice itself, more pretentious in extent and character than the cabins around, was ornamented with green jalousies to the windows, and a dazzling brass knocker surmounting a plate of the same metal, whereupon the name, "Mrs. Jones Fumbally," was legible, even from the road. Some efforts at planting had been made in the two square plots of yellowish grass in front, but they had been lamentable failures; and, as if to show that the demerit was of the soil and not of the proprietors, the dead shrubs were suffered to stand where they had been stuck down, while, in default of leaves or buds, they put forth a plentiful covering of stockings, nightcaps, and other wearables, which flaunted as gaily in the breeze as the owners were doing on the beach.

Across the high road and on the beach, which was scarcely more than fifty yards distant, stood a large wooden edifice on wheels, whose make suggested some secret of its original destination, had not that fact been otherwise revealed, since, from beneath the significant name of "Fumbally," an acute decipherer might read the still unerased inscription of "A Panther with only two spots from the head to the tail," an unhappy collocation which fixed upon the estimable lady the epithet of the animal in question.

Various garden-seats and rustic benches were scattered about, some of which were occupied by lounging figures of gentlemen, in costumes ingeniously a cross between the sporting world and the naval service; while the ladies displayed a no less elegant *négligé*, half sea-nymph, half shepherdess.

So much for the prospect landward, while towards the waves themselves there was a party of bathers, whose flowing hair and lengthened drapery indicated their sex. These maintained through all their sprightly gambols an animated conversation with a party of gentlemen on the rocks, who seemed, by the telescopes and spy-glasses which lay around them, to be equally prepared for the inspection of near and distant objects, and alternately turned from the criticism of a fair naiad beneath to a Scotch collier working "north about" in the distance.

Darcy could not help feeling that if the cockneyism of a boarding-house, and the blinds and the brass knocker, were sadly repugnant to the sense of admiration the scene itself would excite, there was an ample compensation in the primitive simplicity of the worthy inhabitants, who seemed to revel in all the unsuspecting freedom of our first parents themselves; for while some stood on little promontories of the rocks in most Canova-like drapery, little frescoes of naked children flitted around and about, without concern to themselves, or astonishment to the beholders.

Never was the good Knight more convinced of his own prudence in paying his first visit alone, and he stood for some time in patient admiration of the scene, until his eye rested on a figure who, seated at some dis tance off on a little eminence of the rocky coast, was as coolly surveying Darcy through his telescope. The mutual inspection continued for several minutes, when the stranger, deliberately shutting up his glass, advanced towards the Knight.

The gentleman was short, but stoutly knit, with a walk and a carriage of his head that, to Darcy's observant eye, bespoke an innate sense of self-importance; his dress was a green coat, cut jockey fashion, and ornamented with very large buttons, displaying heads of stags, foxes, and badgers, and other emblems of the chase, short Russia duck trousers, a wide-leaved straw hat, and a very loose cravat, knotted sailor-fashion on his breast. As he approached the Knight, he came to a full stop about half a dozen paces in front, and putting his hand to his hat, held it straight above his head, pretty much in the way stage imitators of Napoleon were wont to perform the salutation.

"A stranger, sir, I presume?" said he, with an insinuating smile and an air of dignity at the same moment. Darcy bowed a courteous assent, and the other went on: "Sweet scene, sir—lovely nature—animated and grand."

"Most impressive, I confess," said Darcy, with difficulty repressing a smile.

"Never here before, I take it?"

"Never, sir."

"Came from Coleraine, possibly? Walked all the way, eh?"

"I came on foot, as you have divined," said Darcy, dryly.

"Not going to make any stay, probably; a mere glance, and go on again. Isn't that so?"

"I believe you are quite correct; but may I, in return for your considerate inquiries, ask one question on my own part? You are, perhaps, sufficiently acquainted with the locality to inform me if a Miss Daly resides in this village, and where?"

"Miss Daly, sir, did inhabit that cottage yonder, where you see the oars on the thatch, but it has been let to the Moors of Ballymena; they pay two ten a week for the three rooms and the use of the kitchen; smart that, ain't it?"

"And Miss Daly resides at present——"

"She's one of us," said the little man, with a significant jerk of his thumb to the blue board with the gilt letters; "not much of that after all; but she lives under the sway of 'Mother Fum,' though, from one caprice or another, she don't mix with the other boarders. Do you know her yourself?"

"I had that honour some years ago."

"Much altered, I take it, since that; down in the world, too! She was an heiress in those days, I've heard, and a beauty. Has some of the good looks still, but lost all the shiners."

"Am I likely to find her at home at this hour?" said Darcy, moving away, and anxious for an opportunity to escape his communicative friend.

"No, not now; never shows in the morning. Just comes down to dinner, and disappears again. Never takes a hand at whist—penny points tell up, you know—seem a trifle at first, but hang me if they don't make a figure in the budget afterwards. There, do you see that fat lady with the black bathing-cap?—no, I mean the one with the blue baize patched on the shoulder, the Widow Mackie—she makes a nice thing of it—won twelve and fourpence since the first of the month. Pretty creature that yonder, with one stocking on, Miss Boyle, of Carrick-ma-clash."

"I must own," said Darcy, dryly, "that, not having the privilege of knowing these ladies, I do not conceive myself at liberty to regard them with due attention."

"Oh! they never mind that, here; no secrets among us."

"Very primitive, and doubtless very delightful; but I have trespassed too long on your politeness. Permit me to wish you a very good morning."

"Not at all; have nothing in the world to do. Paul Dempsey—that's my name—was always an idle man; Paul Dempsey, sir, nephew of old Paul Dempsey, of Dempsey Grove, in the county of Kilkenny; a snug place, that I wish the proprietor felt he had enjoyed sufficiently long. And your name, if I might make bold, is——?"

"I call myself Gwynne," said Darcy, after a slight hesitation.

"Gwynne—Gwynne—there was a Gwynne, a tailor, in Ballyragget; a connexion, probably?"

"I am not aware of any relationship," said Darcy, smiling.

"I'm glad of it; I owe your brother or your cousin there—that is, if he was either—a sum of seven-and-nine for these ducks. There are Gwynnes in Ross besides, and Quins; are you sure it is not Quin? Very common name Quin."

"I believe we spell our name as I have pronounced it."

"Well, if you come to spend a little time here, I'll give you a hint or two. Don't join Leonard—that blue-nosed fellow, yonder, in whisky. He'll be asking you, but don't—at it all day." Here Mr. Dempsey pantomimed the action of tossing off a dram. "No whist with the widow! If you were younger, I'd say no small plays with Bess Boyle—has a brother in the Antrim militia, a very quarrelsome fellow."

"I thank you sincerely for your kind counsel, although not destined to by it. I have one favour to ask: could you procure me the means to enclose my card for Miss Daly, as I must relinquish the hope of seeing her on this occasion?"

"No, no—stop and dine. Capital cod and oysters—always good. The mutton *rayther* scraggy, but with a good will and good teeth manageable enough; and excellent malt——"

"I thank you for your hospitable proposal, but cannot accept it."

"Well, I'll take care of your card; you'll probably come over again soon. You're at M'Grotty's, ain't you?"

"Not at present; and as to the card, with your permission I'll enclose it." This Darcy was obliged to insist upon; as, if he left his name as Gwynne, Miss Daly might have failed to recognise him, while he desired to avoid being known as Mr. Darcy.

"Well, come in here; I'll find you the requisites. But I wish you'd stop and see the 'Panther.'"

Had the Knight overheard this latter portion of Mr. Dempsey's invitation he might have been somewhat surprised, but it chanced that the words were lost; and, preceded by honest Paul, he entered the little garden in front of the house.

When Darcy had enclosed his card and committed it to the hands of Mr. Dempsey, that gentleman was far too deeply impressed with the importance of his mission to delay a moment in executing it, and then the Knight was at last left at liberty to retrace his steps unmolested towards home. If he had smiled at the persevering curiosity and eccentric communicativeness of Mr. Dempsey, Darcy sorrowed deeply over the fallen fortunes which condemned one he had known so courted and so flattered once, to companionship like this. The words of the classic satirist came full upon his memory, and never did a sentiment meet more ready acceptance than the bitter, heart-wrung confession—"Unhappy poverty! you have no heavier misery in your train than that you make men seem ridiculous." A hundred times he wished he had never made the excursion; he would have given anything to be able to think of her as she had been, without the detracting influence of these vulgar associations. "And yet," said he, half aloud, "a year or so more, if I am still living, I shall probably have forgotten my former position, and shall have conformed myself to the new and narrow limits of my lot, doubtless as she does."

The quick tramp of feet on the heather behind him aroused him, and, in turning, he saw a person coming towards, and evidently endeavouring to overtake, him. As he came nearer, the Knight perceived it was the gentleman already alluded to by Dempsey as one disposed to certain little traits of conviviality—a fact which a nose of a deep copper colour, and two blood-shot, bleary eyes, corroborated. His dress was a blue frock with a standing collar, military fashion, and dark trousers; and, although bearing palpable marks of long wear, were still neat and clean-looking. His age, as well as appearances might be trusted, was probably between fifty and sixty.

"Mr. Gwynne, I believe, sir," said the stranger, touching his cap as he spoke. "Miss Daly begged of me to say that she has just received your card, and will be happy to see you."

Darcy stared at the speaker fixedly, and appeared, while unmindful of his words, to be occupied with some deep emotion within him. The other, who had delivered his message in a tone of easy unconcern, now fixed his eyes on the Knight, and they continued for some seconds to regard each other. Gradually, however, the stranger's face changed; a sickly pallor crept over the features stained by long intemperance, his lip trembled, and two heavy tears gushed out and rolled down his seared cheeks.

"My G—d!—can it be? It surely is not!" said Darcy, with almost tremulous earnestness.

"Yes, Colonel, it is the man you once remembered in your regiment as Jack Leonard; the same who led a forlorn hope at Quebec—the man broke with disgrace and dismissed the service for cowardice at Trois Rivières."

"Poor fellow!" said Darcy, taking his hand; "I heard you were dead."

"No, sir, it's very hard to kill a man by mere shame; though if suffering could do it, I might have died."

"I have often doubted about that sentence, Leonard," said Darcy, eagerly. "I wrote to the Commander-in-Chief to have inquiry made, suspecting that nothing short of some affection of the mind, or some serious derangement of health, could make a brave man behave badly."

"You were right, sir; I was a drunkard, not a coward. I was unworthy of the service; I merited my disgrace, but not on the grounds for which I met it."

"Good Heaven! then I was right!" said Darcy, in a burst of passionate grief; "my letter to the War Office was unanswered. I wrote again, and received for reply that an example was necessary, and Lieutenant Leonard's conduct pointed him out as the most suitable case for heavy punishment."

"It was but just, Colonel; I was a poltroon when I took more than half a bottle of wine. If I were not sober now I could not have the courage to face you here where I stand."

"Poor Jack!" said Darcy, wringing his hand cordially; "and what have you done since?"

Leonard threw his eyes down upon his threadbare garments, his patched boots, and the white-worn seams of his old frock, but not a word escaped his lips. They walked on for some time side by side without speaking, when Leonard said,

"They know nothing of me here, Colonel. I need not ask you to be—cautious." There was a hesitation before he uttered the last word.

"I do not desire to be recognised either," said Darcy, "and prefer being called Mr. Gwynne to the name of my family; and here, if I mistake not, comes a gentleman most eager to learn anything of anybody."

Mr. Dempsey came up at this moment with a lady leaning on each of his arms.

"Glad to see you again, sir; hope you've thought better of your plans, and are going to try Mother Fum's fare. Mrs. M'Quirk, Mr. Gwynne—Mr. Gwynne, Miss Drew. Leonard will do the honours till we come back." So saying, and with a princely wave of his straw hat, Mr. Dempsey resumed his walk with the step of a conqueror.

"That fellow must be a confounded annoyance to you," said Darcy, as he looked after him.

"Not now, sir," said the other, submissively; "I'm used to him; besides, since Miss Daly's arrival, he is far quieter than he used to be, he seems afraid of her. But I'll leave you now, Colonel. He touched his cap respectfully, and was about to move away, when Darcy, pitying the confusion which overwhelmed him, caught his hand cordially, and said,

"Well, Jack, for the moment, good-by; but come over and see me; I live at the little cottage called 'the Corvy.'"

"Good Heaven, sir! and is it true what I read in the newspaper about your misfortunes?"

"I conclude it is, Jack, though I have not read it; they could scarcely have exaggerated."

"And you bear it like this!" said the other, with a stare of amazement; then added, in a broken voice, "though, to be sure, there's a wide difference between loss of fortune and ruined character."

"Come, Jack, I see you are not so good a philosopher as I thought you. Come and dine with me to-morrow at five."

"Dine with *you*, Colonel!" said Leonard, blushing deeply.

"And why not, man? I see you have forgotten the injustice I once did you, and I am happier this day to know it was I was in the wrong than that a British officer was a coward."

"Oh, Colonel Darcy, I did not think this poor broken heart could ever throb again with gratitude, but you have made it do so; you have kindled the flame of pride where the ashes were almost cold." And with a burning blush upon his face he turned away. Darcy looked after him for a second and then entered the house.

Darcy had barely time to throw one glance around the scanty furniture of the modest parlour into which he was ushered, when Miss Daly entered,

She stopped suddenly short, and for a few seconds each regarded the other without speaking; time had, indeed, worked many changes in the appearance of each for which they were unprepared, but no less were they unprepared for the emotions this sudden meeting was to call up.

Miss Daly was plainly but handsomely dressed, and wore her silvery hair beneath a cap in two long bands on either cheek, with something of an imitation of a mode she followed in youth; the tones of her voice, too, were wonderfully little changed, and fell upon Darcy's ear with a strange, melancholy meaning.

"We little thought, Knight," said she, "when we parted last, that our next meeting would have been as this, so many years and many sorrows have passed over us since that day!"

"And a large measure of happiness, too, Maria," said Darcy, as, taking her hand, he led her to a seat; "let us never forget, amid all our troubles, how many blessings we have enjoyed."

Whether it was the words themselves that agitated her, or something in his manner of uttering them, Miss Daly blushed deeply and was silent. Darcy was not slow to see her confusion, and suddenly remembering how inapplicable his remark was to her fortunes, though not to his own, added, hastily, "I, at least, would be very ungrateful if I could not look back with thankfulness to a long life of prosperity and happiness; and if I bear my present reverses with less repining, it is, I hope and trust, from the sincerity of this feeling."

"You have enjoyed the sunny path in life," said Miss Daly, in a low, faint voice, "and it is, perhaps, as you say, reason for enduring altered fortunes better." She paused, and then, with a more hurried voice, added, "One does not bear calamity better from habit, that is all a mistake; when the temper is soured by disappointment the spirit of endurance loses its firmest ally. Your misfortunes will, however, be but short-lived, I hope; my brother writes me he has great confidence in some legal opinions, and certain steps he has already taken in Chancery."

"The warm-hearted and the generous are always sanguine," said Darcy, with a sad smile; "Bagenal would not be your brother if he could see a friend in difficulty without venturing on everything to rescue him. What an old friendship ours has been! class fellows at school, companions in youth, we have run our race together, to end with fortune how similar! I was thinking, Maria, as I came along, of Castle Daly, and remembering how I passed my holidays with you there. Is your memory as good as mine?"

"I scarcely like to think of Castle Daly," said she, almost pettishly, "it reminds me so much of that wasteful, reckless life which laid the foundation of our ruin; tell me how Lady Eleanor Darcy bears up, and your daughter, of whom I have heard so much, and desire so ardently to see; is she more English or Irish?"

"A thorough Darcy," said the Knight, smiling, "but yet with traits of soft submission and patient trust our family has been but rarely gifted with; her virtues are all the mother's, every blemish of her character has come from the other side."

"Is she rash and headstrong? for those are Darcy failings."

"Not more daring or courageous than I love her to be," said Darcy, proudly. "Not a whit more impetuous in sustaining the right, or denouncing the wrong, than I glory to see her; but too ardent, perhaps, too easily carried away by first impressions, than is either fashionable or frequent in the colder world."

"It is a dangerous temper," said Miss Daly, thoughtfully.

"You are right, Maria: such people are for the most part like the gamester who has but one throw for his fortune, if he loses which, all is lost with it."

"Too true! too true!" said she, in an accent whose melancholy sadness seemed to come from the heart. "You must guard her carefully from any rash attachment; a character like hers is strong to endure, but not less certain to sink under calamity."

"I know it; I feel it," said Darcy; "but my dear child is still too young to have mixed in that world which is already closed against her; her affections could never have strayed beyond the limits of our little home circle; she has kept all her love for those who need it most."

"And Lady Eleanor?" said Miss Daly, as if suddenly desirous to change the theme; "Bagenal tells me her health has been but indifferent: how does she bear our less genial climate, here?"

"She's better than for many years past; I could even say she's happier. Strange it is, Maria, but the course of prosperity, like the calms in the ocean, too frequently steep the faculties in an apathy that becomes weariness, but when the clouds are drifted along faster, and the waves rustle at the prow, the energies of life are again excited, and the very occasion of danger begets the courage to confront it. We cannot be happy when devoid of self-esteem, and there is but little opportunity to indulge this honest pride when the world goes fairly with us, without any effort of our own; reverses of fortune——"

"Oh, reverses of fortune!" interrupted Miss Daly, rapidly, "people think much more about them than they merit; it is the world itself makes them so difficult to bear; one can think and act as freely beneath the thatch of a cabin as the gilded roof of a palace. It is the mock sympathy, the affected condolence for your fallen estate, that tortures you; the never-ending recurrence to what you once were contrasted with what you are, the cruelty of that friendship that is never content, save when reminding you of a station lost for ever, and seeking to unfit you for your humble path in the valley, because your step was once proudly on the mountain-top."

"I will not concede all this," said the Knight, mildly; "my fall has been too recent not to remind me of many kindnesses."

"I hate pity," said Miss Daly; "it is like a recommendation to mercy after the sentence of an unjust judge! Now tell me of Lionel."

"A fine, high-spirited soldier, as little affected by his loss as though it touched him not, and yet, poor boy, to all appearance a bright career was about to open before him—well received by the world, honoured by the personal notice of his Prince."

"Ha! now I think of it, why did you not vote against the Minister?"

"It was on that evening," said Darcy, sorrowfully—"on that very evening—I heard of Gleeson's flight."

"Well"—then suddenly correcting herself, and restraining the question that almost trembled on her lip, she added, "and you were, doubtless, too much shocked to appear in the House?"

"I was ill," said Darcy, faintly; "indeed, I believe I can say with truth, my own ruin preyed less upon my mind than the perfidy of one so long confided in."

"And they made this accidental illness the ground of a great attack against your character, and sought to discover in your absence the secret of your corruption. How basely-minded men must be, when they will invent not only actions, but motives to calumniate." She paused, and then muttered to herself, "I wish you had voted against that Bill."

"It would have done little good," said the Knight, answering her soliloquy; "my vote could neither retard nor prevent the measure, and as for myself, personally, I am proud enough to think I have given sufficient guarantees by a long life of independent action, not to need this crowning test of honesty. Now to matters nearer to us both: when will you come and visit my wife and daughter? or shall I bring them here to you?"

"No, no, not here. I am not ashamed of this place for myself, though I should be so if they were once to see it."

"But you feel less lonely," said Darcy, in a gentle tone, as if anticipating the reason of her choice of residence.

"Less lonely!" replied she, with a haughty laugh; "what companionship or society have I with people like these? It is not that!—it is my poverty compels me to live here. Of them and of their habits I know nothing; from me and from mine they take good care to keep aloof. No with your leave I will visit Lady Eleanor at your cottage—that is, if she has no objection to receive me."

"She will be but too happy," said Darcy, "to know and value one of her husband's oldest and warmest friends."

"You must not expect me soon, however," said she, hastily; "I have grown capricious in everything, and never can answer for performing a pledge at any stated time, and therefore never make one."

Abrupt and sudden as had been the changes of her voice and manner through this interview, there was a tone of unusual harshness in the way this speech was uttered; and as Darcy rose to take his leave, a feeling of sadness came over him to think that this frame of mind must have been the slow result of years of heart-consuming sorrow.

"Whenever you come, Maria," said he, as he took her hand in his, "you will be most welcome to us."

"Have you heard any tidings of Forester?" said Miss Daly, as if suddenly recalling a subject she wished to speak on.

"Forester of the Guards? Lionel's friend, do you mean?"

"Yes; you know that he has left the army, thrown up his commission, and gone no one knows where?"

"I did not know of that before. I am sincerely sorry for it. Is the cause surmised?"

Miss Daly made no answer, but stood with her eyes bent on the ground, and apparently in deep thought; then looking up suddenly, she said, with more composure than ordinary, "Make my compliments to Lady Eleanor, and say, that at the first favourable moment I will pay my personal respects to her—kiss Helen for me—good-by." And, without waiting for Darcy to take his leave, she walked hastily by, and closed the door after her.

"This wayward manner," said Darcy, sorrowfully, to himself, "has a deeper root than mere capriciousness; the heart has suffered so long, that the mind begins to partake of the decay." And with this sad reflection he left the village, and turned his solitary steps towards home.

If Darcy was grieved to find Miss Daly surrounded by such unsuitable companionship, he was more than recompensed at finding that her taste rejected nearer intimacy with Mrs. Fumbally's household. More than once the fear crossed his mind that, with diminished circumstances, she might have lapsed into habits so different from her former life, and he could better look upon her struggling as she did against her adverse fortune, than assimilating herself to those as much below her in sentiment as in station. He was happy to have seen his old friend once more, he was glad to refresh his memory of long-forgotten scenes by the sight of her who had been his playfellow and his companion, but he was not free of a certain dread that

Miss Daly would scarcely be acceptable to his wife, while her wayward, uncertain temper would form no safe companionship for his daughter. As he pondered on these things, he began to feel how altered circumstances beget suspicion, and how he, who had never known the feeling of distrust, now found himself hesitating and doubting, where formerly he had acted without fear or reserve.

"Yes," said he, aloud, "when wealth and station were mine, the consciousness of power gave energy to my thoughts, but now I am to learn how narrow means can fetter a man's courage."

"Some truth in that," said a voice behind him; "would cut a very different figure myself if old Bob Dempsey, of Dempsey Grove, were to betake himself to a better world."

Darcy's cheek reddened between shame and anger to find himself overheard by his obtrusive companion, and, with a cold salute, he passed on. Mr. Dempsey, however, was not a man to be so easily got rid of; he possessed that happy temper that renders its owner insensible to shame and unconscious of rebuke; besides that, he was always "going your way," quite content to submit to any amount of rebuff rather than be alone. If you talked, it was well; if you listened, it was better; but if you affected open indifference to him, and neither exchanged a word nor vouchsafed the slightest attention, even that was supportable. for he could give the conversation a character of monologue or anecdote which occupied himself at least.

CHAPTER XXXIX.

A TALE OF MR. DEMPSEY'S GRANDFATHER.

THE Knight of Gwynne was far too much occupied in his own reflections to attend to his companion, and exhibited a total unconcern to several piquant little narratives of Mrs. Mackie's dexterity in dealing the cards—of Mrs. Fumbally's parsimony in domestic arrangements—of Miss Boyle's effrontery—of Leonard's intemperance—and even of Miss Daly's assumed superiority.

"You're taking the wrong path," said Mr. Dempsey, suddenly interrupting one of his own narratives, at a spot where the two roads diverged, one proceeding inland, while the other followed the line of the coast.

"With your leave, sir," said Darcy, coldly, "I will take this way, and, if you'll kindly permit it, I will do so alone."

"Oh! certainly," said Dempsey, without the slightest sign of umbrage; "would never have thought of joining you had it not been from overhearing an expression so exactly pat to my own condition, that I thought we were brothers in misfortune; you scarcely bear up as well as I do, though."

Darcy turned abruptly round, as the fear flashed across him, and he muttered to himself, "This fellow knows me; if so, the whole county will soon be as wise as himself, and the place become intolerable." Oppressed with this unpleasant reflection, the Knight moved on, nor was it till after a considerable interval that he was conscious of his companion's presence, for Mr. Dempsey still accompanied him, though at the distance of several paces, and as if following a path of his own choosing.

Darcy laughed good-humouredly at the pertinacity of his tormentor; and half amused by the man, and half ashamed of his own rudeness to him, he made some casual observation on the scenery to open a reconciliation.

"The coast is much finer," said Dempsey, "close to your cottage."

This was a home-thrust for the Knight, to show him that concealment was of no use against so subtle an adversary.

"'The Corvy' is, as you observe, very happily situated," replied Darcy, calmly; "I scarcely know which to prefer, the coast-line towards Dunluce, or the bold cliffs that stretch away to Bengore."

"When the wind comes north-by-west," said Dempsey, with a shrewd glance of his greenish grey eyes, "there's always a wreck or two between the Skerries and Portrush."

"Indeed! Is the shore so unsafe as that?"

"Oh, yes. You may expect a very busy winter here when the homeward-bound Americans are coming northward."

"D—n the fellow! does he take me for a wrecker?" said Darcy to himself, not knowing whether to laugh or be angry.

"Such a curiosity that old 'Corvy' is, they tell me," said Dempsey, emboldened by his success; "every species of weapon and arm in the world, they say, gathered together there."

"A few swords and muskets," said the Knight, carelessly, "a stray dirk or two, and some harpoons, furnish the greater part of the armoury."

"Oh, perhaps so! The story goes, however, that old Daly—brother, I believe, of our friend at Mother Fum's—could arm twenty fellows at a moment's warning, and did so on more than one occasion, too."

"With what object, in Heaven's name?"

"Buccaneering, piracy, wrecking, and so on," said Dempsey, with all the unconcern with which he would have enumerated so many pursuits of the chase.

A hearty roar of laughter broke from the Knight, and when it ceased, he said, "I would be sincerely sorry to stand in your shoes, Mr. Dempsey, so near to yonder cliff, if you made that same remark in Mr. Daly's hearing."

"He'd gain very little by me," said Mr. Dempsey; "one and eightpence, an old watch, an oyster-knife, and my spectacles, are all the property in my possession, except when, indeed," added he, after a pause, "Bob remits the quarter's allowance."

"It is only just," said Darcy, gravely, "to a gentleman who takes such pains to inform himself on the affairs of his neighbours, that I should tell you that Mr. Bagenal Daly is not a pirate, nor am I a wrecker. I am sure you will be generous enough for this unasked information not to require of me a more lengthened account either of my friend or myself."

"You're in the Revenue, perhaps?" interrupted the undaunted Dempsey; "I thought so when I saw you first."

Darcy shook his head in dissent.

"Wrong again. Ah! I see it all, the old story. Saw better days—you have just come down here to lie snug and quiet, out of the way of writs and latitats—went too fast—by Jove, that touches myself, too! If I hadn't happened to have had a grandfather, I'd have been a rich man this day. Did you ever chance to hear of Dodd and Dempsey, the great wine-merchants? My father was son of Dodd and Dempsey—that is Dempsey, you know--and it was his father, Sam Dempsey, ruined him."

"No very uncommon circumstance," said the Knight, sorrowfully, "for an Irish father."

"You've heard the story, I suppose?—of course you nave, every one knows it."

"I rather think not," said the Knight, who was by no means sorry to turn Mr. Dempsey from cross-examination into mere narrative.

"I'll tell it to you; I am sure I ought to know it well, I've heard my father relate it something like a hundred times."

"I fear I must decline so pleasant a proposal," said Darcy, smiling. "At this moment I have an engagement."

"Never mind. To-morrow will do just as well," interrupted the inexorable Dempsey. "Come over and take your mutton-chop with me at five, and you shall have the story into the bargain."

"I regret that I cannot accept so very tempting an invitation," said Darcy, struggling between his sense of pride and a feeling of astonishment at his companion's coolness.

"Not come to dinner!" exclaimed Dempsey, as if the thing was scarcely credible. "Oh, very well, only remember"—and here he put an unusual gravity into his words—"only remember the *onus* is now on you."

The Knight burst into a hearty laugh at this subtle retort, and, willing as he ever was to go with the humour of the moment, replied,

"I am ready to accept it, sir, and beg that you will dine with *me*."

"When and where?" said Dempsey.

"To-morrow, at that cottage yonder: five is your hour, I believe—we shall say five."

"Booked!" exclaimed Dempsey, with an air of triumph; while he muttered, with a scarcely subdued voice, "Knew I'd do it!—never failed in my life!"

"Till then, Mr. Dempsey," said Darcy, removing his hat courteously, as he bowed to him—"till then——"

"Your most obedient," replied Dempsey, returning the salute; and so they parted.

"The Corvy," on the day after the Knight's visit to Port Ballintray, was a scene of rather amusing bustle; the Knight's dinner-party, as Helen quizzingly called it, affording occupation for every member of the household. In former times, the only difficult details of an entertainment were in the selection of the guests—bringing together a company likely to be suitable to each other, and endowed with those various qualities which make up the success of society; now, however, the question was the more material one, the dinner itself.

It is always a fortunate thing when whatever absurdity our calamities in life excite should be apparent only to ourselves. The laugh which is so difficult to bear from the world, is then an actual relief from our troubles. The Darcys felt this truth, as each little embarrassment that arose was food for mirth; and Lady Eleanor, who least of all could adapt herself to such contingencies, became as eager as the rest about the little preparations of the day.

While the Knight hurried hither and thither, giving directions here and instructions there, he explained to Lady Eleanor some few circumstances respecting the character of his guests. It was, indeed, a new kind of company he was about to present to his wife and daughter; but while conscious of the disparity in every respect, he was not the less eager to do the hospitalities of his humble house with all becoming honour. It is true his invitation to Mr. Dempsey was rather forced from him than willingly accorded; he was about the very last kind of person Darcy would have asked to his table, if perfectly free to choose; but, of all men living, the Knight knew least how to escape from a difficulty the outlet to which should cost him any sacrifice of feeling.

"Well, well, it is but once and away; and, after all, the talkativeness of our little friend Dempsey will be so far a relief to poor Leonard, that he will be brought less prominently forward himself, and be suffered to escape unremarked—a circumstance which, from all that I can see, will afford him sincere pleasure."

At length all the preparations were happily accomplished; the emissary despatched to Kilrush at daybreak had returned with a much-coveted turkey; the fisherman had succeeded in capturing a lordly salmon; oysters and lobsters poured in abundantly; and Mrs. M'Kerrigan, who had been left as a fixture at "the Corvy," found her only embarrassment in selection from that profusion of "God's gifts," as she phrased it, that now surrounded her. The hour of five drew near, and the ladies were seated in the hall, the doors of which lay open, as the two guests were seen making their way towards the cottage.

"Here they come, papa," said Helen; "and now for a guess. Is not the short man with the straw hat Mr. Dempsey, and his tall companion Mr. Leonard?"

"Of course it is," said Lady Eleanor; "who could mistake the garrulous pertinacity of that little thing that gesticulates at every step, or the plodding patience of his melancholy associate?"

The next moment the Knight was welcoming them in front of the cottage. The ceremony of introduction to the ladies being over, Mr. Dempsey, who probably was aware that the demands upon his descriptive powers would not be inconsiderable when he returned to "Mother Fum's," put his glass to his eye, and commenced a very close scrutiny of the apartment and its contents.

"Quite a show-box, by Jove!" said he, at last, as he peered through a glass cabinet, where Chinese slippers, with models in ivory and carvings in box were heaped promiscuously together; "upon my word, sir, you have a very remarkable collection. And who may be our friend in the boat here?" added he, turning to the grim visage of Bagenal Daly himself, who stared with a bold effrontery that would not have disgraced the original.

"The gentleman you see there," said the Knight, "is the collector himself, and the other is his servant. They are represented in the costumes in which they made their escape from a captivity among the Red Men."

"Begad!" said Dempsey, "that fellow with the tortoise painted on his forehead has a look of our old friend Miss Daly; shouldn't wonder if he was a member of her family."

"You have well guessed it—he is the lady's brother."

"Ah, ah!" muttered Dempsey to himself, "always thought there was something odd about her—never suspected Indian blood, however. How Mother Fum will stare when I tell her she's a Squaw! Didn't they show these things at the Rooms in Mary's-street? I think I saw them advertised in the papers."

"I think you must mistake," said the Knight; "they are the private collection of my friend."

"And where may Woc-woc—confound his name—the 'Howling Wind,' as he is pleased to call himself, be passing his leisure hours just now?"

"He is at present in Dublin, sir; and, if you desire, he shall be made aware of your polite inquiries."

"No, no—hang it, no—don't like the look of him! Should have no objection, though, if he'd pay old Bob Dempsey a visit, and frighten him out of this world for me."

"Dinner, my Lady," said old Tate, as he threw open the doors into the dining-room, and bowed with all his accustomed solemnity.

"Hum," muttered Dempsey, "my Lady, won't go down with me!—too old a soldier for that!"

"Will you give my daughter your arm?" said the Knight to the little man, for already Lady Eleanor had passed on with Mr. Leonard.

As Mr. Dempsey arranged his napkin on his knee, he endeavoured to catch Leonard's eye, and telegraph to him his astonishment at the elegance of the table equipage which graced the board. Poor Leonard, however, seldom looked up; a deep sense of shame, the agonising memory of what he once was, recalled vividly by the sight of those objects, and the appearance of persons which reminded him of his past condition, almost stunned him. The whole seemed like a dream; even though intemperance had degraded him, there were intervals in which his mind, clear to see and reflect, sorrowed deeply over his fallen state. Had the Knight met him with a cold and repulsive deportment, or had he refused to acknowledge him altogether, he could better have borne it than all the kindness of his present manner. It was evident, too, from Lady Eleanor's tone to him, that she knew nothing of his unhappy fortune, or that if she did, the delicacy with which she treated him was only the more benevolent. Oppressed by such emotions, he sat endeavouring to eat, and trying to listen and interest himself in the conversation around him, but the effort was too much for his strength, and a vague, half-whispered assent, or a dull, unmeaning smile, were about as much as he could contribute to what was passing.

The Knight, whose tact was rarely at fault, saw every struggle that was passing in Leonard's mind, and adroitly contrived that the conversation should be carried on without any demand upon him, either as talker or listener. If Lady Eleanor and Helen contributed their aid to this end, Mr. Dempsey was not backward on his part, for he talked unceasingly. The good things of the table, to which he did ample justice, afforded an opportunity for catechising the ladies in their skill in household matters, and Miss Darcy, who seemed immensely amused by the novely of such a character, sustained her part to admiration, entering deeply into culinary details, and communicating receipts invented for the occasion. At another time, perhaps, the Knight would have checked the spirit of *persiflage* in which his daughter indulged, but he suffered it now to take its course, well pleased that the mark of her ridicule was not only worthy of the scarcasm, but insensible to its arrow.

"Quite right—quite right not to try Mother Fum's when you can get up a little thing like this—and such capital sherry; look how Tom takes it in —slips like oil over his lip!"

Leonard looked up; an expression of rebuking severity for a moment crossed his features, but his eyes fell the next instant, and a low, faint sigh escaped him.

"I ought to know what sherry is—'Dodd and Dempsey's' was the great house for sherry."

"By the way," said the Knight, "did not you promise me a little narrative of Dodd and Dempsey, when we parted yesterday?"

"To be sure I did. Will you have it now?"

Lady Eleanor and Helen rose to withdraw, but Mr. Dempsey, who took the movement as significant, immediately interposed, by saying,

"Don't stir, ma'am—sit down, ladies, I beg; there's nothing broad in the story—it might be told before the Maids of Honour."

Lady Eleanor and Helen were thunderstruck at the explanation, and the Knight laughed till the tears came.

"My dear Eleanor," said he, "you really must accept Mr. Dempsey's assurance, and listen to his story now."

The ladies took their seats once more, and Mr. Dempsey having filled his glass, drank off a bumper; but whether it was that the narrative itself demanded a greater exertion at his hands, or that the cold quietude of Lady Eleanor's manner abashed him, but he found a second bumper necessary before he commenced his task.

"I say," whispered he to the Knight, "couldn't you get that decanter out of Leonard's reach before I begin?—he'll not leave a drop in it while I am talking."

As if he felt that, after his explanation, the tale should be more particularly addressed to Lady Eleanor, he turned his chair round so as to face her, and thus began:

"There was once upon a time, ma'am, a Lord-Lieutenant of Ireland who was a Duke. Whether he was Duke of Rutland, or Bedford, or Portland, or any other title it was he had, my memory doesn't serve me; it is enough, however, if I say he was immensely rich, and, like many other people in the same way, immensely in debt. The story goes that he never travelled through England, and caught sight of a handsome place, or fine domain, or a beautiful cottage, that he didn't go straightway to the owner and buy it down out of the face, as a body might say, whether he would or no. And so in time it came to pass that there was scarcely a county in England without some magnificent house belonging to him. In many parts of Scotland he had them too, and, in all probability, he would have done the same in Ireland if he could. Well, ma'am, there never was such rejoicings as Dublin saw the night his Grace arrived to be our Viceroy! To know that we had got a man with one hundred and fifty thousand a year, and a spirit to spend double the money, was a downright blessing from Providence, and there was no saying what might not be the prosperity of Ireland under so auspicious a ruler.

"To do him justice, he didn't baulk public expectation. Open house at the Castle, ditto at the Lodge in the Park, a mansion full of guests in the county Wicklow, a pack of hounds in Kildare, twelve horses training at the Curragh, a yacht like a little man-of-war in Dunleary harbour, large subscriptions to everything like sport, and a pension for life to every man that could sing a jolly song, or write a witty bit of poetry! Well, ma'am, they say, who remember those days, that they saw the best of Ireland, and surely I believe, if his Grace had only lived, and had his own way, the Peerage would have been as pleasant, and the Bench of Bishops as droll, and the Ladies of Honour as——Well, never mind, I'll pass on." Here Mr. Dempsey, to console himself for the abruptness of his pause, poured out and drank another bumper of sherry. "Pleasant times they were," said he, smacking his lips, "and faith, if Tom Leonard himself was alive then, the colour of his nose might have made him Commander of the Forces; but, to continue, it was Dodd and Dempsey's house supplied the sherry—only the sherry, ma'am; old Stewart, of Belfast, had the port, and Kinnahan the claret and lighter liquors. I may mention, by the way, that my grandfather's contract included brandy, and that he wouldn't have given it up for either of the other two. It was just about this time that Dodd died, and my grandfather was left alone in the firm, but whether it was out of respect for his late partner or that he might have felt himself lonely, but he always kept up the name of Dodd on the brass plate, and signed the name along with his own; indeed, they say that he once saluted his wife by the name of Mrs. Dodd and Dempsey. But, as I was saying, it was one of those days when my grandfather was seated on a high stool in the back office of his house in Abbey-street, that a fine, tall young fellow, with a blue frock-coat, all braided with gold, and an elegant cocked-hat, with a plume of feathers in it, came tramping into the room, his spurs jingling, and his brass sabre clinking, and his sabretash banging at his legs.

"'Mr. Dempsey?' said he.

"'D. and D.,' said my grandfather; 'that is, Dodd and Dempsey, your Grace,' for he half suspected it was the Duke himself.

"'I am Captain M'Claverty, of the Scots Greys,' said he, 'first aide-de-camp to his Excellency.'

"'I hope you may live to be colonel of the regiment,' said my grandfather, for he was as polite and well-bred as any man in Ireland.

"'That's too good a sentiment,' said the captain, 'not to be pledged in a glass of your own sherry.'

"'And we'll do it, too,' said old Dempsey. And he opened the desk, and took out a bottle he had for his own private drinking, and uncorked it with a little pocket corkscrew he always carried about with him, and he produced two glasses, and he and the captain hob-nobbed and drank to each other.

"'Begad!' said the captain, 'his Grace sent me to thank you for the delicious wine you supplied him with, but it's nothing to this—not to be compared to it.'

"'I've better again,' said my grandfather. 'I've wine that would bring the tears into your eyes when you saw the decanter getting low.'

The captain stared at him, and maybe it was that the speech was too much for his nerves, but he drank off two glasses one after the other as quick as he could fill them out.

"'Dempsey,' said he, looking round, cautiously, 'are we alone?'

"'We are,' said my grandfather.

"'Tell me, then,' said M'Claverty, 'how could his Grace get a taste of this real sherry, for himself, alone, I mean? Of course, I never thought of his giving it to the Judges, and old Lord Dunboyne, and such like.'

"'Does he ever take a little sup in his own room, of an evening?'

"'I am afraid not, but I'll tell you how I think it might be managed; you're a snug fellow, Dempsey, you've plenty of money muddling away in the bank at three-and-a-half per cent., couldn't you contrive, some way or other, to get into his Excellency's confidence, and lend him ten or fifteen thousand, or so?'

"'Ay, or twenty,' said my grandfather—'or twenty, if he likes it.'

"'I doubt if he would accept such a sum,' said the captain, shaking his head; 'he has bags of money rolling in upon him every week or fortnight; sometimes we don't know where to put them.'

"'Oh of course,' said my grandfather; 'I meant no offence, I only said twenty, because, if his Grace would condescend, it isn't twenty, but a fifty thousand I could give him, and on the nail, too.'

"'You're a fine fellow, Dempsey—a devilish fine fellow; you're the very kind of fellow the Duke likes—open-handed, frank, and generous.'

"'Do you really think he'd like me?' said my grandfather; and he rocked on the high stool, so that it nearly came down.

"'Like you! I'll tell you what it is,' said he, laying his hand on my grandfather's knee, 'before one week was over, he couldn't do without you. You'd be there morning, noon, and night; your knife and fork always ready for you, just like one of the family.'

"'Blood alive!' said my grandfather, 'do you tell me so?'

"'I'll bet you a hundred pounds on it, sir!'

"'Done,' said my grandfather, 'and you must hold the stakes;' and with that he opened his black pocket-book, and put a note for the amount into the captain's hand.

"'This is the 31st of March,' said the captain, taking out his pencil and tablets. 'I'll just book the bet.'

"'And, indeed,' added Mr. Dempsey, 'for that matter, if it was a day later it would have been only more suitable.'

"Well, ma'am, what passed between them afterwards I never heard said, but the captain took his leave, and left my grandfather so delighted and overjoyed, that he finished all the sherry in the drawer, and when the head clerk came in to ask for an invoice, or a thing of the kind, he found old Mr.

Dempsey with his wig on the high stool, and he bowing round it, and calling it your Grace. There's no denying it, ma'am, he was blind drunk.

"About ten days or a fortnight after this time, my grandfather received a note from Teesum and Twist, the solicitors, stating that the draft of the bond was already drawn up for the loan he was about to make to his Grace, and begging to know to whom it was to be submitted.

"'The captain will win his bet, devil a lie in it,' said my grandfather; 'he's going to bring the Duke and myself together.'

"Well, ma'am, I won't bother you with the law business, though if my father was telling the story he would not spare you one item of it all, who read this, and who signed the other, and the objections that was made by them thieving attorneys! and how the Solicitor-General struck out this and put in that clause; but to tell you the truth, ma'am, I think that all the details spoil, what we may call, the poetry of the narrative; it is finer to say he paid the money, and the Duke pocketed it.

"Well, weeks went over and months long, and not a bit of the Duke did my grandfather see, nor M'Claverty either; he never came near him. To be sure his Grace drank as much sherry as ever; indeed, I believe out of love to my grandfather they drank little else; from the bishops and the chaplain, down to the battle-axe guards, it was sherry, morning, noon, and night; and though this was very pleasing to my grandfather, he was always wishing for the time when he was to be presented to his Grace, and their friendship was to begin. My grandfather could think of nothing else, daylight and dark; when he walked, he was always repeating to himself what his Grace might say to him, and what he would say to his Grace; and he was perpetually going up at eleven o'clock, when the guard was relieved in the Castle-yard, suspecting that every now and then a footman in blue and silver would come out, and, touching his elbow, whisper in his ear, 'Mr. Dempsey, the Duke's waiting for you.' But, my dear ma'am, he might have waited till now, if Providence had spared him, and the devil a taste of the same message would ever have come near him, or a sight of the same footman in blue! It was neither more nor less than a delusion, or an illusion, or a confusion, or whatever the name of it is. At last, ma'am, in one of his prowlings about the Phœnix Park, who does he come on but M'Claverty; he was riding past in a great hurry, but he pulled up when he saw my grandfather, and called out, 'Hang it! who's this? I ought to know *you.*'

"'Indeed you ought,' said my grandfather; 'I'm Dodd and Dempsey, and by the same token there's a little bet between us, and I'd like to know who won and who lost.'

"'I think there's small doubt about that,' said the captain; 'did Grace borrow twenty thousand of you?'

"'He did, no doubt of it.'

"'And wasn't it *my* doing?'

"'Upon my conscience, I can't deny it.'

"'Well, then, I won the wager, that's clear.

"'Oh! I see now,' said my grandfather; 'that was the wager, was it? Oh, bedad! I think you might have given me odds, if that was our bet.'

"'Why, what did you think it was?'

"'Oh, nothing at all, sir; it's no matter now; it was another thing was passing in my mind. I was hoping to have the honour of making his acquaintance, flattered as I was by all you told me about him.'

"'Ah! that's difficult, I confess,' said the captain, 'but still one might do something. He wants a little money just now; if you could make interest to be the lender, I wouldn't say that what you suggest is impossible.'

"Well, ma'am, it was just as it happened before. The old story, more parchment, more comparing of deeds, and a heavy cheque on the bank for the amount.

"When it was all done, M'Claverty came in one morning in plain clothes to my grandfather's back office.

"'Dodd and Dempsey,' said he, 'I've been thinking over your business, and I'll tell you what my plan is. Old Vereker, the Chamberlain, is little better than a beast, thinks nothing of anybody that isn't a Lord or a Viscount, and, in fact, if he had his will, the Lodge in the Phœnix would be more like Pekin in Tartary than anything else; but I'll tell you, if he won't present you at the Levee, which he flatly refuses at present, I'll do the thing in a way of my own. His Grace is going to spend a week up at Ballyriggan House, in the county of Wicklow, and I'll contrive it, when he's taking his morning walk through the shrubbery, to present you. All you've to do is to be ready at a turn of the walk; I'll show you the place, you'll hear his foot on the gravel, and you'll slip out, just this way. Leave the rest to me.'

"'It's beautiful,' said my grandfather; 'begad, that's elegant.'

"'There's one difficulty,' said M'Claverty—'one infernal difficulty.'

"'What's that?' asked my grandfather.

"'I may be obliged to be out of the way. I lost five fifties at Daly's the other night, and I may have to cross the water for a few weeks.'

"'Don't let that trouble you,' said my grandfather; 'there's the paper.' And he put the little bit of music into his hand, and sure enough a pleasanter sound than the same crisp squeak of a new note no man ever listened to.

"'It's agreed upon now?' said my grandfather.

"'All right,' said M'Claverty; and with a jolly slap on the shoulder, he said, 'Good morning, D. and D.,' and away he went.

"He was true to his word; that day three weeks my grandfather received a note in pencil; it was signed J. M'C., and ran thus: 'Be up at Ballyriggan at eleven o'clock on Wednesday, and wait at the foot of the hill, near the birch copse, beside the wooden bridge. Keep the left of the path, and lie still.' Begad, ma'am, it's well nobody saw it but himself, or they might have thought that Dodd and Dempsey was turned highwayman.

"My grandfather was prouder of the same note, and happier that morning, than if it was an order for fifty butts of sherry. He read it over and over, and he walked up and down the little back office, picturing out the whole scene, settling the chairs till he made a little avenue between them, and practising the way he'd slip out slyly and surprise his Grace. No doubt, it would have been as good as a play to have looked at him.

"One difficulty preyed upon his mind, what dress ought he to wear? Should he be in a Court suit, or ought he rather to go in his robes as an Alderman? It would never do to appear in a black coat, a light grey spencer, punch-coloured shorts and gaiters, white hat with a strip of black crape on it, mere Dodd and Dempsey! That wasn't to be thought of. If he could only ask his friend M'Hale, the fishmonger, who was knighted last year, he could tell all about it. M'Hale, however, would blab; he'd tell it to the whole Livery, every Alderman of Skinner's-alley would know it in a week! No, no, the whole must be managed discreetly; it was a mutual confidence between the Duke and 'D. and D.' 'At all events,' said my grandfather, 'a Court dress is a safe thing;' and out he went and bespoke one, to be sent home that evening, for he couldn't rest till he tried it on, and felt how he could move his head in the straight collar, and bow, without the sword tripping him up and pitching him into the Duke. I've heard my father say, that in the days that elapsed till the time mentioned for the interview, my grandfather lost two stone in weight. He walked half over the county Dublin, lying in ambush in every little wood he could see, and jumping out whenever he could see or hear any one coming; little surprises which were sometimes taken as practical jokes, very unbecoming a man of his age and appearance.

"Well, ma'am, Wednesday morning came, and at six o'clock my grandfather was on the way to Ballyriggan, and at nine he was in the wood, posted at the very spot M'Claverty told him, as happy as any man could be whose expectations were so overwhelming. A long hour passed over, and another; nobody passed but a baker's boy with a bulldog after him, and an old woman that was stealing brushwood in the shrubbery. My grandfather remarked her well, and determined to tell his Grace of it, but his own business soon drove that out of his head, for eleven o'clock came, and now there was no knowing the moment the Duke might appear. With his watch in his hand, he counted the minutes, ay, even the seconds if he was a thief going to be hanged, and looking out over the heads of the crowd for a fellow to gallop in with a reprieve, he couldn't have suffered more: his heart was in his mouth. At last, it might be about half-past eleven, he heard a footstep on the gravel, and then a loud, deep cough, 'a fine kind of cough,' my grandfather afterwards called it; he peeped out, and there, sure enough, at about sixty paces, coming down the walk, was a large, grand-looking man—not that he was dressed as became him, for, strange as you may think it, the Lord-Lieutenant had on a shooting-jacket, and a pair of plaid trousers, and cloth boots, and a big lump of a stick in his hand—and lucky it was that my grandfather knew him, for he bought a picture of him. On he came nearer and nearer, every step on the gravel-walk drove out of my grandfather's head half a dozen of the fine things he had got off by heart to say during the interview, until at last he was so overcome by joy, anxiety, and a kind of terror, that he couldn't tell where he was, or what was going to happen to him, but he had a kind of instinct that reminded him he was to jump out when the Duke was near him, and 'pon my conscience so he did, clean and clever, into the middle of the walk, right in front of his Grace. My grandfather used to say, in telling the story, that he verily believed his feelings at that moment would have made him burst a blood-vessel, if it wasn't that the Duke put his hands to his sides and laughed till the woods rang again but between shame and fright, my grandfather didn't join in the laugh.

"'In Heaven's name!' said his Grace, 'who or what are you?—this isn't May-day.'

"My grandfather took this speech as a rebuke for standing so bold in his Grace's presence, and being a shrewd man, and never deficient in tact, what does he do, but drops down on his two knees before him. 'My Lord,' said he, 'I am only Dodd and Dempsey.'

"Whatever there was droll about the same house of Dodd and Dempsey, I never heard, but his Grace laughed now till he had to lean against a tree. 'Well, Dodd and Dempsey, if that's your name, get up. I don't mean you any harm. Take courage, man; I am not going to knight you. By the way, are you not the worthy gentleman who lent me a trifle of twenty thousand more than once?'

"My grandfather couldn't speak, but he moved his lips, and he moved his hands, this way, as though to say the honour was too great for him, but it was all true.

"'Well, Dodd and Dempsey, I've a very high respect for you,' said his Grace; 'I intend, some of these fine days, when business permits, to go over and eat an oyster at your villa on the coast.'

"My grandfather remembers no more; indeed, ma'am, I believe that at that instant his Grace's condescension had so much overwhelmed him, that he had a kind of vision before his eyes of a whole wood full of Lord-Lieutenants, with about thirty thousand people opening oysters for them as fast as they could eat, and he himself running about with a pepper-caster, pressing them to eat another 'black fin.' It was something of that kind, for when he got on his legs, a considerable time must have elapsed, as he found all silent around him, and a smart rheumatic pain in his knee-joints from the cold of the ground.

"The first thing my grandfather did when he got back to town, was to remember that he had no villa on the sea-coast, nor any more suitable place to eat an oyster than his house in Abbey-street, for he couldn't ask his Grace to go to 'Killeen's.' Accordingly he set out next day in search of a villa, and before a week was over he had as beautiful a place about a mile below Howth as ever was looked at; and that he mightn't be taken short, he took a lease of two oyster-beds, and made every preparation in life for the Duke's visit. He might have spared himself the trouble. Whether it was that somebody had said something of him behind his back, or that politics were weighing on the Duke's mind—the Catholics were mighty troublesome then—or, indeed, that he forgot it altogether, clean, but so it was, my grandfather never heard more of the visit, and if the oysters waited for his Grace to come and eat them, they might have filled up Howth harbour.

"A year passed over, and my grandfather was taking his solitary walk in the Park, very nearly in the same place as before—for you see, ma'am, he couldn't bear the sight of the sea-coast, and the very smell of shell-fish made him ill—when somebody called out his name. He looked up, and there was M'Claverty in a gig.

"'Well, D. and D., how goes the world with you?'

"'Very badly, indeed,' says my grandfather; his heart was full, and he just told him the whole story.

"'I'll settle it all,' said the captain; 'leave it to me. There's to be a review to-morrow in the Park: get on the back of the best horse you can find—the Duke is a capital judge of a nag—ride him briskly about the field, he'll notice you, never fear, the whole thing will come up before his memory, and you'll have him to breakfast before the week's over.'

"'Do you think so?—do you really think so?'

"'I'll take my oath of it. I say, D. and D., could you do a little thing at a short date just now?'

"'If it wasn't too heavy,' said my grandfather, with a faint sigh.

"'Only a hundred.'

"'Well,' said he, 'you may send it down to the office. Good-by.' And with that he turned back towards town again; not to go home, however, for he knew well there was no time to lose, but straight he goes to Dycer's—it was old Tom was alive in those days, and a shrewder man than Tom

Dycer there never lived. They tell you, ma'am, there's chaps in London, that if you send them your height, and your width, and your girth round the waist, they'll make you a suit of clothes that will fit you like your own skin, but, 'pon my conscience, I believe, if you'd give your age and the colour of your hair to old Tom Dycer, he could provide you a horse the very thing to carry you. Whenever a stranger used to come into the yard, Tom would throw a look at him out of the corner of his eye—for he had only one, there was a feather on the other—Tom would throw a look at him, and he'd shout out, 'Bring out 42; take out that brown mare with the white fetlocks.' That's the way he had of doing business, and the odds were five to one but the gentleman rode out half an hour after on the beast Tom intended for him. This suited my grandfather's knuckle well, for when he told him that it was a horse to ride before the Lord-Lieutenant he wanted, 'Bedad,' says Tom, 'I'll give you one you might ride before the Emperor of Chaney—here, Dennis, trot out 176.' To all appearance, ma'am, 176 was no common beast, for every man in the yard, big and little, set off, when they heard the order, down to the stall where he stood, and at last two doors were flung wide open, and out he came with a man leading him. He was seventeen hands two if he was an inch, bright grey, with flea-bitten marks all over him; he held his head up so high at one end, and his tail at the other, that my grandfather said he'd have frightened the stoutest fox-hunter to look at him; besides, my dear, he went with his knees in his mouth when he trotted, and gave a skelp of his hind-legs at every stride, that it wasn't safe to be within four yards of him.

"'There's action!' says Tom—'there's bone and figure! Quiet as a lamb, without stain or blemish, warranted in every harness, and to carry a lady.'

"'I wish he'd carry a wine-merchant safe for about one hour and a half,' said my grandfather to himself. 'What's his price?'

"But Tom wouldn't mind him, for he was going on reciting the animal's perfections, and telling him how he was bred out of Kick the Moon, by Moll Flanders, and that Lord Dunraile himself only parted with him because he didn't think him showy enough for a charger. 'Though, to be sure,' said Tom, 'he's greatly improved since that. Will you try him in the school, Mr. Dempsey?' said he; 'not but I tell you that you'll find him a little mettlesome or so there; take him on the grass, and he's gentleness itself—he's a kid, that's what he is.'

"'And his price?' said my grandfather.

"Dycer whispered something in his ear.

"'Blood alive!' said my grandfather.

"'Devil a farthing less. Do you think you're to get beauty and action, ay, and gentle temper, for nothing?'

"My dear, the last words, 'gentle temper,' wasn't well out of his mouth when 'the kid' put his two hind-legs into the little pulpit where the auctioneer was sitting, and sent him flying through the window behind him into the stall.

"'That comes of tickling him,' said Tom; 'them blackguards never will let a horse alone.'

"'I hope you don't let any of them go out to the reviews in the Park, for I declare to Heaven, if I was on his back then, Dodd and Dempsey would be D. D. sure enough.'

"'With a large snaffle, and the saddle well back,' says Tom, 'he's a lamb.'

"'God grant it,' says my grandfather; 'send him over to me to-morrow, about eleven.' He gave a cheque for the money—we never heard how much it was—and away he went.

"That must have been a melancholy evening for him, for he sent for old Rogers, the attorney, and after he was measured for breeches and boots, he made his will and disposed of his effects, 'For there's no knowing,' said he, 'what 176 may do for me.' Rogers did his best to persuade him off the excursion:

"'Dress up one of Dycer's fellows like you; let him go by the Lord-Lieutenant prancing and rearing, and then, you yourself can appear on the ground, all splashed and spurred, half an hour after.'

"'No,' says my grandfather, 'I'll go myself.'

"For, so it is, there's no denying, when a man has got ambition in his heart it puts pluck there. Well, eleven o'clock came, and the whole of Abbey-street was on foot to see my grandfather; there wasn't a window hadn't five or six faces in it, and every blackguard in the town was there to see him go off, just as if it was a show.

"'Bad luck to them,' says my grandfather; 'I wish they had brought the horse round to the stable-yard, and let me get up in peace.'

"And he was right there; for the stirrup, when my grandfather stood beside the horse, was exactly even with his chin; but somehow, with the help of the two clerks and the book-keeper, and the office stool, he got up on his back with as merry a cheer as ever rung out to welcome him, while a dirty blackguard, with two old pocket-handkerchiefs for a pair of breeches, shouted out, 'Old Dempsey's going to get an appetite for the oysters!'

"Considering everything, 176 behaved very well; he didn't plunge, and he didn't kick, and my grandfather said, 'Providence was kind enough not to let him rear!' but somehow, he wouldn't go straight, but sideways, and kept lashing his long tail on my grandfather's legs, and sometimes round his body, in a way that terrified him greatly, till he became used to it.

"'Well, if riding be a pleasure,' says my grandfather, 'people must be made different from me.'

"For, saving your favour, ma'am, he was as raw as a griskin, and there wasn't a bit of him the size of a half-crown he could sit on without a cry out; and no other pace would the beast go but this little jig, jig, from side to side, while he was tossing his head and flinging his mane about, just as if to say, 'Couldn't I pitch you sky-high, if I liked? Couldn't I make a Congreve-rocket of you, Dodd and Dempsey?'

"When he got on the 'Fifteen Acres,' it was only the position he found himself in that destroyed the grandeur of the scene; for there was fifty thousand people assembled at least, and there was a line of infantry of two miles long, and the artillery was drawn up at one end, and the cavalry stood beyond them, stretching away towards Knockmaroon.

"My grandfather was now getting accustomed to his sufferings, and he felt that, if 176 did no more, with God's help he could bear it for one day, and so he rode on quietly outside the crowd, attracting, of course, a fair share of observation, for he wasn't always in the saddle, but sometimes a little behind or before it. Well, at last there came a cloud of dust, rising at the far end of the field, and it got thicker and thicker, and then it broke, and there were white plumes dancing, and gold glittering, and horses all shaking their gorgeous trappings, for it was the Staff was galloping up, and then there burst out a great cheer, so loud that nothing seemed possible to be louder, until bang—bang—bang, eighteen large guns went thundering together, and the whole line of infantry let off a clattering volley, till you'd think the earth was crashing open.

"'Devil's luck to ye all—couldn't you be quiet a little longer?' says D. and D., for he was trying to get an easy posture to sit in, but just at this moment 176 pricked up his ears, made three bounds in the air, as if something lifted him up, shook his head like a fish, and away he went: wasn't it wonderful that my grandfather kept his seat? He remembers, he says, that at each bound he was a yard over his back, but as he was a heavy man, and kept his legs open, he had the luck to come down in the same place, and a sore place it must have been! for he let a screech out of him each time that would have pierced the heart of a stone. He knew very little more what happened, except that he was galloping away somewhere, until at last he found himself in a crowd of people, half dead with fatigue and fright, and the horse thick with foam.

"'Where am I?' says my grandfather.

"'You're in Lucan, sir,' says a man.

"'And where's the review?' says my grandfather.

"'Five miles behind you, sir.'

"'Blessed Heaven!' says he; 'and where's the duke?'

"'God knows,' said the man, giving a wink to the crowd, for they thought he was mad.

"'Won't you get off and take some refreshment?' says the man, for he was the owner of a little public.

"'Get off!' says my grandfather; 'it's easy talking! I found it hard enough to get on. Bring me a pint of porter where I am.' And so he drained off the liquor, and he wiped his face, and he turned the beast's head once more towards town.

"When my grandfather reached the Park again, he was, as you may well believe, a tired and a weary man; and, indeed, for that matter, the beast didn't seem much fresher than himself, for he lashed his sides more rarely, and he condescended to go straight, and he didn't carry his head higher than his rider's. At last they wound their way up through the fir copse at the end of the field, and caught sight of the review, and, to be sure, if poor D. and D. left the ground before under a grand salute of artillery and small arms, another of the same kind welcomed him back again. It was an honour he'd have been right glad to have dispensed with, for when 176 heard it, he looked about him to see which way he'd take, gave a loud neigh, and, with a shake that my grandfather said he'd never forget, he plunged forward, and went straight at the thick of the crowd: it must have been a cruel sight to have seen the people running for their lives. The soldiers that kept the line laughed heartily at the mob, but they hadn't the joke long to themselves, for my grandfather went slap at them into the middle of the field; and he did that day what I hear has been very seldom done by cavalry, he broke a square of the 79th Highlanders, and scattered them over the field. In truth, the beast must have been the devil himself, for wherever he saw most people, it was there he always went. There were, at this time, three heavy dragoons and four of the horse-police, with drawn swords, in pursuit of my grandfather; and, if he were the enemy of the human race, the cries of the multitude could not have been louder, as one universal shout arose of 'Cut him down! Cleave him in two!' And do you know, he said, afterwards, he'd have taken it as a mercy of Providence if they had. Well, my dear, when he had broke through the Highlanders, scattered the mob, dispersed the band, and left a hole in the big drum you could have put your head through, 176 made for the Staff, who, I may remark, were all this time enjoying the confusion immensely. When, however, they saw my grandfather heading towards them, there was a general cry of 'Here he comes! here he comes! Take care, your Grace!' And there arose among the group around the Duke a scene of plunging, kicking, and rearing, in the midst of which in dashed my grandfather. Down went an aide-de-camp at one side; 176 plunged, and off went the town-major at the other, while a stroke of a sabre, kindly intended for my grandfather's skull, came down on the horse's back and made him give plunge the third, which shot his rider out of the saddle, and sent him flying through the air like a shell, till he alighted under the leaders of a carriage, where the Duchess and the Ladies of Honour were seated.

"Twenty people jumped from their horses now to finish him; if they were hunting a rat, they couldn't have been more venomous.

"'Stop! stop!' said the Duke; 'he's a capital fellow, don't hurt him. Who are you, my brave little man? You ride like Chifney for the Derby.'

"'God knows who I am!' says my grandfather, creeping out, and wiping his face. 'I was Dodd and Dempsey when I left home this morning; but I am bewitched, devil a lie in it.'

"'Dempsey, my Lord Duke,' said M'Claverty, coming up at the moment. 'Don't you know him?' and he whispered a few words in his Grace's ear.

"'Oh, yes, to be sure,' said the Viceroy. 'They tell me you have a capital pack of hounds, Dempsey. What do you hunt?'

"'Horse, foot, and dragoons, my Lord,' said my grandfather; and, to be sure, there was a jolly roar of laughter after the words, for poor D. and D. was just telling his mind, without meaning anything more.

"'Well, then,' said the Duke, 'if you've always as good sport as to-day, you've capital fun of it.'

"'Oh! delightful, indeed!' said my grandfather; 'never enjoyed myself more in my life.'

"'Where's his horse?' said his Grace.

"'He jumped down into the sand quarry and broke his neck, my Lord Duke.'

"'The Heavens be praised!' said my grandfather; 'if it's true, I am as glad as if I got fifty pounds.'

"The trumpets now sounded for the cavalry to march past, and the Duke was about to move away, when M'Claverty again whispered something in his ear.

"'Very true,' said he; 'well thought of. I say, Dempsey, I'll go over some of these mornings and have a run with your hounds.'

"My grandfather rubbed his eyes and looked up, but all he saw was about twenty Staff-officers with their hats off, for every man of them saluted my father as they passed, and the crowd made way for him with as much respect as if it was the Duke himself. He soon got a car to bring him home, and notwithstanding all his sufferings that day, and the great escape he had of his life, there wasn't as proud a man in Dublin as himself.

"'He's coming to hunt with my hounds!' said he; ''tisn't to take an oyster and a glass of wine, and be off again!—no, but he's coming down to spend the whole day with me.'

"The thought was ecstasy; it only had one drawback. Dodd and Dempsey's house had never kept hounds. Well, ma'am, I needn't detain you long about what happened; it's enough if I say that in less than six weeks my grandfather had bought up Lord Tyrawley's pack, and his hunting-box, and his horses, and I believe his grooms; and though he never ventured on the back of a beast himself, he did nothing from morning to night but listen and talk about hunting, and try to get the names of the dogs by heart, and practise to cry, 'Tally-ho!' and 'Stole away!' and 'Ho-ith! ho-ith!' with which, indeed, he used to start out of his sleep at night, so full he was of the sport. From the 1st of September he never had a red coat off his back. 'Pon my conscience, I believe he went to bed in his spurs, for he didn't know what moment the Duke might be on him, and that's the way the time went on till spring; but not a sign of his Grace, not a word, not a hint that he ever thought more of his promise! Well, one morning my grandfather was walking very sorrowfully down near the Curragh, where his hunting-lodge was, when he saw them roping-in the course for the races, and he heard the men talking of the magnificent cup the Duke was to give for the winner of the three-year old stakes, and the thought flashed on him, 'I'll bring myself to his memory that way.' And what does he do, but he goes back to the house and tells his trainer to go over to the racing stables, and buy, not one, nor two, but the three best horses that were entered for the race. Well, ma'am, their engagements were very heavy, and he had to take them all on himself, and it cost him a sight of money. It happened that this time he was on the right scent, for down comes M'Claverty the same day with orders from the Duke to take the odds, right and left, on one of the three, a little mare called Let-Me-Alone-Before-the-People; she was one of his own breeding, and he had a conceit out of her. Well, M'Claverty laid on the money here and there, till he stood what between the Duke's bets and all the officers of the Staff and his own the heaviest winner or loser on that race.

"'She's Martin's mare, isn't she?' said M'Claverty.

"'No, sir, she was bought this morning by Mr. Dempsey, of Tear Fox Lodge.'

"'The devil she is,' said M'Claverty; and he jumped on his horse, and he cantered over to the Lodge.

"'Mr. Dempsey at home?' says he.

"'Yes, sir.'

"'Give him this card, and say, I beg the favour of seeing him for a few moments.'

"The man went off, and came back in a few minutes, with the answer, 'Mr. Dempsey is very sorry, but he's engaged.'

"'Oh, oh! that's it!' says M'Claverty to himself; 'I see how the wind blows. I say, my man, tell him I've a message from his Grace the Lord-Lieutenant.'

"Well, the answer came for the captain to send the message in, for my grandfather couldn't come out.

"'Say it's impossible,' said M'Claverty; 'it's for his own private ear.'

"Dodd and Dempsey was strong in my grandfather that day! he would listen to no terms.

"'No,' says he, 'if the goods are worth anything, they never come without an invoice. I'll have nothing to say to him.'

"But the captain wasn't to be baulked; for, in spite of everything, he passed the servant, and came at once into the room where my grandfather was sitting—ay, and before he could help it, was shaking him by both hands as if he was his brother.

"'Why the devil didn't you let me in?' said he; 'I came from the Duke with a message for you.'

"'Bother!' says my grandfather.

"'I did though,' says he; 'he's got a heavy book on your little mare, and he wants you to make your boy ride a waiting race, and not win the first heat—you understand?'

"'I do,' says my grandfather, 'perfectly; and he's got a deal of money on her, has he?'

"'He has,' said the captain; 'and every one at the Castle, too, high and low, from the chief secretary down to the second coachman—we are all backing her.'

"'I am glad of it!—I am sincerely glad of it,' said my grandfather, rubbing his hands.

"'I knew you would be, old boy,' cried the captain, joyfully.

"'Ah, but you don't know why; you'd never guess.'

"M'Claverty stared at him, but said nothing.

"'Well, I'll tell you,' resumed my grandfather; 'the reason is this: I'll not let her run, no, divil a step! I'bring her up to the ground, and you may look at her, and see that she's all sound and safe, in top condition, and with a skin like a looking-glass, and then I'll walk her back again! And do you know why I'll do this?' said he, while his eyes flashed fire, and his lip trembled; 'just because I won't suffer the house of Dodd and Dempsey to be humbugged as if we were greengrocers! Two years ago, it was to "eat an oyster with me;" last year, it was a "day with my hounds;" maybe now his Grace would join the race dinner; but that's all past and gone—I'll stand it no longer.'

"'Confound it, man,' said the captain, 'the Duke must have forgotten it. You never reminded him of his engagement. He'd have been delighted to have come to you if he only recollected.'

"'I am sorry my memory was better than his,' said my grandfather, 'and I wish you a very good morning.'

"'Oh, don't go; wait a moment; let us see if we can't put this matter straight. You want the Duke to dine with you?'

"'No, I don't; I tell you I've given it up.'

"'Well, well, perhaps so; will it do if you dine with him?'

"My grandfather had his hand on the lock—he was just going—he turned round, and fixed his eyes on the captain.

"'Are you in earnest? or is this only more of the same game?' said he, sternly.

"'I'll make that very easy to you,' said the captain; 'I'll bring the invitation to you this night; the mare doesn't run till to-morrow; if you don't receive the card, the rest is in your own power.'

"Well, ma'am, my story is now soon told; that night, about nine o'clock, there comes a footman all splashed and muddy, in a Castle livery, up to the door of the Lodge, and he gave a violent pull at the bell, and when the servant opened the door, he called out in a loud voice, 'From his Excellency the Lord-Lieutenant,' and into the saddle he jumped, and away he was like lightning; and, sure enough, it was a large card, all printed, except a word here and there, and it went something this way:

"'I am commanded by his Excellency the Lord-Lieutenant to request the pleasure of Mr. Dempsey's company at dinner on Friday, the 23rd instant, at the Lodge, Phœnix Park, at seven o'clock.

"'GRANVILLE VEREKER, Chamberlain.

'Swords and Bags.

"'At last!' said my grandfather, and he wiped the tears from his eyes; for to say the truth, ma'am, it was a long chase without ever getting once a 'good view.' I must hurry on; the remainder is easy told. Let-Me-Alone-Before-the-People won the cup, my grandfather was chaired home from the course in the evening, and kept open house at the Lodge for all comers while the races lasted; and at length the eventful day drew near on which he was to realise all his long-coveted ambition. It was on the very morning before, however, that he put on his Court suit for about the twentieth time, and the tailor was standing trembling before him while my grandfather complained of a wrinkle here, or a pucker there.

"'You see,' said he, 'you've run yourself so close that you've no time now to alter these things before the dinner'

"'I'll have time enough, sir,' says the man, 'if the news is true.'

"'What news?' says my grandfather, with a choking in his throat, for a sudden fear came over him.

"'The news they have in town this morning.'

"'What is it?—speak it out, man!'

"'They say——But sure you've heard it, sir?'

"'Go on!' says my grandfather; and he got him by the shoulders and shook him. 'Go on, or I'll strangle you

"'They say, sir, that the Ministry is out, and——'

"'And well——'

"'And that the Lord-Lieutenant has resigned, and the yacht is coming round to Dunleary to take him away this evening, for he won't stay longer than the time to swear in the Lords Justices—he's so glad to be out of Ireland.'

"My grandfather sat down on the chair, and began to cry, and well he might, for not only was the news true, but he was ruined besides. Every farthing of the great fortune that Dodd and Dempsey made was lost and gone—scattered to the winds; and when his affairs were wound up, he, that was thought one of the richest men in Dublin, was found to be something like nine thousand pounds worse than nothing. Happily for him, his mind was gone too, and though he lived a few years after, near Finglass, he was always an innocent, didn't remember anybody, nor who he was, but used to go about asking the people if they knew whether his Grace the Lord-Lieutenant had put off his dinner-party for the 23rd; and then he'd pull out the old card to show them, for he kept it in a little case, and put it under his pillow every night till he died."

While Mr. Dempsey's narrative continued, Tom Leonard indulged freely and without restraint in the delights of the Knight's sherry, forgetting not only all his griefs, but the very circumstances and people around him. Had the party maintained a conversational tone, it is probable that he would have been able to adhere to the wise resolutions he had planned for his guidance on leaving home; unhappily, the length of the tale, the prosy monotony of the speaker's voice, the deepening twilight which stole on ere the story drew to a close, were influences too strong for prudence so frail; an instinct told him that the decanter was close by, and every glass he drained either drowned a care or stifled a compunction.

The pleasant buzz of voices which succeeded to the anecdote of Dodd and Dempsey aroused Leonard from his dreary stupor. Wine, and laughter, and merry voices, were adjuncts he had not met for many a day before, and, strangely enough, the only emotions they could call up were some vague, visionary sorrowings over his fallen and degraded condition.

"By Jove:" said Dempsey, in a whisper to Darcy, "the lieutenant has more sympathy for my grandfather than I have myself—I'll be hanged if he isn't wiping his eyes! So you see, ma'am," added he, aloud, "it was a taste for grandeur ruined the Dempseys; the same ambition that has destroyed states and kingdoms has brought your humble servant to a trifle of thirty-eight pounds four and nine per annum for all his worldly comforts and virtuous enjoyments; but, as the old ballad says,

Though classic 'tis to show one's grief,
And cry like Carthaginian Marius,
I'll not do this, nor ask relief
Like that ould beggar Belisarius.

No, ma'am, 'Never give in while there's a score behind the door,'—that's the motto of the Dempseys. If it's not on their coat-of-arms, it's written in their hearts."

"Your grandfather, however, did not seem to possess the family courage," said the Knight, slyly.

"Well, and what would you have? Wasn't he brave enough for a wine-merchant?"

"The ladies will give us some tea, Leonard," said the Knight, as Lady Eleanor and her daughter had, some time before, slipped unobserved from the room.

"Yes, colonel, always ready."

"That's the way with him," whispered Dempsey; "he'd swear black and blue this minute that you commanded the regiment he served in. He very often calls me the quartermaster."

The party rose to join the ladies, and while Leonard maintained his former silence, Dempsey once more took on himself the burden of the conversation by various little anecdotes of the Fumbally household, and sketches of life and manners at Port Ballintray.

So perfectly at ease did he find himself, so inspired by the happy impression he felt convinced he was making, that he volunteered a song "if the young lady would only vouchsafe a few chords on the piano" by way of accompaniment—a proposition Helen acceded to.

Thus passed the evening, a period in which Lady Eleanor more than once doubted if the whole were not a dream, and the persons before her the mere creations of disordered fancy; an impression certainly not lessened as Mr. Dempsey's last words at parting conveyed a pressing invitation to a "little thing he'd get up for them at Mother Fum's."

CHAPTER XL.

SOME VISITORS AT GWYNNE ABBEY.

It is a fact not only well worthy of mention, but pregnant with its own instruction, that persons who have long enjoyed all the advantages of an elevated social position better support the reverses which condemn them to humble and narrow fortunes, than do the vulgar-minded, when, by any sudden caprice of the goddess, they are raised to a conspicuous and distinguished elevation.

There is in the Gentleman, and still more in the Gentlewoman—as the very word itself announces—an element of placidity and quietude that suggests a spirit of accommodation to whatever may arise to ruffle the temper or disturb the equanimity. Self-respect and consideration for others are a combination not inconsistent or unfrequent, and there are few who have not seen, some time or other, a reduced gentleman dispensing in a lowly station the mild graces and accomplishments of his order, and, while elevating others, sustaining himself.

The upstart, on the other hand, like a mariner in some unknown sea without chart or compass, has nothing to guide him; impelled hither or thither as caprice or passion dictate, he is neither restrained by a due sense of decorum, nor admonished by a conscientious feeling of good breeding. With the power that rank and wealth bestows he becomes not distinguished, but eccentric; unsustained by the companionship of his equals, he tries to assimilate himself to them rather by their follies than their virtues, and thus presents to the world that mockery of rank and station which makes good men sad, and bad men triumphant.

To these observations we have been led by the altered fortunes of those two families of whom our story treats. If the Darcys suddenly found themselves brought down to a close acquaintanceship with poverty and its fellows, they bore the change with that noble resignation that springs from true regard for others at the sacrifice of ourselves. The little shifts and straits of narrowed means were ever treated jestingly, the trials that a gloomy spirit had converted into sorrows, made matters of merriment and laughter, and as the traveller sees the Arab tent in the desert spread beside the ruined temple of ancient grandeur, and happy faces and kind looks beneath the shade of ever-vanished splendour, so did this little group maintain in their fall the kindly affection and the high-souled courage that made of that humble cottage a home of happiness and enjoyment.

Let us now turn to the west, where another and very different picture presented itself. Although certain weighty questions remained to be tried at law between the Darcys and the Hickmans, Bicknell could not advise the Knight to contest the mortgage under which the Hickmans had now taken possession of the abbey.

The reputation for patriotism and independence so fortunately acquired by that family came at a most opportune moment. In no country of Europe are the associations connected with the proprietorship of land more regarded than in Ireland; this feeling, like most others truly Irish, has the double property of being either a great blessing or a great curse, for while it can suggest a noble attachment to country, it can also, as we see it in our own day, be the fertile source of the most atrocious crime.

Had Hickman O'Reilly succeeded to the estate of the Darcys at any other moment than when popular opinion called the one a "patriot" and the other a "traitor," the consequences would have been serious; all the disposable force, civil and military, would scarcely have been sufficient to secure possession. The thought of the "ould ancient family" deposed and exiled by the men of yesterday, would have excited a depth of feeling enough to stir the country far and near. Every trait that adorned the one, for generations, would be remembered, while the humble origin of the other would be offered as the bitterest reproach, by those who thought in embodying the picture of themselves and their fortune they were actually summing up the largest amount of obloquy and disgrace. Such is mob principle in everything! Aristocracy has no such admirers as the lowly born, just as the liberty of the press is inexpressibly dear to that part of the population who know not how to read.

When last we saw Gwynne Abbey the scene was one of mourning, the parting hour of those whose affections clung to the old walls, and who were to leave it for ever. We must now return there for a brief space under different auspices, and when Mr. Hickman O'Reilly, the high-sheriff of the county, was entertaining a large and distinguished company in his new and princely residence.

It was the Assize week, and the Judges, as well as the leading officers of the Crown, were his guests; many of the gentry were also there, some from indifference to whom their host might be; others, from curiosity to see how the upstart, Bob Hickman, would do the honours; and there were many who felt far more at their ease in the abbey now, than when they had the fears of Lady Eleanor Darcy's quietude and coldness of manner before them.

No expense was spared to rival the style and retinue of the abbey under its former owners. O'Reilly well knew the value of first impressions in such matters, and how the report that would soon gain currency would decide the matter for or against him. So profusely, and with such disregard to money was everything done, that, as a mere question of cost, there was no doubt that never in the Knight's palmiest days had anything been seen more magnificent than the preparations. Luxuries, brought at an immense cost, and by contraband, from abroad; wines, of the rarest excellence, abounded at every entertainment; equipages, more splendid than any ever seen there before, appeared each morning; and troops of servants without number moved hither and thither, displaying the gorgeous liveries of the O'Reillys.

The guests were for the most part the neighbouring gentry, the military, and the members of the Bar; but there were others also, selected with peculiar care, and whose presence was secured at no inconsiderable pains. These were the leading "diners-out" of Dublin, and recognised "men about town," whose names were seen on club committees, and whose word was law on all questions of society. Among them, the chief was Con Heffernan, and he now saw himself for the first time a guest at Gwynne Abbey. The invitation was made and accepted with a certain coquetting that gave it the character of a reconciliation; there were political differences to be got over, mutual recriminations to be forgotten; but as each felt, for his own reasons, not indisposed to renew friendly relations, the matter presented little difficulty, and when Mr. O'Reilly received his guest, on his arrival, with a shake of both hands, the action was meant and taken as a receipt in full for all past misunderstanding, and both had too much tact ever to go back on "bygones."

There had been a little correspondence between the parties, the early portions of which were marked "Confidential," and the latter, "Strictly Confidential and Private." This related to a request made by O'Reilly to Heffernan to entreat his influence in behalf of Lionel Darcy. Nothing could exceed the delicacy of the negotiation, for after professing that the friendship which had subsisted between his own son and young Darcy was the active motive for the request, he went on to say, that in the course of certain necessary legal investigations, it was discovered that young Lionel, in the unguarded carelessness of a young and extravagant man, had put his name to bills of a large amount, and even hinted that he had not stopped there, but had actually gone the length of signing his father's name to documents for the sale of property. To obtain an appointment for him in some regiment serving in India would at once withdraw him from the likelihood of any exposure in these matters. To interest Heffernan in the affair was the object of O'Reilly's correspondence, and Heffernan was only too glad, at so ready an opportunity, to renew their ruptured relations.

Lions were not as fashionable in those days as at present, but still the party had its share in the person of Counsellor O'Halloran, the great orator of the Bar, and the great speaker at public meetings, the rising patriot who, not being deemed of importance enough to be bought, was looked on as incorruptible. He had come down special to defend O'Reilly in a record of Darcy *versus* Hickman, the first case submitted for trial by Bicknell, and one which, small in itself, would yet, if determined in the Knight's favour, form a rule of great importance respecting those that were to follow.

It was in the first burst of Hickman O'Reilly's indignation against Government that he had secured O'Halloran as his counsel, never anticipating that any conjuncture would bring him once more into relations with the Ministry. His appointment of high-sheriff, however, and his subsequent correspondence with Heffernan, ending with the invitation to the abbey, had greatly altered his sentiments, and he more than once regretted the precipitancy with which he had selected his advocate.

Whether "the Counsellor" did or did not perceive that his reception was one of less cordiality and more embarrassment than might be expected, it is not easy to say, for he was one of those persons who live too much out of themselves to betray their own feelings to the world. He was a large and well-looking man, but whose features would have been coarse in their expression were it not for the animated intelligence of his eye, and the quaint humour that played about the angles of his mouth, and added to the peculiar drollery of an accent to which Kerry had lent all its native archness. His gestures were bold, striking, and original; his manner of speaking, even in private, impressive—from the deliberate slowness of his utterance, and the air of truthfulness sustained by every agency of look, voice, and expression. The least observant could not fail to remark in him a conscious power, a sense of his own great gifts either in argument or invective, for he was no less skilful in unravelling the tangled tissue of a knotted statement, than in overwhelming his adversary with a torrent of abusive eloquence. The habits of his profession, but, in particular, the practice of cross-examination, had given him an immense insight into the darker recesses of the human heart, and made him master of all the subtleties and evasions of inferior capacities. This knowledge he brought with him into society, where his powers of conversation had already established for him a high repute. He abounded in anecdote, which he introduced so easily and naturally, that the *à propos* had as much merit as the story itself. Yet with all these qualities, and in a time when the members of his profession were more than ever esteemed and courted, he himself was not received, save on sufferance, into the better society of the capital. The stamp of a "low tone," and the assertion of democratic opinions, were two insurmountable obstacles to his social acceptance; and he was rarely, if ever, seen in those circles which arrogated to themselves the title of best. Whether it was a conscious sense of what was "in him" powerful enough to break down such barriers as these, and that, like Nelson, he felt the day would come when he would have a "*Gazette of his own*," but his manner at times displayed a spirit of haughty daring and effrontery that formed a singular contrast with the slippery and insinuating softness of his *nisi prius* tone and gesture.

If we seem to dwell longer on this picture than the place the original occupies in our story would warrant, it is because the character is not fictitious, and there is always an interest to those who have seen the broad current of a mighty river rolling onward in its mighty strength, to stand beside the little streamlet which, first rising from the mountain, gave it origin—to mark the first obstacles that opposed its course—and to watch the strong impulses that moulded its destiny to overcome them.

Whatever fears Hickman O'Reilly might have felt as to how his counsel, learned in the law, would be received by the Government agent, Mr. Heffernan, were speedily allayed. The gentlemen had never met before, and yet, ere the first day went over, they were as intimate as old acquaintances, each, apparently, well pleased with the strong good sense and natural humour of the other. And so, indeed, it may be remarked in the world, that when two shrewd, far-reaching individuals are brought together, the attraction of quick intelligence and craft is sufficient to draw them into intimate relations at once. There is something wonderfully fraternal in roguery.

This was the only social difficulty O'Reilly dreaded, and happily it was soon dispelled, and the general enjoyment was unclouded by even the slightest accident. The Judges were *bon vivants*, who enjoyed good living and good wine; he of the Common Pleas, too, was an excellent shot, and always exchanged his robes for a shooting-jacket on entering the park, and despatched hares and woodcocks as he walked along, with as much unconcern as he had done Whiteboys half an hour before. The Solicitor-General was passionately fond of hunting, and would rather any day have drawn a cover than an indictment; and so with the rest, they seemed all of them sporting gentlemen of wit and pleasure, who did a little business at law by way of "distraction." Nor did O'Halloran form an exception: he was as ready as the others to snatch an interval of pleasure amid the fatigues of his laborious day. But, somehow, he contrived that no amount of business should be too much for him; and while his ruddy cheek and bright eye bespoke perfect health and renewed enjoyment, it was remarked that the lamp burned the whole night long unextinguished in his chamber, and that no morning found him ever unprepared to defend the interest of his client.

There was, as we have said, nothing to throw a damper on the general joy; fortune was bent on dealing kindly with Mr. O'Reilly, for while he was surrounded with distinguished and delighted guests, his father, the doctor, the only one whose presence could have brought a blush to his cheek, was confined to his room by a severe cold, and unable to join the party.

The Assize calendar was a long one, and the town the last in the circuit, so that the Judges were in no hurry to move on; besides, Gwynne Abbey was a quarter which it was very unlikely would soon be equalled in style or living and resources. For all these several reasons the business of the law went on with an easy and measured pace, the Court opening each day at ten, and closing about three or four, when a magnificent procession of carriages and saddle-horses drew up in the main street to convey the guests back to the abbey.

While the other trials formed the daily subject of table-talk, suggesting those stories of fun, anecdote, and incident, with which no other profession can enter into rivalry, the case of Darcy *versus* Hickman was never alluded to, and, being adroitly left last on the list for trial, could not possibly interfere with the freedom so essential to pleasant intercourse.

The day fixed on for this record was a Saturday. It was positively the last day the Judges could remain, and having accepted an engagement to a distant part of the country for that very day at dinner, the Court was to sit early, and there being no other cause for trial, it was supposed the cause would be concluded in time to permit their departure. Up to this morning the high-sheriff had never omitted, as in duty bound, to accompany the Judges to the Court-house, displaying in the number and splendour of his equipages a costliness and magnificence that excited the wonder of the assembled gentry. On this day, however, he deemed it would be more delicate, on his part, to be absent, as the matter in litigation so nearly concerned himself. And half seriously, and half in jest, he made his apologies to the learned Baron who was to try the cause, and begged for permission to remain at the abbey. The request was most natural, and at once acceded to, and although Heffernan had expressed the greatest desire to hear the

Counsellor, he determined to pass the morning, at least, with O'Reilly, and endeavour afterwards to be in time for the address to the jury.

At last the procession moved off; several country gentlemen, who had come over to breakfast, joining the party, and making the cavalcade, as it entered the town, a very imposing body. It was the market-day, too, and thus the square in front of the Court-house was crowded with a frieze-coated and red-cloaked population, earnestly gesticulating and discussing the approaching trial, for to the Irish peasant the excitement of a law process has the most intense and fascinating interest. All the ordinary traffic of the day was either neglected or carelessly performed, in the anxiety to see those who dispensed the dread forms of justice, but more particularly to obtain a sight of the young "Counsellor," who, for the first time, had appeared on this circuit, but whose name as a patriot and an orator was widely renowned.

"Here he comes !—Here he comes !—Make way there !" went from mouth to mouth, as O'Halloran, who had entered the inn for a moment, now issued forth in wig and gown, and carrying a heavily-laden bag in his hand. The crowd opened for him respectfully and in dead silence, and then a hearty cheer burst forth, that echoed through the wide square, and was taken up by hundreds of voices in the neighbouring streets.

It needed not the reverend companionship of Father John M'Enerty, the parish priest of Curraghglass, who walked at his side, to secure him this hearty burst of welcome, although of a truth the circumstance had its merit also, and many favourable comments were passed upon O'Halloran for the familiar way he leaned on the priest's arm, and the kindly intelligence that subsisted between them.

If anything could have added to the pleasure of the assembled crowd at the instant, it was an announcement by Father John, who, turning round on the steps of the Court-house, informed them in a kind of confidential whisper that was heard over the square, that "if they were good boys, and didn't make any disturbance in the town," the Counsellor would give them a speech when the trial was over.

The most deafening shout of applause followed this declaration, and whatever interest the questions of law had possessed for them before, was now merged in the higher anxiety to hear the great Counsellor himself discuss the "veto," that long-agitated question each had taught himself to believe of nearest importance to himself.

"When last I visited this town," said Bicknell to the senior counsel employed in the Knight's behalf, "I witnessed a very different scene. Then we had triumphal arches, and bonfire illuminations, and addresses. It was young Darcy's birthday, and a more enthusiastic reception it is impossible to conceive than he met in these very streets from these very people."

"There is only one species of interest felt for dethroned monarchs," said the other, caustically—"how they bear their misfortunes."

"The man you see yonder waving his hat to young O'Reilly, was one of a deputation to congratulate the heir of Gwynne Abbey! I remember him well—his name is Mitchell."

"I hope not the same I see upon our jury-list here," said the Counsellor, as he unfolded a written paper, and perused it attentively.

"The same man; he holds his house under the Darcys, and has received many and deep favours at their hands."

"So much the worse, if we should find him in the jury-box. But have we any chance of young Darcy yet? Do you give up all hope of his arrival?"

"The last tidings I received from my clerk were, that he was to follow him down to Plymouth by that night's mail, and still hoped to be in time to catch him ere the transport sailed."

"What a rash and reckless fellow he must be, that would leave a country where he has such interests at stake."

"If he felt that a point of honour or duty was involved, I don't believe he'd sacrifice a jot of either to gain this cause, and I'm certain that some such plea has been made use of on the present occasion."

"How they cheer! What's the source of their enthusiasm at this moment? There it goes, that carriage with the green liveries and the Irish motto round the crest. Look at O'Halloran, too! how he shakes hands with the townsfolk; canvassing for a verdict already! Now, Bicknell, let us move on; but, for my part, I feel our cause is decided outside the Court-house. If I'm not very much mistaken, we are about to have an era of 'popular justice' in Ireland, and our enemies could not wish us worse luck."

CHAPTER XLI.

A SCENE AT THE ASSIZES.

Although Mr. Hickman O'Reilly affected an easy unconcern regarding he issue of the trial, he received during the morning more than one despatch from the Court-house narrating its progress. They were brief but significant; and when Heffernan, with his own tact, inquired if the news were satisfactory, the reply was made by putting into his hands a slip of paper with a few words written in pencil: "They are beaten—the verdict is certain."

"I concluded," said Heffernan, as he handed back the paper, "that the case was not deemed by you a very doubtful matter."

"Neither doubtful nor important," said Hickman, calmly; "it was an effort, in all probability suggested by some crafty lawyer, to break several leases on the ground of forgery in the signatures. I am sure nothing short of Mr. Darcy's great difficulties would ever have permitted him to approve of such a proceeding."

"The shipwrecked sailor will cling to a hen-coop," said Heffernan. "By the way, where are these Darcys? What has become of them?"

"Living in Wales, or in Scotland, some say."

"Are they utterly ruined?"

"Utterly, irretrievably; a course of extravagance maintained for years at a rate of about double his income—loans obtained at any sacrifice—sales of property effected without regard to loss, have overwhelmed him, and the worst of it is, the little remnant of fortune left is likely to be squandered in vain attempts to recover at law what he has lost by recklessness."

Heffernan walked on for some moments in silence, and, as if pondering over Hickman's words, repeated several times, half aloud: "No doubt of it—no doubt of it." Then added, in a louder tone: "The whole history of this family, Mr. O'Reilly, is a striking confirmation of a remark I heard made, a few days since, by a distinguished individual—to *you* I may say it was Lord Cornwallis. 'Heffernan,' said he, 'this country is in a state of rapid transition; everything progresses but the old gentry of the land; they alone seem rooted to ancient prejudices, and fast confirmed in bygone barbarisms.' I ventured to ask him if he could suggest a remedy for the evil, and I'll never forget the tone with which he whispered in my ear, 'Yes; supersede them!' And that, sir," said Heffernan, laying his hand confidentially on O'Reilly's arm—"that is and must be the future policy regarding Ireland."

Mr. Heffernan did not permit himself to risk the success of his stroke by a word more, nor did he even dare to cast a look at his companion and watch how his spell was working. As the marksman feels when he has shot his bolt that no after-thought can amend the aim, so did he wait quietly for the result, without a single effort on his part.

"The remark is a new one to me," said O'Reilly, at length; "but so completely does it accord with my own sentiments, I feel as if I either had, or might have, made it myself. The old school you speak of were little calculated to advance the prosperity of the country; the attachment of the people to them was fast wearing out."

"Nay," interposed Heffernan, "it was that very same attachment, that rude remnant of feudalism, made the greatest barrier against improvement. The law of the land was powerless in comparison with the obligations of this clanship. It is time, full time, that the people should become English in feeling, as they are in law and in language, and to make them so, the first step is, to work the reformation in the gentry. Now, at the hazard of a liberty which you may deem an impertinence, I will tell you frankly, Mr. O'Reilly, that you, you yourself, are admirably calculated to lead the van of this great movement. It is all very natural, and perhaps very just, that in a moment of chagrin with a Minister or his party, a man should feel indignant, and—although acting under a misconception—throw himself into a direct opposition; yet a little reflection will show that such a line involves a false position. Popularity with the masses could never recompense a man like you for the loss of that higher esteem you must sacrifice for it; the *devoirs* of your station impose a very different class of duties from what this false patriotism suggests; besides, if from indignation—a causeless indignation I am ready to prove it—you separate yourself from the Government, you are virtually suffering your own momentary anger to decide the whole question of your son's career. You are shutting the door of advancement against a young man with every adventitious aid of fortune in his favour—handsome—accomplished—wealthy—what limit need there be to his ambition? And finally, some fellow, like our friend 'the Counsellor,' without family, friends, or fortune, but with lungs of leather, and a ready tongue, will beat you hollow in the race, and secure a wider influence over the mass of the people than a hundred gentlemen like you! You will deem it, probably, enough to spend ten or fifteen thousand on a contested election, and to give a vote for your party in Parliament; he, on the other hand, will write letters, draw up petitions, frame societies, meetings, resolutions, and make speeches, every word of which will sink deeply into the hearts of men whose feelings are his own. You, and others in your station, will be little better than tools in his hands, and powerful as you think yourselves to-day, with your broad acres and your cottier freeholders, the time may come when these men will be less at *your* bidding than *his*, and for this simple reason, the man of nothing will always be ready to bid higher for mob support than he who has a fortune to lose."

"You have put a very strong case," said O'Reilly; "perhaps I should think it stronger, if I had not heard most of the arguments before, from yourself; and know by this time how their application to me has not sustained your prophecy."

"I am ready to discuss that with you, too," said Heffernan. "I know how it all happened: had I been with you the day you dined with Castlereagh, the misunderstanding never could have occurred; but there was a fatality in it all. Come," said he, familiarly, and he slipped his arm, as he spoke, within O'Reilly's, "I am the worst diplomatist in the world, and I fear I never should have risen to high rank in the distinguished corps of engineers if such had been my destination. I can lay down the parallels and the trenches patiently enough, I can even bring up my artillery and my battering-train, but, hang it! somehow, I never can wait for a breach to storm through. The truth is, if it were not for a very strong feeling on the subject I have just spoken of, you never would have seen me here this day. No man is happier or prouder to enjoy your hospitality than I am, but, I acknowledge, it was a higher sentiment induced me to accept your invitation. When your note reached me, I showed it to Castlereagh.

"'What answer have you sent?' said he.

"'Declined, of course,' said I.

"'You are wrong, Heffernan,' said his Lordship, as he took from me the note which I held ready sealed in my hand; 'in my opinion, Heffernan, you are quite wrong.'

"'I may be so, my Lord; but I confess to you I always act from the first impulse, and if it suggests regret afterwards, it at least saves trouble at the time.'

"'Heffernan,' said the Secretary, as he calmly read over the lines of your letter, 'there are many reasons why you should go; in the first place, O'Reilly has really a fair grudge against us, and this note shows that he has the manliness to forget it. Every line of it bespeaks the gentleman, and I'll not feel contented with myself until you convey to him my own sorrow for what is past, and the high sense I entertain of his character and conduct.'

"He said a great deal more; enough, if I tell you he induced me to rescind my first intention, and to become your guest; and I may say, that I never followed advice the consequences of which have so thoroughly sustained my expectations."

"This is very flattering," said O'Reilly; "it is, indeed, more than I looked for; but, as you have been candid with me, I will be as open with you: I had already made up my mind to retire, for a season at least, from politics. My father, you know, is a very old man, and not without the prejudices that attach to his age; he was always adverse to those ambitious views a public career would open, and a degree of coldness had begun to grow up between us in consequence. This estrangement is now happily at an end; and, in his consenting to our present mode of life, and its expenditure, he is, in reality, paying the recompense of his former opposition. I will not say what changes time may work in my own opinions, or my line of acting, but I will pledge myself that, if I do resume the path of public life, you are the very first man I will apprise of the intention."

A cordial shake-hands ratified this compact, and Heffernan, who now saw that the fortress had capitulated, only stipulating for the honours of war, was about to add something very complimentary, when Beecham O'Reilly galloped up, with his horse splashed and covered with foam.

"Don't you want to hear O'Halloran, Mr. Heffernan?" cried he.

"Yes, by all means."

"Come along, then; don't lose a moment; there's a phaeton ready for you at the door, and, if we make haste, we'll be in good time."

O'Reilly whispered a few words in his son's ear, to which the other replied, aloud,

"Oh! quite safe—perfectly safe. He was obliged to join his regiment, and sail at a moment's notice."

"Young Darcy, I presume?" said Heffernan, with a look of malicious intelligence. But no answer was returned, and O'Reilly continued to converse eagerly in Beecham's ear.

"Here comes the carriage, Mr. Heffernan," said the young man, "so slip in, and let's be off;" and, giving his horse to a servant, he took his seat beside Heffernan, and drove off at a rapid pace towards the town.

After a quick drive of some miles they entered the town, and had no necessity to ask if O'Halloran had begun his address to the jury. The streets which led to the square before the Court-house, and the square itself, was actually crammed with country-people, of all sexes and ages; some standing with hats off, or holding their hands close to their ears, but all, in breathless silence, listening to the words of "the Counsellor," which were not less audible to those without than within the building.

Nothing short of Beecham O'Reilly's present position in the county, and the fact that the gratification they were then deriving was of his family's procuring for them, could have enabled him to force a passage through that dense crowd, which wedged up all the approaches. As it was, he could only advance step by step, the horses and even the pole of the carriage actually forcing the way through the throng.

As they went thus slowly, the rich tones of the speaker swelled on the air with a clear, distinct, and yet so soft and even musical intonation, that they fell deeply into the hearts of the listeners. He was evidently bent as much on appealing to those outside the court as to the jury, for his speech was less addressed to the legal question at issue, than to the social condition of the peasantry; the all but absolutism of a landlord—the serf-like slavery of a tenantry, dependent on the will or the caprice of the owners of the soil! With the consummate art of a rhetorician, he first drew the picture of an estate happily circumstanced, a benevolent landlord surrounded by a contented tenantry, the blessings of the poor man, "rising like the dews of the earth, and descending again in rain to refresh and fertilise the source it sprang from." Not vaguely nor unskilfully, but with thorough knowledge of his subject, he descanted on the condition of the peasant, his toils, his struggles against poverty and sickness borne with long suffering and patience, from the firm trust that, even in this world, his destinies were committed to no cruel or unfeeling task-master. Although generally a studied plainness and even homeliness of language pervaded all he said, yet, at times, some bold figure, some striking and brilliant metaphor would escape him, and then, far from soaring—as it might be suspected he had—above the comprehension of the hearers, a subdued murmur of delight would follow the words, and swelling louder and louder, burst forth at last into one great roar of applause. If a critical ear might cavil at the incompleteness or inaptitude of his similes, to the warm imagination and excited fancy of the Irish peasant they had no such blemishes.

It was at the close of a brilliant peroration on this theme, that Heffernan and Beecham O'Reilly reached the Court-house, and with difficulty forcing their way, obtained standing-room near the bar.

The orator had paused, and turning round, he caught Beecham's eye: the glance exchanged was but of a second's duration, but, brief as it was, it did not escape Heffernan's notice, and with a readiness he knew well how to profit by, he assumed a quiet smile, as though to say that he, too, had read its meaning. The young man blushed deeply; whatever his secret thoughts were, he felt ashamed that another should seem to know them, and in a hesitating whisper, said,

"Perhaps my father has told you——?"

A short nod from Heffernan—a gesture to imply anything or nothing—was all his reply, and Beecham went on:

"He's going to do it, now."

Heffernan made no answer, but, leaning forward on the rail, settled himself to listen attentively to the speaker.

"Gentlemen of the Jury," said O'Halloran, in a low and deliberate tone, "if the only question I was interested in bringing before you this day was the cause you sit there to try, I would conclude here. Assured as I feel what your verdict will and must be, I would not add a word more, nor weaken the honest merit of your convictions by anything like an appeal to your feelings. But I cannot do this. The law of the land, in the plenitude of its liberty, throws wide the door of justice, that all may enter and seek redress for wrong, and with such evident anxiety that he who believes himself aggrieved should find no obstacle to his right, and that even he who frivolously and maliciously advances a charge against another, suffers no heavier penalty for his offence than the costs of the suit. No, my Lords, for the valuable moments lost in a vexatious cause, for the public time consumed, for insult and outrage cast upon the immutable principles of right and wrong, you have nothing more severe to inflict than the costs of the action!—a pecuniary fine, seldom a heavy one, and not unfrequently to be levied upon insolvency! What encouragement to the spirit of revengeful litigation! How suggestive of injury is the system! How deplorable would it be if the Temple could not be opened without the risk of its altar being desecrated! But, happily, there is a remedy—a great and noble remedy—for an evil like this. The same glorious institutions that have built up for our protection the bulwark of the law, have created another barrier against wrong—grander, more expansive, and more enduring still; one neither founded on the variable basis of nationality or of language, not propped by the artifices of learned, or the subtleties of crafty men; not following the changeful fortunes of a political condition, or tempered by the tone of the judgment-seat, but of all lands, of every tongue, and nation, and people, great, enduring, and immutable—the law of Public Opinion. To the bar of this judgment-seat, one higher and greater than even your Lordships, I would now summon the plaintiff in this action. There is no need that I should detail the charge against him, the accusation he has brought this day is our indictment—his allegation is his crime."

The reader, by this time, may partake of Mr. Heffernan's prescience, and divine what the secret intelligence between the Counsellor and Beecham portended, and that a long-meditated attack on the Knight of Gwynne, in all the relations of his public and private life, was the chief duty of Mr. O'Halloran in the action. Taking a lesson from the great and illustrious chief of a neighbouring state, O'Reilly felt that Usurpation can never be successful till Legitimacy becomes odious. The "prestige" of the "old family" clung too powerfully to every class in the county to make his succession respected. His low origin was too recent, his moneyed dealings too notorious, to gain him acceptance, except on the ruins of the Darcys. The new edifice of his own fame must be erected out of the scattered and broken materials of his rival's house. If any one was well calculated to assist in such an emergency, it was O'Halloran.

It was by—to use his own expression—"weeding the country of such men" that the field would be opened for that new class of politicians who were to issue their edicts in newspapers, and hold their parliaments in public meetings. Against exclusive or exaggerated loyalty the struggle would be violent, but not difficult; while against moderation, sound sense and character, the Counsellor well knew the victory was not so easy of attainment. He himself, therefore, had a direct personal object in this attack on the Knight of Gwynne, and gladly accepted the special retainer that secured his services.

By a series of artful devices, he so arranged his case that the Knight of Gwynne did not appear as an injured individual seeking redress against the collusive guilt of his agent and his tenantry, but as a ruined gambler, endeavouring to break the leases he had himself granted and guaranteed, and, by an act of perfidy, involve hundreds of innocent families in hopeless beggary. To the succour of these unprotected people Mr. Hickman O'Reilly was represented as coming forward, this noble act of devotion being the first pledge he had offered of what might be expected from him as the future leader of a great county.

He sketched with a masterly but diabolical ingenuity the whole career of the Knight, representing him at every stage of life as the pampered voluptuary seeking means for fresh enjoyment, without a thought of the consequences; he exhibited him dispensing, not the graceful duties of hospitality, but the reckless waste of a tasteless household, to counterbalance by profusion the insolent hauteur of his wife, "that same Lady Eleanor who would not deign to associate with the wives and daughters of his neighbours!" "I know not," cried the orator, "whether you were more crushed by *his* gold or by *her* insolence: it was time that you should weary of both. You took the wealth on trust, and the rank on guess—what now remains of either?"

He drew a frightful picture of a suffering and poverty-enslaved tenantry, sinking fast into barbarism from hopelessness—unhappily, no Irishman need depend upon his imagination for the sketch. He contrasted the hours of toil and sickness with the wanton spendthrift in his pleasures—the gambler setting the fate of families on the die, reserving for his last hope the consolation that he might still betray those whom he had ruined, and that when he had dissipated the last shilling of his fortune, he still had the resource of putting his honour up to auction! "And who is there will deny that he did this?" cried O'Halloran. "Is there any man in the kingdom has not heard of his conduct in Parliament, that foul act of treachery which the justice of Heaven stigmatised by his ruin! How on the very night of the debate he was actually on his way to inflict the last wound upon his country, when the news came of his own overwhelming destruction! And, like as you have seen some time in our unhappy land the hired informer transferred from the witness-table to the dock, this man stands now forth to answer for his own offences!

"It was full time that the rotten edifice of this feudalist gentry should fall—honour to you on whom the duty devolves to roll away the first stone!"

A slight movement in the crowd behind the bar disturbed the silence in which the Court listened to the speaker, and a murmur of disapprobation was heard, when a hand, stretched forth, threw a little slip of paper on the table before O'Halloran. It was addressed to him; and believing it came from the attorney in the cause, he paused to read it. Suddenly his features became of an ashy paleness, his lip trembled convulsively, and in a voice scarcely audible from emotion, he addressed the Bench.

"My Lords—I ask the protection of this Court. I implore your Lordships to see that an advocate, in the discharge of his duty, is not the mark of an assassin. I have just received this note——" He attempted to read it, but, after a pause of a second or two, unable to utter a word, he handed the paper to the Bench.

The Judge perused the paper, and immediately whispered an order that the writer, or, at least, the bearer of the note, should be taken into custody.

"You may rest assured, sir," said the senior Judge, addressing O'Halloran, "that we will punish the offender, if he be discovered, with the utmost penalty the law permits. Mr. Sheriff, let the Court be searched."

The sub-sheriff was already, with the aid of a strong police force, engaged in the effort to discover the individual who had thus dared to interfere with the administration of justice; but all in vain. The Court and the galleries were searched without eliciting anything that could lead to detection; and although several were taken up on suspicion, they were immediately afterwards liberated on being recognised as persons well known and in repute. Meanwhile the business of the trial stood still, and O'Halloran, with his arms folded, and his brows bent in a sullen frown, sat without speaking, or noticing any one around him.

The curiosity to know the exact words the paper contained was meanwhile extreme, and a thousand absurd versions gained currency, for, in the absence of all fact, invention was had recourse to: "Young Darcy is here—he was seen this morning on the mail—it was he himself gave the letter." Such were among the rumours around, while Con Heffernan, coolly tapping his snuff-box, asked one of the lawyers near him, but in a voice plainly audible on either side, "I hope our friend Bagenal Daly is well; have you seen him lately?"

From that moment an indistinct murmur ran through the crowd that it was Daly had come back to "the West" to challenge the whole Bar, and the Bench, if necessary. Many added that there could no longer be any doubt of the fact, as Mr. Heffernan had seen and spoken to him.

Order was at last restored, but so completely had this new incident absorbed all the interest of the trial, that already the galleries began to thin, and of the great crowd that filled the body of the Court, many had taken their departure. The Counsellor arose, agitated, and evidently disconcerted, to finish his task: he spoke, indeed, indignantly of the late attempt to coerce the free expression of the advocate "by a brutal threat," but the theme seemed one he felt no pleasure in dwelling upon, and he once more addressed himself to the facts of the case.

The Judge charged briefly, and the Jury, without retiring from the box, brought in a verdict for Hickman O'Reilly.

When the Judges retired to unrobe, a messenger of the Court summoned O'Halloran to their chamber. His absence was very brief, but when he returned his face was paler, and his manner more disturbed than ever, notwithstanding an evident effort to seem at ease and unconcerned. By this time Hickman O'Reilly had arrived in the town, and Heffernan was complimenting the Counsellor on the admirable display of his speech.

"I regret sincerely that the delicate nature of the position in which I stood prevented my hearing you," said O'Reilly, shaking his hand.

"You have indeed had a great loss," said Heffernan; "a more brilliant display I never listened to."

"Well, sir," interposed the little priest of Curraghglass, who, not altogether to the Counsellor's satisfaction, had now slipped an arm inside of his, "I hope the evil admits of remedy; Mr. O'Halloran intends to address few words to the people before he leaves the town."

Whether it was the blank look that suddenly O'Reilly's features assumed, or the sly malice that twinkled in Heffernan's grey eyes, or that his own feelings suggested the course, but the Counsellor hastily whispered a few words in the priest's ear, the only audible portion of which was the conclusion: "Be that as it may, I'll not do it."

"I'm ready now, Mr. O'Reilly," said he, turning abruptly round.

"My father has gone over to say 'Good-by' to the Judges," said Beecham; "but I'll drive you back to the abbey—the carriage is now at the door."

With a few more words in a whisper to the priest, O'Halloran moved on with young O'Reilly towards the door.

"Only think, sir," said Father John, dropping behind with Heffernan, from whose apparent intimacy with O'Halloran he augured a similarity of politics, "it is the first time the Counsellor was ever in our town, the people have been waiting since two o'clock to hear him on the 'veto'—sorra one of them knows what the same 'veto' is—but it will be a cruel disappointment to see him leave the place without so much as saying a word."

"Do you think a short address from *me* would do instead?" said Heffernan, slyly; "I know pretty well what's doing up in Dublin."

"Nothing could be better, sir," said Father John, in ecstasy; "if the Counsellor would just introduce you in a few words, and say that, from great fatigue, or a sore-throat, or anything that way, he deputed his friend Mr.——"

"Heffernan's my name."

"His friend Mr. Heffernan to state his views about the 'veto'—mind, it must be the 'veto'—you can touch on the reform in Parliament, the oppression of the penal laws, but the 'veto' will bring a cheer that will beat them all."

"You had better hint the thing to the Counsellor," said Heffernan; "I am ready whenever you want me."

As the priest stepped forward to make the communication to O'Halloran, that gentleman, leaning on Beecham O'Reilly's arm, had just reached the steps of the Court-house, where now a considerable police force was stationed, a measure possibly suggested by O'Reilly himself.

The crowd, on catching sight of "the Counsellor," cheered vociferously, and, although they were not without fears that he intended to depart without speaking, many averred that he would address them from the carriage. Before Father John could make known his request, a young man, dressed in a riding costume, burst through the line of police, and, springing up the steps, seized O'Halloran by the collar.

"I gave you a choice, sir," said he, "and you made it;" and, at the same instant, with a heavy horsewhip, struck him several times across the shoulders, and even the face. So sudden was the movement, and so violent the assault, that, although a man of great personal strength, O'Halloran had received several blows almost before he could defend himself, and when he had rallied, his adversary, though much lighter and less muscular, showed in skill, at least, he was his superior. The struggle, however, was not to end here, for the mob, now seeing their favourite champion attacked, with a savage howl of vengeance dashed forward, and the police, well aware that the youth would be torn limb from limb, formed a line in front of him with fixed bayonets. For a few moments the result was doubtful; nor was it until more than one retired into the crowd bleeding and wounded, that the mob desisted, or limited their rage to yells of vengeance.

Meanwhile "the Counsellor" was pulled back within the Court-house by his companions, and the young man secured by two policemen; a circumstance which went far to allay the angry tempest of the people without.

As, pale and powerless from passion, his livid cheek marked with a deep blue welt, O'Halloran sat in one of the waiting-rooms of the Court, O'Reilly and his son endeavoured, as well as they could, to calm down his rage: expressing, from time to time, their abhorrence of the indignity offered, and the certain penalty that awaited the offender. O'Halloran never spoke; he tried twice to utter something, but the words died away without sound, and he could only point to his cheek with a trembling finger, while his eyes glared like the red orbs of a tiger.

As they stood thus, Heffernan slipped noiselessly behind O'Reilly, and said in his ear,

"Get him off to the abbey; your son will take care of him. I have something for yourself to hear."

O'Reilly nodded significantly, and then, turning, said a few words in a low, persuasive tone to O'Halloran, concluding thus: "Yes, by all means, leave the whole affair in my hands. I'll have no difficulty in making a bench. The town is full of my brother magistrates."

"On every account I would recommend this course, sir," said Heffernan, with one of those peculiarly meaning looks by which he so well knew how to assume a further insight into any circumstance than his neighbours possessed.

"I will address the people," cried O'Halloran, breaking his long silence with a deep and passionate utterance of the words; "they shall see in me the strong evidence of the insolent oppression of that faction that rules this country; I'll make the land ring with the tyranny that would stifle the voice of justice, and make the profession of the Bar a forlorn hope to every man of independent feeling."

"The people have dispersed already," said Beecham, as he came back from the door of the Court; "the square is quite empty."

"Yes, I did that," whispered Heffernan in O'Reilly's ear; "I made my servant put on the Counsellor's great-coat, and drive rapidly off towards the abbey. The carriage is now, however, at the back entrance to the Court-house, so, by all means, persuade him to return."

"When do you propose bringing the fellow up for examination, Mr. O'Reilly?" said O'Halloran, as he arose from his seat.

"To-morrow morning. I have given orders to summon a full bench of magistrates, and the affair shall be sifted to the bottom."

"You may depend upon that, sir," said the Counsellor, sternly. "Now I'll go back with you, Mr. Beecham O'Reilly." So saying, he moved towards a private door of the building where the phaeton was in waiting, and, before any attention was drawn to the spot, he was seated in the carriage, and the horses stepping out at a fast pace towards home.

"It's not Bagenal Daly?" said O'Reilly, the very moment he saw the carriage drive off.

"No! no!" said Heffernan, smiling.

"Nor the young Darcy—the captain?"

"Nor him either. It's a young fellow we have been seeking for in vain the last month. His name is Forester."

"Not Lord Castlereagh's Forester?"

"The very man. You may have met him here as Darcy's guest?"

O'Reilly nodded.

"What makes the affair worse is, that the relationship with Castlereagh will be taken up as a party matter by O'Halloran's friends in the press; they will see a Castle plot, where, in reality, there is nothing to blame save the rash folly of a hot-headed boy."

"What is to be done?" said O'Reilly, putting his hand to his forehead, in his embarrassment to think of some escape from the difficulty.

"I see but one safe issue—always enough to any question, if men have resolution to adopt it."

"Let me hear what you counsel," said O'Reilly, as he cast a searching glance at his astute companion.

"Get him off as fast as you can."

"O'Halloran! You mistake him, Mr. Heffernan; he'll prosecute the business to the end."

"I'm speaking of Forester," said Heffernan, dryly; "it is *his* absence is the important matter at this moment."

"I confess I am myself unable to appreciate your view of the case," said O'Reilly, with a cunning smile; "the policy is a new one to me which teaches that a magistrate should favour the escape of a prisoner who has just insulted one of his own friends."

"I may be able to explain my meaning to your satisfaction," said Heffernan, as, taking O'Reilly's arm, he spoke for some time in a low, but earnest manner. "Yes," said he, aloud, "your son Beecham was the object of this young man's vengeance; chance alone turned his anger on 'the Counsellor.' His sole purpose in 'the West' was to provoke your son to a duel, and I know well what the result of your proceedings to-morrow would effect. Forester would not accept of his liberty on bail, nor would he enter into a security on his part to keep the peace. You will be forced, actually forced, to commit a young man of family and high position to a gaol; and what will the world say? That in seeking satisfaction for a very gross outrage on the character of his friend, a young Englishman of high family was sent to prison! In Ireland the tale will tell badly; *we* always have more sympathy than censure for such offenders. In England, how many will know of his friends and connexions, who never heard of your respectable bench of magistrates—will it be very wonderful if they side with their countryman against the stranger?"

"How am I to face O'Halloran if I follow this counsel?" said O'Reilly with a thoughtful but embarrassed air.

"Then, as to Lord Castlereagh," continued Heffernan, not heeding the question, "he will take your interference as a personal and particular favour. There never was a more favourable opportunity for you to disconnect yourself with the whole affair. The hired advocate may calumniate as he will, but he can show no collusion or connivance on your part. I may tell you, in confidence, that a more indecent and gross attack was never uttered than this same speech. I heard it, and from the beginning to the end it was a tissue of vulgarity and falsehood. Oh! I know what you would say: I complimented the speaker on his success, and all that: so I did, perfectly true, and he understood me, too—there is no greater impertinence, perhaps, than in telling a man that you mistook his bad cider for champagne! But enough of him. You may have all the benefit, if there be such, of the treason, and yet never rub shoulders with the traitor. You see I am eager on this point, and I confess I am very much so. Your son Beecham could not have a worse enemy in the world of Club and Fashion than this same Forester; he knows and is known to everybody."

"But I cannot perceive how the thing is to be done," broke in O'Reilly pettishly; "you seem to forget that O'Halloran is not the man to be put off with any lame, disjointed story."

"Easily enough," said Heffernan, coolly; "there is no difficulty whatever. You can blunder in the warrant of his committal; you can designate him by a wrong Christian name, call him Robert, not Richard; he may be admitted to bail, and the sum a low one. The rest follows naturally; or better than all, let some other magistrate—you surely know more than one to aid in such a pinch—take the case upon himself, and make all the necessary errors; that's the best plan."

"Conolly, perhaps," said O'Reilly, musingly; "he is a great friend of Darcy's, and would risk something to assist this young fellow."

"Well thought of," cried Heffernan, slapping him on the shoulder; "just give me a line of introduction to Mr. Conolly on one of your visiting cards, and leave the rest to me."

"If I yield to you in this business, Mr. Heffernan," said O'Reilly, as he sat down to write, "I assure you it is far more from my implicit confidence in your skill to conduct it safely to the end, than from any power of persuasion in your arguments. O'Halloran is a formidable enemy."

"You never were more mistaken in your life," said Heffernan, laughing; "such men are only noxious by the terror they inspire; they are the rattlesnakes of the world of mankind, always giving notice of their approach, and never dangerous to the prudent. He alone is to be dreaded who, tiger-like, utters no cry till his victim is in his fangs."

There was a savage malignity in the way these words were uttered that made O'Reilly almost shudder. Heffernan saw the emotion he had unguardedly evoked, and laughing, said,

"Well, am I to hold over the remainder of my visit to the abbey as a debt unpaid? for I really have no fancy to let you off so cheaply."

"But you are coming back with me—are you not?"

"Impossible! I must take charge of this foolish boy, and bring him up to Dublin; I only trust that I have a vested right to come back and see you at a future day."

O'Reilly responded to the proposition with courteous warmth, and with mutual pledges, perhaps of not dissimilar sincerity, they parted, the one to his own home, the other to negotiate in a different quarter, and in a very different spirit of diplomacy.

CHAPTER XLII.

MR. HEFFERNAN'S COUNSELS.

Mr. Heffernan possessed many worldly gifts and excellences, but upon none did he so much pride himself, in the secret recesses of his heart,—he was too cunning to indulge in more public vauntings,—as in the power he wielded over the passions of men much younger than himself. Thoroughly versed in their habits of life, tastes, and predilections, he knew how much always to concede to the warm and generous temperament of their age, and to maintain his influence over them, less by the ascendancy of ability, than by a more intimate acquaintance with all the follies and extravagances of fashionable existence.

Whether he had, or had not been, a principal actor in the scenes he related with so much humour, it was difficult to say: for he would gloss over his own personal adventures so artfully, that it was not easy to discover whether the motives were cunning or delicacy. He seemed, at least, to have done everything that wildness and eccentricity had ever devised; to have known intimately every man renowned for such exploits; and to have gone through a career of extravagance and dissipation quite sufficient to make him an unimpeachable authority in every similar case. The reserve which young men feel with regard to those older than themselves, was never experienced in Con Heffernan's company; they would venture to tell him anything, well aware that, however absurd the story or embarrassing the scrape, Heffernan was certain to cap it by another, twice as extravagant in every respect.

Although Forester was by no means free from the faults of his age and class, the better principles of his nature had received no severe or lasting injury, and his estimation for Heffernan proceeded from a very different view of his character from that which we have just alluded to. He knew him to be the tried and trusted agent of his cousin, Lord Castlereagh, one for whose abilities he entertained the greatest respect; he saw him consulted and advised with on every question of difficulty, his opinions asked, his suggestions followed; and if, occasionally, the policy was somewhat tortuous, he was taught to believe that the course of politics, like that "of true love, never did run smooth." In this way, then, did he learn to look up to Heffernan, who was too shrewd a judge of motives to risk a greater ascendancy by any hazardous appeal to the weaker points of his character.

Fortune could not have presented a more welcome visitor to Forester's eyes than Heffernan, as he entered the room of the inn where the youth had been conducted by the sergeant of the police; and where he sat, bewildered by the difficulties in which his own rashness had involved him. The first moments of meeting were occupied by a perfect shower of questions, as to how Heffernan came to be in that quarter of the world? when he had arrived? and with whom he was staying? All questions which Heffernan answered by the laughing subterfuge of saying, "Your good genius, I suppose, sent me to get you out of your scrape, and fortunately I am able to do so. But what in the name of everything ridiculous could have induced you to insult this man, O'Halloran? You ought to have known that men like him cannot fight; they would be made riddles of, if they once consented to back by personal daring the insolence of their tongues. They set out by establishing for themselves a kind of outlawry from honour, they acknowledge no debts within the jurisdiction of that court, otherwise they would soon be bankrupt."

"They should be treated like all others without the pale of law, then," said Forester, indignantly.

"Or, like Sackville," added Heffernan, laughing, "when they put their swords 'on the peace establishment,' they should put their tongues on the 'civil list.' Well, well, there are new discoveries made every day; some men succeed better in life by the practice of cowardice, than others ever did, or ever will do, by the exercise of valour."

"What can I do here? Is there anything serious in the difficulty?" said Forester, hurriedly; for he was in no humour to enjoy the abstract speculations in which Heffernan indulged.

"It might have been a very troublesome business," replied Heffernan, quietly; "the Judge might have issued a bench warrant against you, if he did not want your cousin to make him Chief Baron; and Justice Conolly might have been much more technically accurate, if he was not desirous of seeing his son in an infantry regiment. It's all arranged now, however; there is only one point for your compliance, you must get out of Ireland as fast as may be. O'Halloran will apply for a rule in the King's Bench, but the proceedings will not extend to England."

"I am indifferent where I go to," said Forester, turning away; "and provided this foolish affair does not get abroad, I am well content."

"Oh! as to that, you must expect your share of notoriety. O'Halloran will take care to display his martyrdom for the people! It will bring him briefs now; Heaven knows what greater rewards the future may have in store from it!"

"You heard the provocation," said Forester, with an unsuccessful attempt to speak calmly—"the gross and most unpardonable provocation?"

"I was present," replied Heffernan, quietly.

"Well, what say you? Was there ever uttered an attack more false and foul? Was there ever conceived a more fiendish and malignant slander?"

"I never heard anything worse."

"Not anything worse! No, nor ever one-half so bad."

"Well, if you like it, I will agree with you; not one-half so bad. It was untrue in all its details, unmanly in spirit. But, let me add, that such philippics have no lasting effect, they are like unskilful mines, that, in their explosion, only damage the contrivers. O'Reilly, who was the real deviser of this same attack, whose heart suggested, whose head invented, and whose coffers paid for it, will reap all the obloquy he hoped to heap upon another. Take myself, for instance, an old time-worn man of the world, who has lived long enough never to be sudden in my friendships or my resentments, who thinks that liking and disliking are slow processes; well, even I was shocked, outraged at this affair; and, although having no more intimacy with Darcy than the ordinary intercourse of social life, confess I could not avoid acting promptly and decisively on the subject. It was a question, perhaps, more of feeling than actual judgment—a case, in which the first impulse may generally be deemed the right one." Here Heffernan paused, and drew himself up with an air that seemed to say, "If I am confessing to a weakness in my character, it is, at least, one that leans to virtue's side."

Forester awaited with impatience for the explanation, and, not perceiving it to come, said, "Well, what did you do in the affair?"

"My part was a very simple one," said Heffernan. "I was Mr. O'Reilly's guest, one of a large party, asked to meet the Judges and the Attorney-General. I came in, with many others, to hear O'Halloran; but if I did, I took the liberty of not returning again. I told Mr. O'Reilly frankly, that, in point of fact, the thing was false, and, as policy, it was a mistake. Party contests are all very well, they are necessary, because without them there is no banner to fight under; and the man of mock liberality to either side would take precedence of those more honest but less cautious than himself; but these things are great evils when they enlist libellous attacks on character in their train. If the courtesies of life are left at the door of our popular assemblies, they ought at least to be resumed when passing out again into the world."

"And so you actually refused to go back to his house?" said Forester, who felt far more interested in this simple fact than in all the abstract speculation that accompanied it.

"I did so: I even begged of him to send my servant and my carriage after me; and, had it not been for your business, before this time I had been some miles on my way towards Dublin."

Forester never spoke, but he grasped Heffernan's hand, and shook it with earnest cordiality.

"Yes, yes," said Heffernan, as he returned the pressure; "men can be strong partisans, anxious and eager for their own side, but there is something higher and nobler than party." He arose as he spoke, and walked towards the window, and then, suddenly turning round, and with an apparent desire to change the theme, asked, "But how came you here? What good or evil fortune prompted you to be present at this scene?"

"I fear you must allow me to keep that a secret," said Forester, in some confusion.

"Scarcely fair, that, my young friend," said Heffernan, laughing, "after hearing my confession in full."

Forester seemed to feel the force of the observation, but, uncertain how to act, he maintained a silence for several minutes.

"If the affair were altogether my own, I should not hesitate," said he, at length, "but it is not so. However, we are in confidence here, and so I will tell you. I came to this part of the country at the earnest desire of Lionel Darcy. I don't know whether you are aware of his sudden departure for India. He had asked for leave of absence, to give evidence on this trial; the application was made a few days after a memorial he sent in for a change of regiment. The demand for leave was unheeded, but he received a peremptory order to repair to Portsmouth, and take charge of a detachment under sailing-orders for India; they consisted of men belonging to the 11th Light Dragoons, of which he was gazetted to a troop. I was with him at Chatham when the letter reached him, and he explained the entire difficulty to me, showing that he had no alternative, save neglecting the interest of his family, on the one hand, or refusing that offer of active service he had so urgently solicited on the other. We talked the thing over one entire night through, and at last, right or wrong, persuaded ourselves that any evidence he could give would be of comparatively little value; and that the refusal to join would be deemed a stain upon him as an officer, and, probably, be the cause of greater grief to the Knight himself, than his absence at the trial. Poor fellow! he felt far more deeply for quitting England without saying 'Good-by' to his family, than for all the rest."

"And so he actually sailed in the transport?" said Heffernan.

"Yes, and without time for more than a few lines to his father and parting request to me to come over to Ireland and be present at the trial. Whether he anticipated any attack of this kind or not, I cannot say, but he expressed the desire so strongly I half suspect as much."

"Very cleverly done, faith!" muttered Heffernan, who seemed far more occupied with his own reflections than attending to Forester's words; "a deep and subtle stroke, Master O'Reilly, ably planned, and as ably executed."

"I am rejoiced that Lionel escaped this scene, at all events," said Forester.

"I must say, it was neatly done," continued Heffernan, still following out his own train of thought; "'Non contigit cuique,' as the Roman says; it is not every man can take in Con Heffernan—I did not expect Hickman O'Reilly would try it." He leaned his head on his hand for some minutes, then said aloud, "The best thing for you will be to join your regiment."

"I have left the army," said Forester, with a flush, half of shame, half of anger.

"I think you were right," replied Heffernan, calmly, while he avoided noticing the confusion in the young man's manner. "Soldiering is no career for any man of abilities like yours; the lounging life of a barrack-yard, the mock duties of parade, the tiresome dissipations of the mess, suit small capacities and minds of mere routine. But you have better stuff in you, and, with your connexions and family interest, there are higher prizes to strive for in the wheel of fortune."

"You mistake me," said Forester, hastily; "it was with no disparaging opinion of the service I left it. My reasons had nothing in common with such an estimate of the army."

"There's Diplomacy, for instance," said Heffernan, not minding the youth's remark; "your brother has influence with the Foreign-office."

"I have no fancy for the career."

"Well, there are Government situations in abundance. A man must do something in our work-a-day world, if only to be companionable to those who do. Idleness begets *ennui* and falling in love, and although the first only wearies for the time, the latter lays its impress on all a man's after-life, fills him with false notions of happiness, instils wrong motives for exertion, and limits the exercise of capacity to the small and valueless accomplishments that find favour beside the work-table and the piano."

Forester received somewhat haughtily the unasked counsels of Mr. Heffernan respecting his future mode of life, nor was it improbable that he might himself have conveyed his opinion thereupon in words, had not the appearance of the waiter to prepare the table for dinner interposed a barrier.

"At what hour shall I order the horses, sir?" asked the man of Heffernan.

"Shall we say eight o'clock?—or is that too early?"

"Not a minute too early for me," said Forester; "I am longing to leave this place, where I hope never again to set foot."

"At eight, then, let them be at the door, and whenever your cook is ready we dine."

CHAPTER XLIII.

AN UNLOOKED-FOR PROMOTION.

The same post that brought the Knight the tidings of his lost suit, conveyed the intelligence of his son's departure for India, and although the latter event was one over which—if in his power—he would have exercised no control, yet was it by far the more saddening of the two announcements.

Unable to apply any more consolatory counsels, his invariable reply to Lady Eleanor was, "It was a point of duty; the boy could not have done otherwise; I have too often expressed my opinion to him about the 'devoirs' of a soldier to permit of his hesitating here. And as for our suit, Mr. Bicknell says the jury did not deliberate ten minutes on their verdict; whatever right we might have on our side, it was pretty clear we had no law. Poor Lionel is spared the pain of knowing this at least." He sighed heavily and was silent; Lady Eleanor and Helen spoke not either, and except their long-drawn breathings nothing was heard in the room.

Lady Eleanor was the first to speak. "Might not Lionel's evidence have given a very different colouring to our cause if he had been there?"

"It is hard to say; I am not aware whether we failed upon a point of fact or law: Mr. Bicknell writes like a man who felt his words were costly matters, and that he should not put his client to unnecessary expense. He limits himself to the simple announcement of the result, and that the charge of the bench was very pointedly unfavourable. He says something about a motion for a new trial, and regrets Daly's having prevented his engaging Mr. O'Halloran, and refers us to the newspapers for detail."

"I never heard a question of this O'Halloran," said Lady Eleanor, "nor of Mr. Daly's opposition to him before."

"Nor did I either; though in all likelihood, if I had, I should have been of Bagenal's mind myself. Employing such men has always appeared to me on a par with the barbarism of engaging the services of savage nations in a war against civilised ones; and the practice is defended by the very same arguments—if they are not with you, they are against you."

"You are right, my dear father," said Helen, while her countenance glowed with unusual animation; "leave such allies to the enemy if he will, no good cause shall be stained by the scalping-knife and the tomahawk."

"Quite right, my dearest child," said he, fondly; "no defeat is so bad as such a victory."

"And where was Mr. Daly? He does not seem to have been at the trial."

"No; it would appear as if he were detained by some pressing necessity in Dublin. This letter is in his handwriting; let us see what he says."

Before the Knight could execute his intention, old Tate appeared at the door, and announced the name of Mr. Dempsey.

"You must present our compliments," said Darcy, hastily, "and say that a very particular engagement will prevent our having the pleasure of receiving his visit this evening."

"This is really intolerable," said Lady Eleanor, who, never much disposed to look favourably on that gentleman, felt his present appearance anything but agreeable.

"You hear what your master says," said Helen to the old man, who, never having in his whole life received a similar order, felt proportionately astonished and confused.

"Tell Mr. Dempsey we are very sorry, but——"

"For all that, he won't be denied," said Paul, himself finishing the sentence, while, passing unceremoniously in front of Tate, he walked boldly into the middle of the room. His face was flushed, his forehead covered with perspiration, and his clothes, stained with dust, showed that he had come off a very long and fast walk. He wiped his forehead with a flaring cotton handkerchief, and then, with a long-drawn puff, threw himself back into an arm-chair.

There was something so actually comic in the cool assurance of the little man, that Darcy lost all sense of annoyance at the interruption, while he surveyed him and enjoyed the dignified coolness of Lady Eleanor's reception.

"That's the devil's own bit of a road," said Paul, as he fanned himself with a music-book, "between this and Coleraine. Whenever it's not going up a hill, it's down one. Do you ever walk that way, ma'am?"

"Very seldom indeed, sir."

"Faith, and I'd wager, when you do, that it gives you a pain just here below the calf of the leg, and a stitch in the small of the back."

Lady Eleanor took no notice of this remark, but addressed some observation to Helen, at which the young girl smiled, and said, in a whisper,

"Oh, he will not stay long."

"I am afraid, Mr. Dempsey," said the Knight, "that I must be uncourteous enough to say that we are unprepared for a visitor this evening. Some letters of importance have just arrived, and as they will demand all our attention, you will, I am sure, excuse the frankness of my telling you that we desire to be alone."

"So you shall in a few minutes more," said Paul, coolly. "Let me have a glass of sherry-and-water, or, if wine is not convenient, ditto of brandy, and I'm off. I didn't come to stop. It was a letter that you forgot at the Post-office, marked 'with speed,' on the outside, that brought me here; for I was spending a few days in Coleraine with old Hewson."

The kindness of this thoughtful act at once eradicated every memory of the vulgarity that accompanied it, and as the Knight took the letter from his hands, he hastened to apologise for what he said by adding his thanks for the service.

"I offered a fellow a shilling to bring it, but being harvest-time he wouldn't come," said Dempsey. "Phew! what a state the roads are in! dust up to your ankles!"

"Come, now, pray help yourself to some wine-and-water," said the Knight, "and while you do so, I'll ask permission to open my letter."

"There's a short cut down by Port-na-happle mill, they tell me, ma'am," said Dempsey, who now found a much more complaisant listener than at first; "but, to tell you the truth, I don't think it would suit you or me; there are stone walls to climb over and ditches to cross. Miss Helen, there, might get over them, she has a kind of a thorough-bred stride of her own, but fencing destroys me outright."

"It was a very great politeness to think of bringing us the letter, and I trust your fatigues will not be injurious to you," said Lady Eleanor, smiling faintly.

"Worse than the damage to a pair of very old shoes, ma'am, I don't anticipate; I begin to suspect they've taken their last walk this evening."

While Mr. Dempsey contemplated the coverings of his feet with a very sad expression, the Knight continued to read the letter he held in his hand with an air of extreme intentness.

"Eleanor, my dear," said he, as he retired into the deep recess of a window, "come here for a moment."

"I guessed there would be something of consequence in that," said Dempsey, with a sly glance from Helen to the two figures beside the window. "The envelope was a thin one, and I read 'War-office' in the corner of the inside cover."

Not heeding the delicacy of this announcement, but only thinking of the fact, which she at once connected with Lionel's fortunes, Helen turned an anxious and searching glance towards the window, but the Knight and Lady Eleanor had entered a small room adjoining, and were already concealed from view.

"Was he ever in the Militia, miss?" asked Dempsey, with a gesture of his thumb to indicate of whom he spoke.

"I believe not," said Helen, smiling at the pertinacity of his curiosity.

"Well, well," resumed Dempsey, with a sigh, "I would not wish him a hotter march than I had this day, and little notion I had of the same tramp only ten minutes before. I was reading the *Saunders* of Tuesday last, with an account of that business done at Mayo between O'Halloran and the young officer—you know what I mean?"

"No, I have not heard it; pray tell me," said she, with an eagerness very different from her former manner.

"It was a horsewhipping, miss, that a young fellow in the Guards gave O'Halloran, just as he was coming out of Court; something the Counsellor said about somebody in the trial—names never stay in my head, but I remember it was a great trial at the Westport assizes, and that O'Halloran came down special, and faith, so did the young captain too; and if the lawyer laid it on very heavily, within the court, the red-coat made up for it outside. But I believe I have the paper in my pocket, and, if you like, I'll read it out for you."

"Pray do," said Helen, whose anxiety was now intense.

"Well, here goes," said Mr. Dempsey; "but with your permission I'll just wet my lips again. That's elegant sherry!"

Having sipped and tasted often enough to try the young lady's patience to its last limit, he unfolded the paper, and read aloud:

"'When Counsellor O'Halloran had concluded his eloquent speech in the trial of Darcy *v.* Hickman—for a full report of which see our early columns—a young gentleman, pushing his way through the circle of congratulating friends, accosted him with the most insulting and opprobrious epithets, and, failing to elicit from the learned gentleman a reciprocity'—that means, miss, that O'Halloran didn't show fight—'struck him repeatedly across the shoulders, and even the face, with a horsewhip. He was immediately committed under a bench warrant, but was liberated almost at once. Perhaps our readers may understand these proceedings more clearly when we inform them that Captain Forester, the aggressor in this case, is a near relative of our Irish Secretary, Lord Castlereagh.' That's very neatly put, miss, isn't it?" said Mr. Dempsey, with a sly twinkle of the eye; "it's as much as to say that the Castle chaps may do what they please. But it won't end there, depend upon it; the Counsellor will see it out."

Helen paid little attention to the observation, for, having taken up the paper as Mr. Dempsey laid it down, she was deeply engaged in the report of the trial and O'Halloran's speech.

"Wasn't that a touching-up the old Knight of Gwynne got?" said Dempsey, as, with his glass to his eye, he peered over her shoulder at the newspaper. "Faith, O'Halloran flayed him alive! He's the boy can do it!"

Helen scarce seemed to breathe, as, with a heart almost bursting with indignant anger, she read the lines before her.

"Strike him!" cried she, at length, unable longer to control the passion that worked within her; "had he trampled him beneath his feet, it had not been too much?"

The little man started and stared with amazement at the young girl, as, with flashing eyes and flushed cheek, she arose from her seat, and tearing the paper into fragments, stamped upon them with her foot.

"Blood alive, miss, don't destroy the paper! I only got a loan of it from Mrs. Kennedy, of the post-office; she slipped it out of the cover, though it was addressed to Lord O'Neil. Oh, dear! oh, dear! it's a nice article now!"

These words were uttered in the very depth of despair, as kneeling down on the carpet Mr. Dempsey attempted to collect and arrange the scattered fragments.

"It's no use in life! Here's the Widow Wallace's pills in the middle of the Counsellor's speech! and the last day's drawing of the lottery mixed up with that elegant account of old Darcy's——"

A hand which, if of the gentlest mould, now made a gesture to enforce silence, arrested Mr. Dempsey's words, and at the same moment the Knight entered with Lady Eleanor. Darcy started as he gazed on the excited looks and the air of defiance of his daughter, and, for a second, a deep flush suffused his features, as with an angry frown he asked of Dempsey, "What does this mean, sir?"

"D—n me if I know what it means!" exclaimed Paul, in utter despair at the confusion of his own faculties. "My brain is in a whirl."

"It was a little political dispute between Mr. Dempsey and myself, sir," said Helen, with a faint smile. "He was reading for me an article from the newspaper, whose views were so very opposite to mine, and his advocacy of them so very animated, that—in short, we both became warm."

"Yes, that's it," cried Dempsey, glad to accept any explanation of a case in which he had no precise idea wherein lay the difficulty—"that's it; I'll take my oath it was."

"He is a fierce Unionist," said Helen, speaking rapidly to cover her increasing confusion, "and has all the conventional cant by heart, 'old-fashioned opinions,' 'musty prejudices,' and so on."

"I did not suspect you were so eager a politician, my dear Helen," said the Knight, as, half-chidingly, he threw his eyes towards the scattered fragments of the torn newspaper.

The young girl blushed till her neck became crimson; shame, at the imputation of having so far given way to passion; sorrow, at the reproof, whose injustice she did not dare to expose; and regret, at the necessity of dissimulation, all overwhelming her at the same moment.

"I am not angry, my sweet girl," said the Knight, as he drew his arm around her, and spoke in a low, fond accent. "I may be sorry—sincerely sorry—at the social condition that has suffered political feeling to approach our homes and our firesides, and thus agitate hearts as gentle as yours by these rude themes. For your sentiments on these subjects I can scarcely be a severe critic, for I believe they are all my own."

"Let us forget it all," said Helen, eagerly, for she saw that Mr. Dempsey, having collected once more the torn scraps, was busy in arranging them into something like order. In fact, his senses were gradually recovering from the mystification into which they had been thrown, and he was anxious to vindicate himself before the party. "All the magnanimity, however, must not be mine," continued she, "and until that odious paper is consumed, I'll sign no treaty of peace." So saying, and before Dempsey could interfere to prevent it, she snatched up the fragments, and threw them into the fire. "Now, Mr. Dempsey, we are friends again," said she, laughing.

"The Lord grant it!" ejaculated Paul, who really felt no ambition for so energetic an enemy. "I'll never tell a bit of news in your company again, so long as my name is Paul Dempsey. Every officer of the Guards may horsewhip the Irish bar——I was forgetting—not a syllable more."

The Knight, fortunately, did not hear the last few words, for he was busily engaged in reading the letter he still held in his hands; at length he said,

"Mr. Dempsey has conferred one great favour on us by bringing us this letter, and as its contents are of a nature not to admit of any delay——"

"He will increase the obligation by taking his leave," added Paul, rising, and, for once in his life, really well pleased at an opportunity of retiring.

"I did not say that," said Darcy, smiling.

"No, no, Mr. Dempsey," added Lady Eleanor, with more than her wonted cordiality; "you will, I hope, remain for tea."

"No, ma'am, I thank you; I have a little engagement—I made a promise. If I get safe out of the house without some infernal blunder or other, it's only the mercy of Providence." And with this burst of honest feeling, Paul snatched up his hat, and without waiting for the ceremony of leave-taking, rushed out of the room, and was soon seen crossing the wide common at a brisk pace.

"Our little friend has lost his reason," said the Knight, laughing. "What have you been doing to him, Helen?"

A gesture to express innocence of all interference was the only reply, and the party became suddenly silent.

"Has Helen seen that letter?" said Lady Eleanor, faintly; and Darcy handed the epistle to his daughter. "Read it aloud, my dear," continued Lady Eleanor, "for, up to this, my impressions are so confused, I know not which is reality, which mere apprehension."

Helen's eyes glanced to the top of the letter, and saw the words, "War-office;" she then proceeded to read: "'Sir,—In reply to the application made to the Commander-in-Chief of the Forces in your behalf, expressing your desire for an active employment, I have the honour to inform you, that his Royal Highness having graciously taken into consideration the eminent services rendered by you in former years, and the distinguished character of that corps, which, raised by your exertions, still bears your name, has desired me to convey his approval of your claim, and his desire, should a favourable opportunity present itself, of complying with your wish. I have the honour to remain, your most humble and obedient servant,

"'HARRY GREVILLE,

"'Private Secretary.'"

On an enclosed slip of paper was the single line in pencil: "H. G. begs to intimate to Colonel Darcy the propriety of attending the next levee of H. R. H., which will take place on the 14th."

"Now, you, who read riddles, my dearest Helen, explain this one to us. I made no application of the kind alluded to, nor am I aware of any one having ever done so for me. The thought never once occurred to me, that his Majesty or his Royal Highness would accept the services of an old and shattered hulk, while many a glorious three-decker lies ready to be launched from the stocks. I could not have presumed to ask such a favour, nor do I well know how to acknowledge it."

"But is there anything so very strange," said Helen, proudly, "that those highly placed by station should be as highly gifted by nature, and that his Royal Highness, having heard of your unmerited calumnies, should have seen that this was the fitting moment to remember the services you have rendered the Crown? I have heard that there are several posts of high trust and honour conferred on those who, like yourself, have won distinction in the service."

"Helen is right," said Lady Eleanor, drawing a long breath, and as if released of a weighty load of doubt and uncertainty; "this is the real explanation; the phrases of official life may give it another colouring to our eyes, but such, I feel assured, is the true solution."

"I should like to think it so," said Darcy, feelingly; "it would be a great source of pride to me at this moment, when my fortunes are lower than ever they were—lower than ever I anticipated they might be—to know that my benefactor was the Monarch. In any case I must lose no time in acknowledging this mark of favour. It is now the fourth of the month; to be in London by the fourteenth, I should leave this to-morrow."

"It is better to do so," said Lady Eleanor, with an utterance from which a great effort had banished all agitation; "Helen and I are safe and well here, and as happy as we can be when away from you and Lionel."

"Poor Lionel!" said the Knight, tenderly, "what good news for him it would be were they to give me some Staff appointment—I might have him near us. Come, Eleanor," added he, with more gaiety of manner, "I feel a kind of presentiment of good tidings. But we are forgetting Bagenal Daly all this time; perhaps this letter of his may throw some light on the matter."

Darcy now broke the seal of Daly's note, which, even for him, was one of the briefest. This was so far fortunate, since his writing was in his very worst style, blotted and half erased in many places, scarcely legible anywhere. It was only by assembling a "committee of the whole house" that the Darcys were enabled to decipher even a portion of this unhappy document. As well as as it could be rendered, it ran somewhat thus:

"The verdict is against us; old Bretson never forgave you carrying away the medal from him in Trinity some fifty years back; he charged dead against you; I always said he would. *Summum jus, summa injuria.*—The Chief Justice—the greatest wrong! and the Jury the fellows who lived under you, in your own town, and their fathers and grandfathers! at least, as many of the rascals as had such.—Never mind, Bicknell has moved for a new trial; they have gained the 'Habere' this time, and so has O'Halloran—you heard of the thrashing——"

Here two tremendous patches of ink left some words that followed quite unreadable.

"What can this mean?" said Darcy, repeating the passage over three or four times, while Helen made no effort to enlighten him in the difficulty. Baffled in all his attempts, he read on: "'I saw him in his way through Dublin last night.' Who can he possibly mean?" said Darcy, laying down the letter, and pondering for several minutes.

"O'Halloran, perhaps," said Lady Eleanor, in vain seeking a better elucidation.

"Oh, not him, of course!" cried Darcy; "he goes on to say, that 'he is a devilish high-spirited young fellow, and for an Englishman a warm-blooded animal.' Really, this is too provoking; at such a time as this he might have taken pains to be a little clearer," exclaimed Darcy.

The letter concluded with some mysterious hints about intelligence that a few days might disclose, but from what quarter, or on what subject, nothing was said, and it was actually with a sense of relief Darcy read the words "Yours ever, Bagenal Daly," at the foot of the letter, and thus spared himself the torment of further doubts and guesses.

Helen was restrained from at once conveying the solution of the mystery by recollecting the energy she had displayed in her scene with Mr. Dempsey, and of which the shame still lingered on her flushed cheek.

"He adds something here about writing by the next post," said Lady Eleanor.

"But before that arrives I shall be away," said the Knight; and the train of thought thus evoked soon erased all memory of other matters. And now the little group gathered together to discuss the coming journey, and talk over all the plans by which anxiety was to be beguiled and hope cherished till they met again.

"Miss Daly will not be a very importunate visitor," said Lady Eleanor, dryly, "judging at least from the past; she has made one call here since we came, and then only to leave her card."

"And if Helen does not cultivate a more conciliating manner, I scarce think that Mr. Dempsey will venture on coming either," said the Knight, laughing.

"I can readily forgive all the neglect," said Helen, haughtily, "in compensation for the tranquillity."

"And yet, my dear Helen," said Darcy, "there is a danger in that same compact. We should watch carefully to see whether, in the isolation of a life apart from others, we are not really indulging the most refined selfishness, and dignifying with the name of philosophy a solitude we love for the indulgence of our own egotism. If we are to have our hearts stirred and our sympathies strongly moved, let the themes be great ones, but above all things let us avoid magnifying the petty incidents of daily occurrence into much consequence: this is what the life of monasteries and convents teaches, and a worse lesson there need not be."

Darcy spoke with more than usual seriousness, for he had observed some time past how Helen had imbibed much of Lady Eleanor's distance towards her humble neighbours, and was disposed to retain a stronger memory of their failings in manner than of their better and heartier traits of character.

The young girl felt the remark less as a reproof than a warning, and said,

"I will not forget it."

CHAPTER XLIV.

A PARTING INTERVIEW.

When Heffernan, with his charge, Forester, reached Dublin, he drove straight to Castlereagh's house, affectedly to place the young man under the protection of his distinguished relative, but in reality burning with eager impatience to recount his last stroke of address, and to display the cunning artifice by which he had embroiled O'Reilly with the great popular leader. Mr. Heffernan had a more than ordinary desire to exhibit his skill on this occasion; he was still smarting under the conscious sense of having been duped by O'Reilly, and could not rest tranquilly until revenged. Under the mask of a most benevolent purpose, O'Reilly had induced Heffernan to procure Lionel Darcy an appointment to a regiment in India. Heffernan undertook the task, not, indeed, moved by any kindliness of feeling towards the youth, but as a means of reopening once more negotiations with O'Reilly; and now to discover that he had interested himself simply to withdraw a troublesome witness in a suit—that he had been, in his own phrase, "jockeyed"—was an insult to his cleverness he could not endure.

As Heffernan and Forester drove up to the door, they perceived that a travelling-carriage, ready packed and loaded, stood in waiting, while the bustle and movement of servants indicated a hurried departure.

"What's the matter, Hutton?" asked Heffernan of the valet who appeared at the moment; "is his Lordship at home?"

"Yes, sir, in the drawing-room; but my Lord is just leaving for England. He is now a Cabinet Minister."

Heffernan smiled, and affected to hear the tidings with delight, while he hastily desired the servant to announce him.

The drawing-room was crowded by a strange and anomalous-looking assemblage, whose loud talking and laughing entirely prevented the announcement of Con Heffernan's name from reaching Lord Castlereagh's ears. Groups of personal friends come to say good-by—deputations eager to have the last word in the ear of the departing Secretary—tradesmen begging recommendations to his successor—with here and there a disappointed suitor, earnestly imploring future consideration, were mixed up with hurrying servants, collecting the various minor articles which lay scattered through the apartment.

The time which it cost Heffernan to wedge his way through the dense crowd was not wholly profitless, since it enabled him to assume that look of cordial satisfaction at the noble Secretary's promotion which he was so very far from really feeling. Like most men who cultivate mere cunning, he underrated all who do not place the greatest reliance upon it, and in this way conceived a very depreciating estimate of Lord Castlereagh's ability. Knowing how deeply he had himself been trusted, and how much employed in state transactions, he speculated on a long career of political influence, and that, while his Lordship remained as Secretary, his own skill and dexterity would never be dispensed with. This pleasant illusion was now suddenly dispelled, and he saw all his speculations scattered to the wind at once; in fact, to borrow his own sagacious illustration, "he had to submit to a new deal with his hand full of trumps."

He was still endeavouring to disentangle himself from the throng, when Lord Castlereagh's quick eye discovered him.

"And here comes Heffernan," cried he, laughingly; "the only man wanting to fill up the measure of congratulations. Pray, my Lord, move one step and rescue our poor friend from suffocation."

"By Jove! my Lord, one would imagine you were the rising and not the setting sun, from all this adulating assemblage," said Heffernan, as he shook the proffered hand of the Secretary, and held it most ostentatiously in his cordial pressure. "This was a complete surprise for me," added he. "I only arrived this evening with Forester."

"With Dick? Indeed! I'm very glad the truant has turned up again. Where is he?"

"He passed me on the stairs, I fancy to his room, for he muttered something about going over in the packet along with you."

"And where have you been, Heffernan, and what doing?" asked Lord Castlereagh, with that easy smile that so well became his features.

"That I can scarcely tell you here," said Heffernan, dropping his voice to a whisper, "though I fancy the news would interest you." He made a motion towards the recess of a window, and Lord Castlereagh accepted the suggestion, but with an indolence and half-apathy which did not escape Heffernan's shrewd perception. Partly piqued by this, and partly stimulated by his own personal interest in the matter, Heffernan related, with unwonted eagerness, the details of his visit to the West, narrating with all his own skill the most striking characteristics of the O'Reilly household, and endeavouring to interest his hearer by those little touches of native archness in description of which he was no mean master.

But often as they had before sufficed to amuse his Lordship, they seemed a failure now, for he listened, if not with impatience, yet with actual indifference, and seemed more than once as if about to stop the narrative by the abrupt question, "How can this possibly interest *me?*"

Heffernan read the expression, and felt it as plainly as though it were spoken.

"I am tedious, my Lord," said he, whilst a slight flush coloured the middle of his cheek; "perhaps I only weary you."

"He must be a fastidious hearer who could weary of Mr. Heffernan's company," said his Lordship, with a smile so ambiguous that Heffernan resumed with even greater embarrassment:

"I was about to observe, my Lord, that this same member for Mayo has become much more tractable. He evidently sees the necessity of confirming his new position, and, I am confident, with very little notice, might be converted into a staunch Government supporter."

"Your old favourite theory, Heffernan," said the Secretary, laughing; "to warm these Popish grubs into Protestant butterflies by the sunshine of kingly favour, forgetting the while that 'the winter of their discontent' is never far distant. But please to remember besides, that gold mines will not last for ever—the fountain of honour will at last run dry, and if——"

"I ask pardon, my Lord," interrupted Heffernan. "I only alluded to those favours which cost the Minister little, and the Crown still less—that social acceptance from the Court here upon which some of your Irish friends set great store. If you could find an opportunity of suggesting something of this kind, or if your Lordship's successor——"

"Heaven pity him!" exclaimed Lord Castlereagh. "He will have enough on his hands, without petty embarrassments of this sort. Without you have promised, Heffernan," added he, hastily. "If you have already made any pledge, of course we must sustain your credit."

"I, my Lord! I trust you know my discretion better than to suspect me. I merely threw out the suggestion from supposing that your Lordship's interest in our poor concerns here might outlive your translation to a more distinguished position."

There was a tone of covert impertinence in the accent, as well as the words, which, while Lord Castlereagh was quick enough to perceive, he was too shrewd to mark by any notice.

"And so," said he, abruptly changing the topic, "this affair of Forester's shortened your visit?"

"Of course. Having cut the knot, I left O'Reilly and Conolly to the tender mercies of O'Halloran, who, I perceive by to-day's paper, has denounced his late client in round terms. Another reason, my Lord, for looking after O'Reilly at this moment. It is so easy to secure a prize deserted by her crew."

"I wish Dick had waited a day or two," said Lord Castlereagh, not heeding Heffernan's concluding remark, "and then I should have been off. As it is, he would have done better to adjourn the horse-whipping *sine die*. His lady-mother will scarcely distinguish between the two parties in such a conflict, and probably deem the indignity pretty equally shared by both parties."

"A very English judgment on an Irish quarrel," observed Heffernan.

"And you yourself, Heffernan—when are we to see you in London?"

"Heaven knows, my Lord. Sometimes I fancy that I ought not to quit my post here, even for a day; then again I begin to fear lest the new officials may see things in a different light, and that I may be thrown aside as the propagator of antiquated notions."

"Mere modesty, Heffernan," said Lord Castlereagh, with a look of most comic gravity. "You ought to know by this time that no government can go on without you. You are the fly-wheel that regulates motion and perpetuates impulse to the entire machine. I'd venture almost to declare that you stand in the inventory of articles transmitted from one Viceroy to another, and as we read of 'one throne covered with crimson velvet, and one state couch with gilt supporters,' so we might chance to fall upon the item of 'one Con Heffernan, Kildare-place.'"

"In what capacity, my Lord?" said Heffernan, endeavouring to conceal his anger by a smile.

"Your gifts are too numerous for mention. They might better be summed up under the title of 'State Judas.'"

"You forget, my Lord, he carried the bag. Now I was never pursebearer even to the Lord Chancellor. But I can pardon the simile, coming as I see it does, from certain home convictions. Your Lordship was doubtless assimilating yourself to another historical character of the same period and would, like nim, accept the iniquity, but 'wash your hands' of its consequences."

"Do you hear that, my Lord?" said Lord Castlereagh, turning round, and addressing the Bishop of Kilmore. "Mr. Heffernan has discovered a parallel between my character and that of Pontius Pilate." A look of rebuking severity from the prelate was directed towards Heffernan, who meekly said,

"I was only reproving his Lordship for permitting me to discharge *all* the duties of Secretary for Ireland, and yet receive none of the emoluments."

"But you refused office in every shape and form," said Lord Castlereagh, hastily. "Yes, gentlemen, as the last act of my official life amongst you"—here he raised his voice, and moved into the centre of the room—"I desire to make this public declaration, that as often as I have solicited Mr. Heffernan to accept some situation of trust and profit under the Crown, he has as uniformly declined. Not, it is needless to say, from any discrepancy in our political views, for I believe we are agreed on every point, but upon the ground of maintaining his own freedom of acting and judging."

The declamatory tone in which he spoke these words, and the glances of quiet intelligence that were exchanged through the assembly, were in strong contrast with the forced calmness of Heffernan, who, pale and red by turns, could barely suppress the rage that worked within him; nor was it without an immense effort he could mutter a feigned expression of gratitude for his Lordship's panegyric, while he muttered to himself,

"You shall rue this yet!"

CHAPTER XLV.

THE FIRE.

It was late in the evening as the Knight of Gwynne entered Dublin, and took up his abode for the night in an obscure inn, at the north side of the city. However occupied his thoughts up to that time by the approaching event in his own fortune, he could not help feeling a sudden pang as he saw once more the well-known landmarks that reminded him of former days of happiness and triumph. Strange as it may now sound, there was a time when Irish gentlemen were proud of their native city; when they regarded ts University with feelings of affectionate memory, as the scene of early efforts and ambitions; and could look on its Parliament House as the proud evidence of their national independence! Socially, too, they considered Dublin—and with reason—second to no city of Europe; for there was a period, brief but glorious, when the highest breeding of the courtier mingled with the most polished wit and refined conversation, and when the splendour of wealth — freely displayed as it was — was only inferior to the more brilliant lustre of a society richer in genius and in beauty than any capital of the world.

None had been a more favoured participator in these scenes than Darcy himself: his personal gifts, added to the claims of his family and fortune, secured him early acceptance in the highest circles, and if his abilities had not won the very highest distinctions, it seemed rather from his own indifference than from their deficiency.

In those days, his arrival in town was the signal for a throng of visitors to call, all eagerly asking on what day they might secure him to dine or sup, to meet this one, or that. The thousand flatteries society stores up for her favourites, all awaited him. Parties, whose fulfilment hung listlessly in doubt, were now hastily determined on, as "Darcy is come" got whispered abroad; and many a scheme of pleasure but half-planned found a ready advocacy when the prospect of obtaining him as a guest presented itself.

The consciousness of social success is a great element in the victory. Darcy had this, but without the slightest taint of vain boastfulness or egotism; his sense of his own distinction was merely sufficient to heighten his enjoyment of the world, without detracting, ever so little, from the manly and unassuming features of his character. It is true he endeavoured, and even gave himself pains to be an agreeable companion, but he belonged to a school and a time when conversation was cultivated as an art, and when men preferred making the dinner-table and the drawing-room the arena of their powers, to indicting verses for an "Annual," or composing tales for a fashionable "Miscellany."

We have said enough, perhaps, to show what Dublin was to him, once. How very different it seemed to his eyes now! The season was late summer, and the city dusty and deserted, few persons in the streets, scarcely a carriage to be seen, an air of listlessness and apathy was over everything—for it was the period when the country was just awakening after the intoxicating excitement of the Parliamentary struggle—awakening to discover that it had been betrayed and deserted!

As soon as Darcy had taken some slight refreshment he set out in search of Daly. His first visit was to Henrietta-street, to his own house, or rather what had been his, for it was already let, and a flaring brass-plate on the door proclaimed it the office of a fashionable solicitor. He knocked, and inquired if any one "knew where Mr. Bagenal Daly now resided?" but the name seemed perfectly unknown. He next tried Bicknell's; but that gentleman had not returned since the circuit; he was repairing the fatigues of his profession by a week or two's relaxation at a watering-place.

He did not like, himself, to call at the Club, but he despatched a messenger from the inn, who brought word back that Mr. Daly had not been there for several weeks, and that his present address was unknown. Worried and annoyed, Darcy tried in turn each place where Daly had been wont to frequent, but all in vain. Some had seen him, but not lately; others suggested that he did not appear much in public on account of his moneyed difficulties; and one or two limited themselves to a cautious declaration of ignorance, with a certain assumed shrewdness, as though to say that they could tell more if they would.

It was near midnight when Darcy returned to the inn, tired and worn out by his unsuccessful search. The packet in which he was to sail for England was to leave the port early in the morning, and he sat down in the travellers' room, exhausted and fatigued, till his chamber should be got ready for him.

The inn stood in one of the narrow streets leading out of Smithfield, and was generally resorted to by small farmers and cattle-dealers repairing to the weekly market. Of these, three or four still lingered in the public room, conning over their accounts and discussing the prices of "short-horns and black faces" with much interest, and anticipating all the possible changes the new political condition of the country might be likely to induce.

Darcy could scarcely avoid smiling as he overheard some of these speculations, wherein the prospect of a greater export trade was deemed the most certain indication of national misfortune. His attention was, however, suddenly withdrawn from the conversation by a confused murmur of voices, and the tramp of many feet in the street without. The noise gradually increased, and attracted the notice of the others, and suddenly the words "Fire! fire!" repeated from mouth to mouth, explained the tumult.

As the tide of men was borne onward, the din grew louder, and at length the narrow street in front of the inn became densely crowded by a mob hurrying eagerly forward, and talking in loud, excited voices.

"They say that Newgate is on fire, sir," said the landlord, as, hastily entering, he addressed Darcy; "but if you'll come with me to the top of the house, we'll soon see for ourselves."

Darcy followed the man to the upper story, whence, by a small ladder, they obtained an exit on the roof. The night was calm and starlight, and the air was still. What a contrast! that spangled heaven, in all its tranquil beauty, to the dark streets below, where, in tumultuous uproar, the commingled mass was seen by the uncertain glimmer of the lamps, few and dim as they were. Darcy could mark that the crowd consisted of the very lowest and most miserable-looking class of the capital, the dwellers in the dark alleys and purlieus of the ill-favoured region. By their excited gestures and wild accents, it was clear to see how much more of pleasure than of sorrow they felt at the occasion that now roused them from their dreary garrets and damp cellars. Shouts of mad triumph and cries of menace burst from them as they went. The Knight was roused from a moody contemplation of the throng by the landlord saying aloud,

"True enough, the gaol is on fire: see, yonder, where the dark smoke is rolling up, that is Newgate."

"But the building is of stone—almost entirely of stone, with little or no wood in its construction," said Darcy; "I cannot imagine how it could take fire."

"The floors, the window-frames, the rafters are of wood, sir," said the other; "and then," added he, with a cunning leer, "remember what the inhabitants are!"

The Knight little minded the remark, for his whole gaze was fixed on the cloud of smoke, dense and black as night, that rolled forth, as if from the ground, and soon enveloped the gaol and all the surrounding buildings in darkness.

"What can that mean?" said he, in amazement.

"It means that this is no accident, sir," said the man, shrewdly; "it's only damp straw and soot can produce the effect you see yonder; it is done by the prisoners—see, it is increasing! and here come the fire-engines!"

As he spoke, a heavy, cavernous sound was heard rising from the street, where now a body of horse-police were seen escorting the fire-engines. The service was not without difficulty, for the mob offered every obstacle short of open resistance; and once it was discovered that the traces were cut, and considerable delay thereby occasioned.

"The smoke is spreading; see, sir, see how it rolls this way, blacker and heavier than before!"

"It is but smoke, after all," said Darcy; but, although the words were uttered half-contemptuously, his heart beat anxiously as the dense volume hung suspended in the air, growing each moment blacker as fresh masses arose. The cries and yells of the excited mob were now wilder and more frantic, and seemed to issue from the black, ill-omened mass that filled the atmosphere.

"That's not smoke, sir; look yonder!" said the man, seizing Darcy's arm, and pointing to a reddish glare that seemed trying to force a passage through the smoke, and came not from the gaol, but from some building at the side, or in front of it.

"There again!" cried he, "that is fire!"

The words were scarcely uttered, when a cheer burst from the mob beneath; a yell more dissonant and appalling could not have broken from demons than was that shout of exultation, as the red flame leaped up and flashed towards the sky. As the strong host of a battle will rout and scatter the weaker enemy, so did the fierce element dispel the less powerful; and now the lurid glow of a great fire lit up the air, and marked out with terrible distinctness the waving crowd that jammed up the streets—the windows filled with terrified faces—and the very housetops crowded by terror-stricken and distracted groups.

The scene was truly an awful one; the fire raged in some houses exactly in front of the gaol, pouring with unceasing violence its flood of flame through every door and window, and now sending bright jets through the roofs, which, rent with a report like thunder, soon became one undistinguishable mass of flame. The cries for succour, the shouts of the firemen, the screams of those not yet rescued, and the still increasing excitement of the mob, mingling their hellish yells of triumph through all the dread disaster, made up a discord the most horrible; while, ever and anon, the police and the crowd were in collision, vain efforts being made to keep the mob back from the front of the gaol, whither they had fled as a refuge from the heat of the burning houses.

The fire seemed to spread, defying all the efforts of the engines. From house to house the lazy smoke was seen to issue for a moment, and then, almost immediately after, a new cry would announce that another building was in flames. Meanwhile, the smoke, which in the commencement had spread from the court-yard and windows of the gaol, was again perceived to thicken in the same quarter, and suddenly, as if by a preconcerted signal, it rolled out from every barred casement and loopholed aperture—from every narrow and deep cell within the lofty walls—and the agonised yell of the prisoners burst forth at the same moment, and the air seemed to vibrate with shrieks and cries.

"Break open the gaol!" resounded on every side. "Don't let the prisoners be burned alive!" was uttered in accents whose humanity was far inferior to their menace; and, as if with one accord, a rush was made at the strongly barred gates of the dark building. The movement, although made with the full force of a mighty multitude, was in vain. In vain the stones resounded upon the thickly-studded door—in vain the strength of hundreds pressed down upon the oaken barrier. They might as well have tried to force the strong masonry at either side of it!

"Climb the walls!" was now the cry, and the prisoners re-echoed the call in tones of shrieking entreaty. The mob, savage from their recent repulse at the gate, now seized the ladders employed by the firemen, and planted them against the great enclosure-wall of the gaol. The police endeavoured to charge, but, jammed up by the crowd, their bridles in many instances cut, their weapons wrested from them, they were almost at the mercy of the mob. Orders had been despatched for troops, but as yet they had not appeared, and the narrow streets being actually choked up with people, would necessarily delay their progress. If there were any persons in that vast mass disposed to repel the violence of the mob, they did not dare to avow it, the odds were so fearfully on the side of the multitude.

The sentry who guarded the gate was trampled down. Some averred he was killed in the first rush upon the gate; certain it was his cap and coat were paraded on a pole, as a warning of what awaited his comrades within the gaol, should they dare to fire on the people. This horrible banner was waved to and fro above the stormy multitude. Darcy had but time to mark it, when he saw the crowd open, as if cleft asunder by some giant hand, and, at the same instant, a man rode through the open space, and tearing down the pole, felled him who carried it to the earth by a stroke of his whip. The red glare of the burning houses made the scene distinct as daylight, but the next moment a rolling cloud of black smoke hid all from view, and left him to doubt the evidence of his eyesight.

"Did you see the horseman?" asked Darcy, in eager curiosity, for he did not dare to trust his uncorroborated sense.

"There he is!" cried the other. "I know him by a white band on his arm. See, he mounts one of the ladders!—there!—he is near the top!"

A cheer that seemed to shake the very atmosphere now rent the air, as, pressing on like soldiers to a breach, the mob approached the walls. Some shots were fired by the guard, and their effect might be noted by the more savage yells of the mob, whose exasperation was now like madness.

"The shots have told—see!" cried the man. "Now the people are gathering in close groups, here and there."

But Darcy's eyes were fixed on the walls, which were already crowded with the mob, the dark figures looking like spectres as they passed and repassed through the dense canopy of smoke.

"The soldiers! the soldiers!" screamed the populace from below, and at the instant a heavy lumbering sound crept on, and the head of a cavalry squadron wheeled into the square before the gaol. The remainder of the troop soon defiled; but instead of advancing, as was expected, they opened their ranks, and displayed the formidable appearance of two eight-pounders, from which the limbers were removed with lightning speed, and their mouths turned full upon the crowd. Meanwhile, an infantry force was seen entering the opposite side of the square, thus showing the mob that they were taken in front and rear, no escape being open save by the small alleys which led off from the street before the prison. The military preparations took scarcely more time to effect than we have employed to relate; and now began a scene of tumult and terror the most dreadful to witness! The order to prime and load, followed by the clanking crash of four hundred muskets, the close ranks of the cavalry, as if with difficulty restrained from charging down upon them, and the lighted fuses of the artillery, all combined to augment the momentary dread, and the shouts of vengeance so lately heard were at once changed into piercing cries for mercy. The blazing houses, from which the red fire shot up unrestrained, no longer attracted notice—the gaol itself had no interest for those whose danger was become so imminent.

An indiscriminate rush was made towards the narrow lanes for escape, and from these arose the most piercing and agonising cries, for while pressed down and trampled, many were trodden under foot never again to rise; others were wounded or burned by the falling timbers of the blazing buildings, and the fearful cry of "The soldiers! the soldiers!" still goaded them on by those behind.

"Look yonder," cried Darcy's companion, seizing him by the arm—"look there—near the corner of the market! See, the troops have not perceived that ladder, and there are two fellows now descending it."

True enough. At a remote angle of the gaol, not concealed from view by the smoke, stood the ladder in question.

"How slowly they move!" cried Darcy, his eyes fixed upon the figures with that strange anxiety so inseparable from the fate of all who are engaged in hazardous enterprise. "They will certainly be taken."

"They must be wounded," cried the other; "they seem to creep rather than step——I know the reason, they are in fetters."

Scarcely was the explanation uttered when the ladder was seen to be violently moved, as if from above, and the next moment was hurled back from the wall, on which several soldiers were now perceived firing on those below.

"They are lost!" said the Knight; "they are either captured or cut down by this time."

"The square is cleared already," said the other; "how quietly the troops have done their work! And the fire begins to yield to the engines."

The square was indeed cleared; save the groups beside the fire-engines, and here and there a knot gathered around some wounded man, the space was empty, the troops having drawn off to the sides, around which they stood in double file. A dark cloud rested over the gaol itself, but no longer did any smoke issue from the windows, and already the fire, its rage in part expended, in part subdued, showed signs of decline.

"If the wind was from the west," said the landlord, "there's no saying where that might have stopped this night!"

"It is a strange occurrence altogether," said the Knight, musingly.

"Not a bit strange, sir," replied the other, whose neighbourhood made him acquainted with classes and varieties of men of whom Darcy knew nothing; "it was an attempt by the prisoners."

"Do you think so?" asked Darcy.

"Ay, to be sure, sir; there's scarcely a year goes over without one contrivance or another for escape; last autumn two fellows got away by following the course of the sewers and gaining the Liffey; they must have passed two days underground, and up to their necks in water a great part of the time."

"Ay, and besides that," observed another—for already some ten or twelve persons were assembled on the roof as well as Darcy and the landlord—"they had to wade the river at the ebb-tide, when the mud is at least eight or ten feet deep."

"How that was done, I cannot guess," said Darcy.

"A man will do many a thing for liberty, sir," remarked another, who was buttoned up in a frieze coat, although the night was hot and sultry; "these poor devils there were willing to risk being roasted alive for the chance of it."

"Quite true," said Darcy; "fellows that have a taste for breaking the law need not be supposed desirous of observing it as to their mode of death; and yet they must have been daring rascals to have made such an attempt as this."

"Maybe you know the old song, sir," said the other, laughing:

"There's many a man no bolts can keep,
No chains be made to bind him,
And tho' fetters be heavy, and cells be deep,
He'll fling them far behind him."

"I have heard the ditty," answered the Knight, "and if my memory serves me, the last lines run thus:

Though iron bolts may rust and rot,
And stone and mortar crumble;
Freney, beware! for well I wot
Your pride may have a tumble"

"Devil a lie in that, anyhow, sir," said the other, laughing heartily, "and an uglier tumble a man needn't have than to slip through Tom Galvin's fingers. But I see the fire is out now, so I'll be jogging homeward: good night, sir."

"Good night," said Darcy; and then, as the other moved away, turning to the landlord, he asked if he knew the stranger.

"No, sir," was the reply; "he came up with some others to have a look at the fire."

"Well, I'll to my bed," said Darcy; "let me be awakened at four o'clock. I see I shall have but a short sleep, the day is breaking already."

CHAPTER XLVI.

BOARDING-HOUSE CRITICISM.

It was not until after the lapse of several days that Darcy's departure was made known to the denizens of Port Ballintray. If the event was slow of announcement, they endeavoured to compensate for the tardiness of the tidings by the freedom of their commentary on all its possible and impossible reasons. There was not a casualty, in the whole catalogue of human vicissitudes, unquoted; deaths, births, and marriages were ransacked in newspapers; all sudden and unexpected turns of fortune were well weighed; accidents and offences scanned with cunning eyes, and the various paragraphs to which editorial mysteriousness gave an equivocal interpretation were commented on with a perseverance and an ingenuity worthy of a higher theme.

It may be remarked that no class of persons are viewed more suspiciously, or excite more sharp criticism from their neighbours, than those who, with evidently narrow means, prefer retirement and estrangement from the world to mixing in the small circle of some petty locality. A hundred schemes are put in motion to ascertain by what right such superiority is asserted—why, and on what grounds, they affect to be better than their neighbours, and so on; the only offence all the while consisting in an isolation which cannot with truth imply any such imputation.

When the Knight of Gwynne found himself by an unexpected turn of fortune condemned to a station so different from his previous life, he addressed himself at once to the difficulties of his lot; and, well aware that all reserve on his part would be set down as the cloak of some deep mystery, he affected an air of easy cordiality with such of the boarding-house party as he ever met, and endeavoured, by a tone of well-assumed familiarity, to avoid all detection of the difference between him and his new associates.

It was in this spirit that he admitted Mr. Dempsey to his acquaintance, and even asked him to his cottage. In this diplomacy he met with little assistance from Lady Eleanor and his daughter; the former, from a natural coldness of manner and an instinctive horror of everything low and underbred. Helen's perceptions of such things were just as acute, but, inheriting the gay and lively temperament of her father's house, she better liked to laugh at the absurdities of vulgar people than indulge a mere sense of dislike to their society. Such allies were too dangerous to depend on, and hence the Knight conducted his plans unaided and unsupported.

Whether Mr. Dempsey was bought off by the flattering exception made in his favour, and that he felt an implied superiority on being deemed their advocate, he certainly assumed that position in the circle of Mrs. Fumbally's household, and, on the present occasion, sustained his part with a certain mysterious demeanour that imposed on many.

"Well, he's gone, at all events!" said a thin old lady with a green shade over a pair of greener eyes, "that can't be denied, I hope! Went off like a shot on Tuesday morning. Sandy M'Shane brought him into Coleraine, for the Dublin coach, and, by the same token, it was an outside place he took——"

"I beg your pardon, ma'am," interposed a fat little woman, with a choleric red face and a tremulous under-lip—she was an authoress in the provincial papers, and occasionally invented her English as well as her incidents—"it was the Derry mail he went by. Archy M'Clure trod on his toe, and asked pardon for it, just to get him into conversation, but he seemed very much dejected, and wouldn't interlocute."

"Very strange indeed!" rejoined the lady of the shade, "because I had my information from Williams, the guard of the coach."

"And I mine from Archy M'Clure himself."

"And both were wrong," interposed Paul Dempsey, triumphantly.

"It's not very polite to tell us so, Mr. Dempsey," said the thin old lady bridling.

"Perhaps the politeness may equal the voracity," said the fat lady, who was almost boiling over with wrath.

"This Gwynne wasn't all right, depend upon it," interposed a certain little man in pewder; "I have my own suspicions about him."

"Well, now, Mr. Dun'op, what's your opinion? I'd like to hear it."

"What does Mrs. M'Caudlish say?" rejoined the little gentleman, turning to the authoress—for, in the boarding-house, they both presided judicially in all domestic inquisitions regarding conduct and character—"what does Mrs. M'Caudlish say?"

"I prefer letting Mr. Dunlop expose himself before me."

"The case is doubtful—dark—mysterious," said Dunlop, with a solemn pause after each word.

"The more beyond my conjunctions," said the lady. "You remember what the young gentleman says in the Latin poet, 'Sum Davy, non sum Euripides.'"

"I'll tell you my opinion, then," said Mr. Dunlop, who was evidently modified by the classical allusion, and, with firm and solemn gesture, he crossed over to where she sat, and whispered a few words in her ear.

A slight scream, and a long-drawn "Oh!" was all the answer.

"Upon my soul I believe so," said Mr. Dunlop, thrusting both hands into the furthest depths of his coat-pockets; "nay, more, I'll maintain it!"

"I know what you are driving at," said Dempsey, laughing; "you think he's the gauger that went off with Mrs. Murdoch of Ballyquirk——"

"Mr. Dempsey! Mr. Dempsey! the ladies, sir! the ladies!" called out two or three reproving voices from the male portion of the assembly, while, as if to corroborate the justice of the appeal, the thin lady drew her shade down two inches lower, and Mr. Dunlop's face became what painters call "of a warm tint."

"Oh! never talk of a rope where a man's father was hanged," muttered Paul to himself, for he felt all the severity of his condemnation, though he knew that the point of law was against him.

"There's a rule in this establishment, Mr. Dempsey," said Mr. Dunlop, with all the gravity of a judge delivering a charge—"a rule devised to protect the purity, the innocence"—here the ladies held down their heads—"the beauty——"

"Yes, sir, and I will add, the helplessness of that sex——"

"Paul's right, by Jove!" hiccupped Jack Leonard, whose faculties, far immersed in the effects of strong whisky-and-water, suddenly flashed out into momentary intelligence—"I say he's right! Who says the reverse?"

"Oh, Captain Leonard!—oh dear, Mr. Dunlop!" screamed three or four female voices in concert, "don't let it proceed further."

A faint and an anxious group were gathered around the little gentleman, whose warlike indications grew stronger as pacific entreaties increased.

"He shall explain his words," said he, with a cautious glance to see that his observation was not overheard; then, seeing that his adversary had relapsed into oblivion, he added, "he shall withdraw them;" and finally, em boldened by success, he vociferated, "or he shall eat them. I'll teach him," said the now triumphant victor, "that it is not in Mark Dunlop's presence ladies are to be insulted with impunity. Let the attempt be made by whom it will—he may be a lieutenant on half-pay, or on full pay!—I tell him, I don't care a rush."

"Of course not!" "Why would you?" and so on, were uttered in ready chorus around him, and he resumed:

"And as for this Gwynne, or Quin, who lives up at the Corvy yonder, for all the airs he gives himself, and his fine ladies too, my simple belief is he's a Government spy."

"Is that your opinion, sir?" said a deep and almost solemn voice, and at the same instant Miss Daly appeared at the open window. She leaned her arm on the sill, and calmly stared at the now terrified speaker, while she repeated the words, "Is that your opinion, sir?"

Before the surprise her words had excited subsided, she stood at the door of the apartment. She was dressed in her riding-habit, for she had that moment returned from an excursion along the coast.

"Mr. Dunlop," said the lady, advancing towards him, "I never play the eavesdropper; but you spoke so loud, doubtless purposely, that nothing short of deafness could escape hearing you. You were pleased to express a belief respecting the position of a gentleman with whom I have the honour to claim some friendship."

"I always hold myself ready, madam, to render an account to any individual of whom I express an opinion—to himself, personally, I mean."

"Of course you do, sir. It is a very laudable habit," said she, dryly; "but in this case—don't interrupt me—in the present case, it cannot apply, because the person traduced is absent. Yes, sir, I said traduced."

"Oh, madam, I must say the word would better suit one more able to sustain it. I shall take the liberty to withdraw." And so saying, he moved towards the door; but Miss Daly interposed, and by a gesture of her hand, in which she held a formidable horsewhip, gave a very unmistakable sign that the passage was not free.

"You'll not go yet, sir. I have not done with you," said she, in a voice every accent of which vibrated in the little man's heart. "You affect to regret, sir, that I am not of the sex that exacts satisfaction, as it is called; but I tell you, I come of a family that never gave long scores to a debt of honour. You have presumed—in a company, certainly, where the hazard of contradiction was small—to asperse a gentleman of whom you know nothing—not one single fact—not one iota of his life, character, or fortune. You have dared to call him by words, every letter of which would have left a welt on your shoulders if uttered in his hearing. Now, as I am certain he would pay any little debts I might have perchance forgotten in leaving a place where I had resided, so will I do likewise by him, and here, on this spot, and in this fair company, I call upon you to unsay your falsehood, or——" Here she made one step forward, with an air and gesture that made Mr. Dunlop retire with a most comic alacrity. "Don't be afraid, sir," continued she, laughing. "My brother, Mr. Bagenal Daly, will arrive here soon. He's no new name to your ears. In any case, I promise you, that whatever you find objectionable in my proceedings towards you, he will be most happy to sustain. Now, sir, the hand wants four minutes to six. If the hour strike before you call yourself a wanton, gratuitous calumniator, I'll flog you round the room."

A cry of horror burst from the female portion of the assembly at a threat the utterance of which was really not less terrific than the meaning.

"Such a spectacle," continued Miss Daly, sarcastically, "I should scruple to inflict on this fair company; but the taste that could find pleasure in witless, pointless slander, may not, it is possible, dislike to see a little castigation. Now, sir, you have just one minute and a quarter."

"I protest against this conduct, madam. I here declare——"

"Declare nothing, sir, till you have avowed yourself by your real name and character. If you cannot restrain your tongue, I'll very soon convince you that its consequences are far from agreeable. Is what you have spoken false?"

"There may come a heavy reckoning for all this, madam," said Dunlop, trembling between fear and passion.

"I ask you again, and for the last time, are your words untrue? Very well, sir. You held a commission in Germany they say, and probably, as a military man, you may think it undignified to surrender, except on compulsion."

With these words Miss Daly advanced towards him with a firm and determined air, while a cry of horror arose through the room, and the fairer portion intrepidly threw themselves in front of their champion, while Dempsey and the others only restrained their laughter for fear of personal consequences. Pushing fiercely on, Miss Daly was almost at his side, when the door of the room was opened, and a deep and well-known voice called out to her,

"Maria, what the devil is all this?"

"Oh, Bagenal," cried she, as she held out her hand, "I scarcely expected you before eight o'clock."

"But in the name of everything ridiculous, what has happened? Were you about to horsewhip this pleasant company?"

"Only one of its members," said Miss Daly, coolly—"a little gentleman who has thought proper to be more lavish of his calumny than his courage. I hand him over to you, now, and faith, though I don't think that he had any fancy for me, he'll gain by the exchange! You'll find him yonder," said she, pointing to a corner where already the majority of the party were gathered together.

Miss Daly was mistaken, however, for Mr. Dunlop had made his escape during the brief interchange of greetings between the brother and sister. "Come, Bagenal," said she, smiling, "it's all for the best. I have given him a lesson he'll not readily forget—had you been the teacher, he might not have lived to remember it."

"What a place for *you!*" said Bagenal, as he threw his eye superciliously around the apartment and its occupants; then taking her arm within his own, he led her forth, and closed the door after them.

Once more alone, Daly learned with surprise, not unmixed with sorrow, that his sister had never seen the Darcys, and save by a single call, when she left her name, had made no advances towards their acquaintance. She showed a degree of repugnance, too, to allude to the subject, and rather endeavoured to dismiss it by saying shortly,

"Lady Eleanor is a fine lady, and her daughter a wit. What could there be in common between us?"

"But for Darcy's sake?"

"For *his* sake I stayed away," rejoined she, hastily; "they would have thought me a bore, and, perhaps, have told him as much. In a word, Bagenal, I didn't like it, and that's enough. Neither of us were trained to put much constraint on our inclinations. I doubt if the lesson would be easily learned at our present time of life."

Daly muttered some half-intelligible bitterness about female obstinacy and wrong-headedness, and walked slowly to and fro. "I must see Maurice at once," said he, at length.

"That will be no easy task; he left this for Dublin on Tuesday last."

"And has not returned? When does he come back?"

"His old butler, who brought me the news, says not for some weeks."

"Confusion and misery!" exclaimed Daly; "was there ever anything so ill-timed! And he's in Dublin?"

"He went thither, but there would seem some mystery about his ultimate destination; the old man hinted at London."

"London!" said he, with a heavy sigh. "It's now the 18th, and on Saturday she sails."

"Who sails?" asked Miss Daly, with more of eagerness than she yet exhibited.

"Oh, I forgot, Molly, I hadn't told you, I'm about to take a voyage—not a very long one, but still distant enough to make me wish to say 'Good-by' ere we separate. If God wills it, I shall be back early in the spring."

"What new freak is this, Bagenal?" said she, almost sternly; "I thought that time and the world's crosses might have taught you to care for quietness, if not for home."

"Home! repeated he, in an accent the sorrow of which sank into her very heart, "when had I ever a home? I had a house and lands, and equipages, horses, and liveried servants, all that wealth could command, or my own reckless vanity could prompt, but these did not make a home!"

"You often promised we should have such one day, Bagenal," said she, tenderly, while she stole her hand within his; "you often told me that the time would come when we should enjoy poverty with a better grace than ever we dispensed riches."

"We surely are poor enough to make the trial now," said he, with a bitterness of almost savage energy.

"And if we are, Bagenal," replied she, "there is the more need to draw more closely to each other; let us begin at once."

"Not yet, Molly, not yet," said he, passing his hand across his eyes. "I would grasp such a refuge as eagerly as yourself, for," added he, with deep emotion, "I am to the full as weary! but I cannot do it yet."

Miss Daly knew her brother's temper too long and too well, either to offer a continued opposition to any strongly expressed resolve, or to question him about a subject on which he showed any desire of reserve.

"Have you no Dublin news for me?" she said, as if willing to suggest some less touching subject for conversation.

"No, Molly; Dublin is deserted. The few who still linger in town seem only half awake to the new condition of events. The Government party are away to England; they feel, doubtless, bound in honour to dispense their gold in the land it came from; and the Patriots—Heaven bless the mark!—they look as rueful as if they began to suspect that Patriotism was too dear a luxury after all."

"And this burning of Newgate—what did it mean? Was there, as th newspaper makes out, anything like a political plot connected with it?"

"Nothing of the kind, Molly. The whole affair was contrived among the prisoners. Freney, the well-known highwayman, was in the gaol, and, although not tried, his conviction was certain."

"And they say he has escaped. Can it be possible that some persons of influence, as the journals hint, actually interested themselves for the escape of a man like this?"

"Everything is possible in a state of society like ours, Molly."

"But a highwayman—a robber—a fellow that made the roads unsafe to travel!"

"All true," said Daly, laughing. "Nobody ever kept a hawk for a singing bird; but he's a bold villain to pounce upon another."

"I like not such appliances; they scarcely serve a good name, and they make a bad one worse."

"I'm quite of your mind, Molly," said Daly, thoughtfully; "and if honest men were plenty, he would be but a fool who held any dealings with the knaves. But here comes the car to convey me to the Corvy. I will make a hasty visit to Lady Eleanor, and be back with you by supper-time."

CHAPTER XLVII.

DALY'S FAREWELL.

Neither of the ladies was at home when Bagenal Daly, followed by his servant Sandy, reached the Corvy, and sat down in the porch to await their return. Busied with his own reflections, which, to judge from the deep abstraction of his manner, seemed weighty and important, Daly never looked up from the ground, while Sandy leisurely walked round the building to note the changes made in his absence, and comment, in no flattering sense, on the art by which the builder had concealed so many traits of the Corvy's origin.

"Ye'd no ken she was a ship ava!" said he to himself, as he examined the walls over which the trellised creepers were trained, and the latticed windows festooned by the honeysuckle and the clematis, and gazed in sadness over the altered building. "She's no a bit like the auld Corvy!"

"Of course she's not!" said Daly, testily, for the remark had suddenly aroused him from his musings. "What the devil would you have? Are *you* like the raw and ragged fellow I took from this bleak coast, and led over more than half the world?"

"Troth, I am no the same man noo that I was sax-and-forty years agane, and sorry I am to say it."

"Sorry—sorry! not to be half-starved, and less than half-clad; hauling a net one day, and being dragged for yourself the next—sorry!"

"Even sae, sore sorry. Eight-and-sixty may be aye sorry not to be twa-

and-twenty. I ken nae rise in life can pay off that score. It's na ower pleasant to think on, but I'm no the man I was then. No, nor for that matter, yerself neither."

Daly was too long accustomed to the familiarity of Sandy's manner to feel offended at the remark, though he did not seem by any means to relish its application. Without making any reply, he arose and entered the hall. On every side were objects reminding him of the past, strange, and sad commentary on the words of his servant. Sandy appeared to feel the force of such allies, and, as he stood near, watched the effect the various articles produced on his master's countenance.

"A bonnie rifle she is," said he, as if interpreting the admiring look Daly bestowed upon a richly ornamented gun. "Do you mind the day yer honour shot the corbie at the Tegern See?"

"Where the Tyrol fellows set on us, on the road to Innspruck, and I brought down the bird to show them that they had to deal with a marksman as good at least as themselves."

"Just sae, it was a bra' shot; your hand was as firm, and your eye as steady then as any man's."

"I could do the feat this minute," said Daly, angrily, as turning away he detached a heavy broadsword from the wall.

"She was aye over weighty in the hilt," said Sandy, with a dry malice.

"You used to draw that bowstring to your ear," said Daly, sternly, as he pointed to a Swiss bow of portentous size.

"I had twa hands in those days," said the other, calmly, and without the slightest change of either voice or manner.

Not so with him to whom they were addressed. A flood of feelings seemed to pour across his memory, and laying his hand on Sandy's shoulder, he said, in an accent of very unusual emotion, "You are right, Sandy, I must be changed from what I used to be."

"Let us awa to the auld life we led in those days," said the other, impetuously, "and we'll soon be ourselves again! Doesn't that remind yer honour of the dark night on the Ottowa, when you sent the canoe, with the pine-torch burning in her bow, down the stream; and drew all the fire of the Indian fellows on her."

"It was a grand sight," cried Daly, rapturously, "to see the dark river glittering with its torchlight, and the chiefs, as they stood rifle in hand peering into the dense pine copse, and making the echoes ring with their war-cries."

"It was unco near at one time," said Sandy, as he took up the fold of the blanket with which his effigy in the canoe was costumed. "There's the twa bullet-holes, and here, the arrow-head in the plank, where I had my head! If ye had missed the Delaware chap wi' the yellow cloth on his forehead——"

"I soon changed its colour for him," said Daly, savagely.

"Troth did ye; ye gied him a bonny war paint; how he sprang into the air; I think I see him noo; many a night when I'm lying awake, I think I can hear the dreadful screech he gave, as he plunged into the river."

"It was not a cry of pain, it was baffled vengeance," said Daly.

"He never forgave the day ye gripped him by the twa hands in yer ain one, and made the squaws laugh at him. Eh, how that auld deevil they can'd Black Buffalo yelled! Her greasy cheeks shook and swelled over her dark eyes, till the face looked like nothing but a tar lake in Demerara when there's a hurricane blowin' over it."

"You had rather a tenderness in that quarter, if I remember right," said Daly, dryly.

"I'll no deny she was a bra sauncie woman, and kenned weel to mak a haggis wi' an ape's head and shoulders." Sandy smacked his lips, as if the thought had brought up pleasant memories.

"How I escaped that bullet is more than I can guess," said Daly, as he inspected the blanket where it was pierced by a shot; and as he spoke he threw its wide folds over his shoulders, the better to judge of the position.

"Ye aye wore it more on this side," said Sandy, arranging the folds with tasteful pride; "an' troth, it becomes you well. Tak the bit tomahawk in your hand, noo. Ech! but yer like yoursel once more."

"We may have to don this gear again, and sooner than you think," said Daly, thoughtfully.

"Nae a bit sooner than I'd like," said Sandy. "The salvages, as they ca' them, hae neither baillies nor policemen, they hae nae cranks about lawyers and 'tornies; a grip o' a man's hair and a sharp knife is even as mickle a reason as a hempen cord and a gallows tree! Ech, it warms my bluid again to see you stridin' up and doon—if you had but a smudge o yellow ochre, or a bit o' red round your eyes, ye'd look awful well."

"What are you staring at?" said Daly, as Sandy opened a door stealthily, and gazed down the passage towards the kitchen.

"I'm thinking that as there is naebody in the house but the twa lasses, maybe your honour would try a war-cry—ye ken ye could do it bra'ly once."

"I may need the craft soon again," said Daly, thoughtfully.

"Mercy upon us! here's the leddies!" cried Sandy. But before Daly could disencumber himself of his weapons and costume, Helen entered the hall.

If Lady Eleanor started at the strange apparition before her, and involuntarily turned her eye towards the canoe, to see that its occupant was still there, it is not much to be wondered at, so strongly did the real and the coun terfeit man resemble each other. The first surprise over, he was welcomed with sincere pleasure. All the eccentricities of character which in former days were commented on so sharply were forgotten, or their memory replaced by the proofs of his ardent devotion.

"How well you are looking!" was his first exclamation, as he gazed at Lady Eleanor and Helen alternately, with that steady stare which is one of the prerogatives of age towards beauty.

"There is no such tonic as necessity," said Lady Eleanor, smiling, "and it would seem as if health were too jealous to visit us, when we have every other blessing."

"It is worth them all, madam. I am an old man, and have seen much of the world, and I can safely aver, that what are called its trials lie chiefly in our weaknesses. We can all of us carry a heavier load than fortune lays on us——" He suddenly checked himself, as if having unwittingly lapsed into something like rebuke, and then said, "I find you alone; is it not so?"

"Yes; Darcy has left us, suddenly and almost mysteriously, without you can help us to a clearer insight. A letter from the War-office arrived here on Tuesday, acknowledging, in most complimentary terms, the fairness of his claim for military employment, and requesting his presence in London. This was evidently in reply to an application, although the Knight made none such."

"But he has friends, mamma—warm-hearted and affectionate ones—who might have done so," said Helen, as she fixed her gaze steadily on Daly.

"And you, madam, have relatives of high and commanding influence," said he, avoiding to return Helen's glance—"men of rank and station, who might well feel proud of such a *protégé* as Maurice Darcy. And what have they given him?"

"We can tell you nothing; the official letter may explain more to your clear-sightedness, and I will fetch it." So saying, Lady Eleanor arose and left the room. Scarcely had the door closed, when Daly stood up, and, walking over, leaned his arm on the back of Helen's chair.

"You received my letter, did you not?" said he, hurriedly. "You know the result of the trial?"

Helen nodded assent, while a secret emotion covered her face with crimson, as Daly resumed:

"There was ill-luck everywhere: the case badly stated; Lionel absent; I myself detained in Dublin, by an unavoidable necessity—everything unfortunate, even to the last incident. Had I been there, matters would have taken another course. Still, Helen, Forester was right; and, depend upon it, there is no scanty store of generous warmth in a heart that can throb so strongly beneath the aiguiletted coat of an aide-de-camp. The holiday habits of that tinsel life teach few lessons of self-devotion, and the poor fellow has paid the penalty heavily."

"What has happened?" said Helen, in a voice scarcely audible.

"He is disinherited, I hear. All his prospects depended on his mother; she has cast him off, and, as the story goes, is about to marry. Marriage is always the last vengeance of a widow."

"Here is the letter," said Lady Eleanor, entering; "let us hope you can read its intentions better than we have."

"Flattering, certainly," muttered Daly, as he conned over the lines to himself. "It's quite plain they mean to do something generous. I trust I may learn it before I sail."

"Sail! you are not about to travel, are you?" asked Lady Eleanor, in a voice that betrayed her dread of being deprived of such support.

"Oh! I forgot I hadn't told you. Yes, madam, another of those strange riddles which have beset my life compels me to take a long voyage—to America."

"To America!" echoed Helen; and her eye glanced as she spoke to the Indian war-cloak and the weapons that lay beside his chair.

"Not so, Helen," said Daly, smiling, as if replying to the insinuated remark; "I am too old for such follies now. Not in heart, indeed, but in limb," added he, sternly; "for I own I could ask nothing better than the prairie or the pine forest. I know of no cruelty in savage life that has not its counterpart amid our civilisation, and for the rude virtues that are nurtured there, they are never warmed into existence by the hotbed of selfishness."

"But why leave your friends?—your sister?"

"My sister!" He paused, and a tinge of red came to his cheek as he remembered how she had failed in all attention to the Darcys. "My sister, madam, is self-willed and headstrong as myself. She acknowledges none of the restraints or influence by which the social world consents to be bound and regulated; her path has ever been wild and erratic as my own. We sometimes cross, we never contradict, each other." He paused, and then muttered to himself, "Poor Molly! how different I knew you once! And so," added he, aloud, "I must leave without seeing Darcy! and there stands Sandy, admonishing me that my time is already up. Good-by, Lady Eleanor; good-by, Helen." He turned his head away for a second, and then, in a voice of unusual feeling, said: "Farewell is always a sad word, and doubly sad when spoken by one old as I am; but if my heart is heavy at this moment, it is the selfish sorrow of him who parts from those so near. As for you, madam, and your fortunes, I am full of good hope.

When people talk of suffering virtue, believe me, the element of courage must be wanting; but where the stout heart unites with the good cause, success will come at last."

He pressed his lips to the hands he held within his own, and hurried, before they could reply, from the room.

"Our last friend gone!" exclaimed Lady Eleanor, as she sank into a chair.

Helen's heart was too full for utterance, and she sat down silently, and watched the retiring figure of Daly and his servant till they disappeared in the distance.

CHAPTER XLVIII.

THE DUKE OF YORK'S LEVEE.

When Darcy arrived in London, he found a degree of political excitement for which he was little prepared. In Ireland, the Union had absorbed all interest and anxiety, and with the fate of that measure were extinguished the hopes of those who had speculated on national independence. Not so in England; the real importance of the annexation was never thoroughly considered till the fact was accomplished, nor, until then, were the great advantages and the possible evils well and maturely weighed. Then, for the first time, came the anxious question, What next? Was the Union to be the compensation for large concessions to the Irish people, or was it rather the seal of their incorporation with a more powerful nation, who, by this great stroke of policy, would annihilate for ever all dreams of self-existence? Mr. Pitt inclined to the former opinion, and believed the moment propitious to award the Roman Catholic claims, and to a general remission of those laws which pressed so heavily upon them. To this opinion the King was firmly and, as it proved, insurmountably opposed; he regarded the Act of Union as the final settlement of all possible disagreements between the two countries, as the means of uniting the two Churches, and finally, of excluding at once and for ever the admission of Roman Catholics to Parliament. This wide difference led to the retirement of Mr. Pitt, and subsequently to the return of the dangerous indisposition of the King, an attack brought on by the anxiety and agitation this question induced.

The hopes of the Whig party stood high; the Prince's friends, as they were styled, again rallied around Carlton House, where, already, the possibility of a long Regency was discussed. Besides these causes of excitement were others of not less powerful interest; the growing power of Bonaparte, the war in Egypt, and the possibility of open hostilities with Russia, who had now thrown herself so avowedly into the alliance of France.

Such were the stirring themes Darcy found agitating the public mind, and he could not help contrasting the mighty interests they involved with the narrow circle of consequences a purely local Legislature could discuss or decide upon. He felt at once that he trod the soil of a more powerful and more ambitious people, and he remembered with a sigh his own anticipations, that in the English Parliament the Irish members would be but the camp-followers of the Crown or the Opposition.

If he was English in his pride of government and his sense of national power and greatness, he was Irish in his tastes, his habits, and his affections If he gloried in the name of Briton as the type of national honour and truth throughout the globe, he was still more ardently attached to that land where, under the reflected grandeur of the monarchy, grew up the social affections of a poorer people. There is a sense of freedom and independence in the habits of semi-civilisation very fascinating to certain minds, and all the advantages of more polished communities are deemed shallow compensation for the ready compliance and cordial impulses of the less cultivated.

With all his own high acquirements the Knight was of this mind, and if he did not love England less, he loved Ireland more.

Meditating on the great changes of fortune Ireland had undergone even within his own memory, he moved along through the crowded thoroughfares of the mighty city, when he heard his name called out, and at the same instant a carriage drew up close by him.

"How do you do, Knight?" said a friendly voice, as a hand was stretched forth to greet him. It was Lord Castlereagh, who had only a few weeks previous exchanged his office of Irish Secretary for a post at the Board of Trade. The meeting was a cordial one on both sides, and ended in an invitation to dine on the following day, which Darcy accepted with willingness, as a gage of mutual good feeling and esteem.

"I was talking about you to Lord Netherby only yesterday," said Lord Castlereagh, "and, from some hints he dropped, I suspect the time is come that I may offer you any little influence I possess, without it taking the odious shape of a bargain; if so, pray remember that I have as much pride as yourself on such a score, and will be offended if you accept from another what might come equally well through *me*."

The Knight acknowledged this kind speech with a grateful smile and a pressure of the hand, and was about to move on, when Lord Castlereagh asked if he could not drop him in his carriage at his destination, and thus enjoy, a few moments longer, his society.

"I scarcely can tell you, my Lord," said Darcy, laughing, "which way I was bent on following. I came up to town to present myself at the Duke of York's Levee, and it is only a few moments since I remembered that I was not provided with a uniform."

"Oh, step in then," cried Lord Castlereagh, hastily; "I think I can manage that difficulty for you; there is a Levee this very morning; some pressing intelligence has arrived from Egypt, and his Royal Highness has issued a notice for a reception for eleven o'clock. You are not afraid," said Lord Castlereagh, laughing, as Darcy took his seat beside him—"you are not afraid of being seen in such company now."

"If I am not, my Lord, set my courage down to my principle; for I never felt your kindness so dangerous," said the Knight, with something of emotion.

A few moments of rapid driving brought them in front of the Duke's residence, where several carriages and led horses were now standing, and officers in full dress were seen to pass in and out, with signs of haste and eagerness.

"I told you we should find them astir here," said Lord Castlereagh. "Holloa, Fane, have you heard anything new to-day?"

The officer thus addressed touched his hat respectfully, and approaching the window of the carriage, whispered a few words in Lord Castlereagh's ear.

"Is the news confirmed?" said his Lordship, calmly.

"I believe so, my Lord; at least, Edgecumbe says he heard it from Dundas, who got it from Pitt himself."

"Bad tidings these, Knight," said Lord Castlereagh, as the aide-de-camp moved away; "Pulteney's expedition against Ferrol has failed. These conjoint movements of army and navy seem to have a most unlucky fortune."

"What can you expect, my Lord, from an ill-assorted 'Union?'" said Darcy, slyly.

"They'll work better after a time," said Lord Castlereagh, smiling good humouredly at the hit; "for the present, I acknowledge the success is not flattering. The General always discovers that the land batteries can only be attacked in the very spot where the Admiral pronounces the anchorage impossible; each feels compromised by the other; hence envy and every manner of uncharitableness."

"And what has been the result here? Is it a repulse?"

"You can scarcely call it that, since they never attacked. They looked at the place, sailed round it, and, like the King of France in the story, they marched away again. But here we are at length at the door; let us try if we cannot accomplish a landing better than Lork Keith and General Moore."

Through a crowd of anxious faces, whose troubled looks tallied with the evil tidings, Lord Castlereagh and Darcy ascended the stairs and reached the ante-chamber, now densely thronged by officers of every grade of the service. His Lordship was immediately recognised and surrounded by many of the company, eager to hear his opinion.

"You don't appear to credit the report, my Lord," said Darcy, who had watched with some interest the air of quiet incredulity which he assumed.

"It is all true, notwithstanding," said he, in a whisper; "I heard it early this morning at the Council, and came here to see how it would be received. They say that war will be soon as unpopular with the red-coats as with the no-coats; and really to look at these sombre faces, one would say there was some truth in the rumour. But here comes Taylor." And so saying, Lord Castlereagh moved forward, and laid his hand on the arm of an officer in a staff uniform.

"I don't think so, my Lord," said he, in reply to some question from Lord Castlereagh; "I'll endeavour to manage it, but I'm afraid I shall not succeed. Have you heard of Elliot's death? The news has just arrived."

"Indeed! So then the government of Chelsea is to give away. Oh, that fact explains the presence of so many veteran generals! I really was puzzled to conceive what martial ardour stirred them."

"You are severe, my Lord," said Darcy; "I hope you are unjust."

"One is rarely so in attributing a selfish motive anywhere," said the young nobleman, sarcastically. "But, Taylor, can't you arrange this affair? Let me present my friend meanwhile: The Knight of Gwynne—Colonel Taylor."

Before Taylor could more than return the Knight's salutation, he was summoned to attend his Royal Highness, and, at the same moment, the folding-doors at the end of the apartment were thrown open and the reception began.

Whether the sarcasm of Lord Castlereagh was correct, or that a nobler motive was in operation, the number of officers was very great, and although the Duke rarely addressed more than a word or two to each, a considerable time elapsed before Lord Castlereagh, with the Knight following, had entered the room.

"It is against a positive order of his Royal Highness, my Lord," said an aide-de-camp, barring the passage; "none but field-officers, and in full uniform, are received by his Royal Highness."

Lord Castlereagh whispered something, and endeavoured to move on, but again the other interposed, saying, "Indeed, my Lord, I'm deeply grieved at it, but I cannot—I dare not transgress my orders."

The Duke, who had been up to this moment engaged in conversing with a group, suddenly turned, and perceiving that the presentations were not followed up, said, "Well, gentlemen, I am waiting." Then recognising Lord Castlereagh, he added, gaily, "Another time, my Lord, another time: this morning belongs to the service, and the colour of your coat excludes you."

"I ask your Royal Highness's pardon," said Lord Castlereagh, in a tone of great deference, while he made the apology an excuse for advancing a step into the room, "I have but just left the Council, and was anxious to inform you that your Royal Highness's suggestions have been fully adopted."

"Indeed! is that the case?" said the Duke, with an elated look, while he drew his lordship into the recess of a window. The intelligence, to judge from the Duke's expression, must have been both important and satisfactory, for he looked intensely eager and pleased by turns.

"And so," said he, aloud, "they really have determined on Egypt? Well, my Lord, you have brought me the best tidings I've heard for many a day."

"And like all bearers of good despatches," said Lord Castlereagh, catching up the tone of the Duke, "I prefer a claim to your Royal Highness's patronage."

"If you look for Chelsea, my Lord, you are just five minutes too late. Old Sir Harry Belmore has this instant got it."

"I could have named as old and perhaps a not less distinguished soldier to your Royal Highness, with this additional claim—a claim I must say, your Royal Highness never disregards——"

"That he has been unfortunate with the unlucky," said the Duke, laughing, and good naturedly alluding to his own failure in the expedition to the Netherlands; "but who is your friend?"

"The Knight of Gwynne—an Irish gentleman."

"One of your late supporters, eh, Castlereagh?" said the Duke, laughing. "How came he to be forgotten till this hour? Or did you pass him a bill of gratitude payable at nine months after date?"

"No, my Lord, he was an opponent; he was a man that I never could buy, when his influence and power were such as to make the price of his own dictating Since that day, fortune has changed with him."

"And what do you want with him now?" said the Duke, while his eyes twinkled with a sly malice; "are you imitating the man that bowed down before the statues of Hercules and Apollo at Rome, not knowing when the time of those fellows might come up again? Is that your game?"

"Not exactly, your Royal Highness; but I really feel some scruples of conscience that, having assisted so many unworthy candidates to pensions and peerages, I should have done nothing for the most upright man I met in Ireland."

"If we could make him a Commissary-General," said the Duke, laughing, "the qualities you speak of would be of service just now: there never was such a set of rascals as we have got in that department! But come, what can we do with him? What's his rank in the army? Where did he serve?"

"If I dare present him to your Royal Highness without a uniform," said Lord Castlereagh, hesitatingly, "he could answer these queries better than I can."

"Oh! by Jove! it is too late for scruples now—introduce him at once."

Lord Castlereagh waited for no more formal permission, but, hastening to the ante-chamber, took Darcy's hand, and led him forward.

"If I don't mistake, sir," said the Duke, as the old man raised his head after a deep and courteous salutation, "this is not the first time we have met. Am I correct in calling you Colonel Darcy?"

The Knight bowed low in acquiescence.

"The same officer who raised the 28th Light Dragoons, known as Darcy's Light Horse?'"

The Knight bowed once more.

"A very proud officer in command," said the Duke, turning to Lord Castlereagh with a stern expression on his features; "a Colonel, who threatened a Prince of the Blood with arrest for breach of duty."

"He had good reason, your Royal Highness, to be proud," said the Knight, firmly; "first, to have a Prince to serve under his command; and, secondly, to have held that station and character in the service to have rendered so unbecoming a threat pardonable."

"And who said it was?" replied the Duke, hastily.

"Your Royal Highness has just done so."

"How do you mean?"

"I mean, my Lord Duke," said Darcy, with a calm and unmoved look, that your Royal Highness would never have recurred to the theme to one humbled as I am, if you had not forgiven it."

"As freely as I trust you forgive me, Colonel Darcy," said the Duke, grasping his hand and shaking it with warmth. "Now for *my* part: what can I do for you?—what do you wish?"

"I can scarcely ask your Royal Highness; I find that some kind friend has already applied on my behalf. I could not have presumed, old and useless as I am, to prefer a claim myself."

"There's your own regiment vacant," said the Duke, musing. "No, by Jove! I remember Lord Netherby asking me for it the other day for some relative of his own. Taylor, is the Colonelcy of the 28th promised?"

"Your Royal Highness signed it yesterday."

"I feared as much. Who is it?—perhaps he'd exchange."

"Colonel Maurice Darcy, your Royal Highness, unattached."

"What! have I been doing good by stealth? Is this really so?"

"If it be, your Royal Highness," said Darcy, smiling, "I can only assure you that the officer promoted will not exchange."

"The depôt is at Gosport, your Royal Highness," said Taylor, in reply to a question from the Duke.

"Well, station it in Ireland, Colonel Darcy may prefer it," said the Duke; "for, as the regiment forms part of the expedition to Egypt, the depôt need not be moved for some time to come."

"Your Royal Highness can increase the favour by only one concession—dare I ask it?—to permit me to take the command on service."

The Duke gazed with astonishment at the old man, and gradually his expression became one of deep interest, as he said,

"Colonel Darcy could claim as a right what I feel so proud to accord him as a favour. Make a note of that, Taylor," said the Duke, raising his voice, so as to be heard through the room; "'Colonel Darcy to take the command on service at his own special request.' Yes, gentlemen," added he, louder, "these are times when the exigencies of the service demand alike the energy of youth and the experience of age; it is, indeed, a happy conjuncture that finds them united. My Lord Castlereagh and Colonel Darcy, are you disengaged for Wednesday?"

They both bowed respectfully.

"Then on Wednesday I'll have some of your brother officers to meet you, Colonel. Now, Taylor, let us get through our list."

So saying, the Duke bowed graciously, and Lord Castlereagh and the Knight retired, each too full of pleasure to utter a word as he went.

CHAPTER XLIX.

THE TWO SIDES OF A MEDAL.

ALTHOUGH the Knight lost not an hour in writing to Lady Eleanor, informing her of his appointment, the letter hastily written, and entrusted to a waiter to be posted, was never forwarded, and the first intelligence of the event reached her in a letter from her courtly relative, Lord Netherby.

So much depends upon the peculiar tact and skill of the writer, and so much upon our own frame of mind at the time of reading, that it is difficult to say whether we do not bear up better under the announcement of any sudden and sorrowful event from the hand of one less cared for, than from those nearest and dearest to our hearts. The consolations that look like the special pleadings of affection, become, as it were, the mere expressions of impartiality. The points of view being so different, give a different aspect to the picture, and gleams of light fall, where, seen from another quarter, all was shadow and gloom. So it was here. What, if the tidings had come from her husband, had been regarded in the one painful light of separation and long absence, assumed, under Lord Netherby's style, the semblance of a most gratifying event, with, of course, that alloy of discomfort from which no human felicity is altogether free: so very artfully was this done, that Lady Eleanor half felt as if, in indulging in her own sorrow, she were merely giving way to a selfish regret, and as Helen, the better to sustain her mother's courage, affected a degree of pleasure she was really far from feeling, this added to the conviction that she ought, if she could, to regard her husband's appointment as a happy event.

"Truly, mamma," said Helen, as she sat with the letter before her, "'le style c'est l'homme.' His Lordship is quite heroic when describing all the fêtes and dinners of London; all the honours showered on papa in visiting-cards and invitations; how Excellencies called, and Royal Highnesses shook hands: he even chronicles the distinguishing favour of the gracious Prince, who took wine with him. But listen to him when the theme is really one that might evoke some trait, if not of enthusiasm, at least of national pride: 'As for the expedition, my dear cousin, though nobody knows exactly for what place it is destined, everybody is aware that it is not intended to be a fighting one. Demonstrations are now the vogue, and it is become just as bad taste for our army to shed blood, as it would be for a well-bred man to mention a certain ill-conducted individual before ears polite. Modern war is like a game at whist between first-rate players; when either party has four by honours, he shows his hand, and saves the trouble of a contest. The Naval Service is, I grieve to say, rooted to its ancient prejudices, and continues its abominable pastime of broadsides and boardings; hence its mob popularity at this moment! The Army will, however, always be the gentlemanlike cloth, and I thank my stars I don't believe we have a single relative afloat. Guy Herries was the last; he was shot or piked, I forget which, in boarding a Spanish galliot off Cape Verde. "Que diable allait-il faire dans cette galère?" Rest satisfied, therefore, if the gallant Knight has little glory, he will have no dangers; our expeditions never land. Jekyll says they are only intended to give the service an appetite for fresh meat and soft bread, after four months' biscuit and salt beef. At all events, my dear cousin, reckon on seeing my friend the Knight gazetted as Major-General on the very next promotions. The Prince is delighted with him; and I carried a message from his Royal Highness yesterday to the War-office in his behalf. You would not come to see me, despite all the seductions I threw out, and now the season is nigh over. May I hope better things for the next year, when perhaps I can promise an inducement the more, and make your welcome more graceful by dividing its cares with one far more competent than myself to fulfil them.'—What does he mean, mamma?"

"Read on, my dear; I believe I can guess the riddle."

"'The person I allude to was, in former days, if not actually a friend, a favoured intimate of yours; indeed I say that this fact is but another claim to my regard?'—Is it possible, mamma, his Lordship thinks of marrying?"

"Even so, Helen," said Lady Eleanor, sighing, for she remembered how, in his very last interview with her at Gwynne Abbey, he spoke of his resolve on making Lionel his heir; but then, those were the days of their prosperous fortune, the time when, to all seeming, they needed no increase of wealth.

If Helen was disposed to laugh at the notion of Lord Netherby's marrying, a glance at the troubled expression of her mother's features would have checked the emotion. The heritage was a last hope, which was not the less cherished that she had never imparted it to another.

"Shall I read on?" said Helen, timidly; and at a signal from Lady Eleanor she resumed: "'I know how much "badinage" a man at my time of life must expect from his acquaintances, and how much of kind remonstrance from his friends, when he announces his determination to marry. A good deal of this must be set down to the score of envy, some of it proceeds from mere habit on these occasions, and lastly, one's bachelor friends very naturally are averse to the closure against them of a house "où on dîne." I have thought of all this, and, per contra, I have set down the isolation of one, if not deserted, at least somewhat neglected by his relatives, and fancied, that if not exactly of that age when people marry for love, I am not yet quite so old but I may become the object of true and disinterested affection.

"'Lady ——, I have pledged my honour not to write her name, even to you, is, in rank and fortune, fully my equal, in every other quality my superior. The idlers at "Boodle's" can neither sneer at a "mésalliance," nor hint at the "faiblesse" of an "elderly gentleman." It is a marriage founded on mutual esteem, and, so far as station is concerned, on equality; and when I say that his Royal Highness has expressed his unqualified approval of the step, I believe I can add no more. I owe you, my dear cousin, this early and full explanation of my motives on many accounts: if the result should change the dispositions I once believed unalterable, I beg it may be understood as proceeding far more from necessity than the sincere wish of your very affectionate relative,

"'NETHERBY.'

"'My regret at not seeing Helen here this season is, in a measure, alleviated by Lady —— telling me that brunettes were more the rage; her Ladyship, who is no common arbiter, says that no "blonde" attracted any notice: even Lady Georgiana Maydew drew no admiration. My fair cousin is, happily, very young, "et les beaux jours viendront," even before hers have lost their brilliancy.

"'I am sorry Lionel left the Coldstreams; with economy he could very well have managed to hold his ground, and we might have obtained something for him in the Household. As for India, the only influential person I know is my wine-merchant; he is, I am told, a Director of the Honourable Company, but he'd certainly adulterate my Madeira if I condescended to ask him a favour.'"

"Well, Helen, I think you will agree with me, selfishness is the most candid of all the vices; how delightfully unembarrassed is his Lordship's style, how frank, honest, and straightforward!"

"After his verdict upon 'blondes,' mamma," said Helen, laughing, "I dare not record my opinion of him—I cannot come into Court an impartial evidence. This, however, I will say, that if his Lordship be not an unhappy instance of the school, I am sincerely rejoiced that Lionel is not being trained up a Courtier; better a soldier's life with all its hazards and its dangers, than a career so certain to kill every manly sentiment."

I agree with you fully, Helen; life cannot be circumscribed within petty limits and occupied by petty cares, without reducing the mind to the same miniature dimensions; until at last, so immeasurably greater are our own passions and feelings than the miserable interests around us, we end by self-worship and egotism, and fancy ourselves leviathans because we swim in a fish-pond. But who can that be crossing the grass-plot yonder? I thought our neighbours of Port Ballintray had all left the coast?"

"It is the gentleman who dined here, mamma, the man that never spoke—I forget his name——"

Helen had not time to finish, when a modest tap was heard at the door, and the next moment Mr. Leonard presented himself. He was dressed with more than his wonted care, but the effort to make poverty respectable was everywhere apparent; the blue frock was brushed to the very verge of its frail existence, the gloves were drawn on at the hazard of their integrity, and his hat, long inured to every vicissitude of weather, had been cocked into a strange counterfeit of modish smartness. With all these signs of unusual attention to appearances, his manner was modest even to humility, and he took a chair with the diffidence of one who seemed to doubt the propriety of being seated in such a presence.

Notwithstanding Lady Eleanor's efforts at conversation, aided by Helen, who tried in many ways to relieve the embarrassment of their visitor, this difficulty seemed every moment greater, and he seemed, as he really felt, to have summoned up all his courage for an undertaking, and in the very nick of the enterprise, to have left himself beggared of his energy. A vague assent, a look of doubt and uncertainty, a half-muttered expression of acquiescence in whatever was said, was all that could be obtained from him but still, while his embarrassment appeared each instant greater, he evinced no disposition to take his leave. Lady Eleanor, who, like many persons whose ordinary manner is deemed cold and haughty, could exert at will considerable powers of pleasing, did her utmost to put her visitor at his ease, and by changing her topics from time to time, detect, if possible, some clue to his coming. It was all in vain: he followed her, it is true, as well as he was able, and with a bewildered look of constrained attention, seemed endeavouring to interest himself in what she said, but it was perfectly apparent, all the while, that his mind was preoccupied, and by very different thoughts.

At length she remained silent, and resuming the work she was engaged on when he entered, sat for some time without uttering a word, or even looking up. Mr. Leonard coughed slightly, but, as if terrified at his own rashness, soon became mute and still. At last, after a long pause, so long that Lady Eleanor and Helen, forgetful of their visitor, had become deeply immersed in their own reflections, Mr. Leonard arose slowly, and with a voice not free from a certain tremor, said, "Well, madam, then I suppose I may venture to say that I saw you and Miss Darcy both well."

Lady Eleanor looked up with astonishment, for she could not conceive the meaning of the words, nor in what quarter they were to be reported.

"I mean, madam," said Leonard, "that when I present myself to the Colonel, I may take the liberty to mention having seen you."

"Do you speak of my husband, sir—Colonel Darcy?" said Lady Eleanor, with a very different degree of interest in her look and accent.

"Yes, madam," said Leonard, with a kind of forced courage in his manner, "I hope to be under his command in a few days."

"Indeed, sir!" said Lady Eleanor, with animation; "I did not know that you had served, still less that you were about to join the army once more."

Leonard blushed deeply, and he suddenly grew deadly pale, while, in a voice scarcely louder than a mere whisper, he muttered, "So then, madam, Colonel Darcy has never spoken of me to you?"

Lady Eleanor, who misunderstood the meaning of the question, seemed slightly confused as she replied, "I have no recollection of it, sir—I cannot call up at this moment having heard your name from my husband."

"I ought to have known it—I ought to have been certain of it," said Leonard, in a voice bursting from emotion, while the tears gushed from his eyes; "he could not have asked me to his house to sit down at his table as a mere object of your pity and contempt! and yet I am nothing else."

The passionate vehemence in which he now spoke seemed so different from his recent manner, that both Lady Eleanor and Helen had some doubts as to his sanity, when he quickly resumed: "I was broke for cowardice—dismissed the Service with disgrace—degraded! Well may I call it so, to be what I became. I would tell you that I was not guilty—that Colonel Darcy knows—but I dare not choose between the character of a coward and—a drunkard. I had no other prospect before me than a life of poverty and repining—maybe of worse—of shame and ignominy! when, last night, I received these letters; I scarcely thought they could be for me, even when I read my name on them. Yes, madam, this letter from the War-office permits me to serve as a volunteer with the 8th Regiment of Foot; and this, which is without signature, encloses me fifty pounds to buy my outfit and join the regiment. It does not need a name; there is but one man living could stoop to help such as I am, and not feel dishonoured by the contact; there is but one man brave enough to protect him branded as a coward."

"You are right, sir," cried Helen; "this must be my father's doing."

Leonard tried to speak, but could not; a trembling motion of his lips, and a faint sound issued, but nothing articulate. Lady Eleanor stopped him as he moved towards the door, and taking his hand pressed it cordially, while she said, "Be of good heart, sir; my husband is not less quick to perceive than he is ever ready to befriend. Be assured he would not now be your ally if he had not a well-grounded hope that you would merit it. Farewell, then, remember you have a double tie to duty, and that *his* credit, as well as *your own*, is on the issue."

Leonard muttered a faint "I will," and departed.

"How happily timed is this little incident, Helen," said Lady Eleanor, as she drew her daughter to her side; "how full of pleasant hope it fills the heart, at a moment when the worldly selfishness of the courtier's letter had left us low and sorrow-struck. These are indeed the sunny spots in life, that never look so brilliant as when seen amid lowering skies and darkening storms."

CHAPTER L.

AN UNCEREMONIOUS VISIT.

As winter drew near, with its dark and leaden skies, and days and nights of storm and hurricane, so did the worldly prospect of Lady Eleanor and her daughter grow hourly more gloomy. Bicknell's letters detailed new difficulties and embarrassments on every hand. Sums of money, supposed to have been long since paid and acknowledged by Gleeson, were now demanded with all the accruing interest; rights hitherto unquestioned were now threatened with dispute, as Hickman O'Reilly's success emboldened others to try their fortune. Of the little property that still remained to them, the rents were withheld until their claim to them should be once more established by law. Disaster followed disaster, till at length the last drop filled up the measure of their misery, as they learned that the Knight's personal liberty was at stake, and more than one writ was issued for his arrest.

The same post that brought this dreadful intelligence, brought also a few lines from Darcy, the first that had reached them since his departure.

His note was dated from the "*Hermione* frigate, off the Needles," and contained little more than an affectionate farewell. He wrote in health, and apparently in spirits, full of the assurance of a speedy and happy meeting; nor was there any allusion to their embarrassments, save in the vague mention of a letter he had written to Bicknell, and who would himself write to Lady Eleanor.

"It is not, dearest Eleanor," wrote he, "the time we would have selected for a separation, when troubles thicken around us; yet who knows if the incident may not fall happily, and turn our thoughts from the loss of fortune to the many blessings we enjoy in mutual affection and in our children's love, all to thicken around us at our meeting? I confess, too, I have a pride in being thought worthy to serve my country still, not in the tiresome monotony of a depôt, but in the field! among the young, the gallant, and the brave! Is it not enough to take off half this load of years, and make me fancy myself the gay Colonel you may remember cantering beside your carriage in the Park—I shame to say how long ago! I wonder what the French will think of us, for nearly every officer in command might be superannuated, and Abercrombie is as venerable in white hairs as myself! There are, however, plenty of young and dashing fellows to replace us, and the spirit of the whole army is admirable.

"Whither we are destined, what will be our collective force, and what the nature of the expedition, are profound secrets, with which even the Generals of Brigades are not entrusted; so that all I can tell you is, that some seven hundred and fifty of us are now sailing southward, under a steady breeze from the north-north-west; that the land is each moment growing fainter to my eyes, while the Pilot is eagerly pressing me to conclude this last expression of my love to yourself and dearest Helen. Adieu.

"Ever yours,

"Maurice Darcy."

As with eyes half-dimmed by tears Lady Eleanor read these lines, she could not help muttering a thanksgiving that her husband was at least beyond the risk of that danger of which Bicknell spoke—an indignity, she feared, he never could have survived.

"And better still," cried Helen, "if a season of struggle and privation awaits us, that we should bear it alone, and not before *his* eyes, for whom such a prospect would be torture. Now let us see how to meet the evil." So saying, she once more opened Bicknell's letter, and began to peruse it carefully, while Lady Eleanor sat, pale and in silence, nor even by a gesture showing any consciousness of the scene.

"What miserable trifling do all these legal subtleties seem," said the young girl, after she had read for some time; "how trying to patience to canvass the petty details by which a clear and honest cause must be asserted! Here are fees to counsel, briefs, statements, learned opinions, and wise consultations multiplied to show that we are the rightful owners of what our ancestors have held for centuries, while every step of usurpation by these Hickmans would appear almost unassailable. With what intensity of purpose, too, does that family persecute us. All these actions are instituted by them; these bonds are all in their hands. What means this hate?"

Lady Eleanor looked up, and as her eyes met Helen's a faint flush coloured her cheek, for she thought of her interview with the old Doctor, and that proposal by which their conflicting interests were to be satisfied.

"We surely never injured them," resumed the young girl, eagerly; "they were always well and hospitably received by us. Lionel even liked Beecham, when they were boys together—a mild and quiet youth he was."

"So I thought him, too," said Lady Eleanor, stealing a cautious glance at her daughter. "We saw him," continued she, more boldly, "under circumstances of no common difficulty—struggling under the embarrassment of a false social position, with such a grandfather!"

"And such a father! Nay, mamma, of the two you must confess the Doctor was our favourite. The old man's selfishness was not half so vulgar as his son's ambition."

"And yet, Helen," said Lady Eleanor, calmly, "such are the essential transitions by which families are formed; wealthy in one generation, aspiring in the next, recognised gentry—mayhap titled—in the third. It is but rarely that the whole series unfolds itself before our eyes at once, as in the present instance, and consequently it is but rarely that we detect so palpably all its incongruities and absurdities. A few years more," added she, with a deep sigh, "and these O'Reillys will be regarded as the rightful owners of Gwynne Abbey by centuries of descent; and if an antiquary detect the old leopards of the Darcys frowning from some sculptured keystone, it will be to weave an ingenious theory of intermarriage between the houses."

"An indignity they might well have spared us," said Helen, proudly.

"Such are the world's changes," continued Lady Eleanor, pursuing her own train of thought. "How very few remember the origin of our proudest houses, and how little does it matter whether the foundations have been laid by the rude courage of some lawless Baron of the tenth century, or the crafty shrewdness of some Hickman O'Reilly of the nineteenth."

If there was a tone of bitter mockery in Lady Eleanor's words, there was also a secret meaning which, even to her own heart, she would not have ventured to avow. By one of those strange and most inexplicable mysteries of our nature, she was endeavouring to elicit from her daughter some expression of dissent to her own recorded opinion of the O'Reillys, and seeking for some chance word which might show that Helen regarded an alliance with that family with more tolerant feelings than she did herself.

Her intentions on this head were not destined to be successful. Helen's rejudices on the score of birth and station were rather strengthened than shaken by the changes of fortune; she cherished the prestige of their good blood as a source of proud consolation that no adversity could detract from. Before, however, she could reply, the tramp of a horse's feet—a most unusual sound—was heard on the gravel without; and immediately after the heavy foot of some one, as if feeling his way in the dark towards the door. Without actual fear, but not without intense anxiety, both mother and daughter heard the heavy knocking of a loaded horsewhip on the door; nor was it until old Tate had twice repeated his question, that a sign replied he might open the door.

"Look to the pony there!" cried a voice, as the old man peered out into the dark night. And before he could reply or resist, the speaker pushed past him and entered the room. "I crave your pardon, my Lady Eleanor," said she—for it was Miss Daly who, drenched with rain, and all splashed with mud, now stood before them—"I crave your pardon for this visit of so scant ceremony. Has the Knight returned yet?"

The strong resemblance to her brother Bagenal, increased by her gesture and the tones of her voice, at once proclaimed to Lady Eleanor who her visitor was; and as she rose graciously to receive her, she replied, that "the Knight, so far from having returned, had already sailed with the expedition under General Abercrombie."

Miss Daly listened with breathless eagerness to the words, and as they concluded, she exclaimed aloud, "Thank God!" and threw herself into a chair. A pause, which, if brief, was not devoid of embarrassment, followed; and while Lady Eleanor was about to break it, Miss Daly again spoke, but with a voice and manner very different from before. "You will pardon, I am certain, the rudeness of my intrusion, Lady Eleanor, and you, too, Miss Darcy, when I tell you that my heart was too full of anxiety to leave any room for courtesy. It was only this afternoon that an accident informed me that a person had arrived in this neighbourhood with a writ to arrest the Knight of Gwynne. I was five-and-twenty miles from this when I heard the news, and although I commissioned my informant to hasten thither with the tidings, I grew too full of dread, and had too many fears of a mischance, to await the result, so that I resolved to come myself."

"How full of kindness!" exclaimed Lady Eleanor, while Helen took Miss Daly's hand and pressed it to her lips. "Let our benefactress not suffer too much in our cause. Helen, dearest, assist Miss Daly to a change of dress. You are actually wet through."

"Nay, nay, Lady Eleanor, you must not teach me fastidiousness. It has been my custom for many a year not to care for weather, and in the kind of life I lead such training is indispensable." Miss Daly removed her hat as she spoke, and, pushing back her dripping hair, seemed really insensible to the discomforts which caused her hosts so much uneasiness.

"I see clearly," resumed she, laughing, "I was right in not making myself known to you before; for though you may forgive the eccentricities that come under the mask of good intentions, you'd never pardon the thousand offences against good breeding and the world's prescription, which spring from the wayward fancies of an old maid who has lived so much beyond the pale of affection, she has forgotten all the arts that win it."

"If you are unjust to yourself, Miss Daly, pray be not so to us; nor think that we can be insensible to friendship like yours."

"Oh, as for this trifling service, you esteem it far too highly; besides, when you hear the story, you'll see how much more you have to thank your own hospitality than my promptitude."

"This is, indeed, puzzling me," exclaimed Lady Eleanor.

"Do you remember having met and received at your house a certain Mr. Dempsey?"

"Certainly, he dined with us on one occasion, and paid us some three or four visits. A tiresome little vulgar man, with a most intense curiosity devouring him to know everything of everybody."

"To this gift, or infirmity, whichever it be, we are now indebted. Since the breaking-up of the boarding-house at Port Ballintray, which, this year, was somewhat earlier than usual"—here Miss Daly smiled slightly, as though there lay more in the words than they seemed to imply—"Mr. Dempsey betook himself to a little village near Glenarm, where I have been staying, and where the chief recommendation as a residence lay possibly in the fact that the weekly mail-car to Derry changed horses there. Hence, an opportunity of communing with the world he valued at its just price. It so chanced that the only traveller who came for three weeks, arrived the night before last, drenched to the skin, and so ill from cold, hunger, and exhaustion, that, unable to prosecute his journey further, he was carried from the car to his bed. Mr. Dempsey, whose heart is really as kind as inquisitive, at once tendered his services to the stranger, who, after some brief intercourse, commissioned him to open his portmanteau, and taking out writing materials, to inform his friends in Dublin of his sudden indisposition, and his fears that his illness might delay, or perhaps render totally abortive, his mission to the north. Here was a most provoking mystery for Mr. Dempsey. The very allusion to a matter of importance, in this dubious half-light, was something more than human nature should be tried with, and if the patient burned with the fever of the body, Mr. Dempsey suffered under the less tolerable agony of mental torment—imagining every possible contingency that should bring a stranger down into a lonely neighbourhood, and canvassing every imaginable inducement, from seduction to highway robbery. Whether the sick man's sleep was merely the heavy debt of exhausted nature, or whether Mr. Dempsey aided his repose by adding a few drops to the laudanum prescribed by the doctor, true it is, he lay in a deep slumber, and never awoke till late the following day; meanwhile Mr. Dempsey recompensed his Samaritanism by a careful inspection of the stranger's trunk and its contents; and, in particular, made a patient examination of two parchment documents, which, fortunately for his curiosity, were not sealed, but simply tied with red tape. Great was his surprise to discover that one of these was a writ to arrest a certain Paul Dempsey, and the other directed against the resident of the Corvy, whom he now, for the first time, learned was the Knight of Gwynne.

"Self-interest, the very instinct of safety itself, weighed less with him than his old passion for gossip; and no sooner had he learned the important fact of who his neighbour was, than he set off straight to communicate the news to me. I must do him the justice to say, that when I proposed his hastening off to you with the tidings, that the little man acceded with the utmost promptitude, but as his journey was to be performed on foot, and by certain mountain paths not always easily discovered in our misty climate, it is probable he could not reach this for some hours."

When Miss Daly concluded, Lady Eleanor and her daughter renewed their grateful acknowledgments for her thoughtful kindness. "These are sad themes by which to open our acquaintance," said Lady Eleanor; "but it is among the prerogatives of friendship to share the pressure of misfortune, and Mr. Daly's sister can be no stranger to ours."

"Nor how undeserved they were," added Miss Daly, gravely.

"Nay, which of us can dare say so much?" interrupted Lady Eleanor "we may well have forgotten ourselves in that long career of prosperity we enjoyed—for ours was, indeed, a happy lot! I need not speak of my husband to one who knew him once so well. Generous, frank, and noble-hearted as he always was—his only failing the excessive confidence that would go on believing in the honesty of others, from the prompting of a spirit that stooped to nothing low or unworthy—he never knew suspicion."

"True," echoed Miss Daly, "he never did suspect!"

There was such a plaintive sadness in her voice, that it drew Helen's eyes towards her; nor could all her efforts conceal a tear that trickled along her cheek.

"And to what an alternative are we now reduced!" continued Lady Eleanor, who, with all the selfishness of sorrow, loved to linger on the painful theme,—"to rejoice at separation, and to feel relieved in thinking that he is gone to peril life itself, rather than endure the lingering death of a broken heart!"

"Yes, young lady," said Miss Daly, turning towards Helen, "such are the recompenses of the most endearing affection—such the penalties of loving. Would you not almost say, 'It were better to be such as I am, unloved, uncared for—without one to share a joy or grief with.' I half think so myself," added she, suddenly rising from her chair. "I can almost persuade myself that this load of life is easier borne when all its pressure is one's own."

"You are not about to leave us?" said Lady Eleanor, taking her hand affectionately.

"Yes," replied she, smiling sadly, "when my heart has disburdened itself of an immediate care, I become but sorry company, and sometimes think aloud. How fortunate I have no secrets!—Bring my pony to the door," said she, as Tate answered the summons of the bell.

"But wait at least for daylight," said Helen, eagerly; "the storm is increasing, and the night is dark and starless. Remember what a road you've come."

"I often ride at this hour, and with no better weather," said she, adjusting the folds of her habit; "and as to the road, Puck knows it too well to wander from the track, daylight or dark."

"For our sakes, I entreat you not to venture till morning," cried Lady Eleanor.

"I could not if I would," said Miss Daly, steadily. "By to-morrow, at noon, I have an engagement at some distance hence, and much to arrange in the mean time. Pray do not ask me again. I cannot bear to refuse you, even in such a trifle, and as to me or my safety, waste not another thought about it. They who have so little to live for are wondrous secure from accident."

"When shall we see you? Soon, I hope and trust!" exclaimed both mother and daughter together.

Miss Daly shook her head; then added, hastily, "I never promise anything. I was a great castle-builder once, but time has cured me of the habit, and I do not like, even by a pledge, to forestal the morrow. Farewell, Lady Eleanor. It is better to see but little of me, and think the better, than grow weary of my waywardness on nearer acquaintance. Adieu, Miss Darcy; I am glad to have seen you; don't forget me." So saying, she pressed Helen's hands to her lips, but ere she let them drop, she squeezed a letter into her grasp; the moment after, she was gone.

"Oh then, I remember her the beauty wonst!" said Tate, as he closed the door, after peering out for some seconds into the dark night; "and proud she was, too—riding a white Arabian, with two servants in scarlet liveries after her! The world has quare changes; but hers is the greatest ever I knew!"

CHAPTER LI.

A TETE-A-TETE AND A LETTER.

LONG after Miss Daly's departure, Lady Eleanor continued to discuss the eccentricity of her manners, and the wilful abruptness of her address, for although deeply sensible and grateful for her kindness, she dwelt on every peculiarity of her appearance with a pertinacity that more than once surprised her daughter. Helen, indeed, was very far from being a patient listener, not only because she was more tolerant in her estimate of their visitor, but because she was eager to read the letter so secretly entrusted to her hands. A dread of some unknown calamity, some sad tidings of her father or Lionel, was ever uppermost in her thoughts, nor could she banish the impression that Miss Daly's visit had another and very different object than that which she alleged to Lady Eleanor.

It may be reckoned among the well-known contrarieties of life, that our friends are never more disposed to be long-winded and discursive than at the very time we would give the world to be alone and to ourselves. With a most malicious intensity they seem to select that moment for indulging in all those speculations by which people while away the weary hours. In such a mood was Lady Eleanor Darcy. Not only did she canvass and criticise Miss Daly, as she appeared before them, but went off into long rambling reminiscences of all she had formerly heard about her, for, although they had never met before, Miss Daly had been the reigning Belle of the West before her own arrival in Ireland.

"She must have been handsome, Helen, don't you think so?" said she, at the end of a long enumeration of the various eccentricities imputed to her.

"I should say very handsome," replied Helen.

"Scarcely feminine enough, perhaps," resumed Lady Eleanor; "the features too bold, the expression too decided; but this may have been the fault of a social tone, which required everything in exaggeration, and would tolerate nothing save in excess."

"Yes, mamma," said Helen, vaguely assenting to a remark she had not attended to.

"I never fancied that style, either in beauty or in manner," continued

Lady Eleanor "It wants, in the first place, the great element of pleasing; it is not natural."

"No, mamma!" rejoined Helen, mechanically as before.

"Besides," continued Lady Eleanor, gratified at her daughter's ready assent, "for one person to whom these mannerisms are becoming, there are at least a hundred slavish imitators ready to adopt without taste, and follow without discrimination. Now Miss Daly was the fashion once. Who can say to what heresies she has given origin, to what absurdities in dress, in manner, and in bearing?"

Helen smiled, and nodded an acquiescence without knowing to what.

"There is one evil attendant on all this," said Lady Eleanor, who, with the merciless ingenuity of a thorough poser, went on ratiocinating from her own thoughts; "one can rarely rely upon even the kindest intentions of people of this sort, so often are their best offices but mere passing, fitful impulses; don't you think so?"

"Yes, mamma," said Helen, roused by this sudden appeal to a more than usual acquiescence, while totally ignorant as to what.

"Then, they have seldom any discretion, even when they mean well."

"No, mamma."

"While they expect the most implicit compliance on your part with every scheme they have devised for your benefit."

"Very true," chimed in Helen, who assented at random.

"Sad alternative," sighed Lady Eleanor, "between such rash friendship and the lukewarm kindness of our courtly cousin."

"I think not!" said Helen, who fancied she was still following the current of her mother's reflections.

"Indeed!" exclaimed Lady Eleanor, in astonishment, while she looked at her daughter for an explanation.

"I quite agree with you, mamma," cried Helen, blushing, as she spoke, for she was suddenly recalled to herself.

"The more fortunate is the acquiescence, my dear," said Lady Eleanor, dryly, "since it seems perfectly instinctive. I find, Helen, you have not been a very attentive listener, and as I conclude I must have been a very unamusing companion, I'll even say good night; nay, my sweet child, it is late enough not to seek excuse for weariness—good night."

Helen blushed deeply, dissimulation was a very difficult task to her, and for a moment seemed more than her strength could bear. She had resolved to place the letter in her mother's hands, when the thought flashed across her, that if its contents might occasion any sudden or severe shock, she would never forgive herself. This mental struggle, brief as it was, brought the tears to her eyes, an emotion Lady Eleanor attributed to a different cause, as she said,

"You do not suppose, my dearest Helen, that I am angry, because you thoughts took a pleasanter path than my own."

"Oh, no! no!" cried Helen, eagerly, "I know you are not. it is my own——" She stopped, another word would have revealed everything, and with an affectionate embrace she hurried from the room.

"Poor child!" exclaimed her mother; "the courage that sustained us both so long is beginning to fail her now; and yet I feel as if our trials were but commencing."

While Lady Eleanor dwelt on these sad thoughts, Helen sat beside her bed weeping bitterly.

"How shall I bear up," thought she, "if deprived of that confiding trust a mother's love has ever supplied—without one to counsel or direct me?"

Half fearing to open the letter, lest all her resolves should be altered by its contents, she remained a long time balancing one difficulty against another. Wearied and undecided, she turned at last to the letter itself, as if for advice. It was a strange hand, and addressed to "Miss Daly." With trembling fingers she unfolded the paper, and read the writer's name—"Richard Forester."

A flood of grateful tears burst forth as she read the words: a sense of relief from impending calamity stole over her mind, while she said, "Thank God! my father and Lionel——" She could say no more, for sobbing choked her utterance. The emotions, if violent, passed rapidly off; and as she wiped away her tears, a smile of hope lit up her features. At any other time she would have speculated long and carefully over the causes which made Forester correspond with Miss Daly, and by what right she herself should be entrusted with his letter. Now her thoughts were hurried along too rapidly for reflection. The vague dread of misfortune, so suddenly removed, suggested a sense of gratitude, that thrilled through her heart like joy. In such a frame of mind she read the following lines:

"At Sea

"My dear Miss Daly,

"I cannot thank you enough for your letter, so full of kindness, of encouragement, and of hope. How much I stand in need of them! I have strictly followed every portion of your counsel—would that I could tell you as successfully as implicitly! The address of this letter will, however, be the shortest reply to that question. I write these lines from the *Hermione* frigate. Yes, I am a volunteer in the expedition to the Mediterranean; and only think who is my commanding officer—'the Knight himself.' I had enrolled myself under the name of Conway; but when called up on deck this morning for inspection, such was my surprise on seeing the Knight of Gwynne, or, as he is now called, Colonel Darcy, I almost betrayed myself. Fortunately, however, I escaped unnoticed—a circumstance I believe I owe chiefly to the fact that several young men of family are also volunteers, so that my position attracted no unusual attention. It was a most anxious moment for me as the Colonel came down the line, addressing a word here and there as he went; he stopped within one of me, and spoke for some seconds to a young fellow, whose appearance indicated delicate health. How full of gentleness and benevolence were his words; but when he turned and fixed his eyes on me, my heart beat so quick, my head grew so dizzy, I thought I should have fainted. He remained at least half a minute in front of me, and then asked the orderly for my name.—'Conway! Conway!' repeated he more than once. A very old name. I hope you'll do it credit, sir,' added he, and moved on; how much to my relief I need not say. What a strange rencontre! Often as I wonder at the singular necessity that has made me a private soldier, all my astonishment is lost in thinking of the Knight of Gwynne's presence amongst us; and yet he looks the soldier even as much as he did the country gentleman, when I first saw him, and, strangely too, seems younger and more active than before. To see him here, chatting with the officers under his command, moving about, taking interest in everything that goes on, who would suspect the change of fortune that has befallen him! Not a vestige of discontent; not even a passing look of impatience on his handsome features; and yet, with this example before me, and the consciousness that my altered condition is nothing in comparison with his, I am low-spirited and void of hope! But a few weeks ago, I would have thought myself the luckiest fellow breathing, if told that I were to serve under Colonel Darcy and now, I feel ashamed and abashed, and dread a recognition every time I see him. In good truth, I cannot forget the presumption that led me first to his acquaintance. My mind dwells on that unhappy mission to the West, and its consequences. My foolish vanity in supposing that I, a mere boy, uninformed, and without reflection, should be able to influence a man, so much my superior in every way! and this, bad as it is, is the most favourable view of my conduct, for I dare not recal the dishonourable means by which I was to buy his support. Then, I think of my heedless and disreputable quarrel. What motives and what actions in the eyes of her whose affection I sought! How worthily am I punished for my presumption!

"I told you that I strictly followed the advice of your last letter. Immediately on receiving it I wrote a few lines to my mother, entreating her permission to see and speak to her, and expressing an earnest hope that our interview would end in restoring me to the place I so long enjoyed in her affection. A very formal note, appointing the following day, was all the reply.

"On arriving at Berkeley-square, and entering the drawing-room, I found, to my great astonishment, I will not say more, that a gentleman, a stranger to me, was already there, seated at the fire, opposite my mother, and with that easy air that bespoke his visit was not merely accidental, but a matter of pre-arrangement. Whatever my looks might have conveyed, I know not, but I was not given the opportunity for a more explicit inquiry, when my mother, in her stateliest of manners, arose and said,

" 'Richard, I wish to present you to my esteemed friend, Lord Netherby; a gentleman to whose kindness you are indebted for any favourable construction I can put upon your folly, and who has induced me to receive you here to-day.'

" 'If I knew, Madam, that such influence had been necessary, I should have hesitated before I laid myself under so deep an obligation to his Lordship, to whose name and merits I confess myself a stranger.'

" 'I am but too happy, Captain Forester,' interposed the Earl, 'if any little interest I possess in Lady Wallincourt's esteem enables me to contribute to your reconciliation. I know the great delicacy of an interference, in a case like the present, and how officious and impertinent the most respectful suggestions must appear, when offered by one who can lay no claim, at least to *your* good opinion.'

"A very significant emphasis on the word 'your,' a look towards my mother, and a very meaning smile from her in reply, at once revealed to me what, till then, I had not suspected; that his Lordship meditated a deeper influence over her Ladyship's heart than the mere reconciliation of a truant son to her esteem.

" 'I believe, my Lord,' said I, hastily, and I fear not without some anger—'I believe I should not have dared to decline your kind influence in my behalf, had I suspected the terms on which you would exert it. I really was not aware before that you possessed, so fully, her Ladyship's confidence.'

" 'If you read the morning papers, Captain Forester,' said he, with the blandest smile, 'you could scarcely avoid learning that my presence here is neither an intrusion nor an impertinence.'

" 'My dear mother,' cried I, forgetting all, save the long-continued grief by which my father's memory was hallowed, 'is this really the case?'

" 'I can forgive your astonishment,' replied she, with a look of anger, 'that the qualities you hold so highly in your esteem should have met favour from one so placed and gifted as the Earl of Netherby.'

" 'Nay, madam; on the contrary. My difficulty is to think, how any new proffer of attachment could find reception in a heart I fondly thought closed against such appeals; too full of its own memories of the past to profane the recollection by——'

"I hesitated and stopped. Another moment, and I would have uttered a word which for worlds I would not have spoken!

"My mother became suddenly pale as marble; and lay back in her chair as if faint and sick. His Lordship adjusted his neckcloth and his watch-chain, and walked towards the window, with an air of much awkwardness as so very courtly a personage could exhibit.

"'You see, my Lord,' said my mother—and her voice trembled at every word—'you see, I was right: I told you how much this interview would agitate and distress me.'

"'But it need not, madam,' interposed I; 'or, at all events, it may be rendered very brief. I sought an opportunity of speaking to you, in the hope, that whatever impressions you may have received of my conduct in Ireland, were either exaggerated or unjust: that I might convince you, however I may have erred in prudence or judgment, I have transgressed neither in honour nor good faith.'

"'Vindications,' said my mother, 'are very weak things in the face of direct facts. Did you, or did you not, resign your appointment on the Viceroy's staff—I stop not to ask with what scant courtesy—that you might be free to rove over the country, on some knight-errant absurdity? Did you, after having one disreputable quarrel in the same neighbourhood, again involve yourself and your name in an affair with a notorious mob-orator and disturber, and thus become the "celebrity" of the newspapers for at least a fortnight? And lastly, when I hoped, by absence from England, and foreign service, to erase the memory of these follies—to give them no harsher name—did you not refuse the appointment, and, without advice or permission, sell out of the army altogether?'

"'Without adverting to the motives, madam, you have so kindly attributed to me, I beg to say "yes" to all your questions. I am no longer an officer in his Majesty's service.'

"'Nor any longer a member of *my* family, sir,' said my mother, passionately; 'at least so far as the will rests with me. A gentleman so very independent in his principles is doubtless not less so in his circumstances. You are entitled to five thousand pounds only, by your father's will: this, if I mistake not, you have received and spent many a day ago. I will not advert to what my original intentions in your behalf were; they are recorded, however, in this paper, which you, my Lord, have read.' Here her Ladyship drew forth a document, like a law-paper, while the Earl bowed a deep acquiescence, and muttered something like—

"'Very generous and noble-minded, indeed!'

"'Yes, sir,' resumed my mother, 'I had no other thought or object, save in establishing you in a position suitable to your name and family; you have thought fit to oppose my wishes on every point, and here I end the vain struggle.' So saying, she tore the paper in pieces, and threw the fragments into the fire.

"A deep silence ensued, which I, for many reasons, had no inducement to break. The Earl coughed and hemmed three or four times, as though endeavouring to hit upon something that might relieve the general embarrassment, but my mother was again the first to speak.

"'I have no doubt, sir, you have determined on some future career. I am not indiscreet enough to inquire what, but that you may not enter upon it quite unprovided, I have settled upon you the sum of four hundred pounds yearly. Do not mistake me, nor suppose that this act proceeds from any lingering hope on my part that you will attempt to retrace your false steps, and recover the lost place in my affection. I am too well acquainted with the family gift of determination, as it is flatteringly styled, to think so. You owe this consideration entirely to the kind interference of the Earl of Netherby Nay, my Lord, it is but fair that you should have any merit the act confers, where you have incurred all the responsibility.'

"'I will relieve his Lordship of both,' said I. 'I beg to decline your Ladyship's generosity and his Lordship's kindness, with the self-same feeling of respect.'

"'My dear Captain Forester, wait one moment,' said Lord Netherby, taking my arm. 'Let me speak to you, even for a few moments.'

"'You mistake him, my Lord,' said my mother, with a scornful smile while she arose to leave the room—'you mistake him much.'

"'Pray hear me out,' said Lord Netherby, taking my hand in both his own. 'It is no time, nor a case for any rash resolves,' whispered he; 'Lady Wallincourt has been misinformed—her mind has been warped by stories of one kind or other. Go to her, explain fully and openly everything.'

"'Her Ladyship is gone, my Lord,' exclaimed I, stopping him.

"Yes, she had left the room while we were yet speaking. This was my last adieu from my mother! I remember little more, though Lord Netherby detained me still some time, and spoke with much kindness; indeed, throughout, his conduct was graceful and good-natured."

"Why should I weary you longer? Why speak of the long dreary night, and the longer day that followed this scene—swayed by different impulses—now hoping and fearing alternately—not daring to seek counsel from my friends, because I well knew what worldly advice would be given—I was wretched. In the very depth of my despondency, like a ray of sunlight darting through some crevice of a prisoner's cell, came your own words to me, 'Be a soldier in more than garb or name, be one in the generous ardour of a bold career. Let it be your boast that you started fairly in the race, and so distanced your competitors.' I caught at the suggestion with avidity. I was no more depressed or downhearted. I felt as if, throwing off my load of care, a better and a brighter day was about to break for me; the same evening I left London for Plymouth, and became a Volunteer.

"Before concluding these lines, I would ask why you tell me no more of

Miss Darcy than that 'she is well, and, the reverse of her fortune considered, in spirits.' Am I to learn no more than that? will you not say if my name is ever spoken by, or before her? How am I remembered? Has time, have my changed fortunes softened her stern determination towards me? Would that I could know this—would that I could divine what may lurk in her heart of compassionate pity for one who resigned all for her love, and lost With all my gratitude for your kindness, when I well-nigh believed none remained in the world for me,

"I am, yours in sincere affection,
"RICHARD FORESTER.

"I forgot to ask if you can read one strange mystery of this business, at least so the words seem to imply? Lord Netherby said, when endeavouring to dissuade me from leaving my mother's house, 'Remember, Captain Forester, that Lady Wallincourt's prejudices regarding your Irish friends have something stronger than mere caprice to strengthen them. You must not ask her to forget as well as forgive, all at once.' Can you interpret this riddle for me? for although at the time it made little impression, it recurs to my mind now twenty times a day."

Here concluded Forester's letter. A single line in pencil was written at the foot, and signed "M. D.:" "I am a bad prophet, or the Volunteer will turn out better than the Aide-de-camp."

CHAPTER LII.

A DINNER AT CON HEFFERNAN'S.

WHEN the Union was carried, and the new order of affairs in Ireland assumed an appearance of permanence, a general feeling of discontent began to exhibit itself in every class in the capital. The Patriots saw themselves neglected by the Government, without having reaped in popularity a recompense for their independence. The mercantile interest perceived, even already, the falling off in trade from the removal of a wealthy aristocracy: and the supporters of the Minister, or such few as still lingered in Dublin, began to suspect how much higher terms they might have exacted for their adhesion, had they only anticipated the immensity of the sacrifice to which they contributed.

Save that comparatively small number, who had bargained for English Peerages and English rank, and had thereby bartered their nationality, none were satisfied.

Even the moderate men—that intelligent fraction who believe that no changes are fraught with one-half the good or evil their advocates or opponents imagine—even they were disappointed on finding that the incorporation of the Irish Parliament with that of England was the chief element of the new measure, and no more intimate or solid Union contemplated. The shrewd men of every party saw, not only how difficult would be the future government of the country, but that the critical moment was come which should decide into whose hands the chief influence would fall. Among these speculators on the future, Mr. Heffernan held a prominent place. No man knew better the secret machinery of office, none had seen more of that game, half fair, half foul, by which an administration is sustained. He knew, moreover, the character and capability of every public man in Ireland, had been privy to their waverings and hesitations, and even their bargains with the Crown; he knew where gratified ambition had rendered a new Peer indifferent to a future temptation, and also, where abortive negotiations had sowed the seeds of a lingering disaffection.

To construct a new Party from these scattered elements—a Party which, possessing wealth and station, had not yet tasted any of the sweets of patronage, was the task he now proposed to himself. By this Party, of whom he himself was to be the organ, he hoped to control the minister, and support him by turns. Of those already purchased by the Government, few would care to involve themselves once more in the fatigue of a public life. Many would gladly repose on the rewards of their victory—many would shrink from the obloquy their reappearance would inevitably excite. Mr. Heffernan had then to choose his friends either from that moderate section of politicians, whom scruples of conscience or inferiority of ability had left unbought, or the more energetic faction, suddenly called into existence by the success of the French Revolution, and of which O'Halloran was the leader. For many reasons his choice fell on the former. Not only because they possessed that standing and influence which, derived from property, would be most regarded in England, but that their direction and guidance would be an easier task; whereas the others, more numerous and more needy, could only be purchased by actual place or pension, while in O'Halloran, Heffernan would always have a dangerous rival, who, if he played subordinate for a while, it would only be at the price of absolute rule, hereafter.

From the moment Lord Castlereagh withdrew from Ireland, Mr. Heffernan commenced his intrigue. At first, by a tour of visits through the country, in which he contrived to sound the opinions of a great number of persons, and subsequently, by correspondence, so artfully sustained, as to induce many to commit themselves to a direct line of action, which, when discussing, they had never speculated on seeing realised.

With a subtlety of no common kind, and an indefatigable industry, Heffernan laboured in the cause during the summer and autumn, and with such success, that there was scarcely a county in Ireland where he had not secured some leading adherent, while for many of the boroughs he had already entered into plans for the support of new candidates of his own opinions.

The views he put forward were simply these: Ireland can no longer be governed by an Oligarchy, however powerful. It must be ruled either by the weight and influence of the country gentlemen, or left to the mercy of the Demagogue. The Gentry must be rewarded for their adhesion, and enabled to maintain their pre-eminence, by handing over to them the patronage, not in part or in fractions, but wholly and solely. Every civil appointment must be filled up by them—the Church—the Law—the Revenue—the Police, must all be theirs. "The great aristocracy," said he, "have obtained the Marquisates and Earldoms; Bishoprics and Governments have rewarded their services. It is now *our* turn, and if our prizes be less splendid and showy, they are not devoid of some sterling qualities.

"To make Ireland ungovernable without us, must be our aim and object—to embarrass and confound every administration—to oppose the Ministers—pervert their good objects and exaggerate their bad. Pledged to no distinct line of acting, we can be Patriotic when it suits us, and declaim on popular rights when nothing better offers. Acting in concert, and diffusing an influence in every county and town and corporation, what Ministry can long resist us, or what Government anxious for office would refuse to make terms with us? With station to influence society—wealth to buy the press—activity to watch and counteract our enemies, I see nothing which can arrest our progress. We must and will succeed."

Such was the conclusion of a letter he wrote to one of his most trusted allies; a letter written to invite his presence in Dublin, where a meeting of the leading men of the new party was to be held, and their engagements for the future determined upon.

For this meeting Heffernan made the greatest exertions, not only that it might include a great portion of the wealth and influence of the land, but that a degree of *éclat* and splendour should attend it, the more likely to attract notice, from the secrecy maintained as to its object and intention. Many were invited on the consideration of the display their presence would make in the capital; and not a few were tempted by the opportunity for exhibiting their equipages and their liveries at a season when the recognised leaders of fashion were absent.

It is no part of our object here to dwell on this well-known intrigue, one which at the time occupied no small share of public attention, and even excited the curiosity and the fears of the Government. Enough when we say that Mr. Heffernan's disappointments were numerous and severe. Letters of apology, some couched in terms of ambiguous cordiality, others less equivocally cold, came pouring in for the last fortnight. The Noble Lord destined to fill the chair regretted deeply that domestic affairs of a most pressing nature would not permit of his presence. The Baronet who should move the first resolution would be compelled to be absent from Ireland; the Seconder was laid up with the gout. Scarcely a single person of influence had promised his attendance; the greater number had given vague and conditional replies, evidently to gain time and consult the feeling of their country neighbours.

These refusals and subterfuges were a sad damper to Mr. Heffernan' hopes. To any one less sanguine, they would have led to a total abandonment of the enterprise. He, however, was made of sterner stuff, and resolved, if the demonstration could effect no more, it could at least be used as a threat to the Government—a threat of not less power because its terrors were involved in mystery. With all these disappointments time sped on, the important day arrived, and the great room of the Rotunda, hired specially for the occasion, was crowded by a numerous assemblage, to whose proceedings no member of the public press was admitted. Notice was given that in due time a declaration, drawn up by a Committee, would be published, but until then the most profound secrecy wrapped their objects and intentions.

The meeting, convened for one o'clock, separated at five; and, save the unusual concourse of carriages, and the spectacle of some liveries, new to the capital, there seemed nothing to excite the public attention. No loud-tongued orator was heard from without; nor did a single cheer mark the reception of any welcome sentiment; and as the members withdrew, the sarcastic allusions of the mob intimated that they were supposed to be a new sect of "Quakers." Heffernan's carriage was the last to leave the door, and it was remarked, as he entered it, that he looked agitated and ill—signs which few had ever remarked in him before. He drove rapidly home, where a small and select party of friends had been invited by him to dinner.

He made a hasty toilet, and entered the drawing-room a few moments after the first knock at the street door announced the earliest guest. It was an old and intimate friend, Sir Giles St. George, a south-country Baronet of old family, but small fortune, who for many years had speculated on Heffernan's interest in his behalf. He was a shrewd, coarse man, who, from eccentricity and age, had obtained, a species of moral "writ of ease," absolving him from all observance of the usages in common among all well-bred people—a privilege he certainly did not seem disposed to let rust from disuse.

"Well, Con," said he, as he stood with his back to the fire, and his hands deeply thrust into his breeches-pockets—"well, Con, your Convention has been a damnable failure. Where the devil did you get up such a rabble of briefless barristers, ungowned attorneys, dissenting ministers, and illegitimate sons? I'd swear, out of your seven hundred, there were not five-and-twenty possessed of a fifty-pound freehold—not five who could defy the sheriff in their own county."

Heffernan made no reply, but with arms crossed, and his head leaned forward, walked slowly up and down the room, while the other resumed,

"As for old Killowen, who filled the chair, that was enough to damn the whole thing. One of King James's Lords, forsooth!—why, man, what country gentleman of any pretension could give precedence to a fellow like that, who neither reads, writes, nor speaks the King's English—and your great gun, Mr. Hickman O'Reilly——"

"False-hearted scoundrel!" muttered Heffernan, half aloud.

"Faith he may be, but he's the cleverest of the pack. I liked his speech well. There was good common sense in his asking for some explicit plan of proceeding—what you meant to do, and how to do it. Eh, Con, that was to the point."

"To the point!" repeated Heffernan, scornfully; "yes, as the declaration of an informer, that he will betray his colleagues, is to the point!"

"And then his motion to admit the reporters," said St. George, as with a malignant pleasure he continued to suggest matter of annoyance.

"He's mistaken, however," said Heffernan, with a sarcastic bitterness that came from his heart. "The day for rewards is gone by. He'll never get the Baronetcy by supporting the Government in this way. It is the precarious, uncertain ally they look more after. There is consummate wisdom, Giles, in not saying one's last word. O'Reilly does not seem aware of that. Here come Godfrey and Hume," said he, as he looked out of the window. "Burton has sent an apology."

"And who is our sixth?"

"O'Reilly—and here's his carriage. See how the people stare admiringly at his green liveries; they scarcely guess that the owner is meditating a change of colour. Well, Godfrey, in time for once. Why, Robert, you seem quite fagged by your day's exertion. Ah! Mr. O'Reilly, delighted to find you punctual. Let me present you to my old friend Sir Giles St. George. I believe, gentlemen, you need no introduction to each other. Burton has disappointed us—so we may order dinner at once."

As Mr. Heffernan took the head of the table, not a sign of his former chagrin remained to be seen. An air of easy conviviality had entirely replaced his previous look of irritation, and in his laughing eye and mellow voice there seemed the clearest evidence of a mind perfectly at ease, and a spirit well disposed to enjoy the pleasures of the board. Of his guests, Godfrey was a leading member of the Irish bar, a man of good private fortune and a large practice, who, out of whim rather than from any great principle, had placed himself in continual opposition to the Government, and felt grievously injured and affronted when the Minister, affecting to overlook his enmity, offered him a silk gown. Hume was a Commissioner of Customs, and had been so for some thirty years; his only ambition in life being to retire on his full salary, having previously filled his department with his sons and grandsons. The gentle remonstrances of the Secretary against his plan had made him one of the disaffected, but without courage to avow or influence to direct his animosity. Of Mr. O'Reilly the reader needs no further mention. Such was the party who now sat at a table most luxuriously supplied; for although Heffernan was very far from a frequent inviter, yet his dinners were admirably arranged, and the excellence of his wine was actually a mystery among the *bon-vivants* of the capital. The conversation turned of course upon the great event of the day, but so artfully was the subject managed by Heffernan that the discussion took rather the shape of criticism on the several speakers, and their styles of delivery, than on the matter of the meeting itself.

"How eager the Castle folks will be to know all about it," said Godfrey. "Cooke is, I hear, in a sad taking to learn the meaning of the gathering."

"I fancy, sir," said St. George, "they are more indifferent than you suppose. A meeting held by individuals of a certain rank and property, and convened with a certain degree of ostentation, can scarcely ever be formidable to a government."

"You forget the Volunteers," said Heffernan.

"No; I remember their assembling well enough, and a very absurd business they made of it. The Bishop of Downe was the only man of nerve amongst them; and as for Lord Charlemont, the thought of an attainder was never out of his head till the whole association was disbanded."

"They were very formidable, indeed," said Heffernan, gravely. "I can assure you that the Government were far more afraid of their defenders than of the French."

"A government that is ungrateful enough to neglect its supporters," chimed in Hume, "men that have spent their best years in its service, can scarcely esteem itself very secure. In the department I belong to myself, for instance——"

"Yours is a very gross case," interrupted Heffernan, who from old experience knew what was coming, and wished to arrest it.

"Thirty-four years, come November next, have I toiled as a commissioner."

"Unpaid!" exclaimed St. George, with a well-simulated horror—"unpaid!"

"No, sir; not without my salary, of course. I never heard of any man holding an office in the Revenue for the amusement it might afford him. Did you, Godfrey?"

"As for me," said the lawyer, "I spurn their patronage. I well know the price men pay for such favours."

"What object could it be to *you*," said Heffernan, "to be made Attorney-General or placed on the Bench, a man independent in every sense; so I said to Castlereagh, when he spoke to me on the subject: 'Never mind Godfrey,' said I, 'he'll refuse your offers; you'll only offend him by solicitation;' and when he mentioned the 'Rolls'——" here Heffernan paused, and filled his glass leisurely. An interruption contrived to stimulate Godfrey's curiosity, and which perfectly succeeded, as he asked, in a voice of tremulous eagerness—"Well, what did you say?"

"Just as I replied before—'he'll refuse you.'"

"Quite right, perfectly right—you have my unbounded gratitude for the answer," said Godfrey, swallowing two bumpers as rapidly as he could fill them.

"Very different treatment from what I met—an old and tried supporter of the party," said Hume, turning to O'Reilly, and opening upon him the whole narrative of his long-suffering neglect.

"It's quite clear, then," said St. George, "that we are agreed—the best thing for us would be a change of Ministry."

"I don't think so at all," interposed Heffernan.

"Why, Con," interrupted the Baronet, "they should have *you* at any price—however, these fellows have learned the trick—the others know nothing about it. You'd be in office before twenty-four hours."

"So I might to-morrow," said Heffernan. "There's scarcely a single post of high emolument and trust that I have not been offered and refused. The only things I ever stipulated for in all my connexion with the Government were certain favours for my personal friends." Here he looked significantly towards O'Reilly, but the glance was intercepted by the Commissioner, who cried out, "Well, could they say I had no claim? Could they deny thirty-four years of toil and slavery?"

"And in the case for which I was most interested," resumed Heffernan, not heeding the interruption, "the favour I sought would have been more justly bestowed from the rank and merits of the party, than as a recompense for any services of mine."

"I won't say that, Heffernan," said Hume, with a look of modesty, who with the most implicit good faith supposed he was the party alluded to; "I won't go that far; but I will and must say, that after four-and-thirty years' service as a Commissioner——"

"A man must have laid by a devilish pretty thing for the rest of his life," said St. George, who felt all the bitterness of a narrow income augmented by the croaking complaints of the well-salaried official.

"Well, I hope better days are coming for all of us," said Heffernan, desirous of concluding the subject ere it should take an untoward turn.

"You have got a very magnificent seat in the West, sir," said St. George addressing O'Reilly, who during the whole evening had done little more than assent or smile concurrence with the several speakers.

"The finest thing in Ireland," interrupted Heffernan.

"Nay, that is saying too much," said O'Reilly, with a look of half-real, half-affected bashfulness. "The abbey certainly stands well, and the timber is well grown."

"Are you able to see Clew Bay from the small drawing-room still, for I remember remarking that the larches on the side of the glen would eventually intercept the prospect?"

"You know the abbey, then?" asked O'Reilly, forgetting to answer the question addressed to him.

"Oh, I know it well. My family is connected—distantly, I believe, with the Darcys, and in former days we were intimate. A very sweet place it was; I am speaking of thirty years ago, and of course it must have improved since that."

"My friend here has given it every possible opportunity," said Heffernan with a courteous inclination of the head.

"I've no doubt of it," replied St. George, "but neither money nor bank securities will make trees grow sixty feet in a twelvemonth. The improvements I allude to were made by Maurice Darcy's father; he sunk forty thousand pounds in draining, planting, subsoiling, and what not. He left a rent-charge in his will to continue his plans, and Maurice and his son—what's the young fellow called—Lionel, isn't it? well, they are, or rather they were, bound to expend a very heavy sum annually on the property."

A theme less agreeable to O'Reilly's feelings could scarcely have been started, and though Heffernan saw as much, he did not dare to interrupt it suddenly, for fear of any unpalatable remark from St. George. Whether from feeling that the subject was a painful one, or that he liked to indulge his loquacity in detailing various particulars of the Darcys and their family circumstances, the old man went on without ceasing. Now, narrating some strange caprice of an ancestor in one century; now, some piece of good fortune that occurred to another. "You know the old prophecy in the family, I suppose, Mr. O'Reilly?" said he, "though to be sure you are not very likely to give it credence."

"I scarcely can say I remember what you allude to."

"By Jove, I thought every old woman in the West would have told it to you. How is this the doggrel runs—ay, here it is,—

A new name in this house shall never begin
Till twenty-one Darcys have died in Gwynne.

Now, they say that, taking into account all of the family who have fallen in battle, been lost at sea, and so on, only eleven of the stock died at the abbey."

Although O'Reilly affected to smile at the old rhyme, his cheek became deadly pale, and his hand shook as he lifted the glass to his lips. It was no vulgar sense of fear, no superstitious dread that moved his cold and calculating spirit, but an emotion of suppressed anger that the ancient splendour of the Darcys should be thus placed side by side with his own unhonoured and unknown family.

"I don't think I ever knew one of these good legends have even so much of truth—though the credit is now at an end," said Heffernan, gaily.

"I'll engage old Darcy's butler wouldn't agree with you," replied St. George. "Ay, and Maurice himself had a great dash of old Irish superstition in him, for a clever, sensible fellow as he was."

"It only remains for my friend here, then, to fit up a room for the Darcys and invite them to die there at their several conveniences," said Con, laughing. "I see no other mode of fulfilling the destiny."

"There never was a man played his game worse," resumed St. George, who with a pertinacious persistence continued the topic. "He came of age with a large unencumbered estate, great family influence, and a very fair share of abilities. It was the fashion to say he had more, but I never thought so, and now, look at him!"

"He had very heavy losses at play," said Heffernan, "certainly."

"What if he had? They never could have materially affected a fortune like his. No, no. I believe 'Honest Tom' finished him—raising money to pay off old debts, and then never clearing away the liabilities. What a stale trick! and how invariably it succeeds!"

"You do not seem, sir, to take into account an habitually expensive mode of living," insinuated O'Reilly, quietly.

"An item, of course—but only an item in the sum total," replied St. George. "No man can eat and drink above ten thousand a year, and Darcy had considerably more. No; he might have lived as he pleased, had he escaped the acquaintance of honest Tom Gleeson. By-the-by, Con, is there any truth in the story they tell about this fellow, and that he really was more actuated by a feeling of revenge towards Darcy than a desire for money?"

"I never heard the story. Did you, Mr. O'Reilly?" asked Heffernan.

"Never," said O'Reilly, affecting an air of unconcern, very ill consorting with his pale cheek and anxious eye.

"The tale is simply this. That as Gleeson waxed wealthy, and began to assume a position in life, he one day called on the Knight to request him to put his name up for ballot at 'Daly's.' Darcy was thunderstruck, for it was in those days when the Club was respectable—but still the Knight had tact enough to dissemble his astonishment, and would, doubtless, have got through the difficulty, had it not been for Bagenal Daly, who was present, and called out, 'Wait till Tuesday, Maurice, for I mean to propose M'Cleery, the breeches-maker, and then the thing won't seem so remarkable!' Gleeson smiled, and slipped away, with an oath to his own heart, to be revenged on both of them. If there be any truth in the story, he did ruin Daly, by advising some money-lender to buy up all his liabilities."

"I must take the liberty to correct you, sir," said O'Reilly, actually trembling with anger. "If your agreeable anecdote has no better foundation than the concluding hypothesis, its veracity is inferior to its ingenuity. The gentleman you are pleased to call a money-lender, is my father; the conduct you allude to was simply the advance of a large sum on mortgage."

"Foreclosed, like Darcy's, perhaps," said St. George, his irascible face becoming blood-red with passion.

"Come, come, Giles, you really can know nothing of the subject you are talking of—besides, to Mr. O'Reilly the matter is a personal one."

"So it is," muttered St. George; "and if report speaks truly, as unpleasant as personal."

This insulting remark was not heard by O'Reilly, who was deeply engaged in explaining to the lawyer beside him the minute legal details of the circumstance.

"Shrewd a fellow as Gleeson was," said St. George, interrupting O'Reilly, by addressing the lawyer, "they say he has left some flaw open in the matter, and that Darcy may recover a very large portion of the lost estate."

"Yes; if for instance this bond should be destroyed. He might move in Equity——"

"He'd move Heaven and Earth, sir, if it's Bagenal Daly you mean," said St. George, who had stimulated his excitement by drinking freely. "Some will tell you that he is a steadfast, firm friend; but I'll vouch for it, a more determined enemy never drew breath."

"Very happily for the world we live in, sir," said O'Reilly, "there are agencies more powerful than the revengeful and violent natures of such men as Mr. Daly."

"He's every jot as quick-sighted as he's determined, and when he wagered a hogshead of claret that Darcy would one day sit again at the head of his table in Gwynne Abbey——"

"Did he make such a bet?" asked O'Reilly with a faint laugh.

"Yes; he walked down the club-room, and offered it to any one present, and none seemed to fancy it; but young Kelly, of Kilclare, who being a new member just come in, perhaps thought there might be some *éclat* in booking a bet with Bagenal Daly."

"Would you like to back his opinion, sir?" said O'Reilly, with a simulated softness of voice, "for although I rarely wager, I should have no objection to convenience you, here, leaving the amount entirely at your option."

"Which means," said St. George, as his eyes sparkled with wine and passion, "that the weight of *your* purse is to tilt the beam against that of *my* opinion. Now, I beg leave to tell you——"

"Let me interrupt you, Giles; I never knew my Burgundy disagree with any man before, but I'd smash every bottle of it to-morrow if I thought it could make so pleasant a fellow so wrong-headed and unreasonable. What say you if we qualify it with some cognac and water?"

"Maurice Darcy is my relative," said St. George, pushing his glass rudely from him, "and I have yet to learn the unreasonableness of wishing well to a member of one's own family. His father and mine were like brothers! Ay, by Jove! I wonder what either of them would think of the changes time has wrought in their sons' fortunes:" his voice dropped into a low, muttering sound, while he mumbled on, "one, a beggar and an exile, the other"—here his eye twinkled with a malicious intelligence as he glanced around the board—"the other the guest of Con Heffernan." He arose as he spoke, and fortunately the noise thus created prevented his words being overheard. "You're right, Con," said he, "that Burgundy has been too much for me. The wine is unimpeachable, notwithstanding."

The others rose also; although pressed in all the customary hospitality of the period to have "one bottle more," they were resolute in taking leave, doubtless not sorry to escape the risk of any unpleasant termination to the evening's entertainment.

The lawyer and the commissioner agreed to see St. George home, for although long seasoned to excesses, age had begun to tell upon him, and his limbs were scarcely more under control than his tongue. O'Reilly had dropped his handkerchief, he was not sure whether in the drawing or the dinner-room, and this delayed him a few moments behind the rest, and although he declared, at each moment, the loss of no consequence, and repeated his "good night," Heffernan held his hand and would not suffer him to leave.

"Try under Mr. O'Reilly's chair, Thomas.—Singular specimen of a by-gone day, the worthy Baronet!" said he, with a shrug of his shoulders. "Would you believe it, he and Darcy have not been on speaking terms for thirty years, and yet how irritable he showed himself in his behalf!"

"He seems to know something of the family affairs, however," said O'Reilly, cautiously.

"Not more than club gossip: all that about Daly and his wager is a week old."

"I hope my father may never hear it," said O'Reilly, compassionately: "he has all the irritability of age, and these reports invariably urge him on to harsh measures, which, by the least concession, he would never have pursued. The Darcys, indeed, have to thank themselves for any severity they have experienced at our hands. Teasing litigation and injurious reports of us have met all our efforts at conciliation."

"A compromise would have been much better, and more reputable for all parties," said Heffernan, as he turned to stir the fire, and thus purposely averted his face while making the remark.

"So it would," said O'Reilly, hurriedly; then stopping abruptly short, he stammered out, "I don't exactly know what you mean by the word, but if it implies a more amicable settlement of all disputed points between us, I perfectly agree with you."

Heffernan never spoke: a look of cool self-possession and significance was all his reply. It seemed to say, "Don't hope to cheat *me*; however, you may rely on my discretion."

"I declare my handkerchief is in my pocket all this while," said O'Reilly, trying to conceal his rising confusion with a laugh. "Good night, once more—you're thinking of going over to England to-morrow evening?"

"Yes, if the weather permits, I'll sail at seven. Can I be of any service to you?"

"Perhaps so: I may trouble you with a commission. Good night."

"So, Mr. Hickman, you begin to feel the hook! Now let us see if we cannot play the fish, without letting him know the weakness of the tackle!" said Heffernan, as he looked after him, and then slowly retraced his steps to the now deserted drawing-room.

"How frequently will chance play the game more skilfully for us than all our cleverness," said he, while he paced the room alone. "That old bear, St. George, who might have ruined everything, has done me good service. O'Reilly's suspicions are awakened—his fears are aroused: could I only find a clue to his terror I could hold him as fast by his fears as by this same Baronetcy. This Baronetcy," added he, with a sneering laugh, "that I am to negotiate for, and—be refused!"

With this sentiment of honest intentions on his lips, Mr. Heffernan retired to rest, and, if this true history is to be credited, to sleep soundly till morning.

CHAPTER LIII.

PAUL DEMPSEY'S WALK.

WITH the most eager desire to accomplish his mission, Paul Dempsey did not succeed in reaching the Corvy until late on the day after Miss Daly's visit. He set out originally by paths so secret and circuitous that he lost his way, and was obliged to pass his night among the hills, where, warned by the deep thundering of the sea that the cliffs were near, he was fain to await daybreak ere he ventured further. The trackless waste over which his way led was no bad emblem of poor Paul's mind, as, cowering beneath a sand-hill, he shivered through the long hours of night. Swayed by various impulses, he could determine on no definite line of action, and wavered, and doubted, and hesitated, till his very brain was addled by its operations.

At one moment he was disposed, like good Launcelot Gobbo, to "run for it," and, leaving Darcy and all belonging to him to their several fates, to provide for his own safety; when suddenly a dim vision of meeting Maria Daly in this world, or the next, and being called to account for his delinquency, routed such determinations. Then he revelled in the glorious opportunity for gossip afforded by the whole adventure. How he should astonish Coleraine and its neighbourhood by his revelations of the Knight and his family. Gossip in all its moods and tenses, from the vague indicative of mere innuendo, to the full subjunctive of open defamation! Not indeed that Mr. Dempsey loved slander for itself; on the contrary, his temperament was far more akin to kindliness than its opposite; but the passion for retailing one's neighbour's foibles or misfortunes is an impulse that admits no guidance; and, as the gambler would ruin his best friend at play, so would the professed gossip calumniate the very nearest and dearest to him on earth. There are in the social, as in the mercantile world, characters who never deal in the honest article of commerce, but have a store of damaged, injured, or smuggled goods, to be hawked about surreptitiously, and always to be sold in the "strictest secrecy." Mr. Dempsey was a pedlar in this wise, and, if truth must be told, he did not dislike his trade.

And yet, at moments, thoughts of another and more tender kind were wafted across Paul's mind, not resting indeed long enough to make any deep impression, but still leaving behind them, as pleasant thoughts always will, little twilights of happiness. Paul had been touched—a mere graze—skin deep—but still touched, by Helen Darcy's beauty and fascinations. She had accompanied him more than once on the piano while he sang, and whether the long-fringed eyelashes and the dimpled cheek had done the mischief, or that the thoughtful tact with which she displayed Paul's good notes and glossed over his false ones had won his gratitude, certain is it, he had already felt a very sensible regard for the young lady, and more than once caught himself, when thinking about her, speculating on the speedy demise of Bob Dempsey, of Dempsey's Grove, and all the consequences that might ensue therefrom.

If the enjoyment Mr. Dempsey's various peculiarities afforded Helen suggested on her part the semblance of pleasure in his society, Paul took these indications all in his own favour, and even catechised himself how far he might be deemed culpable in winning the affections of a charming young lady, so long as his precarious condition forbid all thought of matrimony. Now, however, that he knew who the family really were, such doubts were much allayed, for, as he wisely remarked to himself, "Though they are ruined, there's always nice picking in the wreck of an Indiaman!" Such were the thoughts by which his way was beguiled, when late in the afternoon he reached the Corvy.

Lady Eleanor and her daughter were out walking when Mr. Dempsey arrived, and, having cautiously reconnoitred the premises, ventured to approach the door. All was quiet and tranquil about the cottage; so, reassured by this, he peered through the window into the large hall, where a cheerful fire now blazed and shed a mellow glow over the strange decorations of the chamber. Mr. Dempsey had often desired an opportunity of examining these curiosities at his leisure. Not indeed prompted thereto by any antiquarian taste, but, from a casual glance at the inscriptions, he calculated on the amount of private history of the Dalys he should obtain. Stray and independent facts, it is true, but to be arranged by the hand of a competent and clever commentator.

With cautious hand he turned the handle of the door and entered.

There he stood, in the very midst of the coveted objects, and never did humble bookworm gaze on the rich titles of an ample library with more enthusiastic pleasure. He drew a long breath to relieve his overburdened heart, and glutted his eyes in ecstasy on every side. Enthusiasm takes its tone from individuality, and doubtless Mr. Dempsey felt at that moment something as Belzoni might, when, unexpectedly admitted within some tomb of the Pyramids, he found himself about to unravel some secret history of the Pharaohs.

"Now for it," said he, half aloud; "let us do the thing in order; and first of all, what have we here?" He stooped and read an inscription attached to a velvet coat embroidered with silver:

"Coat worn by B. D. in his duel with Colonel Matthews—62—the puncture under the sword-arm being a tierce outside the guard; a very rare point, and which cost the giver seriously."

"He killed Matthews, of course," added Dempsey; "the passage can mean nothing else, so let us be accurate as to fact and date." So saying, he proceeded to note down the circumstance in a little memorandum-book. "So!" added he, as he read his note over; "now for the next. What can this misshapen lump of metal mean?"

"A piece of brute gold, presented with twelve female slaves by the chiefs of Doolawochyeekeka on B. D.'s assuming the sovereignty of the island."

"Brute gold," said Mr. Dempsey; "devilish little of the real thing about it, I'll be sworn! I suppose the ladies were about equally refined and valuable."

"Glove dropped by the Infanta Donna Isidora within the arena at Madrid, a few moments after Ruy Peres da Castres was gored to death."

A prolonged low whistle from Mr. Dempsey was the only comment he made on this inscription, while he stooped to examine the fragment of a bull's horn, from which a rag of scarlet cloth was hanging. The inscription ran, "Portion of horn broken as the bull fell against the barrier of the Circus. The cloth was part of Da Castres' vest."

A massive antique helmet, of immense size and weight, lay on the floor beside this. It was labelled, "Casque of Rudolp v. Hapsbourg, presented to B. D. after the tilt at Regensburg by Edric Conrad Wilhelm Kur Furst von Bayern. A.D. 1750."

A splendid goblet of silver gilt, beautifully chased and ornamented, was inscribed on the metal as being the gift of the Doge of Venice to his friend Bagenal Daly, and underneath was written on a card, "This cup was drained to the bottom at a draught by B. D. after a long and deep carouse, the liquor strong 'Vino di Cypro.' The Doge tried it and failed; the mark within shows how far he drank."

"By Jove! what a pull," exclaimed Dempsey, who, as he peered into the capacious vessel, looked as if he would not object to try his own prowess at the feat.

Wonderment at this last achievement seemed completely to have taken possession of Mr. Dempsey, for while his eyes ranged over weapons of every strange form and shape—armour, idols, stuffed beasts and birds, they invariably came back to the huge goblet with an admiring wonder, that showed that here at least there was an exploit whose merits he could thoroughly appreciate.

"A half-gallon can is nothing to it!" muttered he, as he replaced it on its bracket.

The reflection was scarcely uttered, when the quick tramp of a horse and the sound of wheels without startled him. He hastened to the window just in time to perceive a jaunting-car drive up to the wicket, from which three men descended. Two, were common-looking fellows in dark upper coats and glazed hats; the third, better dressed, and with a half-gentlemanlike air, seemed the superior. He threw off a loose travelling coat, and discovered, to Mr. Dempsey's horror, the features of his late patient at Larne, the sheriff's officer from Dublin. Yes, there was no doubt about it. That smart conceited look, the sharp and turned-up nose, the scrubby whisker, proclaimed him as the terrible Anthony Nickie, of Jervas-street, a name which Mr. Dempsey had read on his portmanteau, before guessing how its owner was concerned in his own interests.

What a multitude of terrors jostled each other in his mind as the men approached the door! and what resolves did he form and abandon in the same moment! To escape by the rear of the house while the enemy was assailing the front—to barricade the premises, and stand a siege—to arm himself—and there was a choice of weapons, and give battle, were all rapid impulses, no sooner conceived than given up. A loud summons of the door-bell announced his presence, and, ere the sounds died away, Tate's creaking footstep and winter cough resounded along the corridor. Mr. Dempsey threw a last despairing glance around, and the thought flashed across him, how happily would he exchange his existence with any of the grim images and uncouth shapes that grinned and glared on every side: ay, even with that saw-mouthed crocodile that surmounted the chimney! Quick as his eye traversed the chamber, he fancied that the savage animals were actually enjoying his misery, and Sandy's counterpart appeared to show a diabolical glee at his wretched predicament. It was at this instant he caught sight of the loose folds of the Indian blanket which enveloped Bagenal Daly's image. The danger was too pressing for hesitation; he stepped into the canoe, and cowering down under the warlike figure, awaited his destiny. Scarcely had the drapery closed around him when Tate admitted the new arrival.

"The Corvy?" said Mr. Nickie to the old butler, who with decorous ceremony bowed low before him. "The Corvy, ain't it?"

"Yes, sir," replied Tate.

"All right, Mac," resumed Nickie, turning to the elder of his two followers, who had closely dogged him to the door. "Bring that carpet-bag and the small box off the car, and tell the fellow he'll have time to feed his horse at that cabin on the road-side."

He added something in a whisper, too low for Tate to hear, and then taking the carpet-bag, he flung it carelessly in a corner, while he walked forward and deposited the box on the table before the fire.

His honour is coming to dine, maybe?" asked Tate, respectfully; for old habit of his master's hospitality had made the question almost a matter of course, while age had so dimmed his eyesight, that even Anthony Nickie, passed with him for a gentleman.

"Coming to dine," repeated Nickie, with a coarse laugh; "that's a bar gain there's always two words to, my old boy. I suppose you've heard it is manners to wait to be asked, eh? without," added he, after a second's pause—"without I'm to take this as an invitation."

"I believe your honour might, then," said Tate, with a smile. "'Tis many a one I kept again the family came home for dinner, and sorrow word of it they knew till they seen them dressed in the drawing-room! And the dinner-table!" said Tate, with a sigh, half in regret over the past, half preparing himself with a sufficiency of breath for a lengthened oration—"the dinner-table! it's wishing it I am still! after laying for ten, or maybe twelve, his honour would come in and say, 'Tate, we'll be rather crowded here, for here's Sir Gore Molony and his family. You'll have to make room for five more.' Then Miss Helen would come springing in with, 'Tate, I forgot to say, Colonel Martin and his officers are to be here at dinner.' After that it would be my Lady herself, in her own quiet way, 'Mr. Wilkinson'—she nearly always called me that—'couldn't you contrive a little space here for Lady Burke and Miss Mac Donnel?' But the Captain beat all, for he'd come in after the soup was removed, with five or six gentlemen from the hunt, splashed and wet up to their necks; over he'd go to the side-table, where I'd have my knives and forks, all beautiful, and may I never, but he'd fling some here, others there, till he'd clear a space away, and then he'd cry, 'Tate, bring back the soup, and set some sherry here.' Maybe that wasn't the table for noise, drinking wine with every one at the big table, and telling such wonderful stories, that the servants didn't know what they were doing, listening to them. And the master!—the Heavens be about him!—sending me over to get the names of the gentlemen, that he might ask them to take wine with him. Oh, dear—oh, dear, I'm sure I used to think my heart was broke with it; but sure it's nigher breaking now that it's all past and over."

"You seem to have had very jolly times of it in those days," said Nickie.

"Faix, your honour might say so if you saw forty-eight sitting down to dinner every day in the parlour for seven weeks running; and Master Lionel—the Captain that is—at the head of another table in the library, with twelve or fourteen more—nice youths they wor!"

While Tate continued his retrospections, Mr. Nickie had unlocked his box, and cursorily throwing a glance over some papers, he muttered to himself a few words, and then added aloud,

"Now for business."

CHAPTER LIV.

MR. ANTHONY NICKIE, ATTORNEY-AT-LAW.

We have said that Mr. Dempsey had barely time to conceal himself when the door was opened—so narrow indeed was his escape, that had the new arrival been a second sooner, discovery would have been inevitable; as it was, the pictorial Daly and Sandy rocked violently to and fro, making their natural ferocity and grimness something even more terrible than usual. Mr. Nickie remarked nothing of this. His first care was to divest himself of certain travelling encumbrances, like one who purposes to make a visit of some duration, and then, casting a searching look around the premises, he proceeded,

"Now for Mr. Darcy——"

"If ye'r maning the Knight of Gwynne, sir,—his honour——"

"Well, is his honour at home?" said the other, interrupting with a saucy laugh.

"No, sir," said Tate, almost overpowered at the irreverence of his questioner.

"When do you expect him then—in an hour or two hours?"

"He's in England," said Tate, drawing a long breath.

"In England! What do you mean, old fellow? he has surely not left this lately?"

"Yes, sir, 'twas the King sent for him, I heerd the mistress say."

A burst of downright laughter from the stranger stopped poor Tate's explanation.

"Why, it's *you* his Majesty ought to have invited," cried Mr. Nickie, wiping his eyes, "*you yourself*, man; devilish fit company for each other you'd be."

Poor Tate had not the slightest idea of the grounds on which the stranger suggested his companionship for Royalty, but he was not the less insulted at the disparagement of his master thus implied.

"'Tis little I know about Kings or Queens," growled out the old man "but they must be made of better clay than ever I seen yet, or they're not too good company for the Knight of Gwynne."

After a stare for some seconds, half surprise, half insolence, Nickie said, "You can tell me, perhaps, if this cottage is called the 'Corvy?'"

"Ay, that's the name of it."

"The property of one Bagenal Daly, Esquire, isn't it?"

Tate nodded an assent.

"Maybe he is in England too," continued Nickie. "Perhaps it was the Queen sent for him—he's a handsome man, I suppose?"

"Faix, you can judge for yourself," said Tate, "for there he is, looking at you this minute."

Nickie turned about hastily, while a terrible fear shot through him that his remarks might have been heard by the individual himself; for, though a stranger to Daly personally, he was not so to his reputation for hare-brained daring and rashness, nor was it till he had stared at the wooden representative for some seconds that he could dispel his dread of the original.

"Is that like him?" asked he, affecting a sneer.

"As like as two pays," said Tate, "barring about the eyes; Mr. Daly's is brighter and more wild-looking. The Blessed Joseph be near us!" exclaimed the old man, crossing himself devoutly, "one would think the crayture knew what we were saying. Sorra lie in't, there's neither luck nor grace in talking about you!"

This last sentiment, uttered in a faint voice, was called forth by an involuntary shuddering of poor Mr. Dempsey, who, feeling that the whole scrutiny of the party was directed towards his hiding-place, trembled so violently, that the plumes nodded, and the bone necklace jingled with the motion.

While Mr. Nickie attributed these signs to the wind, he at the same time conceived a very low estimate of poor Tate's understanding, an impression not altogether unwarranted by the sidelong and stealthy looks which he threw at the canoe and its occupants.

"You seem rather afraid of Mr. Daly," said he, with a sneering laugh.

"And so would you be, too, if he was as near you as that chap is," replied Tate, sternly. "I've known braver-looking men than either of us not like to stand before him. I mind the day——"

Tate's reminiscences were brought to a sudden stop by perceiving his mistress and Miss Darcy approaching the cottage; and hastening forward, he threw open the door, while by way of introduction he said,

"A gentleman for the master, my Lady."

Lady Eleanor flushed up, and as suddenly grew pale. She guessed at once the man and his errand.

'The Knight of Gwynne is from home, sir," said she, in a voice her efforts could not render firm.

"I understand as much, madam," said Nickie, who was struggling to recover the easy self-possession of his manner with the butler, but whose awkwardness increased at every instant. "I believe you expect him in a day or two?

This was said to elicit if there might be some variance in the statement of Lady Eleanor and her servant.

"You are misinformed, sir. He is not in the kingdom, nor do I anticipate his speedy return."

"So I told him, my Lady," broke in the old butler. "I said the King wanted him——"

"You may leave the room, Tate," said Lady Eleanor, who perceived with annoyance the sneering expression old Tate's simplicity had called up in the stranger's face. "Now, sir," said she, turning towards him, "may I ask if your business with the Knight of Gwynne is of that nature that cannot be transacted in his absence, or through his law agent?"

"Scarcely, madam," said Nickie, with a sententious gravity, who, in the 'vantage ground his power gave him, seemed rather desirous of prolonging the interview. "Mr. Darcy's part can scarcely be performed by deputy, even if he found any one friendly enough to undertake it."

Lady Eleanor never spoke, but her hand grasped her daughter's more closely, and they both stood pale and trembling with agitation. Helen was the first to rally from this access of terror, and with an assured voice she said,

"You have heard, sir, that the Knight of Gwynne is absent; and as you say your business is with him alone, is there any further reason for your presence here?"

Mr. Nickie seemed for a moment taken aback by this unexpected speech, and for a few seconds made no answer; his nature and his calling, however, soon supplied presence of mind, and with an air of almost insolent familiarity, he answered,

"Perhaps there may be, young lady." He turned, and opening the door gave a sharp whistle, which was immediately responded to by a cry of "Here we are, sir," and the two followers already mentioned entered the cottage.

"You may have heard of such a thing as an execution, ma'am," said Nickie, addressing Lady Eleanor, in a voice of mock civility. "The attachment of property for debt. This is part of my business at the present moment."

"Do you mean here, sir—in this cottage?" asked Lady Eleanor, in an accent scarcely audible from terror.

"Yes, ma'am, just so. The law allows fourteen days for redemption, with payment of costs, until which time these men here will remain on the premises; and although these gimcracks will scarcely pay my client's costs, we must only make the best of it."

"But this property is not ours, sir. This cottage belongs to a friend."

"I am aware of that, ma'am. And that friend is about to answer for his own sins on the present occasion, and not yours. These chattels are attached as the property of Bagenal Daly, Esquire, at the suit of Peter Hickman, formerly of Loughrea, surgeon and apothecary."

"Is Mr. Daly aware—does he know of these proceedings?" gasped Lady Eleanor, faintly.

"In the multiplicity of similar affairs, ma'am, it is quite possible he may have let this one escape his memory; for, if I don't mistake, he has two actions pending in the King's Bench—an answer in equity—three cases of common assault—and a contempt of court—all upon his hands for this present session, not to speak of what this may portend."

Here he took a newspaper from his pocket, and having doubled down a paragraph, handed it to Lady Eleanor.

Overwhelmed by grief and astonishment, she made no motion to take the paper, and Mr. Nickie, turning to Helen, read aloud:

"'There is a rumour prevalent in the capital this morning, to which we cannot, in the present uncertainty as to fact, make any more than a guarded allusion. It is indeed one of those strange reports which we can neither credit nor reject—the only less probable thing than its truth, being, that any one could deliberately fabricate so foul a calumny. The story in its details we forbear to repeat; the important point, however, is, to connect the name of a well-known and eccentric late M.P. for an Irish borough with the malicious burning of Newgate, and the subsequent escape of the robber Freney.

"'The reasons alleged for this most extraordinary act are so marvellous, absurd, and contradictory, that we will not trifle with our readers' patience by recounting them. The most generally believed one, however, is, that the senator and the highwayman had maintained, for years past, an intercourse of a very confidential nature, the threat to reveal which, on his trial, Freney used as compulsory means of procuring his escape.'

"Carrick goes further," added Mr. Nickie, as he restored the paper to his pocket, "and gives the name of Bagenal Daly, Esq., in full; stating, besides, that he sailed for Halifax on Sunday last."

Lady Eleanor and Helen exchanged looks of intelligent meaning, as he finished the paragraph. To them Daly's hurried departure had a most significant importance.

"This, ma'am, among other reasons," resumed Nickie, "was another hint to my client to press his claim; for Mr. Daly's departure once known, there would soon be a scramble for the little remnant of his property. With your leave, I'll now put the keepers in possession. Perhaps you'll not be offended," added he, in a lower tone, "if I remark that it's usual to offer the men some refreshment. Come here, M'Dermot," said he, aloud—"a very respectable man, and married, too—the ladies will make you comfortable, Mick, and I'm sure you'll be civil and obliging."

A grunt and a gesture with both hands was the answer.

"Falls, we'll station you in the kitchen; mind you behave yourself."

"I'll just take a slight inventory of the principal things—a mere matter of form, ma'am—I know you'll not remove one of them," said Mr. Nickie, who, like most coarsely minded people, was never more offensive than when seeking to be complimentary. He did not notice, however, the indignant look with which his speech was received, but proceeded regularly in his office.

There is something insupportably offensive and revolting in the business-like way of those who execute the severities of the law. Like the undertaker, they can sharpen the pangs of misfortune by vulgarising its sorrows. Lady Eleanor gazed, in but half consciousness, at the scene; the self-satisfied assurance of the chief, the ruffian contentedness of his followers, grating on every prejudice of her mind. Not so Helen: more quick to reason on impressions, she took in, at a glance, their sad condition, and saw that in a few days, at furthest, they should be houseless as well as friendless in the world—no one near to counsel or to succour them! Such were her thoughts as almost mechanically her eyes followed the sheriff's officer through the chamber.

"Not that, sir," cried she, hastily, as he stopped in front of a miniature of her father, and was noting it down in his list, among the objects of the apartment—"not that, sir."

"And why not, miss?" said Nickie, with a leer of impudent familiarity.

"It is a portrait of the Knight of Gwynne, sir, and *our* property."

"Sorry for it, miss, but the law makes no distinction with regard to property on the premises. You can always recover by a replevin."

"Come, Helen, let us leave this," said Lady Eleanor, faintly; "come away, child."

"You said, sir," said Helen, turning hastily about—"you said, sir, that these proceedings were taken at the suit of Doctor Hickman. Was it his desire that we should be treated thus?"

"Upon my word, young lady, he gave no special directions on the subject nor, if he had, would it signify much. The law, once set in motion, must take its course; I suppose you know that."

Helen did not hear his speech out, for, yielding to her mother, she quitted the apartment.

Mr. Nickie stood for a few moments gazing at the door by which they had made their exit, and then, turning towards M'Dermot, with a knowing wink he said, "We'll be better friends before we part, I'll engage, little as she likes me now."

"Faix, I never seen yer equal at getting round them," answered the sub., in a voice of fawning flattery, the very opposite of his former gruff tone.

"That's the way I always begin, when they take a saucy way with them," resumed Nickie, who felt evidently pleased at the other's admiration. "An when they're brought down a bit to a sense of their situation. I can just be as kind as I was cruel."

"Never fear ye!" said M'Dermot, with a sententious shake of the head "Devil a taste of her would lave the room, if it wasn't for the mother."

"I saw that plain enough," said Nickie, as he threw a self-approving look at himself in a tall mirror opposite.

"She's a fine young girl, there's no denying it," said M'Dermot, who anticipated, as the result of his chief's attention, a more liberal scale of treatment for himself. "But I don't know how ye'll ever get round her, though to be sure if *you* can't, who can?"

"This inventory will keep me till night," said Nickie, changing the theme quite suddenly, "and I'll miss Dempsey, I'm afraid."

"I hope not; sure you have his track—haven't you?"

"Yes, and I have four fellows after him, along the shore here, but they say he's cunning as a fox. Well, I'll not give him up in a hurry, that's all. Is that rain I hear against the glass, Mick?"

"Ay, and dreadful rain, too!" said the other, peeping through the window, which now rattled and shook with a sudden squall of wind. "You'll not be able to leave this so late."

"So I'm thinking, Mick," said Nickie, laying down his writing materials, and turning his back to the fire: "I believe I must stay where I am."

"'Tis yourself is the boy!" cried Mick, with a look of admiration at his master.

"You're wrong, Mick," said he, with a scarce repressed smile, "all wrong; I wasn't thinking of her."

"Maybe not," said M'Dermot, shaking his head doubtfully; "maybe she's not thinking of you this minute! But aither all, I don't know how ye'll do it. Any one would say the vardic was again you."

"So it is, man, but can't we move for a new trial?" So saying, he turned suddenly about, and pulled the bell.

M'Dermot said nothing, but stood staring at his chief, with a well-feigned expression of wonderment, as though to say, "What is he going to do next?"

The summons was speedily answered by old Tate, who stood in respectful attention within the door. Not the slightest suspicion had crossed the butler's mind of Mr. Nickie's calling, or of his object with the Knight, or his manner would certainly have displayed a very different politeness. "Didn't you ring, sir?" said he, with a bow to Nickie, who now seemed vacillating, and uncertain how to proceed.

"Yes—I did—ring—the—bell," replied he, hesitating between each word of the sentence. "I was about to say that, as the night was so severe—a perfect hurricane it seems—I should remain here. Eh, did you speak?"

"No, sir," replied Tate, respectfully.

"You can inform your mistress, then, and say, with Mr. Nickie's respectful compliments—mind that—that if they have no objection, he would be happy to join them at supper."

Tate stood as if transfixed, not a sign of anger, not even of surprise in his features. The shock had actually stupified him.

"Do ye hear what the gentleman's saying to you?" asked Mick, in a stern voice.

"Sir?" said Tate, endeavouring to recover his routed faculties—"sir!"

"Tell the old fool what I said," muttered Nickie, with angry impatience; and then, as if remembering that his message might, possibly, be not over courteously worded by Mr. M'Dermot, he approached Tate, and said, "Give your mistress Mr. Nickie's compliments, and say, that not being able to return to Coleraine, he hopes he may be permitted to pass the evening with her and Miss Darcy." This message, uttered with great rapidity, as if the speaker dare not trust himself with more deliberation, was accompanied by a motion of the hand, which half pushed the old butler from the room.

Neither Mr. Nickie nor his subordinate exchanged a word during Tate's absence. The former, indeed, seemed far less confident of his success than at first, and M'Dermot waited the issue, for his cue, what part to take in the transaction.

If Tate's countenance, when he left the room, exhibited nothing but confusion and bewilderment, when he re-entered it his looks were composed and steadfast.

"Well?" said Nickie, as the old butler stood for a second without speaking—"well?"

"Her Ladyship says that you and the other men, sir, may receive any accommodation the house affords." He paused for a moment or two, and then added, "Her Ladyship declines Mr. Nickie's society."

"Did she give you that message herself?" asked Nickie, hastily; "are those her own words?"

"Them's her words," said Tate, dryly.

"I never heerd the likes——"

"Stop, Mick, hold your tongue," said Nickie, to his over-zealous follower, while he muttered to himself, "My name isn't Anthony Nickie, or I'll make her repent that speech! Ay, faith," said he, aloud, as turning to the portrait of the Knight he appeared to address it, "you shall come to the hammer as the original did before you." If Tate had understood the purport of this sarcasm, it is more than probable the discussion would have taken another form; as it was, he listened to Mr. Nickie's orders about the supper with due decorum, and retired to make the requisite preparations. "I will make a night of it, by——" exclaimed Nickie, as with clenched fist he struck the table before him. "I hope you know how to sing, Mick?"

"I can do a little that way, sir," grinned the ruffian, "when the company pressin'. If it wasn't too loud——"

"Too loud! you may drown the storm out there, if ye're able. But wait till we have the supper and the liquor before us, as they might cut off the supplies." And with this prudent counsel, they suffered Tate to proceed in his arrangements, without uttering another word.

CHAPTER LV.

A CONVIVIAL EVENING.

While Tate busied himself in laying the table, Mr. Nickie, with bent brows and folded arms, passed up and down the apartments, still ruminating on the affront so openly passed upon him, and cogitating how best to avenge it. As passing and repassing he cast his eyes on the preparations, he halted suddenly, and said, "Lay another cover here." Tate stood, uncertain whether he had heard aright the words, when Nickie repeated, "Don't you hear me? I said, lay another cover. The gentleman will sup here."

"Oh! indeed," exclaimed Tate, as, opening his eyes to the fullest extent, he appeared to admit a new light upon his brain; "I beg pardon, sir, I was thinking that this gentleman might like to sup with the other gentleman, out in the kitchen beyond!"

"I said he'd sup here," said Nickie, vehemently, for he felt the taunt in all its bitterness.

"I say, old fellow," said M'Dermot in Tate's ear, "you needn't be sparin' of the liquor. Give us the best you have, and plenty of it. It is all the same to yer master, you know, in a few days. I was saying, sir," said he to Nickie, who, overhearing him, turned sharply round—"I was saying, sir, that he might as well give up the ould bin with the cobweb over it. It's the creditors suffers now, and we've many a way of doin' a civil turn."

"His mistress has shut the door on that," said Nickie, savagely, "and she may take the consequences."

"Oh, never mind him," whispered M'Dermot to Tate; "he's the best-hearted crayture that ever broke bread, but passionate, d'ye mind, passionate."

Poor Tate, who had suddenly become alive to the characters and objects of his guests, was now aware that his mistress's refusal to admit the chief might possibly be productive of very disastrous consequences; for, like all low Irishmen, he had a very ample notion of the elastic character of the law.

and thought that its pains and penalties were entirely at the option of him who executed it.

"Her Ladyship never liked to see much company," said he, apologetically.

"Well, maybe so," rejoined M'Dermot, "but in a quiet homely sort of a way, sure she needn't have refused Mr. Anthony; little she knows, there's not the like of him for stories about the Court of Conscience and the Sessions."

"I don't doubt it," exclaimed Tate, who, in assenting, felt pretty certain that his fascinations would scarcely have met appreciation in the society of his mistress and her daughter.

"And if ye heerd him sing 'Hobson's Choice,' with a new verse of his own at the end!"

Tate threw a full expression of wondering admiration into his features, and went on with his arrangements in silence.

"Does he know anything of Dempsey, do you think?" said Nickie, in a whisper to his follower.

"Not he," muttered the other, scornfully: "the crayture seems half a nat'ral." Then, in a voice pitched purposely loud, he said, "Do you happen to know one Dempsey in these parts?"

"Paul Dempsey?" added Nickie.

"A little, short man, with a turned-up nose, that walks with his shoulders far back and his hands spread out? Ay, I know him well; he dined here one day with the master, and sure enough he made the company laugh hearty!"

"I'd be glad to meet him, if he's as pleasant as you say," said Nickie, slyly.

"There's nothing easier, then," said Tate; "since the boarding-house is closed there at Ballintray, he's up in Coleraine for the winter. I hear he waits for the Dublin mail, at M'Grotty's door, every evening, to see the passengers, and that he has a peep at the way-bill before the agent himself."

"Has he so many acquaintances that he is always on the look out for one?"

"Faix, if they'd let him," cried Tate, laughing, "I believe he'd know every man, woman, and child in Ireland. For curiosity he beats all ever I seen."

As Tate spoke, a sudden draught of wind seemed to penetrate the chamber—at least the canoe and its party shook perceptibly.

"We'll have a rare night of it," said Nickie, drawing nearer to the fire. Then resuming, added, "And you say I'll have no difficulty to find him?"

"Not the least, bedad! It would be far harder to escape him, from all I hear. He watches the coach, and never leaves it till he sees the fore boot and the hind one empty; not only looking the passengers in the face, but tumbling over the luggage, reading all the names, and where they're going. Oh, he's a wonderful man for knowledge!"

"Indeed," said Nickie, with a look of attention to draw on the garrulity of the old man.

"I've reason to remember it well," said Tate, putting both hands to his loins. "It was the day he dined here I got the rheumatiz in the small of my back. When I went to open the gate without there for him, he kept me talking for three-quarters of an hour in the teeth of an east wind that would shave a goat—asking me about the master and the mistress, and Miss Helen, ay, and even about myself at last—if I had any brothers—and what their names was—and who was Mister Daly—and whether he didn't keep a club-house. By my conscience, it's well for him ould Bagenal didn't hear him!"

A clattering sound from the canoe suddenly interrupted Tate's narrative; he stopped short, and muttered, in a tone of unfeigned terror,

"That's the way always—may I never see glory! ye can't speak of him but he hears ye!"

A rude laugh from Nickie, chorused still more coarsely by M'Dermot, arrested Tate's loquacity, and he finished his arrangements without speaking, save in a few broken sentences.

If Mr. Nickie could have been conciliated by material enjoyments, he might decidedly have confessed that the preparations for his comfort were ample and hospitable. A hot supper diffused its savoury steam on a table where decanters and flasks of wine of different sorts and sizes attested that the more convivial elements of a feast were not forgotten. Good humour was, however, not to be restored by such amends. He was wounded in his self-love, outraged in his vanity, and he sat down in a dogged silence to the meal, a perfect contrast in appearance to the coarse delight of his subordinate.

While Tate remained to wait on them, Nickie's manner and bearing were unchanged. A sullen, sulky expression sat on features which, even when at the best, conveyed little better than a look of shrewd keenness; nor could the appetite with which he eat suggest a passing ray of satisfaction to his face.

"I am glad we are rid of that old fellow at last," said he, as the door closed upon Tate. "Whether fool or knave, I saw what he was at; he would have been disrespectful if he dared."

"I didn't mind him much, sir," said M'Dermot, honestly confessing that the good cheer had absorbed his undivided attention.

"I did, then; I saw his eyes fixed on us—on you particularly. I thought he would have laughed outright when you helped yourself to the entire duck."

Nickie spoke this with an honest severity, meant to express his discontent with his companion fully as much as with the old butler.

"Well, it was an excellent supper, anyhow," said M'Dermot taking the bottle which Nickie pushed towards him somewhat rudely, "and here's wishing health and happiness and long life to ye, Mr. Anthony. May ye always have as plentiful a board, and better company round it."

There was a fawning humility in the fellow's manner that seemed to gratify the other, for he nodded a return to the sentiment, and, after a brief pause, said,

"The servants in these grand houses—and that old fellow, you may remark, was with the Darcys when they were great people—they give themselves airs to everybody they think below the rank of their master."

"Faix, they might behave better to *you*, Mr. Anthony," said M'Dermot.

"Well, they're run their course now," said Nickie, not heeding the remark. 'Both master and man have had their day. I've seen more executions on property in the last six months than ever I did in all my life before. Creditors won't wait now as they used to do. No influence now to make gaugers, and tide-waiters, and militia officers! no privilege of Parliament to save them from arrest."

"My blessings on them for that, anyhow," said M'Dermot, finishing his glass. "The Union's a fine thing."

"The fellows that got the bribes—and to be sure there was plenty of money going—won't stay to spend it in Ireland; devil a one will remain here, but those that are run out and ruined."

"Bad luck to it for a Bill!" said M'Dermot, who felt obliged to sacrifice his consistency in his desire to concur with each new sentiment of his chief.

"The very wine we're drinking, maybe, was given for a vote. Pitt knew well how to catch them."

"Success attend him," chimed in M'Dermot.

"And just think of them now," continued Nickie, whose ruminations were never interrupted by the running commentary—"just think of them! selling the country—trade—prosperity—everything, for a few hundred pounds."

"The blackguards!"

"Some, to be sure, made a fine thing out of it. Not like old Darcy here; they were early in the market, and got both rank and money too."

"Ay, that was doin' it in style!" exclaimed Mike, who expressed himself this time somewhat equivocally, for safety's sake.

"There's no denying it, Castlereagh was a clever fellow!"

"The best man ever I seen—I don't care who the other is."

"He knew when to bid, and when to draw back; never became too pressing, but never let any one feel himself neglected; watched his opportunities slyly and when the time came, pounced down like a hawk on his victim."

"Oh, the thieves' breed! What a hard heart he had!" muttered M'Dermot, perfectly regardless of whom he was speaking.

Thus did Mr. Nickie ramble on, in the popular cant, over the subject of the day; for, although the Union was now carried, and its consequences—whatever they might be—so far inevitable, the men whose influence effected the measure were still before the bar of public opinion—an ordeal not a whit more just and discriminating than it usually is. While the current of these reminiscences ran on, varied by some anecdote here, or some observation there, both master and man drank deeply. So long as good liquor abounded, Mr. M'Dermot could have listened with pleasure, even to a less entertaining companion; and as for Nickie, he felt a vulgar pride in discussing, familiarly and by name, the men of rank and station who took a leading part in Irish politics. The pamphlets and newspapers of the day had made so many private histories public, had unveiled so many family circumstances before the eyes of the world, that his dissertations had all the seeming authenticity of personal knowledge.

It was at the close of a rather violent denunciation of the "Traitors"—as the Government party was ever called—that Nickie, striking the table with his fist, called on M'Dermot to sing.

"I say, Mac," cried he, with a faltering tongue, and eyes red and bleared from drinking—"the old lady—wouldn't accept my society—she didn't think --An-tho-ny Nickie, Esquire—good enough—to sit down—at her table. Let us show her what she has lost, my boy. Give her 'Bob Uniake's Boots,' or 'The Major's Prayer.'"

"Or what d'ye think of the new ballad to Lord Castlereagh, sir?" suggested M'Dermot, modestly. "It was the last thing Rhoudlim had when I left town."

"Is it good?" hiccupped Nickie.

"If ye heerd Rhoudlim——"

"D—n Rhoudlum!—she used to sing that song Parsons made on the attorneys. Parsons never liked us, Mac. You know what he said to Holmes, who went to him for a subscription of five shillings, to help to bury Mat Costegan. 'Wasn't he an attorney?' says Parsons. 'He was,' says the other. 'Well, here's a pound,' says he; 'take it and bury four!'"

"Oh, by my conscience, that was mighty nate!" said M'Dermot, who completely forgot himself.

Nickie frowned savagely at his companion, and for a moment seemed about to express his anger more palpably, when he suddenly drank off his glass, and said, "Well, the song—let us have it now."

"I'm afraid—I don't know more than a verse here and there," said Mac, bashfully stroking down his hair, and mincing his words—"but with the help of a chorus——"

'Trust me for that,' cried Nickie, who now drank glass after glass with out stopping; "I'm always ready for a song." So saying, he burst out into a half lachrymose chant—

An old maid had a roguish eye!
  And she was call'd the great Ramshoodera!
Rich was she and poor was I!
          Fol de dol de die do!

"I forget the rest, Mickie, but it goes on about a Nabob and a bear, and—a—what's this ye call it, a pottle of green gooseberries that Lord Claugoff sold to Mrs. Kelfoyle."

"To be sure; I remember it well," said Mac, humouring the drunken lucubrations; "but my chant is twice as aisy to sing—the air is the 'Black Joke;' any one can chorus."

"Well, open the proceedings," hiccupped Nickie; "state the case."

And thus encouraged, Mr. M'Dermot cleared his throat, and in a voice loud and coarse enough to be heard above the howling din, began:

Though many a mile he's from Erin away,
Here's health and long life to my Lord Castlereagh,
    With his bag full of guineas so bright!
'Twas he that made Bishops and Deans by the score,
And Peers, of the fashion of Lord Donoughmore!
And a Colonel of horse, of our friend Billy Lake,
And Wallscourt, a Lord—t'other day but Joe Blake,
    With his bag full of guineas so bright.

Come Beresford, Bingham, Luke Fox, and Tyrone,
Come Kearney, Bob Johnston, and Arthur Malone,
    With your bag full of guineas so bright;
Lord Charles Fitzgerald and Kit Fortescue,
And Henry Deane Grady—we'll not forget you,
Come Cuffe, Isaac Corry, and General Dunne,
—And you Jemmy Vandeleur—come every one,
    With your bag full of guineas so bright.

Come Talbot and Townsend. Come Toler and Trench,
Tho' made for the gallows! ye're now on the Bench,
    With your bag full of guineas so bright.
But if ever again this black list I'll begin,
The first name I'll take is the ould Knight of Gwynne,
Who robb'd of his property, stripp'd of his pelf,
Would be glad to see Erin as poor as himself,
    With no bag full of guineas so bright.

If the Parliament's gone, and the world it has scoff'd us,
What a blessing to think that we've Tottenham Loftus,
    With his bag full of guineas so bright.
Oh what consolation through every disaster,
To know that your Lordship is made our Postmaster,
And your uncle a Bishop, your aunt—but why mention
Two thousand a year, "of a long service pension"
    Of a bag full of guineas so bright.

But what is the change, since your Lordship appears!
You found us all Paupers, you left us all Peers,
With your bag full of guineas so bright.
Not a man in the island, however he boast,
But has a good reason to fill to the toast—
From Cork to the Causeway, from Howth to Clue Bay,
A health and long life to my Lord Castlereagh,
With his bag full of guineas so bright.

The boisterous accompaniment by which Mr. Nickie testified his satisfaction at the early verses had gradually subsided into a low droning sound, which at length, towards the conclusion, lapsed into a prolonged heavy snore. "Fast!" exclaimed M'Dermot, holding the candle close to his eyes. "Fast!" Then taking up the decanter, he added, "And if ye had gone off before, it would have been no great harm. Ye never had the bottle out of yer grip for the last hour and half!" He heaped some wood on the grate, refilled his glass, and then disposing himself so as to usurp a very large share of the blazing fire, prepared to follow the good example of his chief. Long habit had made an arm-chair to the full as comfortable as a bed to the worthy functionary, and his arrangements were scarcely completed, when his nose announced by a deep sound that he was a wanderer in the land of dreams.

Poor Mr. Dempsey—for if the reader may have forgotten him all this while, we must not—listened long and watchfully to the heavy notes, nor was it without considerable fear that he ventured to unveil his head and take a peep under Daly's arm at the sleepers. Reassured by the seeming heaviness of the slumberers, he dared a step further, and, at last, seated himself bolt upright in the canoe, glad to relieve his cramped-up legs, even by this momentary change of position. So cautious were all his movements, so still and noiseless every gesture, that had there been a waking eye to mark him, it would have been hard enough to distinguish between his figure and those of his inanimate neighbours.

The deep and heavy breathing of the sleepers was the only sound to be heard; they snored as if it were a contest between them; still it was long before Dempsey could summon courage enough to issue from his hiding-place, and with stealthy steps approach the table. Cautiously lifting the candle, he first held it to the face of one and then of the other of the sleepers. His next move was to inspect the supper-table, where, whatever the former abundance, nothing remained save the veriest fragments: the bottles too were empty, and poor Dempsey shook his head mournfully, as he poured out and drank the last half-glass of sherry in a decanter. This done, he stood for a few minutes reflecting what step he should take next. A sudden change of position of Nickie startled him from these deliberations, and Dempsey cowered down beneath the table in terror. Scarcely daring to breathe, Paul waited while the sleeper moved from side to side, muttering some short and broken words; at length he seemed to have settled himself to his satisfaction, for so his prolonged respiration bespoke. Just as he had turned for the last time, a heavy roll of papers fell from his pocket to the floor. Dempsey eyed the packet with a greedy look, but did not dare to reach his hand towards it, till well assured that the step was safe.

Taking a candle from the table, Paul reseated himself on the floor, and opened a large roll of documents tied with red tape; the very first he unrolled seemed to arrest his attention strongly, and although passing on to the examination of the remainder, he more than once recurred to it, till at length creeping stealthily towards the fire, he placed it among the burning embers, and stirred and poked until it became a mere mass of blackened leaves.

"There," muttered he, "Paul Dempsey's his own man again. And now what can he do for his friends? Ha, ha! 'Execution against Effects of Bagenal Daly, Esq.,'" said he, reading half-aloud; "and this lengthy affair here, 'Instructions to A. N. relative to the enclosed;' let us see what that may be." And so saying he opened the scroll—a bright flash of flame burst out from among the slumbering embers, and ere it died away Paul read a few lines of the paper. "What scoundrels!" muttered he, as he wiped the perspiration from his forehead, for already had honest Paul's feelings excited him to the utmost. The flame was again flickering, in another moment it would be out, when, stealing forth his hand, he placed an open sheet upon it, and then, as the blaze caught, he laid the entire bundle of papers on the top, and watched them till they were reduced to ashes.

"Maybe it's a felony—I'm sure it's a misdemeanour at least—what I've done now," muttered he; "but there was no resisting it. I wish I thought it was no heavier crime to do the same by these worthy gentlemen here."

Indeed, for a second or two, Paul's hesitation seemed very considerable. Fear, or something higher in principle, got the victory at length, and after a long silence, he said,

"Well, I'll not harm them." And with this benevolent sentiment he stood up, and detaching Darcy's portrait from the wall, thrust it into his capacious pocket. This done, he threw another glance over the table, lest some unseen decanter might still remain; but no, except a water jug of pure element, nothing remained.

"Good night, and pleasant dreams t'ye both," muttered Paul, as, blowing out one candle, he took the other, and slipped, without the slightest noise, from the room.

CHAPTER LVI.

MR. DEMPSEY BEHIND THE SCENES.

No very precise or determined purpose guided Mr. Dempsey's footsteps as he issued from the hall and gained the corridor, from which the various rooms of the cottage opened. Benevolent intentions of the very vaguest kind towards Lady Eleanor were commingled with thoughts of his own safety, and perhaps more strongly than either, an intense curiosity to inspect the domestic arrangements of the family, not without the hope of finding something to eat.

He had now been about twenty-four hours without food, and to a man who habitually lived in a boarding-house, and felt it a point of honour to consume as much as he could for his weekly pay, the abstinence was far from agreeable. If then his best inspirations were blended with some selfishness, he was not quite unpardonable. Mr. Dempsey tried each door as he went along, and although they were all unlocked, the interiors responded to none of his anticipations. The apartments were plainly but comfortably furnished, in some books lay about, and an open piano told of recent habitation. In one, which he judged rightly to be the Knight's dressing-room, a table was covered over with letters and law papers, documents which honest Paul beheld with some feeling akin to Aladdin, when he surveyed the inestimable treasures he had no means of carrying away with him from the mine. A faint gleam of light shone from beneath a door at the end of the corridor, and thither with silent footsteps he now turned. All was still—he listened as he drew near—but except the loud ticking of a clock, nothing was to be heard. Paul tried to reconnoitre by the keyhole, but it was closed. He waited for some time, unable to decide on the most fitting course, and at length opened the door, and entered. Stopping short at the threshold, Paul raised the candle, to take a better view of the apartment. Perhaps any one save himself would have returned on discovering it was a bedroom. A large old-fashioned bed, with a deep and massive curtain closely drawn, stood against one wall; beside it, on a table, was a night-lamp, from which the faint glimmer he had first noticed proceeded. Some well-stuffed arm-chairs were disposed here and there, and on the tables lay articles of female dress. Mr. Dempsey stood for a few seconds, and perhaps some secret suspicion crept over him that this visit might be thought intrusive. It might be Lady

Eleanor's, or perhaps Miss Darcy's chamber. Who was to say she was not actually that instant in bed asleep? Were the fact even so, Mr. Dempsey only calculated on a momentary shock of surprise at his appearance, well assured that his explanation would be admitted as perfectly satisfactory. Thus wrapt in his good intentions, and shrouding the light with one hand, he drew the curtain with the other. The bed was empty—the coverings were smooth—the pillows unpressed. The occupant, whoever it might be, had not yet taken possession. Mr. Dempsey's fatigue was only second to his hunger, and having failed to discover the larder, it is more than probable he would have contented himself with the gratification of a sleep, had he not just at that instant perceived a light flickering beside and beneath the folds of a heavy curtain, which hung over a doorway at the furthest end of the room. His spirit of research once more encouraged, he moved towards it, and drawing it very gently, admitted his eye in the interspace. A glass door intervened between him and a small chamber, but permitted him to see without being heard by those within. Flattening his features on the glass, he stared at the scene, and truly one less inspired by the spirit of inquiry might have felt shocked at being thus placed. Lady Eleanor sat in her dressing gown on a sofa, while, half kneeling, half lying at her feet, was Helen, her head concealed in her mother's lap, and her long hair loosely flowing over her neck and shoulders. Lady Eleanor was pale as death, and the marks of recent tears were on her cheeks; but still her features wore the expression of deep tenderness and pity, rather than of selfish sorrow. Helen's face was hidden, but her attitude, and the low sobbing sounds that at intervals broke the stillness, told how her heart was suffering.

"My dear, dear child," said Lady Eleanor, as she laid her hand upon the young girl's head, "be comforted. Rest assured that in making me the partner in your sorrow, I will be the happier participator in your joy, whenever its day may come. Yes, Helen, and it will come."

"Had I told you earlier——"

"Had you done so," interrupted Lady Eleanor, "you had been spared much grief, for I could have assured you, as I now do, that you are not to blame—that this young man's rashness, however we may deplore it, had no promptings from us."

Helen replied, but in so low a tone, that Mr. Dempsey could not catch the words; he could hear, however, Lady Eleanor uttering at intervals words of comfort and encouragement, and at last she said,

"Nay, Helen, no half-confidence, my child. Acknowledge it fairly, that your opinion of him is not what it was at first; or if you will not confess it, leave me to my own judgment. And why should you not?" added she, in a stronger voice; "wiser heads may reprove his precipitancy—criticise what would be called his folly—but you may be forgiven for thinking that his

Quixotism could deserve another and a fonder title. And I, Helen, grown old and chilly-hearted—each day more distrustful of the world—less sanguine in hope—more prone to suspect—even I, feel that devotion like his has a strong claim on your affection. And shall I own to you that on the very day he brought us that letter, a kind of vague presentiment that I should one day like him, stole across me. What was the noise?—did you not hear something stir?" Helen had heard it, but paid no further attention, for there was no token of any one being near.

Noise, however, there really was, occasioned by Mr. Dempsey, who, in his eagerness to hear, had pushed the door partly open. For some moments back, honest Paul had listened with as much embarrassment as curiosity, sorely puzzled to divine of whom the mother and daughter were speaking. The general tenor of the conversation left the subject no matter of difficulty. The individual was the only doubtful question. Lady Eleanor's allusion to a letter, and her own feelings at the moment, at once reminded him of her altered manner to himself on the evening he brought the epistle from Coleraine, and how she, who up to that time had treated him with unvarying distance and reserve, had as suddenly become all the reverse.

"Blood alive!" said he to himself, "I never as much as suspected it!" His eagerness to hear further was intense; and although he had contrived to keep the door ajar, his curiosity was doomed to disappointment, for it was Helen who spoke, and her words were uttered in a low, faint tone, utterly inaudible where he stood. Whatever pleasure Mr. Dempsey might have at first derived from his contraband curiosity, was more than repaid now by the tortures of anxiety. He suspected that Helen was making a full confession of her feelings towards him, and yet he could not catch a syllable. Lady Eleanor, too, when she spoke again, it was in an accent almost equally faint, and all that Paul could gather was, that the mother was using expressions of cheerfulness and hope, ending with the words—

"His own fortunes look now as darkly as ours—mayhap the same bright morning will dawn for both together, Helen. We have hope to cheer us, for him and for us."

"Ah! true enough," muttered Paul; "she's alluding to old Bob Dempsey, and if the Lord would take him, we'd all come right again."

Helen now arose, and seated herself beside her mother, with her head leaning on her shoulder; and Mr. Dempsey might have been pardoned if he thought she never looked more beautiful. The loose folds of her night-dress less concealed than delineated the perfect symmetry of her form; while, through the heavy masses of the luxuriant hair that fell upon her neck and shoulders, her skin seemed, more than ever, delicately fair. If Paul's mind was a perfect whirl of astonishment, delight, and admiration, his doubts were no less puzzling. What was he to do? Should he at once discover himself

—throw himself at Helen's feet in a rapture, confessing that he had heard her avowal, and declare that the passion was mutual. This, although with evident advantages on the score of dramatic effect, had also its drawback. Lady Eleanor, who scarcely looked as well in dishabille as her daughter, might feel offended. She might take it ill, also, that he had been a listener. Paul had heard of people who actually deemed eavesdropping unbecoming! who knows, among her own eccentricities, if this one might not find place? Paul, therefore, resolved on a more cautious advance, and for his guidance, applied his ear more to the aperture. This time, however, without success, for they spoke still lower than before; nor, after a long and patient waiting, could he hear more than that the subject was their present embarrassment, and the necessity of immediately removing from the Corvy—but where to, and how, they could not determine.

There was no time to ask Bicknell's advice; before an answer could arrive, they would be exposed to all the inconvenience, perhaps insult, which Mr. Nickie's procedure seemed to threaten. The subject appeared one to which all their canvassing had brought no solution, and at last Lady Eleanor said,

"How thankful I am, Helen, that I never wrote to Lord Netherby; more than once, when our difficulties seemed to thicken, I half made up my mind to address him. How much would it add to my present distress of mind, if I had yielded to the impulse! The very thought is now intolerable."

"Pride! pride!" muttered Paul.

"And I was so near it," ejaculated Lady Eleanor.

"Yes," said Helen, sharply; "our noble cousin's kindness would be a sore aggravation of our troubles."

"Worse than the mother, by Jove!" exclaimed Paul. "Oh dear! if I had a cousin a Lord, maybe he'd not hear of me."

Lady Eleanor spoke again, but Paul could only catch a stray word here and there, and again she reverted to the necessity of leaving the cottage at once.

"Could we even see this Mr. Dempsey," said she, "he knows the country well, and might be able to suggest some fitting place for the moment, at least till we could decide on better."

Paul scarcely breathed, that he might catch every syllable.

"Yes," said Helen, eagerly, "he would be the very person to assist us but poor little man, he has his own troubles, too, at this moment."

"She's a kind creature," muttered Paul, "how fond I'm growing of her."

"It is no time for the indulgence of scruples, otherwise, Helen, I'd not place much reliance on the gentleman's taste"

"Proud as Lucifer," thought Paul.

"His good nature, mamma, is the quality we stand most in need of, and I have a strong trust that he is not deficient there."

"What a situation to be placed in!" sighed Lady Eleanor: "that we should turn with a shudder from seeking protection, where it is our due, and yet ask counsel and assistance from a man like this!"

"I feel no repugnance whatever to accepting such a favour from Mr. Dempsey, while I should deem it a great humiliation to be suitor to the Earl of Netherby."

"And yet he is our nearest relative living—with vast wealth and influence, and I believe not indisposed towards us. I go too fast, perhaps," said she, scornfully, "his obligations to my own father were too great and too manifold, that I should say so."

"What a Tartar!" murmured Paul.

"If the proud Earl could forget the services my dear father rendered him, when, a younger son, without fortune or position, he had no other refuge than our house—if he could wipe away the memory of benefits once received—he might perhaps be better minded towards us; but obligation is so suggestive of ill-will."

"Dearest mamma," said Helen, laughing, "if your hopes depend upon his Lordship's forgetfulness of kindness, I do think we may afford to be sanguine. I am well inclined to think that he is not weighed down by the load of gratitude that makes men enemies. Still," added she, more seriously, "I am very averse to seeking his aid, or even his counsel: I vote for Mr. Dempsey."

"How are we to endure the prying impertinence of his curiosity? Have you thought of that, Helen?"

Paul's cheek grew scarlet, and his very fingers' ends tingled.

"Easily enough, mamma. Nay, if our troubles were not so urgent, it would be rather amusing than otherwise—and with all his vulgarity——"

"The little vixen," exclaimed Paul, so much off his guard that both mother and daughter started.

"Did you hear that, Helen? I surely heard some one speak."

"I almost thought so," replied Miss Darcy, taking up a candle from the table, and proceeding towards the door. Mr. Dempsey had but time to retreat behind the curtain of the bed, when she reached the spot where he had been standing. "No, all is quiet in the house," said she, opening the door into the corridor and listening. "Even our respectable guests would seem to be asleep." She waited for a few seconds, and then returned to her place on the sofa.

Mr. Dempsey had either heard enough to satisfy the immediate cravings of his curiosity, or, more probably, felt his present situation too critical, for when he drew the curtain once more close over the glass door he slipped noiselessly into the corridor, and entering the first room he could find, opened the window and sprang out.

"You shall not be disappointed in Paul Dempsey anyhow," said he, as he buttoned up the collar of his coat, and pressed his hat more firmly on his head. "No, my Lady, he may be vulgar and inquisitive, though I confess it's the first time I ever heard of either; but he is not the man to turn his back on a good-natured action, when it lies full in front of him. What a climate to be sure! it blows from the four quarters of the globe all at once—and the rain soaks in and deluges one's very heart's blood. Paul, Paul, you'll have a smart twinge of rheumatism from this night's exploit."

It may be conjectured that Mr. Dempsey, like many other gifted people, had a habit of compensating for the want of society by holding little dialogues or discourses with himself, a custom from which he derived no small gratification, for, while it lightened the weariness of a lonely way, it enabled him to say many more flattering and civil things to himself than he usually heard from an ungrateful world.

"They talk of Demerara," said he, I back Antrim against the world for a hurricane. The rainy season here lasts all the year round, and if practice makes perfect—— There, now I'm wet through, I can't be worse. Ah! Helen, Helen, if you knew how unfit Paul Dempsey is to play Paris! By the way, who was the fellow that swam the Hellespont for love of a young lady? Not Laertes, no—that's not it—Leander, that's the name—Leander."

Paul muttered the name several times over, and by a train of thought, which we will not attempt to follow or unravel, began humming to himself the well-known Irish ditty of

Teddy, ye gander,
Yer like a Highlander.

He soon came to a stop in the words, but continued to sing the air, till at last he broke out in the following version of his own:

Paul Dempsey, ye gander,
You're like that Leander,
Who, for somebody's daughter—for somebody's daughter
Did not mind it one pin
To be wet to the skin,
With a dip in salt water—a dip in salt water

Were you wiser, 'tis plain,
You'd be now in Coleraine,
A nightcap on your head—a nightcap on your head,
With a jorum of rum,
Made by old Mother Fum,
At the side of your bed—at the side of your bed.

For tho' love is divine,
When the weather is fine,
And a season of bliss—a season of bliss:
'Tis a different thing
For a body to sing
On a night such as this—a night such as this.

Paul Dempsey! remember,
On the ninth of December
You'll be just forty-six—you'll be just forty-six,
And the world will say,
That at your time o' day,
You're too old for these tricks—you're too old for these tricks.

And tho' water may show
One's loves, faith, I know
I'd rather prove mine—I'd rather prove mine
With my feet on the fender;
'Tis then I grow tender,
O'er a bumper of wine—o'er a bumper of wine!

"A bumper of wine!" sighed he. "On my conscience, it would be an ugly toast I'd refuse to drink this minute, if the liquor was near.

Ah! when warm and snug,
With my legs on the rug,
By a turf fire red—a turf fire red—
But how can I rhyme it?
With this horrid climate,
Destroying my head—destroying my head?

With a coat full of holes,
And my shoes without soles,
And my hat like a teapot—my hat like a teapot——

"Oh, murther, murther!" screamed he aloud, as his shins came in contact with a piece of timber, and he fell full length to the ground, sorely bruised, and perfectly enveloped in snow. It was some minutes before he could rally sufficiently to get up; and although he still shouted for help, seeing a light in a window near, no one came to his assistance, leaving poor Paul to his own devices.

It was some consolation for his sufferings to discover that the object over which he had stumbled was the shaft of a jaunting-car, such a conveyance being at that moment what he most desired to meet with. The driver at last made his appearance, and informed him that he had brought Nickie and his two companions from Larne, and was now only waiting their summons to proceed to Coleraine.

Paul easily persuaded the man that he could earn a fare in the mean time, for that Nickie would probably not leave the Corvy till late on the following day, and that, by a little exertion, he could manage to drive to Coleraine and back before he was stirring. It is but fair to add, that poor Mr. Dempsey supported his arguments by lavish promises of reward, to redeem which he speculated on mortgaging his silver watch, and, probably, his umbrella, when he reached Coleraine.

It was yet a full hour before daybreak, as Lady Eleanor, who had passed the night in her dressing-room, was startled by a sharp tapping noise at her window; Helen lay asleep on the sofa, and too soundly locked in slumber to hear the sounds. Lady Eleanor listened, and while half fearing to disturb the young girl, wearied and exhausted as she was, she drew near to the window. The indistinct shadow of a figure was all that she could detect through the gloom, but she fancied she could hear a weak effort to pronounce her name.

There could be little doubt of the intentions of the visitor; whoever he should prove, the frail barrier of a window could offer no resistance to any one disposed to enter by force, and, reasoning thus, Lady Eleanor unfastened the casement, and cried, "Who is there?"

A strange series of gestures, accompanied by a sound between a sneeze and the crowing of a cock, was all the reply, and when the question was repeated in a louder tone, a thin quivering voice muttered, "Pau—au—l De—de—dempsey, my La—dy."

"Mr. Dempsey, indeed!" exclaimed Lady Eleanor. "Oh! pray come round to the door at your left hand, it is only a few steps from where you are standing."

Short as the distance was, Mr. Dempsey's progress was of the slowest, and Lady Eleanor had already time to awaken Helen, ere the half-frozen Paul had crossed the threshold.

"He has passed the night in the snow," cried Lady Eleanor to her daughter, as she led him towards the fire.

"No, my Lady," stammered out Paul, "only the last hour and a half; before that I was snug under Old Daly's blanket."

A very significant interchange of looks between mother and daughter seemed to imply that poor Mr. Dempsey's wits were wandering.

"Call Tate; let him bring some wine here at once, Helen."

"It's all drunk; not a glass in the decanter," murmured Paul, whose thoughts recurred to the supper-table.

"Poor creature, his mind is quite astray," whispered Lady Eleanor, her compassion not the less strongly moved, because she attributed his misfortune to the exertions he had made in their behalf. By this time the group was increased by the arrival of old Tate, who, in a flannel nightcap fastened under the chin, and a very ancient dressing-gown of undyed wool, presented a lively contrast to the shivering condition of Mr. Dempsey.

"It's only Mr. Dempsey!" said Lady Eleanor, sharply, as the old butler stood back, crossing himself and staring with sleepy terror at the white figure.

"May I never! But so it is," exclaimed Tate, in return to an attempt at a bow on Dempsey's part, which he accomplished with a crackling noise like reaking glass.

"Some warm wine at once," said Helen, while she heaped two or three logs upon the hearth.

"With a little ginger in it, miss," grinned Paul. But the polite attempt at a smile nearly cut his features, and ended in a most lamentable expression of suffering.

"This is the finest thing in life agin' the cowld," said Tate, as he threw over the shivering figure a Mexican mantle, all worked and embroidered with quills, that gave the gentle Mr. Dempsey the air of an enormous porcupine. The clothing, the fire, and the wine, of which he partook heartily, soon restored him, and ere long he had recounted to Lady Eleanor the whole narrative of his arrival at the Corvy—his concealment in the canoe—the burning of the law papers, and even down to the discovery of the jaunting-car, omitting nothing, save the interview he had witnessed between the mother and daughter.

Lady Eleanor could not disguise her anxiety on the subject of the burnt documents, but Paul's arguments were conclusive in reply:

"Who's to tell of it? Not your Ladyship, not Miss Helen; and as to Paul, meaning myself, my discretion is quite Spanish. Yes, my Lady," said he, with a tragic gesture, that threw back the loose folds of his costume, 'there is an impression abroad, which I grieve to say is wide-spread, that the humble individual who addresses you is one of those unstable, fickle minds that accomplish nothing great; but I deny it, deny it indignantly. Let the occasion but arise—let some worthy object present itself, or herself"—he gave a most melting look towards Helen, which cost all her efforts to sustain without laughter—"and then, madam, Don Paulo Dempsey will come out in his true colours."

"Which I sincerely hope may not be of the snow tint," said Lady Eleanor, smiling. "But pray, Mr. Dempsey, to return to a theme more selfish. You are sufficiently aware of our unhappy circumstances here at this moment, to see that we must seek some other abode, at least for the present. Can you then say where we can find such?"

"Miss Daly's neighbourhood, perhaps," broke in Helen.

"Never do—not to be thought of," interrupted Paul; "there's nothing for it but the Panther——"

"The what, sir?" exclaimed Lady Eleanor, in no small surprise.

"The Panther, my Lady, Mother Fum's! snug, quiet, and respectable social, if you like—selfish, if you please it. Solitary or gregarious; just as you fancy."

"And where, sir, is the Panther?" said Lady Eleanor, who in her innocence supposed this to be the sign of some village inn.

"In the Diamond of Coleraine, my Lady, opposite M'Grotty's, next but one to Kitty Black's hardware, and two doors from the Post-office; central and interesting. Mail-car from Newtown, Lim.—takes up passengers, within view of the windows, at two every day. Letters given out at four—see every one in the town without stirring from your window. Huston's, the apothecary, always full of people at post hour. Gribbin's tobacco-shop assembles all the Radicals at the same time to read the *Patriot*. Plenty of life and movement."

"Is there nothing to be found more secluded, less——"

"Less fashionable, your Ladyship would observe. To be sure there is but there's objections—at least I am sure you would dislike the prying, inquisitive spirit——Eh? Did you make an observation, miss?"

"No, Mr. Dempsey," said Helen, with some difficulty preserving a suitable gravity. "I would only remark that you are perfectly in the right, and that my mother seeks nothing more than a place where we can remain without obtrusiveness or curiosity directed towards us."

"There will always be the respectful admiration that beauty exacts," replied Paul, bowing courteously, "but I can answer for the delicacy of Coleraine as for my own."

If this assurance was not quite as satisfactory to the ladies as Mr. Dempsey might have fancied it ought to be, there was really no alternative: they knew nothing of the country, which side to direct their steps, or whither to seek shelter; besides, until they had communicated with Bicknell, they could not with safety leave the neighbourhood to which all their letters were addressed.

It was then soon determined to accept Mr. Dempsey's suggestion and safe-conduct, and leaving Tate for the present to watch over such of their effects as they could not conveniently carry with them, to set out for Coleraine. The arrangements were made as speedily as the resolve, and day had scarcely dawned ere they quitted the "Corvy."

CHAPTER LVII.

MR. HEFFERNAN OUT-MANŒUVRED.

It was on the very same evening that witnessed these events, that Lord Castlereagh was conducting Mr. Con Heffernan to his hotel, after a London dinner-party. The late Secretary for Ireland had himself volunteered the politeness, anxious to hear some tidings of people and events, which, in the busy atmosphere of a crowded society, were unattainable. He speedily ran over a catalogue of former friends and acquaintances, learning, with that surprise with which successful men always regard their less fortunate contemporaries, that this one was still where he had left him, and that the other jogged on his daily road as before, when he suddenly asked,

"And the Darcys, what of them?"

Heffernan shrugged his shoulders without speaking.

"I am sorry for it," resumed the other; "sorry for the gallant old Knight himself, and sorry for a state of society in which such changes are assumed as evidences of progress and prosperity. These upstart Hickmans are not the elements of which a gentry can be formed."

"O'Reilly still looks to you for the Baronetcy, my Lord," replied Heffernan, with a half sneer. "You have him with or against you on that condition, at least so I hear."

"Has he not had good fortune enough in this world to be satisfied? He has risen from nothing to be a man of eminence, wealth, and county influence; would it not be more reasonable in him to mature his position by a little patience, than endanger it by fresh shocks to public opinion? Even a boa, my dear Heffernan, when he swallows a goat, takes six months to digest his meal. No! no! such men must be taught reserve, if their own prudence does not suggest it."

"I believe you are right, my Lord," said Heffernan, thoughtfully; "O'Reilly is the very man to forget himself in the sunshine of Court favour, and mistake good luck for desert."

"With all his money, too," rejoined Lord Castlereagh, "his influence will just be proportioned to the degree of acceptance his constituents suppose him to possess with us here. He has never graduated as a Patriot, and his slight popularity is only 'special gratia.' His patent of Gentleman has not come to him by birth."

"For this reason the Baronetcy——"

"Let us not discuss that," said Lord Castlereagh, quickly. "There is an objection in a high quarter to bestow honours, which would seem to ratify the downfal of an ancient house." He seemed to have said more than he was ready to admit, and to change the theme turned the conversation on the party they had just quitted.

"Sir George Hannaper always does these things well."

Mr. Heffernan assented blandly, but not over eagerly. London was not "*his* world," and the tone of a society so very different to what he was habituated had not made on him the most favourable impression.

"And after all," said Lord Castlereagh, musingly, "there is a great deal of tact—ability, if you will—essential to the success of such entertainments, to bring together men of different classes and shades of opinion, people who have never met before, perhaps are never to meet again, to hit upon the subjects of conversation that may prove generally interesting, without the risk of giving undue preponderance to any one individual's claims to superior knowledge. This demands considerable skill."

"Perhaps the difficulty is not so great *here*, my Lord," said Heffernan, half timidly, "each man understands his part so well; information and conversational power appear tolerably equally distributed; and when all the instruments are so well tuned, the leader of the orchestra has an easy task."

"Ah! I believe I comprehend you," said Lord Castlereagh, laughing; "you are covertly sneering at the easy and unexciting quietude of our London habits. Well, Heffernan, I admit we are not so fond of solo performances as you are in Dublin; few among us venture on those 'obligato passages' which are so charming to Irish ears; but don't you think the concerted pieces are better performed?"

"I believe, my Lord," said Heffernan, abandoning the figure in his anxiety to reply, "that we would call this dull in Ireland. I'm afraid that we are barbarous enough to set more store by wit and pleasantry than on grave discussion and shrewd table-talk. It appears to me that these gentlemen carry an air of business into their conviviality."

"Scarcely so dangerous an error as to carry conviviality into business," said Lord Castlereagh, slyly.

"There's too much holding back," said Heffernan, not heeding the taunt; "each man seems bent on making what jockeys call 'a waiting race.'"

"Confess, however," said Lord Castlereagh, smiling, "there's no struggle, no hustling at the winning-post: the best horse comes in first——"

"Upon my soul, my Lord," said Heffernan, interrupting, "I have yet to learn that there is such a thing. I conclude from your Lordship's observation that the company we met to-day were above the ordinary run of agreeability."

"I should certainly say so."

"Well, then, I can only affirm that we should call this a failure in our less polished land. I listened with becoming attention; the whole thing was new to me, and I can safely aver I neither heard one remark above the level of common-place, nor one observation evidencing acute perception of passing events or reflection on the past. As to wit or epigram——"

"Oh, we do not value these gifts at *your* price; we are too thrifty a nation, Heffernan, to expend all our powder on fireworks."

"Faith, I agree with you, my Lord; the man who would venture on a rocket would be treated as an incendiary."

"Come, come, Heffernan, I'll not permit you to say so. Did you ever in any society see a man more appreciated than our friend Darcy was the last evening we met him, his pleasantry relished, his racy humour well taken, and his stores of anecdote enjoyed with a degree of zest I have never seen surpassed?"

"Darcy was always too smooth for our present taste," said Heffernan, caustically. "His school was antiquated years ago; there was a dash of the French courtier through the Irishmen of his day."

"That made the most polished gentlemen of Europe, I've been told," said Lord Castlereagh, interrupting. "I know your taste inclines to a less chastened and more adventurous pleasantry, shrewd insight into an antagonist's weak point, a quick perception of the ridiculous——"

"Allied with deep knowledge of men and motives, my Lord," said Heffernan, catching up the sentence, "a practical acquaintance with the world in its widest sense; that cultivated keenness that smacks of reading intentions before they are avowed, and divining plans before they are more than conceived. These solid gifts are all essential to the man who would influence society, whether in a social circle or in the larger sphere of active life."

"Ah! but we were talking of merely social qualities," said Lord Castlereagh, stealing a cautious look of half malice, "the wit that sets the table in a roar."

"And which, like lightning, my Lord, must now and then prove dangerous, or men will cease to be dazzled by its brilliancy. Now, I rather incline to think that the Knight's pleasantry is like some of the claret we were drinking to-day, a little spoiled by age."

"I protest strongly against the judgment," said Lord Castlereagh, with energy; "the man who at his time of life consents to resume the toils and dangers of a soldier's career must not be accused of growing old."

"Perhaps your Lordship would rather shift the charge of senility against the Government which appoints such an officer," said Heffernan maliciously.

"As to that," said Lord Castlereagh, laughingly, "I believe the whole thing was a mistake. Some jealous but indiscreet friend of Darcy's made an application in his behalf, and without his cognisance, pressing the claim of an old and meritorious officer, and directly asking for a restitution to his grade. This was backed by Lord Netherby, one of the Lords in Waiting, and without much inquiry—indeed, I fancy without any—he was named Colonel, in exchange from the unattached list. The Knight was evidently flattered by so signal a mark of favour, and, if I read him aright, would not change his command for a brigade at home. In fact, he has already declined prospects not less certain of success."

"And is this really the mode in which officers are selected for an enterprise of hazard and importance?" said Heffernan, affecting a tone of startled indignation as he spoke.

"Upon my word, Heffernan," said Lord Castlereagh, subduing the rising tendency to laugh outright, "I fear it is too true. We live in days of back-stairs and court favour. I saw an application for the office of Under-Secretary for Ireland, so late as yesterday——"

"You did, my Lord!" interrupted Heffernan, with more warmth than he almost ever permitted himself to feel. "You did, from a man who has rendered more unrewarded services to the Government than any individual in the kingdom."

"The claim was a very suitable one," said Lord Castlereagh, mildly. "The gentleman who preferred it could point to a long list of successful operations, whose conduct rested mainly or solely on his own consummate skill and address; he could even allege the vast benefit of his advice to young and not over-informed Chief Secretaries——"

"I would beg to observe, my Lord——"

"Pray allow me to continue," said Lord Castlereagh, laying his hand gently on the other's arm. "As one of that helpless class so feelingly alluded to, I am ready to evince the deepest sense of grateful acknowledgments. It may be that I would rather have been mentioned more flatteringly; that the applicant had spoken of me as an apter and more promising scholar——"

"My Lord, I must and will interrupt you. The memorial, which was presented in my name, was sent forward under the solemn pledge that it should meet the eyes of Mr. Pitt alone; that whether its prayer was declined or accorded, none, save himself, should have cognisance of it. If, after this, it was submitted to your Lordship's critical examination, I leave it to your good taste and your sense of decorum how far you can avow or make use of the knowledge so obtained."

"I was no part in the compact you allege, nor, I dare to say, was Mr. Pitt," said Lord Castlereagh, proudly; but, momentarily resuming his former tone, he went on: "The Prime Minister, doubtless, knew how valuable the lesson might be to a young man entering on public life which should teach him not to lay too much store by his own powers of acuteness; not to trust too implicitly to his own qualities of shrewdness and perception; and that, by well reflecting on the aid he received from others, he might see how little the subtraction would leave for his own peculiar amount of skill. In this way I have to acknowledge myself greatly Mr. Heffernan's debtor, since, without the aid of this document, I should never have recognised how ignorant I was of every party and every public man in Ireland; how dependent on his good guidance; how I never failed, save in rejecting—never succeeded, save in profiting by his wise and politic counsels."

"Is your Lordship prepared to deny these assertions?" said Heffernan, with an imperturbable coolness.

"Am I not avowing my grateful sense of them?" said Lord Castlereagh, smiling blandly. "I feel only the more deeply your debtor, because, till now, I never knew the debt—both principal and interest must be paid together; but seriously, Heffernan, if you wanted office, was I not the proper channel to have used in asking for it? Why disparage your pupil while extolling your system?"

"You did my system but little credit, my Lord," replied Heffernan, with an accent as unmoved as before; "you bought votes when you should have bought the voters themselves; you deemed the Bill of Union the consummation of Irish policy—it is only the first act of the piece. You were not the first general who thought he beat the enemy when he drove in the pickets."

"Would my tactics have been better had I made one of my spies a Major-General, Mr. Heffernan?" said Lord Castlereagh, sneeringly.

"Safer, my Lord—far safer," said Heffernan, "for he might not have exposed you afterwards. But I think this is my hotel; and I must say it is the first time in my life that I have closed an interview with your Lordship without regret."

"Am I to hope it will be the last?" said Lord Castlereagh, laughing.

"The last interview, my Lord, or the last occasion of regretting its shortness?" said Heffernan, with a slight anxiety of voice.

"Whichever Mr. Heffernan opines most to his advantage," was the cool reply.

"The former, with your permission, my Lord," said Heffernan, as a flush suffused his cheek. "I wish your Lordship a very good night."

"Good night, good night! Stay, Thomas, Mr. Heffernan has forgotten his gloves."

"Thanks, my Lord; they were not left as a gage of battle, I assure you."

"I feel certain of it," said Lord Castlereagh, laughing. "Good night, once more."

The carriage rolled on, and Mr. Heffernan stood for an instant gazing after it through the gloom.

"I might have known it," muttered he to himself; "these Lords are the only people who do stick to each other now-a-days." Then, after a pause, he added, "Drogheda is right, by Jove! there's no playing against 'four by honours.'"

And with this reflection he slowly entered the hotel, and repaired to his chamber.

CHAPTER LVIII.

A BIT OF "BY-PLAY."

REVERSES of fortune might be far more easily supported, if they did not entail, as their inevitable consequence, the association with those, all of whose tastes, habits, and opinions, run in a new and different channel. It is a terrible aggravation to the loss of those comforts which habit has rendered necessaries, to unlearn the usages of a certain condition, and adopt those of a class beneath us—or, what is still worse, engage in the daily, hourly conflict between our means and our requirements.

Perhaps Lady Eleanor Darcy and her daughter never really felt the meaning of their changed condition, nor understood its poignancy, till they saw themselves as residents of Mrs. Fumbally's boarding-house, whither Mr. Dempsey's polite attentions had conducted them. It was to no want of respect on that lady's part that any portion of this feeling could be traced. "The Panther" had really behaved with the most dignified consideration; and while her new guests were presented as Mrs. and Miss Gwynne, intimated, by a hundred little adroit devices of manner, that their real rank and title were regarded by her as inviolable secrets—not the less likely to be respected, that she was herself ignorant of both. Heaven knows what secret anguish the retention of these facts cost poor Paul! secrecy being with him a quality something like Acre's courage, which "oozed out of his fingers' ends." Mr. Dempsey hated those miserly souls that can treasure up a fact for their own personal enjoyment, and yet never invite a neighbour to partake of it; and it was a very inefficient consolation to him, in this instance, to throw a mysterious cloak over the strangers, and, by an air of profound consciousness, seek to impose on the other boarders. He made less scruple about what he deemed his own share of the mystery, and scarcely had Mrs. Fumbally performed the honours of the two small chambers destined for Lady Eleanor and Helen, than Paul followed her to the little apartment familiarly termed her "den," and shutting the door, with an appearance of deep caution, took his place opposite to her at the fire.

"Well, Mr. Dempsey," said Mrs. Fumbally, "now that all is done and settled—now that I have taken these ladies into the 'Establishment' "—a very favourite designation of Mrs. Fum's when she meant to be imposing—"I hope I am not unreasonable in expecting a full and complete account from you of who they are, whence they came, and, in fact, every particular necessary to satisfy me concerning them."

"Mrs. Gwynne! Miss Gwynne! mother and daughter—Captain Gwynne, the father, on the recruiting staff in the Isle of Skye, or, if you like it better, with his regiment at St. John's. Mrs. G—— a Miss Rickaby, one of the Rickabys of Pwhlmdlwmm, North Wales—ancient family—small estate—all spent—obliged to live retired—till—till—no matter what—a son comes of age—to sign something—or anything that way——"

"This is all fiddle-faddle, Mr. Dempsey," said Mrs. Fum, with an expression that seemed to say, "Take care how you trifle with me."

"To be sure it is," rejoined Paul; "all lies, every word of it. What do you say, then, if we have her the Widow Gwynne—husband shot at Bergen-op-Zoom——"

"I say, Mr. Dempsey, that if you wish me to keep your secret before the other boarders——"

"The best way is never to tell it to you—eh, Mrs. Fum? Well, come, I will be open. Name, Gwynne—place of abode unknown—family ditto—means supposed to be ample—daughter charming—so very much so, indeed, that if Paul Dempsey were only what he ought—the Dempsey of Dempsey's Grove——"

"Oh, is that it?" said Mrs. Fumbally, endeavouring to smile—"is that it?"

"That's it," rejoined Paul, as he drew up his shirt-collar, and adjusted his cravat.

"Isn't she very young, Mr. Dempsey?" said Mrs. Fum, slyly.

"Twenty, or thereabouts, I take it," said Paul, carelessly—"quite suitable as regards age."

"I never thought you'd marry, Mr. Dempsey," said Mrs. Fum, with a languishing look, that contrasted strangely with the habitually shrewish expression of the "Panther's" face.

"Can't help it, Mrs. Fum. The last of the Romans! No more Dempseys when I'm gone, if I don't. Elder branch all dropped off—last twig of the younger myself."

"Ah! these are considerations, indeed!" sighed the lady. "But don't you think that a person more like yourself in taste—more similar in opinion of the world? She looks proud, Mr. Dempsey; I should say, overbearingly proud."

"Rather proud myself, if that's all," said Dempsey, drawing himself up, and protruding his chin with a most comic imitation of dignity.

"Only becomingly so, Mr. Dempsey—a proper sense of self-respect, a due feeling for your future position in life—I never saw more than that, I must say. Now, I couldn't help remarking the way that young lady threw herself into the chair, and the glance she gave at the room. It was number eight, Mr. Dempsey, with the chintz furniture, and the looking-glass over the chimney! well, really, you'd say, it was poor Leonard's room, with the settee bed in the corner—the look she gave it!"

"Indeed!" exclaimed Dempsey, who really felt horrified at this undervaluing judgment of what every boarder regarded as the very sanctum of the Fumbally Temple.

"Truth, every word of it!" resumed Mrs. Fum. "I thought my ears deceived me, as she said to her mother, 'Oh, it's all very neat and clean!'—neat and clean, Mr. Dempsey! The elegant rug which I worked myself—the pointer—and the wild duck."

"Like life, by Jove, if it wasn't that the dog has only three legs."

"Perspective, Mr. Dempsey, don't forget its perspective, and if the bird's wings are maroon, I couldn't help it, it was the only colour to be had in the town."

"The group is fine—devilish fine!" said Paul, with the air of one whose word was final.

"'Neat and clean' were the expressions she used! I could have cried as I heard it." Here the lady, probably in consideration for the omission, wiped her eyes, and dropped her voice to a very sympathetic key.

"She meant it well, depend upon it, Mrs. Fum, she meant it well."

"And the old lady," resumed Mrs. Fumbally, deaf to every consolation, "lay back in her chair this way, and said, 'Oh, it will all do very well—you'll not find us troublesome, Mrs. Flumary!' I haven't been the head of this establishment eight-and-twenty years to be called Flumary. How these airs are to be tolerated by the other boarders, I'm sure is more than I can say."

It appeared more than Mr. Dempsey could say also, if one might pronounce from the woe-begone expression of his face; for, up to this moment totally wrapped up in the mysterious portion of the affair, he had lost sight of all the conflicting interests this sudden advent would call into activity.

"That wasn't all," continued Mrs. Fumbally, "for when I told them the dinner hour was five, the old lady interrupted me with—'For the present—

with your permission—we should prefer dining at six.' Did any one ever hear the like? I'll have a pretty rebellion in the house, when it gets out! Mrs. Mackay will have her tea up-stairs every night—Mr. Dunlop will always breakfast in bed. I wouldn't be surprised if Miss Boyle stood out for broth in the middle of the day."

"Oh!" exclaimed Paul, holding up both hands in horror.

"I vow and protest, I expect that next!" exclaimed Mrs. Fum, as folding her arms, and fixing her eyes rigidly on the grate, she sat, the ideal of abused and injured benevolence. "Indeed, Mr. Dempsey," said she, after a long silence on both sides, "it would be a great breach of the regard many years of intimacy with you has formed, if I did not say, that your affections are misplaced. Beauty is a perishable gift."

Paul looked at Mrs. Fumbally, and seemed struck with the truth of her remark.

"But the qualities of the mind, Mr. Dempsey, those rare endowments that make happy the home and hearth. You're fond of beef hash with pickled onions," said she, smiling sweetly; "well, you shall have one to-day."

"Good creature!" muttered Paul, while he pressed her hand affectionately. "The best heart in the world!"

"Ah, yes," sighed the lady, half soliloquising, "conformity of temper—the pliancy of the reed—the tender attachment of the ivy."

Paul coughed, and drew himself up proudly, and, as if a sudden thought occurred to him that he resembled an oak of the forest, he planted his feet firmly, and stood stiff and erect.

"You are not half careful enough about yourself, Mr. Dempsey—never attend to changing your damp clothes—and I assure you the climate here requires it; and when you come in, cold and wet, you should always step in here, on your way up-stairs, and take a little something warm and cordial. I don't know if you approve of this," suiting the action to the words. Mrs. Fum had opened a small cupboard in the wall, and taken out a quaint-looking flask, and a very diminutive glass.

"Nectar, by Jove—downright nectar."

"Made with some white currants and ginger," chimed in Mrs. Fum, simply, as if to imply—See what skill can effect—behold the magic power of intelligence!

"White currants and ginger!" echoed Paul, holding out the glass to be refilled.

"A trifle of spirits, of course."

"Of course! couldn't be comforting without it."

"That's what poor dear Fumbally always called, 'Ye know, ye know!' It was his droll way of saying 'Noyau!'" Here Mrs. F. displayed a conflict of smiles and tears; a perfect April landscape on her features. "He had such spirits."

"I don't wonder, if he primed himself with this, often," said Dempsey, who at last relinquished his glass, but with evident unwillingness.

"He used to say that his was a happy home!" sobbed Mrs. Fum, while she pressed her handkerchief to her face.

Paul did not well know what he should say, or if, indeed, he was called upon to utter a sentiment at all; but he thought he could have drunk another glass, to the late Fum's memory, if his widow hadn't kept such a tight grip of the flask.

"Oh, Mr. Dempsey, who could have thought it would come to this?" The sorrowful drooping of her eyelids, as she spoke, seemed to intimate an allusion to the low state of the decanter, and Dempsey at once replied,

"There's a very honest glass in it still."

"Kind—kind creature!" sobbed Mrs. Fum, as she poured out the last of the liquor. And Paul was sorely puzzled, whether the encomium applied to the defunct or himself. "Do you know, Mr. Dempsey"—here she gave a kind of hysterical giggle, that might take any turn, hilarious, or the reverse, as events should dictate—"do you know, that as I see you there, standing before the fire, looking so pleasant and cheerful, so much at home, as a body might say, I can't help fancying a great resemblance between you and my poor dear Fum. He was older than you," said she, rapidly, as a slight cloud passed over Paul's features;—"older and stouter, but he had the same jocose smile, the same merry voice, and even that little fidgety habit with the hands. I know you'll forgive me—even that was his."

This was in all probability strictly correct, inasmuch as for several years before his demise the gifted individual had laboured under a perpetual "Delirium tremens."

"He rather liked this kind of thing," said Paul, pantomiming the action of drinking with his now empty glass.

"In moderation—only in moderation."

"I've heard that it disagreed with him," rejoined Paul, who, not pleased with his counterpart, resolved on showing his knowledge of his habits.

"So it did," sighed Mrs. Fum; "and he gave it up in consequence."

"I heard that, too," said Paul; and then muttered to himself, "on the morning he died."

A gentle tap at the door now broke in upon the colloquy, and a very slatternly servant woman, with bare legs and feet, made her appearance.

"What d'ye want, Biddy?" asked her mistress, in an angry voice. "I'm just settling accounts with Mr. Dempsey, and you bounce in as if the house was on fire."

"It's just himsel's wanted," replied the northern maiden; "the leddie canna get on ava without him, he maun come up to number 'eight,' as soon as he can."

"I'm ready," quoth Paul, as he turned to arrange his cravat, and run his hand through his hair; "I'm at their service."

"Remember, Mr. Dempsey, remember, that what I've spoken to you this day is in the strictest confidence. If matters have proceeded far with the young lady up-stairs, if your heart, if hers be really engaged, forget everything—forget *me*."

Mrs. Fumbally's emotion had so overpowered her towards the end of her speech, that she rushed into an adjoining closet and clapped-to the door, an obstacle that only acted as a sound-board to her sobs, and from which Paul hastened with equal rapidity to escape.

An entire hemisphere might have separated the small chamber where Mr. Dempsey's late interview took place from the apartment on the first floor, to which he now was summoned, and so, to do him justice, did Paul himself feel; and not all the stimulating properties of that pleasant cordial could allay certain tremors of the heart, as he turned the handle of the door.

Lady Eleanor was seated at a writing-table, and Helen beside her, working, as Mr. Dempsey entered, and, after a variety of salutations, took a chair, about the middle of the room, depositing his hat and umbrella beside him.

"It would seem, Mr. Dempsey," said Lady Eleanor, with a very benign smile, "it would seem that we have made a very silly mistake; one, I am bound to say, you are quite exonerated from any share in, and the confession of which will, doubtless, exhibit my own and my daughter's cleverness in a very questionable light before you. Do you know, Mr. Dempsey, we believed this to be an inn."

"An inn!" broke in Paul, with uplifted hands.

"Yes, and it was only by mere accident we have discovered our error, and that we are actually in a boarding-house. Pray now, Helen, do not laugh, the blunder is quite provoking enough already."

Why Miss Darcy should laugh, and what there could be to warrant the use of the epithet, "provoking," Paul might have been broken on the wheel without being able to guess, while Lady Eleanor went on,

"Now, it would seem customary for the guests to adopt, here, certain hours in common—breakfasting, dining together, and associating like the members of one family."

Paul nodded an assent, and she resumed.

"I need scarcely observe to *you*, Mr. Dempsey, how very unsuited either myself or Miss Darcy would be to such an assembly, if even present circumstances did not more than ever enjoin a life of strict retirement."

"Dear me!" exclaimed Paul, in a tone of deprecation, "there never was anything more select than this. Mother Fum never admits without a reference; I can show you the advertisement in the Derry papers. We kept the Collector out for two months, till he brought us a regular bill of health, as a body might say."

"Could you persuade them to let us remain in 'Quarantine,' then, for a few days?" said Helen, smiling.

"Oh, no! Helen, nothing of the kind; Mr. Dempsey must not be put to any troublesome negotiations on our account. There surely must be an hotel of some sort in the town."

"This is a nice mess!" muttered Paul, who began to anticipate some of the miseries his good nature might cost him.

"A few days, a week at furthest, I hope, will enable us to communicate with our law adviser, and decide upon some more suitable abode. Could you, then, for the meanwhile, suggest a comfortable inn, or if not, a lodging in the town?"

Paul wrung his hands in dismay, but uttered not a syllable.

"To be candid, Mr. Dempsey," said Helen, "my father has a horror of these kind of places, and you could recommend us no country inn, however humble, where he would not be better pleased to hear of our taking refuge."

"But, Fumbally's! the best-known boarding-house in the North."

"I should be sincerely grieved, to be understood as uttering one syllable in its disparagement," rejoined Lady Eleanor; "I could not ask for a more satisfactory voucher of its respectability; but, ours are peculiar circumstances."

"Only a pound a week," struck in Paul, "with extras."

"Nothing could be more reasonable; but pray understand me, I speak of course in great ignorance, but it would appear to me that persons living together in this fashion have a kind of right to know something of those who present themselves, for the first time, amongst them. Now, there are many reasons why neither my daughter nor myself would like to submit to this species of inquiry."

"I'll settle all that," broke in Paul; "leave that to me, and you'll have no further trouble about it."

"You must excuse my reliance even on such discretion," said Lady Eleanor, with more hauteur than before.

"Are we to understand that there is neither inn nor lodging-house to be found?" asked Helen.

"Plenty of both, but full of bagmen," ejaculated Paul, whose contrivances were all breaking down beneath him.

"What is to be done?" exclaimed Lady Eleanor to her daughter.

"Lord bless you!" cried Paul, in a whining voice, "if you only come down amongst them with that great frill round your neck you wore the first day I saw you at the Corvy, you'll scare them so, they'll never have courage to utter a word. There was Miss Daly—when she was here——"

"Miss Daly—Miss Maria Daly!" exclaimed both ladies together.

"Miss Maria Daly," repeated Dempsey, with an undue emphasis on every syllable. "She spent the summer with us on the coast."

"Where had she resided up to that time, may I ask?" said Lady Eleanor, hastily.

"At the Corvy—always at the Corvy, until your arrival."

"Oh! Helen, think of this," whispered Lady Eleanor, in a voice tremulous with agitation. "Think what sacrifices we have exacted from our friends—and now, to learn that while we stand hesitating about encountering the inconveniences of our lot, that we have been subjecting another to that very same difficulty from which we shrink." Then, turning to Mr. Dempsey, she added,

"I need not observe, sir, that while I desire no mystery to be thrown around our arrival here, I will not be the less grateful for any restraint the good company may impose on themselves as to inquiries concerning us. We are really not worth the attention, and I should be sorry to impose upon kind credulity by any imaginary claim to distinction."

"You'll dine below, then?" asked Paul, far more eager to ascertain this fact than any reasons that induced it.

Lady Eleanor bowed, and Dempsey, with a face beaming with delight, arose to withdraw and communicate the happy news to Mrs. Fumbally.

CHAPTER LIX.

A GLANCE AT MRS. FUMBALLY'S.

GREAT as Lady Eleanor's objection was to subjecting herself or her daughter to the contact of a boarding-house party, when the resolve was once taken the matter cost her far less thought or anxiety than it occasioned to the other inmates of the "Establishment." It is only in such segments of the great world that curiosity reaches its true intensity, and the desire to know every circumstance of one's neighbour becomes an absorbing passion. A distrustful impression that nobody is playing on "the square"—that every one has some special cause of concealment—some hidden shame, seems the presiding tone of these places.

Mrs. Fumbally's was no exception to the rule, and now that the residents had been so long acquainted, that the personal character and fortune of each was known to all, the announcement of a new arrival caused the most lively sensations of anxiety.

Directories were ransacked for the name of Gwynne, and every separate owner of the appellation canvassed and discussed. Army lists were interrogated and conned over. Dempsey himself was examined for two hours before a "Committee of the whole house," and though his inventive powers were no mean gifts, certain discrepancies, certain unexplained difficulties, did not fail to strike the acute tribunal, and he was dismissed as unworthy of credit. Baffled, not beaten, each retired to dress for dinner—a ceremony, be it remarked, only in use on great occasions—fully impressed with the conviction that the Gwynne case was a legitimate object of search and discovery.

It is not necessary here to allude to the strange display of costume that day called forth, nor what singular extravagances in dress each drew from the armoury of his fascinations. The collector closed the Custom-house an hour earlier, that he might be properly powdered for the occasion. Miss Boyle abandoned, "for the nonce," her accustomed walk on the Banside, where the officers used to lounge, and in the privacy of her chamber prepared for the event. There is a tradition of her being seen, with a formidable array of curl-papers, so late as four in the afternoon. Mr. Dunlop was in a perpetual trot all day, between his tailor and his bootmaker, sundry alterations being required at a moment's notice. Mrs. Fumbally herself, however, eclipsed all competitors, as, in a robe of yellow satin, spotted with red, she made her appearance in the drawing-room; her head-dress being a turban of the same prevailing colours, but ornamented by a drooping plume of feathers and spangles so very umbrageous and pendant, that she looked like a weeping ash clad in tinsel. A crimson brooch of vast proportions—which, on near inspection, turned out to be a portrait of the departed Fumbally, but whose colours were, unhappily, not "fast ones"—confined a scarf of green velvet, from which envious time had worn off all the pile, and left a "sear and yellow" stubble everywhere perceptible.

Whether Mrs. Fum's robe had been devised at a period when dresses were worn much shorter, or that, from being very tall, a sufficiency of the material could not be obtained—but true it is, her costume would have been almost national in certain Scotch regiments, and necessitated, for modesty's sake, a peculiar species of ducking trip, that, with the nodding motion of her head, gave her the gait of a kangaroo.

Scarcely had the various individuals time to give a cursory glance at their neighbour's finery, when Lady Eleanor appeared leaning on her daughter's arm. Mr. Dempsey had waited for above half an hour outside the door to offer his escort, which being coldly but civilly declined, the ladies entered.

Mrs. Fumbally rose to meet her guests, and was about to proceed in due form with a series of introducings, when Lady Eleanor cut her short by a very slight but courteous salutation to the company collectively, and then sat down.

The most insufferable assumption of superiority is never half so chilling in its effect upon underbred people as the calm quietude of good manners.

And thus the party were more repelled by Lady Eleanor and her daughter's easy bearing than they would have felt at any outrageous pretension. The elegant simplicity of their dress, too, seemed to rebuke the stage finery of the others, and very uneasy glances met and were interchanged at this new companionship. A few whispered words, an occasional courageous effort to talk aloud, suddenly ending in a cough, and an uneasy glance at the large silver watch over the chimney, were all that took place, when the uncombed head of a waiter, hired specially for the day, gave the announcement that dinner was served.

"Mr. Dempsey—Mr. Dunlop," said Mrs. Fumbally, with a gesture towards Lady Eleanor and her daughter. The gentlemen both advanced a step and then stood stock still, as Lady Eleanor, drawing her shawl around her with one hand, slipped the other within her daughter's arm. Every eye was now turned towards Mr. Dunlop, who was a kind of recognised type of high life, and he, feeling the urgency of the moment, made a step in advance, and with extended arm, said, "May I have the honour to offer my arm?"

"With your leave, I'll take my daughter's, sir," said Lady Eleanor, coldly; and without paying the least attention to the various significant glances around her, she walked forward to the dinner-room.

The chilling reserve produced by the new arrivals had given an air of decorous quietude to the dinner, which, if gratifying to Lady Eleanor and Helen, was very far from being so to the others, and as the meal proceeded, certain low mutterings—the ground swell of a coming storm—announced the growing feeling of displeasure amongst them. Lady Eleanor and Miss Darcy were too unconscious of having offered any umbrage to the party, to notice these indications of discontent; nor did they remark that Mr. Dempsey himself was becoming overwhelmed by the swelling waves of popular indignation.

A very curt monosyllable had met Lady Eleanor in the two efforts she had made at conversation with her neighbour, and she was perhaps not very sorry to find that table-talk was not a regulation of the "Establishment."

Had Lady Eleanor or Helen been disposed to care for it, they might have perceived that the dinner itself was not less anomalous than the company, and like them suffered sorely from being over dressed. They, however, affected to eat, and seem satisfied with everything, resolved that having encountered the ordeal, they would go through with it to the last. The observances of the table had one merit in the Fumbally household; they were conducted with no unnecessary tediousness. The courses—if we dare so apply the name to an irregular skirmish of meats, hot, cold, and *réchauffé*—followed rapidly, the guests ate equally so, and the table presented a scene, if not of convivial enjoyment, at least of bustle and animation, that supplied its place. This movement, so to call it, was sufficiently new to amuse Helen Darcy, who, less pained than her mother at their companionship, could not help relishing many of the eccentric features of the scene. Everything in the dress, manner, tone of voice, and bearing of the company, presenting such a striking contrast to all she had been used to. This enjoyment on her part, although regulated by the strictest good breeding, was perceived, or rather suspected, by some of the ladies present, and looks of very unmistakable anger were darted towards her from the end of the table, so that both mother and daughter felt the moment a very welcome one, when a regiment of small decanters were set down on the board, and the ladies rose to withdraw.

If Lady Eleanor had consulted her own ardent wishes, she would at once have retired to her room, but she had resolved on the whole sacrifice, and took her place in the drawing-room, determined to follow in every respect the usages around her. Mrs. Fumbally addressed a few civil words to her, and then left the room to look after the cares of the household. The group of seven ladies who remained, formed themselves into a coterie apart, and producing from sundry bags and baskets little specimens of female handi work, began arranging their cottons and worsteds with a most praiseworthy activity.

While Lady Eleanor sat with folded hands, and half-closed lids, sunk in her own meditations, Helen arose and walked towards a book-shelf, where some well-thumbed volumes were lying. An odd volume of "Delphine," a "Treatise on Domestic Cookery," and "Moore's Zeluco," were not attractive, and she sauntered to the piano, on which were scattered some of the songs from the "Siege of Belgrade," the then popular piece; certain comic melodies lay also among them, inscribed with the name of Lawrence M'Farland, a gentleman whom they had heard addressed several times during dinner. While Helen turned over the music pages, the eyes of the others were riveted on her, and when she ran her fingers over the keys of the cracked old instrument, and burst into an involuntary laugh at its discordant tones, a burst of unequivocal indignation could no longer be restrained.

"I declare, Miss M'Corde," said an old lady with a paralytic shake in her head, and a most villanous expression in her one eye—"I declare I would speak to her, if I was in your place."

"Unquestionably," exclaimed another, whose face was purple with excitement; and thus encouraged, a very thin and very tall personage, with a long, slender nose tipped with pink, and light red hair in ringlets, arose from her seat, and approached where Helen was standing.

"You are perhaps not aware, ma'am," said she, with a mincing, lisping accent, the very essence of gentility, "that this instrument is not a 'house piano.'"

Helen blushed slightly at the address, but could not for her life guess what the words meant. She had heard of grand pianos and square pianos, of cottage pianos, but never of "house pianos," and she answered in the most simple of voices, "Indeed."

"No, ma'am, it is not; it belongs to your very humble servant"—here she curtseyed to the ground—"who regrets deeply that its tone should not have more of your approbation."

"And I, ma'am," said a fat old lady, waddling over, and wheezing as though she should choke, "I have to express my sorrow that the book-shelf, which you have just ransacked, should not present something worthy of your notice. The volumes are mine."

"And perhaps, ma'am," cried a third, a little meagre figure, with a voice like a nutmeg-grater, "you could persuade the old lady, whom I presume is your mother, to take her feet off that worked stool. When I made it I scarcely calculated on the honour it now enjoys!"

Lady Eleanor looked up at this instant, and, although unconscious of what was passing, seeing Helen, whose face was now crimson, standing in the midst of a very excited group, she arose hastily, and said,

"Helen, dearest, is there anything the matter?"

"I should say there was, ma'am," interposed the very fat lady—"I should be disposed to say there was a great deal the matter. That to make use of private articles as if they were for house use—to thump one lady's piano—to toss another lady's books—to make oneself comfortable in a chair specially provided for the oldest boarder—with one's feet on another lady's footstool—these are liberties, ma'am, which become something more than freedom when taken by unknown individuals."

"I beg you will forgive my daughter and myself," said Lady Eleanor, with an air of real regret; "our total ignorance——"

"I thought as much, indeed," muttered she of the shaking head; "there is no other word for it."

"You are quite correct, ma'am," said Lady Eleanor, at once addressing her in the most apologetic of voices—"I cannot but repeat the word; our very great ignorance of the usages observed here is our only excuse, and I beg you to believe us incapable of taking such liberties in future."

If anything could have disarmed the wrath of this Holy Alliance, the manner in which these words were uttered might have done so. Far from it, however. When the softer sex are deficient in breeding, mercy is scarcely one of their social attributes. Had Lady Eleanor assumed towards them the manner with which, in other days, she had repelled vulgar attempts at familiarity, they would, in all probability, have shrunk back, abashed and ashamed; but, her yielding suggested boldness, and they advanced, with something like what in Cossack warfare is termed a "Hurra," an indiscriminate clang of voices being raised, in reprobation of every supposed outrage the unhappy strangers had inflicted on the company. Amid this Babel of accusation, Lady Eleanor could distinguish nothing, and while, overwhelmed by the torrent, she was preparing to take her daughter's arm and withdraw, the door, which led into the dining-room, was suddenly thrown open, and the convivial party entered *en masse.*

"Here's a shindy—by George!" cried Mr. M'Farland—"the Pickle, and the wit of the Establishment—I say, see how the new ones are getting it!"

While Mr. Dempsey hurried away to seek Mrs. Fumbally herself, the confusion and uproar increased. The loud, coarse laughter of the "Gentlemen" being added to the wrathful violence of the softer sex. Lady Eleanor, however, had drawn her daughter to her side, and without uttering a word, proceeded to leave the room. To this course a considerable obstacle presented itself in the shape of the Collector, who, with expanded legs, and hands thrust deep into his side-pockets, stood against the door.

"Against the ninth general rule, ma'am, which you may read in the frame over the chimney!" exclaimed he, in a voice somewhat more faltering and thicker than became a respectable official. "No lady or gentleman can leave the room, while any dispute in which they are concerned remains unsettled. Isn't that it, M'Farland?" cried he, as the young gentleman alluded to took down the law-table from its place.

"All right," replied M'Farland; "the very best rule in the house. Without it, all the rows would take place in private! Now for a court of inquiry. Mr. Dunlop, you are for the prosecution, and can't sit."

"May I beg, sir, you will permit us to pass out?" said Lady Eleanor, in a voice whose composure was slightly shaken.

"Can't be, ma'am; in contravention of all law," rejoined the Collector.

"Where is Mr. Dempsey?" whispered Helen, in her despair; and though the words were uttered in a low voice, one of the ladies overheard them. A general titter ran immediately around, only arrested by the fat lady exclaiming aloud, "Shameless minx!"

A very loud hubbub of voices outside now rivalled the tumult within, amid which one most welcome was distinguished by Helen.

"Oh, mamma, how fortunate, I hear Tate's voice."

"It's me—it's Mrs. Fumbally," cried that lady, at the same moment tapping sharply at the door.

"No matter, can't open the door now. Court is about to sit," replied the Collector. "Mrs. Gwynne stands arraigned for—for what is't? There's no use in making that clatter; the door shall not be opened."

This speech was scarcely uttered, when a tremendous bang was heard, and the worthy Collector, with the door over him, was hurled on his face in the midst of the apartment, upsetting in his progress a round table and a lamp over the assembled group of ladies.

Screams of terror, rage, pain, and laughter, were now commingled, and while some assisted the prostrate official to rise, and sprinkled his temples with water, others bestowed their attentions on the discomfited fair, whose lustre was sadly diminished by lamp-oil and bruises, while a third section, of which M'Farland was chief, lay back in their chairs and laughed vociferously, Meanwhile, how and when, nobody could tell, but Lady Eleanor and her daughter had escaped and gained their apartments in safety.

A more rueful scene than the room presented need not be imagined. The Collector, whose nose bled profusely, sat pale, half fainting, in one corner, while some kind friends laboured to stop the bleeding, and restore him to animation. Lamentations of the most poignant grief were uttered over silks satins, and tabinets, irretrievably ruined; while the paralytic lady, having broken the ribbon of her cap, her head rolled about fearfully, and even threatened to come clean off altogether. As for poor Mrs. Fumbally, she flew from place to place, in a perfect agony of affliction; now, wringing her hands over the prostrate door, now, over the fragments of the lamp, and now endeavouring to restore the table, which, despite all her efforts, would not stand upon two legs. But the most miserable figure of all was Paul Dempsey, who saw no footing for himself anywhere. Lady Eleanor and Helen must detest him to the day of his death. The boarders could never forgive him. Mrs. Fum would as certainly regard him as the author of all evil, and the Collector would inevitably begin dunning him for an unsettled balance of fourteen and ninepence, lost at "Spoiled five," two winters before.

Already, indeed, symptoms of his unpopularity began to show themselves. Angry looks and spiteful glances were directed towards him, amidst muttered expressions of displeasure. How far these manifestations might have proceeded there is no saying, had not the attention of the company been drawn to the sudden noise of a carriage stopping at the street door.

"Going, flitting, evacuating the territory!" exclaimed M'Farland, as from an open window he contemplated the process of packing a post-chaise with several heavy trunks and portmanteaus.

"The Gwynnes!" muttered the Collector, with his handkerchief to his face.

"Even so! flying with camp equipage and all. There stands your victor that little old fellow with the broad shoulders. I say, come here a moment," called he aloud, making a sign for Tate to approach. "The Collector is not in the least angry for what's happened; he knew you didn't mean anything serious. Pray, who are these ladies, your mistresses I mean?"

"Lady Eleanor Darcy and Miss Darcy, of Gwynne Abbey," replied Tate, sturdily, as he gave the names with a most emphatic distinctness.

"The devil it was!" exclaimed M'Farland.

"By my conscience, yer may well wonder at being in such company, sir," said Tate, laughing, and resuming his place just in time to assist Lady Eleanor to ascend the steps. Helen quickly followed, the door was slammed to, and Tate mounting with an alacrity of a town footman, the chaise set out at a brisk pace down the street.

CHAPTER LX.

THE COAST IN WINTER.

ALTHOUGH Tate Wilkinson had arrived in Coleraine, and provided himself with a chaise, expressly to bring his mistress and her daughter back to the Corvy—from which the Sheriff's officers had retired in discomfiture, on discovering the loss of their warrants—Lady Eleanor, dreading a renewal of the law proceedings, had determined never to return thither.

From the postilion they learned that a small but not uncomfortable lodging could be had near the little village of Port Ballintray, and to this spot they now directed their course. The transformation of a little summer watering-place into the dismal village of some poor fishermen in winter, is a sad spectacle; nor was the picture relieved by the presence of the fragments of a large vessel, which, lately lost with all its crew, hung on the rocks, thumping and clattering with every motion of the waves. By the faint moonlight, Lady Eleanor and her daughter could mark the outlines of figures, as they waded in the tide, or clambered along the rocks, stripping the last remains of the noble craft, and contending with each other for the spoils of the dead.

If the scene itself was a sorrowful one, it was no less painful to their eyes from feeling a terrible similitude between their own fortunes and that of the wrecked vessel; the gallant ship meant to float in its pride over the ocean, now a broken and shattered wreck, falling asunder with each stroke of the sea!

"How like, and yet how unlike!" sighed Lady Eleanor; "if these crushed and shattered timbers have no feeling in the hour of adversity, yet are they denied the glorious hopefulness that in the saddest moments clings to humanity. Ours is shipwreck too, but taken at its worst, in only temporary calamity!"

Helen pressed her mother's hands with fervour to her lips—perhaps never had she loved her with more intensity than at that instant.

The chaise drew up at the door of a little cabin, built at the foot of, and, as it actually seemed, against a steep rocky cliff of great height. In summer, it was regarded as one of the best among the surrounding lodgings, but now it looked dreary enough. A fishing-boat, set up on one end, formed a kind of sheltering porch to the doorway, while spars, masts, and oars were lashed upon the thatch, to serve as a protection against the dreadful gales of winter.

A childless widow was the only occupant, whose scanty livelihood was eked out by letting lodgings to the summer visitors, a precarious subsistence, which, in bad seasons, and they were not unfrequent, failed altogether. It was with no small share of wonderment that Mary Spellan, or "old Molly," as the village more usually called her, saw a carriage draw up to the cabin door late of a dark night in winter, nor was this feeling unalloyed by a very strong tincture of suspicion, for Molly was an Antrim woman, and had her proportion of the qualities, good and bad, of the "Black North."

"They'll no be makin' a stay on't," said she to the postboy, who, in his capacity of interpreter, had got down to explain to Molly the requirements of the strangers. "They'll be here to-day and awa to-morrow, I'm thenkin'," said she, with habitual and native distrust. "And what for wull I make a 'hottle' "—(no greater indignity could be offered to the lodging-house keeper than to compare the accommodation in any respect with that of an hotel)—"of my wee bit house, takin' out linen and a' the rest o' it—for maybe a day or twa."

Lady Eleanor, who watched from the window of the chaise the course of the negotiations, without hearing any part of the colloquy, was impatient at the slow progress events seemed to take, and supposing that the postboy's demands were made with more regard to their habits than to old Molly's means of accommodation, called out,

"Tell the good woman that we are easily satisfied, and if the cabin be but clean and quiet——"

"What's the leddie sayin' ?" said Molly, who heard only a stray word, and that not over pleasing to her.

"She's saying it will do very well," said the postboy, conciliatingly, "and tis maybe a whole year she'll stay with you."

"Ech, dearee me !" sighed Molly, "it's wearisome enough to ha' them a the summer, without hae'ing them in the winter too. Tell her to come ben, and see if she likes the place." And with this not over courteous proposal, Molly turned her back, and rolled, rather than walked, into the cabin.

The three little rooms, which comprised the whole suite destined for strangers, were, in all their poverty, scrupulously clean; and Molly, gradually thawed by the evident pretensions of her guests, volunteered little additions to the furniture, as she went along, concluding with the very characteristic remark,

"But ye maun consider, that it's no my habit, or my likin' either, to hae lodgers in the winter, and af ye come, ye maun e'en pay for your whistle, like ither folk."

This was the arrangement that gave Lady Eleanor the least trouble, and though the terms demanded were in reality exorbitant, they were acceded to, without hesitation, by those who never had had occasion to make similar compacts, and believed that the sum was a most reasonable one.

As is ever the case, the many wants and inconveniences of a restricted dwelling were far more placidly endured by those long habituated to every luxury, than by their followers; and so, while Lady Eleanor and Helen submitted cheerfully to daily privations of one kind or other, Tate lived a life of everlasting complaint and grumbling over the narrow accommodation of the cabin, continually irritating old Molly by demands impossible to comply with, and suggesting the necessity of changes, perfectly out of her power to effect. It is but justice to the faithful old butler to state, that to this line of conduct he was prompted by what he deemed due to his mistress, and her high station, rather than by any vain hope of ever succeeding, his complaints being less demands for improvement than after the fashion of those "protests," which dissentient members of a Legislature think it necessary to make, in cases where opposition is unavailing.

These half-heard mutterings of Tate were the only interruptions to a life of sad, but tranquil monotony. Lady Eleanor and her daughter lived as though in a long dream; the realities around them so invested with sameness and uniformity, that days, weeks, and months blended into each other, and became one commingled mass of time, undivided and unmarked. Of the world without they heard but little—of those dearest to them, absolutely nothing. The very newspapers maintained a silence on the subject of the expedition under Abercrombie, so that of the Knight himself they had no tidings whatever. Of Daly they only heard once, at the end of one of Bicknell's letters, one of those gloomy records of the law's delay! that he said, "You will be sorry to learn, that Mr. Bagenal Daly, having omitted to appear personally, or by counsel, in a cause lately called on here, has been cast in heavy damages, and pronounced in contempt, neither of which inflictions will probably give him much uneasiness, if, as report speaks, he has gone to pass the remainder of his days in America. Miss Daly speaks of joining him, when she learns that he has fixed on any spot of future residence." The only particle of consolation extractable from the letter was in a paragraph at the end, which ran thus: "O'Reilly's solicitor has withdrawn all the proceedings lately commenced, and there is an evident desire to avoid further litigation. I hear that for the points now in dispute, an arbitration will be proposed. Would you feel disposed, or free to accept such an offer, if made? Let me know this, as I should be prepared at all events."

Even this half-confession of a claim gave hope to the drooping spirits of Lady Eleanor, and she lost no time in acquainting Bicknell with her opinion, that while they neither could nor would compromise the rights of their son, that, for any interests actually their own, and terminating with their lives, they would willingly adopt any arrangement that should remove the most pressing evils of poverty, and permit them to live united for the rest of their days.

The severe winter of northern Ireland closed in, with all its darkening skies and furious storms—scattered fragments of wrecked vessels, spars, and ship-gear, strewed the rocky coast for miles. The few cottages here and there were closed and barricaded as if against an enemy, the roof fastened down by ropes and heavy implements of husbandry, to keep safe the thatch; the boats of the fishermen drawn up on land, grouped round the shealings in sad, but not unpicturesque confusion. The ever-restless sea, beating like thunder upon that iron shore; the dark impending clouds lowering over cliff and precipice, were all that the eye could mark. No cattle were on the hills, the sheep nestling in the little glens and valleys were almost undistinguishable from the depth of gloom around; not a man was to be seen.

The little village of Port Ballintray, which a few months before abounded in all the sights and sounds of human intercourse, was now perfectly deserted. Most of the cottages were fastened on the inside; in some, the doors, burst open by the storm, showed still more unquestionably that no dwellers remained; the little gardens, tended with such care, were now uprooted and devastated; fallen trellises and ruined porches were seen on every side, and even Mrs. Fumbally's, the pride and glory of the place, had not escaped the general wreck, and the flaunting archway, on which, in bright letters, her name was inscribed, hung pensively by one pillar, and waved like a sad pendulum, "counting the weary minutes over!"

While nothing could less resemble the signs of habitation than the aspect of matters without, within a fire burned on more than one hearth, and a serving-woman was seen moving from place to place, occupied in making those arrangements which bespoke the speedy arrival of visitors.

It was long after nightfall that a travelling carriage and four—a rare sight in such a place, even in the palmiest days of summer—drew up at the front of the little garden, and after some delay, a very old and feeble man was lifted out, and carried between two servants into the house; he was followed by another, whose firm step and erect figure indicated the prime of life; while after him again came a small man, most carefully protected by coats and comforters against the severity of the season. He walked lame, and in the shuddering look he gave around in the short transit from the carriage to the house door, showed that such prospects, however grand and picturesque, had few charms for him.

A short interval elapsed after the luggage was removed from the carriage, and then one of the servants mounted the box, the horses' heads were turned, and the conveyance was seen retiring by the road to Coleraine.

The effective force of Mrs. Kum's furniture was never remarkable, in days of gala and parade; it was still less imposing now, when nothing remained save an invalided garrison of deal chairs and tables, a few curtainless beds, and a stray chest of drawers or two of the rudest fashion.

The ample turf fire on the hearth of the chief sitting-room, cheering and bright as was its aspect, after the dark and rainy scene without doors, could not gladden the air of these few and comfortless movables into a look of welcome, and so one of the newly-arrived party seemed to feel, as he threw his glance over the meagre-looking chamber, and in a half-complaining, half-inquiring tone, said,

"Don't you think, sir, they might have done this a little better? These windows are no defence against the wind or rain, the walls are actually soaked with wet: not a bit of carpet, not a chair to sit upon! I'm greatly afraid for the old gentleman; if he were to be really ill in such a place——"

A heavy fit of coughing from the inner room now seemed to corroborate the suspicion.

"We must make the best of it, Nalty," said the other. "Remember, the plan was of your own devising; there was no time for much preparation here, if even it had been prudent or possible to make it; and as to my father, I warrant you his constitution is as good as yours or mine; anxiety about this business has preyed upon him; but let your plan only succeed, and I warrant him as able to undergo fatigue and privation as either of us."

"His cough is very troublesome," interposed Nalty, timidly.

"About the same I have known it every winter since I was a boy," said the other, carelessly. "I say, sir," added he, louder, while he tapped the door with his knuckles—"I say, sir, Nalty is afraid you have caught fresh cold."

"Tell him, his annuity is worth three years' purchase," said the old man from within, with a strange, unearthly effort at a laugh. "Tell him, if he'll pay five hundred pounds down, I'll let him run his own life against mine in the deed."

"There, you hear that, Nalty! What say you to the proposal?"

"Wonderful old man! astonishing!" muttered Nalty, evidently not flattered at the doubts thus suggested as to his own longevity.

"He doesn't seem to like that, Bob, eh?" called out the old man, with another cackle.

"After that age they get a new lease, sir—actually a new lease of life," whispered Nalty.

Mr. O'Reilly—for it was that gentleman, who, accompanied by his father and confidential lawyer, formed the party—gave a dry assent to the proposition, and drawing his chair closer to the fire, seemed to occupy himself with his own thoughts. Meanwhile, the old doctor continued to maintain a low muttering conversation with his servant, until at length the sounds were exchanged for a deep snoring respiration, and he slept.

The appearance of a supper, which, if not very appetising, was at least very welcome, partially restored the drooping spirits of Mr. Nalty, who now ate and talked with a degree of animation quite different from his former mood.

"The ham is excellent, sir, and the veal very commendable," said he, perceiving that O'Reilly sat with his untouched plate before him, "and a glass of sherry is very grateful after such a journey."

"A weary journey, indeed," said O'Reilly, sighing; "the roads in this part of the island would seem seldom travelled, and the inns never visited; however, if we succeed, Nalty——"

"So we shall, sir, I have not the slightest doubt of it; it is perfectly evident that they have no money to go on. 'The sinews of war' are expended, all Bicknell's late proceedings indicate a failing exchequer; that late record, for instance, at Westport, should never have been left to a common jury."

"All this may be true, and yet we may find them unwilling to adopt a compromise: there is a spirit in this class of men very difficult to deal with."

"But we have two expedients," interrupted Nalty.

"Say, rather, a choice between two; you forget that if we try my father's plan, the other can never be employed."

"I incline to the other mode of procedure," said Nalty, thoughtfully; "it has an appearance of frankness and candour very likely to influence people of this kind; besides, we have such a strong foundation to go upon—the issue of two trials at bar, both adverse to them, O'Grady's opinion on the ejectment cases equally opposed to their views. The expense of a suit in equity to determine the validity of the entail, and show how far young Darcy can be a plaintiff: then the cases for a jury; all costly matters, sir! Bicknell knows this well; indeed, if the truth were out, I suspect Sam is getting frightened about his own costs, he has sold out of the funds twice to pay fees."

"Yet the plan is a mere compromise, after all," said O'Reilly; "it is simply saying, relinquish your right, and accept so much money."

"Not exactly, sir; we deny the right, we totally reject the claim, we merely say, forego proceedings that are useless, spare yourselves and us the cost and publicity of legal measures, whose issue never can benefit you, and, in return for your compliance, receive an annuity or a sum, as may be agreed upon."

"But how is Lady Eleanor to decide upon a course so important, in the absence of her husband and her son? Is it likely, is it possible she would venture on so bold a step?"

"I think so; Bicknell half acknowledged that the funds of the suit were her jointure, and that Darcy, out of delicacy towards her, had left it entirely at her option to continue or abandon the proceedings."

"Still," said O'Reilly, "a great difficulty remains; for supposing them to accept our terms, that they give up the claim and accept a sum in return, what, if at some future day evidence should turn up to substantiate their views—they may not, it is true, break the engagement—though I don't see why they should not—but let us imagine them to be faithful to the contract —what will the world say? in what position shall we stand when the matter gains publicity?"

"How can it, sir?" interposed Nalty, quickly; "how is it possible, if there be no trial? The evidence, as you call it, is no evidence, unless produced in Court. You know, sir," said the little man, with twinkling eyes and pleased expression, "that a great authority at common law only declined the testimony of a ghost because the spirit wasn't in court to be cross-examined. Now all they could bring would be rumour, newspaper allegations and paragraphs, asterisks and blanks."

"There may come a time when public opinion, thus expounded, will be as stringent as the judgments of the law courts," said O'Reilly, thoughtfully.

"I am not so certain of that, sir; the licence of an unfettered press will always make its decisions inoperative; it is 'the chartered libertine' the poet speaks of."

"But what, if yielding to public impression it begins to feel that its weight is in exact proportion to its truth, that well-founded opinions, just judgments, correct anticipations, obtain a higher praise and price than scandalous anecdotes and furious attacks? What if that day should arrive, Nalty? I am by no means convinced that such an era is distant."

"Let it come, sir," said the little man, rubbing his hands, "and when it does there will be enough employment on its hand without going back on our transgressions; the world will always be wicked enough to keep the moralist at his work of correction; but to return to our immediate object, I perceive you are inclined to Dr. Hickman's plan."

"I am so far in its favour," said O'Reilly, "that it solves the present difficulty, and prevents all future danger. Should my father succeed in persuading Lady Eleanor to this marriage, the interest of the two families is inseparably united. It is very unlikely that any circumstance, of what nature soever, would induce young Darcy to dispute his sister's claim, or endanger her position in society. This settlement of the question is satisfactory in itself, and shows a good face to the world, and I confess I am curious to know what peculiar objection you can see against it."

"It has but one fault, sir."

"And that?"

"Simply, it is impossible.

"Is it the presumption of a son of mine seeking an alliance with the daughter of Maurice Darcy, that appears so very impossible?" said Hickman, with a hissing utterance of each word, that bespoke a fierce conflict of passion within him.

"Certainly not, sir," replied Nalty, hastily excusing himself. "I am well aware which party contributes most to such a compact. Mr. Beecham O'Reilly might look far higher——"

"Wherein lies the impossibility you speak of, then?" rejoined O'Reilly, sternly.

"I need scarcely remind *you*, sir," said Nalty, with an air of deep humility, "*you* that have seen so much more of life than I have, of what inveterate prejudices these old families—as they like to call themselves—are made up. That, creating a false standard of rank, they adhere to its distinctions with a tenacity far greater than what they exhibit towards the real attributes of fortune. They seem to adopt for their creed the words of the old song,

The King may make a Baron bold,
Or an Earl of any fool, sir,
But with all his power, and all his gold
He never can make an O'Toole, sir."

"These are very allowable feelings when sustained by wealth and fortune," said O'Reilly, quietly.

"I verily believe their influence is greater in adversity," said Nalty; "they seem to have a force of consolation that no misery can rob them of; besides, in this case—for we should not lose sight of the matter that concerns us most—we must not forget that they regard your family in the light of oppressors. I am well aware that you have acted legally and safely throughout, but still—let us concede something to human prejudices and passions—is it unreasonable to suppose that they charge you and yours with their own downfal?"

"The more natural our desire to repair the apparent wrong."

"Very true on *your* part, but not perhaps the more necessary on theirs to accept the amende."

"That will very much depend, I think, on the way of its being proffered. Lady Eleanor, cold, haughty, and reserved as she is to the world, has always extended a degree of cordiality and kindness towards my father; his age, his infirmities, a seeming simplicity in his character, have had their influence. I trust greatly to this feeling, and to the effect of a request made by an old man, as if from his death-bed. My father is not deficient in the tact to make an appeal of this kind very powerful; at all events, his heart is in the scheme, and nothing short of that would have induced me to venture on this long and dreary journey at such a season. Should he only succeed in gaining an influence over Lady Eleanor, through pity or any other motive, we are certain to succeed. The Knight, I feel sure, would not oppose; and as for the young lady, a handsome young fellow with a large fortune can scarcely be deemed very objectionable."

"How was the proposition met before?" said Nalty, inquiringly; "was their refusal conveyed in any expression of delicacy? Was there any acknowledgment of the compliment intended them?"

"No, not exactly," said O'Reilly, blushing; for, while he hesitated about the danger of misleading his adviser, he could not bear to repeat the insolent rejection of the offer. "The false position in which the families stood towards each other made a great difficulty, but, more than all, the influence of Bagenal Daly increased the complexity; now he, fortunately for us, is not forthcoming, his debts have driven him abroad, they say."

"So, then, they merely declined the honour in cold and customary phrase," said Nalty, carelessly.

"Something in that way," replied O'Reilly, affecting an equal unconcern; "but we need not discuss the point, it affords no light to guide us regarding the future."

If Nalty saw plainly that some concealment was practised towards him, he knew his client too well to venture on pushing his inquiries further, so he contented himself with asking when and in what manner O'Reilly proposed to open the siege.

"To-morrow morning," replied the other; "there's no time to be lost. A few lines from my father to Lady Eleanor will acquaint her with his arrival in the neighbourhood, after a long and fatiguing search for her residence. We may rely upon him performing his part well; he will allude to his own breaking health in terms that will not fail to touch her, and ask permission to wait upon her. As for us, Nalty, we must not be foreground figures in the picture. You, if known to be here at all, must be supposed to be my father's medical friend. I must be strictly in the shade."

Nalty gave a grim smile at the notion of his new professional character, and begged O'Reilly to proceed.

"Our strategy goes no further; such will be the order of battle. We must trust to my father for the mode he will engage the enemy afterwards, for the reasons which have led him to take this step; the approaching close of a long life, unburdened with any weighty retrospect, save that which concerns the Darcy family; for, while affecting to sorrow over their changed fortunes, he can attribute their worst evils to bad counsels and rash advice, and insinuate how different had been their lot had they only consented to regard us—as they might and ought to have done—in the light of friends.—Hush! who is speaking there?"

They listened for a second or two, and then came the sound of the old man's voice, as he talked to himself in his sleep: his accents were low and complaining, as if he were suffering deeply from some mental affliction, and, at intervals, a heavy sob would break from him.

"He is ill, sir; the old gentleman is very ill!" said Nalty, in real alarm.

"Hush!" said O'Reilly, as, with one hand on the door, he motioned silence with the other.

"Yes, my Lady," muttered the sleeper, but in a voice every syllable of which was audible, "eighty-six years have crept to your feet, to utter this last wish and die. It is the last request of one that has already left the things of this world, and I would carry from it nothing but the thought that will track him to the grave!" A burst of grief, too sudden and too natural to admit of a doubt of its sincerity, followed the words, and O'Reilly was about to enter the room, when a low dry laugh arrested his steps, and the old man said,

"Ay! Bob Hickman, didn't I tell you that would do? I knew she'd cry and I told you, if she cried one tear, the day was ours!"

There was something so horrible in the baseness of a mind thus revelling in its own duplicity, that even Nalty seemed struck with dread. O'Reilly saw what was passing in the other's mind, and affecting to laugh at these "effects of fatigue and exhaustion," half led, half pushed him from the room, and said "Good night."

CHAPTER LXI.

THE DOCTOR'S LAST DEVICE.

"TELL Mister Bob—Mr. O'Reilly I mean—to come to me," were the first words of old Doctor Hickman, as he awoke on the following morning.

"Well, sir, how have you slept?" said his son, approaching the bedside, and taking a chair; "have you rested well?"

"Middling, only middling, Bob. The place is like a vault, and the rats have it all their own way. They were capering about the whole night, and made such a noise trying to steal off with one of my shoes."

"Did they venture that far?"

"Ay, did they! but I couldn't let it go with them. I know you're in a hurry to stand in them yourself, Bob, and leave me and the rats to settle it between us, ay!"

"Really, sir, these are jests——"

"Too like earnest to be funny, Bob; so I feel them myself. Ugh! ugh! The damp of this place is freezing the very heart's blood of me. How is Nalty this morning?"

"Like a fellow taken off a wreck, sir, after a week's starvation. He is sitting at the fire there, with two blankets round him, and vows to heaven, every five minutes, that if he was once back in Old Dominick-street, a thousand guineas wouldn't tempt him to such another expedition."

The old doctor laughed till it made him cough, and when the fit was over, laughed again, wiping his weeping eyes, and chuckling in the most unearthly glee at the lawyer's discomfiture.

"Wrapped up in blankets, eh, Bob?" said he, that he might hear further of his fellow-traveller's misery.

O'Reilly saw that he had touched the right key, and expatiated for some minutes upon Nalty's sufferings, throwing out, from time to time, adroit hints that only certain strong and hale constitutions could endure privations like these. Now, you, sir," continued he, "you look as much yourself as ever; in fact, I half doubt how you are to play the sick man, with all these signs of rude health about you."

"Leave that to me, Bob; I think I've seen enough of them things to know them now. When I've carried my point, and all's safe and secure, you'll see me like the Pope we read of, that looked all but dead till they elected him, and then stood up stout and hearty five minutes after—we'll have a miracle of this kind in our own family."

"I suspect, sir, we shall have difficulty in obtaining an interview," said O'Reilly.

"No!" rejoined the old man, with a scarcely perceptible twinkle of his fishy eyes.

"Nalty's of my opinion, and thinks that Lady Eleanor will positively decline it."

"No," echoed he once more.

"And that, without any suspicion of our plan, she will yet refuse to receive you."

"I'm not going to ask her, Bob," croaked the old doctor, with a species of chuckling crow in his voice.

"Then you have abandoned your intention," exclaimed O'Reilly, in dismay, "and the whole journey has been incurred for nothing."

"No!" said the doctor, whose grim old features were lit up with a most spiteful sense of his superior cunning.

"Then I don't understand you, that's clear," exclaimed O'Reilly, testily. "You say that you do not intend to call upon her——"

"Because she's coming here to see me," cried the old man, in a scream of triumph; "read that, it's an answer to a note I sent off at eight o'clock. Joe waited and brought back this reply." As he spoke, he drew from beneath his pillow a small note, and handed it to his son. O'Reilly opened it with impatience, and read: "Lady Eleanor Darcy begs to acknowledge the receipt of Dr. Hickman's note, and, while greatly indisposed to accept of an interview which must be so painful to both parties, without any reasonable prospect of rendering service to either, feels reluctant to refuse a request made under circumstances so trying. She will therefore comply with Dr. Hickman's entreaty, and, to spare him the necessity of venturing abroad in this severe weather, will call upon him at twelve o'clock, should she not learn in the mean while that the hour is inconvenient."

"Lady Eleanor Darcy come out to call upon you, sir!" said O'Reilly, with an amazement in part simulated to flatter the old man's skill, but far more really experienced. "This is indeed success."

"Ay, you may well say so," chimed in the old man; "for besides that I always look ten years older when I'm in bed and unshaved, with my nightcap a little off—this way; the very sight of these miserable walls, green with damp and mould, this broken window, and the poverty-struck furniture, will all help, and I can get up a cough, if I only draw a long breath."

"I vow, sir, you beat us all; we are mere children compared to you. This is a masterstroke of policy."

"What will Nalty say now eh, Bob?"

"Say, sir?—what can any one say, but that the move showed a master's hand, as much above our skill to accomplish, as it was beyond our wit to conceive? I should like greatly to hear how you intend to play the game out," said O'Reilly, throwing a most flattering expression of mingled curiosity and astonishment into his features.

"Wait till I see what trumps the adversary has in hand, Bob; time enough to determine the lead when the cards are dealt."

"I suppose I must keep out of sight, and perhaps Nalty also."

"Nalty ought to be in the house if we want him; as my medical friend, he could assist to draw up any little memorandum we might determine upon; a mere note, Bob, between friends, not requiring the interference of lawyers, eh?" There was something fiendish in the low laugh which accompanied these words. "What brings that fellow into the room so often, putting turf on, and looking if the windows are fast? I don't like him, Bob." This was said in reference to a little chubby man, in a waiter's jacket, who really had taken every imaginable professional privilege to obtrude his presence.

"There, there, that will do," said O'Reilly, harshly; "you needn't come till we ring the bell."

"Leave the turf-basket where it is. Don't you think we can mind the fire for ourselves?"

"Let Joe wait, that will be better, sir," whispered O'Reilly; "we cannot be too cautious here." And with a motion of the hand he dismissed the waiter, who, true to his order, seemed never to hear "an aside."

"Leave me by myself, Bob, for half an hour; I'd like to collect my thoughts —to settle and think over this meeting. It's past eleven now, and she said twelve o'clock in the note."

"Well, I'll take a stroll over the hills, and be back for dinner about three; you'll be up by that time."

"That will I, and very hungry, too," muttered the old man. "This dying scene has cost me the loss of my breakfast; and faith, I'm so weak and low, my head is quite dizzy. There's an old saying, mocking is catching, and sure enough there may be some truth in it, too."

O'Reilly affected not to hear the remark, and moved towards the door, when he turned about and said,

"I should say, sir, that the wisest course would be to avoid anything like coercion, or the slightest approach to it. The more the appeal is made to her feelings of compassion and pity——"

"For great age and bodily infirmity," croaked the old man, while the filmy orbs shot forth a flash of malicious intelligence.

"Just so, sir. To others' eyes you do indeed seem weak and bowed down with years. It is only they who have opportunity to recognise the clearness of your intellect and the correctness of your judgment can see how little inroad time has made."

"Ay, but it has, though," interposed the old man, irritably. "My hand shakes more than it used to do; there's many an operation I'd not be able for as I once was."

"Well, well, sir," said his son, who found it difficult to repress the annoyance he suffered from his continual reference to the old craft. "Remember that you are not called upon now to perform these things."

"Sorry I am it is so," rejoined the other. "I gave up seven hundred a year when I left Loughrea to turn gentleman with you at Gwynne Abbey; and faith, the new trade isn't so profitable as the old one! So it is," muttered he to himself, "and now, there's a set of young chaps come into the town, with their medical halls, and great bottles of pink and blue water in the windows! What chance would I have to go back again?"

O'Reilly heard these half-uttered regrets in silence; he well knew that the safest course was to let the feeble brain exhaust its scanty memories without impediment. At length, when the old doctor seemed to have wearied of the theme, he said,

"If she make allusion to the Dalys, sir, take care not to confess our mistake about that cabin they call the Corvy, and which you remember we discovered that Daly had settled upon his servant. Let Lady Eleanor suppose that we withdrew proceedings out of respect to her."

"I know, I know," said the old man, querulously, for his vanity was wounded by these reiterated instructions.

"It is possible, too, sir, she'd stand upon the question of rank; if so, say that Heffernan—no, say that Lord Castlereagh will advise the King to confer the Baronetcy on the marriage—don't forget that, sir—on the marriage."

"Indeed; then I'll say nothing about it," said he, with an energy almost startling. "It's that weary Baronetcy cost me the loan to Heffernan on his own bare bond; I'm well sick of it! Seven thousand pounds at five and a half per cent., and no security!"

"I only thought, sir, it might be introduced incidentally," said O'Reilly, endeavouring to calm down this unexpected burst of irritation.

"I tell you I won't. If I'm bothered any more about the same Baronetcy, I'll make a clause in my will against my heir accepting it. How bad you are for the coronet with the two balls; faix, I remember when the family arms had three of them; ay, and we sported them over the door, too. Eh, Bob, shall I tell her that?"

"I don't suppose it would serve our cause much, sir," said O'Reilly, repressing with difficulty his swelling anger. Then, after a moment, he added, "I could never think of obtruding any advice of mine, sir, but that I half feared you might, in the course of the interview, forget many minor circumstances, not to speak of the danger that your natural kindliness might expose you to in any compact with a very artful woman of the world."

"Don't be afraid of that anyhow, Bob," said he, with a most hideous grin. "I keep a watchful eye over my natural kindliness, and, to say truth, it has done me mighty little mischief up to this. There, now, leave me quiet and to myself."

When the old man was left alone his head fell slightly forward, and his hands, clasped together, rested on his breast. His eyes, half closed and downcast, and his scarcely-heaving chest, seemed barely to denote life, or at most that species of life in which the senses are steeped in apathy. The grim, hard features, stiffened by years, and a stern nature, never moved; the thin, close-drawn lips never once opened; and to any observer the figure might have seemed a lifeless counterfeit of old age. And yet, within that brain, fast yielding to time and infirmity, where reason came and went like the flame of some flickering taper, and where memory brought up objects of dreamy fancy as often as bygone events—even there, plot and intrigue held their ground, and all the machinery of deception was at work, suggesting, contriving, and devising wiles that in their complexity were too puzzling for the faculties that originated them. Is there a Nemesis in this, and do the passions by which we have swayed and controlled others rise up before us in our weak hours, and become the tyrants of our terror-stricken hearts?

It is not our task, were it even in our power, to trace the strange commingled web of reality and fiction that composed the old man's thoughts. At one time he believed he was supplicating the Knight to accord him some slight favour, as he had done more than once successfully. Then he suddenly remembered their relative stations, so strangely reversed; the colossal fortune he had himself accumulated; the hopes and ambitions of his son and grandson, whose only impediments to rank and favour lay in himself, the humble origin of all this wealth. How strange and novel did the conviction strike him that all the benefit of his vast riches lay in the pleasure of their accumulation. That for him fortune had no seductions to offer. Rank, power, munificence, what were they? he never cared for them.

No; it was the game he loved even more than the stake. That tortuous course of policy, by which he had outwitted this man and doubled on that. The schemes skilfully conducted—the plots artfully accomplished—these he loved to think over; and while he grieved to reflect upon the reckless waste he witnessed in the household of his son, he felt a secret thrill of delight that he, and he alone, was capable of those rare devices and bold expedients by which such a fortune could be amassed. Once and only once did any expression of his features sympathise with these ponderings; and then a low, harsh laugh broke suddenly from him, so fleeting that it failed to arouse even himself. It came from the thought that if, after his death, his son or grandson would endeavour to forget his memory, and have it forgotten by others, that every effort of display, every new evidence of their gorgeous wealth, would as certainly evoke the criticism of the envious world, who, in spite of them, would bring up the "old Doctor" once more, and, by the narrative of his life, humble them to the dust.

This desire to bring down to a level with himself those around him had been the passion of his existence. For this he had toiled and laboured, and struggled through imaginary poverty when possessed of wealth; had endured scoffs and taunts—had borne everything—and to this desire could be traced his whole feeling towards the Darcys. It was no happiness to him to be the owner of their princely estate if he did not revel in the reflection that they were in poverty. And this envious feeling he extended to his very son. If now and then a vague thought of the object of his present journey crossed his mind, it was speedily forgotten in the all-absorbing delight of seeing the proud Lady Eleanor humbled before him, and the inevitable affliction the Knight would experience when he learned the success of this last device. That it would succeed he had little doubt; he had come too well prepared with arguments to dread failure. Nay, he thought, he believed he could compel compliance if such were to be needed.

It was in the very midst of these strangely confused musings that the doctor's servant announced to him the arrival of Lady Eleanor Darcy. The old man looked around him on the miserable furniture, the damp, discoloured walls, the patched and mended window-panes, and for a moment he could not imagine where he was. The repetition of the servant's announcement, however, cleared away the cloud from his faculties, and with a slight gesture of his hand he made a sign that she should be admitted. A momentary pause ensued, and he could hear his servant expressing a hope that her Ladyship might not catch cold, as the snow-drift was falling heavily, and the storm very severe. A delay of a few minutes was caused to remove her wet cloak. What a whole history did these two or three seconds reveal to old Hickman as he thought of that Lady Eleanor Darcy of whose fastidious elegance the whole "West" was full—whose expensive habits and luxurious tastes had invested her with something like an Oriental reputation for magnificence. Of her coming on foot and alone, through storm and snow, to wait upon him.

He listened eagerly, her footstep was on the stairs, and he heard a low sigh she gave, as, reaching the landing-place, she stood for a moment to recover breath.

"Say Lady Eleanor Darcy," said she, unaware that her coming had been already telegraphed to the sick man's chamber.

A faint complaining cry issued from the room as she spoke, and Lady Eleanor said, "Stay. Perhaps Dr. Hickman is too ill; if so, at another time, I'll come this evening, or to-morrow."

"My master is most impatient to see your Ladyship," said the man. "He has talked of nothing else all the morning, and is always asking if it is nigh twelve o'clock."

Lady Eleanor nodded as if to concede her permission, and the servant entered the half-darkened room. A weak, murmuring sound of voices followed, and the servant returned, saying, in a cautious whisper, "He is awake, my Lady, and wishes to see your Ladyship now."

Lady Eleanor's heart beat loudly and painfully; many a sharp pang shot through it, as, with a strong effort to seem calm, she entered.

CHAPTER LXII.

A DARK CONSPIRACY.

Doctor Hickman was so little prepared for the favourable change in Lady Eleanor's appearance since he had last seen her, as almost to doubt that she was the same, and it was with a slight tremor of voice he said,

"Is it age with me, my Lady, or altered health, that makes the difference, but you seem to me not what I remember you? You are fresher, pardon an old man's freedom, and I should say far handsomer, too?"

"Really, Mr. Hickman, you make me think my excursion well repaid by such flatteries," said she, smiling pleasantly, and not sorry thus for a moment to say something that might relieve the awkward solemnity of the scene. "I hope, sir, that this air, severe though it be, may prove as serviceable to yourself. Have you slept well?"

"No, my Lady, I scarcely dozed the whole night; this place is a very poor one. The rain comes in there—where you see that green mark—and the wind whistles through these broken panes—and rats, bother them, they never ceased the night through. A poor, poor spot it is, sure enough!"

It never chanced to cross his mind while bewailing these signs of indigence and discomfort, that she, to whom he addressed the complaint, had been reduced to as bad, even worse hardships, by his own contrivance. Perhaps, indeed, the memory of such had not occurred at that moment to Lady Eleanor, had not the persistence with which he dwelt on the theme somewhat ruffled her patience, and eventually reminded her of her own changed lot. It was then with a slightly irritated tone she remarked,

"Such accommodation is a very unpleasant contrast to the comforts you are accustomed to, sir, and these sudden lessons in adversity are, now and then, very trying things."

"What does it signify?" sighed the old man, heavily, "a day sooner, a few hours less of sunshine, and the world can make little difference to one like me! Happy for me if, in confronting them, I have done anything towards my great purpose, the only object between me and the grave!"

Lady Eleanor never broke the silence which followed these words, and though the old man looked as if he expected some observation or rejoinder, she said not a word. At length he resumed, with a faint moan,

"Ah, my Lady, you have much to forgive us for."

"I trust, sir, that our humbled fortunes have not taught us to forget the duties of Christianity," was the calm reply.

"Much, indeed, to pardon," continued he, "but far less, my Lady, than is laid to our charge. Lawyers and attorneys make many a thing a cause of bitterness, that a few words in kindness would have settled. And what two men of honest intentions could arrange amicably in five minutes, is often worked up into a tedious lawsuit, or a ruinous inquiry in Chancery. So it is!"

"I have no experience in these affairs, sir, but I conclude your remarks are quite correct."

"Faith, you may believe them, my Lady, like the Bible, and yet, knowing these fellows so well, having dealings with them since—since—oh, God knows how long—upon my life, they beat me entirely after all. 'Tis like taking a walk with a quarrelsome dog, devil a cur he sees but he sets on him, and gets you into a scrape at every step you go! That's what an attorney does for you. Take out a writ against that fellow—process this one, distrain the other—get an injunction here—apply for a rule there. Oh dear! —oh dear! I'm well weary of it for law! All the bitterness it has given me in my life long—all the sorrow and affliction it costs me now." He wiped his eyes as he concluded, and seemed as if overcome by grief.

"It must needs be a sorry source of reparation, sir" rejoined Lady

Eleanor, with a calm, steady tone, "when even those so eminently successful can see nothing but affliction in their triumphs."

"Don't call them triumphs, my Lady; that's not the name to give them. I never thought them such."

"I'm glad to hear it, sir—glad to know that you have laid up such store of pleasant memories for seasons like the present."

"There was that proceeding, for instance, in December last.—Now, would you believe it, my Lady, Bob and I never knew a syllable about it till it was all over. You don't know what I'm speaking of; I mean the writ against the Knight."

"Really, Dr. Hickman, I must interrupt you; however gratifying to me to hear that you stand exculpated for any ungenerous conduct towards my husband, the pleasure of knowing it is more than counterbalanced by the great pain the topic inflicts upon me."

"But I want to clear myself, my Lady; I want you to think of us a little more favourably than late events may have disposed you."

"There are few so humble, sir, as not to have opinions of more consequence than mine."

"Ay, but it's yours I want—yours, that I'd rather have than the King's on his throne. 'Tis in that hope I've come many a weary mile far away from my home, maybe never to see it again! and all that I may have your forgiveness, my Lady, and not only your forgiveness, but your approbation."

"If you set store by any sentiments of mine, sir, I warn you not to ask more than I have in my power to bestow. I can forgive, I have forgiven, much; but ask me not to concur in acts which have robbed me of the companionship of my husband and my son."

"Wait a bit; don't be too hard, my Lady; I'm on the verge of the grave a little more, and the dark sleep that never breaks will be on me, and if, in this troubled hour, I take a wrong word, or say a thing too strong—forgive me for it. My thoughts are often before me, on the long journey I'm so soon to go."

"It were far better, Dr. Hickman, that we should speak of something less likely to be painful to us both, and if that cannot be, that you should rest satisfied with knowing, that however many are the sources of sorrow an humbled fortune has opened to us, the disposition to bear malice is not among their number."

"You forgive me, then, my Lady—you forgive me all?"

"If your own conscience can only do so, as freely as I do, believe me, sir, your heart will be tranquil."

The old man pressed his hands to his face, and appeared overcome by emotion. A dead silence ensued, which at length was broken by old Hickman muttering broken words to himself, at first indistinctly, and then more clearly.

"Yes, yes,—I made—the offer—I begged—I supplicated. I did all—all. But no, they refused me! There was no other way of restoring them to their own house and home—but they wouldn't accept it. I would have settled the whole estate—free of debt—every charge paid off, upon them. There's not a Peer in the land could say he was at the head of such a property."

"I must beg, sir, that I may be spared the unpleasantness of overhearing what I doubt is only intended for your own reflection; and, if you will permit me, to take my leave——"

"Oh, don't go—don't leave me yet, my Lady. What was it I said?—where was my poor brain rambling? Was I talking about Captain Darcy?—Ah! that was the most painful part of all."

"My God! what is it you mean?" said Lady Eleanor, as a sickness like fainting crept over her—"speak, sir—tell me this instant!"

"The bills, my Lady—the bills, that he drew in Gleeson's name."

"In Gleeson's name! It is false, sir, a foul and infamous calumny; my son never did this thing—do not dare to assert it before me, his mother."

"They are in that pocket-book, my Lady—seven of them for a thousand pounds each. There are two more somewhere among my papers—and it was to meet the payment that the Captain did this." Here he took from beneath his pillow a parchment document, and held it towards Lady Eleanor, who, overwhelmed with terror and dismay, could not stretch her hand to take it.

"Here—my Lady—somewhere here," said he, moving his finger vaguely along the lower margin of the document—"here you'll see Maurice Darcy written—not by himself, indeed, but by his son. This deed of sale includes part of Westport, and the town-lands of Cooldrennon and Shoughnakelly. Faith and my Lady, I paid my hard cash down on the nail for the same land, and have no better title than what you see! The Knight has only to prove the forgery; of course he couldn't do so against his own son."

"Oh! sir, spare me—I entreat of you to spare me!" sobbed Lady Eleanor, as, convulsed with grief, she hid her face.

A knocking was heard at this moment at the door, and on its being repeated louder, Hickman querulously demanded, "Who was there?"

"A note for Lady Eleanor Darcy," was the reply; "her Ladyship's servant waits for an answer."

Lady Eleanor, without knowing wherefore, seemed to feel that the tidings required prompt attention, and with an effort to subdue her emotion, she broke the seal, and read:

"LADY ELEANOR,—Be on your guard—there is a dark plot against you. Take counsel in time—and if you hear the words, ''Tis eighty-six years have crept to your feet, to die,' you can credit the friendship of this warning."

"Who brought this note?" said she, in a voice that became full and strong, under the emergency of danger.

"Your butler, my Lady."

"Where is he? send him to me." And as she spoke, Tate mounted the stairs.

"How came you by this note, Tate?"

"A fisherman, my Lady, left it this instant, with directions to be given to you at once, and without a moment's delay."

"'Tis nothing bad, I hope and trust, my Lady," whispered the old man "The darling young lady is not ill?"

"No, sir, she is perfectly well, nor are the tidings positively bad ones. There is no answer, Tate." So saying, she once more opened the paper and read it over.

Without seeing wherefore, Lady Eleanor felt a sudden sense of hardihood take possession of her; the accusation by which, a moment previous, she had been almost stunned, seemed already lighter to her eyes, and the suspicion that the whole interview was part of some dark design, dawned suddenly on her mind. Nor was this feeling permanent: a glance at the miserable old man, who, with head bent down, and half-closed eyes, lay before her, dispelling the doubts even more rapidly than they were formed. Indeed, now that the momentary excitement of speaking had passed away, he looked far more wan and wasted than before; his chest, too, heaved with a fluttering, irregular action, that seemed to denote severe and painful effort, while his fingers, with a restless and fidgety motion, wandered here and there, pinching the bed-clothes, and seeming to search for some stray object.

While the conflict continued in Lady Eleanor's mind, the old man's brain once more began to wander, and his lips murmured, half articulately, certain words. "I would give it all!" said he, with a sudden cry; "every shilling of it for that—but it cannot be—no, it cannot be."

"I must leave you, sir," said Lady Eleanor, rising; "and although I have heard much to agitate and afflict me, it is some comfort to my heart to think that I have poured some balm into yours; you have my forgiveness for every thing."

"Wait a second, my Lady, wait one second," gasped he, as with outstretched hands he tried to detain her. "I'll have strength for it in a minute—I want—I want to ask you once more what you refused me once—and it isn't——it isn't that times are changed, and that you are in poverty now, makes me hope for better luck. It is because this is the request of one, on his death-bed—one, that cannot turn his thoughts away from this world, till he has his mind at ease. There, my Lady, take that pocket-book and that deed, throw them into the fire, there. They're the only proofs against the Captain—no eye but yours must ever see them.—If I could see my own beautiful Miss Helen once more in the old house of her fathers——"

"I will not hear of this, sir," interposed Lady Eleanor, hastily. "No time or circumstances can make any change in the feelings with which I have already replied to this proposal."

"Heffernan tells me, my Lady, that the Baronetcy is certain—don't go—don't go—It's the voice of one you'll never hear again calls on you. 'Tis eighty-six years have crept to your feet, to die!"

A faint shriek burst from Lady Eleanor—she tottered, reeled, and fell fainting to the ground.

Terrified by the sudden shock, the old man rung his bell with violence, and screamed for help, in accents where there was no counterfeited anxiety; and in another moment his servant rushed in, followed by Nalty, and in a few seconds later by O'Reilly himself, who, hearing the cries, believed that the effort to feign a death-bed had turned into a dreadful reality.

"There—there—she is ill—she is dying! It was too much—the shock did it!" cried the old man, now horror-struck at the ruin he had caused.

"She is better—her pulse is coming back," whispered O'Reilly; "a little water to her lips—that will do."

"She is coming to—I see it now," said old Hickman; "leave the room, Bob; quick, before she sees you."

As O'Reilly gently disengaged his arm, which, in placing the fainting form on the sofa, was laid beneath her head, Lady Eleanor slowly opened her eyes, and fixed them upon him. O'Reilly suddenly became motionless; the calm and steady gaze seemed to have paralysed him; he could not stir, he could not turn away his own eyes, but stood like one fascinated and spell-bound.

"Oh dear—oh dear!" muttered the old man, "she'll know him now, and see it all!"

"Yes," exclaimed Lady Eleanor, pushing back from her the officious hands that ministered about her. "Yes, sir, I do see it all! Oh, let me be thankful for the gleam of reason that has guided me in this dark hour. And you, too, do you be thankful that you have been spared from working such deep iniquity!"

As she spoke she arose, not a vestige of illness remaining, but a deep flush mantling in the cheek that, but a moment back, was deathly pale. "Farewell, sir. You had a brief triumph over the fears of a poor weak woman; but I forgive you, for you have armed her heart with a courage it never knew before."

With these words she moved calmly towards the door, which O'Reilly in respectful silence held open; and then, descending the stairs with a firm step, left the house.

"Is she gone, Bob?" said the old man, faintly, as the door clapped heavily. "Is she gone?"

O'Reilly made no reply, but leaned his head on the chimney, and seemed lost in thought.

"I knew it would fail," said Nalty, in a whisper to O'Reilly.

"What's that he's saying, Bob?—what's Nalty saying?"

"That he knew it would fail, sir," rejoined O'Reilly, with a bitterness that showed he was not sorry to say a disagreeable thing.

"Ay! but Nalty was frightened about his annuity; he thought, maybe, *I'd* die in earnest. Well, we've something left yet."

"What's that?" asked O'Reilly, almost sternly.

"The indictment for forgery," said Hickman, with a savage energy.

"Then you must look out for another lawyer, sir," said Nalty. "That I tell you frankly and fairly."

"What?—I didn't hear."

"He refuses to take the conduct of such a case," said O'Reilly; "and, indeed, I think on very sufficient grounds."

"Ay!" muttered the old Doctor. "Then I suppose there's no help for it!—Here, Bob, put these papers in the fire."

So saying, he drew a thick roll of documents from beneath his pillow, and placed it in his son's hands. "Put them in the blaze, and let me see them burned."

O'Reilly did as he was told, stirring the red embers till the whole mass was consumed.

"I am glad of that, with all my heart," said he, as the flame died out. "That was a part of the matter I never felt easy about."

"Didn't you?" grunted the old man, with a leer of malice. "What was it you burned, d'ye think?"

"The bills—the bonds with young Darcy's signature," replied O'Reilly, almost terrified by an unknown suspicion.

"Not a bit of it, Bob. The blaze you made there was a costly fire to you, as you'll know one day.—That was my will."

CHAPTER LXIII.

THE LANDING AT ABOUKIR.

We must now ask of our reader to leave for a season this scene of plot and intrigue, and turn with us to a very different picture. The same morning which, on the iron-bound coast of Ireland, broke in storm and hurricane, dawned fair and joyous over the shady shores of Egypt, and scarcely ruffled the long rolling waves as they swept into the deep Bay of Aboukir. Here now a fleet of one hundred and seventy ships lay at anchor, the expedition sent forth by England to arrest the devouring ambition of Buonaparte, and rescue the land of the Pyramids from bondage.

While our concern here is less with the great event than with the fortune of one of its humble followers, we would fain linger a little over the memory of this glorious achievement of our country's arms. For above a week after the arrival of the fleet, the gale continued to blow with unabated fury; a sea mountains high rolled into the bay, accompanied by sudden squalls of such violence that the largest ships of the fleet could barely hold on by their moorings, while many smaller ones were compelled to slip their cables, and stand out to sea. If the damage and injury were not important enough to risk the success of the expedition, the casualties, ever inseparable from such events, threw a gloom over the whole force, a feeling grievously increased by the first tidings that met them—the capture of one of the officers and a boat's crew, who were taken while examining the shore, and seeking out the fittest spot for a landing.

On the 7th of March the wind and sea subsided, the sky cleared, and a glorious sunset gave promise of a calm, so soon to be converted into a storm, not less terrible than that of the elements.

As day closed, the outlying ships had all returned to their moorings, the accidents of the late gale were repaired, and the soaked sails hung flapping in the evening breeze to dry; while the decks swarmed with moving figures, all eagerly engaged in preparation for that event, which each well knew could not now be distant. How many a heart throbbed high with ecstasy and hope, that soon was to be cold—how many an eye wandered over that strong line of defences along the shore, that never was to gaze upon another sunset! And yet, to mark the proud step, the flashing look, the eager speech of all around, the occasion might have been deemed one of triumphant pleasure rather than the approach of an enterprise full of hazard and danger. The disappointments which the storm had excited, by delaying the landing, were forgotten altogether, or only thought of to heighten the delight which now they felt.

The rapid exchange of signals between the line-of-battle ships showed that preparations were on foot, and many were the guesses and surmises current as to the meaning of this or that ensign, each reading the mystery by the light of his inward hopes. On one object, however, every eye was fixed with a most intense anxiety. This was an armed launch, which, shooting out from beneath the shadow of a three-decker, swept across the bay with muffled oars. Nothing louder than a whisper broke the silence on board of her, as they stole along the still water, and held on their course towards the shore. Through the gloom of the falling night, they were seen to track each indenture of the coast—now, lying on their oars to take soundings; now, delaying, to note some spot of more than ordinary strength. It was already midnight before "the reconnoissance" was effected, and the party returned to the ship, well acquainted with the formidable preparations of the enemy, and all the hazard that awaited the hardy enterprise. The only part of the coast approachable by boats, was a low line of beach, stretching away to the left, from the Castle of Aboukir, and about a mile in extent; and this was commanded by a semicircular range of sand-hills, on which the French batteries were posted, and whose crest now glittered with the bivouac fires of a numerous army. From the circumstances of the ground, the guns were so placed as to be able to throw a cross-fire over the bay, while a lower range of batteries protected the shore, the terrible effect of whose practice might be seen on the torn and furrowed sands; sad presage of what a landing party might expect! Besides these precautions, the whole breastwork bristled with cannon and mortars of various calibre, embedded in the sand, nor was a single position undefended, or one measure of resistance omitted, which might increase the hazard of an attacking force.

Time was an important object with the English general; reinforcements were daily looked for by the French; indeed, it was rumoured that tidings had come of their having sailed from Toulon, for, with an unparalleled audacity and good fortune combined, a French frigate had sailed the preceding day through the midst of our fleet, and, amid the triumphant cheerings of the shore batteries, hoisted the tricolor in the face of our assembled ships. Scarcely had the launch reached the Admiral's ship, when a signal ordered the presence of all officers in command to attend a council of war. The proceedings were quickly terminated, and in less than half an hour the various boats were seen returning to their respective ships, the resolution being taken to attack that very morning, or, in the words of the general order, "to bring the troops as soon as possible before the enemy." Never were tidings more welcomed; the delay, brief as it was, had stimulated the ardour of the men to the highest degree, and they actually burned with impatience to be engaged. The dispositions for attack were simple, and easily followed. A sloop of war, anchored just beyond the reach of cannon-shot, was named as the point of rendezvous. By a single blue light at her mizen, the boats were to move towards her—three lights at the maintop would announce that they were all assembled—a single gun would then be the signal to make for the shore.

Strict orders were given that no unusual lights should be seen from the ships, nor any unwonted sight or sound betray extraordinary preparation The men were mustered by the half-light in use on board, the ammunition distributed in silence, and every precaution taken that the attack should have the character of a surprise. These orders were well and closely followed; but so short was the interval, and so manifold the arrangements, it was already daylight before the rendezvous was accomplished.

If the plan of debarkation was easily comprehended, that of the attack was not less so. Nelson once summed up a "general order," by saying, "The captain will not make any mistake who lays his ship alongside of an enemy of heavier metal." So Abercrombie's last instructions were, "Whenever an officer may be in want of orders, let him assault an enemy's battery." These were to be carried by the bayonet alone, and, of the entire force, not one man landed with a loaded musket.

A few minutes after seven the signal was given, and the boats moved off. The sun was high, a light breeze fanned the water, the flags and streamers of the ships-of-war floated proudly out as the flotilla stood for the shore; in glorious rivalry they pulled through the surf, each eager to be first, and all the excitement of a race was imparted to this enterprise of peril.

Conspicuous among the leading boats were two, whose party equipped in a brilliant uniform of blue and silver formed part of the cavalry force. The inferiority of the horses supplied was such that only two hundred and fifty were mounted, and the remainder had asked and obtained permission to serve on foot. A considerable portion of this corps was made up of volunteers, and several young men of family and fortune were said to serve in the ranks; and from the circumstance of being commanded by the Knight of Gwynne, were called "Darcy's Volunteers." It was a glorious sight to see the first boat of this party, in the stern of which sat the old Knight himself, shoot out ahead, and amid the cheering of the whole flotilla, lead the way in shore.

Returning the various salutes which greeted him, the old man sat bare-headed, his silvery hair floating back in the breeze, and his manly face beaming with high enthusiasm.

"A grand spectacle for an unconcerned eye-witness," said an officer to his neighbour.

The words reached Darcy's ears, and he called out, "I differ with you, captain. To enjoy all the thrilling ecstasy of this scene a man must have his stake on the venture. It is our personal hopes and fears are necessary ingredients in the exalted feeling. I would not stand on yonder cliff and look on, for millions; but such a moment as this is glorious." As he spoke, a long line of flame ran along the heights, and at the same instant the whole air trembled as the entire batteries opened their fire. The sea hissed and glittered with round shot and shell; while, in a perfect hurricane, they rained on every side.

The suddenness of the cannonade, and the confusion consequent on the casualties that followed, seemed for a moment to retard the advance, or, as it appeared to the French, to deter the invading force altogether; for as they perceived some of the boats to lie on their oars, and others withdrawn to the assistance of their comrades, a deafening cheer of triumph rang out from the batteries, and was heard over the bay. Scarcely had it been uttered when the British answered by another, whose hoarse roar bespoke the coming vengeance.

The flotilla had now advanced within a line of buoys laid down to direct the fire, and here grape and musketry mingled their clattering with the deeper thunder of cannon.

"This is sharp work, gentlemen," said the Knight, as the spray twice splashed over the boat, from shot that fell close by. "They'll have our range soon. Do you mark how accurately the shots fall over that line of surf?"

"That's a sand-bank, sir," said the cockswain who steered. "There's barely draught of water there for heavy launches."

"I perceive there is some shelter yonder beneath that large battery."

"They can trust that spot," cried the cockswain, smiling. "There's a heavy surf there, and no boat could live through it.—But stay, there is a boat about to try it." Every eye was now turned towards a yawl, which, with twelve oars, vigorously headed on through the very midst of a broken and foam-covered tract of water, where jets of sea sprang up from hidden rocks, and cross currents warred and contended against each other.

The hazardous venture was not alone watched by those in the boats, but, from the crowning ridge of batteries, from every cliff and crag on shore, wondering enemies gazed on the hardihood of the daring.

"They'll do it yet, sir—they'll do it yet," cried the cockswain, wild with excitement. "There's deep water inside that reef."

The words were scarcely out, when a tremendous cannonade opened from the large battery. The balls fell on every side of the boat, and at length one struck her on the stem, rending her open from end to end, and scattering her shivered planks over the surfy sea.

A shout, a cheer, a drowning cry from the sinking crew, and all was over.

So sudden and so complete was this dreadful catastrophe, that they who witnessed it almost doubted the evidence of their senses, nor were the victors long to enjoy this triumph; the very discharge which sunk the boat having burst a mortar, and ignited a mass of powder near, a terrible explosion followed. A dense column of smoke and sand filled the air, and when this cleared away, the face of the battery was perceived to be rent in two.

"We car do it now, lads," cried Darcy. "They'll never recover from the confusion yonder in time to see us." A cheer met his words, and the cockswain turned the boat's head in the direction of the reef.

Closely followed by their comrades in the second boat, they pulled along through the surf like men whose lives were on the venture: four arms to every oar, the craft bounded througn the boiling tide; twice the keel was felt to graze the rocky bed, but the strong impulse of the boat's "way" carried her through, and soon they floated in the still water within the reef.

"It shoals fast here," cried the cockswain.

"What's the depth?" asked Darcy.

"Scarcely above three feet. If we throw over our six-pounder——"

"No, no. It's but wading, after all. Keep your muskets dry, move together, and we shall be the first to touch the shore." As he said this, he sprang over the side of the boat into the sea, and waving his hat above his head, began his progress towards the land. "Come along, gentlemen, we've often done as much when salmon-fishing in our own rivers." Thus, lightly jesting, and encouraging his party, he waded on, with all the seeming carelessness of one bent on some scheme of pleasure.

The large batteries had no longer the range, but a dreadful fire of musketry was poured in from the heights, and several brave fellows fell mortally wounded, ere the strand was reached. Cheered by the approving shouts of thousands from the boats, they at length touched the beach, and wild and disorderly as had been their advance when breasting the waves, no sooner had they landed than discipline resumed its sway, and the words, "Fall in, men," were obeyed with the prompt precision of a parade. A strong body of tirailleurs, scattered along the base of the sand-hills, and through the irregularities of the ground, galled them with a drooping and destructive fire as they formed; nor was it till an advanced party had driven these back, that the dispositions could be well and properly taken. By this time several other boats had touched the shore, and already detachments from the 40th, 28th, and 42nd Regiments were drawn up along the beach, and, from these, frequent cries and shouts were heard, encouraging and cheering the "Volunteers," who alone, of all the force, had yet come to close quarters with the enemy.

A brief but most dangerous interval now followed; for the boats, assailed by a murderous fire, had sustained severe losses, and a short delay inevitably followed, assisting the wounded, or rescuing those who had fallen into the sea. Had the French profited by this pause, to bear down upon the small force now drawn up, inactive on the beach, the fate of that great achievement might have been perilled; as it happened, however, nothing was further rom their thought than coming into immediate contact with the British, and they contented themselves with a distant but still destructive cannonade. It is not impossible that the audacity of those who first landed, and who—a mere handful—assumed the offensive, might have been the reason of this conduct, certain it is, the boats, for a time retarded, were permitted again to move forward and disembark their men, with no other resistance than the fire from the batteries

The three first regiments which gained the land were, strangely enough, representatives of the three different nationalities of the Empire, and scarcely were the words, "Forward! to the assault!" given, when an emulative struggle began, which should first reach the top and cross bayonets with the French. On the left, and nearest to the causeway that led up the heights, stood the Highlanders. These formed under an overwhelming shower of grape and musketry, and, with pibrochs playing, marched steadily forward. The 40th made an effort to pass them, which caused a momentary confusion, ending in an order for this regiment to halt, and support the 42nd, and while this was taking place, the 28th rushed to the ascent in broken parties, and following the direction the "Volunteers" had taken in pursuit of the tirailleurs, they mounted the heights together.

So suddenly was the tirailleur force repelled, that they had scarcely time to give the alarm, when the 28th passed the crest of the hill, and prepared to charge. The Irish regiment, glorying in being the first to reach the top, cheered madly, and bore down. The French poured in a single volley, and fell back; not to retreat, but to entice pursuit. The stratagem succeeded. The 28th pursued them hotly, and almost at once found themselves engaged in a narrow gorge of the sand-hills, and exposed to a terrific cross-fire. To retreat was impossible; their own weight drove them on, and the deafening cheers of their comrades drowned every word of command. Grape at half-musket distance ploughed through their ranks, while one continuous crash of small-arms showed the number and closeness of their foes.

It was at this moment that Darcy, whose party was advancing by a smaller gorge, ascended a height, and beheld the perilous condition of his gallant countrymen. There was but one way to liberate them, and that involved their own destruction: to throw themselves on the French flank, and while devoting themselves to death, enable the 28th to retire or make head against the opposing force. While Darcy, in a few hurried words, made known his plan to those around him, the opportunity for its employment most strikingly presented itself. A momentary repulse of the French had driven a part of their column to the high road leading to Alexandria, where already several baggage carts and ammunition waggons were gathered. This movement seemed so like retreat, that Darcy's sanguine nature was deceived, and calling out, "Come along, lads—they are running already!" he dashed onward, followed by his gallant band. His attack, if inefficient for want of numbers, was critical in point of time. The same instant that the French were assailed by him in flank, the 42nd had gained the summit and attacked them in front; fresh battalions each moment arrived, and now along the entire crest of the ridge the fight raged fiercely. One after the other the batteries were stormed, and carried by our infantry at the bayonet's point, and, in less than an hour from the time of landing, the British flag waved over seven of the nine heavy batteries.

The battle, severe as it was on the heights, was maintained with even greater slaughter on the shore. The French, endeavouring, too late, to repair the error of not resisting the actual landing, had now thrown an immense force by a flank movement on the British battalions; and this attack of horse, foot, and artillery combined, was, for its duration, the great event of the day. For a brief space it appeared impossible for the few regiments to sustain the shock of such an encounter; and had it not been for the artillery of the gun-boats stationed along the shore, they must have yielded. Their fire, however, was terribly destructive, sweeping through the columns as they came up, and actually cutting lanes in the dense squadrons.

Reinforcements poured in, besides, at every instant, and after a bloody and anxious struggle, the British were enabled to take the offensive, and advance against their foes. The French, already weakened by loss, and dispirited by failure, did not await the conflict, but retired slowly, it is true, and in perfect order, on one of the roads leading into the great highway to Alexandria.

Victory had even more unequivocally pronounced for the British on the heights. By this time every battery was in their possession. The enemy were in full flight towards Alexandria, the tumultuous mass, occasionally assailed by our light infantry, to whom, from our deficiency in cavalry, was assigned the duty of harassing the retreat. It was here that Darcy's Volunteers, now reduced to one-third of their original number, highly distinguished themselves, not only attacking the flank of the retiring enemy, but seizing every opportunity of ground to assail them in front, and retard their flight.

In one of these onslaughts, for such they were, the "Volunteers" became inextricably entangled with the enemy, and although fighting with the desperation of tigers, volley after volley tore through them; and the French, maddened by the loss they had already suffered at their hands, hastened to finish them by the bayonet. It was only by the intervention of the French officers, a measure in itself not devoid of peril, that any were spared; and those few, bleeding and mangled, were hurried along as prisoners, the only triumph of that day's battle! The strange spectacle of an affray in the very midst of a retiring column, was seen by the British in pursuit, and the memory of this scene is preserved among the incidents of that day's achievements.

Many and desperate attempts were made to rescue the prisoners. The French, however, received the charges with deadly volleys, and as their flanks were now covered by a cloud of tirailleurs, they were enabled to continue their retreat on Alexandria, protected by the circuitances of the ground, every point of which they had favourably occupied. The battle was now over; guns, ammunition, and stores were all landed; on the heights, the English ensign waved triumphantly; and, far as the eye could reach, the French masses were seen in flight, to seek shelter within the lines of Alexandria.

It was a glorious moment as the last column ascended the cliffs, to find their gallant comrades masters of the French position in its entire extent. Here, now, two brigades reposed with piled arms, guns, mortars, camp equipage, and military chests strewed on every side, all attesting the completeness of a victory which even a French bulletin could hardly venture to disavow. It is perhaps fortunate that, at times like this, the feeling of high excitement subdues all sense of the regret so natural to scenes of suffering: and thus, amid many a sight and sound of woe, glad shouts of triumph were raised, and heartfelt bursts of joyous recognition broke forth as friends met, and clasped each other's hands. Incidents of the battle, traits of individual heroism, were recorded on every side: anecdotes then told for the first time, to be remembered, many a year after, among the annals of regimental glory!

It is but seldom, at such moments, that men can turn from the theme of triumph to think of the more disastrous events of the day; and yet a general feeling of sorrow prevailed on the subject of the brave "Volunteers," of whose fate none could bring any tidings; some asserting that they had all fallen to a man on the road leading to Alexandria, others affirming that they were carried off prisoners by the French cavalry.

A party of light infantry, who had closely followed the enemy till nightfall, had despatched some of their wounded to the rear, and by these the news came, that, in an open space, beside the high road, the ground was covered with bodies in the well-known blue and silver of the "Volunteers." One only of these exhibited signs of life, and him they had placed among the wounded in one of the carts, and brought back with them. As will often happen, single instances of suffering excite more of compassionate pity than wide-spread affliction; and so here. When death and agony were on every hand—whole waggons filled with maimed and dying comrades—a closely-wedged group gathered around the dying volunteer, their saddened faces betraying emotions that all the terrible scenes of the day had never evoked.

"It's no use, sir," said the surgeon to the field-officer who had called him to the spot. "There is internal bleeding, besides this ghastly sabre cut."

"Who knows him?" said the officer, looking around; but none made answer. "Can no one tell his name?"

There was a silence for a few seconds; when the dying man lifted his failing eyes upwards, and turned them slowly around on the group. A slight tremor shook his lips, as if with an effort to speak; but no sound issued. Yet in the terrible eagerness of his features might be seen the working of a spirit fiercely struggling for utterance.

"Yes, my poor fellow," said the officer, stooping down beside him, and taking his hand. "I was asking for your name."

A faint smile and a slight nod of the head seemed to acknowledge the speech.

"He is speaking—hush! I hear his voice," cried the officer.

An almost inaudible murmur moved his lips—then a shivering shook his frame—and his head fell heavily back.

"What is this?" said the officer.

"Death," said the surgeon, with the solemn calm of one habituated to such scenes. "His last words were strange—did you hear them?"

"I thought he said 'Court-martial.'"

The surgeon nodded, and turned to move away.

"See here, sir," said a sergeant, as opening the dead man's coat he drew forth a white handkerchief, "the poor fellow was evidently trying to write his name with his own blood; here are some letters clear enough. L-e-o, and this is an n—— or m——"

"I know him now," cried another. "This was the volunteer who joined us at Malta; but Colonel Darcy got him exchanged into his own corps. His name was Leonard."

CHAPTER LXIV.

THE FRENCH RETREAT.

Let us now turn to the Knight of Gwynne, who, wounded and bleeding, was carried along in the torrent of the retreat. Poor fellow, he had witnessed the total slaughter or capture of the gallant band he had so bravely led into action but a few hours before, and now, with one arm powerless, and a sabre cut in the side, could barely keep up with the hurried steps of the flying army.

From the few survivors among his followers, not one of whom was un wounded, he received every proof of affectionate devotion. If they were proud of the gallant old officer as their leader, they actually loved him like a father. The very last incident of their struggle was an effort to cut through the closing ranks of the French, and secure his escape; and although one of the volunteers almost lifted him into the saddle, from which he had torn the rider, Darcy would not leave his comrades, but cried out, "What signifies a prisoner more or less, lads? The victory is ours, let that console us." The brave fellow, who had perilled his life for his leader, was cut down at the same instant. Darcy saw him bleeding and disarmed, and had but time to throw him his last pistol, when he was driven onward, and, in the mingled confusion of the movement, beheld him no more.

The exasperation of a defeat so totally unlooked for, had made the French almost savage in their vindictiveness, and nothing but the greatest efforts on the part of the officers could have saved the prisoners from the cruel vengeance of the infuriated soldiery. As it was, insulting epithets, oaths, and obnoxious threats, met them at every moment of the halt, and at each new success of the British their fury broke out afresh, accompanied by menacing gestures, that seemed to dare and defy every fear of discipline.

Darcy, whom personal considerations were ever the last to influence, smiled at these brutal demonstrations, delighted at heart to witness such palpable evidence of insubordination in the enemy, nor could he, in the very midst of outrages which perilled his life, avoid comparing to his followers the French troops of former days with these soldiers of the Republic. "I remember them at Quebec," said he, "under Montcalm. It may be too much to say that the spirit of a monarchy had imparted a sense of chivalry to its defenders but certainly it is fair to think, that the bloody orgies of a revolutionary capital have made a ruffian and ruthless soldiery."

Nor was this the only source of consolation open, for he beheld on every side of him, in the disorder of the force, the moral discouragement of the army, and the meagre preparations made for the defence of Alexandria. Wounded and weary, he took full note of these various circumstances, and made them the theme of encouragement to his companions in captivity. "There is little here, lads," said he, "to make us fear a long imprisonment. The gallant fellows, whose watch-fires crown yonder hills, will soon bivouac here. All these preparations denote haste and inefficiency. These stockades will offer faint resistance, their guns seem in many instances unserviceable, and from what we have seen of their infantry to-day, we need never fear the issue of a struggle with them."

In the brief intervals of an occasional halt, he lost no opportunity of remarking the appearance of the enemy's soldiery—their bearing and their equipment—and openly communicated to his comrades his opinion that the French army was no longer the formidable force it had been represented to be and that the first heavy reverse would be its dismemberment. In all the confidence a foreign language suggests, he spoke his mind freely and without reserve, not sparing the officers in his criticisms, which now and then took a form of drollery that drew laughter from the other prisoners. It was at the close of some remark of this kind, and while the merriment had not yet subsided, that a French major, who had more than once shown interest for the venerable old soldier, rode close up to his side and whispered a few words of friendly caution in his ear, while by an almost imperceptible gesture, he pointed to a group of prisoners who accompanied the Knight's party, and persisted in pressing close to where he walked. These were four dragoons of Hompesch's regiment, then serving with the British army, but a corps which had taken no part in the late action. Darcy could not help wondering at their capture, a feeling not devoid of distrust, as he remarked that neither their dress nor accoutrements bore any trace of the fierce struggle, while their manner exhibited a degree of rude assurance and effrontery, rather than the regretful feelings of men taken prisoners.

Darcy's attention was not permitted to dwell much more on the circumstance, for, at the same instant, the column was halted, in order that the wounded might pass on, and in the sad spectacle that now presented itself, all memory of his own griefs was merged. The procession was a long one, and seemed even more so than it was, from the frequent halts in front, the road being choked up by tumbrels and waggons, all confusedly mixed up in the hurry of retreat. Night was now falling fast, but still there was light enough to descry the ghastly looks of the poor fellows, suffering in every variety of agony. Some sought vent to their tortures by shouts and cries of pain; others preserved a silence, that seemed from their agonised features an effort as dreadful as the very wounds themselves; many were already mad with suffering, and sang and blasphemed, with shrieks of mingled recklessness and misery. What a terrible reverse to the glory of war, and how far deeper into the heart do such scenes penetrate than all the triumphs the most successful campaign has ever gathered! While Darcy still gazed on this sad sight, he was gently touched on the arm by the same officer who had addressed him before, saying, "There is an English soldier here among the wounded, who wishes to speak with you; it is against my orders to permit it, but be brief and cautious." With a motion to a litter some paces in the rear, the officer moved on to his place in the column, nor waited for any reply.

The Knight lost not a second in profiting by the kind suggestion, but, in the now thickening gloom, it was some time before he could discover the object of his search. At length he caught sight of the well-known uniform of his corps—the blue jacket slashed with silver—as it was thrown loosely over the figure, and partly over the face of a wounded soldier. Gently removing it, he gazed with steadfastness at the pale and bloodless countenance of a young and handsome man, who, with half-closed eyelids, lay scarcely breathing before him "Do you know me, my poor fellow?" whispered Darcy, bending down over him—"do you know me? For I feel as if we should know each other well, and had met before this." The wounded man met his glance with a look of kind acknowledgment, but made no effort to speak; a faint sigh broke from him, as with a tremulous hand he pushed back the jacket and showed a terrible bayonet stab in the chest, from which, at each respiration, the blood welled out in florid rivulets.

"Where is the surgeon?" said Darcy, to the soldier beside the litter.

"He is here, monsieur," said a sharp-looking man, who, without coat, and with shirt-sleeves tuckėd up, came hastily forward.

"Can you look to this poor fellow for me?" whispered Darcy, while he pressed into the not unwilling hand of the doctor a somewhat weighty purse.

"We can do little more than put a pad on a wounded vessel just now," said the surgeon, as with practised coolness he split up with a scissors the portions of dress around the wound. "When we have them once housed in the hospital—— Parbleu!" cried he, interrupting himself, "this is a severe affair."

Darcy turned away while the remorseless fingers of the surgeon probed the gaping incision, and then whispered low, "Can he recover?"

"Ah! mon Dieu! who knows? There is enough mischief here to kill half a squadron; but some fellows get through anything. If we had him in a quiet chamber of the Faubourg, with a good nurse, and all still and tranquil about him, there's no saying; but here, with some seven hundred others—many as bad, some worse than himself—the chances are greatly against him. Come, however, we'll do our best for him." So saying, he proceeded to pass ligatures on some bleeding arteries; and although speaking rapidly all the while, his motions were even still more quick and hurried. "How old is he?" asked the surgeon, suddenly, as he gazed attentively at the youth.

"I can't tell you," said Darcy. "He belonged to my own corps, and by the lace on his jacket, I see, must have been a Volunteer; but I shame to say I don't remember even his name."

"He knows *you*, then," replied the doctor, who, with the shrewd perception of his craft, watched the working of the sick man's features. "Is't not so?" said he, stooping down and speaking with marked distinctness. "You know your colonel?"

A gesture, too faint to be called a nod of the head, and a slight motion of the eyebrows, seemed to assent to this question; and Darcy, whose labouring faculties struggled to bring up some clue to the memory of a face he was convinced he had known before, was about to speak again, when a mounted orderly, with a led horse beside him, rode up to the spot, and looking round for a few seconds, as if in search of some one, said.

"The English colonel, I believe?" The Knight nodded. "You are to mount this horse, sir," continued the orderly, "and proceed to the head-quarters at once."

The doctor whispered a few hasty sentences, and while promising to bestow his greatest care upon the sick man, assured Darcy that at the head-quarters he would soon obtain admission of the wounded Volunteer into the officers' hospital. Partly comforted by this, and partly yielding to what he knew was the inevitable course of fortune, the Knight took a farewell look of his follower, and mounted the horse provided for him.

Darcy was too much engrossed by the interest of the wounded soldier's case to think much on what might await himself; nor did he notice for some time that they had left the high road by which the troops were marching for a narrower causeway, leading, as it seemed, not into, but at one side of Alexandria. It mattered so little to him, however, which way they followed, that he paid no further attention, nor was he aware of their progress, till they entered a little mud-built village, which swarmed with dogs, and miserable looking, half-clothed Arabs.

"How do they call this village?" said the Knight, speaking now for the first time to his guide.

"El Etscher," replied the soldier; "and here we halt." At the same moment he dismounted at the door of a low, mean-looking house; and h ushered Darcy into a small room dimly lighted by a lamp, departed.

The Knight listened to the sharp tramp of the horses' feet as they moved away, and, when they had gone beyond hearing, the silence that followed fell heavily and drearily on his spirits. After sitting for some time in expectation of seeing some one sent after him, he arose and went to the door, but there now stood a sentry posted. He returned at once within the room, and partly overcome by fatigue, and partly from the confusion of his own harassed thoughts, he leaned his head on the table and slept soundly.

"Pardon, Monsieur le Colonel," said a voice at his ear, as, some hours later in the night, he was awakened from his slumbers. "You will be pleased to follow me." Darcy looked up and beheld a young officer, who stood respectfully before him; and though for a second or so he could not remember where he was, the memory soon came back, and without a word he followed his conductor.

The officer led the way across a dirty, ill-paved court-yard, and entered a building beyond it of greater size, but apparently not less dilapidated than that they had quitted. From the hall, which was lighted with a large lamp, they could perceive through an open door a range of stables filled with horses; at the opposite side a door corresponding with this one, at which a dragoon stood with his carbine on his arm. At a word from the officer the soldier moved aside and permitted them to enter.

The room into which they proceeded was large, but almost destitute of furniture. A common deal table stood in the middle, littered with military cloaks, swords, and chakos. In one corner was a screen, from behind which the only light proceeded, and, with a gesture towards this, the officer motioned Darcy to advance, while with noiseless footsteps he himself withdrew.

Darcy moved forward, and soon came within the space enclosed by the screen, and in front of an officer in a plain uniform, who was busily engaged in writing. Maps, returns, printed orders, and letters lay strewed about him, and in the small brazier of burning wood beside him might be seen the charred remains of a great heap of papers. Darcy had full a minute to contemplate the figure before him ere he was noticed. The Frenchman was short and muscular, with a thick, bushy head of hair, bald in the centre of the head. His features were full of intelligence and quickness, but more unmistakably denoted violence of temper, and the coarse nature of one not born to his present rank, which seemed, at least, that of a field officer. His hands were covered with rings, but their shape and colour scarcely denoted that such ornaments were native to them.

"Ha—the English Colonel—sit down, sir," said he to Darcy, pointing to a chair, without rising from his own. Darcy seated himself with the easy composure of one who felt that in any situation his birth and breeding made him unexceptionable company.

"I wished to see you, sir. I have received orders, that is," said he, speaking with the greatest rapidity and a certain thickness of utterance very difficult to follow, "to send for you here, and make certain inquiries, your answers to which will entirely decide the conduct of the Commander-in-Chief in your behalf. You are not aware, perhaps, how completely you have put this in our power?"

"I suppose," said Darcy, smiling, "my condition as a prisoner of war makes me subject to the usual hardships of such a lot; but I am not aware of anything, peculiar to my case, that would warrant you in proposing even one question which a gentleman and a British officer could refuse to answer."

"There is exactly such an exception," replied the Frenchman, hastily. "The proofs are very easy, and nearer at hand than you think of."

"You have certainly excited my curiosity, sir," said the Knight, with composure; "you will excuse my saying that the feeling is unalloyed by any fear."

"We shall see that presently," said the French officer, rising and moving towards the door of an apartment which Darcy had not noticed. "Auguste," cried he, "is that report ready?" The answer was not audible to the Knight. But the officer resumed, "No matter; it is sufficient for our purpose." And hastily taking a paper from the hands of a subaltern, he returned to his place within the screen. "A gentleman so conversant with our language, it would be absurd to suppose ignorant of our institutions. Now, sir, to make a very brief affair of this, you have, in contravention to a law passed in the second year of the Republic, ventured to apply opprobrious epithets to the forces of France; ridiculing the manner, bearing, and conduct of our troops, and instituting comparisons between the free citizens of a free state and the miserable minions of a degraded monarchy. If a Frenchman, your accusation, trial, and sentence would have probably been nigh accomplished before this time. As a foreigner and a prisoner of war——"

"I conclude such remarks as I pleased to make were perfectly open to me," added Darcy, finishing the sentence.

"Then you admit the charge," said the Frenchman, eagerly, as if he had succeeded in entrapping a confession.

"So far, sir, as the expressions of my poor judgment on the effectiveness of your army, and its chances against such a force as we have yonder, I am not only prepared to avow, but if you think the remarks worth the trouble of hearing, to repeat them."

"As a prisoner of war, sir, according to the eighty-fourth article of the

Code Militaire, the offence must be tried by a court-martial, one-half of whose members shall have the same rank as the accused."

"I ask nothing better, sir, nor will I ever believe that any man who has carried a sword could deem the careless comments of a prisoner on what he sees around him a question of crime and punishment."

"I would advise you to reflect a little, sir, ere you suffer matters to proceed so far. The witnesses against you——"

"The witnesses!" exclaimed the Knight, in amazement.

"Yes, sir; four dragoons of a German regiment, thoroughly conversant with your language and ours, have deposed to the words——"

"I avow everything I have spoken, and am ready to abide by it."

"Take care, sir—take care."

"Pardon me, sir," said Darcy, with a look of quiet irony, "but it strikes me that the exigencies of your army must be far greater than I deemed them, or you had never had recourse to a system of attempted intimidation."

"You are in error there," said the Frenchman. "It was the desire to serve not to injure you, suggested my present course. It remains with yourself to show that my interest was not misplaced."

"Let me understand you more clearly. What is expected of me?"

"The answers to questions, which doubtless every countryman of yours and mine could reply to from the public papers, but which, to us here, remote from intercourse and knowledge, are matters of slow acquirement." While the French officer spoke he continued to search among the papers before him for some document, and at length, taking up a small slip of paper, resumed: "For instance, the *Moniteur* asserts that you meditate sending a force from India, to cross the Red Sea and the Desert, and menace us by an attack in the rear as well as in front. This reads so like a fragment of an Oriental tale, that I can forgive the smile with which you hear it."

"Nay, sir; you have misinterpreted my meaning," said the Knight, calmly. "I am free to confess I thought this intelligence was no secret. The form of our Government, the public discussions of our Houses, the freedom of our Press, are little favourable to mystery. If you have nothing to ask of me more difficult to answer than this——"

"And the expedition of Acre—is this also correct?"

"Perfectly so. A combined movement, which shall compel you to evacuate the country, is in preparation."

"Parbleu! sir," said the Frenchman, stamping his foot with impatience, "these are somewhat bold words for a man in your situation to one in mine."

"I fancy, sir, that circumstance affects the issue I allude to very slightly indeed: even though the officer to whom I address myself should be General Menou, the Commander-in-Chief."

"And if I be, sir, and if you know it," said Menou—for it was he—his face suffused with anger, "is it consistent with the respect due to *my* position, and to *your own* safety, to speak thus?"

"For the first, sir, although a mere surmise on my part, I humbly hope I have made no transgression; for the last, I have very little reason to feel any solicitude, knowing that if you hurt a hair of my head, that a heavy reprisal will await such of your own officers as may be taken, and the events of yesterday may have told you that a contingency of this sort is neither improbable nor remote."

Menou made no answer to this threatening speech, but with folded arms paced the apartment for several minutes. At length he turned hastily round, and, fixing his eyes on the Knight, said, with a rude oath, "You are a fortunate man, sir, that you did not hold this language to my predecessor in the command. General Kleber would have had you in front of a *peloton* of grenadiers within five minutes after you uttered it."

"I have heard as much," said the Knight, with a slight smile.

Menou rang a bell which stood beside him, and an Aide-de-Camp entered.

"Captain le Messurier," said he, in the ordinary tone of discipline, "this officer is under arrest. You will take the necessary steps for his safe keeping, and his due appearance when summoned before a military tribunal." He bowed to Darcy as he spoke, and, reseating himself at the table, took up his pen to write.

"At the hazard of being thought very hardy, sir," said the Knight, as he moved towards the door, "I would humbly solicit a favour."

"A favour!" exclaimed Menou, staring in surprise.

"Yes, sir; it is that the services of a surgeon should be promptly rendered——"

"I have given orders on that score already. My own medical man shall attend to you."

"I speak not of myself, sir. It is of a Volunteer of my corps, a young man who now lies badly wounded; his case is not without hope, if speedily looked to."

"He must take his chance with others," said the General, gruffly, while he made a gesture of leave-taking; and Darcy, unable to prolong the interview, retired.

"I am sorry, sir," said the Aide-de-Camp, as he went along, "that my orders are peremptory, and you must, if the state of your health permit, at once leave this."

"Is it thus your prisoners of war are treated, sir?" said Darcy, scornfully, "or am I to hope—for hope I do—that the exception is created especially for me?"

The officer was silent, and although the flush of shame was on his cheek, the severe demands of duty overcame all personal feeling, and he did not dare to answer.

The Knight was not one of those on whom misfortune can press, without eliciting in return the force of resistance, and, if not forgetting, at least combating, the indignities to which he had been subjected; he resigned himself patiently to his destiny, and after a brief delay, set forth for his journey to Akrish, which he now learned was to be the place of his confinement.

CHAPTER LXV.

TIDINGS OF THE WOUNDED.

The interests of our story do not require us to dwell minutely on the miserable system of intrigue by which the French authorities sought to compromise the life and honour of a British officer. The Knight of Gwynne was committed to the charge of a veteran officer of the Republic, who, though dignified with the title of the Governor of Akrish, was, in reality, invested with no higher functions than that of gaoler over the few unhappy prisoners whom evil destiny had thrown into French hands.

By an alternate system of cruelty and concession, efforts were daily made to entrap Darcy either into some expression of violence or impatience at this outrage on all the custom of war, or, induce him to join a plot for escape, submitted to him by those who, apparently prisoners like himself, were in reality the spies of the Republic. Sustained by a high sense of his own dignity, and not ignorant of the character under which revolutionised France accomplished her triumphs, the Knight resisted every temptation, and in all the gloom of this remote fortress—ominously secluded from the world—denied access to any knowledge of passing events—cut off from all communication with his country and his comrades—he never even for a moment forgot himself, nor became entangled in the perfidious schemes spread for his ruin. It was no common aggravation of the miseries of imprisonment, to know that each day and hour had its own separate machinery of perfidy at work. At one moment, he would be offered liberty on the condition of revealing the plans of the expedition; at another, he would be suddenly summoned to appear before a tribunal of military law, when it was hinted he would be ar raigned for having commanded a force of liberated felons—for in this way were the Volunteers once designated—in the hope that the insult would evoke some burst of passionate indignation. If the torment of these unceasing annoyances preyed upon his health and spirits, already harassed by sad thoughts of home, the length of time to which the intrigues were protracted showed Darcy that the wiles of his enemies had not met success in their own eyes, and this gleam of hope, faint and slender as it was, sustained him through many a gloomy hour of captivity.

While the Knight continued thus to live in the long sleep of a prisoner's existence, events were hastening to their accomplishment by which his future liberty was to be secured. The victorious army of Abercrombie had already advanced and driven the French back beneath the lines of Alexandria. The action which ensued was terribly contested, but ended in the complete triumph of the British, whose glory was, however, dearly bought by the death of their gallant leader.

The Turkish forces now joined the English under General Hutchinson, and a series of combined movements commenced, by which the French saw themselves so closely hemmed in, that no course was open save a retreat upon Cairo.

Whether from the changed fortune of their arms—for the French had now sustained one unbroken series of reverses—or that the efforts to entrap the Knight had shown so little prospect of success, the manner of the Governor had, for some time back, been altered much in his favour, and several petty concessions were permitted, which, in the earlier days of his captivity, were strictly denied. Occasionally, too, little hints of the campaign would be dropped, and acknowledgments made, "that Fortune had not been as uniformly favourable to the 'Great Nation' as was her wont." These significant confessions received a striking confirmation, when, at daybreak one morning, an order arrived for the garrison to abandon the Fort of Akrish, and for the prisoners, under a strong escort, to fall back upon Damanhour.

The movements indicated haste and precipitancy, so much so, indeed, that ere the small garrison had got clear of the town, the head of a retreating column was seen entering it by the road from Alexandria, and now no longer any doubt remained that the British had compelled them to fall back

As the French retired, their forces continued to come up each day, and in the long convoy of wounded, as well as in the shattered condition of gun-carriages and waggons, it was easy to read the signs of a recent defeat. Nor was the matter long doubtful to Darcy, for by some strange anomaly of human nature, the very men who would exaggerate the smallest accident or advantage into a victory and triumph, were now just as loud in proclaiming that they had been dreadfully beaten. Perhaps the avowal was compensated for by the licence it suggested to inveigh against the generals, and in the true spirit of a republican army, to threaten them openly with the speedy judgments of the home Government.

Among those who occasionally halted to exchange a few words or greeting with the officer in conduct of the prisoners, the Knight recognised with satisfaction the same officer who, in the retreat from Aboukir, had so kindly suggested caution to him. At first he seemed half fearful of addressing him, to speak his gratitude, lest even so much might compromise the young captain in the eyes of his countrymen. The hesitation was speedily overcome, however, as the young Frenchman gaily saluted him, and said,

"Ah, mon General, you had scarcely been here to-day if you had but listened to my counsels. I told you that the Republic, one and indivisible, did not admit criticism of its troops."

"I scarcely believed you could shrink from such an ordeal," said the Knight, smiling.

"Not in the *Moniteur*, perhaps," rejoined the Frenchman, laughing. "Yours, however, had an excess of candour, which if only listened to at your own head-quarters, might have induced grave errors.

"I comprehend," interrupted Darcy, gaily catching up the ironical humour of the other. "I comprehend, and you would spare an enemy such an injurious illusion."

"Just so; I wish your army had been equally generous, with all my heart," added he, as coolly as before; "here we are in full retreat on Cairo."

"On Damanhour, you mean," said Darcy.

"Not a bit of it; on Cairo, General. There's no need of mincing the matter; we need fear no eavesdropper here. Ah, by-the-by, your German friends were retaken, and by a detachment of their own regiment, too. We saw the fellows shot the morning after the action."

"Now that you are kind enough to tell me what is going forward, perhaps you could let me know something of my poor comrades, whom you took prisoners on the night of the 9th."

"Yes. They are with few exceptions dead of their wounds, two men exchanged about a week since, and then, what strange fellows your countrymen are! they sent us back a major of brigade in exchange for a wounded soldier, who, when he left our camp, did not seem to have life enough to bring him across the lines!"

"Did you see him?" asked Darcy, eagerly.

"Yes; I commanded the escort. He was a young fellow of scarcely more than four-and-twenty, and must have been good-looking, too."

"Of course you could not tell his name," said the Knight, despondingly.

"No; I heard it, however, but it has escaped me. There was a curious story brought back about him by our brigade-major, and one which, I assure you, furnished many a hearty laugh at your land of noble privileges and aristocratic forms."

"Pray let me hear it."

"Oh, I cannot tell you one half of it; the finale interested the major most, because it concerned himself, and this he repeated to us at least a dozen times. It would seem, then, that this youth—a rare thing, I believe, in your service—was a man of birth, but, according to your happy institutions, was a man of nothing more, for he was a younger son. Is not that your law?"

Darcy nodded, and the other resumed.

"Well, in some fit of spleen, at not being born a year or two earlier, or for some love affair with one of your blonde insensibles, or from weariness of your gloomy climate, or from any other true British cause of despair, our youth became a soldier. Parbleu! your English chivalry has its own queer notions, when it regards the service as a last resource of the desperate! No matter, he enlisted, came out here, fought bravely, and was taken prisoner in the very same attack with yourself; but, while Fortune dealt heavily with one hand, she was caressing with the other, for, the same week she condemned him to a French prison, she made him a Peer of England, having taken off the elder brother, an Ambassador at some Court, I believe, by a fever. So goes the world. Good and ill-luck battling against each, and one, never getting uppermost, without the other, recruiting strength for a victory in turn."

"These are strange tidings, indeed," said the Knight, musing, "and would interest me deeply, if I knew the name of the individual."

"That I am unfortunate enough to have forgotten," said the Frenchman, carelessly; "but I conclude he must be a person of some importance, for we heard that the vessel which was to sail with despatches was delayed several hours in the bay, to take him back to England."

Although the whole recital contained many circumstances which the Knight attributed to French misrepresentation of English habitudes, he was profoundly struck by it, and dwelt fondly on the hope, that if the young Peer should have served under his command, he would not neglect, on arriving in England, to inform his friends of his safety.

These thoughts, mingling with others of his home, and of his son Lionel, far away in a distant quarter of the globe, filled his mind as he went, and made him ponder deeply over the strange accidents of a life that, opening with every promise, seemed about to close in sorrow and uncertainty. Full of movement and interest as was the scene around, he seldom bestowed on it even a passing glance; it was an hour of gloomy reverie, and he neither marked the long train of waggons with their wounded, the broken and shattered gun-carriages, or the miserable aspect of the cavalry, whose starved and galled animals could scarcely crawl. The Knight's momentary indifference was interpreted in a very different sense by the officer who commanded the escort, and who seemed to suspect that this apathy concealed a shrewd insight into the real condition of the troops and the signs of distress and discomfiture so palpable on every side. As, impressed with this conviction, he watched the old man with prying curiosity, a smile, faint and fleeting enough, once crossed Darcy's features. The Frenchman's face flushed as he beheld it, and he quickly said,

"They are the same troops that landed at the Arabs' Tower, and who carry such inscriptions on their standards as these." He snatched a flag from the sergeant beside him as he spoke, and pointed to the proud words embroidered there: "Le Passage de la Scrivia"—"Le Passage de l'Isonzo"—"Le Pont de Lodi." Then, in a low, muttering voice, he added, "But Buonaparte was with us then."

Had he spoken for hours, the confession of their discontent with their generals could not have been more manifest, and a sudden gleam of hope shot through Darcy's breast, to think his captivity might soon be over.

There was every reason to indulge in this pleasing belief; disorganisation had extended to every branch of the service. An angry correspondence, in which even personal chastisement was broadly hinted at, passed between the two officers highest in command, and this not secretly, but publicly known to the entire army. Peculation of the most gross and open kind was practised by the commissaries, and as the troops became distressed by want, they retaliated by daring breaches of discipline, so that at every parade men stood out from the ranks, boldly demanding their rations, and answering the orders of the officers by insulting cries of "Bread! bread!"

All this while the British were advancing steadily, overcoming each obstacle in turn, and with a force whose privations had made no inroad upon the strictest discipline; they felt confident of success. The few prisoners who occasionally fell into the hands of the French, wore all the assurance of men who felt that their misfortunes could not be lasting, and in good-humoured raillery bantered the captors on the British beef and pudding they would receive, instead of horseflesh, so soon as the capitulation was signed.

The French soldiers were, indeed, heartily tired of the war; they were tired of the country, of the leaders, whose incompetency, whether real or not, they believed; tired, above all, of absence from France, from which they felt exiled. Each step they retired from the coast seemed to them another day's journey from their native land, and they did not hesitate to avow to their prisoners, that they had no wish or care save to return to their country.

Such was the spirit of the French army as it drew near Cairo, than which no greater contrast could exist than that presented by the advancing enemy. Let us now return to the more immediate interests of our story, and while we beg to corroborate the brief narrative of the French officer, we hope it is unnecessary to add that the individual whose suddenly changed fortune had elevated him from the ranks of a simple Volunteer to that of a Peer of England, was our old acquaintance Dick Forester.

From the moment when the tidings reached him, to that in which he lay still suffering from his wounds, in the richly-furnished chamber of a London hotel, the whole train of events through which he had so lately passed, seemed like the incoherent fancies of a dream. The excited frame of mind in which he became a volunteer with the army, had not time to subside ere came the spirit-stirring hour of the landing at Aboukir. The fight, in all its terrible but glorious vicissitudes—the struggle in which he perilled his own life to save his leader's—the moments that seemed those of ebbing life in which he lay upon a litter before Darcy's eyes, and yet unable to speak his name—and then the sudden news of his brother's death, overwhelming him at once with sorrow for his loss—and all the thousand fleeting thoughts of his own future, should life be spared him—these were enough, and more than enough, to disturb and overbalance a mind already weakened by severe illness.

Had Forester known more of his only brother, it is certain that the predominance of the feeling of grief would have subdued the others, and given at least the calm of affliction to his troubled senses. But they were almost strangers to each other; the elder having passed his life almost exclusively abroad, and the younger, separated by distance and a long interval of years, being a complete stranger to his qualities and temper.

Dick Forester's grief, therefore, was no more than that which ties of so close kindred will ever call up, but unmixed with the tender attachment of a brother's love. His altered fortunes had not thus the strong alloy of heartfelt sorrow to make them distasteful; but still there was an unreality in everything—a vague uncertainty in all his endeavours at close reasoning, which harassed and depressed him. And when he awoke from each short disturbed sleep, it took several minutes before he could bring back his memory to the last thought of his waking hours. The very title "my Lord," so scrupulously repeated at each instant, startled him afresh at each moment he heard it; and as he read over the names of the high and titled personages whose anxieties for his recovery had made them daily visitors at his hotel, his heart faltered between the pleasure of flattery, and a deeper feeling of almost scorn for the sympathies of a world that could minister to the caprices of rank what it withheld from the real sufferings of the same man in obscurity. His mother he had not yet seen, for Lady Netherby, much attached to her eldest son, and vain of abilities by which she reckoned on his future distinction, was, herself, seriously indisposed. Lord Netherby, however, had been a frequent visitor, and had already seen Forester several times, although always very briefly, and only upon the terms of distant politeness.

Although in a state that precluded everything like active exertion, and which, indeed, made the slightest effort a matter of peril, Forester had already exchanged more than one communication with the Horse Guards on the subject of the Knight's safety, and received the most steady assurances that his exchange was an object on which the authorities were most anxious, and engaged at the very moment in negotiations for its accomplishment. There were two difficulties: one, that no officer of Darcy's precise rank was then a prisoner with the British; and secondly, that any very pressing desire expressed for his liberation would serve to weaken the force of that conviction they were so eager to impress, that the campaign was nearly ended, and that nothing but capitulation remained for the French.

Forester was not more gratified than surprised at the tone of obliging and almost deferential politeness which pervaded each answer to his applications. He had yet to learn how a vote in the "Lords" can make secretaries civil, and under-secretaries most courteous, and while his few uncertain lines were penned with diffidence and distrust, the replies gradually inducted him into that sense of confidence which a few months later he was to feel like a birthright.

How far these thoughts contributed to his recovery it would be difficult to say, nor does it exactly lie in our province to inquire. The likelihood is, that the inducements to live are strong aids to overcome sickness, for, as a witty observer has remarked, "There is no such *manque de savoir vivre* as dying at four-and-twenty.

It is very probable Forester experienced all this, and that the dreams of the future in which he indulged were not only his greatest, but his pleasantest aid to recovery. A brilliant position, invested with rank, title, fortune, and a character for enterprise, are all flattering adjuncts to youth, while in the hope of succeeding, where his dearest wishes were concerned, lay a source of far higher happiness. How to approach this subject again most fittingly, was now the constant object of his thoughts. He sometimes resolved to address Lady Eleanor, but so long as he could convey no precise tidings of the Knight, this would be an ungracious task. Then he thought of Miss Daly, but he did not know her address. All these doubts and hesitations invariably ending in the resolve, that as soon as his strength permitted he would go over to Ireland, and finding out Bicknell, obtain accurate information as to Lady Eleanor's present residence, and also learn if, without being discovered, he could in any way be made serviceable to the interests of the family.

Perhaps we cannot better convey the gradually dawning conviction of his altered fortune on his mind, than by mentioning that while he canvassed these various chances, and speculated on their course, he never dwelt on the possibility of Lady Netherby's power to influence his determination. In the brief note he received from her each morning, the tone of affectionate solicitude for his health was always accompanied by some allusive hint of the "duties" recovery would impose, and each inquiry after his night's rest was linked with a not less anxious question, as to how soon he might feel able to appear in public. Constitutionally susceptible of all attempts to control him, and from his childhood disposed to rebel against dictation, he limited his replies to brief accounts of his progress, or inquiries after her own health, resolved in his heart that now that fortune was his own, to use the blessings it bestows according to the dictates of affection and a conscientious sense of right, and be neither the toy of a faction nor the tool of a party. In Darcy—could he but see him once more—he looked for a friend and adviser, and whatever the fortune of his suit, he felt that the Knight's counsels should be his guidance as to the future, reposing not even more trust on unswerving rectitude, than on the vast range of his knowledge of life, and the common-sense views he could take of the most complex, as of the very simplest questions.

It was now some seven weeks after his return, and Forester, for we would still desire to call him by the name our reader has known him, was sitting upon a sofa, weak and nervous, as the first day of a convalescent's appearance in the drawing-room usually is, when his servant, having deposited on the table several visiting-cards of distinguished inquirers, mentioned that the Earl of Netherby wished to pay his respects. Forester moved his head in token of assent, and his Lordship soon after entered.

CHAPTER LXVI.

THE DAWN OF CONVALESCENCE.

STEPPING noiselesly over the carpet, with an air at once animated and regardful of the sick man, Lord Netherby was at Forester's side before he could arise to receive him; and pressing him gently down with both hands, said, in a voice of most silvery cadence,

"My dear Lord—you must not stir for the world—Halford has only permitted me to see you under the strict pledge of prudence; and now, how are you? Ah! I see—weak and low. Come, you must let me speak for you, or at least interpret your answers to my own liking. We have so much to talk over, it is difficult where to begin."

"How is Lady Netherby?" said Forester, with a slight hesitation be tween the words.

"Still very feeble and very nervous. The shock has been a dreadful one to her. You know that poor Augustus was coming home on leave—when——when this happened."

Here his Lordship sighed, but not too deeply, for he remembered that the law of primogeniture is the sworn enemy to grief.

"There was some talk, too, of his being a sent on special embassy to Paris—a very high and important trust—and so really the affliction is aggravated by thinking what a career was opening to him. But, as the Dean of Walworth beautifully expressed it, 'We are cut down like flowers of the field.' Ah!"

A sigh and a slight wave with a handkerchief, diffusing an odour of Eau-de-Portugal through the chamber, closed this affecting sentiment.

"I trust in a day or two I shall be able to see my mother," said Forester, whose thoughts were following a far more natural channel. "I can walk a little to-day, and before the end of the week Halford promises me that I shall drive out."

"That's the very point we are most anxious about," said Lord Netherby, eagerly; "we want you, if possible, to take your seat in 'the Lords' next week. There is a special reason for it. Rumour runs that the Egyptian expedition will be brought on for discussion on Thursday next. Some malcontents are about to disparage the whole business, and, in particular, the affair at Alexandria. Ministers are strong enough to resist this attack, and even carry the war back into the enemy's camp; but we all think it would be a most fortunate moment for you, when making your first appearance in the House, to rise and say a few words on the subject of the campaign. The circumstances under which you joined—your very dangerous wound—have given you a kind of prerogative to speak, and the occasion is most opportune. Come, what say you? Would such an effort be too great?"

"Certainly not for my strength, my Lord, if not for my shame sake; for really I should feel it somewhat presumptuous in me, a man who carried his musket in the ranks, to venture on a discussion, far more a defence, of the great operations in which he was a mere unit; one of those rank and file who figured, without other designation, in lists of killed and wounded."

"This is very creditable to your modesty, my dear Lord," said the old Peer, smiling most blandly, "but pardon me if I say it displays a great forgetfulness of your present position. Remember that you now belong to the Upper House, and that the light of the Peerage shines on the past as on the future."

"By which I am to understand," replied Forester, laughing, "that the events which would have met a merited oblivion in Dick Forester's life, are to be remembered with honour to the Earl of Wallincourt."

"Of course they are," cried Lord Netherby, joining in the laugh. "If an unlikely scion of Royalty ascends the throne, we look out for the evidences of his princely tastes in the sports of his boyhood. Nay, if a clever writer or painter wins distinction from the world, do we not 'try back' for his triumphs at school, or his chalk sketches on coach-house gates, to warrant the early development of genius?"

"Well, my Lord," said Forester, gaily, "I accept the augury, and as nothing more nearly concerns a man's life than the fate of those who have shown him friendship, let me inquire after some friends of mine, and some relations of yours—the Darcys."

"Ah, those poor Darcys!" said Lord Netherby, wiping his eyes, and heaving a very profound sigh, as though to say that the theme was one far too painful to dwell upon—"theirs is a sad story, a very sad story indeed!"

"Anything more gloomy than the loss of fortune, my Lord?" asked Forester, with a trembling lip, and a cheek pale as death. Lord Netherby stared to see whether the patient's mind was not beginning to wander. That there could be that thing worse than loss of fortune he had yet to learn—assuredly he had never heard of it. Forester repeated his question.

"No, no, perhaps not, if you understand by that phrase what I do," said Lord Netherby, almost pettishly. "If, like me, you take in all the long train of ruin and decay such loss implies: pecuniary distress—moneyed difficulties—fallen condition in society—inferior association——"

"Nay, my Lord, in the present instance, I can venture to answer for it, such consequences have not ensued. You do your relatives scarcely justice to suppose it."

"It is very good and very graceful, both, in you," said Lord Netherby, with an almost angelic smile, "to say so. Unfortunately, these are not merely speculative opinions on my part. While I make this remark, understand me as by no means imputing any blame to them. What could they do?—that is the question—what could they do?"

"I would rather ask of your Lordship, what have they done? When I know that, I shall be, perhaps, better enabled to reply to your question."

In all likelihood it was more the manner than the substance of this question which made Lord Netherby hesitate how to reply to it, and at last he said:

"To say in so many words what they have done, is not so easy. It would, perhaps, give better insight into the circumstances were I to say what they have not done."

"Even as you please, my Lord. The negative charge, then," said Forester, impatiently——

"Lord Castlereagh, my Lord!" said a servant, throwing open the door, for he had already received orders to admit him when he called, though, had Forester guessed how inopportune the visit could have proved, he would never have said so.

In the very different expressions of Lord Netherby and the sick man's face, it might be seen how differently they welcomed the new arrival.

Lord Castlereagh saluted both with a courteous and cordial greeting and although he could not avoid seeing that he had dropped in somewhat mal-à-propos, he resolved rather to shorten the limit of his stay than render it awkward by any expressions of apology. The conversation, therefore, took that easy, careless tone, in which each could join with freedom. It was after a brief pause, when none exactly liked to be the first to speak, that Lord Netherby observed:

"The very moment you were announced, my Lord, I was endeavouring to persuade my young friend here to a line of conduct in which, if I have your Lordship's co-operation, I feel I shall be successful."

"Pray let me hear it," said Lord Castlereagh, gaily, and half interrupting what he feared was but the opening of an over lengthy exposition.

Lord Netherby was not to be defeated so easily, nor defrauded of a theme whereupon to expend many loyal sentiments, and so he opened a whole battery of arguments on the subject of the young Peer's first appearance in the House, and the splendid opportunity, as he called it, of a maiden speech.

"I see but one objection," said Lord Castlereagh, with a well-affected gravity.

"I see one hundred," broke in Forester, impatiently.

"Perhaps *my* one will do," rejoined Lord Castlereagh.

"Which is—if I may take the liberty——" lisped out Lord Netherby.

"That there will be no debate on the subject. The motion is withdrawn."

"Motion withdrawn!—since when?"

"I see you have not heard the news this morning," said Lord Castlereagh, who really enjoyed the discomfiture of one very vain of possessing the earliest intelligence.

"I have heard nothing," exclaimed he, with a sigh of despondency.

"Well, then, I may inform you, that the *Pike* has brought us very stirring intelligence. The war in Egypt is now over. The French have surrendered under the terms of a convention, and a treaty has been ratified that permits their return to France. Hostages for the guarantee of the treaty have been already interchanged, and"—here he turned towards Forester, and added—"it will doubtless interest you to hear that your old friend the Knight of Gwynne is one of them, an evidence that he is not only alive, but in good health also."

"This is, indeed, good news you bring me," said Forester, with a flashing eye and a heightened complexion. "Has any one written? Do Colonel Darcy's friends know of this?"

"I have myself done so," said Lord Castlereagh. "Not that I may attribute the thoughtful attention to myself, for I received his Royal Highness's commands on the subject. I need scarcely say that such a communication must be gratifying to any one."

"Where are they at present?" said Forester, eagerly.

"That was a question of some difficulty to me, and I accordingly called on my Lord Netherby to ascertain the point. I found he had left home, and now have the good fortune to catch him here." So saying, Lord Castlereagh took from the folds of a pocket-book a sealed but unaddressed letter, and dipping a pen in the ink before him, prepared to write.

There were, indeed, very few occurrences in life which made Lord Netherby feel ashamed. He had never been obliged to blush for any solecism in manner, or any offence against high breeding, nor had the even tenor of his days subjected him to any occasion of actual shame, so that the confusion he now felt had the added poignancy of being a new as well as a painful sensation.

"It may seem very strange to you, my Lord," said he, in a broken and hesitating voice; "not but that, on a little reflection, the case will be easily accounted for; but—so it is—I—really must own—I must frankly acknowledge—that I am not at this moment aware of my dear cousin's address."

If his Lordship had not been too much occupied in watching Lord Castlereagh's countenance, he could not have failed to see, and be struck by, the indignant expression of Forester's features.

"How are we to reach them, then, that's the point?" said Lord Castlereagh, over whose handsome face not the slightest trace of passion was visible. "If I mistake not, Gwynne Abbey they have left many a day since."

"I think I can lay my hand on a letter. I am almost certain I had one from a law-agent, called—called——"

"Bicknell, perhaps," interrupted Forester, blushing between shame and impatience.

"Quite right—you are quite right," replied Lord Netherby, with a significant glance at Lord Castlereagh, cunningly intended to draw off attention from himself. "Well, Mr. Bicknell wrote to me a very tiresome and complicated epistle about law affairs—motions, rules, and so forth—and mentioned at the end that Lady Eleanor and Helen were living in some remote village on the northern coast."

"A cottage called the Corvy," broke in Forester, "kindly lent to them by an old friend, Mr. Bagenal Daly."

"Will that address suffice," said Lord Castlereagh, "with the name of the nearest post-town?"

"If you will make me the postman, I'll vouch for the safe delivery," said Forester, with an animation that made him flushed and pale within the same instant.

"My dear young friend—my dear Lord Wallincourt!" exclaimed Lord Netherby, laying his hand upon his arm. He said no more; indeed he firmly believed the enunciation of his new title must be quite sufficient to recal him to a sense of due consideration for himself.

"You are scarcely strong enough, Dick," said Lord Castlereagh, coolly "It is a somewhat long journey for an invalid, and Halford, I'm sure, wouldn't agree to it."

"I'm quite strong enough," said Forester, rising and pacing the room with an attempted vigour that made his debility seem still more remarkable; "if not to-day, I shall be to-morrow. The travelling, besides, will serve me—change of air and scene. More than all, I am determined on doing it."

"Not if I refuse you the despatches, I suppose?" said Lord Castlereagh, laughing.

"You can scarcely do that," said Forester, fixing his eyes steadfastly on him. "Your memory is a bad one, or you must recollect sending me down once upon a time to that family on an errand of a different nature. Don't you think you owe an amende to them and to me?"

"Eh! what was that? I should like to know what you allude to," said Lord Netherby, whose curiosity became most painfully eager.

"A little secret between Dick and myself," said Lord Castlereagh, laughing. "To show I do not forget which, I'll accede to his present request, always provided that he is equal to it."

"Oh, as to that——"

"It must be 'Halfordo non obstante,' or not at all," said Lord Castlereagh, rising. "Well," continued he, as he moved towards the door, "I'll see the doctor on my way homeward, and, if he incline to the safety of the exploit, you shall hear from me before four o'clock. I'll send you some extracts, too, from the official papers, such as may interest your friends, and you may add '*bien des choses de ma part*,' in the way of civil speeches and gratulation."

Lord Netherby had moved towards the window as Lord Castlereagh withdrew, and seemed more interested by the objects in the street than anxious to renew the interrupted conversation.

Forester—if one were to judge from his preoccupied expression—appeared equally indifferent on the subject, and both were silent. Lord Netherby at last looked at his watch, and, with an exclamation of astonishment at the lateness of the hour, took up his hat. Forester did not notice the gesture, for his mind had suddenly become awake to the indelicacy, to say no worse, of leaving London for a long journey without one effort to see his mother. A tingling feeling of shame burned in his cheek and made his heart beat faster, as he said, "I think you have your carriage below, my Lord?"

"Yes," replied Lord Netherby, not aware whether the question might portend something agreeable or the reverse.

"If you'll permit me, I'll ask you to drive me to Berkeley-square. I think the air and motion will benefit me; and perhaps Lady Netherby will see me."

"Delighted—charmed to see you—my dear young friend," said Lord Netherby, who having, in his own person, some experience of the sway and influence her ladyship was habituated to exercise, calculated largely on the effect of an interview between her and her son. "I don't believe you could possibly propose anything more gratifying nor more likely to serve her. She is very weak and very nervous; but to see you will, I know, be of immense service. I'm sure you'll not agitate her," added he, after a pause. If the words had been "not contradict," they would have been nearer his meaning.

"You may trust me, for both our sakes," said Forester, smiling, "By-the-by, you mentioned a letter from a law-agent of the Darcys, Mr. Bicknell was it expressive of any hope of a favourable termination to the suit, or did he opine that the case was a bad one?"

"If I remember aright, a very bad one; bad, from the deficiency of evidence—worse, from the want of funds to carry it on. Of course, I only speak from memory, and the epistle was so cramp, so complex, and with such a profusion of detail intermixed, that I could make little out of it, and retain even less. I must say that, as it was written without my cousin's knowledge or consent, I paid no attention to it. It was, so to say, quite unauthorised."

"Indeed!" exclaimed Forester, in an accent whose scorn was mistaken by the hearer, as he resumed.

"Just so; a mere lawyer's *ruse*, to carry on a suit. He proposed, I own, a kind of security for any advance I should make, in the person of Miss Daly, whose property, amounting to some three or four thousand pounds, was to be given as security! There always is some person of this kind on these occasions—some tame elephant—to attract the rest: but I paid no attention to it. The only thing, indeed, I could learn of the lady was, that she had a fire-eating brother who paid bond debts with a pistol, and small ones with a horsewhip."

"I know Mr. Daly and his sister, too. He is a most honourable and high-minded gentleman; of her, I only needed to hear the trait your Lordship has just mentioned, to say that she is worthy to be his sister in every respect."

"I was not aware that they were acquaintances of yours."

"Friends, my Lord, would better express the relationship between us friends, firm and true, I sincerely believe them. Pray, if not indiscreet may I ask the date of this letter?"

"Some day of June last, I think. The case was to come on for tria next November in Westport, and it was for funds to carry on the suit, it would seem, they were pressed."

"You didn't hear a second time?"

"No, I've told you that I never answered this letter. I was quite willing, I am so at this hour, to be of any service to my dear cousin, Lady Eleanor Darcy, and to aid her to the fullest extent; but, to prosecute a hopeless lawsuit, to throw away some thousands in an interminable Equity investigation—to measure purses, too, against one of the richest men in Ireland, as I hear their antagonist is—this, I could never think of."

"But who has pronounced this claim hopeless?" said Forester, impatiently.

A cold shrug of the shoulders was all Lord Netherby's reply.

"Not Miss Daly, certainly," rejoined Forester, "who was willing to peril everything she possessed in the world upon the issue."

The sarcasm intended by this speech was deeply felt by Lord Netherby, as with an unwonted concession to ill-humour, he replied,

"There is nothing so courageous as indigence!"

"Better never be rich, then," cried Forester, "if cowardice be the first lesson it teaches. But I think better of affluence than this. I saw that same Knight of Gwynne when at the head of a princely fortune, and I never, in any rank of life, under any circumstances, saw the qualities which grace and adorn the humblest, more eminently displayed."

"I quite agree with you; a more perfectly conducted household it is impossible to conceive."

"I speak not of his retinue, nor of his graceful hospitalities, my Lord, nor even of his generous munificence and benevolence; these are rich men's gifts everywhere. I speak of his trusting, confiding temper; the hopeful trust he entertained of something good in men's natures at the moment he was smarting from their perfidy and ingratitude; the forgiveness towards those that injured, the unvarying kindness towards those that forgot him."

"I declare," said Lord Netherby, smiling, "I must interdict a continuance of this panegyric, now that we have arrived, for you know Colonel Darcy was a first love of Lady Netherby."

Nothing but a courtier of Lord Netherby's stamp could have made such a speech, and while Forester became scarlet with shame and anger, a new light suddenly broke upon him, and the rancour of his mother respecting the Knight and his family were at once explained.

"Now to announce you," said Lord Netherby, gaily; "let that be my task." And so saying, he lightly tripped up the stairs before Forester.

CHAPTER LXVII.

A BOUDOIR.

When, having passed through a suite of gorgeously furnished rooms, Forester entered the dimly-lighted boudoir where his lady-mother reclined, his feelings were full of troubled emotion. The remembrance of the last time he had been there was present to his mind, mingled with anxious fears as to his approaching reception. Had he been more conversant with the "world," he needed not to have suffered these hesitations. There are few conditions in life between which so wide a gulf yawns, as that of the titled heir of a house and the younger brother. He was, then, as little prepared for the affectionate greeting that met him, as for the absence of all trace of illness in her Ladyship's appearance. Both were very grateful to his feelings as he drew his chair beside her sofa, and a soft remembrance of former days of happiness stole over his pleased senses. Lord Netherby, with a fitting consideration, had left them to enjoy this interview alone, and thus their emotions were unrestrained by the presence of the only one who had witnessed their parting. Perhaps, the most distinguishing trait of the closest affection is, that the interruptions to its course do not involve the misery of reconciliation to enable us to return to our own place in the heart; but that the moment of grief, or anger, or doubt, over, we feel that we have a right to resume our influence in the breast whose thoughts have so long mingled with our own. The close ties of filial and parental love are certainly of this nature, and it must be a stubborn heart whose instincts do not tend to that forgiveness which as much blots out as it pardons past errors. Such was not Lady Netherby's. Pride of station, the ambition of leadership in certain circles, had so incorporated themselves with the better dictates of her mind, that she rarely, if ever, permitted mere feeling to influence her; but if, for a moment, it did get the ascendancy, her heart could feel as acutely as though it had been accustomed to such indulgence. In a word, she was as affectionate as the requirements of her rank permitted—oh! this Rank—this Rank! how do its conventionalities twine and twist themselves round our natures till love and friendship are actually subject to the cold ordinance of a fashion! How many hide the dark spots of their heart behind the false screen they call their "Rank!" The rich man, in the Bible, clothed in his purple, and faring sumptuously, was but acting in conformity with his "Rank!"—nay, more, he was charitable as became his "Rank," for the poor were fed with the crumbs from his table.

Forester was well calculated by natural advantages to attract a mother's pride. He was handsome and well-bred, had even more than a fair share of abilities, which gained credit for something higher from a native quickness of apprehension, and even already, the adventurous circumstances of his first campaign had invested his character with a degree of interest that promised well for his success in the world. If her manner to him was then kind and affectionate, it was mingled also with something of admiration, which her woman's heart yielded to the romantic traits of the youth.

She listened with eager pleasure to the animated description he gave of the morning at Aboukir, and the brilliant panorama of the attack, nor was the enjoyment marred by the mention of the only name that could have pained her, the last words of Lord Netherby having sealed Forester's lips with respect to the Knight of Gwynne.

The changeful fortunes of his life as a prisoner were mingled with the recital of the news by which his exchange was effected, and this brought back once more the subject by which their interview was opened—the death of his elder brother. Lady Netherby perhaps felt she had done enough for sorrow, for she dwelt but passingly on the theme, and rather addressed herself to the future which was now about to open before her remaining son, carefully avoiding, however, the slightest phrase that should imply dictation, and only seeming to express the natural expectation "the world" had formed of what his career should be.

"Lord Netherby tells me," said she, "that the Duke of York will, in all likelihood, name you as an extra aide-de-camp, in which case you probably would remain in the service. It is an honour that could not well be declined."

"I scarcely like to form fixed intentions which have no fixed foundations," said Forester; "but if I might give way to my own wishes, it would be to indulge in perfect liberty—to have no master."

"Nor any mistress either, to control you, for some time, I suppose," rejoined she, smiling, as if carelessly, but watching how her words were taken. Forester affected to partake in the laugh, but could not conceal a slight degree of confusion. Lady Netherby was too clever a tactician to let even a momentary awkwardness interrupt the interview, and resumed: "You will be dreadfully worried by all the 'Lionising' in store for you, I'm certain; you are to be feasted and fêted to any extent, and will be fortunate if the gratulations on your recovery do not brink back your illness."

"I shall get away from it all, at once," said Forester, rising, and walking up and down, as if the thought had suggested the impatient movement.

"You cannot avoid presenting yourself at the levee," said Lady Netherby anxiously, for already a dread of her son's wilful temper came over her. "His Royal Highness's inquiries after you do not leave an option on this matter."

"What if I'm too ill?" said he, doggedly; "what if I should not be in town?"

"But where else could you be, Richard?" said she, with a resumption of her old imperiousness of tone and manner.

"In Ireland, madam," said Forester, coldly.

"In Ireland! And why, for any sake, in Ireland?"

Forester hesitated, and grew scarlet; he did not know whether to evade inquiry by a vague reply, or at once avow his secret determination. At length, with a faltering, uncertain voice, he said: "A matter of business will bring me to that country; I have already conversed with Lord Castlereagh on the subject. Lord Netherby was present."

"I am sure he could never concur—I'm certain." So far her Ladyship had proceeded, when a sudden fear came over her that she had ventured too far, and, turning hastily, she rang the bell beside her. "Davenport," said she to the grave-looking groom of the chambers, who as instantaneously appeared, "is my Lord at home?"

"His Lordship is in the library, my Lady."

"Alone?"

"No, my Lady, a gentleman from Ireland is with his Lordship."

"A gentleman from Ireland!" repeated she, half aloud, as though the very mention of that country were destined to persecute her; then quickly added, "Say I wish to speak with him here."

The servant bowed and withdrew; and now a perfect silence reigned in the apartment. Forester felt that he had gone too far to retreat, even were he so disposed, and although dreading nothing more than a "scene," awaited, without speaking, the course of events. As much yielding to an involuntary impatience as to relieve the awkwardness of the interval, he arose and walked into the adjoining drawing-room, carelessly tossing over books and prints upon the tables, and trying to affect an ease he was very far from experiencing.

It was while he was thus engaged that Lord Netherby entered the boudoir, and seeing her Ladyship alone, was about to speak in his usual tone, when, at a gesture from her, he was made aware of Forester's vicinity, and hastily subdued his voice to a whisper. Whatever the nature of the tidings which, in a hurried and eager tone, his Lordship retailed, her manner on hearing evinced mingled astonishment and delight, if the word dare be applied to an emotion whose source was in anything rather than an amiable feeling.

"It seems too absurd—too monstrous in every way," exclaimed she, at the end of an explanation which took several minutes to recount. "And why address himself to you? That seems also inexplicable."

"This," rejoined Lord Netherby, aloud—"this was his own inspiration. He candidly acknowledges that no one either counselled or is even aware of the step he has taken."

"Perhaps the *à propos* may do us good service," whispered she, with a glance darted at the room where Forester was now endeavouring, by humming an air, to give token of his vicinity, as well as assume an air of indifference.

"I thought of that," said Lord Netherby, in the same low voice. "Would you see him? A few moments would be enough."

Lady Netherby made no answer, but with closed eyes and compressed lips seemed to reflect deeply for several minutes. At last she said, "Yes, let him come. I'll detain Richard in the drawing-room; he shall hear everything that is said. If I know anything of him, the insult to his pride will do far more than all our arguments and entreaties."

"Don't chill my little friend by any coldness of manner," said his Lordship, smiling, as he moved towards the door; "I have only got him properly thawed within the last few minutes."

"My dear Richard," said she, as the door closed after Lord Netherby, "I must keep you prisoner in the drawing-room for a few minutes, while I receive a visitor of Lord Netherby's. Don't close the doors; I can't endure heat, and this room becomes insupportable without a slight current of air. Besides, there is no secret, I fancy, in the communication. As well as I understand the matter, it does not concern us; but Netherby is always doing some piece of silly good-nature, for which no one thanks him!"

The last reflection was half soliloquy, but said so that Forester could and did hear every word of it. While her Ladyship, therefore, patiently awaited the arrival of her visitor in one room, Forester threw himself into a chair, and taking up a book at hazard, endeavoured to pass the interval without further thought about the matter.

Sitting with his back towards the door of the boudoir, Forester acci dentally had placed himself in such a position, that a large mirror between the windows reflected to him a considerable portion of the scene within. It was then with an amount of astonishment far above ordinary, that he beheld the strange-looking figure who followed Lord Netherby into the apartment of his mother. He was a short, dumpy man, with a bald head, over which the long hairs of either side were studiously combed into an ingenious kind of network, and meeting at an angle above the cranium, looked like the uncovered rafters of a new house. Two fierce-looking grey eyes that seemed ready for fun or malice, rolled and revolved unceasingly over the various decorations of the chamber, while a large thick-lipped mouth, slightly opened at either end, vouched for one who neglected no palpable occasion for self-indulgence or enjoyment. There was, indeed, throughout his appearance, a look of racy satisfaction and contentment, that consorted but ill with his costume, which was a suit of deep mourning; his clothes having all the gloss and shine of a recent domestic loss, and made, as seems something to be expected on these occasions, considerably too large for him, as though to imply that the defunct should not be defrauded in the full measure of sorrow. Deep crape weepers encircled his arms to the elbows, and a very banner of black hung mournfully from his hat.

"Mr. ——" Here Lord Netherby hesitated, forgetful of his name.

"Dempsey, Paul Dempsey, your Grace," said the little man, as, stepping forward, he performed the salutation before Lady Netherby, by which he was accustomed to precede an invitation to dance.

"Pray be seated, Mr. Dempsey. I have just briefly mentioned to her Ladyship the circumstances of our interesting conversation, and with your permission will proceed with my recital, begging, that if I fall into any error, you will kindly set me right. This will enable Lady Netherby, who is still an invalid, to support the fatigue of an interview, wherein her advice and counsel will be of great benefit to us both."

Mr. Dempsey bowed several times, not sorry, perhaps, that in such an awful presence he was spared the office of chief orator.

"I told you, my dear," said Lord Netherby, turning towards her Ladyship, "that this gentleman has for a considerable time back enjoyed the pleasure of intimacy with our worthy relative, Lady Eleanor Darcy——"

The fall of a heavy book in the adjoining room interrupted his Lordship, between whom and Lady Netherby a most significant interchange of glances took place. He resumed, however, without a pause—

"Lady Eleanor and her accomplished daughter. If the more urgent question were not now before us, it would gratify you much to learn, as I have just done, the admirable patience she has exhibited under the severe trials she has met—the profound insight she obtained into the condition, hopeless as it proves to be, of their unhappy circumstances—and the resignation in which, submitting to changed fortune, she not only has, at once, abandoned the modes of living she was habituated to, but actually descended to what I can fancy must have been the hardest infliction of all—vulgar companionship, and the society of a boarding-house."

"A most respectable establishment, though," broke in Paul; "Fumbally's is well known all over Ulster——"

A very supercilious smile from Lady Netherby cut short a panegyric Mr. Dempsey would gladly have extended.

"No doubt, sir, it was the best thing of the kind," resumed his Lordship; "but remember who Lady Eleanor Darcy was; ay, and is. Think of the station she had always held, and then fancy her in daily intercourse with those people——"

"Oh! it is very horrid, indeed," broke in Lady Netherby, leaning back, and looking overcome even at the bare conception of the enormity.

"The little miserable notorieties of a fishing village——"

"Coleraine, my Lord—Coleraine," cried Dempsey.

"Well, be it so. What is Coleraine?"

"A very thriving town on the river Bann, with a smart trade in yarn two breweries, three meeting-houses, a pound, and a Sunday-school," repeated Paul, as rapidly as though reading from a volume of a topographical dictionary.

"All very commendable and delightful institutions, on which I beg heartily to offer my congratulations; but, you will allow me to remark, scarcely enough to compensate for the accustomed appliances of a residence at Gwynne Abbey. But I see we are trespassing on Lady Netherby's strength. You seem faint, my dear."

"It's nothing—it will pass over in a moment or so. This sad account of these poor people has distressed me greatly."

"Well, then, we must hasten on. Mr. Dempsey became acquainted with our poor friends in this their exile; and although from his delicacy and good taste he will not dwell on the circumstance, it is quite clear to me, has shown them many attentions; I might use a stronger word, and say—kindnesses."

"Oh! by Jove, I did nothing. I could do nothing——"

"Nay, sir, you are unjust to yourself; the very intentions by which you set out on your present journey, are the shortest answer to that question. It would appear, my dear, that my fair relative, Miss Darcy, has not forfeited the claim she possessed to great beauty and attraction; for here, is the gentleman before us, is an evidence of their existence. Mr. Dempsey, who 'never told his love,' as the poet says, waited in submission himself for the hour of his changing fortune; and until the death of his mother——"

"No, my Lord; my uncle. Bob Dempsey, of Dempsey's Grove."

"His uncle, I mean. Mr. Dempsey, of Dempsey's Hole."

"Grove—Dempsey's Grove," interpolated Paul, reddening.

"Grove, I should say," repeated Lord Netherby, unmoved. "By which he has succeeded to a very comfortable independence, and is now in a position to make an offer of his hand and fortune."

"Under the conditions, my Lord—under the conditions," whispered Paul.

"I have not forgotten them," resumed Lord Netherby, aloud. "It would be ungenerous not to remember them, even for your sake, Mr. Dempsey, seeing how much my poor, dear relative, Lady Eleanor, is bent on prosecuting this unhappy suit, void of all hope, as it seems to be, and not having any money of her own——"

"Ready money—cash," interposed Paul.

"So I mean—ready money to make the advances necessary—Mr. Dempsey wishes to raise a certain sum by loan, on the security of his property, which may enable the Darcys to proceed with their claim; this deed to be executed on his marriage with Miss Darcy. Am I correct, sir?"

"Quite correct, my Lord; you've only omitted, that, to save expensive searches, lawyers' fees, and other devilments of the like nature, that your Lordship should advance the blunt yourself?"

"I was coming to that point. Mr. Dempsey opines that, taking the interest it is natural we should do in our poor friends, he has a kind of claim to make this proposition to us. He is aware of our relationship—mine, I mean—to Lady Eleanor. She spoke to you, I believe, on that subject, Mr Dempsey?"

"Not exactly to *me*," said Paul, hesitating, and recalling the manner in which he became cognisant of the circumstance; "but I heard her say that your Lordship was under very deep obligation to her own father—that you were, so to say, a little out at elbows once, very like myself, before Bob died, and that, then——"

"We all lived together like brothers and sisters," said his Lordship, reddening. "I'm sure I can't forget how happily the time went over."

"Then, Lady Eleanor, I presume, sir, did not advert to those circumstances as a reason for your addressing yourself to Lord Netherby?" said her Ladyship, with a look of stern severity.

"Why, my Lady, she knows nothing about my coming here. Lord bless us! I wouldn't have told her for a thousand pounds!"

"Nor Miss Darcy either?"

"Not a bit of it! Oh, by Jove! if you think they're not as proud as ever they were, you are much mistaken; and, indeed, on this very same subject I heard her say that nothing would induce her to accept a favour from your Lordship, if even so very improbable an event should occur as your offering one."

"So that we owe the honour of your visit to the most single-minded of motives, sir," said Lady Netherby, whose manner had now assumed all its stateliness.

"Yes, my Lady, I came as you see—Dempsius cum Dempsio—so that if I succeed, I can say, like that fellow in the play, 'Alone, I did it.'"

Lord Netherby, who probably felt that the interview had lasted sufficiently long for the only purpose he had destined or endured it, was now becoming somewhat desirous of terminating the audience, nor was his impatience allayed by those sportive sallies of Mr. Dempsey in allusion to his own former condition as a dependent.

At length he said, "You must be aware, Mr. Dempsey, that this is a matter demanding much time and consideration. The Knight of Gwynne is absent.

"That's the reason there is not an hour to lose," interposed Paul.

"I am at a loss for your meaning."

"I mean, that if he comes home before it's all settled, that the game is up. He would never consent, I'm certain."

"So you think that the ladies regard you with more favourable eyes?" said her Ladyship, smiling a mixture of superciliousness and amusement.

"I have my own reasons to think so," said Paul, with great composure.

"Perhaps you take too hopeless a view of your case, sir," resumed Lord Netherby, blandly; "I am, unhappily, very ignorant of Irish family rank; but I feel assured that Mr. Dempsey, of Dempsey's Hole——"

"Grove—Dempsey's Grove," said Paul, with a look of anger.

"I ask your pardon, humbly—I would say of Dempsey's Grove—might be an accepted suitor in the very highest quarters. At all events, from news I have heard this morning, it is more than likely that the Knight will be in London before many weeks, and I dare not assume either the responsibility of favouring your views, or incurring his displeasure by an act of interference. I think her Ladyship concurs with me."

"Perfectly. The case is really one which, however we may, and do, feel the liveliest interest in, lies quite beyond our influence or control."

"Mr. Dempsey may rest assured that, even from so brief an acquaintance we have learned to appreciate some of his many excellent qualities of hea and heart."

Lady Netherby bowed an acquiescence cold and stately; and his Lordshi rising at the same time, Paul saw that the audience drew to a close. H arose then slowly, and with a faint sigh—for he thought of his long an dreary journey, made to so little profit.

"So I may jog back again as I came," muttered he, as he drew on hi gloves. "Well, well, Lady Eleanor knew him better than I did. Goo morning, my Lady. I hope you are about to enjoy better health. Good-by my Lord."

"Do you make any stay in town, Mr. Dempsey?" inquired his Lordship in that bland voice that best became him.

"'Till I pack my portmanteau, my Lord, and pay my bill at the 'Tavi stock'—not an hour longer."

"I'm sorry for that. I had hoped, and Lady Netherby also expected, we should have had the pleasure of seeing you again."

"Very grateful, my Lord; but I see how the land lies as well as if I was here a month." And with this significant speech Mr. Dempsey repeated his salutations and withdrew.

"What presumption!" exclaimed Lady Netherby, as the door closed behind him. "But how needlessly Lady Eleanor Darcy must have lowered herself to incur such acquaintanceship!"

Lord Netherby made no reply, but gave a glance towards the still open door of the drawing-room. Her Ladyship understood it at once, and said,

"Oh, let us release poor Richard from his bondage. Tell him to come in."

Lord Netherby walked forward; but scarcely had he entered the drawing-room, when he called out, "He's gone!"

"Gone! when?—how?" cried Lady Netherby, ringing the bell. "Did you see Lord Wallincourt when he was going, Davenport?" asked she, at once assuming her own calm deportment.

"Yes, my Lady."

"I hope he took the carriage."

"No, my Lady, his Lordship went on foot."

"That will do, Davenport. I don't receive to-day."

"I must hasten after him," said Lord Netherby, as the servant withdrew. "We have, perhaps, incurred the very hazard we hoped to obviate."

"I half feared it," exclaimed Lady Netherby, gravely; "lose no time, however, and bring him to dinner; say that I feel very poorly, and that his society will cheer me greatly; if he is unfit to leave the house, stay with him; above all things, let him not be left alone."

Lord Netherby hastened from the room, and his carriage was soon heard at a rapid pace proceeding down the square.

Lady Netherby sat with her eyes fixed on the carpet, and her hands clasped closely, lost in thought. "Yes," said she, half aloud, "there is a fate in it! This Lady Eleanor may have her vengeance yet!"

It was about an hour after this, and while she was still revolving her own deep thoughts, that Lord Netherby re-entered the room.

"Well, is he here?" asked she, impatiently.

"No, he's off to Ireland; the very moment he reached the hotel he ordered four horses to his carriage, and while his servant packed some trunks, he himself drove over to Lord Castlereagh's, but came back almost immediately. They must have used immense despatch, for Long told me that they would be nigh Barnet when I called."

"He's a true Wallincourt," said her Ladyship, bitterly. "Their family motto is 'Rash in Danger,' and they have well deserved it."

CHAPTER LXVIII.

A LESSON FOR EAVESDROPPING.

Forester—for so to the end we must call him—but exemplified the old adage in his haste. The debility of long illness was successfully combated for some hours by the fever of excitement, but, as that wore off, symptoms of severe malady again exhibited themselves, and when on the second evening of his journey he arrived at Bangor, he was dangerously ill. With a head throbbing, and a brain almost mad, he threw himself upon a bed, perhaps the thought of his abortive effort to reach Ireland the most agonising feeling of his tortured mind. His first care was to inquire after the sailing of the packet, and learning that the vessel would leave within an hour, he avowed his resolve to go at every hazard. As the time drew nigh, however, more decided evidences of fever set in, and the medical man who had been called to his aid, pronounced that his life would pay the penalty were he to persist in his rash resolve. His was not a temper to yield to persuasion on selfish grounds, and nothing short of his actual inability to endure moving from where he lay at last compelled him to cede; even then he ordered his only servant to take the despatches which Lord Castlereagh had given him, and proceed with them to Dublin, where he should seek out Mr. Bicknell, and place them in his hands, with strict injunctions to have them forwarded to Lady Eleanor Darcy at once. The burning anxiety of a mind weakened by a tedious and severe malady, the fever of travelling, and the impatient struggles he made to be clear and explicit in his directions, repeated as they were full twenty times over, all conspired to exaggerate the worst features of his case, and ere the packet sailed, his head was wandering in wild delirium.

Linwood knew his master too well to venture on a contradiction, and although with very grave doubts that he should ever see him again alive, he set out, resolving to spare no exertions to be back soon again in Bangor. The transit of the Channel forty-five years ago was, however, very different from that at present, and it was already the evening of the following day when he reached Dublin.

There was no difficulty in finding out Mr. Bicknell's residence; a very showy brass-plate on a door in a fashionable street, proclaimed the house of the well-known man of law. He was not at home, however, nor would be for some hours; he had gone out on a matter of urgent business, and left orders that except for some most pressing reason, he was not to be sent for. Linwood did not hesitate to pronounce his business such, and at length obtained the guidance of a servant to the haunt in question.

It was in a street of a third or fourth-rate rank, called Stafford-street, that Bicknell's servant now stopped, and having made more than one inquiry as to name and number, at last knocked at the door of a sombre-looking, ruinous old house, whose windows, broken or patched with paper, bespoke an air of poverty and destitution. A child in a ragged and neglected dress opened the door, and answering to the question "If Mr. Bicknell were there," in the affirmative, led Linwood up-stairs, creaking as they went with rottenness and decay.

"You're to rap there, and he'll come to you," said the child, as they reached the landing, where two doors presented themselves; and so saying, she slipped noiselessly and stealthily down the stairs, leaving him alone in the gloomy lobby. Linwood was not without astonishment at the place in which he found himself, but there was no time for the indulgence of such a feeling, and he knocked at first gently, and then, as no answer came, more loudly, and at last, when several minutes elapsed, without any summons to enter, he tapped sharply at the panel with his cane. Still there was no reply; the deep silence of the old house seemed like that of a church at midnight, not a sound was heard to break it. There was a sense of dreariness and gloom over the ruinous spot, and the fast-closing twilight, that struck Linwood deeply, and it is probable, had the mission with which he was entrusted been one of less moment than his master seemed to think it, that Linwood would quietly have descended the stairs, and deferred his interview with Mr. Bicknell to a more suitable time and place. He had come, however, bent on fulfilling his charge, and so, after waiting what he believed to be half an hour, and which might possibly have been five or ten minutes, he applied his hand to the lock, and entered the room.

It was a large, low-ceilinged apartment, whose motheaten furniture seemed to rival with the building itself, and which, though once not without some pretension to respectability, was now crumbling to decay, or coarsely mended by some rude hand. A door, not quite shut, led into an inner apartment, and from this room the sound of voices proceeded, whose conversation, in all probability, had prevented Linwood's summons from being heard.

Whether the secret instincts of his calling were the prompter—for Linwood was a valet—or that the strange circumstances in which he found himself had suggested a spirit of curiosity, but Linwood approached the door and peeped in. The sin of eavesdropping, like most other sins, would seem only difficult at the first step; the subsequent ones come easily, for, as the listener established himself in a position to hear what went forward, he speedily became interested in what he heard.

By the grey half-light three figures were seen. One was a lady, so at least her position and attitude bespoke her, although her shawl was of a coarse and humble stuff, and her straw bonnet showed signs of time and season. She sat back in a deep leather chair, with hands folded, and her head slightly thrown forward, as if intently listening to the person who, at a distance of half the room, addressed her. He was a thick-set, powerful man, in a jockey-cut coat and top-boots; a white hat, somewhat crushed and travel-stained, was at his feet, and across it a heavy horsewhip; his collar was confined by a single fold of a spotted handkerchief, that thus displayed a brawny throat and a deep beard of curly black hair, that made the head appear unnaturally large. The third figure was of a little, dapper, smart-looking personage, with a neatly-powdered head and a scrupulously white cravat, who, standing partly behind the lady's chair, bestowed an equal attention on the speaker.

The green-coated man, it was clear to see, was of an order in life far inferior to the others, and in the manner of his address, his attitude as he sat and his whole bearing, exhibited a species of rude deference to the listeners.

"Well, Jack," cried the little man, in a sharp, lively voice, "we knew all these facts before; what we were desirous of, was, something like proof—something that might be brought out into open court and before a jury."

"I'm afraid then, sir," replied the other, "I can't help you there. I told Mr. Daly all I knew and all I suspected, when I was up in Newgate, and if he hadn't been in such a hurry that night to leave Dublin for the north, I could have brought him to the very house this fellow Garret was living in."

"Who is Garret?" broke in the lady, in a deep, full voice.

"The late Mr. Gleeson's butler, ma'am," said the little man; "a person we have never been able to come at. To summon him as a witness would avail us nothing; it is his private testimony that might be of such use to us."

"Well, you see, sir," continued the green coat, or, as he was familiarly named by the other, Jack, whom, perhaps, our reader has already recognised as Freney, the others being Miss Daly and Bicknell—"well, you see, sir, Mr. Daly was angry at the way things was done that night—and sure enough he had good cause—and sorra bit of a word he'd speak to me when I was standing with the tears in my eyes to thank him; no, nor he wouldn't take the mare that was ready saddled and bridled in Healey's stables waiting for him, but he turned on his heel with 'D—n you, for a common highwayman; it's what a man of blood and birth ever gets by stretching a hand to save you.'"

"He should have thought of that before," remarked Miss Daly, solemnly.

"Faith, and if he did, ma'am, your humble servant would have had to dance upon nothing!" rejoined Freney, with a laugh that was very far from mirthful.

"And what was the circumstance which gave Mr. Daly so much displeasure, Jack?" asked Bicknell. "I thought that everything went on exactly as he had planned it."

"Quite the contrary, sir: nothing was the way it ought to be. The fire was never thought of——"

"Never thought of! Do you mean to say it was an accident?"

"No, I don't, sir; I mean, that all we wanted was to make believe that the gaol was on fire, which was easy enough with burning straw; the rest was all planned safe and sure. And when we saw the real flames shooting up, sorra one was more frightened than some of ourselves; each accusing the other, cursing and shouting, and crying like mad! Ay, indeed! there was an ould fellow in for sheep-stealing, and nothing would convince him but that it was the 'Devil took us at our word,' and sent his own fire for us. Not one of them was more puzzled than myself. I turned it every way in my mind, and could make nothing of it; for though I knew well that Mr. Daly would burn down Dublin from Barrack-street to the North-wall if he had a good reason for it, I knew also he'd not do it out of mere devilment. Besides, ma'am, the way matters was going, it was likely that none of us would escape. There was I—saving your presence—with eight-pound fetters on my legs. Ay, faix! I went down the ladder in them afterwards."

"But the fire."

"I'm coming to it, sir. I was sitting this way, with my chin on my hands, at the window of my cell, trying to get a taste of fresh air, for the place was thick of smoke, when I seen the flames darting out of the windows of a public-house at the corner, the sign of the 'Cracked Padlock,' and, at the same minute, out came the fire through the roof, a great red spike of flame higher than the chimney. 'That's no accident,' says I to myself, 'whatever them that's doing it means;' and sure enough, the blaze broke out in the other corner of the street just as I said the words. Well, ma'am, of all the terrible yells and cries that was ever heard, the prisoners set up then, for, though there was eight lying for execution on Saturday, and twice as many more very sure of the same end, after the sessions, none of us liked to face such a dreadful thing as fire. Just then, ma'am, at that very minute, there came, as it might be under my window, a screech so loud and so piercing that it went above all the other cries, just the way the yellow fire darted through the middle of the thick, lazy smoke. Sorra one could give such a screech but a throat I knew well, and so I called out at the top of my voice, 'Ah, ye limb of the devil, this is your work!' and as sure as I'm here, there came a laugh in my ears, and whether it was the devil himself gave it or Jemmy, I often doubted since."

"And who is Jemmy?" asked Bicknell.

"A bit of a 'gossoon' I had to mind the horses, and meet me with a beast here and there, as I wanted. The greatest villain for wickedness that was ever pinioned!"

"And so he was really the cause of the fire?"

"Ay, was he! He not only hid the tinder and chips——"

Just as Freney had got thus far, he drew his legs up close beneath him, sunk down his head as if into his neck, and with a spring, such as a tiger might have given, cleared the space between himself and the door, and rolled over on the floor, with the trembling figure of Linwood under him. So terribly sudden was the leap, that Miss Daly and Bicknell scarcely saw the bound ere they beheld him with one hand upon the victim's throat, while with the other he drew forth a clasp-knife, and opened the blade with his teeth.

"Keep back, keep back," said Freney, as Bicknell drew nigh; and the words came thick and guttural, like the deep growl of a mastiff.

"Who are you, and what brings you here?" said Freney, as, setting his knee on the other's chest, he relinquished the grasp by which he had almost choked him.

"I came to see Mr. Bicknell," muttered the nearly lifeless valet.

"What did you want with me——?"

"Wait a bit," interposed Freney. "Who brought you here? how came you to be standing by that door?"

"Mr. Bicknell's servant showed me the house, and a child brought me to this room."

"There, sir," said Freney, turning his head towards Bicknell, without releasing the strong pressure by which he pinned the other down—"there, sir, so much for your caution. You told me if I came to this lady's lodgings here, that I was safe, and now here's this fellow has heard us and everything we've said, maybe these two hours."

"I only heard about Newgate," muttered the miserable Linwood; "I was but a few minutes at the door, and was going to knock. I came from Lord Wallincourt with papers of great importance for Mr. Bicknell. I have them, if you'll let me——"

"Let him get up," said Miss Daly, calmly.

Freney stood back, and retired between his victim and the door, where he stood, with folded arms and bent brows, watching him.

"He has almost broke in my ribs," said Linwood, as he pressed his hand to his side, with a grimace of true suffering.

"So much for eavesdropping. You need expect no pity from me," said Miss Daly, sternly. "Where are these papers?"

"My Lord told me," said the man, as he took them from his breast, "that I was to give them into Mr. Bicknell's own hands, with strictest directions to have them forwarded at the instant. "But for that," added he, whining, "I had never come to this."

"Let it be a lesson to you about listening, sir," said Miss Daly. "Had my brother been here——"

"Oh, by the powers!" broke in Freney, "he'd have pitched you neck and crop into the water-hogshead below, if your master was the Lord-Lieutenant."

"By this time Bicknell was busy reading the several addresses on the packets, and the names inscribed in the corners of each.

"If I'm not mistaken, madam," said he to Miss Daly, "this Lord Wallincourt is the new peer, whose brother died at Lisbon. The name is Forester."

"Yes, sir, you are right," muttered Linwood.

"The same Mr. Richard Forester my brother knew, the cousin of Lord Castlereagh?"

"Yes, ma'am," said Linwood.

"Where is he? Is he here?"

"No, ma'am, he's lying dangerously ill, if he be yet alive, at Bangor. He wanted to bring these papers over himself, but was only able to get so far when the fever came on him again."

"Is he alone?"

"Quite alone, ma'am; no one knows even his name. He would not let me say who he was."

Miss Daly turned towards Bicknell, and spoke for several minutes in a quick and eager voice. Meanwhile, Freney, now convinced that he had not to deal with a spy or a thief-catcher, came near and addressed Linwood.

"I didn't mean to hurt ye till I was sure ye deserved it, but never play that game any more."

Linwood appeared to receive both apology and precept with equal discontent.

"Another thing," resumed Freney; "I'm sure you are an agreeable young man in the housekeeper's room and the butler's parlour, very pleasant and conversable, with a great deal of anecdote and amusing stories, but, mind me, let nothing tempt ye to talk about what ye heard me say to-night. It's not that I care about myself—it's worse than gaol-breaking they can tell of me—but I won't have another name mentioned. D'ye mind me?"

As if to enforce the caution, he seized the listener between his finger and thumb, and whether there was something magnetic in the touch, or that it somehow conveyed a foretaste of what disobedience might cost, but Linwood winced till the tears came, and stammered out,

"You may depend on it, sir, I'll never mention it."

"I believe you," said the robber, with a grin, and fell back to his place.

"I will not lose a post, rely upon it, madam," said Bicknell· "and am I to suppose you have determined on this journey?"

"Yes," said Miss Daly, "the case admits of little hesitation; the young man is alone, friendless, and unknown. I'll hasten over at once—I am too old for slander, Mr. Bicknell. Besides, let me see who will dare to utter it."

There was a sternness in her features as she spoke that made her seem the actual image of her brother. Then, turning to Linwood, she continued,

"I'll go over this evening to Bangor in the packet; let me find you there."

"I'll see him safe on board, ma'am," said Freney, with a leer, while, slipping his arm within the valet's, he half led, half drew him from the room.

CHAPTER LXIX.

A LESSON IN POLITICS.

In the deep bay-window of a long, gloomy-looking dinner-room of a Dublin mansion, sat a party of four persons around a table plentifully covered with decanters and bottles, and some stray remnants of a dessert, which seemed to have been taken from the great table in the middle of the apartment. The night was falling fast, for it was past eight o'clock of an evening in autumn, and there was barely sufficient light to descry the few scrubby-looking ash and alder trees that studded the barren grass-plot between the house and the stables. There was nothing to cheer in the aspect without, nor, if one were to judge from the long pauses that ensued after each effort at conversation, the few and monotonous words of the speakers, were there any evidences of a more enlivening spirit, within doors. The party consisted of Dr. Hickman and his son Mr. O'Reilly, Mr. Heffernan, and "Counsellor" O'Halloran.

At first, and by the dusky light in the chamber, it would seem as if but three persons were assembled, for the old doctor, whose debility had within the last few months made rapid strides, had sunk down into the recess of the deep chair, and save by a low quavering respiration, gave no token of his presence. As these sounds became louder and fuller, the conversation gradually dropped into a whisper, for the old man was asleep. In the subdued tone of the speakers, the noiseless gestures as they passed the bottle from hand to hand, it was easy to mark that they did not wish to disturb his slumbers. It is no part of our task to detail how these individuals came to be thus associated. The assumed object which at this moment drew them together was the approaching trial at Galway of a record brought against the Hickmans by Darcy. It was Bicknell's last effort, and with it must end the long and wearisome litigation between the houses.

The case for trial had nothing which could suggest any fears as to the result. It was on a motion for a new trial that the cause was to come on. The plea was misdirection and want of time, so that, in itself, the matter was one of secondary importance. The great question was, that a General Election now drew nigh, and it was necessary for O'Reilly to determine on the line of political conduct he should adopt, and thus give O'Halloran the opportunity of a declaration of his client's sentiments in his address to the jury.

The conduct of the Hickmans since their accession to the estate of Gwynne Abbey had given universal dissatisfaction to the county gentry. Playing at first the game of popularity, they assembled at their parties people of every class and condition; and while affronting the better-bred by low association, dissatisfied the inferior order by contact with those who made their inferiority more glaring. The ancient hospitalities of the abbey were remembered in contrast with the ostentatious splendour of receptions in which display and not kindness was intended. Vulgar presumption and purse-pride had usurped the place once occupied by easy good breeding and cordiality, and even they who had often smarted under the cold reserve of Lady Eleanor's manner, were now ready to confess that she was born to the rank she assumed, and not an upstart, affecting airs of superiority The higher order of the county gentry accordingly held aloof, and at last discontinued their visits altogether; of the second-rate, many who were flattered at first by invitations, became dissatisfied at seeing the same favours extended to others below them, and they, too, ceased to present themselves, until, at last, the society consisted of a few sycophantic followers, who swallowed the impertinence of the host with the aid of his claret, and buried their own self-respect, if they were troubled with such a quality, under the weight of good dinners.

Hickman O'Reilly, for a length of time, affected not to mark the change in the rank and condition of his guests, but as one by one the more respectable fell off, and the few left were of a station that the fine servants of the house regarded as little above their own, he indignantly declined to admit any company in future, reduced the establishment to the few merely necessary for the modest requirements of the family, and gave it to be known that the uncongenial tastes and habits of his neighbours made him prefer isolation and solitude to such association.

For some time he had looked to England as the means of establishing for himself and his son a social position. The refusal of the Minister to accord the Baronetcy was a death-blow to this hope, while he discovered that mere wealth, unassisted by the sponsorship of some one in repute, could not suffice to introduce Beecham into the world of fashion. Although these things had preyed on him severely, there was no urgent necessity to act in respect of them till the time came, as it now had done, for a General Election.

The strict retirement of his life must now give way before the requirements of an Election candidate, and he must consent to take the field once more as a public man, or, by abandoning his seat in Parliament, accept a condition of what he knew to be complete obscurity. The old doctor was indeed favourable to the latter course—the passion for hoarding had gone on increasing with age. Money was, in his estimation, the only species of power above the changes and caprice of the world. Bank-notes were the only things he never knew to deceive; and he took an almost fiendish delight in contrasting the success of his own penurious practices with all the disappointments his son O'Reilly had experienced in his attempts at what he called "high life." Every slight shown him, each new instance of coldness or aversion of the neighbourhood, gave the old man a diabolical pleasure, and seemed to revive his youth in the exercise of a malignant spirit.

O'Reilly's only hope of reconciling his father to the cost of a new Election was in the prospect held out that the seat might at last be secured in perpetuity for Beecham, and the chance of a rich marriage in England thus provided. Even this view he was compelled to sustain by the assurance that the expense would be a mere trifle, and that, by the adoption of popular principles, he should come in almost for nothing. To make the old doctor a convert to these notions, he had called in Heffernan and O'Halloran, who both, during the dinner, nad exerted themselves with their natural tact, and now that the doctor had dropped asleep, were reposing themselves, and recruiting the energies so generously expended.

Hence the party seemed to have a certain gloom and weight over it, as the shadow of coming night fell on the figures seated, almost in silence, around the table. None spoke, save an occasional word or two, as they passed round the bottle. Each retreated into his own reflections, and communed with himself. Men who have exhibited themselves to each other, in a game of deceit and trick, seem to have a natural repugnance to any recurrence to the theme when the occasion is once over. Even they whose hearts have the least self-respect will avoid the topic if possible.

"How is the bottle?—with you, I believe," said O'Reilly to Heffernan, in the low tone to which they had all reduced the conversation.

"I have just filled my glass; it stands with the Counsellor."

O'Halloran poured out the wine and sipped it slowly. "A very remarkable man," said he, sententiously, with a slight gesture of his head to the chair where the old doctor lay coiled up asleep. "His faculties seem as clear, and his judgment as acute, as if he were only five-and-forty, and I suppose he must be nearly twice that age."

"Very nearly," replied O'Reilly; "he confesses commonly to eighty-six, but when he is weak or querulous, he often says ninety-one or two."

"His memory is the most singular thing about him," said Heffernan. "Now, the account of Swift's appearance in the pulpit with the gown thrust back, and his hands stuck in the belt of the cassock, browbeating the Lord Mayor and Aldermen for coming in late to church; it came as fresh as if he were talking of an event of last week.

"How good the imitation of voice was, too," added Heffernan: "'Giving two hours to your dress, and twenty minutes to your devotions, you come into God's house looking more like mountebanks than Christian men!'"

"I've seldom seen him so much inclined to talk and chat away as this evening," said O'Reilly; "but I think you chimed in so well with his humour, it drew him on."

"There was something of dexterity," said Heffernan, "in the way he kept bringing up these reminiscences and old stories, to avoid entering upon the subject of the Election. I saw that he wouldn't approach that theme, no matter how skilfully you brought it forward."

"You ought not to have alluded to the Darcys, however," said O'Halloran. "I remarked that the mention of their name gave him evident displeasure; indeed, he soon after pushed his chair back from the table and became silent."

"He always sleeps after dinner," observed O'Reilly, carelessly. "It was about his usual time."

Another pause now succeeded, in which the only sounds heard were the deep-drawn breathings of the sleeper.

"You saw Lord Castlereagh, I think you told me?" said O'Reilly, anxious to lead Heffernan into something like a declaration of opinion.

"Oh, repeatedly; I dined either with him, or in his company, three or four times every week of my stay in town."

"Well, is he satisfied with the success of his measure?" asked O'Halloran, caustically. "Is this Union working to his heart's content?"

"It is rather early to pass a judgment on that point, I think."

"I'm not of that mind," rejoined O'Halloran, hastily. "The fruits of the measure are showing themselves already. The men of fortune are flying the country; their town houses are to let; their horses are advertised for sale at Dycer's. Dublin is, even now, beginning to feel what it may become when the population has no other support than itself."

"Such will always be the fortune of a province. Influence will and must converge to the capital," rejoined Heffernan.

"But what, if the great element of a province be wanting? what, if we have not that inherent respect and reverence for the Metropolis, Provincials always should feel? what, if we know that our interests are misunderstood our real wants unknown, our peculiar circumstances either undervalued or despised?"

"If the case be as you represent it——"

"Can you deny it? Tell me that."

"I will not deny or admit it. I only say, if it be such, there is still a remedy, if men are shrewd enough to adopt it."

"And what may that remedy be?" said O'Reilly, calmly.

"An Irish party!"

"Oh, the old story; the same plot over again we had this year at the Rotunda?" said O'Reilly, contemptuously.

"Which only failed from our own faults," added Heffernan, angrily. "Some of us were lukewarm and would do nothing; some waited for others to come forward; and some again wanted to make their hard bargain with the Minister, before they made him feel the necessity of the compact."

O'Reilly bit his lip in silence, for he well understood at whom this reproof was levelled.

"The cause of failure was very different," said O'Halloran, authoritatively. "It was one which has dissolved many an association, and rendered many a scheme abortive, and will continue to do so, as often as it occurs You failed for want of a 'Principle.' You had rank and wealth, and influence more than enough to have made your weight felt and acknowledged, but you had no definite object or end. You were a Party, and you had not a Purpose."

"Come, come," said Heffernan, "you are evidently unaware of the nature of our association, and seem not to have read the resolutions we adopted."

"No—on the contrary, I read them carefully; there was more than sufficient in them to have made a dozen Parties. Had you adopted one steadfast line of action, set out with one brief intelligible proposition—I care not what—Slave Emancipation, or Catholic Emancipation, Repeal of Tests Acts, or Parliamentary Reform—any of them, taken your stand on that, and that alone, you must have succeeded. Of course, to do this, is a work of time and labour; some men will grow weary and sink by the way, but others take up the burden, and the goal is reached at last. There must be years long of writing and speaking, meeting, declaring, and plotting; you must consent to be thought vulgar and low-minded—ay, and to become so, for active partisans are only to be found in low places. You will be laughed at and jeered, abused, mocked, and derided at first; later on, you will be assailed more powerfully, and more coarsely; but, all this while, your strength is developing, your agencies are spreading. Persuasion will induce some; notoriety others; hopes of advantage, many more, to join you. You will then have a Press as well as a Party, and the very men that sneered at your beginnings, will have to respect the persistence and duration of your efforts. I don't care how trumpery the arguments used; I don't value one straw the fallacy of the statements put forward. Let one great question, one great demand for anything be made for some five-and-twenty or thirty years. Let the Press discuss, and the Parliament debate it. You are sure of its being accorded in the end. Now, it will be a Party ambitious of power that will buy your alliance at any price. Now, a tottering Government anxious to survive the session and reach the snug harbour of the long vacation. Now, it will be the high 'bid' of a Popular Administration. Now, it will be the last hope of second-rate capacities, ready to supply their own deficiencies, by incurring a hazard. However it come, you are equally certain of it."

There was a pause as O'Halloran concluded. Heffernan saw plainly to what the Counsellor pointed, and that he was endeavouring to recruit for that party of which he destined the future leadership for himself, and Con had no fancy to serve in the ranks of such an army. O'Reilly, who thought that the profession of a popular creed might be serviceable in the emergency of an Election, looked with more favour on the exposition, and after a brief interval, said,

"Well, supposing I were to see this matter in your light, what support could you promise me? I mean at the Hustings."

"Most of the small freeholders, now—all of them, in time. The Priests to a man, the best election agents that ever canvassed a constituency. By degrees the forces will grow stronger, according to the length and breadth of the Principle you adopt—make it Emancipation and I'll ensure you lease of the County." Heffernan smiled dubiously. "Ah, never mind Mr. Heffernan's look, these notions don't suit him. He's one of the petty traders in politics, who like small sales and quick returns."

"Such dealing makes fewest bankrupts," said Heffernan, coolly.

"I own to you," said O'Halloran, "the rewards are distant, but they're worth waiting for. It is not the miserable bribe of a situation, or a title, both beneath what they would accord to some state apothecary; but power, actual power, and real patronage are in the vista."

A heavy sigh and a rustling sound in the deep arm-chair announced that the doctor was awaking, and, after a few struggles to throw off the drowsy influence, he sat upright, and made a gesture that he wished for wine."

"We've been talking about political matters, sir," said O'Reilly. "I hope we didn't disturb your doze?"

"No; I was sleeping sound," croaked the old man, in a feeble whine, "and I had a very singular dream! I dreamed I was sitting in a great kitchen of a big house, and there was a very large, hairy turnspit sitting opposite to me, in a nook beside the fire, turning a big spit with a joint of meat on it. 'Who's the meat for?' says I to him. 'For my Lord Castlereagh,' says he, 'devil a one else.' 'For himself alone?' says I. 'Just so,' says he; 'don't you know, that's the Irish Parliament that we're roasting and basting, and, when it's done,' says he, 'we'll sarve it up to be carved.' 'And who are you?' says I to the turnspit. 'I'm Con Heffernan,' says he, 'and the devil a bit of the same meat I'm to get after cooking it, till my teeth's watering.' "

A loud roar of laughter from O'Halloran, in which Heffernan endeavoured to take a part, met this strange revelation of the doctor's sleep nor was it for a considerable time after that the conversation could be resumed without some jesting allusion of the Counsellor to the turnspit and his office.

"Your dream tallies but ill, sir, with the rumours through Dublin," said O'Reilly, whose quick glance saw through the mask of indifference by which Heffernan concealed his irritation.

"I didn't hear it. What was it, Bob?"

"That the Ministry had offered our friend here the Secretaryship for Ireland."

"Sure, if they did——" He was about to add, "That he'd have as certainly accepted it," when a sense of the impropriety of such a speech arrested the words.

"You are mistaken, sir," interposed Heffernan, answering the unspoken sentence. 'I did refuse. The conditions on which I accorded my humble support to the bill of the Union have been shamefully violated, and I could not, if I even wished it, accept office from a Government that have been false to their pledges."

"You see my dream was right, after all," chuckled the old man. "I said they kept him working away in the kitchen, and gave him none of the meat afterwards."

"What if I had been stipulating for another, sir?" said Heffernan, with a forced smile. "What if the breach of faith I allude to had reference not to me, but to your son yonder, for whom, and no other, I asked—I will not say a favour—but a fair and reasonable acknowledgment of the station he occupies?"

"Ah! that weary title," exclaimed the Doctor, crankily. "What have we to do with these things?"

"You are right, sir," chimed in O'Halloran. "Your present position, self-acquired and independent, is a far prouder one than any to be obtained by ministerial favour."

"I'd rather he'd help us to crush these Darcys," said the old man, as his eyes sparkled and glistened like the orbs of a serpent. "I'd rather my Lord Castlereagh would put his heel upon *them*, than stretch out the hand to *us*."

"What need to trouble your head about them?" said Heffernan, conciliatingly; "they are low enough in all conscience now."

"My father means," said O'Reilly, "that he is tired and sick of the incessant appeals to law this family persist in following; that these trials irritate and annoy him."

"Come, sir," cried O'Halloran, encouragingly, "you shall see the last of them in a few weeks. I have reason to know that an old maiden sister of Bagenal Daly's has supplied Bicknell with the means of the present action. It's the last shot in the locker. We'll take care to make the gun recoil on the hand that fires it."

"Darcy and Daly are both out of the country," observed the old man, cunningly.

"We'll call them up for judgment, however," chimed in O'Halloran "That same Daly is one of those men who infested our country in times past, and by the mere recklessness of their hold on life, bullied and oppressed all who came before them. I am rejoiced to have an opportunity of showing up such a character."

"I wish we had done with them all," sighed the Doctor.

"So you shall, with this record. Will you pledge yourself not to object to the Election expenses if I gain you the verdict?"

"Come, that's a fair offer," said Heffernan, laughing.

"Maybe, they'll come to ten thousand," said the Doctor, cautiously.

"Not above one half the sum, if Mr. O'Reilly will consent to take my advice."

"And why wouldn't he?" rejoined the old man, querulously. "What signifies which side he takes, if it saves the money?"

"Is it a bargain, then?"

"Will you secure me against more trials at law? Will you pledge yourself that I'm not to be tormented by these anxieties and cares?"

"I can scarcely promise that much; but I feel so assured that your annoyance will end here, that I am willing to pledge myself to give you my own services without fee or reward in future, if any action follow this one."

"I think that is most generous," said Heffernan.

"It is as much as saying, he'll enter into recognisances for an indefinite series of five-hundred pound briefs," added O'Reilly.

"Done, then. I take you at your word," said the Doctor, while stretching forth his lean and trembling hand, he grasped the nervous fingers of the Counsellor in token of ratification.

"And now woe to the Darcys!" muttered O'Halloran, as he arose to say good night. Heffernan rose at the same time, resolved to accompany the Counsellor, and try what gentle persuasion could effect in the modification of views, which, he saw, were far too explicit to be profitable.

CHAPTER LXX.

THE CHANCES OF TRAVEL.

NEITHER our space nor our inclination prompt us to dwell on Forester's illness; enough when we say that his recovery, slow at first, made at length good progress, and within a month after the commencement of the attack, he was once more on the road, bent on reaching the North, and presenting him self before Lady Eleanor and her daughter.

Miss Daly, who had been his kind and watchful nurse for many days and nights ere his wandering faculties could recognise her, contributed more than all else to his restoration. The impatient anxiety under which he suffered was met by her mild but steady counsels; and although she never ventured to bid him hope too sanguinely, she told him that his letter had reached Helen's hand, and that he himself must plead the cause he had opened.

"Your greatest difficulty," said she, in parting with him in Dublin, "will be in the very circumstance which, in ordinary cases, would be the guarantee of your success. Your own rise in fortune has widened the interval between you. This, to your mind, presents but the natural means of overcoming the obstacles I allude to; but remember there are others whose feelings are to be as intimately consulted—nay, more so than your own. Think of those who never yet made an alliance without feeling that they were on a footing of perfect equality; and reflect that even if Helen's affections were all your own, Maurice Darcy's daughter can enter into no family, however high and proud it may be, save as the desired and sought-for by its chief members. Build upon anything lower than this, and you fail. More still," added she, almost sternly, "your failure will meet with no compassion from me. Think not, because I have gone through life a lone, uncared-for thing, that I undervalue the strength and power of deep affection, or that I could counsel you to make it subservient to views of worldliness and advantage. You know me little if you think so. But I would tell you this; that no love, deserving of the name, ever existed without those high promptings of the heart that made all difficulties easy to encounter—ay, even those worst of difficulties, that spring from false pride and prejudice. It is by no sudden outbreak of temper, no selfish threat of this or that insensate folly, that your lady-mother's consent should be obtained. It is by the manly dignity and consistency of a character that in the highest interests of a higher station give a security for sound judgment and honourable motives. Let it appear from your conduct that you are not swayed by passion or caprice. You have already won men's admiration for the gallantry of your daring. There is something better still than this, the esteem and regard that are never withheld from a course of honourable and independent action. With these on your side, rely upon it, a mother's heart will not be the last in England to acknowledge and glory in your fame. And now, good-by—you have a better travelling companion than me—you have hope with you."

She returned the cordial pressure of his hand, and was turning away, when, after what seemed a kind of struggle with her feelings, she added,

"One word more, even at the hazard of wearying you. Above all and everything, be honest, be candid; not only with others, but with yourself! Examine well your heart, and let no sense of false shame, let no hopes of some chance or accident deceive you, by which your innermost feelings are to be guessed at, and not avowed. This is the blackest of calamities; this can even embitter every hour of a long life."

Her voice trembled at the last words, and as she concluded she wrung his hand once more affectionately, and moved hurriedly away. Forester looked after her with a tender interest. For the first time in his life he heard her sob. "Yes," thought he, as he lay back and covered his eyes with his hand, "she, too, has loved, and loved unhappily."

There are few sympathies stronger, not even those of illness itself, than connect those whose hearts have struggled under unrequited affection; and so, for many an hour as he travelled, Forester's thoughts recurred to Miss Daly, and the last troubled accents of her parting speech. Perhaps he did not dwell the less on that theme because it carried him away from his own immediate hopes and fears—emotions that rendered him almost irritable by their intensity.

While on the road, Forester travelled with all the speed he could accomplish. His weakness did not permit of his being many hours in a carriage, and he endeavoured to compensate for this by rapid travelling at the time. His impatience to get forward was, however, such, that he scarcely arrived at any halting-place without ordering horses to be at once got ready; so that, when able, he resumed the road without losing a moment.

In compliance with this custom, the carriage was standing all ready with its four posters at the door of the inn of Castle Blayney, while Forester, overcome by fatigue and exhaustion, had thrown himself on a bed and fallen asleep. The rattling crash of a mail-coach and its deep-toned horn suddenly awoke him: he started, and looked at his watch. Was it possible? It was nearly midnight; he must have slept more than three hours! Half gratified by the unaccustomed rest, half angry at the lapse of time, he arose to depart. The night was the reverse of inviting; a long-threatened storm had at last burst forth, and the rain was falling in torrents, while the wind, in short and fitful gusts, shook the house to its foundation, and scattered tiles and slates over the dreary street.

So terrible was the hurricane, many doubts were entertained that the mail could proceed further; and when it did at length set forth, gloomy prognostics of danger—dark pictures of precipices—swollen torrents and broken bridges, were rife in the bar and the landlord's room. These arguments, if they could be so called, were all renewed when Forester called for his bill, as a preparation to depart, and all the perils that ever happened by land or by water, recapitulated to deter him.

"The middle arch of the Slaney Bridge was tottering when the up-mail passed three hours before. A horse and cart were just fished out of Mooney's pond, but no driver as yet discovered. The forge at the cross roads was blown down, and the rafters were lying across the highway." These, and a dozen other like calamities, were bandied about, and pitched like shuttlecocks from side to side, as the impatient traveller descended the stairs.

Had Forester cared for the amount of the reckoning, which he did not, he might have entertained grave fears of its total, on the principle well known to travellers, that the speed of its coming is always in the inverse ratio of the sum, and that every second's delay is sure to swell its proportions. Of this he never thought once, but he often reflected on the tardiness of waiters, and the lingering tediousness of the moments of parting.

"It's coming, Sir: he's just adding it up," said the head waiter, for the sixth time within three minutes, while he moved to and fro, with the official alacrity that counterfeits despatch. "I'm afraid you'll have a bad night, sir. I'm sure the horses won't be able to face the storm over Grange Connel."

Forester made no reply, but walked up and down the hall in moody silence.

"The gentleman that got off the mail thought so too," added the waiter; "and now he's pleasanter at his supper, in the coffee-room, than sitting out there, next to the guard, wet to the skin, and shivering with cold."

Less to inspect the stranger thus alluded to, than to escape the impertinent loquacity of the waiter, Forester turned the handle of the door, and entered the coffee-room. It was a large, dingy-looking chamber, whose only bright spot seemed within the glow of a blazing turf fire, where, at a little table, a gentleman was seated at supper. His back was turned to Forester; but even in the cursory glance the latter gave, he could perceive that he was an elderly personage, and one who had not abandoned the almost by gone custom of a queue.

The stranger, dividing his time between his meal and a newspaper—which he devoured more eagerly than the viands before him—paid no attention to Forester's entrance; nor did he once look round. As the waiter approached, he asked hastily, "What chance there was of getting forward?"

"Indeed, sir, to tell the truth," drawled out the man, "the storm seems getting worse, instead of better. Miles Finerty's new house, at the end of the street, is just blown down."

"Never mind Miles Finerty, my good friend, for the present," rejoined the old gentleman, mildly, "but just tell me, are horses to be had?"

"Faith! and to tell your honour no lie, I'm afraid of it." Here he dropped to a whisper. "The sick-looking gentleman, yonder, has four waiting for him, since nine o'clock; and we've only a lame mare and a pony in the stable."

"Am I never to get this bill?" cried out Forester, in a tone that illness had rendered peculiarly querulous. "I have asked, begged for it, for above an hour—and here I am still."

"He's bringing it now, sir," cried the waiter, stepping hastily out of the room, to avoid further questioning. Forester, whose impatience had now been carried beyond endurance, paced the room with hurried strides, muttering, between his teeth, every possible malediction on the whole race of innkeepers, barmaids, waiters—even down to Boots himself. These imprecating expressions had gradually assumed a louder and more vehement tone, of which he was by no means aware, till the old gentleman, at the pause of a somewhat wordy denunciation, gravely added,

"Insert a clause upon postboys, sir, and I'll second the measure."

Forester wheeled abruptly round. He belonged to a class, a section of society, whose cherished prestige is neither to address or be addressed by an unintroduced stranger; and had the speaker been younger, or of any age more nearly his own, it is more than likely a very vague stare of cool astonishment would have been his only acknowledgment of the speech. The advanced age, and something in the very accent of the stranger, were, how ever, guarantees against this conventional rudeness, and he remarked, with a smile, "I have no objection to extend the provisions of my bill in the way you propose, for perhaps half an hour's experience may teach me how much they deserve it."

"You are fortunate, however, to have secured horses. I perceive that the stables are empty."

"If you are pressed for time, sir," said Forester, on whom the quiet, well-bred manners of the stranger produced a strong impression, "it would be a very churlish thing of me to travel with four horses while I can spare a pair of them."

"I am really very grateful," said the old gentleman, rising, and bowing courteously; "if this be not a great inconvenience——"

"By no means; and if it were," rejoined Forester, "I have a debt to acquit to my own heart on this subject. I remember once, when travelling down to the west of Ireland, I reached a little miserable country town at nightfall, and, just as here, save that then there was no storm——" The entrance of the long-expected landlord, with his bill, here interrupted Forester's story. As he took it, and thus afforded time for the stranger to fix his eyes steadfastly upon him, unobserved, Forester quickly resumed: "I was remarking that, just as here, there were only four post-horses to be had, and that they had just been secured by another traveller a few moments before my arrival. I forget the name of the place——"

"Perhaps I can assist you," said the other, calmly. "It was Kilbeggan."

Had a miracle been performed before his eyes, Forester could not have been more stunned—and stunned he really was, and unable to speak for some seconds. At length, his surprise yielding to a vague glimmering of belief, he called out, "Great Heavens! it cannot be—it surely is not——"

"Maurice Darcy, you would say, sir," said the Knight, advancing with an offered hand. "As surely as I believe you to be my son Lionel's brother officer and friend, Captain Forester."

"Oh, Colonel Darcy! this is, indeed, happiness," exclaimed the young man, as he grasped the Knight's hand in both his own, and shook it affectionately.

"What a strange rencontre," said the Knight, laughing; "quite the incident of a comedy! One would scarcely look for such meetings twice—so like in every respect. Our parts are changed, however; it is your turn to be generous, if the generosity trench not too closely on your convenience?"

Forester could but stammer out assurances of delight and pleasure, and so on, for his heart was too full to speak calmly or collectedly.

"And Lionel, sir, how is he—when have you heard from him?" said the young man, anxious, by even the most remote path, to speak of the Knight's family.

"In excellent health. The boy has had the good fortune to be employed in a healthy station, and, from a letter which I found awaiting me at my army agent's, is as happy as can be. But to recur to our theme: will you forgive my selfishness if I say that you will add indescribably to the favour if you permit me to take these horses at once? I have not seen my family for some time back, and my impatience is too strong to yield to ceremony."

"Of course—certainly; my carriage is, however, all ready, and at the door. Take it as it is, you'll travel faster and safer."

"But you yourself," said Darcy, laughing—"you were about to move forward when we met."

"It's no matter; I was merely travelling for the sake of change," said Forester, confusedly.

"I could not think of such a thing," said Darcy. "If our way led together, and you would accept of me as a travelling companion, I should be but too happy, but to take the long-boat, and leave you on the desolate rock, is not to be thought of." The Knight stopped, and although he made an effort to continue, the words faltered on his lips, and he was silent. At last, and with an exertion that brought a deep blush to his cheek, he said, "I am really ashamed, Captain Forester, to acknowledge a weakness, which is as new to me as it is unmanly. The best amends I can make for feeling, is to confess it. Since we met that same night circumstances of fortune have considerably changed with me. I am not, as you then knew me, the owner of a good house and a good estate. Now, I really would wish to have been able to ask you to come and see me; but, in good truth, I cannot tell where or how I should lodge you if you said 'yes.' I believe my wife has a cabin on this northern shore, but, however it may accommodate us, I need not say I could not ask a friend to put up with it. There is my confession, and now that it is told, I am only ashamed that I should hesitate about it."

Forester once more endeavoured, in broken, disjointed phrases, to express his acknowledgment, and was in the very midst of a mass of contradictory explanations, hopes, and wishes, when Linwood entered with, "The carriage is ready, my Lord."

The Knight heard the words with surprise, and as quickly remarked that the young man was dressed in deep mourning. "I have been unwittingly addressing you as Captain Forester," said he, gravely; "I believe I should have said——"

"Lord Wallincourt," answered Forester, with a slight tremour in his voice; "the death of my brother——" Here he hesitated, and at length was silent.

The Knight, who read in his nervous manner and sickly appearance the signs of broken health and spirits, resolved at once to sacrifice mere personal feeling in a cause of kindness, and said, "I see, my Lord, you are scarcely as strong as when I had the pleasure to meet you first, and I doubt not that you require a little repose and quietness. Come along with me then, and if even this cabin of ours be inhospitable enough not to afford you a room, we'll find something near us on the coast, and I have no doubt we'll set you on your legs again."

"It is a favour I would have asked, if I dared," said Forester, feebly. He then added, "Indeed, sir, I will confess it, my journey had no other object than to present myself to Lady Eleanor Darcy. Through the kindness of my relative, Lord Castlereagh, I was enabled to send her some tidings of yourself, of which my illness prevented my being the bearer, and I was desirous of adding my own testimony, so far as it could go." Here again he faltered.

"Pray continue," said the Knight, warmly; "I am never happier than when grateful, and I see that I have reason for the feeling here."

"I perceive, sir, you do not recognise me," said the young man, thoughtfully, while he fixed his deep, full eyes upon the Knight's countenance.

Darcy stared at him in turn, and, passing his hand across his brow, looked again. "There is some mystification here," said he, quickly, "but I cannot see through it."

"Come, Colonel Darcy," said Forester, with more animation than before "I see that you forget me; but perhaps you remember this." So saying, he walked over to a table where a number of cloaks and travelling gear were lying, and taking up a pistol, placed it in Darcy's hand. "This you certainly recognise?"

"It is my own!" exclaimed the Knight; "the fellow of it is yonder. I had it with me the day we landed at Aboukir."

"And gave it to me when a French dragoon had his sabre at my throat," continued Forester.

"And is it to your gallantry that I owe my life, my brave boy?" cried the old man, as he threw his arm around him.

"Not one half so much as I owe my recovery to your kindness," said

Forester. "Remember the wounded Volunteer you came to see on the march. The surgeon you employed never left me till the very day I quitted the camp, and although I have had a struggle for life twice since then, I never could have lived through the first attack but for his aid."

"Is this all a dream?" said the Knight, as he leaned his head upon his hand, "or are these events real? Then you were the officer whose exchange was managed, and of which I heard soon after the battle?"

"Yes, I was exchanged under a cartel, and sailed for England the day after. And you, sir—tell me of your fate?"

"A slight wound and a somewhat tiresome imprisonment tells the whole story—the latter a good deal enlivened by seeing that our troops were beating the French day after day, and the calculation that my durance could scarcely last till winter. I proved right, for last month came the Capitulation, and here I am. But all these are topics for long evenings to chat over. Come with me; you can't refuse me any longer. Lady Eleanor has the right to speak *her* gratitude to you; I see you won't listen to *mine*."

The Knight seized the young man's arm and led him along as he spoke. "Nay," said he, "there is another reason for it. If you suffered me to go off alone, nothing would make me believe that what I have now heard was not some strange trick of fancy. Here, with you beside me, feeling your arm within my own, and hearing your voice, it is all that I can do to believe it. Come, let me be convinced again. Where did you join us?"

Forester now went over the whole story of his late adventures, omitting nothing from the moment he had joined the frigate at Portsmouth to the last evening, when, as a prisoner, he had sent for Darcy to speak to him before he died. "I thought then," said he, "I could scarcely have more than an hour or two to live; but when you came and stood beside me, I was not able to utter a word, I believe, at the time. It was rather a relief to me than otherwise that you did not know me."

"How strange is this all!" said the Knight, musing. "You have told me a most singular story; only one point remains yet unelucidated. How came you to volunteer—you were in the Guards?"

"Yes," said Forester, blushing and faltering; "I had quitted the Guards, intending to leave the army some short time previous—but—but——"

"The thought of active service brought you back again. Out with it, and never be ashamed. I remember now having heard from an old friend of mine, Miss Daly, how you had left the service; and, to say truth, I was sorry for it—sorry for *your* sake, but sorrier because it always grieves me when men of gentle blood are not to be found where hard knocks are going. None ever distinguish themselves with more honour, and it is a pity that they should lose the occasion to show the world that birth and blood inherit higher privileges than stars and titles."

While the miles rolled over they thus conversed, and as each became more intimately acquainted, and more nearly interested in the other, they drew towards the journey's end. It was late on the following night when they reached Port Ballintray, and as the darkness threatened more than once to mislead them, the postilion halted at the door of a little cabin to procure a light for his lamps.

While the travellers sat patiently awaiting the necessary preparation, a voice from within the cottage struck Darcy's ear; he threw open the door as he heard it, and sprang out, and rushing forward, the moment afterwards pressed his wife and daughter in his arms.

Forester, who in a moment comprehended the discovery, hastened to withdraw from a scene where his presence could only prove constraint, and leaving a message to say that he had gone to the little inn, and would wait on the Knight next morning, he hurried from the spot, his heart bursting with many a conflicting emotion.

CHAPTER LXXI.

HOME.

Perhaps, in the course of a long, and, till its very latter years, a most prosperous life, the Knight of Gwynne had never known more real unbroken happiness, than now that he laid his head beneath the lowly thatch of a fisherman's cottage, and found a home beside the humble hearth, where daily toil had used to repose. It was not that he either felt, or assumed to feel, indifferent to the great reverse of his fortune, and to the loss of that station to which all his habits of life and thought had been conformed. Nor had he the innate sense that his misfortunes had been incurred without the culpability of, at least, neglect on his own part. No, he neither deceived nor exonerated himself. His present happiness sprang from discovering in those far dearer to him than himself, powers of patient submission, traits of affectionate forbearance, signs of a hopeful, trusting spirit, that their trials were not sent without an aim and object—all gifts of heart and mind, higher, nobler, and better than the palmiest days of prosperity had brought forth.

It was that short and fleeting season, the late autumn, a time in which the climate of Northern Ireland makes a brief but brilliant amende for the long dreary months of the year. The sea, at last calm and tranquil, rolled its long waves upon the shore in measured sweep, waking the echoes in a thousand caves, and resounding with hollow voice beneath the very cliffs. The wild and fanciful outlines of the Skerry Islands were marked, sharp and distinct, against the dark blue sky, and reflected not less so in the unruffled water at their base. The White Rocks, as they are called, shone with a lustre like dulled silver, and above them, the ruined towers of old Dunluce hung, balanced over the sea, and, even in decay, seemed to defy dissolution.

The most striking feature of the picture was, however, the myriad of small boats, amounting in some instances to several hundreds, which filled the little bay at sunset. These were the fishermen from Innisshowen, coming to gather the seaweed on the western shore their eastern aspect denied them; a hardy and a daring race, who braved the terrible storms of that fearful coast without a thought of fear. Here were they now, their little skiffs crowded with every sail they could carry—for it was a trial of speed, who should be first up after the turn of the ebb tide—their taper masts bending and springing like whips, the white water curling at the bows, and rustling over the gunwales; while the fishermen themselves, with long harpoon spears, contested for the prizes—large masses of floating weed, which not unfrequently were seized upon by three or four rival parties at the same moment.

A more animated scene cannot be conceived than the bay thus presented. The boats tacking and beating in every direction, crossing each other so closely as to threaten collision—sometimes, indeed, carrying off a bowsprit or a rudder; while, from the restless motions of those on board, the frail skiffs were at each instant endangered—accidents that occurred continually, but whose peril may be judged by the hearty cheers and roars of laughter they excited. Here might be seen a wide-spreading surface of tangled seaweed, vigorously towed in two different directions by contending crews, whose exertions to secure it were accompanied by wildest shouts and cries. There a party were hauling in the prey, while their comrades, with spars and spears, kept the enemy aloof, and here, on the upturned keel of a capsized boat, were a dripping group, whose heaviest penalty was the ridicule of their fellows.

Seated in front of the little cottage, the Darcys and Forester watched this strange scene with all the interest its moving, stirring life could excite; and while the ladies could enjoy the varying picture only for itself, to the Knight and the youth it brought back the memory of a more brilliant and a grander display, one to which heroism and danger had lent the most exciting of all interests.

"I see," said Darcy, as he watched his companion's countenance—"I see whither your thoughts are wandering. They are off to the old castle of Aboukir, and the tall cliffs at Marmorica." Forester slightly nodded an assent, but never spoke, while the Knight resumed—"I told you it would never do to give up the service. The very glance of your eyes at yonder picture, tells me how the great original is before your mind. Come, a few weeks more of rest and quiet, you will be yourself again. Then, must you present yourself before the gallant Duke, and ask for a restitution to your old grade. There will be sharp work ere long. Buonaparte is not the man to forgive Alexandria and Cairo. If I read you aright, you prefer such a career to all the ambition of a political life."

Forester was still silent, but his changing colour told that the Knight's words had affected him deeply, but whether as they were intended, it was not so plain to see. The Knight went on: "I am not disposed to vain regrets; but if I were to give way to such, it would be, that I am not young enough to enter upon the career I now see opening to our arms. Our insular position seems to have moulded our destiny, in great part; but, rely on it, we are as much a nation of soldiers as of sailors." Warming with his theme, Darcy continued, while sketching out the possible turn of events, to depict the noble path open to a young man, who, to natural talents and acquirements, added the high advantages of fortune, rank, and family influence.

"I told you," said he, smiling, "that I blamed you once, unjustly as it happened, because, as a Guardsman, you did not seize the occasion to exchange guard-mounting for the field. But now I shall be sorely grieved if you suffer yourself to be withdrawn from a path that has already opened so brightly, by any of the seductions of your station, or the fascinations of mere fashion."

"Are you certain," said Lady Eleanor, speaking in a voice shaken by agitation—"are you certain, my dear, that these same counsels of yours would be in strict accordance with the wishes of Lord Wallincourt's friends, or is it not possible that *their* ambitions may point very differently for his future?"

"I can but give the advice I would offer to Lionel," said Darcy, "if my son were placed in similarly fortunate circumstances. A year or two, at least, of such training, will be no bad discipline to a young man's mind, and help to fit him to discuss those terms, which, if I see aright, will be rife in our assemblies for some years to come——" Darcy was about to continue, when Tate advanced with a letter, whose address bespoke Bicknell's hand. It was a long-expected communication, and anxious to peruse it carefully, the Knight arose, and making his excuses, re-entered the cottage.

The party sat for some time in silence. Lady Eleanor's mind was in a state of unusual conflict, since, for the first time in her life, had she practised any concealment with her husband, having forborne to tell him of Forester's former addresses to Helen. To this course she had been impelled by various reasons, the most pressing among which were the evident change in the young man's demeanour since he last appeared amongst them, and, consequently, the possibility that he had outlived the passion he then professed; and secondly, by observing that nothing in Helen betrayed the slightest desire to encourage any renewal of those professions, or any chagrin at the change in his conduct. As a mother and as a woman, she hesitated to avow what should seem to represent her daughter as being deserted, while she argued that if Helen were as indifferent as she really seemed, there was no occasion whatever for the disclosure. Now, however, that the Knight had spoken his counsels so strongly, the thought occurred to her, that Forester might receive the advice in the light of a rejection of his former proposal, and suppose that these suggestions were only another mode of refusing his suit. Hence a struggle of doubt and uncertainty arose within her, whether she should at once make everything known to Darcy, or still keep silence, and leave events to their own development. The former course seemed the most fitting, and entirely forgetful of all else, she hastily arose, and followed her husband into the cabin.

Forester was now alone with Helen, and for the first time since that well-remembered night when he had offered his heart and been rejected. The game of dissimulating feelings is almost easiest before a numerous audience. It is rarely possible in a *tête-à-tête*. So Forester soon felt, and although he made several efforts to induce a conversation, they were all abrupt and disjointed, as were Helen's own replies to them. At length came a pause, and what a thing is a pause at such a moment! The long lingering seconds in which a duellist watches his adversary's pistol, wavering over the region of his heart or brain, is less torturing than such suspense. Forester arose twice, and again sat down—his face pale and flushed alternately. At length, with a thick and rapid utterance, he said,

"I have been thinking over the Knight's counsels—dare I ask if they have Miss Darcy's concurrence?"

"It would be a great, a very great presumption in me," said Helen, tremulously, "to offer an opinion on such a theme. I have neither the knowledge to distinguish between the opposite careers, nor have I any feeling for those sentiments which men alone understand in warfare."

"Nor, perhaps," added Forester, with a sudden irony, "sufficient interest in the subject to give it a thought."

Helen was silent; her slightly compressed lips and heightened colour showed that she was offended at the speech, but she made no reply.

"I crave your pardon, Miss Darcy," said he, in a low, submissive accent, that told how heartfelt it was. "I most humbly ask you to forgive my rudeness. The very fact that I had no claim to that interest, should have protected you from such a speech. But see what comes of kindness to those who are little used to it. They get soon spoiled, and forget themselves."

"Lord Wallincourt will have to guard himself well against flattery, if such humble attentions as ours disturb his judgment."

"I will get out of the region of it," said he, resolutely; "I will take the Knight's advice. It is but a plunge, and all is over."

"If I dare to say so, my Lord," said Helen, archly, "this is scarcely the spirit in which my father hoped his counsels would be accepted. His chivalry on the score of a military life may be overstrained, but it has no touch of that recklessness your Lordship seems to lend it."

"And why should not this be the spirit in which I join the army?" said he, passionately; "the career has not for me those fascinations which others feel. Danger I like, for its stimulus, as other men like it; but I would rather confront it when, and where, and how I please, than at the dictate of a colonel, and by the ritual of a despatch."

"Rather be a letter of marque, in fact, than a ship-of-the-line—more credit to your Lordship's love of danger than discipline."

Forester smiled, but not without anger, at the quiet persiflage of her manner. It took him some seconds ere he could resume.

"I perceive," said he, in a tone of deeper feeling, "that whatever my resolves, to discuss them must be an impertinence, when they excite no other emotion than ridicule——"

"Nay, my Lord," interposed Helen, eagerly; "I beg you to forgive my levity. Nothing was further from my thoughts than to hurt one to whom we owe our deepest debt of gratitude. I can never forget you saved my father's life; pray do not let me seem so base, to my heart, as to undervalue this."

"Oh! Miss Darcy," said he, passionately, "it is I who need forgiveness—

I, whose temper, rendered irritable by illness, suspect reproach and sarcasm in every word of those who are kindest to me."

"You are unjust to yourself," said Helen, gently; "unjust, because you expect the same powers of mind and judgment that you enjoyed in health. Think how much better you are, than when you came here. Think what a few days more may do. How changed——"

"Has Miss Darcy changed since last I met her?" asked he, in a tone that sank into the very depth of her heart.

Helen tried to smile, but emotions of a sadder shade spread over her pale features, as she said,

"I hope so, my Lord; I trust that altered fortunes have not lost their teaching. I fervently hope that sorrow and suffering have left something behind them better than unavailing regrets and heart repinings."

"Oh! believe me," cried Forester, passionately, "it is not of this change I would speak. I dared to ask with reference to another feeling."

"Be it so," said Helen, trembling, as if nerving herself for a strong and long-looked-for effort—"be it so, my Lord, and is not my answer wide enough for both? Would not any change—short of a dishonourable one—make the decision I once came to, a thousand times more necessary now?"

"Oh! Helen, these are cold and cruel words. Will you tell me that my rank and station are to be like a curse upon my happiness?"

"I spoke of *our* altered condition, my Lord. I spoke of the impossibility of your Lordship recurring to a theme which the sight of that thatched roof should have stifled. Nay, hear me out. It is not of *you* or *your* motives that is here the question. It is of *me*, and *my* duties. They are there, my Lord—they are with those whose hearts have been twined round mine from infancy. Mine, when the world went well and proudly with us; doubly, trebly mine when affection can replace fortune, and the sympathies of the humblest home make up for all the flatteries of the world. I have no reason to dwell longer on this, to one who knows those of whom I speak, and can value them too."

"But is there no place in your heart, Helen, for other affections than these? or is that place already occupied?"

"My Lord, you have borne my frankness so well, I must even submit to yours with a good grace. Still, this is a question you have no right to ask, or I to answer. I have told you that whatever doubt there might be as to *your* road in life, *mine* offered no alternative. That ought surely to be enough."

"It shall be," said Forester, with a low sigh, as, trembling in every limb, he arose from the seat. "And yet, Helen," said he, in a voice barely above a whisper, "there might come a time, when these duties, to which you cling with such attachment, should be rendered less needful by altered fortunes. I have heard that your father's prospects present more of hope than heretofore, have I not? Think, that if the Knight should be restored to his own again, that then——"

"Nay—it is scarcely worthy of your Lordship to exact a pledge, which is to hang upon a decision like this. A verdict may give back my father's estate; it surely should not dispose of his daughter's hand?"

"I would exact nothing, Miss Darcy," said Forester, stung by the tone of this reply. "But I see you cannot feel for the difficulties which beset him who has staked his all upon a cast. I asked, what might your feelings be, were the circumstances which now surround you altered?"

Helen was silent for a second or two; and then, as if having collected all her energy, she said, "I would that you had spared me—had spared yourself—the pain I now must give us both; but to be silent longer, would be to encourage deception." It was not till after another brief interval that she could continue: "Soon after you left this, my Lord, you wrote a letter to Miss Daly. This letter—I stop not now to ask with what propriety towards either of us—she left in my hands. I read it carefully; and if many of the sentiments it contained served to elevate your character in my esteem, I saw enough to show me that your resolves were scarcely less instigated by outraged pride, than what you fancied to be a tender feeling. This perhaps might have wounded me, had I felt differently towards you. As it was, I thought it for the best: I deemed it happier that your motives should be divided ones, even though you knew it not. But as I read on, my Lord—as I perused the account of your interview with Lady Wallincourt—then a new light broke suddenly upon me; I found what, had I known more of life, should not have surprised, but what, in my ignorance, did indeed astonish me, that my father's station was regarded as one which could be alleged as a reason against your feeling towards his daughter. Now, my Lord, *we* have our pride too; and had your influence over me been all that ever you wished it, I tell you freely that I never would permit my affection to be gratified at the price of an insult to my father's house. If I were to say that your sentiments towards me should not have suffered it, would it be too much?"

"But, dearest Helen, remember that I am no longer dependent on my mother's will—remember that I stand in a position and a rank, which only needs you to share with me to make it all that my loftiest ambition ever coveted."

"These are, forgive me if I tell you, very selfish reasonings, my Lord. They may apply to *you;* they hardly address themselves to *my* position. The pride which could not stoop to ally itself with our house in our days of prosperity, should not assuredly be wounded by suing us in our humbler fortunes."

"Your thoughts dwell on Lady Netherby, Miss Darcy," said Forester, irritably: "she is scarcely the person most to be considered here."

"Enough for me, if I think so," said Helen, haughtily. "The Lady your Lordship's condescension would place in the position of a mother, should at least be able to regard me with other feelings than those of compassionate endurance. In a word, sir, it cannot be. To discuss the topic longer, is but to distress us both. Leave me to my gratitude to you, which is unbounded. Let me dwell upon the many traits of noble heroism I can think of in your character with enthusiasm—ay, and with pride—pride that one so high and so gifted should have ever thought of one so little worthy of him. But do not weaken my principle by hoping that my affection can be won at the cost of my self-esteem."

Forester bowed with a deep, respectful reverence; and when he lifted up his head, the sad expression of his features was that of one who had heard an irrevocable doom pronounced upon his dearest, most cherished hopes. Lady Eleanor at the same moment came forward from the door of the cottage, so that he had barely time to utter a hasty good-by ere she joined her daughter.

"Your father wishes to see Lord Wallincourt, Helen. Has he gone?" But before Helen could reply the Knight came up.

"I hope you have not forgotten to ask him to dinner, Eleanor?" said he. "We did so yesterday, and he never made his appearance the whole evening."

"Helen, did you?" But Helen was gone while they were speaking; so that Darcy, to repair the omission, hastened after his young friend with all the speed he could command.

"Have I found you?" cried Darcy, as, turning an angle of the rocky shore, he came behind Forester, who, with folded arms and bent-down head, stood like one sorrow-struck. "I just discovered that neither my wife nor daughter had asked you to stop to dinner; and as you are punctilious, fully as much as they are forgetful, there was nothing for it but to run after you."

"You are too kind, my dear Knight—but not to-day; I'm poorly—a headache."

"Nay; a headache always means a mere excuse. Come back with me:

you shall be as stupid a *convive* as you wish, only be a good listener, for I have got a great budget from my man of law, Mr. Bicknell, and am dying for somebody to inflict it upon."

With the best grace he could muster—which was still very far from a good one—Forester suffered himself to be led back to the cottage, endeavouring, as he went, to feel or feign an interest in the intelligence the Knight was full of. It seemed that Bicknell was very anxious not only for the Knight's counsel on many points, but for his actual presence at the trial. He appeared to think that Darcy being there, would be a great check upon the line of conduct he was apprised O'Halloran would adopt. There was already a very strong reaction in the West in favour of the old gentry of the land, and it would be, at least, an evidence of willingness to confront the enemy, were the Knight to be present.

"He tells me," continued the Knight, "that Daly regretted deeply not having attended the former trial—why, he does not exactly explain, but he uses the argument to press me now to do so."

Forester might, perhaps, have enlightened him on this score, had he so pleased, but he said nothing.

"Of course, I need not say, nothing like intimidation is meant by this advice. The days for such are, thank God, gone by in Ireland; and it was, besides, a game I never could have played at; but yet, it might be what many would expect of me, and, at all events, it can scarcely do harm. What is your opinion?"

"I quite agree with Mr. Bicknell," said Forester, hastily; "there is a certain licence these gentlemen of wig and gown enjoy, that is more protected by the Bench than either good morals or good manners warrant."

"Nay, you are now making the very error I would guard against," said Darcy, laughing. "This legal sparring is rather good fun, even though they do not always keep the gloves on. Now, will you come with me?"

"Of course; I should have asked your leave to do so, had you not invited me."

"You'll hear the great O'Halloran, and I suspect that is as much as I shall gain myself by this action. We have merely some points of law to go upon; but, as I understand, nothing new or material in evidence to adduce. You ask, then, why persist? I'll own to you I cannot say; but there seems the same punctilio in legal matters as in military; and it is a point of honour to sustain the siege until the garrison have eaten their boots. I am not so far from that contingency now, that I should be impatient; but, meanwhile, I perceive the savour of something better, and here comes Tate to say it is on the table."

CHAPTER LXXII.

AN AWKWARD DINNER-PARTY.

When the reader is informed that Lady Eleanor had not found a fitting moment to communicate to the Knight respecting Forester, nor had Helen summoned courage to reveal the circumstances of their late interview, it may be imagined that the dinner itself was as awkward a thing as need be. It was, throughout, a game of cross purposes, in which Darcy alone was not a player, and therefore more puzzled than the rest, at the constraint and reserve of his companions, whose efforts at conversation were either mere unmeaning common-places, or half-concealed retorts to inferred allusions.

However quick to perceive, Darcy was too well versed in the tactics of society to seem conscious of this, and merely redoubled his efforts to interest and amuse. Never had his entertaining qualities less of success. He could scarcely obtain any acknowledgment from his hearers; and stores of pleasantry, poured out in rich profusion, were listened to with a coldness bordering upon apathy.

He tried to interest them by talking over the necessity of their speedy removal to the capital, where, for the advantages of daily consultation, Bicknell desired the Knight's presence. He spoke of the approaching journey to the West, for the trial itself—he talked of Lionel, of Daly, of their late campaigns—in fact, he touched on everything, hoping by some passing gleam of interest to detect a clue to their secret thoughts. To no avail. They listened with decorous attention, but no signs of eagerness or pleasure marked their features; and when Forester rose to take his leave, it was full an hour and a half before his usual time of going.

"Now for it, Eleanor," said the Knight, as Helen soon after quitted the room, "what's your secret, for all this mystery must mean something? Nay, don't look so impenetrable, my dear; you'll never persuade any man who displayed all his agreeability to so little purpose, that his hearers had not a hidden source of preoccupation to account for their indifference. What is it, then?"

"I am really myself in the dark, without my conjectures have reason, and that Lord Wallincourt may have renewed to Helen the proposal he once made her, and with the same fortune."

"Renewed—proposal!"

"Yes, my dear Darcy, it was a secret I had intended to have told you this very day, and went for the very purpose of doing so, when I found you engaged with Bicknell's letters and advices, and scrupled to break in upon your occupied thoughts. Captain Forester did seek Helen's affections, and was refused; and I now suspect Lord Wallincourt may have had a similar reverse."

"This last is, however, mere guess," said Darcy.

"No more. Of the former Helen herself told me—she frankly acknowledged that her affections were disengaged, but that he had not touched them. It would seem that he was deeper in love than she gave him credit for. His whole adventure as a Volunteer sprang out of this rejected suit, and higher fortunes have not changed his purpose."

"Then Helen did not care for him?"

"That she did not, once, I am quite certain; that she does not, now, is not so sure. But I know that even if she were to do so, the disparity of condition would be an insurmountable barrier to her assent."

Darcy walked up and down with a troubled and anxious air, and at length said,

"Thus is it, that the pride we teach our children, as the defence against low motives and mean actions, displays its false and treacherous principles; and all our flimsy philosophy is based less on the affections of the human heart, than on certain conventional usages we have invented for our own enslavement. There is but one code of right and wrong, Eleanor, and that one neither recognises the artificial distinctions of grade, nor makes a virtual of the self-denial; that is a mere offering to worldly pride."

"You would scarcely have our daughter accept an alliance with a house that disdains our connexion?" said Lady Eleanor, proudly.

"Not, certainly, when the consideration had been once brought before her mind. It would then be but a compromise with principle. But why should she have ever learned the lesson? Why need she have been taught to mingle notions of worldly position and aggrandisement with the emotions of her heart? It was enough—it should have been enough—that his rank and position were nearly her own, not to trifle with feelings immeasurably higher and holier than these distinctions suggest."

"But the world, my dear Darcy; the world would say——"

"The world would say, Eleanor, that her refusal was perfectly right, and if the world's judgments were purer, they might be a source of consolation against the year-long bitterness of a sinking heart. Well, well!" said he, with a sigh, "I would hope that her heart is free: go to her

Eleanor—learn the truth, and if there be the least germ of affection there. I will speak to Wallincourt to-morrow, and tell him to leave us. These half-kindled embers are the slow poison of many a noble nature, and need but daily intercourse to make them deadly."

While Lady Eleanor retired to communicate with her daughter, the Knight paced the little chamber in moody reverie. As he passed and repassed before the window, he suddenly perceived the shadow of a man's figure as he stood beside a rock near the beach. Such an apparition was strange enough to excite curiosity in a quiet, remote spot, where the few inhabitants retired to rest at sunset. Darcy, therefore, opened the window, and moved towards him; but ere he had gone many paces, he was addressed by Forester's voice:

"I was about to pay you a visit, Knight, and only waited till I saw you alone."

"Let us stroll along the sands, then," said Darcy, "the night is delicious." And so saying, he drew his arm within Forester's, and walked along at his side.

"I have been thinking," said Forester, in a low, sad accent—"I have been thinking over the advice you lately gave me, and although, I own, at the time, it scarcely chimed in with my own notions, now, the more I reflect upon it, the more plausible does it seem. I have lived long enough out of fashionable life to make the return to it anything but a pleasure: for politics I have neither talent nor temper, and soldiering, if it does not satisfy every condition of my ambition, offers more to my capacity and my hopes than any other career."

"I would that you were more enthusiastic in the cause," said Darcy, who was struck by the deep depression of his manner; "I would that I saw you embrace the career more from a profound sense of duty and devotion, than as a 'pis aller.'"

"Such it is," sighed Forester, and his arm trembled within Darcy's as he spoke; "I own it frankly, save in actual conflict itself, I have no military ardour in my nature. I accept the road in life, because one must take some path."

"Then, if this be so," said Darcy, "I recal my counsels. I love the service, and you also, too well, to wish for such a mésalliance; no, campaigning will never do with a spirit that is merely not averse. Return to London, consult your relative, Lord Castlereagh—I see you smile at my recommendation of him, but I have learned to read his character very differently from what I once did. I can see now, that however the tortuous course of a difficult policy may have condemned him to stratagems wherein he was an agent—often an unwilling one—that his nature is eminently chivalrous and noble. His education and his prejudices have made him less rash than we, in our nationality, like to pardon, but the honour of the empire lies next his heart. Political profligacy, like any other, may be leniently dealt with, while it is fashionable, but there are minds that never permit themselves to be enslaved by fashion, when once they have gained a consciousness of their own power; such is his. He is already beyond it, and ere many years roll over, he will be equally beyond his competitors too. And now, to yourself. Let him be your guide. Once launched in public life, its interests will soon make themselves felt, and you are young enough to be plastic. I know that every man's early years, particularly those who are the most favoured by fortune, have their clouds and dark shadows. You must not seek an exemption from the common lot; remember how much you have to be grateful for; think of the advantages for which others strive a life-long, and never reach; all yours, at the very outset; and then, if there be some sore spots, some secret sorrows under all, take my advice, and keep them for your own heart. Confessions are admirable things for old ladies, who like the petty martyrdom of small sufferings, but men should be made of sterner stuff. There is a high pride in bearing one's load alone, don't forget that."

Forester felt that if the Knight had read his inmost feelings, his counsels could not have been more directly addressed to his condition; he had, indeed, a secret sorrow, and one which threw its gloom over all his prosperity. He listened attentively to Darcy's reasonings, and followed him, as in the full sincerity of his nature he opened up the history of his own life, now, commenting on the circumstances of good fortune, now, adverting to the mischances which had befallen him. Never had the genial kindness of the old man appeared more amiable. The just judgments, the high and honourable sentiments, not shaken by what he had seen of ingratitude and wrong, but hopefully maintained and upheld, the singular modesty of his character, were all charms that won more and more upon Forester; and when, after a *tête-à-tête* prolonged till late in the night, they parted, Forester's muttered ejaculation was, "Would that I were his son!"

"It is as I guessed," said Lady Eleanor, when the Knight re-entered the chamber; "Helen has refused him. I could not press her on the reasons, nor ask whether her heart approved all that her head determined. But she seemed calm and tranquil; and if I were to pronounce from appearance, I should say that the rejection has not cost her deeply."

"How happy you have made me, Eleanor," exclaimed Darcy, joyfully; "for while, perhaps, there is nothing in this world I should like better than to see such a man my son-in-law, there is no misery I would not prefer to witnessing my child's affections engaged where any sense of duty, or pride, rendered the engagement hopeless. Now, the case is this, Helen can afford to be frank and sisterly towards the poor fellow, who really did love her, and after a few days he leaves us."

"I thought he would go to-morrow," said Lady Eleanor, somewhat anxiously.

"No; I half hinted to him something of the kind, but he seemed bent on accompanying me to the West, and really I did not know how to say nay."

Lady Eleanor appeared not quite satisfied with an arrangement that promised a continuation of restraint, if not of positive difficulty, but made no remark about it, and turned the conversation on their approaching removal to Dublin.

CHAPTER LXXIII.

AN UNEXPECTED PROPOSAL.

Our time is now brief with our reader, and we would not trespass on him longer by dwelling on the mere details of those struggles to which Helen and Forester were reduced by daily association and companionship.

One hears much of Platonism, and, occasionally, of those brother and sisterly affections which are adopted to compensate for dearer and tenderer ties. Do they ever really exist? Has the world ever presented one single successful instance of the compact? We are far, very far, from doubting that friendship, the truest and closest, can subsist between individuals of opposite sex. We only hazard the conjecture that such friendships must not spring out of "Unhappy Love." They must not be built out of the ruins of wrecked affection. No—no; when Cupid is bankrupt, there is no use in attempting to patch up his affairs by any composition with the creditors.

We are not quite so sure that this is exactly the illustration Forester would have used to convey his sense of our proposition; but that he was thoroughly of our opinion, there is no doubt. Whether Helen was one of the same mind or not, she performed her task more easily and more gracefully. We desire too sincerely to part with our fair readers on good terms, to venture on the inquiry whether there is not more frankness and candour in the character of men than women? There is certainly a greater difficulty in the exercise of this quality in the gentler sex, from the many restraints imposed by delicacy and womanly feeling; and the very habit of keeping within this artificial barrier of reserve, gives an ease and tranquillity to female manner under circumstances where men would expose their troubled and warring emotions. So much, perhaps, for the reason that Miss Darcy displayed an equanimity of temper very different from the miserable Forester, and exerted powers of pleasing and fascination which, to him at least, had the singular effect of producing even more suffering than enjoyment.

The intimacy hitherto subsisting between them was rather increased than otherwise. It seemed as if their relations to each other had been fixed by a treaty, and now that transgression or change was impossible. If this was Slavery in its worst form to Forester, to Helen it was Liberty unbounded. No longer restrained by any fear of misconception, absolved, in her own heart, of any designs upon his, she scrupled not to display her capacity for thinking and reflecting with all the openness she would have done to her brother Lionel; while, to relieve the deep melancholy that preyed upon him, she exerted herself by a thousand little stratagems of caprice or fancy, that, however successful at the time, were sure to increase his gloom when he quitted her presence. Such, then, with its varying vicissitudes of pleasure and pain, was the condition of their mutual feeling for the remainder of their stay on the Northern coast. Many a time had Forester resolved on leaving her for ever, rather than perpetuate the lingering torture of an affection that increased with every hour; but the effort was more than his strength could compass, and he yielded, as it were, to a fate, until at last her companionship had become the whole aim and object of his existence.

As winter closed in, they removed to Dublin, and established themselves temporarily in an old-fashioned family hotel, selected by Bicknell, in a quiet, unpretending street. Neither their means nor inclination would have prompted them to select a more fashionable resting-place, while the object of strict seclusion was here secured. The ponderous gloom of the staid old house, where, from the heavy sideboard of almost black mahogany, to the wrinkled visage of the grim waiter, all seemed of a bygone century were rather made matters of mutual pleasantry among the party, than sources of dissatisfaction; while the Knight assured them that this was in his younger days the noisy resort of the gay and fashionable of the capital

"Indeed," added he, "I am not quite sure that this is not where the

'Townsends,' as the club was then called, used to meet in Swift's time. Bicknell will tell us all about it, for he's coming to dine with us."

Forester was the first to appear in the drawing-room before dinner. It is possible that he hurried his toilet in the hope of speaking a few words to Helen, who not unfrequently came down before her mother. If so, he was doomed to disappointment, as the room was empty when he entered, and there was nothing for it but to wait, impatiently indeed, and starting at every footstep on the stairs and every door that shut or opened.

At last he heard the sound of approaching steps, softened by the deep old carpet. They came—he listened—the door opened, and the waiter announced a name, what, and whose, Forester paid no attention to, in his annoyance that it was not hers he expected. The stranger, a very plump, joyous little personage in deep black, did not appear quite unknown to Forester, but as the recognition interested him very little, he merely returned a formal bow to the other's more cordial salute, and turned to the window where he was standing.

"The Knight, I believe, is dressing?" said the new arrival, advancing towards Forester.

"Yes—but I have no doubt he will be down in a few moments."

"Time enough—no hurry in life. They told me below stairs that you were here, and so I came up at once. I thought that I might introduce myself. Paul Dempsey—Dempsey's Grove. You've heard of me before, eh?"

"I have had that pleasure," said Forester, with more animation of manner, for now he remembered the face and figure of the worthy Paul, as he had seen both in the large mirror of his mother's drawing-room.

"Ha! I guessed as much," rejoined Paul, with a chuckling laugh; "the ladies are here, too, ain't they?"

Forester assented, and Paul went on.

"Only heard of it from Bicknell half an hour ago. Took a car, and came off at once. And when did *you* come?"

Forester stared with amazement at a question whose precise meaning he could not guess at, and to which he could only reply by a half-smile, expressive of his difficulty.

"You were away, weren't you?" asked Dempsey.

"Yes; I have been out of England," replied Forester, more than ever puzzled how this fact could or ought to have any interest for the other.

"Never be ashamed of it. Soldiering's very well in its way, though I'd never any taste for it myself—none of that martial spirit that stirred the umpkin as he sang—

Perhaps a recruit
Might chance to shoot
Great General Buonaparte!

Well, well! it seems you soon got tired of glory, of which, from all I hear, a little goes very far with any man's stomach; and no wonder. Except a French bayonet, there's nothing more indigestible than commissary bread."

"The service is not without some hardships," said Forester, blandly, and preferring to shelter himself under a generality, than invite further inquisitiveness.

"Cruelties, you might call them," rejoined Dempsey, with energy. "The frightful stories we read in the papers!—and I suppose they are all true. Were you ever touched up a bit yourself?" This Paul said in his most insinuating manner, and as Forester's stare showed a total ignorance of his meaning, he added—"A little four-and-twenty, I mean," mimicking, as he spoke, the action of flogging.

"Sir!" exclaimed Forester, with an energy almost ferocious. And Dempsey made a spring backwards, and entrenched himself behind a sofa-table.

"Blood alive!" he exclaimed, "don't be angry. I wouldn't offend you for the world; but I thought——"

"Never mind, sir—your apology is quite sufficient," said Forester, who had no small difficulty to repress laughing at the terrified face before him. "I am quite convinced there was no intention to give offence."

"Spoke like a man," said Dempsey, coming out from his ambush with an outstretched hand; and Forester, not usually very unbending in such cases, could not help accepting the salutation so heartily proffered.

"Ah! my excellent friend, Mr. Dempsey," said the Knight, entering at the same moment, and gaily tapping him on the shoulder. "A man I have long wished to see, and thank for many kind offices, in my absence.—I'm glad to see you are acquainted with Mr. Dempsey.—Well, and how fares the world with you?"

"Better, rather better, Knight," said Paul, who had scarcely recovered the fright Forester had given him. "You've heard that Old Bob's off? Didn't go till he couldn't help it, though; and now your humble servant is the head of the house."

While the Knight expressed his warm congratulations, Lady Eleanor and Helen came in, and by their united invitation, Paul was persuaded to remain for dinner—an event which, it must be owned, Forester could not possibly comprehend.

Bicknell's arrival, soon after, completed the party which, however discordant in some respects, soon exhibited signs of perfect accordance and mutual satisfaction. Mr. Dempsey's presence having banished all business topics for discussion, he was permitted to launch out into his own favourite themes, not the least amusing feature of which was the perfect amazement of Forester at the man and his intimacy.

As the ladies withdrew to the drawing-room, Paul became more moody and thoughtful, now and then interchanging glances with Bicknell, and seeming as if on the verge of something, and yet half doubting how to approach it. Two or three hastily swallowed bumpers, and a look, which he believed of encouragement, from Bicknell, at length rallied Mr. Dempsey, and after a slight hesitation, he said,

"I believe, Knight, we are all friends here; it is, strictly speaking, a cabinet council?"

If Darcy did not fathom the meaning of the speech, he had that knowledge of the speaker which made his assent to it almost a matter of course.

"That's what I thought," resumed Paul; "and it is a moment I have been anxiously looking for. Has our friend here said anything?" added he, with a gesture towards Bicknell.

"I, sir? I said nothing, I protest!" exclaimed the man of law, with an air of deprecation. "I told you, Mr. Dempsey, that I would inform the Knight of the generous proposition you made about the loan; but, till the present moment, I have not had the opportunity."

"Pooh, pooh! a mere trifle," interrupted Paul. "It is not of that I was thinking: it is of a very different subject I would speak. Has Lady Eleanor, or Miss Darcy—has she told you nothing of me?" said he, addressing the Knight.

"Indeed they have, Mr. Dempsey, both, spoken of you repeatedly, and always in the same terms of grateful remembrance."

"It isn't that, either," said Paul, with a half-sigh of disappointment.

"You are unjust to yourself, Mr. Dempsey," said Darcy, good-humouredly, "to rest a claim to our gratitude on any single instance of kindness; trust me, that we recognise the whole debt."

"But it's not that," rejoined Paul, with a shake of the head. "Lord bless us! how close women are about these things," muttered he to himself. "There is nothing for it but candour, I suppose, eh?"

This being put in the form of a direct question, and the Knight having as freely assented, Paul resumed:

"Well, here it is. Being now at the head of an ancient name, and very pretty independence—Bicknell has seen the papers—I have been thinking of that next step a man takes who would wish to—wish to—hand down little race of Dempseys. You understand?" Darcy smiled approvingly, and Paul continued: "And, as conformity of temper, taste, and habits are the surest pledges of such felicity, I have set the eyes of my affections upon —Miss Darcy."

So little prepared was the Knight for what was coming, that up to that moment he had been listening with a smile of easy enjoyment; but when the last word was spoken, he started as if he had been stung by a reptile, nor could all his habitual self-control master the momentary flush of irritation that covered his face.

"I know," said Paul, with a dim consciousness that his proposition was but half acceptable, "that we are not exactly, so to say, the same rank and class, but the Dempseys are looking up, and——"

"'The Darcys looking down,' you would add," said the Knight, with a gleam of his habitual humour in his eye.

"And, like the buckets in a well, the full and empty ones meet half way," added Dempsey, laughing. "I know well, as I said before, we are not the same kind of people, and perhaps this would have deterred me from indulging any thoughts on the subject, but for a chance, a bit of an accident, as a body may call it, that gave me courage."

"This is the very temple of candour, Mr. Dempsey," said the Knight, smiling. "Pray proceed, and let us hear the source of your encouragement; what was it?"

"Say, who was it, rather," interposed Paul.

"Be it so, then. Who was it? You have only made my curiosity stronger."

"Lady Eleanor—ay, and Miss Helen herself."

A start of anger and a half-spoken exclamation, were as quickly interrupted by a fit of laughing, and the Knight leaned back in his chair, and shook with the emotion.

"You doubt it; you think it absurd," said Dempsey, himself laughing, and not exhibiting the slightest irritation. "What if they say it's true—will that content you?"

"I'm afraid it would not," said Darcy, equivocally; "there's nothing less likely to do so. Still, I assure you, Mr. Dempsey, if the ladies are of the mind you attribute to them, I shall find it very difficult to disbelieve anything I ever hear hereafter."

"I'm satisfied to stand or fall by their verdict," said Paul, resolutely. "I'm not a fool, exactly; and do you think if I had not something stronger than mere suspicion to guide me, that I'd have gone that same journey to London. Oh, I forgot—I did not tell you about my going to Lord Netherby."

"You went to Lord Netherby, and on this subject?" said Darcy, whose face became suffused with shame, an emotion doubly painful from Forester's presence.

"That I did," rejoined the unabashed Paul, "and a long conversation we had over the matter. He introduced me to his wife, too. Lord bless us, but that is a bit of pride!"

"You are aware that the lady is Lord Wallincourt's mother," interposed Darcy, sternly.

"Faith, so that she isn't mine," said the inexorable Paul, "I don't care! There she was, lying in state, with a greyhound with silver bells on his neck at her feet; and when I came into the room, she lifts up her head and gives me a look, as much as to say, 'Oh, that's him.'—'Mr. Dempsey, of Dempsey's Hole'—for hole he would call it, in spite of me,—'Mr. Dempsey, my love,' said my Lord, bowing as ceremoniously as if he never saw her before; and so, taking the hint, I began a little course of salutations, when she called out, 'Tell him not to do that, Netherby—tell him not to do that——'"

This was too much for Mr. Dempsey's hearers, who, however differently minded as to the narrative, now concurred in one outbreak of hearty laughter.

"Well, my Lord," said Darcy, turning to Forester, "you certainly have shown evidence of a most enviable good temper. Had your Lordship——"

"His Lordship!" exclaimed Paul, in amazement. "Isn't that your son—Captain Darcy?"

"No, indeed, Mr. Dempsey," said the Knight; "I thought, as I came into the drawing-room, that you were acquainted, or I should have presented you to the Earl of Wallincourt."

"Oh, ain't I in it now!" cried Paul, in an accent of grief, most ludicrously natural. "Oh! by the powers, I'm up to the knees in trouble! And that was your mother! oh dear! oh dear!"

"You see, my worthy friend," said Darcy, smiling, "how easy a thing deception is. Is it not possible that your misconceptions do not end here?"

"I'll never get over it, I know I'll not!" exclaimed Paul, wringing his hands as he arose from the table. "Bad luck to it for grandeur," muttered he between his teeth; "I never had a minute's happiness since I got the taste for it." And with this honest avowal he rushed out of the room.

It was some time before the party in the dining-room adjourned up-stairs; but when they did, they found Mr. Dempsey seated at the fire, recounting to the ladies his late unhappy discomfiture—a narrative which even Lady Eleanor's gravity was not enabled to withstand. A kind audience was always a boon of the first water to honest Paul, and very little pressing was needed to induce him to continue his revelations, for the Knight wisely felt that such pretensions as his could not be buried so satisfactorily as beneath the load of ridicule.

Mr. Dempsey's scruples soon vanished and thawed under the warmth of encouraging voices and smiles, and he began the narrative of his night at the "Corvy," his painful durance in the canoe, his escape, the burning of the law papers, and each step of his progress to the very moment that he stood a listener at Lady Eleanor's door. Then he halted abruptly and said, "Now I'm dumb! racks and thumb-screws wouldn't get more out of me."

"You cannot mean, sir," said Lady Eleanor, calmly but haughtily, "that you overheard the conversation that passed between my daughter and myself?"

"Every word of it!" replied Paul, bluntly.

"Oh, really sir, I can scarcely compliment you on the spirit of your curiosity; for although the theme we talked on, if I remember aright, was the speedy necessity of removing—the urgency of seeking some place of refuge——"

"If I hadn't heard which, I could not have assisted you in your departure," rejoined the unabashed Paul; "the old Loyola maxim, 'Evil, that Good may come of it.' "

Helen sat pale and terrified all this time; for although Lady Eleanor had forgotten the discussion of any other topic on that night save that of their legal difficulties, she well remembered a theme nearer and dearer to her heart. Whether from the distress of these thoughts, or in the hope of propitiating Mr. Dempsey to silence, so it was, she fixed her eyes upon him with an expression Paul thought he could read, and he gave a look of such conscious intelligence in return, as brought the blush to her cheek. "I'm not going to say one word about it," said he, in a stage whisper, that even the Knight himself overheard.

"Then I must myself insist upon Mr. Dempsey's revelations," said Darcy, not at all satisfied with the air of mystery Dempsey threw around his intercourse.

Another look from Helen here met Paul's, and he stood uncertain how to act.

"Really, sir," said Lady Eleanor, "however little the subject we discussed was intended for other ears than our own, I must beg of you now to repeat what you remember of it."

"Well, what can I do?" exclaimed Paul, looking at Helen with an expression of the most helpless misery; "I know you are angry, and I know that, when you like it, you can blaze up like a Congreve rocket. Oh, faith! I don't forget the day I showed you the newspaper about the English officer thrashing O'Halloran!"

Helen grew scarlet, and turned away, but not before Forester had caught her eyes, and read in them more of hope than his heart had known for many a day before.

"These are more mysteries, Mr. Dempsey, and if you continue to scatter riddles as you go, we shall never get to the end of this affair."

"Perhaps," interposed Bicknell, hoping to close the unpleasant discussion, "perhaps Mr. Dempsey, feeling that he had personally no interest in the conversation between Lady Eleanor and Miss Darcy——"

"Hadn't he, then?" exclaimed Paul—"maybe not. If I hadn't, then, who had?—tell me that. Wasn't it then and there I first heard of the kind intentions towards me?"

"Towards you, sir! Of what are you speaking?"

"Blood alive! will you tell me that I'm not Paul Dempsey, of Dempsey's Grove?" exclaimed he, driven beyond all patience by what he deemed equivocation. "Will you tell me that your Ladyship didn't allude to the day I brought the letter from Coleraine, and say that you actually began to like me from that hour? Didn't you tell Miss Helen not to be downhearted, because there were better days in store for us? Miss Darcy remembers it, I see—ay, and your Ladyship does now. Didn't you call me rash, and headstrong, and ambitious? I forgive it all; I believe it is true. And wasn't I your bond-slave from that hour? Oh, mercy on me! the pleasant time I had of it at Mother Fum's! And then came the days and nights I was watching over you at Ballintray. Ay, faith, and money was very scarce with me when I gave old Denny Nolan five shillings for the loan of his nankeen jacket to perform the part of waiter at the little inn. Do you remember a little note in the shape of a friendly warning? Eh, now, my Lady, I think your memory is something fresher."

If the confusion of Lady Eleanor and her daughter was extreme at this outpouring of Mr. Dempsey's confessions, the amazement of Darcy and the utter stupefaction of Forester were even greater; to throw discredit upon him, would be to acknowledge the real bearing of the circumstances, which would be far worse than all his imputations. So there was no alternative but to lie under every suspicion his narrative might suggest.

Forester felt annoyed as much that such a person should have obtained this assumed intimacy, as by the pretensions he well knew were only absurd, and took an early leave under the pretence of fatigue. Bicknell soon followed; and now the Knight, arresting Dempsey's preparations for departure, led him back towards the fire, and placing a chair for him between Lady Eleanor and himself, obliged him to recount his scattered reminiscences once more, and, what was a far less pleasing duty to him, to listen to Lady Eleanor while she circumstantially unravelled the web of his delusion, and, in order, explained on what unsubstantial grounds he had built the edifice of his hope. Perhaps honest Paul was not more afflicted at any portion of the disentanglement than that which, in disavowing his pretensions, yet confessed that some other held the favourable place, while that other's name was guarded as a secret. This was, indeed, a sore blow, and he couldn't rally from it; and willingly would he have bartered all the gratitude they expressed for his many friendly offices to know his rival's name.

"Well," exclaimed he, as Lady Eleanor concluded, "it's clear I wasn't the man; only think of my precious journey to London, and the interview with that terrible old Countess! all for nothing. No matter—it's all past and over. As for the loan, I've arranged it all; you shall have the money when you like."

"I must decline your generous offer, not without feeling your debtor for it; but I have determined to abandon these proceedings. The Government have promised me some staff appointment, quite sufficient for my wishes and wants; and I will neither burden my friends, nor wear out myself by tiresome litigation."

"That's the worst of all," exclaimed Dempsey; "I thought you would not refuse me this."

"Nor would I, my dear Dempsey, but that I have no occasion for the sum. To-morrow I set out to witness the last suit I shall ever engage in, and, as I believe there is little doubt of the issue, I have nothing of sanguine feeling to suffer by disappointment."

"Well, then, to-morrow I'll start for Dempsey's Grove," said Paul, sorrowfully. "With very different expectations I quitted it a few days ago. Good-by, Lady Eleanor; good-by, Miss Helen. I suppose there's no use in guessing?"

Mr. Dempsey's leave-taking was far more rueful than his wont, and woe seemed to have absorbed all other feeling; but when he reached the door, he turned round and said,

"Now, I am going—never like to see me again; do tell me the name."

A shake of the head, and a merry burst of laughter, was all the answer, and Paul departed.

CHAPTER LXXIV.

THE LAST STRUGGLE.

THAT the age of chivalry is gone, we are reminded some twenty times in each day of our common-place existence. Perhaps the changed tone of society exhibits nowhere a more practical, but less picturesque advantage, than in the fact that the "joust" of ancient times is now replaced by the combat of the law court. Some may regret—we will not say if we are not of the number—that the wigged Baron of the Exchequer is scarcely so pleasing an arbiter as the Queen of Love and Beauty. Others may deem the knotted subtleties of black-letter a sorry recompense for the "wild crash and tumult of the fray." The Crier of the Common Pleas would figure to little advantage beside the gorgeously clad Herald of the Lists; nor are the artificial distinctions of service so imposing that a patent of precedency could vie with the white cross on the shield of a Crusader. Still there are certain counterbalancing interests to be considered; and it is possible that the veriest decrier of the law's uncertainty "would rather stake life and fortune on the issue of a 'trial of law,' than on the thews and sinews of the doughtiest champion that ever figured in an 'ordeal of battle.'"

In one respect there is a strong similarity between the two institutions. Each, in its separate age, possessed the same sway and influence over men's minds, investing with the deepest interest events of which they were hitherto ignorant, and enlisting partisans of opinion, in cases where, individually, there was nothing at stake.

An important trial has all the high interest of a most exciting narrative, whose catastrophe is yet to come, and where so many influential agencies are in operation to mould it. The proofs themselves, the veracity of witnesses, their self-possession and courage under the racking torture of cross-examination, the ability and skill of the advocate, the temper of the judge, his character of rashness or patience—of doubt or decisiveness; and then, more vague than all besides, the verdict of twelve perhaps rightly-minded, but as certainly very ordinarily endowed men, on questions sometimes of the greatest subtlety and obscurity. The sum of such conflicting currents makes up a "cross sea," where everything is possible, from the favouring tide that leads to safety, to the swell and storm of utter shipwreck.

At the winter assizes of Galway, in the year 1802, all the deep sympathies of a law-loving population were destined to be most heartily engaged by the record of Darcy *versus* Hickman, now removed by a change of *venue* for trial to that city. It needed not the unusual compliment of Galway being selected as a likely spot for the due administration of justice, to make the plaintiff somewhat popular on this occasion. The reaction, which for some time back had taken place in favour of the "Real Gentry," had gone on gaining in strength, so that public opinion was already inclining to the side of those who had earned a sort of prescriptive right to public confidence. The Clap-traps of Patriotism, associated as they were often found to be with cruel treatment of tenants and dependents, were contrasted with the independent bearing of men who, rejecting dictation and spurning mob popularity, devoted the best energies of mind and fortune to the interests of all belonging to them. All the vindictiveness and rancour of a party press could not obliterate these traits, and character sufficed to put down calumny.

Hickman O'Reilly, accompanied by the old doctor, had arrived in Galway the evening before the trial, in all the pomp of a splendid travelling carriage, drawn by four posters. The whole of "Nolan's" Head Inn had been already engaged for them and their party, who formed a tolerably numerous suite of lawyers, solicitors, and clerks, together with some private friends, curious to witness the proceedings.

In a very quiet but comfortable old inn called the "Devil and the Bag of Nails"—a corruption of the ancient Satyr and the Bacchanals—Mr. Bicknell had pitched his camp, having taken rooms for the Knight and Forester, who were to arrive soon after him, but whose presence in Ireland was not even suspected by the enemy.

There was a third individual who repaired to the West on this occasion, but who studiously screened himself from observation, waiting patiently for the issue of the combat to see on which side he should carry his congratulation: need we say his name was Con Heffernan.

Bicknell had heard of certain threats of the opposite party, which, while he did not communicate them to Darcy, were sufficient to give him deep uneasiness, as they went so far as to menace a very severe reprisal for these continued proceedings by a criminal action against Lionel Darcy. Of what nature, and on what grounds sustained, he knew not, but he was given to understand that, if his principal would even now submit to some final adjustment out of court, that the Hickmans would treat liberally with him, and, while abandoning these threatened proceedings against young Darcy, show Bicknell all the grounds for such a procedure.

It was past midnight when Darcy and Forester arrived; but before the Knight retired to rest he had learnt all Bicknell's doubts and scruples, and unhesitatingly decided on proceeding with his suit. He felt that a compromise would now involve the honour of his son, of which he had not the slightest dread of any investigation; and, however small the prospect of success, the trial must take place to evidence his utter disregard—his open defiance of this menace.

Morning came, and long before the judges took their seat, the court was crowded in every part. The town was thronged with the equipages of the neighbouring gentry, all eager to witness the trial; while the country people, always desirous of an exciting scene, thronged every avenue and passage of the building, and even the wide area in front of it. Nothing short of that passion for law and its interests, so inherent in an Irish heart, could have held that vast multitude thus enchained, for the day was one of terrific storm, the rain beating, the wind howling, and the sea roaring as it swept into the bay, and broke in showers of foam upon the rocky shore. Each moment ran the rumour of some new disaster in the town—now it was a chimney fallen, now a roof blown in, now an entire house, with all its inmates, destroyed; fires, too, the invariable accompaniment of hurricane, had broken out in various quarters, and cries for help and screams of wretchedness were mingled with the wilder uproar of the elements. Yet of that dense mob, few, if any, quitted their places for these sights and sounds of woe. The whole interest lay within that sombre building, and on the issue of an event of whose particulars they knew absolutely nothing, and the details of which it was impossible they could follow did they even hear them.

The ordinary precursors to the interest of these scenes are the chance appearances of those who are to figure prominently in them, and such, indeed, attracted far more of attention on this occasion than all the startling accidents by fire and storm then happening on every side. Each lawyer of celebrity on the circuit was speedily recognised, and greeted by tokens of welcome or expressions of disfavour, as politics or party inclined. The attorneys were treated with even greater familiarity, themselves not disdaining to exchange a repartee as they passed, in which combats, be it said, they were not always the victors. At last came old Dr. Hickman, feebly crawling along, leaning one arm on his son's, and the other on the stalwart support of Counsellor O'Halloran. The already begun cheer for the popular "Counsellor," was checked by the arrival of the Sheriff, preceding and making way for the Judges, whose presence ever imposed a respectful demeanour. The buzz and hum of voices, subdued for a moment, had again resumed its sway, when once more the police exerted themselves to make a passage through the throng, calling out, "Make way for the Attorney-General!" and a jovial, burly personage, with a face redolent of convivial humour and rough merriment, came up, rather dragging than linked with the thin, slight figure of Bicknell, who with unwonted eagerness was whispering something in his ear.

"I'll do it with pleasure, Bicknell," rejoined the full, mellow voice, loud enough to be heard by those on either side; "I know the Sheriff very well, and he will take care to let him have a seat on the Bench. What's the name?"

"The Earl of Wallincourt," whispered Bicknell, a little louder.

"That's enough, I'll not forget it." So saying, he released his grasp of the little man, and pursued his vigorous course. In a few moments after, Bicknell was seen, accompanied by Forester alone, "the Knight" having determined not to present himself till towards the close of the proceedings, if even then.

The buzz and din, incident to a tumultuous assembly, had just subsided to the decorous quietude of a Court of Justice, by the Judges entering and taking their seats, when, after a few words interchanged between the Attorney-General and the Sheriff, the latter courteously addressed Lord Wallincourt, and made way for him to ascend the steps leading to the Bench. The incident was in itself too slight and unimportant for mention, save that it speedily attracted the attention of O'Halloran, whose quick glance at once recognised his ancient enemy. So sudden was the shock, and so poignant did it seem, that he actually desisted from the occupation he was engaged in, of turning over his brief, and sat down pale and trembling with passion.

"You are not ill?" asked O'Reilly, eagerly, for he had not remarked the incident.

"Not ill," rejoined O'Halloran, in a low, deep whisper; "but do you see who is sitting next Judge Wallace, on the left of the Bench?"

"Forester, I really believe," exclaimed O'Reilly; for so separated were the two "United" Countries at that period, that his accession to rank and title was a circumstance of which neither O'Reilly nor his lawyer had ever heard.

"We'll change the *venue* for him, too, before the day is over," said O'Halloran, with a savage leer. "Do not let him see that we notice him."

While these brief words were interchanged, the business of the Court was opened, and some routine matters over, the record of Darcy *versus* Hickman called on. After this, the names of the Special Jury List were recited, and the invariable scene of dispute and wrangling, incident to their choice, followed. In Law, as in War, the combat opens by a skirmish; a single cannon-shot, or a leading question, if thrown out, are meant rather to ascertain "the range," than with any positive intention of damage; but, gradually, the light troops fall back, forces concentrate, and a mighty movement is made. In the present instance, the preliminaries were unusually long, the plaintiff's counsel not only stating all the grounds of the present suit, but recapitulating, with painful accuracy, the reasons for the change of *venue,* and reviewing, and, of course, rebutting by anticipation every possible or impossible objection that might be made by his learned friend on "the other side." For our purpose, it is enough if we condense the matter into a single statement, that the action was to show that Hickman, in purchasing portions of the Darcy estate, was, and must have been, aware that the Knight of Gwynne's signature appended to the deed of sale was a forgery, and that he never had concurred in, nor was even cognisant of, this disposal of his property. A single case was selected to establish this fact, on which, if proved, further proceedings in Equity would be founded.

The plaintiff's case opened by an examination of a number of witnesses, old tenants of the Darcy property. These were not only called to prove the value of their holdings, as being very far above the price alleged to have been paid by Hickman, but also that they themselves were in total ignorance that the estate had been conveyed away to another proprietor, and never knew till the flight and death of Gleeson took place, that for many years previous they had ceased to be tenants of Maurice Darcy, to become those of Dr. Hickman.

The examination and cross-examination of these witnesses presented all the varying and changeful fortunes ever observable in such scenes. At one moment, some obdurate old farmer resisting, with ludicrous pertinacity, all the efforts of the examining counsel to elicit the very testimony he himself wished to give; at another, the native humour of the peasant was seen baffling and foiling all the trained skill and practised dexterity of the pleader. Many a merry burst of laughter, many a jest that set the Court in a roar, were exchanged. It was in Ireland, remember; but still the business of the day advanced, and a great weight of evidence was adduced, which, however suggestive to common intelligence, went legally only so far as to show that the tenantry were, almost to a man, of an opinion which, whether well-founded or not in reason, turned out to be incorrect.

Darcy's counsel, a man of quickness and intelligence, made a very able speech, summing up the evidence, and commenting on every leading portion of it. He dwelt powerfully on the fact, that at the time of this alleged sale, the Knight, so far from being a distressed and embarrassed man, and consequently likely to effect a sale at a great loss, was, in reality, in possession of a princely fortune, his debts few and insignificant, and his income far above any possible expenditure. If he studiously avoided adverting to Gleeson's perfidy, as solely in fault, he assumed to himself credit for the forbearance, alleging that less scrupulous advisers might have gone perhaps further, and inferred connivance in a case so dubious and dark. "My client, however," said he, "gave me but one instruction in this cause, and it was this: 'If the law of the land, justly administered, as I believe it will be, restores to me my own, I shall be grateful; but if the pursuit of what I feel my right, involve the risk of reflecting on one honest man's fame, or imputing falsely aught of dishonour to an unblemished reputation, I tell you frankly, I don't think a verdict so obtained can carry with it anything but shame and disgrace.' "

With these words he sat down, amid a murmur of approving voices, for there were many there who knew the Knight by reputation, if not personally, and were aware how well such a speech accorded with every feature of his character.

There was a brief delay as he resumed his seat. It was already late, the Court had been obliged to be lighted up a considerable time previous, and the question of an adjournment was now discussed. The probable length of O'Halloran's reply would best guide the decision, and the Chief Baron asked if the learned counsel's statement were likely to be long.

"Yes, my Lord," replied he; "it is not a case to be dismissed briefly and I have many witnesses to call."

Another brief discussion took place on the Bench, and the Chief Baron announced that, as there were many important causes still standing over for trial, they should best consult public convenience by proceeding, and that, after a few moments devoted to refreshment, the case should go on.

The Judges retired, and many of the leading counsel took the same opportunity to recruit strength exhausted by several hours of severe toil. The Hickmans and O'Halloran never quitted their places; a decanter of sherry and a sandwich from the hotel were served where they sat, but the old man took nothing. The interest of the scene appeared too absorbing to admit of even a sense of hunger or weariness, and he sat with his hands folded, and his eyes mechanically fixed upon the now empty jury-box, for there, the whole day, were his looks riveted, to read, if he might, the varying emotions in the faces of those who held so much of his fortune in their keeping.

While the noise and hubbub which characterise a Court at such intervals was at its highest, a report was circulated that increased in no small degree the excitement of the scene, and gave a character of intense anxiety to an assemblage so lately broken up by varied and dissimilar passions. It was this: a large vessel had struck on a reef in the bay, and the sea was now breaking over her. She had been seen from an early hour endeavouring to beat to the southward; but the wind had drawn more to the westward as the storm increased, and a strong shore current had also drawn her on land. In a last endeavour to clear the headlands of Clare, she missed stays, and being struck by a heavy sea, her rudder was carried away. Totally unmanageable now, she was drifted along, till she struck on a most dangerous reef about a mile from shore. Signals of distress were seen at her mast-head, but no boat could venture out. The storm was already a hurricane, and even in the very harbour two fishing-boats had sunk.

As the dreadful tidings flew from mouth to mouth, a terrible confirmation was heard in the booming of guns of distress, which at brief intervals sounded amid the crashing of the storm.

It was at this moment of intense excitement that the crier proclaimed silence for the approaching entry of the Judges. If the din of human voices became hushed and low, the deafening thunder of the elements seemed to increase, and the roaring of the enraged sea appeared to fill the very atmosphere.

As the Judges resumed their seats, and the vast crowd ceased to stir or speak, O'Halloran arose. His voice was singularly low and quiet; but yet every word he uttered was distinctly heard through all the clamour of the storm. "My Lords," said he, "before entering upon my client's case, I would bespeak the kind indulgence of the Court in respect to a matter purely personal to myself. Your Lordships are too well aware that I should insist upon it, that in a cause where the weightiest interests of property are engaged, the mind of the advocate should be disembarrassed and free—not only free as regards the exercise of whatever knowledge and skill he may possess—not merely free from the supposition of any individual hazard the honest discharge of his duty might incur—but free from the greater thraldom of disturbed and irritated emotions, originating in the deepest sense of wounded honour.

"Far be it from me, my Lords, long used in the practice of these Courts, and long intimate with the righteous principle on which the laws are administered in them, to utter a syllable that in the remotest degree might seem to impugn the justice of the Bench; but, a mere frail and erring creature, with feelings common to all around me, I wish to protest against continuing my client's case while your Lordships' Bench is occupied by one who, in my person, has grossly outraged the sanctity of the law. Yes, my Lords," said he, raising his voice, till the deep tones swelled and floated through the vast space, "as the humble advocate of a cause, I now proclaim, that in addressing that Bench, I am incapable to render justice to the case before me, so long as I see associated with your Lordships a man more worthy to figure in the dock than to take his seat among the ermined Judges of the land. A moment more, my Lords. I am ready to make oath, that the individual on your Lordships' left is Richard Forester, commonly called the Honourable Richard Forester;—how suitable the designation, your Lordships shall soon hear——"

"I beg to interrupt my learned friend," interposed the Attorney-General, rising. "He is totally in error; and I would wish to save him from the embarrassment of misdescription. The gentleman he alludes to is the Earl of Wallincourt, a Peer of the realm."

"Proceed with your client's case, Mr. O'Halloran," said the Chief Baron, who saw that to discuss the question further was now irrelevant. O'Halloran sat down, overwhelmed with rage; a whispered communication from behind told him that the Attorney-General was correct, and that Forester was removed beyond the reach of his vengeance. After a few moments, he rallied, and again rose. Turning slowly over the pages of a voluminous brief, he stood waiting, with practised art, till expectancy had hushed each murmur around, when suddenly the crier called, "Way, there,—make way for the High Sheriff!" and that functionary, with a manner of excessive agitation, leaned over the bar, and addressed the Bench. "My Lords, I most humbly entreat your Lordships' forgiveness for thus interrupting the business of the Court; but the extreme emergency will, I hope, pardon the indecorum A large vessel has struck on the rocks in the bay: each moment it is expected she must go to pieces. A panic seems to prevail among even our hardy fishermen; and my humble request is, that if there be any individual in this crowded assembly possessing naval knowledge, or any experience in calamities of this nature, he will aid us by his advice and co-operation."

The senior Judge warmly approved the humane suggestion of the Sheriff; and several persons were seen now forcing their way through the dense mass,—the far greater part, be it owned, more excited by curiosity than stimulated by any hope of rendering efficient service. Notwithstanding Bicknell's repeated entreaties, and remembrances of his late severe illness, Forester also quitted the Court, and accompanied the Sheriff to the beach. And now O'Halloran, whose impatience during this interval displayed little sympathy with the sad occasion of the interruption, asked, in a manner almost querulous, if their Lordships were ready to hear him? The Court assented, and he began. Without once adverting to the subject on which he so lately addressed them, he opened his case by a species of narrative of the whole legal contest which for some time back had been maintained between the opposite parties in the present suit. Nothing could be more calm or more dispassionate than the estimate he formed of such struggles; neither inclining the balance to one party nor the other, but weighing with impartiality all the reasons that might prompt men, on one side, to continue a course of legal investigations, and the painful necessity, on the other, to provide a series of defences—costly, onerous, and harassing. "I have only to point out to the Court the defendant in this action, to show how severe such a duty may become. Here, my Lords, beside me, sits the gentleman, bowed down with more years than are allotted to humanity generally. Look on him, and say if it be not difficult to determine what course to follow—the abandonment of a just right, or its maintenance, at the cost of rendering the few last years—why do I say years?—days, hours of a life, careworn, distracted, and miserable!"

Dwelling long enough on this theme to interest without wearying the Jury, he adroitly addressed himself to the case of those who, by a system of litigious persecution, would seek to obtain by menace what they must despair of by law. Beginning by vague and wide generalities, he gradually accumulated a mass of allegations and inferences, which, concentrating to a point, he suddenly checked himself, and said, "Now, my Lords, it may be supposed that I will imitate the delicate reserve of my learned friend opposite; and, while filling your minds with dark and mysterious suspicions, profess a perfect ignorance of all intention to apply them. But I will not do this: I will be candid and free-spoken; nay, more, my Lords, I will finish what my learned friend has left incomplete; and I will proclaim to the Court, and this Jury, what he wished, but did not dare, to say, that we, the defendants in this action, were not only cognisant of a forgery, but were associated in the act! There it is, my Lords; and I accept my learned friend's bland smile as the warm acknowledgment of the truth of my assertion. My learned friend is obliged to me. I see that he cannot conceal his joy at the inaptitude of my avowal. But we have a case, my Lords, that can happily dispense with the dexterity of an advocate, and make its truth felt, even through means as unskilful as mine. They disclaimed, it is true —they disclaimed in words the wish to make this inference; but even take their disclaimer as such, and what is it? An avowal of their weakness —an open expression of the poverty of their proofs. Yes, my Lords, their disclaimers were like the ominous sounds which break from time to time upon our ear—but signal-guns of distress. Like that fated vessel, whose sad destiny is perhaps this moment accomplishing, they have been storm tossed and cast away—their proud ensign torn, and their rudder gone, but, unlike her, they cannot brave their fate without seeking to involve others in the calamity."

A terrible gust of wind, so sudden and violent as to be like a thunder-clap, now struck the building, and with one tremendous crash the great window of the Court-house was driven in, and scattered in fragments of glass and timber throughout the Court. A scene of the wildest confusion ensued, for almost immediately the lights became extinguished, and from the dark abyss arose a terrible chaos of voices in every agony of fear and suffering. Some announced that the roof was giving way and was about to crush them; others, in all the bodily torture of severe wounds, cried for help.

It was nearly an hour before the Court could resume its sitting, which at length was done in one of the adjoining courts, the usual scene of the criminal trials. Here, now, lights were procured, and after a considerable delay the cause proceeded. If the various events of the night, added to the fatigue of the day, had impressed both the Bench and the Jury with signs of greatest exhaustion, O'Halloran showed no evidence of abated vigour. On the contrary, like one whose vengeance had been thwarted by opposing accident, he exhibited a species of impatient ardour to resume his work of defamation. With a brief apology for any want of due coherence in an argument so frequently interrupted, he launched out into the most ferocious attack upon the plaintiff in the suit; and while repudiating the affected reserve of the opposite counsel, boldly proclaimed that they would not imitate it. Nay, further, that they were only awaiting the sure verdict in their favour, to commence a criminal action against the parties for the very crime they dared to insinuate against them.

"I shall now call my witnesses, my Lord; and if the Grand Cross of the Bath, which this day's paper tells me is to be conferred upon the plaintiff, be not meant, like the brand which foreign justice impresses on its felons, as a mark of ignominy, I am at a loss to understand how it has descended on this man. Call Nathaniel Leery."

The examination of the witnesses was in perfect keeping with the infamous scurrility of the speech, and the testimony elicited went to prove everything the advocate desired. Though exposed by cross-examination, and their perjury proved, O'Halloran kept a perpetual recapitulation of their assertions before the jury, and so artfully, that few, save the practised minds of a legal auditory, could have distinguished in that confused web of truth and falsehood.

The business proceeded with difficulty, for, added to the uproar of the storm, was a continued tumult of voices in the outer hall of the Court, and where now several sailors, saved from the wreck, had been brought for shelter. By frequent loud cries from this quarter the Court was interrupted, and more than once its proceedings completely arrested—inconveniences which the Judges submitted to with the most tolerant patience—when at length a loud murmur arose, which gradually swelling louder and louder, all respect for the sacred precincts of the judgment-seat seemed lost in the wild tumult. In a tone of sharp reproof the Chief Baron called on the Sheriff to allay the uproar, and, if necessary, to clear the hall. The order was scarcely given, when one deafening shout was raised from the street, and, soon caught up, echoed by a thousand voices, while shrill cries of—"He has saved them! he has saved them!" rent the air.

"What means this, Mr. Sheriff?"

"It is my Lord Wallincourt, my Lord, who has just rescued from the wreck three men who persisted in being lost together, rather than separate. Hitherto only one man was taken at each trip of the boat, but this young nobleman offered a thousand pounds to the crew who would accompany him, and it appears they have succeeded."

"Really, my Lords," said O'Halloran, who had overheard the honourable mention of a hated name, "I must abandon my client's cause. These interruptions, which I conclude your influence is powerless to remove, have so interfered with the line of defence I had laid down for adoption, and have so confused the order of the proofs I had prepared, that I should but injure, and not serve, my respected client by continuing to represent his interests."

A bland assurance from the Court that order should be rigidly enforced, and a pressing remonstrance from O'Reilly, overcame a resolve scarcely maturely taken, and he consented to go on.

"We will now, my Lords," said he, "call a very material witness—a respectable tenant on the property—who will prove that on a day in November, antecedent to Gleeson's death, he had a conversation with the Knight of Gwynne—— Really, my Lords, I cannot proceed; this is no longer a Court of Justice."

The remainder of his words were lost in an uproar like that of the sea itself, and like that element, the great mass swelled forward, and a rush of people from the outer hall bore into the Court, till seats and barriers gave way before that overwhelming throng.

For some minutes the scene was one of almost personal conflict. The mob, driven forward by those behind, were obliged to endure a buffeting by the more recognised possessors of the place; nor was it till police and military had lent their aid that the Court was again restored to quiet, while several of the rioters were led off in custody.

"Who are these men, and to what purpose are they here?" said the Chief Baron, as Bicknell officiously exerted himself to make way for some persons behind.

"I come to tender my evidence in this cause," said a deep, solemn voice, as a man advanced to the witness-table, displaying to the amazed assembly a bold, intrepid countenance, on which streaks of blue and yellow colour were fantastically mingled, like the war-paint of a savage.

"Who are you, sir?" rejoined O'Halloran, with his habitual scowl.

"My name is Bagenal Daly. I believe their Lordships are not ignorant of my rank and station; and this gentleman at my side is also here to afford his testimony. This, my Lords, is Thomas Gleeson!"

One cry of amazement rang through the assembly, through which a wild shriek pierced with a clear and terrible distinctness; and now the attention was suddenly turned towards old Hickman, who had fallen forward senseless on the table.

"My client is very ill—he is dangerously ill, my Lord. I beg to suggest an adjournment of the cause," said O'Halloran; while O'Reilly, with a face like death, continued to whisper eagerly in his ear. "I appeal to the plaintiff himself, if he be here, and is not devoid of the feelings attributed to him, and I ask that the cause may be adjourned."

"It is not a case in which the defendant's illness can be made use of to press such a demand," said one of the Judges, mildly; "but if the opposite party consent——"

"He is worse, my Lord."

"I say, if the opposite party——"

"He is dead!" said O'Halloran, solemnly; and letting go the lifeless hand, it fell with a heavy bang upon the table.

"Take your verdict," said O'Halloran, with the look of a demon; and, bursting his way through the crowd, disappeared.

CHAPTER LXXV.

CONCLUSION.

When Forester entered the Knight's room in the inn, where, in calm quietude, he sat awaiting the verdict, he hesitated for a moment how he should break the joyful tidings of Daly's arrival.

"Speak out," said Darcy. "If not exactly without hope, I am well prepared for the worst."

"Can you say you are equally ready to hear the best?" asked Forester, eagerly.

"The best is a very strong word, my young friend," said Darcy, gravely.

"And yet, I speak advisedly—the best."

"If so, perhaps I am not so prepared. My heart has dwelt so long on these troubles, recognising them as I felt they must be, that I would, perhaps, ask a little time to think how I should hear tidings so remote from all expectation. Of course, I do not speak of the mere verdict here."

"Nor I," interposed Forester, impatiently. "I speak of what restores you to your ancient house and rank, your station, and your fortune."

"Can this be true?"

"Ay, Maurice, every word of it," broke in Daly, who, having listened so far, could no longer restrain himself. The two old men fell into each other's arms with all the cordial affection with which they had embraced as schoolfellows sixty years before.

Great as was Darcy's amazement at seeing his oldest friend thus suddenly restored, it was nothing in comparison to what he felt as Daly narrated the event of the shipwreck, and his rescue from the sinking vessel by Forester.

"And your companions, who were they?" asked Darcy, eagerly.

"You shall hear."

"I guess one of them already," interposed the Knight. "The trusty Sandy. Is it not so?"

"The other you will never hit upon," said Daly, nodding an assent.

"I'm thinking over all our friends, and yet none seem likely."

"Come, Maurice, prepare yourself for surprise. What think you, if he to whose fate I had linked myself, resolving that, live or die, we should not separate, if this man was—Gleeson—honest Tom Gleeson?"

The words seemed stunning in their effect, for Darcy leaned back, and passing his hands over his closed lids, murmured, "I hope my poor faculties are not wandering—I trust this may be no delusion."

"He is yonder," said Daly, taking the Knight's hand in his strong grasp "Sandy mounts guard over him. Not that the poor devil thinks of, or desires escape. He was too weary of a life of deception and sin when we caught him, to wish to prolong it. Now rouse yourself, and listen to me."

It would, doubtless, be a heavy tax on our kind reader's patience were we to relate, circumstantially, the conversation that, now commencing, lasted during the entire night, and till late in the following morning. Enough if we say that Daly, having, through Freney's instrumentality, discovered that Gleeson had not committed suicide, but only spread this rumour for concealment's sake, resolved to pursue him to America. Fearing that any suspicion of his object might escape, he did not even trust Bicknel with the secret; but, by suffering him to continue law proceedings as before, totally blinded the Hickmans as to the possibility of the event.

It would in itself be a tale of marvel to recount the strange adventures which Daly encountered in his search and pursuit of Gleeson, who had originally taken up his residence in the States—was recognised there, and fled into Canada, where he wandered about from place to place, conscience-stricken and miserable. He was wretchedly poor, besides, for on the bills and securities he carried away, many being on eminent houses in America, payment was stopped, and being unable to risk proceedings, he was reduced to beggary.

It now appeared, that at a very early period of life, when a clerk in the office of old Hickman's agent, he had committed a forgery. It was for a small sum, and only done in anticipation of meeting the bill by his salary due a few weeks later. So far the fraud was palliated by the intention.

By some mischance the document fell into the possession of Dr. Hickman, whose name it falsely bore. He immediately took steps to trace its origin, and having succeeded, he sent for Gleeson. When the youth, pale and terror-stricken by suspicion, made his appearance, he was amazed that, instead of finding a prosecutor ready prepared for his ruin, he discovered a benevolent patron, who, having long watched the zeal and assiduity with which he discharged his duties, desired to be of use to him in life. Hickman told him, that if he were disposed to make the venture on his own account, he would use his influence to procure him some small agencies, and even assist him with funds, to make advances to those landlords who might employ him. The interview lasted long. There was much excellent advice and wise admonition on one side, profuse expression of gratitude and lasting fidelity on the other. "Very well, very well," said old Hickman, at the close of a very devoted speech, in which Gleeson professed the most attached, and the most honourable motives—for he was not at all aware that his bill was known of—"I am not ignorant of mankind; they are rarely, if ever, very bad or very good; they can be occasionally faithful to their friends; but there is one thing they are always—careful of themselves. See this"—here he took from his pocket-book the forged paper, and held it before the almost sinking youth—"there is what can bring you to the gallows any day! Is this the first time?"

"It is, so help me——" cried he, falling on his knees.

"Never mind swearing. I believe you. And the last also?"

"And the last!"

"I see it must be, by the date," rejoined Hickman.

"I can pay it, sir; I have the money ready—on Tuesday——"

"Never mind that," replied Hickman, folding it up, and replacing it in the pocket-book. "You shall pay me in something better than money—in gratitude. Come and dine with me alone to-day, and we'll talk over the future."

It has never been our taste to present pictures of depravity to our readers; we would more willingly turn from them, or, where that is impossible, make them as sketchy as may be. It will be sufficient, then, if we say that Gleeson's whole career was the plan and creation of Hickman. The rigid and scrupulous honour, the spotless decorum, the unshaken probity, were all devices to win public confidence and esteem. That they were eminently successful, the epithet of "honest Tom Gleeson," by which he was universally known, is the guarantee. The union of such qualities with consummate skill, and the most unwearied zeal, soon made him the most distinguished man in his walk, and made his services not only an evidence of success, but of a rectitude in obtaining success that men of character prized still more highly.

Possessed of the titles of immense estates, invested with unbounded confidence by the owners, cognisant of every legal flaw that could excite uneasiness, aware of every hitch and strait of their circumstances, he was less the servant than the master of those who employed him.

It was a period when habits of extravagance prevailed to the widest extent. The proprietors of estates deemed spending their incomes their only duty, and left its cares to the agents. The only reproach, then, ever laid to Gleeson's door was, that when a question of a sale or a loan was agitated, honest Tom's scruples were often a most troublesome impediment to his less scrupulous employer. In fact, Gleeson stood before the public as a kind of guardian of estated property! the providence of dowagers, widows, and younger children!

Such a man, with his neck in a halter, at any moment at the mercy of old Dr. Hickman, was an agent for ruin almost inconceivable. Through his instrumentality the old usurer laid out his immense stores of wealth at enormous interest, obtained possession of vast estates at a mere fraction of their worth, till at length, grown hardy by long impunity, and daring by the recognition of the world, bolder expedients were ventured on. Darcy's ruin was long the cherished dream of Hickman; and when, after many a wily scheme and long negotiation, he saw Gleeson engaged as his agent, he felt certain of victory. His first scheme was to make Gleeson encourage young Lionel in every project of extravagance, by putting his name to bills, assuring him that his father permitted him an almost unlimited expenditure. This course once entered upon, and well aware that the young man kept no record of such transactions, his name was forged to several acceptances of large amount, and, subsequently, to sales of property to meet them.

Meanwhile, great loans were raised by Darcy to pay off encumbrances, and never so employed. Till, at length, the Knight decided upon the negotiation which was to clear off Hickman's mortgage, the debt, of all others, he hated most to think of. So quietly was this carried on, that Hickman heard nothing of it; for Gleeson, long wearied by a life of treachery and perfidy, and never knowing the day or the hour when disclosure might come, had resolved on escaping to America with this large sum of money, leaving his colleague in crime to carry on business alone.

"The Doctor" was not, however, to be thus duped. Secret and silent as the arrangements for flight were, he heard of them all; and hastening out to

Gleeson's house, coolly told him that any attempt at escape would bring him to the gallows. Gleeson attempted a denial. He alleged that his intended going over to England was merely on account of this sum, which Darcy was negotiating for, to pay off the mortgage.

A new light now broke on Hickman. He saw that his terrified confederate could not much longer be relied upon, and it was agreed between them that Gleeson should pay the money to redeem the mortgage, and, having obtained the release, show it to the Knight of Gwynne. This done, he was to carry it back to Hickman, and, for the sum of 10,000*l.*, replace it in his hands, thus enabling the doctor to deny the payment and foreclose the mortgage, while honest Tom, weary of perfidy, and seeking repose, should follow his original plan, and escape to America.

The money was paid, as Freney surmised, and Daly believed; but Gleeson, still dreading some act of treachery, instead of returning the release, and claiming the price, started a day earlier than he promised. The rest is known to the reader. Whether the Hickmans credited the story of the suicide or not, they were never quite free of the terror of a disclosure; and, in pressing the matrimonial arrangement, hoped for ever to set at rest the disputed possession.

It would probably not interest our readers were we to dwell longer on Gleeson or his motives. That some vague intention existed of one day restoring to Darcy the release of his mortgage, is perhaps not unlikely. A latent spark of honour, long buried beneath the ashes of crime, often shines out brightly in the last hour of existence. There might be, too, a cherished project of vengeance against the man that tempted and destroyed him. Be it as it may, he guarded the document as though it had been his last hope; and, when tracked, pursued, and overtaken near Fort Erie by a party of the Delawares, of whom the Howling Wind, alias Bagenal Daly, was chief, it was found stitched up in the breast of his waistcoat.

Our space does not permit us to dwell upon Bagenal Daly's adventures, though we may assure our readers that they were both wild and wonderful. One only regret darkened the happiness of his exploit. It was that he was compelled so soon to leave the pleasant society of the Red Skins, and the intellectual companionship of "Blue Fox" and "Hissing Lightning;" while Sandy, discovering himself to be a widower, would gladly have contracted new ties, to cement the alliance of the ancient house of M'Grane with that of the royal family of Hickinbooki, or the "Slimy Whip Snake," a fair princess of which had bid high for his affections. Indeed, the worthy Sandy had become romantic on the subject, and suggested that, if the lady would condescend to adopt certain articles of attire, he would have no objection to take her back to the Corvy. These were sacrifices, however, that not even love was called upon to make, and the project was abortive.

So far have we condensed Bagenal Daly's narrative, which, orally delivered, lasted till the sun was high, and the morning fine and bright. He had only concluded, when a servant in O'Reilly's livery brought a letter, which he sai was to be given to the Knight of Gwynne, but required no answer. Its contents were the following:

"SIR,—The melancholy catastrophe of yesterday evening might excuse me in your eyes from any attention to the claims of mere business. But the discovery of certain documents lately in the possession of my father, demand at my hands the most prompt and complete reparation. I now know, sir, that we were unjustly possessed of an estate and property that were yours. I also know that severe wrongs have been inflicted upon you through the instrumentality of my family. I have only to make the best amende in my power, by immediately restoring the one, and asking forgiveness for the other. If you can and will accord me the pardon I seek, I shall, as soon as the sad duties which devolve upon me here are completed, leave this country for the Continent, never to return. I have already given directions to my legal adviser to confer with Mr. Bicknell, and no step will be omitted to secure a safe and speedy restoration of your house and estate to its rightful owner. In deep humiliation, I remain,

"Your obedient servant,

"H. O'REILLY."

"Poor fellow!" said Darcy, throwing down the letter before Daly, "he seems to have been no party to the fraud, and yet all the penalty falls upon him."

"Have no pity for the upstart rascal, Maurice; I'll wager a hundred —thank Heaven, Mr. Gleeson has put me in possession of a few—that he was as deep as his father. Give me this paper, and I'll ask honest Tom the question."

"Not so, Bagenal; I should be sorry to think worse of any man than I must do. Let him have at least the benefit of a doubt; and as to honest Tom, set him at liberty; we no longer want him; the papers he has given are quite sufficient—more than we are ever like to need."

Daly had no fancy for relinquishing his hold of the game that cost him so much trouble to take, but the Knight's words were usually a law to him, and with a muttering remark of "I'll do it, because I'll have my eye on him," he left the room to liberate his captive.

"There he goes," exclaimed Daly, as, re-entering the room, he saw a chaise rapidly drive from the door. "There he goes, Maurice, and I own to you I have an easier conscience for having let loose Freney on the world, than for liberating honest Tom Gleeson; but who have we here, with four smoking posters?—ladies, too!"

A travelling carriage drew up at the door of the little inn, and immediately three ladies descended. "That's Maria!" cried Daly, rushing from the room, and at once returned with his sister, Lady Eleanor, and Miss Darcy.

Miss Daly had, three days before, received a letter from Bagenal, detailing his capture of Gleeson, and informing her that he hoped to be back in Ireland almost as soon as his letter. With these tidings she hastened to Lady Eleanor, and concerted the journey which now brought them all together.

Story tellers have but scant privilege to linger where all is happiness, unbroken and perfect. Like Mother Cary's chickens, their province is rather with menacing storm than the signs of fair weather. We have, then, but space to say, that a more delighted party never met than those who now assembled in that little inn; but one face showed any signs of passing sorrow—that was poor Forester's. The general joy, to which he had so much contributed by his exertions, rather threw a gloomier shade over his own unhappiness, and in secret he resolved to say "Good-by" that same evening.

Amid a thousand plans for the future, all tinged with their own bright colour, they sat round the fire at evening, when Miss Daly, whose affection for the youth was strengthened by what she had seen during his illness, remarked that he alone seemed exempt from the general happiness.

"To whom we owe so much," said Lady Eleanor, kindly. "My husband is indebted to him for his life."

"I can say as much, too," said Daly; "not to speak of Gleeson's gratitude."

"Nay!" exclaimed the young man, blushing, "I did not know the service I was rendering. I little guessed how grateful I should myself have reason to be, for being its instrument."

"All this is very well," said Miss Daly, abruptly, "but it is not honest—no, it is not honest. There are other feelings concerned here than such amiable generalities as Joy, Pity, and Gratitude. Don't frown, Helen,—that is better, love—a smile becomes you to perfection."

"I must stop you," said Forester, blushing deeply. "It will be enough if I say, that any observation you can make must give me the deepest pain,—not for myself——"

"But for Helen? I don't believe it. You may be a very sharp politician, and a very brave soldier, but you know very little about young ladies. Yes, there's no denying it,—their game is all deceit."

"Oh! Colonel Darcy—Lady Eleanor, will you not speak a word?" exclaimed Forester, pale and agitated.

"A hundred, my dear boy," cried the Knight, "if they would serve you· but Helen's one is worth them all."

"Miss Darcy, dare I hope? Helen, dearest," added he, in a whisper, as, taking her hand, he led her towards a window.

"My Lord, the carriage is ready," said his servant, throwing wide the door.

"You may order the horses back again," said Daly, dryly; "my Lord is not going this evening."

HAS our reader ever made a long voyage? Has he ever experienced in himself the strange but most complete alteration in all his sentiments and feelings when far away from land—on the wild, bleak waters—and that same "himself," when in sight of shore, with seaweed around the prow, and land-breezes on his cheek. But a few hours back, and that ship was his world; he knew her from "bow to taffrail;" he greeted the cook's galley as though it were the "Restaurant" his heart delighted in; he even felt a kind of friendship for the pistons as they jerked up and down into a bowing acquaintance. But, now, how changed are his sentiments; how fixedly are his eyes turned to the pier of the harbour! and how impatient is he at those tacking zig-zag approaches by which nautical skill and care approximate the goal.

Already landed in imagination, the cautious manœuvres of the crew are an actual martyrdom; he has no bowels for anything save his own enfranchisement, and he cannot comprehend the tiresome detail of preparations, which, after all, perhaps, are scarcely five minutes in endurance. At last, the gangway launched, see him, how he elbows forward, fighting his way, carpet-bag in hand, regardless of passport-people, police, and porters; he'll scarce take time to mutter a "Good-by, Captain," in the haste to leave a scene all whose interest is over, and whose adventure is past

Such is the end of a voyage, and such, or very nearly such, the end of a novel! You, most amiable reader, are the passenger—we, the skipper. A few weeks ago you deemed us tolerable company, *faute de mieux*, perhaps. We'll not ask why, at all events. We had you out on the wide, wild waters of uncertainty, free to sail where'er our fancy listed. In our very waywardness there was a mock semblance of power, for the creatures we presented to you were our own, their lives and fortunes in our hands. Now all that is over—we have neared the shore—and all our hold on you is bygone.

How can we hope to excite interest in events already accomplished? Why linger over details which you have already filled up? Of course, say you, all ends happily now. Virtue is rewarded—as novelists understand rewarding—by matrimony; and vice punished in single blessedness. The Hero marries the Heroine, and if they don't live happy—&c.

But what became of Bagenal Daly? says some one, who would compliment us by expressing so much of interest. Bagenal, then, only waited to see the Knight restored to his own, to retire with his sister to the "Corvy," where, attended by Sandy, he passed the remainder of his days in peace and quietude; his greatest enjoyment being to seize on a chance tourist to the Causeway, and make him listen to narratives of his early life, but which age had now so far commingled, that the merely strange became actually marvellous.

Paul Dempsey grieved for a week, but consoled himself on hearing that his rival had been a "Lord;" and subsequently, in a "moment of enthusiasm," he married Mrs. Fumbally. The Hickmans left Ireland for the Continent, where they are still to be found, rambling about from city to city, and expressing the utmost sympathy with their country's misfortunes, but, to avoid any admixture of meaner feeling, suffering no taint of lucre to mingle with their compassion.

As for Lionel Darcy, his name is to be found in the despatches from the East, and with a mention that shows that he has derogated in nothing from the proud character of his race.

Of all those who figured before our reader, but one remains on the stage where they all performed; and he, perhaps, has no claim to be especially remembered. There is always, however, somewhat of respectability attached to the oldest inhabitant, that chronicler of cold winters and warm summers, of rainy springs and stormy Octobers. Con Heffernan, then, lives, and still wields no inconsiderable share of his ancient influence. Each party has discovered his treachery, but neither can dispense with his services

He is the last link remaining between the men of Ireland's "great day" and the very different race who now usurp the direction of her destiny.

Of the period of which we have endeavoured to picture some meagre resemblance, unhappily the few traces remaining are those most to be deplored. The Poverty, the Misery, and the Anarchy survive; the Genial Hospitality, the warm attachment to Country, the cordial generosity of Irish feeling, have sadly declined. Let us hope that from the depth of our present sufferings better days are about to dawn, and a period approaching when Ireland shall be "Great" in the happines of her people, "Glorious" in the development of her inexhaustible reso ces, and "Free," by that best of freedom, free from the trammels of an unmeaning party warfare, which has ever subjected the welfare of the country to the miserable intrigues of a few adventurers.

THE END

S. Cowan & Co., Strathmore Printing Works, Perth.

3-20-56q-4-82.

EVERYBODY'S LAWYER (Beeton's Law Book). Entirely New Edition, Revised by a BARRISTER. A Practical Compendium of the General Principles of English Jurisprudence: comprising upwards of 14,600 Statements of the Law. With a full Index, 27,000 References, every numbered paragraph in its particular place, and under its general head. Crown 8vo, 1,680 pp., cloth gilt, 7*s*. 6*d*.

⁂ *The sound practical information contained in this voluminous work is equal to that in a whole library of ordinary legal books, costing many guineas. Not only for every non-professional man in a difficulty are its contents valuable, but also for the ordinary reader, to whom a knowledge of the law is more important and interesting than is generally supposed.*

BEETON'S DICTIONARY OF GEOGRAPHY: A Universal Gazetteer. Illustrated by Maps—Ancient, Modern, and Biblical, and several Hundred Engravings in separate Plates on toned paper. Containing upwards of 12,000 distinct and complete Articles. Post 8vo, cloth gilt, 7*s*. 6*d*.; half-calf, 10*s*. 6*d*.

BEETON'S DICTIONARY OF BIOGRAPHY: Being the Lives of Eminent Persons of All Times. Containing upwards of 10,000 distinct and complete Articles, profusely Illustrated by Portraits. With the Pronunciation of Every Name. Post 8vo, cloth gilt, 7*s*. 6*d*.; half-calf, 10*s*. 6*d*.

BEETON'S DICTIONARY OF NATURAL HISTORY: A Popular and Scientific Account of Animated Creation. Containing upwards of 2,000 distinct and complete Articles, and more than 400 Engravings. With the Pronunciation of Every Name. Crown 8vo, cloth gilt, 7*s*. 6*d*.; half-calf, 10*s*. 6*d*.

BEETON'S BOOK OF HOME PETS: How to Rear and Manage in Sickness and in Health. With many Coloured Plates, and upwards of 200 Woodcuts from designs principally by HARRISON WEIR. With a Chapter on Ferns. Post 8vo, half-roan, 7*s*. 6*d*.; half-calf, 10*s*. 6*d*.

THE TREASURY OF SCIENCE, Natural and Physical. Comprising Natural Philosophy, Astronomy, Chemistry, Geology, Mineralogy, Botany, Zoology and Physiology. By F. SCHOEDLER, Ph.D. Translated and Edited by HENRY MEDLOCK, Ph.D., &c. With more than 500 Illustrations. Crown 8vo, cloth gilt, 7*s*. 6*d*.; half-calf, 10*s*. 6*d*.

A MILLION OF FACTS of Correct Data and Elementary Information concerning the entire Circle of the Sciences, and on all subjects of Speculation and Practice. By Sir RICHARD PHILLIPS. Carefully Revised and Improved. Crown 8vo, cloth gilt, 7*s*. 6*d*.; half-calf, 10*s*. 6*d*.

THE TEACHER'S PICTORIAL BIBLE AND BIBLE DICTIONARY. With the most approved Marginal References, and Explanatory Oriental and Scriptural Notes, Original Comments, and Selections from the most esteemed Writers. Illustrated with numerous Engravings and Coloured Maps. Crown 8vo, cloth gilt, red edges, 8*s*. 6*d*.; French morocco, 10*s*. 6*d*.; half-calf, 10*s*. 6*d*.; Turkey morocco, 15*s*.

THE SELF-AID CYCLOPÆDIA, for Self-Taught Students. Comprising General Drawing; Architectural, Mechanical, and Engineering Drawing; Ornamental Drawing and Design; Mechanics and Mechanism; the Steam Engine. By ROBERT SCOTT BURN, F.S.A.E., &c. With upwards of 1,000 Engravings. Demy 8vo, half-bound, price 10*s*. 6*d*.

London: WARD, LOCK & CO., Salisbury Square, E.C.

Printed in Great Britain
by Amazon.co.uk, Ltd.,
Marston Gate.